He's the last man she would ever want.
She is definitely not his type.
They're virtual strangers...but suddenly they're

Stranded!

Lucas and Jessica have survived tragedy;
Ryan and Ariel are bound by a secret;
Jonathan and Anne are trapped by the elements;
what will happen when they can't turn away?

Three sets of unlikely lovers—thrown together
by chance...or by fate?

Relive the romance...

by Request™

Three complete novels by your favorite authors!

About the Authors

STEPHANIE JAMES

has been writing romance for over a decade and she loves what she does. Some of you may know her as Jayne Ann Krentz. Others may be familiar with the pen name she uses for historical romance, Amanda Quick. "Those of us who read and write romance know that it is a vital and enduring part of women's fiction," she says. "These are tales that celebrate the life-affirming power of love. This world needs more of our kind of stories."

PATRICIA GARDNER EVANS

has lived in New Mexico all her life, and has traveled extensively throughout the West, exploring old ghost towns, Indian ruins and abandoned homesteads. She spends much of her free time outdoors fishing and raises her own fruits and vegetables. She gets inspiration for her plots and characters from the land and people around her.

KATHLEEN KORBEL

lives in St. Louis with her husband and two children. She devotes her time to enjoying her family, writing, avoiding anyone who tries to explain the intricacies of the computer and searching for the fabled housecleaning fairies. She's had her best luck with her writing—for which she's garnered *Romantic Times* Career Achievement awards in Category Romance and Suspense, and four RITA awards from the Romance Writers of America—and her family, without whom she couldn't have managed any of the other. She hasn't given up on those fairies, though.

Stranded!

Stephanie James
Patricia Gardner Evans
Kathleen Korbel

Silhouette Books

Published by Silhouette Books

America's Publisher of Contemporary Romance

SILHOUETTE BOOKS

by Request

STRANDED!

Copyright © 1995 by Harlequin Enterprises B.V.

ISBN 0-373-20108-7

THE SILVER SNARE
Copyright © 1983 by Jayne Krentz, Inc.

FLASHPOINT
Copyright © 1986 by Patricia Gardner Evans

A STRANGER'S SMILE
Copyright © 1986 by Eileen Dreyer

CONTENTS

A Note from Stephanie James

Dear Reader,

I'm delighted that Silhouette has reissued one of my early books, *The Silver Snare,* for this collection. I hope you enjoy it.

For a man and a woman who strike sparks off each other under even the most civilized conditions, there's nothing like getting stranded to bring out the real people beneath the well-mannered facades.

Jessie and Lucas, the heroine and hero of *The Silver Snare,* are two strong people who clash from the start. A battle of wills ensues when they find themselves stranded in the desert. But love has a way of negotiating a passionate truce.

The underlying theme of this collection, that of finding oneself stranded with the person one is fated to love, is an enduring element in romance. You'll soon see why.

Yours,

Stephanié James

THE SILVER SNARE

Stephanie James

For my brother Jim

One

The clash of wills occurred within hours after the commuter plane shuddered to a jarring halt on the floor of the desert canyon. Jessica Travers lost the battle—decisively.

She had moved instinctively into the power vacuum that had developed among the handful of frightened passengers, operating with the calm authority of a woman who was accustomed to bringing order out of chaos. It had been her fate to have the seat closest to the small door of the de Havilland Twin Otter; she had gotten it open almost before the plane had skewed to a halt. Then she had reached for the seat belts of the two children sitting on the opposite side of the twenty-passenger craft. Thank God there are only seven people on board beside the pilot and co-pilot, she thought as she hustled the two wide-eyed children out the door and turned to give quiet, forceful orders to the pair of elderly women seated farther forward.

The women obeyed with compelling urgency, assisted by the young man ahead of them. As the three of them exited the cabin, Jessica glanced back with a frown, mentally counting heads. There should have been one more passenger, she thought, bracing herself for the leap onto the ground.

Then she saw him, the quiet man with the iron-gray eyes who had been sitting far forward. He had ducked into the cockpit and now he was hurrying back down the narrow aisle.

"Pilot's dead. Can't tell about the other one. Get the hell out!"

Jessica hitched up the skirt of the ivory gabardine suit and jumped, her high-heeled sandals clutched in one hand. The man with the iron-colored eyes was right behind her. Together they raced to join the others, who hovered at a safe distance. The entire evacuation had taken only seconds.

For a critical few moments everyone stood in shaky, stunned silence, waiting to see if the plane would explode into flames. Then, without a word, Jessica joined the quiet man when he started purposefully back toward the stricken aircraft.

"Stay here," he ordered, as he realized she was accompanying him.

Jessica ignored him. "If the co-pilot's injured you'll need help getting him out. It doesn't look as if the plane's going to catch fire."

The co-pilot was unconscious. Together they pulled him from the cockpit and settled him gently on the ground. The waning desert sun beat down on the small group as they gathered around anxiously. Jessica knelt beside the injured man and examined him, using the basic first aid techniques she had learned in a course given to her staff of hotel employees two years earlier. Her gently probing fingers found the swelling bulge on the back of his head.

"We'll have to assume concussion at this point," she sighed, getting to her feet. "Let's see if we can get him into the shade."

It was obvious the rest of the group was accepting her leadership and that of the man beside her. Jessica took the implied responsibility with an equanimity born of experience. She was accustomed to being the one in charge.

"I'm Lucas Kincaid," the gray-eyed man told her as they worked together that afternoon supervising the unloading of the aircraft and soothing the anxieties of the others.

"Jessica Travers. Call me Jessie," she offered in return.

For a time they had worked in harmony, each assuming different chores. It was Lucas who, with the aid of the young man named Dave, took charge of burying the pilot. Jessica assigned the two elderly sisters to soothe the children's fears and then climbed back into the plane to see how many sandwiches had been packed on board as snacks for the passengers. They were in luck. Most commuter planes this size carried no food at all, but the airline had been competing for customers, apparently, and had started offering some light fare. The co-pilot was to have passed out the plastic-wrapped sandwiches at midpoint in the flight, together with a canned drink.

Water, fortunately, was not going to be a problem. The stream running through the desert canyon flowed clear and clean.

Sensing the innate authority in the two strong-minded people who had taken charge, the other passengers seemed more than willing to do as they were told. The trouble didn't start until the instructions Jessica and Lucas were giving began to conflict.

Confusion was the first response when Lucas calmly countermanded an order Jessica had given for the collection of firewood. Several other incidents followed until a new and more immediate tension began to ripple through the small group. Jessica felt it almost at once. She had enough experience handling people to know what was happening. The group would follow the strongest leader. It was as if they were a herd of wild animals waiting for the order of dominance to be clearly established.

The clash of wills grew steadily more imminent during the afternoon. Even the children were looking confused and anxious, their eyes moving questioningly from one adult to the other. It was clear a battle was shaping up over the issue of who would be in charge.

Jessica, accustomed to the refinements of an established corporate structure, which frowned on open warfare in favor of subtle behind-the-scenes maneuvering, was unprepared for the manner of confrontation Lucas forced upon her, however. Instead of a quiet argument carried out away from the others, he brought matters to a head in front of the rest of the passengers.

She knew instinctively that he'd done it that way on purpose. The man wanted no question as to which of them had won the battle. His primitive approach to leadership angered her.

In the end Lucas chose a relatively minor issue, an excuse really, to bring the conflict out into the open. Later Jessica remembered only that the war had been conducted over an insignificant discussion about what to use for boiling stream water.

"That's enough, Jessie," Lucas had announced in his soft, gravelly voice as he rose slowly to his feet beside the fire he'd been building. "I think it's time we solved the problem which seems to be developing here."

There was enough steel buried in his words to catch the attention of the others at once. A taut, curious silence descended on the small group. Everyone, including Jessica, knew the showdown had arrived.

Slowly she eyed the man who was challenging the authority she wielded so automatically. As if in response to an invitation for physical battle, her senses leaped into full alert, the adrenaline pouring into her bloodstream.

Lucas Kincaid was not particularly tall, probably about five-foot ten or eleven inches, but there was a compact, lean strength in him that registered itself at once. The faded jeans he was wearing rode low on narrow hips, fitting closely to the smoothly muscled thighs. The khaki shirt stretched across sinewy shoulders and the hard planes of his chest. The clothing didn't reveal an ounce of fat and Jessica doubted there was any to be found on that strong, well-coordinated frame.

The quiet power in his body was mirrored in the bluntly carved lines of a fiercely unhandsome face and in the cool, watchful depths of iron-gray eyes. Lucas Kincaid was probably around thirty-five or thirty-six, Jessica estimated; he exuded masculine authority. He exerted it now with the confident dominance of a man who was accustomed to command. Military? she wondered fleetingly. Perhaps someone who had once captained a ship? Certainly he wasn't from her own polished world of sophisticated hotels and beautifully organized conventions.

She knew what he saw when he looked at her, and the knowledge didn't add to her composure. The ivory business suit was dusty and stained, although the narrow skirt and the tiny-collared yellow blouse revealed the full curve of her hips, her small waist, and the gentle shape of her small, tip-tilted breasts. Her tawny brown hair was straggling free from the sleek twist at the back of her head, and curling tendrils fell down around her shoulders.

No, she wasn't looking her executive suite best, but the disarray in her appearance did nothing to hide the clear intelligence in her aquamarine eyes or the feminine strength in a face which, while certainly not beautiful, was capable of drawing the attention of the discerning. There was a striking energy and competence in the firm lines of her nose and chin and, underlying those qualities, a gentleness that she rarely allowed to surface. Gentleness and softness were not qualities that would have stood her in good stead in her world, so Jessica had learned early to restrain them. She was twenty-nine years old, but she had been accustomed to positions of responsibility since she had been graduated from college and had gone into hotel management.

Jessica faced her opponent, for that was how she now thought of Lucas, with a steady authority that spoke volumes and rendered her tousled appearance unimportant.

"We're all in this together," she declared forcefully. "Therefore the decisions that affect our future should be mutually agreed upon."

"This is not the sort of situation where consensus will work," Lucas told her flatly, his hands planted implacably on his lean hips as he regarded her with narrowed eyes. "Not even a consensus of two. Since I am not prepared to put my life in your hands and let you make the decisions which will be called for until we're rescued, we're left with only one viable option."

"I'm to put my life in *your* hands, is that it? Let you make the decisions which will decide our fate?" she demanded scornfully. Why did he have to handle it this way in front of the others? Why couldn't he have been a gentleman about the situation? There were more subtle ways of conducting such infighting.

"Yes." His answer was totally unyielding.

"Why should I do that? I see no reason why matters can't be evaluated and discussed as they arise." She felt the tension mount as she tossed the challenge back at him. This man wasn't going to back down. She knew it with sudden certainty. And if he wasn't going to retreat, that left her with little alternative. To drag out the war would be stupid and harmful to the others. Common sense told her as much, even as her pride urged rebellion.

"We're not going to conduct town-hall meetings on every issue which comes up. We don't have that luxury. Take my word for it, if you don't already know it; things can fall apart very quickly in a situation like this. More important, *people* can fall apart. We have no way of knowing how long we're going to be stuck here and that fact alone will contribute to a breakdown in morale. Discipline and a clearly established line of authority are our best defense. When you get back to civilization you can sue me for assuming command without benefit of a vote! But from now until help arrives, this is the way it's going to be. I'm in charge. You will take orders from me and you will not counter any of my instructions."

"Give me one good reason for appointing you our unquestioned leader!"

"I know how to survive out here. I know what we can eat and what will poison us. I know how to shelter us from the sun during the day and how to keep us warm at night. I know how to use the materials from the plane to best advantage and," he paused in the rapid-fire list so that the next words would have greater impact, "I am tougher and stronger than you are, Jessie Travers. If you want a knock-down drag-out battle to prove it, I'm willing to demonstrate."

Jessica caught her breath in amazement, a flush of anger surging into her cheeks as she realized he meant it. Lucas Kincaid was assuming control and he was prepared to enforce his rule with violence.

The resentment in her soared, but there was another element with which to contend. She was intelligent enough to believe him when he said he knew what he was doing out here in the middle of the California desert mountains. It was Lucas who had determined earlier that there was no hope of getting the plane back off the ground. Too much damage had been done during the emergency landing. And it was Lucas who had revealed the treasures in his fishing tackle box, which he had unloaded from the baggage compartment. Jessica knew the knife and other assorted implements might make all the difference in how well they ate during the next few days. And it was Lucas who knew how to use those essential tools. He knew what he was doing and he had the innate air of command that would make the others follow his orders. She might not like the way he was handling matters, but if this was the only way in which he would give the group the benefit of his knowledge, there wasn't much choice for her. She acknowledged to herself that on some very basic level she trusted him. Jessica didn't particularly like the man, but she *trusted* him.

"I'm not going to fight you for the role of exalted leader, Lucas," she told him coolly. She could almost hear the relief that went through the other passengers.

"You're accepting my authority?" he pressed.

Jessica arched one eyebrow. "You can do as you like. I wouldn't dream of engaging in a wrestling match with the one person in the crowd who owns a knife. As you suggested, I'll wait until we're rescued before I sue!"

He ignored her attempt at flippancy. "That's not good enough. Not nearly good enough, Jessie," Lucas told her very quietly. The iron in his eyes sent a shiver along her nerve endings.

"What do you want from me?" she blazed, embarrassed and infuriated over the fact that he was dragging out the scene, now that he had what he sought.

"I want absolute and unquestioning acceptance of my authority. I want to know you'll obey me without any argument or prolonged discussion. I want to know that if I tell you to jump you'll jump. Without complaining! Do I make myself very clear?"

"Very," she breathed angrily. "But I fail to see why you have to take such a feudal approach!"

"Because if I don't, you'll cause trouble from day one," he growled. "You have enough power to split the group into two factions and I think you know it. You can sow dissension and discontent. That sort of thing could cost us our lives if we're here very long. I'm taking steps to ensure our survival by ensuring your obedience."

He was right, Jessica admitted silently, as they faced each other. His way might anger her, but it might also stand the best chance of working. Lucas Kincaid's survival skills might be all that stood between them and disaster. Out of the corner of her eye she saw the frightened, anxious expressions on the children's faces. The elderly women waited tight-lipped for the results of the showdown and the young man focused his whole attention on Lucas, which didn't particularly surprise Jessica. Dave was sporting a military-style haircut and appeared to be only recently out of boot camp. He was responding readily to the dominance in the older man.

"There's no need to play feudal lord," Jessica began determinedly, but even she could hear the surrender in her voice.

"There's every need," Lucas countered roughly. "Everyone in the group has to know exactly where you stand. I want to hear you say you'll follow orders and give me your full support."

She could feel the waves of his willpower lapping at her, reaching out to drag her under. There was no real choice, not in this time and in this place. The stakes were too basic, too critical. Lucas Kincaid wanted complete power and in exchange he offered the best hope of survival.

With a small exclamation of disgust aimed mostly at herself for the act of surrender, she nodded her head once in submission.

"All right, Lucas. You're in charge. I will do as you say."

"No arguments?"

"When you get back home, I suggest you sign up for some of the new management training techniques," she said dryly. "Your approach is a little unpolished."

"Answer me!" he grated.

Jessica blinked. "No arguments," she agreed softly. Inwardly she was seething.

He studied her coldly for a moment longer, as if assessing the depths of her submission; then apparently satisfied, he turned away on one booted heel to issue a series of instructions that sent the others scurrying in several directions. When he'd finished, he turned back to Jessica. "You can get those sandwiches ready. We'll have them for dinner. Not much large enough to eat in that stream."

Jessica resisted the urge to say "Yes, Sir!" Without a word she started toward the box of food. She felt the iron eyes following her for a moment longer, but she didn't glance back.

Later as they sat around the fire on the seat cushions they had removed from the plane's cabin, Lucas explained that they would stay with the plane.

"Our best bet is the ELT," he said quietly in response to a query from Dave.

"What's an ELT?" Abby, one of the two older women, asked. Sharon and Matt, the children, listened solemnly.

"It stands for *Emergency Locating Transmitter*. All aircraft are required to carry them now. I checked earlier and it's functioning, putting out a signal which can be detected for about a hundred and fifty miles. That's the way the searchers will home in on us."

Before she could stop herself, Jessica asked the first question which popped into her head. "But won't the walls of the canyons block that signal?"

"To some extent, yes. It may take a while for people to find us, but they *will* find us. All we have to do is stay alive and healthy until someone picks up that signal."

The others nodded, accepting his certainty of rescue with gratitude. Jessica frowned thoughtfully, glancing across at the co-pilot who had been swimming in and out of consciousness all afternoon. "What killed the pilot? The rest of us survived the landing."

"My guess is he was dead before we hit the ground," Lucas said. "He didn't appear to be injured. A heart attack, perhaps. We probably owe our lives to the co-pilot, who had to take over at the last minute."

Jessica said nothing further. She was keeping her communications with Lucas short and to the point. The memory of the humiliating scene he had put her through earlier would stay with her a long, long time, regardless of how soon help arrived. She felt his eyes on her from time to time during the evening, but she was careful to give him no opportunity to complain about her behavior. Her submission had at least one good side benefit, she noted wryly. The rest of the small group had relaxed and were now functioning as a team, their confidence in Lucas plain to see.

She awoke often during that first night, shifting uncomfortably on the bed of seat cushions and adjusting the makeshift covers. From time to time she crawled stiffly out of bed to check on the condition of the co-pilot, whose name, according to the small tag on his uniform, was Gary Franklin. She had changed earlier into a pair of fashionable mocha suede pants. She'd packed them for the resort to which she had been heading when the plane went down; she was glad now of the added warmth. They weren't in any danger of freezing here in the canyon, but the night was chill, nevertheless.

The fire was burning low, but it gave off a certain primitive comfort just by its presence. Jessica knelt beside Gary and automatically checked his pulse. He didn't seem to be getting any worse, she thought in relief. Placing her hand on his brow, she noted a faint warmth, though, and hoped he wasn't in danger of developing a fever.

About to crawl back to her crude bed, Jessica realized that the little girl, Sharon, was watching her, a silent plea in her blue eyes as she lay very still beneath the sheepskin jacket Lucas had provided as a blanket.

Responding to that ancient call for comfort, Jessica moved over to the child.

"Warm enough, honey?" she whispered, adjusting the jacket with a soothing touch.

Mutely, the little girl nodded. Then a tiny tear trickled down her cheek, reflecting in the firelight. "Do you think my daddy will be looking for Matt and me? We were on our way to visit him."

"Oh, yes; by now he'll be looking very hard for you and Matt," Jessica murmured, her heart going out to the frightened child. "He'll have a lot of people helping him look, too, you know. They'll find us, don't worry. And until they do find us, Lucas will take care of everything." She amazed herself with the ready way the assurance came to her lips. Strange how you could trust a man you never wanted to see again!

"Lucas was mad at you this afternoon, wasn't he?" Sharon whispered anxiously.

With a stifled sigh, Jessica responded to the need for reassurance. "Yes, he was," she said calmly. "I was arguing with him, you see. I won't argue with him anymore."

"My mommy and daddy used to argue a lot. Then Daddy went away. Now Matt and I only get to visit him when school is over for the year."

The unspoken question behind the words came through to Jessica and her mouth curved ruefully. "You don't have to worry, honey. I won't argue with Lucas and he won't go away and leave us."

"Good." Sharon yawned and settled down into the cushions. "Matt hates arguments," she explained with the maturity of an older sister.

"I know how he feels," Jessica grumbled under her breath as she gave in to the impulse to bend down and kiss the girl's forehead.

Then she climbed to her feet and moved silently back toward her own pile of cushions, the socks Dave had loaned her giving little protection against the hard ground. It was going to be a long night.

She was halfway back around the fire, moving past Lucas's quiet form, when he snaked out a strong hand and encircled her ankle. Startled, Jessica swallowed an exclamation of surprise and glanced down. In the dancing firelight she saw the intent gray eyes studying her. She came to a halt and waited obediently.

"Thanks for the vote of confidence," he muttered in that dark, gravelly voice.

"Hardly necessary," she drawled softly. "You're not running this show by putting matters to a vote." The fingers around her ankle tightened dangerously.

"No arguments, remember? You promised me and you just promised Sharon."

Jessica closed her eyes for a few seconds, drawing strength and patience.

"No arguments. You're welcome to the vote of confidence." She opened her eyes again and waited for him to release her.

"Thanks. When this is all over are you ever going to speak to me again?" he demanded, almost whimsically, examining her shadowed features.

"When this is all over," Jessica responded carefully, "I doubt that we shall ever see each other again. The issue won't arise."

He let that pass. "About what happened this afternoon..."

Jessica waited. Was he going to apologize?

"I had to do it, you know. You're a strong-willed woman. You could have been very dangerous."

"Don't worry, I'm not going to play Mr. Christian to your Captain Bligh." No, there wouldn't be any apology from this man. An explanation perhaps, from time to time, but never an apology.

"Good. I'd hate to have to order you to be tied to the mast and flogged!" he said wryly, releasing her ankle as if her skin had become overly warm to the touch. He turned his back on her, apparently going back to sleep without any effort at all. Cautiously, feeling as if she'd had a near miss, Jessica made her way back to her bedding. She fell asleep with the memory of strong fingers wrapped around her ankle, chaining her.

During the next three days, Lucas saw to it that their lives were orderly and disciplined. Everyone had jobs, even the children, and the work was excellent therapy, Jessica acknowledged privately. Each person felt as if he or she were making a contribution to the group's survival, although there was never any question but that each looked to Lucas for leadership and direction. The co-pilot seemed to be recovering, although Jessica kept him quiet and firmly ensconced on his pile of cushions. He occasionally complained of double vision and headaches, but there seemed to be no

fever or other problem. He was content to rest. He agreed
with Lucas's guess about the pilot.

"Right after we got into trouble, he told me he might not
make it. He was in a lot of pain during the last few minutes.
I'm sure it was his heart," Gary said quietly at one point as
he sipped the tea they had made from some leaves off a
scrubby bush Lucas had identified and pronounced safe. "I
did a hell of a job on that landing, didn't I?" he added with
a regretful sigh as he morosely viewed the crippled de Havilland.

"Yes," Lucas told him firmly, "you did. We all walked
away from it, didn't we?" He slapped the younger man on
the shoulder and got to his feet.

"Lucky he was along on the flight, wasn't it?" Gary asked
thoughtfully as he finished his tea and watched Lucas moving off toward the stream.

Jessica, who was waiting to take the soft drink can she had
given him to use as a cup, nodded once, saying nothing.

The sandwiches ran out the second day and when Lucas
disappeared with Dave for an entire afternoon and returned
to camp with a brace of dead rabbits, there was mixed reaction. The children were horrified. Abby and her sister
Mabel nodded appreciatively. Gary viewed the returning
hunters hungrily. Jessica went forward to take the small,
furry bodies with practical nonchalance.

"Here, give me those. You guys look exhausted."

"You know what to do with them?" Lucas asked in surprise, releasing the trophies.

"You're looking at someone who routinely plans food for
five hundred people or more," she told him wryly. "I've
done my stint in the Scanlon kitchens. Management likes its
executives to get *involved* in the basic elements of the hotel
business."

"Scanlon?" he questioned curiously. "The Scanlon hotel chain?"

She nodded. "I'll take them down to the stream and clean
them." She lifted one brow with silent taunting. "Women's
work, I'd say, wouldn't you?"

He let that one go, probably because he didn't want to
have to clean the rabbits himself, Jessica concluded.

It wasn't until the meat was broiling over the fire that
Sharon and Matt finally made known their feelings on the
matter of eating rabbits.

"Yuck." That was from Matt, who nevertheless sniffed the smell of the sizzling meat with an attitude of expectancy.

"You're not supposed to eat rabbits," Sharon remarked reproachfully.

"One eats what is available," Abby Morgan told the child calmly. "I've eaten many a rabbit in my day." It was she who was in charge of roasting the creatures.

The two children turned faintly accusing eyes on Lucas, who surprised Jessica by throwing up his hands in mock defense. "Don't look at me like that," he begged solemnly. "This is as hard on me as it is on you. Back in San Diego I run a pet shop. How do you think I'm going to go home and look the bunnies in the face again?"

For an instant Jessica stared at him and then, unable to resist the impulse, she broke into unexpected, outright laughter. "A pet shop! I don't believe it!"

He glanced up, catching her eye over the top of Sharon's mop of blond hair. "It's true. What did you think I do for a living?" But there was a new element in the iron-gray eyes, something approaching laughter, perhaps, and something more, something infinitely dangerous to a woman.

"I hadn't given it much thought," she said quickly, turning back to the wild roots she was cooking on a sheet of metal retrieved from the plane. It was Lucas, of course, who had dug up the roots and pronounced them edible. "But I certainly wouldn't have guessed that you run a pet shop!"

"But, then, you don't know much about me, do you?" he pointed out quietly.

A faint tremor went through Jessica and she concentrated very hard on the cooking roots. "No." And I don't want to know very much, she added silently to herself. It's better if I don't. Safer.

She couldn't have explained how she had reached that conclusion, but a part of her was firmly convinced it was nothing less than the truth. It was important that she didn't relax around Lucas Kincaid. There was a tension between the two of them which, while it grew out of their initial conflict, seemed to encompass far more than a mere clash between two strong-willed people. She had known that when she'd found herself watching him in idle moments, found herself aware of him as more than a fellow survivor of a disaster. God help her, she was seeing him as a man, a male animal, and that was frightening. What made it worse and far more dangerous, was that some instinct told her he had begun to see her as more than a woman for whom he had assumed temporary responsibility. Was he seeing her as a woman who now belonged to him?

Whatever was happening between them must be firmly squelched, Jessica knew. Her mind resisted the words, for it was as if naming the tension would make it more lethal; more real. But her body recognized it with an unerring instinct that was older than time. No, she must walk carefully around this threatening element that had crept into the atmosphere between them. Lucas Kincaid had assumed absolute control over the group, but his power didn't extend to claiming her for his bed.

On the afternoon of the third day, the females in the crowd opted for a bath in the upper reaches of the cold stream. The men were banished and Sharon, Abby, Mabel, and Jessica frolicked, naked, in the chill waters, reveling in the opportunity to wash their hair and feel clean once more. There was a great deal of giggling and splashing before they emerged one by one to dry themselves on the cotton flower-print dress Mabel had designated as a towel.

"I never did like this dress," she admitted engagingly, as she used it to vigorously rub a laughing Sharon.

Dressed once again, they were striding, single-file, back toward camp, where the men waited to take their places in the stream, when the faintest movement at the edge of her vision caused Jessica to glance curiously up at the rugged canyon wall.

For an instant she could see nothing against the bright glare of desert sunlight. Then her breath caught in her throat as she halted, unnoticed, at the rear of the line. Lucas was up there, lounging with deceptive casualness on a sun-warmed rock. There was another dead rabbit dangling from the belt at his waist.

His eyes met hers as she stood staring up at him. He had been watching, Jessica realized, stricken. He had watched her bathing among the others and she knew now beyond a shadow of a doubt that he wanted her.

The knowledge surged through her senses, devastating them. For an eternity she stood in the sand beside the stream feeling singled out, earmarked, and trapped by the dominant male in the herd. Her wet hair gleamed in the sunlight, dampening the poppy-colored blouse she was wearing. A feeling of panic gripped her as she read the implacable expression carved in harsh lines on his tanned face.

The panic, she realized, horrified, wasn't so much over her patent helplessness if he chose to pursue her; rather, it was being generated by the reaction she was experiencing. There was a sense of primitive rightness about the silent claim his eyes told her he was staking. Her body was choosing to recognize that claim and accept it.

Shocked, Jessica tore her gaze away from the silent hunter on the rock. Hurrying, she trotted after the other women, instinctively seeking safety in a crowd. My God, she thought frantically, what's happening to me? I'm not a . . . a female animal to be claimed by the strongest male in the group! I don't even like the man!

Nothing was said as the afternoon turned into evening. Once again there was rabbit for supper and this time the children didn't complain. Jessica, who had been avoiding Lucas's eyes since he had returned to camp, sat tensely on her pile of cushions, eating the meat he had trapped in a snare made of fishing line.

She was chewing the sizzling, juicy food with actual enjoyment, when the inevitable occurred. Her aquamarine gaze accidentally collided with the waiting iron trap of his eyes across the flickering flames of the fire.

Jessica froze at the message she read in those cool gray depths. She could feel him willing her to acknowledge that somehow, by some primitive right, she belonged to him. He had assumed the responsibility for protecting her. He had hunted and killed to put food in her mouth. He had forced her to accept his authority. Now he was staking the most fundamental of claims.

How long before he came to her bed?

Two

The inevitable occurred on the fourth night of the ordeal and none of Jessica's lectures to herself, none of her mental preparation, quite readied her to handle the situation when the moment arrived.

It had been a difficult day. The novelty of the experience, as well as the fear, had worn off for the children. They were feeling restless and it required considerable effort on the part of everyone to keep them occupied and out of trouble. Abby was worried about a flareup of her sister's arthritis. Dave seemed unusually morose until Lucas dispatched him to check the rabbit snares, and Gary, the co-pilot, worried Jessica by sleeping more than he had the previous day.

But Lucas held his small clan together with firmness, reassurance, and an underlying element of discipline. By dinner he had managed to exhaust everyone with a variety of chores. Each member of the group, including Jessica, was more than ready for bed.

She crawled onto the arrangement of seat cushions, fleeting thoughts of the warmth and comfort of her own bed at home going through her head. After this she would no longer complain about the problems of living in a hotel apartment provided by management!

Lucas had disappeared a few minutes earlier on a nightly walk in the moonlight, which was becoming routine for him. Jessica was deeply aware of his absence and knew she would not fall asleep until he had slipped silently back into camp and taken his own bed. Last night she had lain awake nearly an hour waiting for him to return.

She understood his need for the time to himself after the others were asleep. Lucas gave a considerable amount to the group during the day. The responsibility he had assumed was enormous and he discharged it faithfully. Jessica could well comprehend his desire for some solitude to recharge his energies. The loneliness of command, she thought to herself with a wry smile.

Again, he didn't return for almost an hour and when Jessica finally sensed his presence at the edge of the firelight, she knew that something was different tonight. This time he would not go quietly to his bed on the other side of the fire. Jessica's pulse began to beat more quickly at the telltale points of throat and wrist. Her body was reacting to the dangerous element in the atmosphere before her mind had fully understood it.

She lay with the stillness of a small animal in hiding, watching Lucas through her lashes. He stood silently in the shadows, gazing steadily at the outline of her body. She didn't dare move as a wave of electrical tension flickered between them. The others around the campfire slept peacefully, unaware of the elemental drama being played out in the moonlight.

Then he started toward her, his booted feet making barely a sound on the desert sand. Eyes half-closed and veiled with tawny lashes, Jessica watched him approach, knowing what was on his mind. Her body sang its knowledge of what he wanted.

It was up to her, she told herself. If she called out, made a small scene and awoke the others, Lucas would stop. God help her, what was she going to do? Why wasn't she arousing Abby or Mabel? Perhaps if she pretended to be asleep he would turn back to his own bed.

Before she could sort out a logical course of action, Lucas was beside her, crouching down on one knee and reaching out to finger a curling tendril of her hair as it lay across the cushion. Wordlessly she stared up at him, all pretence of sleep gone. Her nerves were thrillingly alert and wary and alive. It would have been totally impossible to fake sleep.

He knelt with his back to the firelight and his rugged face was in deep shadow even as the dying flames flared revealingly across her own taut features.

Slowly he dropped the coil of hair and moved his rough fingertips gently to the line of her cheek. Lucas traced the contours of her face deliberately, as if he would later be modeling them in clay. Jessica trembled as he stroked her jaw to her chin and then shaped the outline of her lips. She realized with exquisite sensitivity that she wasn't the only one trembling. The force of his desire communicated itself on a fundamental level, calling to her senses. He wanted her. More than that, Lucas wanted her to reciprocate the emotion.

The swelling, flashing response in her veins sent another shudder along her nerves and Jessica was appalled at the strength of her reaction. Here in the shadows, warmed by the fading fire and the power of his need, she *did* want him. Her body ached to meet the sensual demand in the man kneeling beside her, longed to please and satisfy her mate.

Unthinkingly she turned her lips into his palm as he cupped her face and dropped the gentlest of small kisses against his skin.

"Jessie!"

Her name was a tight, near-silent plea and command as his hand slid down to find her wrist. The gray depths of his eyes reflected the silver of moonlight as he slowly straightened, tugging her up beside him. Helpless in the grip of the twin trap of her own strange longing and his undeniable desire, Jessica rose obediently beside him, her eyes never leaving his face.

Without a word he reached down to snag the lightweight windbreaker she had spread over her clothed figure as a blanket; then he was moving off with her in tow, leading her away from the safety and comfort of the campfire. Jessica wasn't sure that anything could have broken the grip of those strong fingers around her wrist at that moment. Nor was she certain she would have welcomed any attempt to do so.

What was happening seemed right and inevitable. She found herself trailing Lucas in silent acquiescence as he led her along the stream to a sandy clearing swathed in privacy and moonlight. There, far out of sight and sound of the others, he halted and turned to her.

She looked up at him, her wrist still chained in his grasp, her mouth slightly parted in unconscious invitation. Her sea-colored eyes were heavy-lidded with sensual need. The longing in her sent repeated shivers through her body.

"Jessie! Jessie, I need you tonight. I want you so badly," he rasped, his voice thick and husky. His iron-gray gaze pored over her face and the fingers of his free hand came up to probe the corner of her mouth.

"I know," she managed in a bare whisper. "I know." Jessica could not have said exactly what she was acknowledging, whether it was his desire or her own. But he read the acceptance in her eyes and with a muffled groan Lucas found her mouth with his own.

The force of his kiss seemed to strangle the breath in her body. Jessica put up her hands instinctively, trying to steady herself against his shoulders as her legs weakened dangerously. The invasion of her mouth was unlike anything she had ever experienced, wiping out the memory of other men's kisses as if they had never taken place.

Lucas wrapped his arms around her fiercely, molding her to his strong, lean length with an urgency that would not now be denied. His lips moved across hers, shaping them, dampening them so that the electrical contact seemed to flow more freely from one to the other. And when she moaned softly in reaction, he seized the moment to deepen the kiss, letting his tongue surge aggressively into the dark warmth behind her lips.

Jessica's nails sank into the fabric of the khaki shirt he wore. Only that morning she had washed that shirt along with others at the stream and left it to dry on a sun-heated rock. She had chided herself for letting him force her so easily into the stereotyped female role. Now she felt as if, having washed his clothes and cooked the food he had hunted, she had some sort of claim on him—a claim equal to the one he was exerting over her.

The deeply masculine scent of him filled her nostrils as Lucas searched the interior of her mouth, conquering and coaxing and claiming. Slowly he dropped to his knees in the sand, pulling her with him. Forcing her head gently back beneath the onslaught of his kiss, he let his fingers seek out the vulnerable line of her throat.

"Lucas! Oh, Lucas..."

The sound of his name on her lips seemed to heighten the urgency in him. He tore his mouth reluctantly from hers and buried it against her throat as he found the first button of her shirt. His hand trembled slightly as he fumbled with the

fastening and his lack of finesse somehow touched the
womanly gentleness Jessica had learned to conceal. She
sighed and leaned into him, absorbing the warmth of his
body and giving him her own in return.

Slowly, a little clumsily, he undressed her, pushing aside
the material of her shirt and finding the small curves of her
breasts with a muted exclamation of need.

"When I saw you bathing yesterday it was all I could do
not to come down and snatch you away from the others and
carry you off," he breathed shakily as he discovered the
hardening bud of her nipple with his thumb. "I saw the water glistening on your thighs and the way the sunlight colored your hair and I told myself you must have been meant
for me. Tonight I tried to walk you out of my mind and I
couldn't. I just couldn't wait any longer, Jessie."

She touched her lips to the tanned column of his neck and
then nibbled experimentally at the sensitive earlobe. "I
know," she said again. "When I saw you watching me I
knew what was going to happen."

"God, Jessie!"

He slipped her shirt off entirely and then he began to
awkwardly undo the zipper of the suede pants in which she
had been sleeping. Her own fingers moving with even less
assurance than his, Jessica undid the buttons of the khaki
shirt, sliding her fingertips inside to find the hard planes of
his chest.

She sighed as she encountered the curling crispness of hair,
tracing its outline down to the flat hardness of his taut
stomach. He whispered her name again and again as he
shaped the outline of her hips with his palms and slid the
suede pants down to her knees. Then he wrenched himself
away to spread their clothing out in a semblance of a bed and
settled her down onto it.

Slowly, kneeling beside her, he removed the last of her
garments, exposing her slender body to the light of the desert moon. She watched him through heavy lashes as he ran
his hands lightly, possessively from her throat, down across
her taut breasts, to the curve of her thigh. The thrill her
senses experienced at his touch confused and shocked her.
Her reaction to this man was uncanny and a little stunning.

Lucas stood up then and impatiently unbuckled the carved
leather belt at his waist. He shoved aside his own clothes
until he towered over her, naked and strong in the silvery
light. Wonderingly, Jessica let her eyes follow the sinewy line

of shoulder and chest and then sink lower to the uncompromising male hardness of his thighs. Her nails curved into the vulnerable inner part of her palm as she absorbed the impact of him there in the moonlight.

He came down beside her, his eyes never leaving her face. She was gathered close against his power and she hid her too-expressive features against his shoulder, arching luxuriously as he stroked the line of her spine down to its base.

He caressed her body with increasing aggression, drawing tantalizing circles on her hips one moment and clenching his fingers tightly into her curving buttocks the next. Under his touch, Jessica began to writhe and twist, seeking to get closer and closer so that she could lose herself in him.

One heavy thigh trapped her languidly shifting legs, holding her still for a moment as Lucas moved his scorching touch along the division of her rounded bottom to the flowing warmth between her thighs.

Jessica gasped at the intimate caress, but before she could respond he was pushing her onto her back, his lips going to the hard peaks of her tip-tilted breasts.

"You're perfect for me," he muttered. His tongue curled around each nipple, urging it into an even tighter bud. Then his teeth nipped excitingly until Jessica was a shivering, moaning bundle of aroused femininity beneath him.

"Lucas!"

The chill of the night was an incredible contrast to the heat of his body, she thought vaguely. It was as if all her nerves, all her senses were being brought into play for this sensual act. She was thrillingly aware of everything about the man above her, from the teasing rasp of his chest hair against her swollen breasts to the strength in the leg thrown across her thighs.

Her hands fluttered across his shoulders, her torn nails digging into the contours here and there before flitting off to explore another zone. When she found the small of his back, he pulled away slightly.

"Touch me," he half-ordered, half-pleaded and caught hold of her hand. With an aching groan he lowered it to his thigh, releasing it only when she obediently began to trace erotic little patterns there.

As if mesmerized by the wonder of him, Jessica's fingers moved closer and closer to the satin-tipped hardness of his manhood until, as if he could no longer wait for her exploring touch to find him, Lucas arched his hips, thrusting himself against her soft palm.

She gasped as he slipped into her hand, startled by the force and strength in him even as she delighted in it. For a long moment he held her close, reveling in her tender caresses, and then he freed himself to begin raining fierce kisses across her breasts and down to the curve of her stomach. Slowly he slid down her body between her legs, his fingers thrusting deeply into the silky flesh of her thighs as his kisses became more and more intimate.

When he nibbled passionately at the inside of her leg, Jessica thought she would go wild with need of him. Her fists locked violently in the pelt of his hair and she lifted her hips off the hard bed in silent confirmation of her arousal.

"Please, Lucas. Please. Now!"

Never had she felt such a stirring of violent emotion. Never had she known a man who could excite her body to such an astounding degree. Never had she known the primitive level of desire she was discovering tonight. Jessica was beyond questioning her own need. She only knew that here in the desert moonlight she must give herself to this man who was claiming her. She was his and he had every right to his claim. By the same token he belonged to her. The passion of her own claim on him was as mind-shaking as his on her. She could not, in that electric moment, conceive of ever wanting any other man but this one.

His teeth teased the silk of her inner thigh once more and then, with a low muttered cry of desire, Lucas moved back up her body, letting his fingers probe the tangle of tawny hair which shadowed the heart of her desire. She called his name with aching softness as he dazzled the most intimate secrets of her with his hand, while he kissed the curve of her shoulder hungrily.

"My woman," he breathed.

Jessica wrapped her arms around his neck. "Yes. Yes, Lucas!"

He shifted his weight, coming tightly against her softness as he covered her length with his own. Jessica gasped as she felt him slowly, inevitably fill her completely. The thrusting impact of him made her mind swirl in a sensual vertigo. Her body accepted the invasion eagerly.

He locked them together and held them both unbearably still for a long moment as if savoring the experience to the utmost. And then, as if he could no longer restrain himself,

Lucas moved against her, establishing a primeval rhythm that captured her body and chained it to his own.

Jessica gave herself up to the thrilling pattern of his lovemaking, her body responding joyously on all levels. She wrapped him close, letting him make them as one being. The coiling tension in her loins made it difficult to breathe as it tightened unbelievably. Her eyes squeezed tightly shut; her world revolved completely now around the man above her. Past and future were unimportant. Only this shivering, explosive need to satisfy and be satisfied counted in this tiny, enthralling universe.

He was losing himself in her. Jessica knew it and gloried in the knowledge. She wanted Lucas as tightly bound to her as she was to him. Together they obeyed the quickening beat of their passion until the ultimate conclusion came flashing toward them, engulfing both before they knew exactly what was happening. It was a sweeping, shattering sensation that seemed to explode the universe around them into bursting fragments of light and power.

Through the shimmering, convulsive finale, Lucas held her as if he would never let her go, her name a muffled cry on his lips that was both an endearment and an exclamation of masculine triumph and satisfaction.

Down, down they floated, their bodies still tightly locked together as the aftermath of their passion made it impossible to move for timeless moments. Slowly, eventually, reality returned there on the floor of the desert canyon. The soft gurgle of the stream, the quiet sounds of the night, the even breathing of the man in whose arms she lay, all impinged on Jessica's sense of awareness. Tentatively, she shifted beneath the heavy weight of him, her eyes opening languidly.

As if her small stirring were the catalyst needed to pull him back to reality, too, Lucas raised his head from her breast to gaze down at her softened, vulnerable face. The silver moonlight glanced off the roughly hewn planes of his cheek and jaw and his iron-gray eyes seemed to drink in her features with a deep possessiveness.

Gently, Lucas raised his hands to cup her face. It seemed a long time before he found the words he wanted. "Things won't ever be the same between us again. You know that, don't you, Jessie?" he finally grated heavily.

"Yes," she agreed very quietly. "I know that."

It was the truth and it was shattering. She had given herself to this man completely. And for no other reason than that he had reached out to take her! He had wanted her and had claimed her as if she were his by right.

Even as he rolled reluctantly to one side and helped her stumble awkwardly to her feet, Jessica began the mental tirade she knew she would be castigating herself with for a long time to come. But nothing could change what had happened between them tonight. As long as she was a part of his small tribe, subject to his leadership, Jessica knew she would be his.

She winced as her bare foot encountered a small rock and then she submitted to being dressed by her lover. No, she thought dazedly, not my lover. The dominant male in the herd. I have given myself to the male who holds the most power in this corner of the world. What did that make her?

Lucas said little as he finished getting both of them dressed and then he pulled her close against his side and started back toward the campsite. Dazed and bemused, Jessica allowed herself to be guided along the edge of the stream. Although her mind was churning with the knowledge of what had happened, her body still remembered the lovemaking and it protested the exertion. Some small voice said she should be lying in Lucas's arms until morning, not going back to her own bed alone.

Just beyond the range of the nearly dead fire with its circle of sleeping people, Lucas drew her to a halt and turned her to face him. "Whatever happens now," he murmured deeply, "you belong to me." He bent his head to brush her lips.

She stared up at him wordlessly, knowing that for the duration of the ordeal she had no choice. In this time and in this place she did, indeed, belong to him.

He released her then, returning her to the cushions that were her bed and making his way back to his own. Across the glowing embers that were all that remained of the fire, his eyes met hers as they both settled beneath makeshift blankets. Knowing herself hunted and trapped, Jessica stifled a cry deep in her throat and turned to bury her face in the cushion. She could no longer meet the masculine possession in that steady gray gaze. Morning became a time to dread. . . .

But the brilliant glow of a desert dawn brought with it the distant drone of an aircraft engine. For Jessica there was no time to think about what had happened during the night. She joined the others as they slowly awakened to the import of the plane. In taut silence the sleepy passengers sat up in their makeshift beds one by one, staring up at the pearl-bright sky.

Lucas spoke first, glancing over at Gary. "They'll hit the ELT signal any minute now."

Gary exchanged a man-to-man glance with him as he sat erect amid his array of cushions and clothes: "None too soon, either."

Sensing the undercurrent of grim understanding that was running between the two men, Jessica stared from one to the other. "What do you mean?" she asked.

Lucas shrugged, his gaze shifting to her questioning face. "The ELT runs on batteries. The signal doesn't go on forever," he replied simply.

"How long?" she managed tensely, as it began to dawn on her that the instrument in which they had all put so much trust might not have been infallible after all.

"Six to eight days maximum for that model in the Otter," Gary told her ruefully.

He had the full attention of the group now. Mabel stared at him. "You mean Lucas and you knew there was a time limit on that device? And you didn't tell us?"

"Wasn't much point in scaring everyone," Lucas drawled firmly, throwing back his covers and surging lithely to his feet.

"Do you think my daddy will be in the plane?" Matt inquired eagerly, leaping off his cushions excitedly. His question served to redirect the attention of the group and everyone once again stared skyward.

"If he's not in the plane, it's a sure bet he'll be waiting for you after the helicopter picks us up," Lucas assured the boy, ruffling the youngster's hair affectionately.

"Helicopter?" Dave asked interestedly.

"That's about all they can use to get us out of this canyon," Gary responded seriously. "It was a stroke of luck the Otter made it down in one piece. No reasonable pilot would try it if there were alternatives!"

"And here I was hoping they would send jeeps or mules at the very least!" Jessica grumbled, getting stiffly to her feet. She hid a small wince at the unfamiliar twinges in her body. Souvenirs of last night, she thought wryly; memories of what it meant to be the only available female in a herd being dominated by a virile male. She bent down to fold clothing in an attempt to hide the rush of red into her cheeks.

"Why did you want them to send out jeeps or mules, Jessie?" Sharon demanded.

"Because I have no desire to ever fly again!" Jessica forced herself to retort with a grin at the little girl. "I'll go out by helicopter if that's the only alternative, but after this, I'm sticking to ground transportation!"

"Nonsense," Gary groaned, his hand going to his head. "Don't you know statistics prove you're far safer in an airplane than you are in a car?"

"Statistics don't always outweigh emotions," Lucas put in wryly, his eyes seeking out Jessica's gaze. "I know how Jessie feels."

Before she was able to find a suitably light response, the approaching search plane swept overhead.

"They didn't see us!" Sharon yelped, stricken.

"They'll have the signal now," Lucas told her calmly. "The plane will be back. Just wait."

Sure enough, the increasing drone of the engine heralded another pass and this time the plane waggled its wingtips in recognition of their presence.

"Won't be long now," Gary sighed in satisfaction.

"Does this mean no more rabbit stew?" Abby chuckled as she climbed to her feet.

"This means Lucas has to start working on explanations to give his bunnies at the pet shop," Jessica couldn't resist putting in.

"I think I'll keep my murderous deeds a secret from them if possible," Lucas said dryly. "Something tells me they wouldn't understand."

The rescuing helicopter arrived two hours later. In the flurry and excitement of the operation, there was no time for Jessica to dwell on the events of the previous evening. She threw herself into preparations for being rescued with a vengeance, gathering up the various items of clothing and repacking the suitcases. As far as Sharon and Matt were concerned, they now regarded the whole event as a camping trip. Abby and Mabel expressed their relief in more subtle ways, but it was blatantly evident. Gary and Dave helped Lucas ensure that the fire was well and truly out.

In a way it *had* been a camping trip, Jessica reflected with a small, disbelieving shake of her head. No one had gone hungry and no one had gotten cold, thanks to Lucas. Everyone and everything was well organized and ready for the helicopter, but no one ran forward with cries of relief when

it landed. The happiness was genuine but not hysterical.
There was an unspoken knowledge that they could have held
out much longer for rescue if it had been necessary. They all
boarded rather sedately.

Jessica, seated in the noisy craft, saw the nod of cool, male
admiration the pilot gave Lucas as he came through the door
last. The man had obviously assessed the difference between the morale and health of this group and others he had
been obliged to assist during the years and knew with unerring instinct who was responsible for it. Lucas took a seat
beside Jessica as the 'copter lifted back off the canyon floor.
She was eternally grateful that the roar of whirling blades
made it impossible to talk.

Matt's and Sharon's daddy wasn't the only one waiting
when the helicopter set down on the tarmac of the small
desert town from which the search crews had been dispatched. The children's mother was also there, the quarrel
with her husband evidently forgotten, at least for the duration of the ordeal. The two ran forward to embrace their
laughing, excited offspring.

Abby and Mabel found an entire entourage of senior cit-
izens, all friends, plus two generations of family gathered in
the glaring heat of the sun. Dave was met by his father, a tall
man with the carriage of a retired military officer, who
greeted his son with barely disguised emotion.

No one came running forward to meet Lucas and as she
walked beside him toward the small waiting room, Jessica
realized that until that moment she hadn't even considered
the possibility that he might have been married. Was the rush
of relief she now experienced only because she wouldn't have
to feel guilty about having slept with a married man?

"No family here to greet you?" he asked quietly, surveying the crowd waiting at the gate.

"Scanlon will undoubtedly have sent someone," she returned calmly, searching the sea of faces.

"The hotel is your family?" He smiled wryly.

"I'm afraid so. My parents died several years ago and I
don't have any close relatives," she told him honestly.
"What about you?"

"Similar sob story, I'm afraid," he chuckled. "I doubt the
bunnies sent anyone."

That brought a smile to her lips and Jessica's eyes sparkled for a moment in genuine humor and warmth. But be-

fore she could say anything, the crowd, consisting mostly of reporters, as it turned out, was upon them.

"Jessie! Jessie! Over here!"

She turned her head at the shouted greeting, recognizing Lee Simon's worried face. The handsome man in the three-piece suit hurried forward. Behind him, parked at the curb, Jessica could see a waiting black limousine with a chauffeur standing nearby.

"Scanlon always does things with style," she had time to tell Lucas as Simon made his way through the throng of reporters and television crews. "Lee manages a resort hotel not far from here."

"I see." Lucas was ignoring the barrage of questions being aimed his way as he watched Lee Simon greet Jessica with restrained enthusiasm.

"Thank God you're all right, Jessie! Scanlon management has been deeply worried, I assure you!"

"Afraid the convention plans for the next twelve months were going to disintegrate without me to supervise them?" she teased, grateful for the greeting, even if it wasn't quite the same as having a real family member present.

"There were dire rumors to the effect that, if anything permanent had happened to you, I was going to have to fill your shoes!" Lee grinned. "God! I can't believe it! We were all so damned scared! Listen, I've got a car waiting as soon as the authorities turn you loose. I'm taking you straight back to the resort. Scanlon management left strict instructions for you to rest for two weeks before even thinking about going back to work!"

"Thanks, Lee, I intend to do exactly that!"

"You all look fairly healthy," broke in an urgent voice at her elbow. She turned to see a reporter thrusting a microphone in her face. "In fact none of you really seems to need a rest cure! How did it go out there, Miss Travers?"

Aware of Lucas standing close at her side, Jessica remembered her duty to the Scanlon hotel chain. If she was to be a source of publicity for them, she must handle it adroitly.

"We're all in excellent shape, Mr. Richardson," she announced calmly, reading the man's name tag as she spoke. "Thanks to Lucas Kincaid. Mr. Kincaid here was in charge the entire time. We all owe him our lives."

That was all it took to send the reporters swarming over Lucas. Jessica watched him virtually disappear in a sea of microphones and recording machines. Then she realized that this was her chance.

"Take me away from here, Lee," she whispered gruffly. "I'll talk to the authorities later if necessary. I just want to get away."

"You bet," he agreed instantly, taking her elbow. "Right this way, Jessie. I can't wait to get to a phone to let everyone know you're really okay."

She moved off with him, Lucas lost in the crowd behind her. She had no way of knowing, of course, how he intended to treat her now that they were safely back in civilization. Perhaps he would have lost interest immediately. Or perhaps he would have pursued her in an attempt to reestablish his claim. Either way, she knew she must escape. The memory of the past five days would be difficult enough to handle as it was.

Safe in the cushioned luxury of the air-conditioned limousine, Jessica settled back into the seat with a sigh. No, she never wanted to see Lucas Kincaid again. The man had stripped away the trappings of her sophisticated, polished world, humiliating her by forcing her to submit to his authority in front of the others and then reducing her to the status of a primitive female animal in his arms. Last night, she told herself again and again, should never have happened. She would never forgive herself for allowing it to occur. As if she'd had any choice in the matter!

That last thought brought a wave of color into her cheeks and she sat staring sightlessly out the window at the dry landscape. Lucas Kincaid had approached her on the most primitive of levels and she had accepted his right to do so. She was furious and disgusted with herself. No, she never wanted to see the man again.

Three

Three days later, Jessica surged up through the sun-warmed water of the cruise ship's pool with a feeling of incredible exhilaration. A two-week cruise from Los Angeles to Mexico, courtesy of Scanlon Hotels! No one could say her company didn't have a heart, she thought, smiling to herself as she tossed back the wet tendrils of tawny hair and braced herself lightly at the edge of the pool.

It seemed that management couldn't bring itself to believe that five days spent surviving a plane crash in a desert canyon wouldn't exhaust one of its prized executives. She had been offered the choice of two weeks in one of Scanlon's luxurious hotels on the coast or the cruise to Mexico. Knowing that she'd only end up working if she went to one of the hotels, Jessica had opted for the first available cruise.

Today was the first day of the voyage. The elegant white ship had set out with a full quota of eager passengers and a good number of them, like Jessica, had already made their way to one of the two pools on board.

Water dripped from the sleek lines of the brilliant persimmon swimsuit with its halter neckline and high-on-the-thigh cut as Jessica climbed the ladder at the edge of the pool. At one end of the pool a convenient bar was already crowded with a variety of passengers in bare feet and sunclothes. Catching up the full-sized white bathsheet which had the words "Scanlon Hotels" woven into the nap of the fabric, she quickly brushed the water from her skin and headed toward the outdoor bar.

More than one man hovering on a barstool watched her approach. Jessica ignored them, aware that they were assessing everything that went by in a swimsuit that afternoon. Sinking into one of the webbed chairs beside a small table, Jessie ordered a glass of iced tea from the whiteuniformed steward who hurried toward her.

When it arrived, it was not brought by the steward. Jessica glanced up, one eyebrow arched inquiringly, a cool smile on her lips as a man who had been seated at the bar delivered the drink with a flourish.

"I hope you don't mind. I took the liberty of having it put on my tab. I'm Kirk Randall." The man's blue eyes, set in a handsome, tennis-tanned face beneath stylishly windblown near-blond hair, smiled down at her.

Jessica hesitated and then shrugged. "Thank you," she said demurely, accepting the glass and, in so doing, his presence. "Jessica Travers. Call me Jessie."

"I was thinking of calling you a fellow hotel towel thief." Kirk grinned, sitting down beside her with alacrity. He was wearing monogrammed white shorts and a red polo shirt with a horrid little animal embroidered on the left breast. Combined with the fashionable deck shoes, his attire and manner spelled politely stated success. He was probably in his early thirties, Jessica guessed as he nodded at her white bathsheet.

"I'm afraid my collection of stolen towels is limited to those with 'Scanlon' on them," she chuckled.

"Specializing?"

"Only the best. I have an inside track, though. I work for the chain."

"That definitely gives you an unfair edge," Kirk complained good-naturedly. "I have to work much harder to collect mine. Are you, uh, traveling alone?"

No sense wasting time, is there? Jessica asked silently. Then she smiled. "Yes. I'm recuperating," she added dryly.

"Nothing serious, I hope."

"An unscheduled landing in a desert canyon."

Kirk snapped his fingers as if something had clicked mentally. "I thought you looked vaguely familiar! That little commuter plane that went down in the desert a few days ago? You and some others were stranded for four or five days, weren't you? Saw you on T.V. just before you climbed into a car and were whisked away."

"Scanlon takes good care of its own," she murmured, sipping at the iced tea. "I was protected from publicity and reporters until I could be ushered quietly on board this ship. By the time we get back to L.A. everyone will have forgotten about the whole thing."

"I won't mention it to anyone else. What a hell of an experience it must have been, though," Kirk said, shaking his head in awe.

"You know what they say about landings," Jessica quipped. "Any one you can walk away from is a good one!" The words reminded her of Lucas's reassurance to the copilot and that, in turn, reminded her that the real reason she had let Scanlon protect her from publicity was that she wanted to stay hidden from Lucas Kincaid.

Lee Simon had arranged to keep her incognito at his resort for the first twenty-four hours after the return to civilization and then he had turned her over to others from Scanlon, who had sheltered her in privacy at one of the coastal hotels. Jessica would never really know if Lucas had made any attempt to find her, but she had considered it prudent to take precautions. The feeling of running scared was a new and unwelcome one to her, but she was intelligent enough to obey her instincts. And they all screamed "run."

"Have you arranged your dinner seating?" Kirk inquired politely.

"I'll be eating at the second seating. I figure I'll need the extra time to work off all the rest of the food they serve during the day," she said smiling.

"I mean, have you arranged to share your table with anyone in particular?" he asked carefully.

"No, I said I'd be glad to mix and mingle," Jessica said with a determined airiness. Kirk Randall seemed nice enough, but the last thing she wanted to do on this voyage was tie herself to any one person for the duration of the trip.

"Well, it's probably too late to do anything about this evening, but perhaps tomorrow night we can arrange to be seated at the same table," Kirk went on hopefully.

"We'll see."

The dress Jessica chose for dinner that night was a flamboyant statement of her intention to have fun on the cruise. In red silk, it was bare at the top, ruffled at the knee-length, diagonal hem and wrapped at the hip for a dramatic effect of which she was totally aware. She paired it with strappy red heels and dangling red-and-white earrings. Then she pulled her hair into a severe knot at the nape of her neck which set off the strong, feminine lines of her face to perfection. There was nothing soft or submissive in the overall look she had achieved, Jessica told herself as she took one last look in the mirror. Instead there was sophistication, poise, and cool control sparked with a flare of independence. She nodded decisively, satisfied. Definitely not a herd doe waiting to be singled out and overcome by the head buck!

That analogy made her cringe and she turned away from her image, firmly repressing her self-disgust. She would never see Lucas Kincaid again. Now all she had to do was make herself forget what he had done to her. And the best way to forget that was to throw herself into the shipboard fun and games.

The elegant dining room was a sea of gleaming crystal, snowy tablecloths, and silver with the cruise line's crest engraved on it. White-jacketed stewards stood at the ready as the passengers who had elected the second seating filed into the paneled room. Jessica found her table readily and greeted the middle-aged couple who had already been seated there. With a friendly smile she took her seat and wondered who would be the fourth at the small table.

Around her the beautifully dressed diners assumed seats, and a pleasant hum of conversation filled the room. Jessica turned to the couple beside her and began an introductory conversation. One thing about being in the hotel business, she thought, one learned how to talk to strangers!

"This is our first cruise," Mrs. Howard confided after introductions had been made. "Bill and I have been promising it to ourselves for years. Finally, this year I told him we were going to stop putting it off!"

"Good idea." Jessica agreed and reached for the menu in front of her plate.

"Are you traveling alone?" the balding Mr. Howard inquired politely as he, too, reached for a menu.

"Yes. I'm taking a vacation. Will you just look at all this food! Knowing it's already been paid for in the cruise fare makes for a terrible temptation to have something from every category, doesn't it? Normally I would never think of ordering an appetizer and a salad and a soup and an entrée and dessert and cheese!"

Ann Howard chuckled delightedly. "We'd heard about the quantity of food we'd be receiving on board, so Bill and I took off five pounds during the past month getting ready."

Jessica laughed. "Smart thinking. I'll just have to make up my mind to take off the five pounds *after* we return to L.A.!"

"I wonder where our fourth is at this table?" Ann remarked, glancing around.

"Perhaps there isn't one." Jessica shrugged, trying to choose between the raw marinated squid and the escargot from the list of appetizers. Squid sounded good.

"Perhaps not," Ann agreed slowly and then brightened as she glanced toward the dining room entrance. "Oh, that must be him now. He's heading this way. How lucky! Another man for this table!"

Jessica glanced up automatically and abruptly the choice between squid and escargot was rendered insignificant. Lucas Kincaid was gliding purposefully across the room, his gray eyes watching her with unwavering intent.

Jessica's fingers clenched the little menu in her hand with a fierceness that wrinkled it as she watched the approach of the man with the jungle-cat hair. Her mind was a sudden whirl of chaotic reaction. Anger, fear, and dread were all mixed into the witch's brew of her emotions. Her first instinct was to run and then her blazing fury took over, keeping her firmly in her seat.

She was back in civilization now. This man no longer had any power over her. She repeated the litany again and again as Lucas came toward the table.

Unlike the other men in the room, who were wearing expensive evening jackets or dashing blazers, Lucas had on a fawn-colored corduroy jacket, which looked as if it had seen better days. The button-down shirt was of cotton instead of a more elegant fabric and the plain, dark tie appeared to be about two years out of style. The slacks, which fit his lean body well enough, were of an inexpensive polyester blend and Jessica could have sworn the low, worn boots he had on were the same ones he'd been wearing the day of the crash. Quite suddenly, as she sat there in her sophisticated red silk dress, Jessica began to regain a measure of her self-control. Lucas Kincaid had fit the rough desert scene quite well. In fact, he had dominated it. But here among the expensively attired cruise passengers, he looked out of place and out of his element.

It was that knowledge that enabled Jessica to meet his eyes as he came to a halt, one strong, short-nailed hand on the back of the vacant chair across from her.

"Hello, Jessie," he said with a smoothness which didn't quite mask the gravel in his voice. "It's lucky for me you picked a ship, isn't it? Chasing you from one Scanlon hotel to another for the past three days has been something of a chore. At least here you can't run any farther than the end of the boat!"

The color washed out of her face and then surged back, a mingling of fury and determination to maintain her control at all costs. "Hello, Lucas. I would have thought you'd have been busy putting down a bunny rebellion during the past few days, not chasing after me," she said very carelessly.

That took him back. The dark lashes lowered, hooding the iron-gray eyes speculatively. He had grown accustomed to her obedience, she realized with soaring pleasure. Lucas hadn't been expecting flippancy. Slowly he sat down, his gaze never leaving her serenely controlled features.

"I couldn't think of a good enough story to give the bunnies. It seemed safer to go after you, instead," he surprised her by saying calmly.

Ann Howard interrupted cheerfully. "Oh, how wonderful! You two know each other. I'm Ann Howard and this is my husband, Bill. Who are you and how do you happen to know Jessie, here?"

Lucas tore his eyes away from Jessie's face and managed a small smile for Ann Howard and her husband. "Lucas Kincaid. Jessie and I met a few days ago. We, uh, got separated before we could finish some business we had started. I was lucky enough to learn she was scheduled to be on this cruise."

"Lucky?" Jessica drawled, her voice implying that she thought luck had probably had little to do with his finding her.

His eyes swung back to her. "Let's just say Scanlon employees don't come cheap. I'm going to have to sell an unbelievable number of parakeets and tropical fish to cover the cost of the bribe I was forced to use!"

"Who did you bribe?" she inquired with acid sweetness.

"Why? You want to thank him?"

"I'll have his job when I return!" she shot back grimly.

He nodded, picking up his menu. "You'd do that, wouldn't you? I've learned a lot about you in the past few days, Jessie. You're very high up in the Scanlon chain, aren't you? You hold a great deal of authority."

"You were fortunate in being able to get a place on this cruise on such short notice," Bill Howard put in, clearly feeling some responsibility to lighten the atmosphere. "Wasn't it sold out?"

"There are always a few cancellations at the last minute, I guess. Since I didn't have the clout of Scanlon behind me when I booked, I was, indeed, fortunate." The iron eyes glittered as Lucas lifted his gaze to look at Jessica over the top of his menu.

He wasn't really furious, she decided, avoiding his accusing glare, just annoyed with her. That gave her one more psychological edge. Her emotions were far more violent!

The steward appeared at their table a moment later, saving Jessica from having to make further conversation. "I'll have the squid, the broccoli and red pepper salad, a small bowl of gazpacho soup and the veal with mushrooms," she ordered briskly when her turn came. Damned if she would let Lucas's presence ruin her meal!

"And for dessert?" the steward prompted helpfully.

"Well, I was going to have both the chocolate soufflé and the selection of cheeses, but I think I'll just have the cheese," she decided slowly.

"Very good." The man nodded. "And you, sir?" He turned to Lucas, who smiled wryly. "A steak and salad, please. With a baked potato on the side. Oh, and I'll try the chocolate soufflé she just turned down."

"I'm with you," Bill announced. "A good steak suits me just fine any day. Ann and I aren't all that adventurous in our eating habits, I guess. Soup, salad, and steak. Sounds good." He handed over the menu with satisfaction as his wife nodded in agreement.

"Would you care for wine?" the steward inquired before taking his leave. Having summed up the culinary expertise at the table, he turned to Jessica as he spoke. So did the others. Feeling three sets of eyes on her, as well as those of the steward, Jessica dutifully chose a soft French burgundy she hoped the others would enjoy.

The dinner conversation went rather well, all things considered, thanks chiefly to the cheerful enthusiasm of Bill and

Ann. Jessica ate her food with a relish that surprised her. Perhaps it was because the more exotic fare put one more subtle barrier between herself and Lucas. Out on the desert the basics might assume monumental importance, she told herself with an air of superiority, but here in the civilized world there was room for the finer things of life. She fully intended to enjoy them. Let Lucas eat steak and salad; she had learned to appreciate more interesting food! And the marinated raw squid tasted even better than usual.

It wasn't until she had eaten the last bite of rich Stilton cheese and realized the Howards were rising and preparing to leave that Jessica allowed herself to worry about what happened next. She caught the anticipatory gleam in Lucas's gray eyes and knew he was readying himself for a private confrontation. She had learned to read him well out there on the desert. There was no doubt but that he was going to make an attempt now to corner her.

Well, she wasn't going to sit around and wait for him to pounce! Getting quickly to her feet, Jessica smiled aloofly at the others. "I shall see you tomorrow morning at breakfast," she said politely to Bill and Ann.

"Maybe we'll run into the two of you in one of the lounges later on this evening," Ann responded warmly, glancing at Lucas as she spoke.

"Perhaps," Jessica said dryly, turning on her heel to sweep out of the dining room in a flounce of polished red silk. Her mind was made up before she reached the door. A stroll on one of the decks should serve to separate her sufficiently from Lucas. It was, after all, a big ship.

The thought that what she was doing was tantamount to running away flickered through her mind more than once, but Jessica pushed it aside. She needed a little time to think.

Lucas, however, chose not to allow her that time. He caught up with her just as she stepped outside into the balmy night air.

"A little like a night back on the desert, isn't it?" he inquired quietly as he loomed up behind her and took her elbow.

Jessica's anger and fear flared with unexpected force as she felt the strength in the hand on her arm. "No, Lucas, it's not at all like a night out on the desert," she hissed, halting to face him. "It's another world entirely. My world. And in my world you don't have any right to hound me like this! In my world you don't have any rights over me at all!"

He sighed, forcing her gently over to the railing. "I had a feeling you were going to be madder than hell."

"What did you expect?" she demanded stiffly, gazing out to sea as he lounged against the rail on one elbow and studied her tense profile. "If the situation had been reversed, how would you be feeling?"

"I can't imagine the situation in reverse," he admitted honestly.

"You can only see it from a man's point of view, is that it?"

"I am a man." He shrugged. "How else could I see it?"

Jessica heard the quiet, masculine statement of fact and shut her eyes briefly against the impossibility of ever making him understand. Then she opened them very wide and turned to look at him. "Given that insurmountable barrier," she began with emphatic steadiness, "I can only try to spell out my position very slowly and carefully and hope you can find some method of comprehending matters."

"I don't think I want to hear this."

"Your only option is to turn around and walk away. I'm flexible. If you choose that alternative I will understand!"

"After that first day on the desert you didn't yell at me like this," he complained gently.

"I am not yelling! Listen to me, Lucas," she said tightly. "I meant what I said. What happened after the crash occurred in another time and in another place. I'm home now and back to operating under my own rules, not those of some self-appointed master who thinks he has the right to take what he wants."

He nodded morosely, staring down at the foaming wake of the ship far below. "I was afraid it might take you a while to get over that little scene we went through after the landing. I knew at the time that you weren't used to taking orders and I've learned since then that you're very accustomed to giving them. It must have been difficult for you, but you're intelligent enough to realize I didn't have much choice, Jessie."

Her fingers tightened on the railing, the knuckles going white. "That *little* scene, as you so lightly put it, was only the beginning, Lucas Kincaid," she blazed fiercely. "It's going to take me a while to get over it, all right, a *long* while. But I just might manage it, eventually. I will never believe it was necessary, however. Things could have been settled between us privately, away from the others. We could have formed a leadership team, taking advantage of each other's expertise."

"Damn it, Jessie! That wasn't management training school out there! It wasn't the kind of position in which you can experiment with new theories of leadership! At least admit that the plan I instituted had the virtue of working!"

"It worked," she allowed coolly. "I'll give you that much. But don't expect me to thank you for making a fool out of me in front of six other people, and don't expect me to forgive you for the way you assumed that winning that battle gave you the right to watch me bathing, or the right to force yourself on me!"

He looked up quickly, eyes narrowing in sudden understanding. "Oh, my God," he muttered disgustedly. "So that's it. You're equating your surrender to my authority with your surrender later in my arms."

"The fact that you even use words like *surrender* to describe both instances shows how impossible it will be for us to ever establish any kind of reasonable relationship. You've wasted your time and money coming along on this cruise, Lucas Kincaid. You no longer have any rights or any power over me, do you understand? I'm not going to follow meekly as you lead me off to bed!"

"The way you did last time?" he drawled with a crooked little grin.

She looked away from the memories in those gray eyes, infuriated with herself for even bothering with the discussion. "Leave me alone, Lucas."

"I can't," he said starkly, the small grin fading as he watched her face. "I want you. You belong to me, sweetheart," he added almost gently. "And I think you know it. Do you really expect me to walk away and leave you alone?"

"Is it so hard for pet shop owners to find female companionship, then?" she challenged, appalled at his claim and just as appalled at the way she had been expecting it.

"I imagine it's tough for any man to find the right woman," Lucas acknowledged blandly. "But when he does he'd be a complete fool to let her go, wouldn't he?"

Jessica spun around to lean against the rail with all the mocking nonchalance she could muster. Arrogantly she let her eyes rove over his lean, unfashionably dressed frame. "What in hell," she asked softly, "makes you think I'm the right woman for you?"

His face hardened at the icy condescension in her words, but he undertook to answer the question. "You think the fact that you have chic, sophisticated clothes, or the fact that you order things like marinated squid instead of steak makes any real difference? Don't forget, lady, I've seen the other side of you. I've seen you get up half a dozen times in the middle of the night to check an injured man's pulse and soothe a worried kid. I've seen you wash clothes in a stream and I've seen you amuse an elderly lady by playing a game of checkers in the sand with pebbles for markers. I've also seen you looking dirty and disheveled and fighting mad but able to surrender gracefully when your common sense told you it was for the best. And last, but not least, I've known what it's like to hold you in my arms and have you give yourself completely to me when I needed you more than I've ever needed any woman in my life. Oh, yes, Jessie Travers. You're the right woman for me. Whether you realize it seems to be an issue at the moment, but I'll make sure you do before this cruise is over!"

"Your caveman tactics won't work on board this ship, Lucas!" But at the bottom of her defiance, Jessica could feel the rush of fear. He had mastered her so easily less than a week ago!

"I don't see why not. They worked once before!" His annoyance flared briefly as he reacted to the rebellion in her. "Oh, hell, Jessie," he went on disgustedly. "Don't make me say things I don't mean!"

Jessica found herself strangely gratified at the slip in his composure. Very slowly but steadily she was convincing her senses of what her mind already knew to be true: She *was* safe on this ship. Quite out of his reach. It was good to see the growing frustration in him, she realized. She wanted him to know that what had happened after the plane crash had been an aberration in her behavior. She would never again play the weak, submissive role to his dominant, aggressive one.

"I think you meant what you just said," she stated evenly. "Why not? It's the truth. Your tactics did work in that particular situation. What you're going to have to learn, Lucas, is that such situations do not constitute a normal way of life for me! It is highly unlikely that you and I will ever find ourselves in such circumstances again."

He looked at her for a long moment. "You're telling me that it takes such dramatic circumstances to release the softer side of your nature?" he finally asked silkily.

Jessica flushed. "I do not consider what happened an example of the softer side of my nature," she bit out. "I consider it an example of the primitive, female animal side of my nature!"

"You're ashamed of your behavior, aren't you?" he demanded gently. "Ashamed of not doing a better job of standing up to me immediately after the crash and ashamed of the way you gave yourself to me that night. Jessie, you've got it all wrong in your head, you little idiot! Let me show you that everything is the same between us and always will be regardless of the circumstances or the surroundings—"

She stepped back with the movement of a startled cat as he reached out, her aquamarine eyes widening with fear. When his hands fell back to his sides, Jessica forced herself to relax. He wouldn't dare try to force himself on her here, she thought. He wouldn't *dare!*

"I told you those tactics won't work," she told him with a spirited rush of confidence. "You can't just reach out and take what you want this time, Lucas."

He swore softly. "You make it sound as if you were some helpless, mindless creature I used for my own pleasure. Is that the way it was, Jessie? Are you going to stand there and tell me you would have let any man make love to you in those circumstances? Are you going to claim you would have let any male lead you off into the sand the way I did that night? Would you really have given yourself so completely to just *any* man who asked it of you the way I did?"

When Jessica flinched he relentlessly pursued his advantage, subtly closing the small gap between them at the rail. "What about it, Jessie? Going to say you were so browbeaten you would have let whichever male happened to be in charge take advantage of you?"

It was too much. Jessica lost her temper and her self-control in a flash of sheer fury. Her palm lashed out, hitting the side of his face with branding force.

For an instant stunned silence hung heavily between the two rigid figures on the deck. For her part Jessica knew an instinctive urge to run as if her life depended on it. But pride made flight impossible. Instead she faced the iron-eyed man who stood staring down at her in anger.

Eventually Lucas spoke, his fingers lifting gingerly to his reddened cheek. The tension seemed to fade a little from the lean lines of his body. "I deserved that, I suppose. My only excuse was that I was losing my temper rapidly."

"I noticed," she remarked scathingly. But her courage was flooding back as she realized he wasn't going to retaliate. "One of the many advantages of being back in civilization," she went on sweetly, "is that I don't have to fear your temper."

A slow, rueful smile unexpectedly touched the corners of his mouth. "Meaning you wouldn't have dared try that little stunt if we were still stranded out in the desert?"

Jessica lifted one shoulder in seemingly casual dismissal, a feeling of being back on top of the situation coming over her. "I would have been too terrified of cutting off the supply of rabbits."

"Well at least you had more sense than to bite the hand that fed you," he allowed, his expression softening with wry humor.

Jessica lifted her chin firmly. "In any event the situation won't arise again. History isn't likely to repeat itself. You shouldn't have come after me, Lucas."

"I had no choice," he said simply. "I want you."

Restlessly, her body reacting uneasily to his words, Jessica moved one hand in an impatient arc. "What do you want from me? An affair? Is that what you need to satisfy your ego?"

"Will you give me that much?" he countered almost whimsically.

"No!"

"You're really scared of me, aren't you?" he muttered, shaking his head in disbelief. "Jessie, that's idiotic. You can't go on holding what happened a week ago against me!"

"I don't see why not," she tossed back gamely.

"Honey, it's yourself you're trying to punish. Don't you see? I think the reason you're so angry is because during those few days you were forced into a role that revealed a side of your nature you've tried to conceal. I told you I've been learning something about you during the past few days as I chased you from one hotel to another. You're smart, you're aggressive, you've got a lot of natural authority that you've channeled into a successful career with Scanlon. Everyone I met admires you and respects you. They're also a little in awe of you, a little wary. I think for the most part they would obey you in a crisis—right down to the last man in the last ditch. You're a natural leader. But I think that none of the people I talked to has ever seen the other side of your nature. You've kept that well concealed, haven't you? To make it in a man's world you had to keep it repressed. But back in the desert I gave you no choice except to make a different kind of contribution to the group."

Jessica caught her breath. "Thank you for the elementary analysis. I'm sure you'll understand if I don't put a lot of faith in the psychoanalytical capabilities of a pet shop owner! Go home and try your skills on a parakeet!"

He grimaced. "I didn't learn my analysis techniques running the pet shop," he admitted ruefully. "I learned them in a much more instructive environment!"

She blinked in surprise, unable to stifle the deep curiosity which sprang to life at his words. Before Jessica could stop herself, she was asking the inevitable question. "Where did you learn them?"

"In the streets of L.A. I was with the LAPD for eight years," he sighed, glancing down again at the foaming water far below.

"The Los Angeles Police Department? You were a cop?" she asked, astonished.

"A classic case of job burnout," he told her, his mouth skewing wryly. "Eight years of dealing with L.A. crazies and street gangs was enough to convince me I needed a career change! I got out before the job got me."

"I see," she whispered slowly. It explained a lot, Jessica thought wonderingly. It explained his tough, take-charge attitude when the chips were down and it probably explained why he thought himself qualified to analyze her behavior. An L.A. cop undoubtedly picked up a lot of basic psychology in the streets. Or *thought* he did!

"But I don't come from that world, Lucas. I come from a much more civilized, more sophisticated environment. You can't apply what you learned there to me."

"Jessie, you can't ignore what happened between us!"

"I don't see why not!"

"Damn it! I'll show you why not!" He moved, then, coming away from the rail with the effortless swiftness of a gray-eyed leopard. She was in his arms before she had time to realize she was trapped.

Four

The sweeping impact of his embrace riveted Jessica's senses. She stood perfectly still beneath the onslaught, her fingers splayed against his chest. Lucas caught her mouth as it was turned upward, lips slightly parted in astonishment. The small cry of protest was stifled in her throat.

The first impression that roared through Jessica's mind was that this kiss was from a different end of the spectrum than the ones to which she had been exposed that night in the desert. That night there had been primitive seduction and need blended with the mastery and demand. Tonight the attempt at mastery was washing out everything else.

It was as if Lucas had tired of trying to talk her back into his arms and had opted for a more direct approach. Which was, Jessica knew, precisely the case.

Initially he didn't ask for a response. Instead he seemed intent on restaking the claim he felt he'd made a few nights previously. His hands locked against the red silk dress as he pulled her firmly into place against the hardening line of his body.

When Jessica resisted, he swung halfway around, setting his back against the rail, legs braced aggressively apart. Then he propelled her intimately between the strength of his thighs so that she was off balance and cradled in the heat of him.

Through the thin silk material of her dress, Jessica was made violently aware of the arousal Lucas had no intention of concealing. He wanted her to know, wanted her to feel the masculine challenge with every fiber of her body.

The stars began to spin overhead and the gentle, rhythmic motion of the huge ship threatened to sweep Jessica into a sensuous pattern that was as old as the sea itself.

Lucas dampened her lips with the aggressive tip of his tongue and when she once again tried to make a muffled sound of protest, he seized the opportunity to swiftly invade the territory he had once before conquered so thoroughly. Jessica trembled as he established a surging, thrusting cadence within her mouth that imitated the authority with which the ship plowed through the soft swells of the Pacific.

But no ship could totally conquer the sea, she told herself fleetingly. And here with the lights and sounds of seven hundred passengers nearby, she was safe. She was safe.

That knowledge blunted the arrow of fear and wariness, which would have caused her to struggle more violently. Instead, Jessica leaned passively against him, feeling his hands begin to slide along her spine up to the bareness at her shoulders and then back to the sensitive area at the base. Her short nails sank into the fabric of the corduroy jacket with the force of little claws as her entire body began to search for something it had once known there in Lucas's arms.

"Jessie, Jessie, please don't put up unnecessary barriers between us," he ground out raggedly as he reluctantly lifted his mouth a fraction of an inch from hers. "I'll only have to tear them down and it's such a waste of time!"

"The barriers are real," she managed throatily, trying to recover from the whirling vertigo his kiss had induced. "I only want to forget everything that happened back there in the desert. Can't you understand that? I don't want to think about how I let you humiliate me, even if it did assist in my own survival! I don't want to think about the way you made me feel like a cornered doe who belongs by right to the strongest male in the herd."

"That's not the way it was!"

"That's the way I remember it!" she flung back angrily.

Instead of arguing, he sealed her mouth once more beneath his own, but this time, as if the earlier kiss had assuaged some of his immediate hunger, he let his lips move slowly, invitingly on hers. Jessica felt the deliberate seduction and knew that it was far more dangerous than the attempt at dominance.

When several happy passengers spilled out of the doorway and onto the open deck behind her, she knew she would have to take advantage of the opportunity to escape. Lucas slackened his grasp as the laughter and the good-natured comments filtered through the balmy night. His head came up slowly, freeing her mouth. When she began to pull away, he let her go, but in the process his hands slid around her rib cage, momentarily gliding possessively across her unconfined breasts.

Jessica stepped back hurriedly at the intimate touch. Her mouth was sensuously softened by his kisses. Her body tingled warmly where he had touched it and even the peak of her breast was tautening beneath the soft red silk. She knew he must have felt the budding nipple when he'd lightly passed his hand across her softness.

For a long moment they stared at each other in the shadows and Jessica knew well the memories in the gray eyes. She was very much afraid they were reflected in her own.

"You should never have come after me, Lucas," she admonished uneasily; then she turned on her heel and moved swiftly away toward the reassuring sounds of laughter and music drifting out to the deck from one of the three lounges.

Jessica threw herself into the darkened, smoky room, the red flounce of her dress swirling around her knees. Her eyes scanned the interior, searching for a vacant table. At the far end a small musical group energetically turned out dance music for the couples crowding the dance floor. A huge, circular padded bar dominated the opposite end of the room.

Concerned with the possibility that Lucas would pursue her and try to commandeer a few dances, Jessica turned toward the right, seeking some refuge in the boisterous crowd. She nearly collided with Kirk Randall, who was wearing a white evening jacket and well-tailored dark trousers. He looked every inch the elegantly casual cruise passenger, she thought fleetingly, remembering Lucas's rather battered corduroy jacket.

"I've been looking for you. How about dancing off some of that dinner? Or didn't you give in to the temptation to sample something from every section of the menu?" he grinned.

"Guilty as charged." Jessica fixed her most charming smile on her face and let him take her hand to lead her out onto the dance floor.

"I wasn't sure if you were going to end up spending the evening with that guy I saw seated at your table," Kirk remarked as he drew her into his arms. "Am I wrong or does his face seem familiar, too? Sorry," he added quickly when Jessica glanced up quizzically. "I'm one of those unlucky folks blessed with a memory for faces!"

"I'm afraid you probably saw Lucas in some of the same pictures where you saw me," she admitted with a smile. "He seems to have opted for a recuperative vacation, too."

"Kincaid, wasn't that the name?" When Jessica nodded mutely Kirk went on thoughtfully. "Quite a coincidence, his winding up on the same ship."

"Quite!"

"You two must, uh, have a lot to talk about," he suggested hesitantly.

"Not really," Jessica stated firmly. "Other than finding ourselves aboard the same ill-fated airplane, we have very little in common."

"Five days of being stranded together didn't provide enough fodder for conversation?" Kirk persisted quietly.

Jessica knew what he was getting at and her eyes hardened. "There were six other people around, Kirk. All the time."

He had the grace to redden slightly. "Sorry, I didn't mean to imply . . ."

"That we spent the five days making passionate love in the sand?" Damn! Why did she have to sound so defensive? Probably because it was too close to the truth.

"I guess the two of you really don't look like each other's type," Kirk allowed consideringly.

"We're not. Now if you don't mind, I'd rather not discuss him."

"My pleasure," he agreed readily and pulled her a little closer.

Jessica didn't spot Lucas in the lounge until after her second dance with Kirk and when she did it wasn't so much a case of spotting him as it was a feeling of awareness that prickled the skin at the nape of her neck. It was an irresistible, tingling sensation, which made her turn her head toward the far end of the crowded room, as Kirk walked her back to their small table. Lucas was at the bar, one elbow braced against the upholstered edge, one heel hooked casually over a rung of the stool he occupied with negligent ease.

He was watching her, a brooding expression in the shadowed eyes which met hers across the intervening space. He was nursing a glass of what looked like bourbon and water. Even as Jessica's glance slid away from his she saw the tall, attractive redhead slip gracefully onto the stool beside Lucas. A single man on board a cruise ship was fair game.

When Jessica saw him again he was dancing with the redhead. There was a slow, somewhat stilted style to his movements that surprised her. It was not at all the way she would have expected him to dance. Her memories were of a lean, coordinated strength that could master a woman in bed or on a dance floor. She would have expected him to be a smooth, forceful partner. Well, it was none of her business. Resolutely she tried to pick up the thread of Kirk's polished conversation.

The next time Jessica happened to see Lucas in the crowd, he was no longer with the redhead. A slightly older, sophisticated blonde was in his arms on the floor. The sight was oddly annoying.

As the evening progressed, Lucas appeared with one new woman after another. Jessica knew that statistically women outnumbered men on most cruises, so it was no wonder he seemed to have a wide choice of dancing partners. Still, it was curious that he showed no sign of settling down with any one woman for the evening. Perhaps that rather stilted style he was exhibiting was the reason!

"Looks like your friend is making up for his five days of enforced abstinence in the desert," Kirk remarked with a small chuckle as he nodded in Lucas's direction.

Jessica ignored the comment and the warmth that washed up under her cheeks at the memory of at least one night that had not exactly been a model of abstinence. She made a subtle point of shifting her gaze derisively away from the sight of Lucas partnering a very determined-looking woman who seemed weighted down in Mexican silver jewelry and little else.

"If he doesn't make a choice fairly soon, he's going to wind up spending the night alone," Kirk went on knowingly.

"Meaning you don't intend to?" Jessica demanded coolly, her head coming around sharply in automatic hauteur.

"Take it easy," Kirk soothed. "I didn't mean..." He broke off abruptly as a strong, square hand descended on Jessica's shoulder.

"Excuse me," Lucas murmured. "I'd like to dance with Jessica." The iron eyes were on Kirk's, daring him to refuse permission. Under the branding touch of his hand, Jessica froze.

Then, when Kirk made the only possible response and nodded brusquely, she sighed inwardly and got slowly to her feet. Her mouth thinned in resigned acceptance of the situation, but there was nothing particularly resigned about the unexpected flutter in the pit of her stomach. As Lucas took her wrist and led her out onto the floor without a word, Jessica was unable to halt the rush of unwelcome fantasy. She remembered only too well how he had once led her just as silently away from the safety of camp and into a dangerous embrace.

The fantasy, unfortunately, was reinforced when Lucas drew her into his arms and wrapped her possessively close. There was none of the stiff formality in his dancing now. Jessica was molded into his warmth, left no option but to accept the sensuous glide of his body.

"If you go back to his stateroom tonight, I swear I'll throttle you, Jessie."

"Nothing like a bright, charming opening conversational gambit to set a pleasant mood on the dance floor, Lucas. Have you been using that line all evening?" she inquired frostily. "Perhaps that's the reason you haven't gotten any of your other dance partners to stick around for more than one number."

"Jessie, I'm not kidding. Your preppy friend is looking for an amusing bedmate tonight and that's all!"

"I tell great jokes in bed, Lucas," she dared in sugary, reassuring tones. "I know you didn't get a full sample of my bedroom wit because of the unusual circumstances in which we found ourselves last week, but don't worry. I do try to be amusing."

His fingers dug violently into her flesh through the thin material of the silk and Jessica sucked in her breath sharply.

"Honey, I know you're only trying to provoke me, but please use another technique. I can't guarantee I'll handle that one very well," he groaned.

Safe in the crowded room, feeling an irritation which seemed to have its roots in the thought of all the women she had witnessed Lucas with that evening, Jessica purred mischievously, "I thought you could handle anything, Lucas."

He looked down at her, apparently attempting to analyze her mood. The note of caution in him was very welcome, Jessica decided. "I'm beginning to think life was simpler back there in the desert where you knew..." his voice trailed off.

"Where I knew and kept my place?" she concluded pertly, sea-green eyes gleaming now with poorly suppressed laughter. "But Lucas, I do know my place. And this time I'm going to maintain it. Out there on the desert the real problem was that I let you usurp my position. I let you put me in another place altogether. One I didn't care for and one I'll never accept again from any man!"

"Damn it, Jessie, will you stop harping on the past? I had no option last week but to do what was best for everyone. Let's just forget about it!" he snapped.

"Agreed," she drawled smoothly. "Consider it forgotten. That suits me just fine."

He stared at her warily before drawing a careful, steady breath. "Then we can start from scratch? Go on from here?"

"Why not?" She smiled brilliantly.

"Jessie, don't tease me," he growled warningly.

"I'm not. I'm willing to forget everything that happened a week ago."

He slid his hands up and down her slender back, sighing heavily with relief. Then he gently pushed her neat head down onto his shoulder. "Thank you, Jessie. It's going to be all right. I promise you."

"I'm sure it will be and now if you'll excuse me, the dance seems to be over and I must be getting back to Kirk." Her head popped up off his shoulder and her eyes burned brightly as she looked up at him.

Lucas stiffened as they came to a halt in the middle of the floor. "Jessie, I mean it! Don't tease me!" It was half a plea, half a warning.

"I wouldn't think of it. We're going to start over, remember? Pretend we've just met? You've danced one dance with every single woman in the room tonight, including me; now I must be getting back to my table. Thank you, Lucas."

She stepped away from him, but he caught her wrist. "You can't go back to him. He's only going to try to get you into his bed tonight."

"Why should you care? We've only just met. What possible difference could it make to you whom I spend the night with?" she mocked, waiting to spring her trap.

"Jessie, don't play this game," he gritted. "You know damn good and well I can't let you spend the night with him or anyone else now!"

"Why should one dance make you feel so possessive, Lucas?" she murmured.

"You're mine," he rasped softly.

"On what do you base that kind of claim?" she challenged gently.

"On the fact that I made you mine that night in the desert when I laid you down on the sand and made love to you!" His hard face was taut and rigid with the force of his muttered words.

Jessica sensed the power in him, acutely aware of the manacle-like grip encircling the small bones of her wrist. "But that's impossible, Lucas. We just met, remember? By mutual agreement we share no past!"

He must have seen the yawning trap, but he was too angry to avoid it. "I won't let you forget that part of what happened last week!"

"It was your idea," she retorted. "But I'm inclined to agree with you. It would be impossible to truly forget the whole mess. I can, however, put it behind me and ignore it. And that's exactly what I intend to do. Don't feel bad, Lucas. Starting over wouldn't have worked, anyway." She touched the side of his tense cheek with teasing fingers and felt as if she were deliberately provoking a leopard.

"Why not?" he asked vengefully.

"You're not my type. Good night, Lucas." Snatching her hand free, Jessica pivoted on one high heel and made for the small table in the corner where Kirk still waited.

She only caught scattered glimpses of him for the rest of the evening. By the time the fabulous midnight buffet was opened, Jessica thought Lucas must have given up and gone to bed. Her attention, which had been divided all evening between trying to enjoy herself with Kirk and an uneasy awareness of Lucas's presence, began to focus on the manner in which she intended to end this first night on board ship.

To give the devil his due, Lucas had a point when he claimed Kirk was hoping for a quick shipboard encounter of the sexual kind. But Jessica had been handling a wide variety of men for several years and she knew how to deal with one like Kirk Randall. Although the temptation to bait Lucas had been irresistible, she certainly had no intention of going to bed with Kirk. By the time he had walked her to her stateroom door, he had realized as much and took the sophisticated rebuff with reasonably good grace. As a gesture of appreciation for the fact that he wasn't going to be difficult, Jessica lifted her face for a goodnight kiss.

It was a warm, polished sort of kiss and it did absolutely nothing for her. She was much too polite to show it, however, as they stepped apart.

"Shall I see the purser about adjusting the dining room seating reservations?" Kirk asked tentatively, searching her face for some enthusiasm for the idea.

"Let's not bother," Jessica said quietly. "I'm sure we'll be seeing enough of each other as it is and you don't want everyone to think you're paired off with me."

"Pairing off with you doesn't seem like such a bad idea," he tried coaxingly.

"I'm sure you'd think it was by the end of the cruise," she countered dryly.

"Why?"

"Because I didn't come on board looking for a romantic fling. I'm supposed to be recuperating, remember?"

His mouth turned down wryly at the corner. "Meaning you're not interested in sharing one of these skinny little stateroom beds?"

"I'm afraid not," she said in graceful apology. There was no need to point out that her bed wasn't particularly skinny or uncomfortable. Nor was her stateroom cramped and small. Scanlon had shipped her out first class. As usual.

"Well, I've still got a lot of time to help you change your mind," Kirk said gallantly, but they both knew he would be prowling elsewhere the next day. A cruise lasted for far too short a period of time to allow a man the luxury of wasting time on elaborate courtship. "Good-night, Jessie. I'll see you around, I'm sure."

She watched him walk down the carpeted corridor and then stepped into her room and closed the door.

The sight of the dark male figure standing in the shadows and gazing out the wide stateroom window made her breath catch in her throat. "Lucas! What are you doing here? How did you get inside my room? And what the hell gives you the right in the first place?" As if to lessen the aura of masculine menace in the shadowy room, Jessica stabbed a finger at the light switch as he turned to face her. Furiously she confronted him, not wanting to admit, even to herself, how much his unexpected presence had shaken her.

"Thank you, Jessie," he said simply.

"For what?"

"For not bringing him inside your room."

"It would have served you right if we'd gone to his room instead!" she choked out.

"That wasn't likely," he returned with a rueful grimace. "I checked. His stateroom is on the same deck as mine. Inside and very small. Not even a porthole. Definitely not in the same class as the one Scanlon booked for you." He flicked an amused glance at the luxurious surroundings of her room. "I figured if you were thinking of flinging your independence in my face, you'd insist on doing it with style and in some comfort!"

"That's true," she managed seethingly. "I'm definitely not into 'roughing it.'" She hoped he got the gibe. He did.

"Except when there's no alternative?" Lucas questioned gently.

"A Scanlon employee is trained to cope. With anything!"

"And is, in turn, rewarded well by the company, I can see. What's your home like? Full of French furniture and Oriental rugs?"

"I have an apartment in a Scanlon hotel in downtown L.A. Not that it's any of your business."

"You *live* in a hotel?" He appeared somewhat staggered at the thought.

"Why not? It's a beautiful place and I'm near my work," she pointed out with a dismissing shrug.

"But a hotel! No one lives in a hotel. That's not a home!"

"It is to me and has been for some time. Look, Lucas, I'd appreciate it if you'd get out of here. It's late and I'd like to get some sleep. I signed up for that early morning aerobics dance class."

"You live in a hotel," he was saying, ignoring her request. "Scanlon has the power to whisk you away from an airport in the middle of nowhere after a media event like a plane crash, keep you incognito for three solid days, and then give you two weeks on a luxury cruise. The only person who greets you after you've been missing for five days is a representative of Scanlon. Your pool towel is embroidered with Scanlon's logo and your luggage carries a Scanlon hotel address. Tell me, if we'd had better lighting that night in the desert would I have been able to find a Scanlon tattoo somewhere on your very soft body? Do they own you? It's beginning to sound as if the firm plays the role of family in your life!''

"It does!" she shot back, annoyed.

"And when you marry?" he pursued relentlessly, appearing vastly curious.

Jessica's chin came up aggressively. "If and when I decide to marry," she emphasized carefully, "it will undoubtedly be to someone within the 'family'!''

"You really mean that, don't you?" he breathed.

"Yes!"

"That man who met you at the airport?"

"Lucas, I want you out of here! Now!" she hissed furiously.

He dismissed that, striding forward abruptly to cup her face between rough palms. "Honey, this is incredible and intolerable. You can't make a company like Scanlon into your family. You can't live in a hotel for the rest of your life! Hell, I'll bet they don't even allow you to have pets! You're too soft and womanly and gentle. I've had a chance to learn about the other side of you, don't forget. If you deny that part of your nature, you'll regret it," he told her earnestly.

"You know nothing about me. What you saw of me last week was not a normal or even a very real side of my nature. How many times do I have to tell you that?" Jessica retorted wearily; then a flash of humor lit her blue-green gaze. "Besides, I don't want a pet. Too much trouble."

He saw the warning gleam in her expression and backed down. "Okay, okay, Jessie, I don't want to send you up in flames again. Believe it or not I waited for you tonight because I wanted to tell you I'm sorry." He released her to run a hand through his dark hair. "I'm sorry," he repeated helplessly.

"About what?" she asked suspiciously.

"About making you afraid of me. About having to do what I did a week ago when I took command after the plane went down. About not realizing until now how alienated you are from the gentler side of your own nature. About trying to enforce a claim on you that you're clearly not ready to accept. About a lot of things, Jessie."

"That's quite a list. What's all this leading up to, Lucas?"

"Jessie, give me another chance. Let me show you that the part of me you saw in the desert last week isn't all there is to my nature. Honey, let me show you we're right for each other." He smiled crookedly. "I'm quite domesticated, you know. Good company, well-mannered, housebroken, and not inclined to wander."

"Any obedience training?" she heard herself ask wryly, responding to the humor in him in spite of herself.

One heavy brow lifted. "You prefer your men on a leash?"

"With a choke-chain collar!"

"Well, I'm not exactly a lap dog," he hedged carefully, "but unless I'm unduly provoked I can guarantee a certain level of obedience. I *am* anxious to please. Doesn't that count?"

"Oh, Lucas, this is ridiculous. You sound like some dog at the city pound looking for a home!"

"You're the one who seems to need a home," he countered. "Jessie, Jessie, please give yourself a chance to get to know me. Surely you don't have to fear me on board this boat. You said as much, yourself. Let me show you I'm not the man you fled from the day the helicopter picked us up and carried us back to civilization."

"Lucas, I don't..."

"Just give me your word you'll stop avoiding me. Please, sweetheart. If nothing else, at least let me have that much!"

Jessica moved uneasily. "I'm not avoiding you, Lucas," she began, and then halted the blatantly untrue protest before she could perjure herself further. "All right, I suppose I was avoiding you. But if I stop doing that, you're liable to think I want to spend my free time with you, and I don't!"

"I'll take it one step at a time, honey," he promised soothingly. "Think of me as a cute, cuddly, obedient, good-natured pet. When was the last time you owned a pet?"

"When I was six. It was a fish and it never did learn to come when I called it!" she snapped spiritedly.

He grinned. "You won't have that problem with me, I promise."

"Don't give me that spaniel look," she protested with budding laughter. She stepped away from the door and opened it for him. "Goodnight, Lucas. See if you can't scent your way back to your own room. Pretend there's a rabbit waiting there for you!"

He hesitated and then obediently moved toward the door. He paused at the threshold to stare searchingly down at her for a long moment. "I'll go. You give me your word you won't spend tomorrow running away from me again?"

Jessica's eyes chilled. "I'm not running from you, Lucas. I never run from any man!"

For a minute she feared he might call her on the lie, but then he seemed to come to a decision. Bending his head Lucas brushed his mouth against hers in the lightest of kisses and then he was gone.

For a long time Jessica stood leaning back against the door she had closed behind him. She knew she didn't dare release her grip on the knob, because then she would have to confront the unpleasant fact that her fingers were trembling. From fear? From anger? From annoyance?

The answer was that her fingers trembled from excitement. Somehow that seemed far more dangerous to acknowledge than any of the other emotions. It was an excitement she had never experienced with any other man and it made absolutely no sense at all that she should feel it around Lucas Kincaid.

The next morning, dressed in a black leotard and tights, which outlined the slender curves of her figure, Jessica threw herself energetically into following the aerobic dance instructions of a female member of the ship's entertainment staff. The before-breakfast exercise class was filled with women and one masculine, cheerfully gay couple. Among the women, Jessica was quite certain she spotted several of the singles with whom Lucas had danced the night before in the lounge. She couldn't resist sizing them up covertly. Even at this hour, their bodies growing damp with perspiration, most of them appeared quite attractive.

When the class drew to a close, it was the redhead who smiled at Jessica and crossed the deck to speak to her. "I saw you give that interesting man at the bar a whirl last night," she chuckled. "I did, too. My name's Selena Harris, by the way. Waste of time, wasn't it?"

"He, uh, did ask me to dance," Jessica admitted quietly, wiping the sheen of dampness from the back of her neck with a towel.

"Did he step all over your feet and spend the whole time apologizing?" the other woman asked, with a knowing grin.

"Well, he did apologize about a few things." Jessica hid a strange smile.

"I should have realized from the way he was dressed that he wasn't quite what I'd hoped to run into on a cruise. Not exactly the polished, sophisticated type, was he? When he wasn't apologizing, did he talk to you about such exciting topics as the care and feeding of Angel Fish?"

"We did discuss pets at one point during the evening," Jessica agreed dryly.

"Unfair, isn't it? I mean, there's something rather intriguing about the man. A certain appeal in that hard, rugged look. I was hoping he'd turn out to be a dynamic corporate executive," Selena sighed regretfully. "I fantasized about him being a ruthless fighter who had surged up the corporate ladder and now desperately needed a mate to help him share life at the top. Of course, when I got a closer look at the clothes he was wearing, I realized he had a way to go to get to the top, but, by then it was too late. I'd already committed myself to a dance."

A rich, throaty feminine laugh interrupted before Jessica was obliged to answer. She turned to see one of the blondes approaching, a rueful smile in her beautifully made-up eyes. Jessica wondered why anyone would make up her eyes for an early morning exercise class. "Sorry, couldn't help overhearing that last remark. I have a hunch we're talking about the same man. Lucas Kincaid? Personally I was hoping he'd turn out to be a wildly successful lawyer. Recently divorced, of course, and in need of consolation. But a pet shop owner? Listen, friends, I now know more about the dietary habits of hamsters than I ever really wanted to know. Where's the justice in this world when the one man in the lounge who looked like he might be terrific in bed turns out to be the meek, mild owner of a pet shop who's on a cruise for his health!"

Jessica blinked, swallowing her astonishment and the curious wave of intrigue that followed. Were they discussing the same man? Didn't they realize Lucas Kincaid was quite capable of making a woman feel stalked, cornered, and possessed? That if he chose, he could master people or situations with a will that was laced with iron?

No, she realized a second later, these two didn't know what she had learned the hard way. They had no idea of the existence of another side of Lucas's personality.

The knowledge that only she was aware of the secret sent a thrill along her nerve endings, together with a flash of dark humor. Lucas had promised her he was housebroken and reasonably obedient. These women wouldn't have doubted such a promise for an instant. The image of a leopard on a leash flashed through Jessica's mind as she walked back to her cabin for a shower before breakfast. The notion of Lucas Kincaid leashed and under control was deeply challenging.

Five

The enticing mental picture of a dangerous jungle cat on a leash, the end of which was held in her hand, was still flickering in and out of Jessica's head later that morning as she took her seat at breakfast. Lucas and the Howards were already there, sipping coffee and poring over the extensive menu.

"Good morning, everyone," she sang out with a cheerfulness which appeared to take all three of her seatmates by surprise. Of one accord they all glanced up.

"Good morning, Jessie. You look as if you had a restful night," Mrs. Howard ventured hopefully. Jessica felt a pang of remorse. Had she intimidated these nice people by making them witnesses to the undeniable tension between herself and Lucas?

"Must be the sea air and an early morning exercise class," she told Ann Howard with mock gravity as she sat down and picked up the menu. "What's for breakfast?"

"Just about everything you can possibly imagine," Lucas said politely. "Except marinated squid. Mercifully, the chef seems willing to save that for dinner. I'm not sure the three of us could stand to watch you eat it at this hour of the day." His gray gaze moved over her with a veiled expression, taking in the attractive picture she made, invigorated and lively from the aerobics class.

Jessica had changed into a rakish white cotton camp shirt and white pants. Her tawny hair was brushed straight back and caught with a clip at the nape of her neck. She looked and felt carefree and prepared to enjoy her vacation to the fullest. When Lucas's gaze settled questioningly on her face, Jessica returned the glance with a charming smile. "One should always be open to new experiences, Lucas," she admonished in response to his remark about the squid. "As someone once said, one eats what's available." It had been Abby Morgan's comment to the children about the suitability of eating rabbit and Jessica saw at once that he remembered it.

Humor replaced the shuttered, watchful gleam in Lucas's eyes and she could almost see him relaxing as he realized she was going to banter with him. He looked very good to her this morning, she found herself thinking vaguely. Automatically she tried to put the face of the man she knew into the frame her dance-class companions had created. It didn't fit very well. Lucas was wearing a pair of jeans and a white cotton shirt, open at the throat and with the sleeves rolled casually up on his forearms. His hair appeared to have been first tossed by the wind and then combed roughly with his hand and she guessed he'd been for an early morning jog around the upper deck. Some mornings his hair had looked precisely the same way out in the desert when he'd risen early to start a small fire for the brush tea.

There was something infinitely compelling about the conflicting image of a domesticated cat and a sleek wild animal. She had been so certain that Lucas was the latter, yet those other women had been equally sure they had been dancing with a rather dull tabby. Perhaps they were all correct. Perhaps there was more than one side to Lucas, just as he had claimed. What would it be like for a woman to know both sides?

"Is something unfastened that shouldn't be?" Lucas inquired, breaking into her reverie.

"What?" Jessica lowered her lashes, confused. Across the table Bill Howard chuckled.

"You were staring at me and I wondered if I'd forgotten to do up something crucial," Lucas explained helpfully.

"No, no, of course not," Jessica mumbled and concentrated on the menu. "I think I'll start with the papaya and lime. What are you going to have, Ann?"

A discussion of the menu got Jessica through the next few minutes and by the time everyone at the table was digging into various egg dishes the conversation was flowing smoothly.

"I've done a little deep-sea fishing off the coast at Mazatlán," Lucas remarked in regard to a question from Bill. "I think we're due to stop there on the way back from Acapulco. We should make it a point to try to charter a boat for the day we'll be in port. It's quite an adventure."

Remembering the fishing tackle box that he'd been carrying on the plane, a spark of mischief made Jessica put in easily, "Isn't your hobby of fishing a bit difficult to justify to all the tropical fish you sell as pets?"

"Fish have a very straightforward sort of philosophy," Lucas retorted equably, eyes glinting. "They'll eat anything smaller than themselves. They would be the first to understand my right to go after what I want."

"Cold-blooded creatures," she murmured.

"Me or the fish?" he challenged gently. He was practically daring her to call him cold-blooded. If she did, Jessica knew instinctively, he would say or do something to remind her of that night in the desert sand.

"I was speaking of the fish," she demurred.

"Umm." He nodded wisely. "Rather like lady hotel executives in that the only thing they fear is something or someone bigger and stronger than they are."

Jessica's aquamarine gaze narrowed fractionally as she realized Lucas was more than willing to respond to the taunting. "Surely that's not a totally irrational fear?"

"Not for a fish," he admitted readily. "But it is for a lady executive."

"Why?"

"Because she has other means of defense besides fleeing." He took a huge bite out of a biscuit slathered with honey.

Jessica hesitated, pouring cream into her coffee. "You may be right," she said lightly.

Before Lucas could respond, Ann Howard was interrupting with a comment to the effect that they would be reaching Acapulco in two more days. Jessica had the impression the Howards had silently decided to act as referees at the dining table. "Are you going to attend that lecture on buying Mexican crafts and products, Jessie?" the older woman asked brightly.

"Yes, I think I will. I've heard the horror stories about people who thought they were getting fabulous deals on silver only to find out it was really tin!"

When the foursome broke up after breakfast, Jessica didn't try to evade Lucas as he fell into step beside her. "Where are you headed?" he asked, sliding his fingers firmly through hers.

"The pool, I think. I'm going to direct my energies into building up an appetite for the mid-morning bouillon break!

He grimaced. "Then comes lunch and then afternoon tea with scones and then dinner again. Where will it all end?"

"In a size larger swimsuit if I'm not careful," she laughed.

Lucas grinned, clearly enjoying the pleasure on her face. "No harm in that. You're a little too much on the fashionably thin side as it is."

"You could be right. Perhaps if I were a little bigger and a little stronger I wouldn't have to worry about being swallowed up."

Lucas halted, tugging her to a stop beside him, the humor vanishing immediately from his gaze as he stood looking down at her. "Jessie, you're not really afraid of me, are you?"

Jessica took a deep, considering breath. Afraid of this man who had succeeded in boring some of the most beautiful women on the ship? Afraid of him when she was surrounded by nearly a thousand other people, a large proportion of which were ship's officers? Afraid of a man who looked at her so anxiously?

"No," she declared positively. "Why should I be afraid of an ex-cop? You're no longer in a position to arrest me, are you?"

"Definitely not," he affirmed, relaxing again at the obvious humor in her. "And even if I were, at the moment I'm clearly outside my jurisdiction."

With that a new mood settled on the relationship and the day. Jessica was well aware of it. For the rest of the afternoon she found herself quite content to spend her time with Lucas. They lazed by the pool until lunch, soaking up the sun and talking idly of a variety of things, none of which included their adventure the previous week. The other women in her dancing class had been right, Jessica was forced to admit with an inner smile, Lucas did like to discuss his pet shop business.

The difference was that, unlike the other women, Jessica was astonished to discover that the subject didn't bore her at all. "What about snakes?" she inquired curiously as she lay on her back, the huge white Scanlon towel beneath her, eyes closed behind dark glasses.

"I tried one and I have a feeling I'm going to be stuck with him forever. His main appeal seems to be for small boys. I must have sold that damn snake ten different times during the past six months!"

"Ten times!" she exclaimed.

"I keep having to refund the money when the kid returns it," Lucas sighed.

"Ah, let me guess. Boy buys snake and takes it home. Mom sees snake. Kid returns snake the next day," Jessica outlined wisely.

"Usually within a few hours. Poor Clarence doesn't know whether he's coming or going." Lucas levered himself lazily up on one elbow to sip from his iced tea. "Maybe he'd be good marinated like that squid," he added thoughtfully as he lay back down on his lounger.

"Clarence is the snake?"

"Yeah."

"What does Clarence eat?"

There was silence from the next lounger for a moment. Then Lucas finally said dryly, "Snakes aren't exactly vegetarians, you know."

"Oh, no!" Jessica made a face behind her dark glasses. "Live food? You have to sacrifice cute little white mice?"

"I can usually locate a small kid to feed him for me. Kids seem to have a rather morbid scientific bent. And there's usually any number of them hanging around a pet shop."

"Snakes?"

"Kids," he corrected with a chuckle.

Jessica thought about that, her eyes still closed. "You like kids, don't you? You were terrific with Sharon and Matt." It was the first reference she had made to the five days they had spent in the desert, and she wasn't totally surprised when again there was a pause from the lounger beside her.

Jessica turned her head to glance curiously at Lucas. He was lying on his back, his lean, tanned body stretched out in the sun, and she shifted her gaze rather quickly at the sight of him clad only in sleek swim trunks. The image sent a re-

membered and unwelcome shiver of desire through her own
slender frame. Hastily she tried to bank the glowing spark.

"I like kids," Lucas finally said, slowly.

She remembered the night he'd patiently pointed out the
constellations in the desert sky to the children. "Kids and
pets," she chuckled wonderingly. "Anyone who likes kids
and pets…" She let the sentence trail off, astounded by what
she had been about to say.

"Can't be all bad?" he concluded hopefully. "What
about you, Jessie? You were pretty good with the young-
sters, yourself. I had the feeling they accepted you in the role
of surrogate mother during the five days."

"And you as the surrogate father?" she put in wryly.

"Yes," he said steadily. "When you and I, uh, hashed out
our differences of opinion, poor Sharon was afraid it was a
repeat of the kind of arguments her parents had indulged in,
wasn't she?"

"Hashed out our differences of opinion!" Jessica echoed mockingly. "That's a euphemistic phrase if ever I heard
one!"

"Well, at least you can laugh about it now," Lucas shot
back quietly. "That's a good sign."

"There's nothing like getting back to the real world to put
things into proper perspective, is there?" she returned in
liquid tones. It was the truth.

Again a pause from Lucas. "You never answered my
question."

"About kids? I don't know, Lucas," she replied honestly. "I've never spent much time around them."

"The Scanlon hotel world doesn't cater to children?" he
drawled.

"Not particularly. We aim more for the international
traveler and the vacationing, two-income couple. We get kids
into the hotels, of course, but I rarely encounter them."

"Or pets?"

She laughed. "I'm afraid we don't encourage pets, either."

"Doesn't it seem like a fantasy world sometimes?" he
persisted gently.

"Perhaps, but it's a very pleasant fantasy and it's been
good to me," she told him firmly. Her tone of voice was
meant to warn him off; he backed down at once, letting the
subject drop immediately.

The knowledge that Lucas was going out of his way not to antagonize her or push controversial subjects pleased Jessica. He was trying very hard not to offend. She relaxed a little more beneath the hot sun as the ship moved with stately grace toward its destination.

In fact, Jessica told herself as the afternoon came and went, the whole situation was becoming downright amusing. Lucas was acting as if he were walking on eggs around her. He was considerate, attentive, and careful to please, obviously determined to prove himself a charming companion. Charming to her, at least, Jessica clarified silently at one point. What would her aerobic dance companions think about him if they were in her position?

After all, nothing could alter the fact that Lucas wasn't a wealthy and recently divorced businessman or lawyer. A pet shop owner wasn't very likely to be deemed a "good catch" by some women. But Jessica knew that she, personally, had never been so deeply aware of, or intrigued by, a man in her life. Now that she seemed to have him and the situation under control, she could free her mind to examine the curious electricity that sparked between them.

That night she danced once more in Lucas's arms after dinner, amused at the benevolent smiles the Howards had showered on them during the meal. It was easy to give herself to the masculine grace of his body on the dance floor, perhaps a little too easy. Lucas held her close, folding her into the heat of his body. Later they made their way through the small, glittering casino on a lower deck. Lucas teased her into throwing several coins into a gleaming slot machine and then they wound up the evening with a walk around the moonlit deck.

Jessica was still asking herself how she would deal with him at the end of the evening as they approached her stateroom door. He silently took the key from her hand, unlocked the door and stood aside.

As he shut out the corridor behind them, she turned, pivoting smoothly around to find herself in his arms. Jessica felt the possessive but still-lashed strength in his arms as they circled her, heard her name whispered in a husky, masculine plea, and then all thought of firmly dismissing him faded from her mind as his mouth found hers. There was no harm in letting him kiss her, she thought wildly. After all, there had been no harm in him all day.

Whatever she had been subconsciously expecting from his embrace, however, one thing was immediately clear. Lucas was still bent on practicing restraint in every aspect of the relationship. For some obscure reason, that annoyed her. Jessica realized belatedly that she wanted him to want her.

Deliberately she leaned against him, her hands sliding around his neck as she let herself respond to the pull of the undeniable attraction they shared. His mouth seemed to harden with heightened desire, slowly increasing its demands. Jessica knew a part of her reveled in the reaction she was provoking. Here it was safe to indulge some of the passion that was flooding through her. Surrounded by the luxury and built-in protection of her sophisticated lifestyle, Jessica began to examine the tantalizing idea that had crept insidiously into her mind during the day. What would it be like to have an affair with Lucas Kincaid?

An affair with Lucas Kincaid. The temptation began to flicker in her head like an internal, beckoning fire. Surely such an idea should have been the last thing on her mind, given past circumstances. Or had the seed been planted out there on the desert, waiting for safe, fertile soil to grow?

"Jessie, Jessie," he groaned, prying his mouth from hers. "You're going to drive me crazy tonight and I've already spent so many sleepless nights recently!"

Confused by her own reactions and the wild notion of an affair, Jessica pulled slightly away from him, her hands fluttering with unconscious sensuality down his neck to his shoulders. "Why am I going to drive you crazy?" she whispered as his palms moved across the expanse of her back, which was bared by the small, black evening dress she had worn that evening. There had been something delightfully unexpected and mildly shocking about wearing black in the warmth of a balmy summer night. But the gown was cut with the sparseness of a sundress and it had made a dashing statement at dinner and later on the dance floor.

"Because you're going to send me away tonight, aren't you?" he answered knowingly. There was a note of resignation underlying his words. His eyes roved her face, clearly expecting to find no hope.

"Lucas," Jessica heard herself say with surprising honesty, "I'm confused. Everything is happening too quickly. This morning I never expected to find myself in this position tonight!"

"I know. Even though I'm going to lie in my bed staring at the bulkhead until dawn, I'm not complaining." His hard mouth crooked gently. "Much," he amended dryly. "I'm just grateful we've finally made a start. Goodnight, Jessie. Sleep well."

With a last, lingering caress, Lucas released her and let himself out the door, leaving Jessica staring in bemused silence at the solid sheet of painted metal.

What did she want from Lucas Kincaid? Why was she beginning to fantasize about something as dangerous as an affair with the man? Not very long ago she had told herself she never wanted to see him again!

Slowly she undressed and crawled into bed, trying to analyze her emotions. What was she trying to prove? That here in her world she could deal with a man like Lucas? That she could subtly master him the way he had once mastered her?

Restlessly she raised herself to a kneeling position on the bed, turning to gaze out at the moonlit sea beyond her stateroom window. That must be it. A part of her wanted to prove something, now that it seemed safe to do so. She wanted to know she could go to bed with the man without feeling as if she'd surrendered. She wanted to put their relationship on a sophisticated, modern, thoroughly manageable level, a level she could control beyond any question.

Jessica blinked in the darkness as the full realization hit her. There were two things she wanted now from Lucas Kincaid. She wanted to wipe out the memory of how it had been between them that night in the desert and she wanted to prove to herself that in the real world she could handle Lucas Kincaid.

Her motives clear to herself at last, Jessica had no trouble at all going straight to sleep.

The next day was spent with Lucas in a round of pleasant shipboard activities. The undemanding nature of cruise life allowed plenty of time for the subtle, teasing sensuality that flickered between Lucas and Jessica. At times she thought her delicate feminine provocation confused him. At other times he seemed grateful for it, as if he were determined not to question the reason behind her willingness to dance the intricate steps which led toward a sophisticated, modern affair. He was too good a fisherman to question his luck, Jessica thought with wry humor.

There were occasions during the day when she would find him watching her with a strangely hooded expression that would clear the instant he realized she noticed it. The expression was a little too intent, too searching, and it disturbed her, but she told herself it was a manifestation of his desire to play the game as cautiously as possible. His caution pleased her. It was as if they had changed roles and he was now the one who must wait to be chosen. That last thought occurred to her late in the afternoon as they lay once again beside the pool, recovering from tea and scones.

"What's so amusing?" Lucas suddenly demanded.

"Nothing really, I'm just relaxing," she lied. There was no way she could tell him she'd been imagining him in such a role reversal!

"Umm." He seemed skeptical and she slid a glance across at him from behind the safety of the sunglasses. "I thought you might be smiling back at one of those two guys sitting across the pool in deck chairs," he admitted.

Automatically Jessica glanced up. Two very attractive men, wearing incredibly tiny designer swim trunks, sat gazing toward Lucas and herself from behind dark glasses. Jessica's smile widened gleefully. "I'm afraid it's you they're watching, not me," she chuckled, shutting her eyes again. "I met them both in my aerobic class. Very charming and very gay."

"What?" He sounded mildly startled and then he grinned ruefully. "Oh, I see." He hesitated and then asked devilishly, "Jealous?"

Jessica pitched an ice cube from her soft drink onto his bare, warm stomach. Lucas's yelp was quite satisfying. He jackknifed erect, grabbing for her in the same motion. Before she quite realized what had happened, he had picked her up and surged to his feet, intent on tossing her into the pool.

"Lucas!" A physical shock went through her as his strong arms closed around her, rendering her helpless. Instantly the laughter died in her eyes and she went rigid in his arms. He was only teasing her, she reminded herself frantically, and she could control him. "Put me down. And not in the water!" she ordered with a fierceness unwarranted by the situation.

He halted immediately, the humor fading from his iron-colored eyes as he looked down at her in his arms and realized she meant business. "You deserve this, Jessie," he tried lightly, but he didn't open his arms and let her fall. She knew in that moment that he didn't quite dare, and a combination of relief and exhilaration soared through her. The tension seeped out of her as Jessica looked up into his face.

"Put me back on the lounger, Lucas. I have no intention of going back into the water just yet." It was a test and they both knew it. The small clash of wills would be fateful, but she knew with rising certainty that she would win it.

Without a word he swung around and set her gently back on the lounger, his face taut and concerned. She had given him a scare, Jessica thought coolly. Her mouth curved in satisfaction and relief. "Good boy," she drawled impudently, resisting the urge to reach out and pat him on the head like a puppy.

Without taking his eyes off her face, Lucas sank down on the pool chair next to hers, leaning forward with his elbows resting on his knees, his large hands clasped together. She had the feeling he had entwined his fingers in an effort to keep himself from taking hold of her. Perhaps by the throat. For a taut moment, silence reigned between them; then Lucas relaxed sufficiently to smile wryly and tug at an imaginary collar around his neck.

"I think I just felt the choke-chain," he growled.

Jessica's smile widened and then she was grinning at him. "You can't get away with some of the tactics you used a week ago. Not here in the real world," she said lightly.

He sighed and leaned back in the chair. "Jessie, I was only teasing."

"I know."

"And you were only testing?" he quipped.

"Yes." Settling herself more comfortably, Jessica decided to change the subject. "Tell me, did you see any of the others after we were rescued?"

"Sharon and Matt left the airport with their parents. I didn't see them again. I'm afraid the kids read a little too much into the fact that both parents came to meet them, though," he added sadly.

"You mean they started hoping that somehow Mommy and Daddy would forgive each other?" Jessica sympathized.

"It looked that way to me. I'm afraid they'll all have to go through the break again. Do you remember how Sharon was afraid that our argument was analogous to the ones her parents apparently had had?"

"I remember. She was afraid I would make you so angry that you'd leave us all on our own out there," Jessica murmured wryly.

"But you assured her I wouldn't abandon any of you because of an argument." He turned his head to trap her gaze. "It's the truth, Jessie. I wouldn't walk out on you because of an argument."

"Well, it was a pretty safe bet you weren't the type to leave all of us alone in the desert and go off in search of personal rescue!" she retorted, deliberately misunderstanding him.

"Jessie, I'm talking about us. You and me. You can't drive me away. Do you understand what I'm saying?"

"You're saying you're the persistent type," she mocked, refusing to let him turn the conversation in such a personal direction. She wasn't ready for it. "What about the others? Did you see them?"

He hesitated and then apparently gave up his attempt to discuss their relationship. "I talked to Dave for a few minutes before he left with his father. Told him to keep in touch. He's stationed at Camp Pendleton near San Diego, so I'll probably see him again one of these days."

"He was nice. I liked him. He idolized you."

Lucas ignored that. "Abby and Mabel claim they're going to write a cookbook on a hundred and one ways to cook rabbit."

"I'll be sure to get an autographed copy," Jessica chuckled. "Even though I don't ever intend to eat rabbit again in my lifetime! What about Gary, the co-pilot?"

"Desolate at not seeing you before you cut out on us," Lucas told her bluntly.

"What do you mean?"

"The poor guy had a crush on you. You must have been aware of it. Perfectly logical, of course. You were the one he saw bending over him every time he woke up in the middle of the night with a splitting headache!"

"You're kidding!" Jessica was genuinely startled. "A crush? On me?"

"He'll get over it," Lucas decided laconically.

Jessica shook her head once in disbelief. She had been aware of no other man in that sense except Lucas.

"I would probably have been jealous as hell if I hadn't realized you were treating him strictly as a nurse treats a patient!"

"Oh, I doubt that he would have represented any sort of real threat to you, even if he hadn't been ill!" Jessica said without thinking. There was a tinge of bitterness in her words that Lucas heard immediately. "You were indisputably in charge!"

"Until I'm sure of you, any other man represents a threat," he admitted calmly.

"Fortunately here in civilization there's not much you can do about potential *threats,* is there?" she asked caustically. He just looked at her for a long moment, saying nothing, and then he signaled the steward for another iced tea.

The strange tension that had developed during their conversation had not disappeared when Jessica joined her tablemates again that evening for dinner. It was a subtle thing and she wasn't even sure the Howards were aware of it. But Lucas was, Jessica knew. He was aware of it and fearful of it, afraid that she would use it as an excuse to give him the cold shoulder. Realizing that, she took great pleasure in doing just the opposite. It was a delicious challenge, this business of keeping Lucas Kincaid hanging on tenterhooks, she decided as she ignored the wary glances of the others and eagerly consumed a plate of sashimi. The selection of raw fish served Japanese style had never tasted better. The ship's chef was excellent. After two glasses of the elegant German Riesling wine she had chosen for the table, the challenge of Lucas became more and more irresistible.

"Would you like to go see the cabaret act?" he inquired politely as they left the dining room an hour later. His hand slid possessively under her arm as she walked beside him.

"Yes, I would," Jessica said smiling. "And then perhaps some dancing?"

He nodded quickly, accepting her wishes unhesitatingly. The floor show was a well-staged production, which included comedy and magic as well as some good song-and-dance numbers. By the time the performance had ended, Jessica had made up her mind. When Lucas took her into his arms later on the dance floor, she went with a willingness that seemed to surprise him. Once again, however, he didn't ask any questions, apparently content to take whatever was offered.

She could feel the sensual tension radiating from his body as the night deepened around them and knew that her own body was vibrating in response. Her decision had been made and now she allowed her excitement full scope. It thrilled her to know that he was as aware of the gathering storm as she, but still trying desperately to keep himself under control. Was he so afraid she would turn away again tonight? Jessica thought wonderingly.

"Jessie?" he rasped heavily as he led her out of the lounge and into the soft, sea-scented night on the open deck. She said nothing, not trusting herself to speak, but nestled into the hard warmth of his shoulder. Wordlessly he held her, his strong hands working against her skin with violently repressed desire. Feeling it, she moved against him, her fingertips sliding up along the sleeve of his corduroy jacket. He groaned and held her lower body against his hardening thighs, letting her know the full extent of his need.

"Oh, Lucas," she finally whispered as a shiver of anticipation and flaring heat raced through her. "Lucas, do you want me?"

"More than anything else on this earth," he breathed shakily and buried his lips in the curve of her neck. "I've never wanted any woman the way I want you. Please, darling...!"

Tonight he must beg for her. He could not simply lead her off into the wilderness and lay her down beneath the stars. Tonight the power to bestow herself rested solely in her own hands. Jessica lifted her face and the moonlight reflected softly in her aqua eyes, darkening them with ancient mystery and the glint of feminine desire. Tonight the power was hers and she could use it to obliterate the memory of how it had been between herself and Lucas a week ago. Tonight she could even the relationship; put it on a proper, modern level. Tonight she would prove to herself and to him that she could handle Lucas Kincaid.

"If I go with you," she began very softly, "it will be because I wish it."

"Yes." He didn't argue with her right to make the decision. She felt the hardness of his body and knew that it was aching for the release of a woman, but he would not argue with her right. Lucas was back in civilization now. He had no option but to play by the rules of society. "Jessie, please come to me. Let me make love to you tonight. Don't turn me away again at your door, sweetheart, I need you so badly!"

She closed her eyes and took a deep breath and then she relaxed against his tough frame. "Yes, Lucas."

She felt the shudder which went through him and then he gently lifted her chin for the softest of kisses. Very carefully, as if she were made of crystal and he was terrified of dropping her on the hard deck, Lucas wrapped her close to his side and started toward the entrance nearest to her stateroom.

balance. If she were under a spell and he was terrified of destroying her, on the hand of she, I was wracked her close to the ride and Jessica. Jessica. She ruled her the Jessica's stateroom.

Six

The red-carpeted corridor which led to Jessica's stateroom was empty at this hour. Everyone else on board was busy enjoying the extensive nightlife available. In silence Lucas walked her down the hall, reached wordlessly for her key, and opened the door. As she stepped inside her room, a sense of the inevitability of the moment assailed her, reminding her forcibly of her emotions that night under the desert sky.

The sensation alarmed her briefly. This wasn't how she wanted to feel! This time was to be different. This time everything would be on her terms. Jessica turned to confront Lucas as he shut the door behind them.

He stood still for a moment, the hard planes of his face visible in the glow of the room's soft light. The iron-colored eyes were shadowed and deep with desire. But she saw that the tension in him was more than sexual and knew he was wary. The knowledge eased the nervous uncertainty which had sprung alive in the pit of her stomach and Jessica's mouth lifted into a gentle, inviting curve. She was still in control of this moment and this man. That was the only thing that mattered.

"Jessie!" He saw the smile and stepped forward abruptly, enclosing her in his arms for long, silent seconds. They stood together, unmoving, savoring the heat of passion that was building in their bodies, and then Lucas lifted his hands to the smooth knot of her tawny hair. Slowly, reverently, he began to undo the thick mass.

"Sweetheart," he grated huskily, "you won't regret this. I'll show you everything's right between us."

"Will you, Lucas?" she breathed in soft, liquid accents. A thrill of desire rippled along her nerves as the last of her hair came down and he raked his strong hands through the tendrils.

"Yes!" The word was a groan of virile promise. Jessica felt the faint trembling in his fingers as he sensuously began to massage the delicate nape of her neck.

Slowly, in response to the spiraling anticipation uncoiling in her body, Jessica lifted her hands to Lucas's shoulders, her peach-tinted nails sinking luxuriously, tantalizingly into the roughness of his corduroy jacket. Her head arched backward as his fingers traced increasingly sensual designs on the incredibly sensitive area just above her shoulders.

"Jessie, I want you so badly. Please, please, don't ever again be frightened of me!"

"I'm not frightened of you, Lucas. Why should I be?" she dared very softly, her lips parting in a summons as old as time.

"Maybe I've got it all backward," he growled thickly as he lowered his head. "Maybe I'm the one who's scared. Of you."

"Yes," she got out huskily and then his mouth was on hers, probing, persuading, pleading. Jessica felt her entire being come shimmeringly awake to the promise of that kiss. Her nails dug more deeply into the fabric of his jacket and her mouth blossomed like a flower to invite the exquisite sting of his hovering tongue.

Lucas groaned as he surged into the dark velvet behind her lips and the strong fingers at the nape of her neck displayed an amazing sensitivity as they slid inside the low neckline of her dress. Jessica's skin seemed to tingle everywhere his hands touched her. Of her own accord she crowded closer into the furnace of his body.

The hard muscles of his taut thighs seemed to cradle her softness as Lucas found the fastening of her dress and slowly undid it. Jessica shivered as his fingers slipped inside the material and gently stroked the skin of her back. The bodice of the gown fell to her waist as she twisted urgently against him, revealing the soft swell of her unconfined breasts.

"God, Jessie!"

The thick desire in his hoarsely uttered words made her slide her hands inside the opening of his jacket, where she found the buttons of his white shirt. Lucas buried his face in the cascading fall of her hair as she exposed his hair-roughened chest to her touch. When they both stood naked from the waist up, he lifted his head to gaze down at her in wonder and still-controlled need.

Slowly he moved his hands from the base of her spine, around her waist, and up her rib cage to the point just beneath the curving weight of her breasts. The iron-colored eyes were dark pools of passion as, his gaze never leaving hers, Lucas carefully rasped his palms across the tautness of her budding nipples.

"Lucas!" She stared up at him from beneath the heavy veil of her lashes, suddenly unable to break the bonds of the iron in his eyes. There was something unbelievably seductive about the way he held her gaze as he explored the delicate tips of her breasts. Jessica knew she could have stepped back at any time, but all she wanted to do was move closer and closer to his touch.

"You're so perfect for me," he whispered, bending his head once more to find her mouth. Instead of sweeping back inside, however, he used the tip of his tongue to outline the shape of her parted lips, until she was moaning far back in the depths of her throat.

Then he swooped and picked her up in his arms, carrying her the short distance to the stateroom bed. There he set her down, still treating her as if he were handling the finest glass. Jessica lay looking up at him, hungry for the look in his eyes which told her of his desire. It fed something in her, something she told herself was a sophisticated, modern form of passion, something totally unlike what she had experienced in the desert.

Lucas stood towering above her in the soft light, drinking in the sight of her sprawled sensuously on the bed, and then his hands went to the buckle of his slacks. Jessica's hooded gaze swept over his blatantly aroused maleness as Lucas stepped out of the remainder of his clothing. Her body trembled in response.

"I could still stop this if I wished," she found herself saying with an unexpected urgency. It was as if she must convince herself as well as him about the truth of the statement.

The words had all the devastating effect she could have wished, and yet Jessica was shocked at the contrition she felt as the color surged up under Lucas's skin. His whole body stiffened and the look in his gray gaze was enough to bring tears to her eyes.

"Jessie, no!" he grated, not moving.

Impulsively, knowing a desperate urge to banish the stunned expression in that hard face, Jessica put out her hand to him and lay back against the pillow. "Come to me, Lucas. I'm not going to send you away. Not tonight."

With a muffled groan he was beside her in a heavy rush, gathering her into his arms with fierce desperation. His lips found the curve of her shoulder and he began dropping quick, stinging little kisses along it up to the pulsepoint at the base of her throat. "Jessie, I would have gone out of my mind if you'd sent me away tonight."

It was the admission she wanted, wasn't it? So why did she bite her lip in a wave of remorse and tenderly stroke his smoothly muscled shoulders? Forget it, Jessica told herself quickly, you have what you want. Everything will be equal this time. Stop worrying about it and take what you need from him now.

Lucas left her throat, moving his mouth down to the swell of her breast, his hands going ahead to slide off the rest of her clothing until she lay naked beside him. When his mouth fastened deliberately on one taut nipple, Jessica moaned again and her legs shifted with languid desire.

As if in response, his hard thigh moved against her softer ones, urging them apart and opening her to his touch more completely. She felt the nip of his teeth on the aroused nipple now as he flattened his hand on her stomach and slowly began tracing circles of tightening ecstasy on her skin. They were not delicate, teasing circles; rather the rough palm of his hand moved with strong, possessive motions, asking a response from her that was answered with an arching tension in her lower body.

"Honey, you're all on fire," he muttered in tones of almost violent satisfaction. "You want me. Please say it!" he pleaded.

"I want you, Lucas." It was the truth and Jessica no longer told herself she had to deny it. Her hips lifted again against the firm touch of his hand and the silkiness of her inner thighs was teased by the roughness of the hard leg inserted between them. It was a heady combination of sensations that washed through her and they were all underlined by the subdued, but ever-present motion of the huge ship. The background throb of its engines seemed to echo the racing pulse that pounded through her veins.

"Jessie, you're the only woman in the world for me now," Lucas confessed raggedly. His stroking hand moved lower, searching out the heated center of her passion until he found his goal.

"Oh, Lucas!" At the intimate touch, Jessica cried out in a voice choked with unbelievable wonder and desire. Her mind cleared of all but the immediate sensations and the immediate knowledge of his presence. Nothing else mattered in this moment. She began to explore the contours of the hard, lean body she remembered so well, her nails circling delicately one moment, kneading deeply into his flesh the next. He gasped aloud at her touch, whispering words of encouragement that made her increasingly eager.

When she cried out once more and began to pull him closer, he suddenly drew back, however.

"Lucas?" she murmured, not understanding as he rolled onto his back. Then she saw the undiminished fire in his eyes and smiled, knowing now what he was doing. He was accepting her right to take the lead tonight, right down to the final ending. With a tight exclamation of passion, Jessica sprawled in sensual abandon across the enticing strength in him, her hair sweeping briefly across his shoulders as she lowered herself to his body.

"Jessie, you're a witch. My desert witch," he muttered, threading his hands through her hair and then sliding them down to her waist. "Make love to me, witch. I need your magic!"

She obeyed with joyous certainty, settling herself so that his body filled hers. He sucked in his breath, his fingers tightening at her hips as she brought them together with taunting, exquisite slowness. She knew he longed to complete the union in a single, thrusting movement, but Jessica took heightened pleasure in forcing a slow, mocking, intimate love-play. Lucas's body was trembling and rigid with the torture to which she was putting him, but he made no move to alter her provocative approach.

Then, when her own need overcame the urge to tantalize, Jessica sighed and succumbed to it. She could feel the shuddering groan deep in his chest as she collapsed fully against him and Lucas's arms came around her with such strength that she wondered how he had tolerated the earlier teasing. But the fleeting thought was pushed aside as he began to move under her, pulling her into the rhythm that found its echo in that of the ship that surrounded them. In tune with the sea, their bodies merged, surging together and then drawing slightly apart. It was the primitive motion of the waves that guided the pattern of their lovemaking and it was as undeniable as the sea itself.

"Jessie, my own!"

She heard her name on his lips, knew the depths of his desire, and it fed her own, stoking it to ever higher levels. The tempo of their union increased, forming now a counterpoint to the waves that rocked them so gently. The strong, muscular hips beneath her lifted with gathering force and Jessica felt Lucas's fingers dig deeply into the resilient curve of her buttocks.

Together they gave themselves up to the moment with an elemental abandon that seemed right. Jessica ceased thinking of the past or the future, throwing herself completely into the reality of the here and now. The man in whose arms she lay was the only being in the universe who counted.

When Lucas felt the small, rippling convulsion that suddenly swept over Jessica, heard his name on her lips, he tensed for one last surge of power and then followed her into the heart of the swirling storm that captured them both completely.

Down, down they tumbled, locked in each other's arms, onto the safety of the seabed. The warm water seemed to cover them both, insulating them for a time and then withdrawing its protective cloak, leaving Lucas and Jessica washed ashore.

It was several long, languorous moments before Lucas broke the filmy silence, shifting slightly to pull her gently closer as he spoke. "What are you thinking about, sweetheart?" He nibbled lazily at her earlobe, which happened to be within reach of his strong, white teeth.

"I'm wondering why you brought me back to my own stateroom instead of taking me down to yours," Jessica murmured lightly. It wasn't quite the truth, but it would serve to set a safe, easy note to the conversation. Some returning sense of caution warned her that that would be best.

"I told you the other night I'm not traveling first class," he chuckled. "And you seem to be very much a first-class sort of woman."

"So we came to my place instead of yours?" she teased, trailing her fingertips through the curling hair on his chest and playing delicately with his flat brown nipples. A sudden thought crossed her mind and she frowned. "Lucas, this trip must have cost you a fortune!"

"About a million parakeets and God knows how many hamsters," he agreed, his mouth crooking humorously. "But you're worth it."

"Thanks!" she giggled.

The laughter faded from his eyes as he gazed down into her upturned face. "Jessie, are you happy here with me tonight?"

She smiled. "Yes, Lucas. I'm happy."

He sighed heavily and his lashes closed briefly in evident relief. "You've really put me through some hoops during the past few days. Ever since you left me to face that damn crowd of newspaper reporters at the airport after we were rescued!"

"Ah, but you were the hero of the episode. It was your duty to handle the publicity afterward," she retorted deliberately.

"I had the impression you weren't terribly impressed with me in the role of hero!" he complained good-naturedly, nuzzling the soft area behind the ear he had been nibbling.

Jessica lifted one brow as she considered that. "I'd rather not talk about it, Lucas," she finally declared firmly.

"Okay. What would you like to talk about?"

"The midnight buffet?" she suggested teasingly.

"My God, woman! You just ate a few hours ago!"

"I want you to get your money's worth out of this cruise," she chuckled. "That means eating everything in sight."

"I think I'm going to need a little more exercise before I can stomach the thought of watching you gobble down raw oysters or stuffed octopus at midnight," he told her reflectively.

"Are they serving stuffed octopus at the midnight buffet?" she demanded ingenuously. "How exciting!"

"When was the last time you had some good, plain food?" he growled, his hands beginning to move enticingly on her arm.

"Several days ago, as a matter of fact. I lived off roasted rabbit for quite some time. Remember?" she shot back dryly.

"Ouch. I'd forgotten." He shrugged. "Well, that doesn't count. I'm talking about a good meat loaf and a baked potato."

She laughed. "I never eat meat loaf when I can get lobster."

"And working for Scanlon assures you the choice, right?" he concluded bluntly, pulling his head away to eye her curiously.

Jessica nodded. It was the truth. "Scanlon takes good care of me."

Lucas shook his head admonishingly. "*I'll* take good care of you," he corrected a little roughly and drew her back into his arms with a forcefulness Jessica told herself she should protest but couldn't. Not just then.

Jessica awoke the next morning with the feeling that something had been radically altered in her shipboard world. The heavy weight of a man's arm across her breasts was part of the change and she gingerly slid out from under it, turning on her side to search the sleeping face of the man next to her. In the new light filtering through the stateroom curtain, Lucas had the air of a relaxed and contented predator. The thought made Jessica uneasy and she reminded herself that he was no longer any such thing. There was no menace now in Lucas Kincaid. Last night she had proven that here in the real world she could mold more than hold her own. A strange smile tilted the edge of her mouth. She could make him jump through hoops! Hadn't he admitted as much?

"A smile like that on a woman's face first thing in the morning is enough to make any sane man refuse to face the remainder of the day!" Lucas grumbled.

"Makes you nervous?" she hazarded brightly, realizing he was studying her through his dark lashes.

"Very."

"Lucas, does something about the ship feel different?" she asked, glancing around as she realized that escaping the confinement of his arm hadn't altered her sense of change.

"We're in port," he yawned. "They've shut down the engines."

"Oh!" Kneeling excitedly, Jessica pulled back the window curtain. "We're anchored in the bay. I can see Acapulco. Come on, let's get going. I have a thousand things to look for in the shops!''

Lucas glanced idly at the watch he still wore. "They won't start ferrying people ashore for another couple of hours. There's no rush, honey.''

But he gave in to her excitement and sense of anticipation with indulgent grace and Jessica made certain they were both among the first group of passengers conveyed ashore in the small lifeboat used for that purpose.

Gleaming high-rise hotels lined the shore of Acapulco, concealing in their shadows the far poorer dwellings and shops of the people who lived in the Mexican Riviera city. They hadn't been ashore more than a few minutes when Jessica was eagerly accosted by a street vendor selling rings. She smiled aloofly and shook her head, having taken to heart the lecture on buying Mexican jewelry that had been given to the ship's passengers. But the man, undaunted, continued to entreat her to look at his wares. He spoke only a few words of English and Jessica knew only a similar number of Spanish phrases. It was Lucas who handled the situation with a rapid spate of Spanish, which surprised her.

"I didn't know you spoke the language," she observed interestedly as the vendor faded into the crowd, searching out another likely tourist.

"I've spent a lot of vacation time fishing down here," he explained easily.

"You know your way around Acapulco?" she demanded, eyes lighting.

"Reasonably well. Why?" He slid a half-amused, half-suspicious glance at her intrigued features.

"Then you must know where all the best shops are!"

"I spent my vacation time fishing, not shopping!" he protested with a grin. But nevertheless, he took her hand and hailed a taxi. Within a few hair-raising moments, they were deposited in an old section of the city and Jessica was enthralled with the collection of chic boutiques mixed in with less sophisticated but just as appealing shops.

"Jessie," he said quite seriously as she started into the nearest boutique. "Some of this part of town is pretty rough. Don't go wandering off, okay?"

She glanced around, one sandaled foot already on the first step leading to the open door. "It looks all right to me." Her brightly patterned cotton wrap dress fluttered around her knees, caught by a small breeze.

"Just take my word for it, honey," he advised, following her into the shop.

Jessica frowned at the tone of command that had surfaced momentarily in his voice. A leopard didn't change its spots overnight, she reminded herself, as she began searching through a pile of beautifully printed cotton fabrics.

But maybe this particular leopard hadn't fully realized that his spots had been changed for him!

Jessica spent the next hour wandering happily through the shops, Lucas trailing faithfully in her wake. It was drawing near lunchtime and she was carrying several packages, when she paused in front of a leathercraft store window. The shop was part of a rambling collection of such places filling every corner of a large, open-air building.

"Going to look at hand-tooled bags?" Lucas asked, seeing her fascination with an item in the window.

"What do you think of that purse?" she demanded earnestly, pointing out an elaborately carved, heavy leather bag.

"I think it looks like something you'd only wear on vacation in Mexico!" he chuckled. "Look, take your time. I'm going to check out that silver display over there. Yell if you need me," he added casually and wandered across the old terraced floor to where another vendor had set up a glittering array of polished silver items.

Jessica nodded at his back, smiling as she realized that he was finally leaving her on her own for a while. Not that there could be any danger in this particular building, with its crowds of tourists and hordes of shops. She took another look at the leather bag, her mouth turning downward doubtfully. Perhaps Lucas was right. It might be the sort of thing which looked terrific on location but would be a totally useless addition to her wardrobe back home. Abandoning the purse with a sigh of mild regret, she went on to the next shop in the open-air building.

Twenty minutes later she had come to the end of the wide hall and was about to start working her way up the opposite side of the building when she decided to glance out into the alley behind the market. She was delighted to find that several vendors had set up displays just beyond the door of the large building. A quick glance back down the hall of indoor displays did not reveal Lucas, so Jessica shrugged dismissingly and stepped out into the alley. She would just take a quick look outside and then start back toward where she had left Lucas.

It wasn't long before she realized that one intriguing alley was going to lead to another. Jessica lost track of time as she moved among the collections of pottery, crafts, and the inevitable silver, real and fake, which were set out on brightly colored cloths on the ground. Everywhere enthusiastic vendors praised their wares and her intelligence for stopping to examine them. At least, it sounded like praise to her untutored ears.

She had just declined an interestingly designed hammock, which she knew she'd never be able to hang in her hotel apartment, and had decided to go back into the main building when one last narrow alley caught her attention. She would take a quick look at the tiny shop housed at the opposite end and then she would go find Lucas. She was getting hungry.

Jessica hadn't gone more than a few steps into the warm, shadowy interior of the alley when her senses warned her she'd made a serious mistake. Uneasily, she turned but saw no one behind her. Nevertheless, the impression of being followed persisted. The shop wasn't that important, she decided quickly. She would skip it and return to the main building.

Her sandaled feet carried her quickly back the way she had come, but not quickly enough. A figure in a wide-brimmed hat and a colorful serape stepped into her path, blocking the only exit. Eyes that glittered with malice and a cold smile of evil anticipation flashed from under the hat.

"The señorita is lost?" the man inquired boldly with a totally false solicitousness as he glided forward. The accent was horrible, but Jessica understood every word.

"The señorita is *not* lost," she stated firmly, lifting her chin and walking toward the alley entrance with a self-confidence she was far from feeling. One had to be firm and unafraid in front of a man like this. Lucas had been right this time, though. She shouldn't have ventured so far from the safety of her fellow tourists. Well, she would just have to bluff her way out of the mess and then discreetly not mention anything about it to Lucas!

"I will help the señorita find her way," the man told her, far too smoothly, eyes gleaming as he took in the sight of her packages and the purse that dangled from her shoulder. "But there is a price, you understand."

"I don't need your help," she bit out, aware that the distance between herself and the man was narrowing rapidly.

So far he showed no sign of retreating. "Kindly get out of my way," she ordered briskly. Her pulse was beginning to pound with what could only be described as fear. The knowledge thoroughly annoyed her.

"There is a price for that, too, señorita," the man drawled, and quite suddenly the dappled sunlight was glinting off a knife in his hand.

Jessica halted. She wasn't prepared to try walking full tilt into a knife blade. Her heart was racing now as the adrenaline surged into her bloodstream. She would have to try screaming, she told herself. Perhaps if she threw her packages at the man and screamed loudly there would be an opportunity to escape in the confusion.

"The price for leaving this alley is your purse," the man told her coolly. He jerked the tip of the knife upward threateningly. The false smile was gone now, leaving only the hard, shadowed eyes. "Give me the purse, señorita!"

It was going to be now or never. Jessica took a tight grip on her fear and gathered herself to hurl the packages in the general direction of her accoster. The scream wouldn't take much preparation; it would come out quite naturally!

For a split-second Jessica and the man formed a frozen tableau as they confronted each other in the old alley, each waiting for the reaction of the other. And then a third figure stepped into the stark scene.

"Lucas!" Jessica's widening eyes and accompanying exclamation of relief were enough to convince her would-be assailant that there was another factor with which to contend. He spun around and saw Lucas standing, feet braced slightly apart, at the alley entrance.

In that moment Jessica knew that her jungle cat was more than capable of matching the thief when it came to sheer menace. There was a cold, dangerous aura radiating from Lucas Kincaid. The iron in his eyes had never been more evident and the assured strength in his stance spoke volumes to the man who had tried to rob Jessica. Instinctively he seemed to react to the dominance in the stranger, eyes narrowing as he backed away a pace or two.

Lucas spoke, his voice as dark and arrogantly threatening as his stance; then his hand moved in the shadows and Jessica realized with a shock that he also carried a knife. Stunned, she could only stare, listening to the sharp slice of his language as he gave commands to the other man. She didn't understand a word of the Spanish, but the effect on her assailant was immediate and electric.

Without a backward glance at Jessica, the man edged toward the front of the alley. Smoothly, slowly, Lucas stood aside and allowed him to pass, his eyes never leaving the tense figure. The other man dropped the knife in front of Lucas, who said something else and kicked the blade out into the street beyond. A moment later the thief had vanished into the maze of twisting alleys.

When he seemed convinced the would-be attacker had truly disappeared, Lucas turned back to face Jessica, who still stood, her arms piled high with packages, her eyes still wide from fright. He stared at her for a very long moment and she had the impression he was struggling for self-control.

"Are you all right?" he finally grated in a voice that was far too civil. Lowering his eyes, he knelt to slip the knife back into his low-cut boot.

"Yes. Yes, I'm fine. A little scared, but otherwise okay." What was he thinking? Why wasn't he yelling at her? He must be furious with her for disobeying his order and going off by herself to explore the far corners of the market. If the situation had been reversed, she would have been tearing a wide strip off the offender! Hadn't Lucas warned her that parts of town were very unsafe? Jessica lowered her lashes anxiously as he came toward her, preparing herself for the tirade to come. "Lucas, I'm sorry, I didn't..."

"Forget it," he got out very carefully, reaching to take some of the packages. "Are you hungry?"

"Hungry? Well, I was a few minutes ago," she acknowledged uneasily. Why didn't he get it over? Why wasn't he reading her the riot act? She could feel the palpable tension in him, could almost touch the anger that she knew simmered just under the surface. He must be absolutely enraged at her stupidity!

"Good. I know an excellent little restaurant not too far from here," he said tightly. "I think we both need a place to sit down and cool off, don't you?"

Unable to think of anything to say to that, Jessica closed her mouth and walked silently beside him as he led the way out of the alley and back toward the main thoroughfare. Desperately she tried to figure out what was happening between them. If she had done something this stupid back in the desert, Lucas would have flayed her alive; she was positive of it.

Warily she darted him a questioning sideways glance, taking in the harsh set of his face as he walked alongside her. She had the distinct impression he was practically gritting his teeth to keep from yelling at her!

And then the truth hit her with the force of a lightning bolt. Lucas Kincaid, who had just successfully faced down a thief in an alley, who had been responsible for seeing himself and seven others safely through the aftermath of a plane crash, and who had helped patrol the dangerous streets of Los Angeles for eight years, was afraid to give her the simple tongue-lashing she undoubtedly deserved!

It was ludicrous, Jessica decided dazedly. The man had nerves of iron to match his eyes, and yet he didn't quite dare to vent his wrath on her! Was he really so terrified of angering her? Had she intimidated him so completely?

The confusion that that thought created in her mind kept Jessica silent until they had been seated in a small café. She remained silent as Lucas gave their order in a tightly controlled tone of voice that totally subdued the otherwise garrulous waitress.

Finally Jessica could stand it no longer. Impulsively she reached across the table and touched his hand. He glanced down at her fingers lying over his whitened knuckles and then up at her repentant expression. "Lucas, you were right. I should never have ventured off on my own like that. My only excuse is that I never intended to wander so far. One thing led to another and I just . . ." She broke off, unable to think of any reasonable excuse under the circumstances. "Thank you," she concluded more firmly. "I was never so relieved to see anyone in my life as I was to see you standing at the entrance of that alley!"

He took a deep, steadying breath and she sensed some of the tension leave his hard frame. His eyes cleared a little and the large hand she had been touching curled around her fingers with just the smallest hint of violence.

"The important thing is that you're all right," he tried to say gallantly. Jessica knew he wanted to say a great deal more that was a great deal less than gallant, and she hid an inward smile when he so obviously bit it back. "Please, Jessie, don't ever do that to me again!"

"No, Lucas," she promised, meaning it.

He relaxed a little further as they ate spicy enchiladas and tacos and by the time they started back to the ship, Lucas was almost back to normal. Jessica kept a wary eye on him from time to time and it came to her that she probably would have felt better if he had given in to the flaring temper that had gripped him. A streak of self-honesty forced her to admit she certainly deserved a stern lecture at the least. He probably would have felt much better afterward, too.

But he was too nervous of alienating her to risk it. Incredible. Jessica wondered at that knowledge again and again during the course of the long, hot afternoon. Lucas wanted her good will so badly he had clamped down on his own perfectly natural reaction to her inexcusable actions.

Another piece of surprising self-knowledge struck Jessica later as he left her at her stateroom door to dress for dinner. She glanced in the mirror as she analyzed it critically.

It was difficult to define, but it had something to do with her own emotions when Lucas had arrived to rescue her. She had experienced more than the natural and overwhelming relief. It was something beyond gratitude, too.

It had something to do with the fact that she had a claim on his protection. When she had looked up to find him standing in the alley, prepared to defend her, Jessica had known a fierce feeling of rightness about the situation. He would take care of her. Because she belonged to him?

With a tight-lipped uneasiness, Jessica pushed that thought out of her mind and reached for the dress she intended to wear to dinner.

Seven

The message from Raul Estrada was waiting for Jessica at the purser's desk that evening. On the way into dinner with Lucas, she picked it up, slitting open the small white envelope curiously.

"From someone in Acapulco?" Lucas inquired, unabashedly trying to read over her shoulder, which was delightfully bared by the halter-necked, peacock-toned gown she wore.

"Raul Estrada. He's the manager of the Scanlon hotel here in Acapulco. He's apparently learned from someone at headquarters in L.A. that I'm on board this ship and is inviting me to spend tomorrow at the hotel." She lifted her eyes from the small note and smiled. "That will work out perfectly, won't it?" Lucas just looked at her, his gaze shuttered, and Jessica went on very brightly. "We don't sail until tomorrow evening and it would be interesting to see the local operation. I'll send word that we'll be happy to accept the invitation. Raul is an excellent host."

"He should be," Lucas observed sardonically as he took her arm and continued toward the dining room. "It's his profession, isn't it?"

"You've got a point," Jessica laughed. "You'd like to go, then?"

"I'll go. Have you met this Estrada character before?"

"Oh, yes. I've run into him occasionally at regional Scanlon meetings. He's very charming."

"A member of the family, in other words?" Lucas murmured dryly as they took their seats and greeted the Howards.

"Definitely." Jessica's smile was a little too brilliant, holding almost a hint of challenge. Lucas did not attempt to respond to it.

In fact, he remained unusually quiet throughout dinner, managing a minimum of polite conversation with Ann and Bill Howard, but little else. He eyed Jessica's order of *seviche* suspiciously, but refrained from commenting on the popular South American concoction, which consisted of raw scallops, onions, and peppers drenched in lime juice. Jessica found herself missing his teasing remarks about her choice of food. Was he still brooding about the scene in Acapulco that afternoon?

When he kissed her goodnight at her stateroom door later that evening and then turned to stride off down the carpeted corridor to his own deck, Jessica was thoroughly perplexed. She had spent most of the day in excited anticipation of how the night would end. It had never occurred to her that she wouldn't be waking in Lucas's arms the next morning.

Confused and unexpectedly annoyed by the turn of events, she shut the door behind him with undue force and locked it. If he wanted to sulk because he hadn't dared chew her out for her behavior earlier in the day, that was his problem!

Raul Estrada sent a car for them the next morning after breakfast. It was waiting on the dock when the ship's tender deposited its first load of passengers.

"I thought perhaps you might have changed your mind about coming with me this morning, Lucas," Jessica remarked a little coolly as she climbed into the back seat of the chauffeured black Mercedes with the Scanlon crest on the door.

"I wouldn't have missed this opportunity for the world," Lucas told her politely as the chauffeur shut the door crisply and slid into the driver's seat. "After all, it's a chance to get an inside look at your world. That's the Scanlon hotel at the far end of the beach, isn't it?"

From the pleasant coolness of the air-conditioned car, Jessica glanced out and saw, far in the distance, the familiar Scanlon symbol on top of a huge, white gleaming tower. "Yes, that's the slice of the Scanlon world here in Acapulco. I keep telling you, Lucas," she added, with a tiny smile, "it's a very enjoyable world. Careful you don't get seduced by it."

He turned his head to give her a sober, straight glance. "I can be seduced only by you, Jessie. Not a hotel."

She swallowed under the impact of his gaze. "Really?" she managed very bravely, "I didn't notice that you were, uh, overcome last night!" Damn! What had made her say that?

But Lucas's hard mouth, which hadn't smiled much thus far that morning began to curve into a suddenly indulgent smile. "Last night I had to work a few things out in my head. Miss me?"

Goaded, Jessica glared at him. "I'm hardly likely to admit a thing like that, am I?" Then, determined to produce an airy counterattack, she went on lightly. "What were you working out in your head, Lucas? All the things you didn't quite dare to say after you rescued me in that alley?"

"Was it so obvious?" he groaned wryly.

Impulsively Jessica patted his leg. "Don't worry, Lucas. I called myself every name in the book. I was probably harder on me than you would have been! Consider the riot act as having been read. Let's just forget the whole thing, shall we?"

He slanted her an oblique glance, ignoring her touch. "What would you have done if I'd lost my temper yesterday, Jessie?"

"Probably lost mine in turn! This way you managed to make me feel terribly guilty. Much more effective, I'm sure." She grinned.

"Does it strike you that you're becoming a little condescending?"

She heard the thin edge of sharpened steel under the words and withdrew her hand from his leg immediately. Then she went very still for a moment as her eyes locked with his. "It strikes me," she stated very carefully, "that I'm trying to make a joke out of the tension caused by yesterday's unfortunate occurrence. If you'd rather not take that approach then by all means start screaming abuse at me. I'm sure the chauffeur will be happy to turn around and take you back to the ship.''

The atmosphere inside the Mercedes was suddenly charged with the full force of their silent clash of wills. Jessica sat tensely, knowing she would win, because there was no option for Lucas other than to back down. She knew that, but even so she couldn't prevent an inward sigh of relief when he nodded his head.

"I agree. Let's forget it,'' he said quietly. "Tell me about Raul Estrada."

Jessica accepted the surrender graciously. What else could the man have done under the circumstances? She smiled with warmth and enthusiasm as the heavy car slowed in front of the ornate hotel entrance.

"You'll see for yourself in a minute. There he is now."

Raul Estrada came down the tiled steps, skirted the huge fountain in the center of the drive, and strode toward the car with a gleaming smile of urbane welcome on his handsome face. He was nearly forty and there was the smallest hint of a paunch beneath the immaculately tailored white tropical jacket he wore, but the handsome, dark face bequeathed to him by his Spanish ancestors remained well molded and attractive. He greeted Jessica as she stepped out of the car with a kiss which, by a deft twist of her head, she managed to place on her cheek, and perfect, California-accented English. Raul was totally bilingual.

"Jessie, my dear! It's so good to see you again. You certainly gave everyone a scare last week. We heard about the plane crash all the way down here! When I learned from Paul Tanner in L.A. that you were sailing down to Acapulco, I took a chance and called the ship in the harbor. Ah! And this is the gentleman you said would accompany you. A friend of Jessie's is always welcome, señor!"

"I'm close to Jessie, but I'm not sure you could really call me a friend of the family," Lucas murmured, obligingly taking the proffered palm and shaking it firmly as he eyed the other man.

Raul blinked uncertainly. "I beg your pardon?"

"A little joke, Raul," Jessica put in quickly as she made introductions. "Nothing important. What a lovely facility," she added gaily, surveying the beautiful building. "Scanlon certainly did itself proud here in Acapulco. I so wanted to come down for the opening ceremonies a year ago, but I couldn't get away at the time."

Raul beamed proudly as all Scanlon managers tended to do when someone complimented the hotels they managed. "Come inside, both of you. I have arranged for lunch later. I thought perhaps you might enjoy seeing the hotel first, though, eh, Jessie?" He smiled at her expectantly.

"Naturally. I'm sure Lucas will enjoy a backstage tour, too."

" 'Know the enemy,' that's my motto," Lucas murmured just loud enough for Jessica to hear. "Yes, I would appreciate a tour of the facilities."

"Good, good, right this way, then," Raul commanded cheerfully. "We'll start with the grounds." He led the way through the circular, open-air lobby with its gleaming brass and tile toward the inviting gardens, which faced the beach.

In spite of his rather sarcastic comment, Lucas did, indeed, appear fascinated with the detailed tour they received. "You have your own water purification plant?" he asked at one point as they walked through the kitchens.

"We want the tourists to feel perfectly comfortable about any water used within the hotel, whether it be in the restaurant or the bar or the shower. It is simpler and more reliable to process all the water in the building to ensure that it is clean than to rely on the city facilities. In some of the smaller hotels, bottled water must be provided in every room. American tourists don't care for that! They keep forgetting and turning on the tap."

"Nothing but the best from Scanlon," Jessica chuckled.

"So I'm continually reminded," Lucas growled.

They followed Raul through the tropical grounds to view the two swimming pools, one of which had a built-in bar at one end where guests sat on stools in the water and sipped fruit-based drinks served by bartenders on the other side of a barrier. The other pool had been designed to closely resemble a jungle pool, complete with artificial waterfall. Tourists luxuriated in the elegant environs, soaking up the sun and spending a great deal of money on cooling drinks.

"We try to ensure that everything a visitor could wish is housed under the Scanlon roof. Shops, sports, the beach, nightclubs, and three restaurants—all are provided," Raul explained to Lucas as they concluded the tour and walked toward a private garden terrace which overlooked the sea.

" 'Scanlon is a world apart,' " Jessica quoted from a company brochure.

"A fantasy world," Lucas put in meaningfully. "Nice for a vacation, but surely a little cloying to live in all the time? It's like the ship we're on."

It was Raul who responded with a laugh and a conspiratorial wink at Jessica as he seated them in his private garden and signaled a nearby white-coated waiter who stood in readiness. "Scanlon makes it well worth our while to live in a gilded cage, doesn't it, Jessie?"

"Very much so," she responded, meeting Lucas's narrowed eyes.

It was Lucas who looked away. "Are you married, Raul? Does your wife share this, uh, cage with you?"

There was a short pause and then Raul said quietly, his dark eyes on Jessica, "My wife died some years ago, Lucas. I have not, as yet, remarried."

Lucas glanced from Raul's face to Jessica's cool features. "But when you do it will be within the family?" he suggested deliberately.

"I'm afraid I don't understand." Raul finally glanced back at his guest as the waiter brought in a fresh-fruit salad sprinkled with coconut.

"I meant you would prefer to marry a Scanlon employee if you were to remarry?" Lucas persisted even though Jessica had begun to frown at him from the other side of the table.

Raul smiled at once and nodded. "The idea has its merits, hasn't it, Jessie? Just imagine how happy Scanlon would be to have someone like you marry someone like me, hmmm? In one fell swoop they would have all the basic management needs of the hotel covered by a husband-and-wife team!"

Jessica forced a light laugh, her feminine intuition warning her that this was more than a casual conversation, at least on Lucas's part. With a firm hand she turned the discussion in another direction, inquiring about Raul's current staffing needs and problems.

For the remainder of lunch the tactic seemed to work. Lucas participated occasionally in the conversation, but for the most part he seemed to watch Raul's face as if he were studying the man. It made Jessica increasingly uneasy. It was as if she'd brought a wild animal to the table and now had to live with the knowledge that it might choose to dine off one of the guests instead of what was placed before it on a plate.

Over and over again she told herself that that was ridiculous. Lucas wouldn't, he *couldn't* do anything too awful. Could he? But she didn't care for the way he patiently watched the older man. After lunch, when Raul temporarily excused himself on a matter that had arisen at the front desk, she told Lucas as much.

"You keep staring at him!" she hissed as they strolled through one of the lush gardens. "It's embarrassing."

"Sorry."

"You're not sorry! What's the matter with you, anyway? He's our host!"

"He's thinking what an asset you'd be to his career," Lucas countered easily, pausing beside a huge bloom to inhale the scent.

"What?" she squeaked. "That's ridiculous!" But she glanced away quickly as he turned to stare at her.

"No, it's not. And what's more you knew it before we even accepted the invitation, didn't you? How well do you know Raul Estrada, Jessie?" Lucas asked in a cool voice.

"I told you, we've met on a few occasions over the years..."

"Tell me something," Lucas interrupted interestedly, "does the idea of being married for business reasons appeal to you?"

"That doesn't deserve an answer!"

"Does he know exactly how good a deal he'd be getting? That you're not only good in business but that you're also good in..."

"Don't say it, Lucas, I'm warning you!" she snapped before he could finish the sentence.

He held her cold eyes for a second longer and then sighed. "I'm sorry, Jessie. I'm jealous as hell."

Instantly she was contrite. How could this man manage to infuriate her one moment and then make her anxious to forgive him the next? "Lucas, there's nothing to be concerned about. If you want the truth, I know that Raul would not be adverse to marrying me. It's been hinted at before. But he'd never push it unless I encouraged him." She hastened on quickly, seeing Lucas's gaze darken. "He's very much the gentleman!"

"Unlike me?" Lucas growled sardonically.

A slow smile crept across her face. "Oh, I don't know. You've been behaving yourself fairly decently lately. Come on, let's go back to the main lobby. Raul should be finished with his business soon."

She turned to start back along the path, but came to an abrupt halt as Lucas stretched out a hand and snagged her by the wrist. "Jessie," he said very seriously as she looked back at him with an inquiringly lifted eyebrow, "I'm going to take you away from all this."

"Back to the ship, you mean?" she taunted lightly, alarmed by the sudden rush of excitement in her veins and by the degree of certainty in his set face.

"No, that's just more of the same," he said impatiently. "We'll finish the cruise, all right, but when we get back I'm going to give you a place where you can be a woman as well as a prized hotel executive. A place where you'll know beyond any doubt that you're wanted for yourself, not just because you'll advance a man's career. We'll make our own reality, you and I, Jessie Travers. You're going to come and live with me."

Aquamarine eyes wide and startled, her heart pounding the way it had the day before when she'd been trapped in the alley, Jessie stared at him, speechless. This wasn't the way she had planned it. Lucas held an attraction for her, she could not deny it, but she certainly had no intention of giving in to it so completely. She had only wanted to prove that she could conduct the relationship on her own terms. Hadn't she?

Scrambling for a response to the unexpected move he had just made, Jessica smiled with belated perception. "It's not really Raul you're jealous of, is it? It's Scanlon."

"Do you blame me? You've made that company your life, your family and your world!"

And he saw no lasting place for himself in that world, Jessica realized. Well, what had he expected? "So I'm absorbed in my job. Is that so bad? Weren't you wrapped up in your work with the police department? I've always heard that that particular profession demands everything from an individual. The department becomes the most important thing in life."

"It was a prison of a job, all right, but at least it was an honest prison," he gritted. "One can see the bars for what they are and for some people, like me, it becomes obvious that escape is the only answer. But you don't even want to acknowledge your own pretty cage. Scanlon has brainwashed you!"

"That's not true!"

"It's given you a perfect outlet for the naturally aggressive, dynamic side of your nature and you've rushed to grab it. If you had another side to your life, that wouldn't be so bad. But somehow you've lost your options or cut them off. Have you ever been in love, Jessie?" he concluded harshly. "Have you ever really come alive in a man's arms the way you do in mine? Is that why you're so afraid of me? Because I'm opening doors that you're afraid to walk through?"

"Stop it, Lucas!" she blazed.

"Are you afraid of me?" he persisted, surveying her critically, as if he would find the answer in her cold, angry, yet composed face.

"Should I be?" she bit out scathingly.

"Perhaps," he said. "I'm a threat to your neat, charming little world, aren't I? But maybe you haven't fully realized that yet."

"You have no business threatening me! If you don't stop it this minute, I swear, I'll..."

"Jessie," he whispered, tugging her rigid figure into his arms. "I'm sorry. I didn't mean to frighten you."

"I'm not frightened, damn it!" she muttered fiercely into his shirt.

But he held her there in the garden for a few minutes as if she had been very frightened, indeed, and Jessica's tense body slowly began to relax. His hands gentled her and Jessica told herself the only emotion he was successfully soothing away was her extreme sense of irritation. Certainly not fear. She did not fear Lucas Kincaid. Not here in her world.

"Is this a form of apology?" she finally got out dryly.

"Something like that, I suppose. I didn't mean to upset you, honey. You know that, don't you?" He pulled away to search her eyes. "I'm trying so damn hard to be on my best behavior!"

The earnest entreaty in his face brought Jessica's sense of humor back to life. Poor Lucas. How much more of this frustration with her would he take before he realized he wasn't ever again going to find the woman he'd found so briefly out there in the desert?

"I know, Lucas, I know." Then she summoned up a small grin. "But don't you realize it's not terribly modern to be jealous of a woman's job?"

"I won't be after I know for certain you'll be coming home to me at night and not to a hotel room!" he told her confidently, his large hands moving with unconscious sensuality on her shoulders.

"Lucas," she protested, realizing he was deadly serious, "please don't push me like this. We have no commitment to each other and you have no right to talk as if we do!"

"Okay, honey, calm down. I know you aren't ready for a commitment yet."

"Most definitely not! I'm on vacation, remember?" she parried, using her brightest, most dazzling smile to hide her inner uncertainty. "I'm recuperating from five miserable days spent in a desert!"

"Were they really so miserable?" he questioned gently.

"From my point of view, yes! Or did you somehow gain the impression I actually enjoyed washing clothes by hand in a stream and eating bunnies four nights in a row?" she demanded flippantly.

"Jessie, this isn't the first time you've made a joke about the experience. Don't you see that it can't have been that devastating for you if you can laugh about it now?"

Jessica considered that briefly. "As I said before, time and distance always add perspective. Now that I'm back in the real world I am able to see the more amusing side of things. I've regained my equilibrium, I suppose. Shows what a few good meals and a dose of Scanlon-oriented reality can do for a person!" Her eyes lit with mischief. "But, Lucas, you must understand that the reason I can laugh about washing your clothes in a desert stream is that I know the odds are vastly in favor of my never having to do it again, not because it was intrinsically enjoyable or amusing!"

"Jessie, what you and I had together in that desert *was* real."

"No," she denied, turning her face toward the ocean. "It had nothing to do with reality. Come on, Lucas, Raul will be waiting."

As the time for their departure drew near, Raul seemed to create an increasingly intimate air between himself and Jessica. He did nothing overt, merely assumed a sense of familiarity, which somehow managed to continually exclude Lucas.

Aware of Lucas's growing tension, Jessica tried resolutely to lighten the situation. She knew she could handle Raul Estrada, but Lucas didn't seem to know it. As the afternoon progressed, she found herself trying to pacify him in subtle ways.

"I'll be in L.A. next month, Jessie," Raul announced calmly as they sat chatting on the scented terrace outside his luxuriously furnished apartment. "You will be in town, won't you?" he asked suavely.

"As far as I know," Jessica responded, conscious of Lucas's hardening glance as he toyed with his glass of iced coffee. "I'll be back at work in another week and there will undoubtedly be a lot of catching up to do."

"Excellent! We'll make it a point to get together for dinner then, hmmm?"

"Uh, perhaps." Belatedly Jessica saw the cold iron in Lucas's gaze. "I'm going to be rather busy for most of the summer, though," she heard herself add quickly. "Several major conventions, including a political affair, are booked. You know what those are like!"

"Ah, yes. But I'm sure there will be time for us," Raul noted gently. "How is Sam, by the way? Is he still in charge of L.A. food and beverage?"

"Yes and as far as I know he's fine." Warily Jessica eyed Lucas; he hadn't said a word for the past twenty minutes. It was like waiting for a volcano to blow, she thought disgustedly. Perhaps she'd better see about getting him out of there before the sky fell. The last thing she wanted was to have him embarrass her in front of another Scanlon employee!

"Raul, it's been great seeing you again," she began firmly, setting down her glass of coffee, "but I think it's time Lucas and I got back to the ship. I seem to recall the captain saying over the loudspeaker this morning that his ship would wait for no one when sailing time arrived!"

"Not even a Scanlon employee," Lucas drawled, restlessly getting to his feet.

Whatever Raul Estrada might have said in response was lost as the peaceful quiet was suddenly interrupted by a short, sharp yip from an excited dog. Automatically all three people glanced toward a nearby hedge just as a scrawny, tan mutt came flying through. It paused a moment to examine the three humans and then bounded happily toward Jessica, floppy ears bouncing.

"Where the devil did that creature come from?" Raul muttered in annoyance. "I'll have Fernando get rid of him. There are so many strays here in Acapulco! All my employees have instructions to keep them off the grounds, but occasionally one slips through. Be careful, Jessie, he'll get your white slacks filthy.''

Amused at the dog's unabashed enthusiasm, Jessica leaned down to pat him carefully on the head. It was the wrong thing to do. The cheerful animal chose to interpret the sign as one of welcome and, with a joyous bark, reared up to plant muddy paws squarely on the front of the pristine white slacks.

"Oh, no!" Jessica laughed ruefully, going ahead and petting the dog, anyway.

Instantly Raul was at her side, aiming a well-shod foot at the offending animal.

"Hey!" Lucas objected harshly, starting forward with a frown. He needn't have worried. The tan dog had survived long enough on the handouts of Acapulco tourists to have learned something about human nature. He had encountered Raul's approach often enough. With a quick twist of his thin body, the animal avoided the kick, dodging around behind Jessica. An instant later, Lucas reached him and swept him safely up under one arm.

Knowing a sucker when he saw one, the dog enthusiastically began to lick Lucas's face. "Jessie and I are on our way out. We'll see that the dog is removed from your fantasy world, Estrada!"

"As you wish," Raul replied, losing interest as he turned back to Jessica. "I am sorry about the damage done to your clothing, my dear."

Jessica shook her head in easy dismissal. "Forget it. I've endured worse. Remember the time the assistant chef dumped an entire kettle of hollandaise down the front of my gown just before that important dinner in San Francisco last year? I assure you I'll survive a couple of paw prints." She glanced over at Lucas. He still held the wriggling dog, which was still madly attempting to lick its benefactor's face.

All might have gone well at that point if Raul hadn't presumed a little too far. "Goodbye, Jessie," he murmured, ignoring Lucas to bend forward and kiss Jessica full on her surprised mouth. "I will definitely see you next month. Be sure to hold several evenings free for me, my dear."

Startled by the unexpected degree of affection from a man she'd always thought of as a business friend, Jessica stepped back and opened her lips to say something very noncommittal.

She never got the chance. Lucas was moving toward her, the dog tucked under one arm, his free hand extended to grasp Jessica's wrist. Roughly he spoke to Raul. The harsh, uncompromising stream of Spanish which flowed from his lips was cold and lethal, even to Jessica's ears, and she didn't have the faintest idea of what was being said. The impact on Raul, however, was immediate and obvious.

The older man fell back a pace, astonished, as Lucas finished speaking and yanked abruptly on his captive's hand. Dog and woman safely chained to him, he started toward the exit.

"Jessie!" Raul called after her retreating figure. "What's going on? Is what he just said true?"

"Is what true?" Unable to free herself, Jessica stumbled a little as she tried to glance back at her friend. Lucas never looked back and never slackened his forward momentum.

"Do you belong to him?" Raul called anxiously. "He says you are his woman!"

Shocked, Jessica tried to summon a hasty protest, but it was too late. Lucas hauled them around the corner and then they were hurrying through the elegant, airy lobby, causing amused and curious expressions to appear on the faces of clerks and guests alike.

Outside Lucas tossed his companions into the back seat of a waiting cab and climbed in beside them, shutting the door with a vicious slam and issuing quick instructions in Spanish to the obliging driver.

Then he leaned back in the seat and turned to meet Jessica's accusing gaze. The dog was happily ensconced on her lap, completing the ruination of the white slacks, and she unthinkingly lifted a hand to pat its dirty, tan fur.

"How dare you?" she hissed at Lucas. "If you were an employee of mine I'd have you fired for embarrassing me like that! How dare you make such an unforgivable scene! Raul Estrada is a friend of mine; nothing more—and even if he were something more, that still wouldn't give you the right to behave so outrageously!"

"He shouldn't have tried to kick the dog and kiss you." Lucas sank more deeply into the battered seat as the cab rocketed toward the docks. "I was doing okay up to that point. God knows I wanted to tell him to keep his hands off you often enough during the day, but I knew you'd be furious."

"I am furious! You had absolutely no right to tell him such things!"

"That you're my woman?" Lucas slanted her an iron glance and then refocused his attention on the colorful street scene outside the car's window. "It's the truth, Jessie. You only seem willing to admit it when you're in my arms, but it's the truth and you know it."

"It is not the truth! Damn it, Lucas, if the whole thing weren't so ludicrous, I'd hire someone to skin you alive! I have never been so furious in my life!"

"Jessie," he said placatingly, "I'm sorry about what happened. If you'd just gotten us out of there a little earlier . . ."

"So it's my fault, is it?"

"Well, yes, in a way. I know you think you can handle Estrada, but you weren't doing a very good job there toward the end. You were practically promising to meet him next month in Los Angeles!"

"I fully intend to meet him. I shall be looking forward to it, in fact! It will be a pleasure to go out with a gentleman!"

"Honey, don't say things like that. You're just upset," he soothed.

"You're impossible," she groaned, some of her anger seeping out of her as the dog on her lap swiped her cheek with his tongue and looked at her with such hope in his eyes she couldn't resist him. "Your dog is hungry. What are you going to do about him? We can't take him on board ship!"

"I know. We'll stop and buy him some tacos before we turn him loose. He'll survive, as long as he steers clear of Estrada's perfect garden!" There was a significant pause. "Jessie, I'm sorry I embarrassed you."

"Are you, Lucas?" she asked tightly.

"Sweetheart, we were making so much progress," he murmured pleadingly. "Please don't ruin it all now because of what just happened back at the hotel!"

"Progress!" she exploded, turning the full force of her glowering gaze on him. "*Progress! Is* that what you thought was happening?"

"You know it was," he said levelly. "You were beginning to see the other side of me. You were getting over some of your anger and you were even starting to laugh at some of the things that happened back there in the desert!" He broke off to narrow his eyes at her as she began to chuckle softly. "What's so amusing?" he demanded stiffly.

"You are, Lucas," she managed wickedly. "For thinking you were making progress with me."

"Jessie," he began on a sudden note of warning.

"Lucas, I'm the one who was making progress with you. Or thought I was. It's obvious there are still some rough spots." She grinned.

He didn't move, but his eyes were suddenly watchful and the grooves at the edge of his mouth tightened. "What are you trying to say, Jessie?" he asked very softly.

"Isn't it obvious? I'm conducting an affair with you, Lucas Kincaid," she murmured with saccharine sweetness. "On my terms, not yours. And for future reference, please take note of the fact that I do not want you flying off the handle and making wild claims every time another man sees fit to be nice to me. Is that understood?"

But even as she spoke the haughty, arrogant words, Jessica was regretting them.

Eight

Unfortunately, the feeling of regret didn't disappear. Why had she let her temper get the better of her? Jessica asked herself that question for the rest of the afternoon and was still asking it as she dressed for dinner.

Surely she had only told him the truth, she argued with herself. Hadn't she already proven whatever it was she had set out to prove? A long-term affair had never been a goal of hers, anyway, so what did it matter if her precipitous words had ended the situation sooner than she had expected? She ought to be content with having made her point in no uncertain terms and then letting Lucas off her hook. He hadn't really deserved to be misled for very long.

When all was said and done, Lucas Kincaid was an honest, straightforward man. Jessica knew first-hand that she could trust him with her life. Still, he'd pushed her into her defensive posture. He was the one who'd followed her on board the ship and set out to ruin her vacation!

But she hadn't meant to hurt him. She'd only wanted to put him in his place. Well, she had done that this afternoon in the taxi and she was still feeling an emotion suspiciously like guilt. Jessica chewed her lip in an agony of frustration as she pulled the little black dress from the small stateroom closet. The frustration and the guilt had been building steadily ever since that scene in the taxi, and they weren't pleasant sensations. She should have been feeling satisfaction, not remorse!

Perhaps if he'd lost his own temper and raged at her in turn she might have felt better about her own taunting words; more justified, at least. As it was, Lucas had merely stared at her for a long moment, his expression totally unreadable, and then he'd asked the driver to find a place where they could buy food for the dog.

The creature had last been seen happily wolfing down several spicy tamales on a sidewalk as the taxi driver, shaking his head over the actions of the crazy gringos, drove Jessica and Lucas on to the docks.

Jessica hadn't seen Lucas for the rest of the afternoon and had told herself several times that it didn't matter. Now, as she slipped into the dashing little dress, she acknowledged that it did matter. "You're not supposed to be cruel to people who rescue little dogs," she announced to her image in the mirror. Tonight she would face him and explain what she had been doing and why. Then she would apologize and that would be the end of the matter. She really didn't *owe* him an apology, but maybe it would relieve her own gnawing sense of guilt if she gave him one. After all, whatever she'd had to prove to herself had been proven. Surely Lucas would no longer be interested in pursuing a relationship when he understood what she had been doing. She could end the whole thing tonight. It was messy, but at least this time they would be parting as equals.

How would Lucas react to her explanation? she wondered as she brushed her hair into a gleaming coil at the nape of her neck. Would he understand why she had acted as she did? That he had more or less pushed her into it by following her on board? Damn it! She was beginning to feel toward him the way he'd felt toward that small dog when Raul had attempted to kick the creature: protective.

Her emotions were in an incredibly complex tangle, she realized. There was a simple explanation, of course: Out in the desert she had been playing out of her league; here in her civilized, safe world, Lucas had been playing out of his. Neither one of them had wanted to hurt the other. Jessica straightened her shoulders determinedly as she left the stateroom. Tonight she would explain everything and put an end to the matter. That was assuming she could find him, she added wryly. Where had Lucas been keeping himself since they had returned from the Scanlon hotel?

He wandered into the dining room right on time, however, dark hair still damp from a shower, eyes cool and remote as they had been in the taxi. The Howards appeared to notice nothing particularly out of the ordinary. Perhaps they were growing accustomed to the unpredictable tension that flowed between their two tablemates.

In any event, they made the necessary dinner conversation, telling tales of what they had seen and done and bought in Acapulco.

"And how about you two?" Bill wound up jovially, as dessert was served.

Jessica nibbled her Brie as the others dug into apple pie, and attempted a small smile. "We saved a small dog from a terrible fate." Her eyes caught Lucas's cool gaze, inviting him to join in that humor. "Or rather Lucas did."

The Howards laughed good-naturedly as she gave a highly expurgated version of the story. Lucas listened to the light tale without comment, concentrating on his apple pie. Jessica couldn't tell if he was angry or simply bored. What in the world was he thinking? Was he sulking again?

That last notion pushed her into trying to goad him out of his self-imposed silence. "I suppose the urge to rescue little dogs in distress is an occupational hazard which comes with being a pet shop owner?"

He looked up and she had the feeling his thoughts had been on something else entirely. "It was also an occupational hazard while I was a cop," he remarked and went back to his pie.

Jessica's eyes narrowed in astonishment as she realized he had just given her a major clue to what had led him to quit the LAPD. He had said he was a victim of job burnout, but she hadn't prodded any more deeply at the time. Now she knew what had led to that burnout. Lucas Kincaid, she was willing to bet, had grown frustrated and angry at being unable to save all the small, helpless people he was supposed to protect.

The flash of insight unnerved her, making it impossible to pick up the thread of the conversation and take it firmly in another direction. Fortunately, Ann Howard plunged to the rescue with a frivolous remark about the silver she had managed to find in what she hoped was a reliable shop in

Acapulco. Jessica finished the excellent, perfectly ripened Brie without tasting the expensive cheese at all.

Lucas remained quiet for the rest of the meal, finishing his coffee in silence. But the inevitable could not be put off indefinitely. If he wasn't going to give her an opening, Jessica decided gamely, she would have to take the initiative. As he rose to leave the dining room, she did the same and placed her fingertips lightly but firmly on the sleeve of his corduroy jacket.

"I'd like to talk to you," Jessica murmured.

He glanced down at her hand and then nodded once. "Yes."

Without a word he led her out onto the upper deck, just as the ship's engines thrummed to life. They were under way again. The next port on the way back to Los Angeles would be Mazatlán. Jessica stood beside Lucas at the rail, watching the lights of Acapulco slowly recede. She took the moment to gather herself for what she had to say.

"I'm sorry, Lucas."

He didn't move. With one foot hooked on the bottom rail, he leaned forward, resting on his elbows, and watched the shoreline. The balmy breeze ruffled his hair and the faint light from the ship cast his face into a hard, unreadable profile. Determined to get the scene over and done with as efficiently as possible, Jessica took another breath.

"When I saw you again after the accident all I could think about was how I didn't want to be reminded of what had happened out there in the desert. When you insisted on trying to reestablish a relationship, I decided I would use the opportunity to prove to myself that here in the real world I wouldn't react to you the way I had after the crash. Here you wouldn't be able to dominate me and if we went to bed together it would be as equals."

"With you being a little more equal than me?" he interposed softly.

Jessica slid a sideways glance at his face as she stood stiffly beside him. What was he thinking? Damn it! She couldn't tell if he was depressed, furious, or totally uncaring about the whole situation!

"Perhaps," she admitted in a voice that was every bit as cool as the one he had used.

"Revenge?" he suggested mildly, apparently undisturbed by the notion.

Jessica's mouth firmed as he asked her the question she had asked herself earlier. "No, it was far more complicated than that, I think. But that may have been a part of it. I was more interested in trying to prove something to myself than in trying to punish you, though. Do you see the difference?"

"And now?" he prompted.

He hadn't answered her question, she realized wryly. Here she was attempting to explain, even apologize, and he was already beginning to arouse her irritation again. Deliberately?

"I knew this afternoon that what I wanted to prove had already been established. In my world I can handle you, Lucas. I'm not boasting. It's the simple truth. I think you've known that all along, haven't you? You can't treat me the way you did out on the desert. Back here in civilization there are rules which neither of us can ignore. The point has been made. There's no reason to drag it out any further."

"You've had enough revenge?" he queried blandly.

"It wasn't revenge! At least, not all of it. That's what I'm trying to explain," she snapped. "Damn it, Lucas, don't be deliberately obtuse!"

"To explain something, you first have to understand it completely yourself," he noted idly.

"I do understand it! I'm saying I've satisfied myself and now I want to call the whole thing off. I don't want to punish you, Lucas!"

"Why not?"

Jessica sighed. "Because you're basically a sincere, honest man. Even a compassionate one. You've never attempted to deceive me. You're not really guilty of anything criminal or vicious. We were both caught in a unique situation and it affected us in a way that we couldn't control. The situation, thank heaven, is highly unlikely to ever arise again. It left me feeling disgusted with myself, though, and when you showed up on this ship I felt very uncomfortable."

"So you decided to prove to yourself that here in your fantasy world you aren't trapped the way you were out in the desert. Here you're safe."

"Something like that. I'm glad you're beginning to understand, Lucas," she told him earnestly. "We both know that everything is different here in real life."

"Do we?" His eyes were still on the receding shoreline, but Jessica's nerves suddenly tingled with unexpected warning.

"Of course," she affirmed as much to herself as to him. "Just look at the kid-glove treatment you've given me lately. A week ago if I'd disobeyed orders the way I did yesterday afternoon you would have done something very emphatic about it. Probably in front of all the others, too, as an example!" She tried to inject just the proper amount of rueful humor into the words. "I knew the other night when we . . ." The next sentence trailed off weakly as a rush of warmth assailed her.

"When we made love?" he finished helpfully.

"Yes," she managed to get out, staring at the lights in the distance. "I knew then that everything was certainly normal again. I didn't feel as though I'd been . . . Oh, never mind, you know what I'm trying to say." She was glad the shadows hid the flush which was undoubtedly painting her throat and cheeks.

"You didn't feel as though you'd surrendered to the dominant male in the herd," he concluded dryly. "I believe that was how you described our first night together."

"Lucas, do you understand what I'm trying to say?" she demanded with a hint of asperity. This had gone far enough. She'd apologized, even though there had been no real need, and she'd explained the motives behind her actions. She didn't owe him anything else. Lucas Kincaid might be a sincere and basically honest man, but he was also a thoroughly exasperating one!

He turned slowly at last to face her, continuing to lean negligently against the rail as he did so. For the first time that evening the shutters were opened and Jessica had a good look at the emotions he had been hiding for the past several hours.

The sight was enough to make her shiver in uneasy surprise. Good God! She had wondered what he was thinking all evening, but she hadn't expected this!

There was no sign that he had been sulking. There was also no indication that he had been hurt by her words. Nor was there anger in that abruptly clear gaze. Having expected some variation on those emotions, Jessica was totally unprepared for the piercing certainty with which he pinned her.

"I understand what you're trying to say, Jessie. But you haven't got the vaguest idea of what you're talking about."

His mouth was edged with a faint, masculine humor which disturbed her as nothing else could have done. It said as clearly as his words that she had just made a fool out of herself.

"Lucas, I don't know what game you're playing, but I..."

"I'm not playing any games. You're the one who's been doing that, honey, and I think it's time we put a stop to them. You've been operating under a slight misconception, Jessie."

"What misconception?" she flared, the wariness she thought long banished springing to life within her as if it had never been far below the surface. The knowledge angered her.

"The notion that everything's different between us just because you're back in your gilded cage. The reality of what happened between you and me, sweetheart, is independent of our environment. I was hoping that you'd come to that conclusion on your own, but it looks as if you've been using the time I gave you to 'prove' something to yourself. Apparently you've been so busy drawing stupid conclusions from my actions that you've overlooked one important fact."

"Which is?"

"Which is that you're no safer from me here in what you choose to call civilization than you were out in the desert." He made no move to touch her, but Jessica flinched and retreated a step as if he had. Her eyes widened and her lips parted in shock.

"No!" she whispered.

Lucas watched her with detached curiosity.

"You couldn't run fast enough to get back to the security of Scanlon, could you, Jessie? I'll bet you've never run from a man in your life the way you ran from me."

"I did not run!"

"You couldn't wait to get back inside your cage," he went on calmly, as if he were analyzing an interesting phenomenon. "Couldn't wait to slam the door in my face. I've been trying to coax you back outside, Jessie. Didn't you realize that? I know I've been treating you with kid gloves. I was hoping you'd relax and begin to feel more secure in my presence if I didn't push you too hard, too fast. I knew that what happened after the crash was something you weren't quite ready to accept. But I thought that, given a little time and not too much pressure, you'd see that what took place between us was real, not some form of strange, animalistic behavior for which you don't have to accept responsibility. I wanted you to open the cage door yourself, Jessie, but you're not going to do that, are you? You're going to hide inside and play sophisticated little games designed to make yourself feel secure and in control."

"I'm not in a cage, Lucas, I'm in my own world, the *real* world, and there's nothing you can do to get me back out of it!" she exclaimed, her fingers digging into the rail at her side as she faced him proudly.

"Well, it's obvious I'm not going to coax you out of it, I'll grant that," he admitted with surprising ease. "But I've been giving it some serious thought since you made your position clear in the taxi this afternoon."

Was that what he'd been dwelling on? she wondered frantically.

"Lucas, I don't know what momentous conclusion you've reached, but I do know this discussion has gone far enough. I've apologized for something which probably didn't merit an apology in the first place and I've . . ."

"It didn't. But you had to do it, didn't you? That's what comes of being soft under the surface, honey. You thought you'd made me suffer and you felt guilty. Poor Jessie. You thought you might have hurt me with your clever little plans, didn't you? Honey, you didn't crush me, you just made me realize I'm wasting my time with the walking-on-eggs approach. It might work eventually, but I'm not sure I'll last out the process now. When I found you in that alley yesterday it was all I could do not to turn you over my knee for having gotten yourself into such a stupid scrape. And this afternoon I thought I'd really lose control watching that slick Estrada oozing charm all over you. The dog saved both your necks, by the way, did you know that? It provided a reason to get you out of his garden before I lost my temper completely."

"You said enough, as I recall!" she charged bitterly.

"You'll remember I did restrain myself to simply talking?" he murmured. "Still, it was an educational experience. If Estrada is the kind of man with whom you normally associate, I can see why falling for me must have been somewhat of a shock. After all, a man who has seen both sides of you, a man who knows who you really are is a threat, isn't he?"

"Damn you, Lucas, I'm not afraid of you!"

"Yes you are, and you're going to be even more afraid of me before you learn to accept the reality of our relationship. But there's no other way that I can see to manage things. I tried the gentling approach and you abused it."

Jessica gasped in outrage at his interpretation of events. "Gentling! Lucas, I don't know where this is leading, but I swear, if you don't stop threatening me, I'll call a ship's officer!"

"I'm not threatening you, sweetheart," he soothed as if she were a fractious puppy. "And I'll be more than happy to enlighten you about where the conversation is leading. It's simple. I'm putting you on notice, Jessie. I'm through trying to persuade you to come back out of your gilded cage by yourself. I'm going to show you that the bars you think are protecting you are useless between us. You're not safe now that you're back in the Scanlon world. You're still as vulnerable to me as you ever were out in that desert because I'm still the man I was out there and you, thank God, are still the same woman. What happened between us is independent of time and circumstance. I'm going to reach into your safe little cage, honey, and pull you out into my arms."

"Don't you dare touch me!" She stepped back another pace, thoroughly alarmed now.

"I won't. Not tonight," he drawled, straightening away from the rail. "Tonight I'm going to let you worry about the whole thing. You're an intelligent woman and with intelligence comes imagination. Use it, Jessie, to think about how far you can run on a ship this size." Strong, white teeth gleamed in a smile of savage amusement and then Lucas swung around on one heel and walked toward the entrance to the interior of the ship.

"I will never run from you or any other man," she couldn't resist calling after him.

"If you don't, things will end even sooner than I'd planned," he retorted mockingly, his hand on the door he was about to enter. "No, you'll run for a while. But eventually it's going to dawn on you that you're feeling the same things here in the middle of your so-called *real* world that you felt out in the desert. And when you make that connection, everything will be all right."

Before she could catch her breath for a scathing response, Lucas was gone. Jessica stood staring after him, trying to assess what had happened to her. One thing was for certain, she decided irately, she no longer had to suffer any guilt over using him! Lucas had just threatened her, hadn't he? That made her the injured party! Or should that read *hunted* party?

That last thought sent another shiver through her. Hunted? Again? No, not here on this ship. He couldn't do such a thing to her!

Slowly Jessica left the rail, brows drawn together in a frown of intense concentration. The expression gave the strong, firm lines of her profile a look of cold severity in the moonlight. Unaware of where she was headed, Jessica walked slowly toward the bow of the ship. She was angry, restless, and confused, a combination potent enough to make a woman a little reckless. Deliberately she avoided the few other passengers who were out walking on deck.

There was a warmth and a freshness about the night air which put her too forcibly in mind of the clear desert nights she had known several days ago. It brought with it too many other associated memories. Dangerous memories.

He couldn't do this to her, Jessica told herself again and again as she stopped once more at the rail and stared down at the softly foaming water below. His latest campaign would only work if she were silly enough to let it work!

She was not the same unprotected female she had been the last time. Surrounding her now were all the accoutrements of civilized society. She would be safe and she had already proven as much, hadn't she?

Spinning angrily around, Jessica fled the shadows of the quiet deck and went in search of laughter and company. She didn't want to ask herself why she needed the security of a crowd just then. The answer might have been too unnerving.

It wasn't hard to find what she sought. It all awaited her on the next deck down, where the lively dance band was entertaining in the largest of the three nightclubs. The defiant recklessness that had begun out on deck drove her to take a red leather stool at the bar, instead of a small table. It seemed important to find an escort for the evening and the direct approach was the quickest. Was she somehow looking for protection?

No! She merely wanted to enjoy the cruise. Coolly she ordered an after-dinner liqueur and swiveled halfway around on the stool to eye the crowded dance floor. One well-arched foot in a high-heeled black sandal swung in the manner of a prowling cat's tail.

Jessica didn't even see Lucas as he approached from the far side of the huge, curving bar. By the time she was aware of his presence, it was too late. He was already sliding lithely onto the empty stool beside her, a glass of the now-familiar bourbon-and-water in his hand.

As her head whipped around, he smiled kindly. "It won't work, Jessie." He waved his free hand in a shallow arc which took in the whole room. "I don't think there's a man out there tonight who will have the courage to try to pick you up. Not as long as your eyes are as hard and glittering as diamonds and your smile is so brilliantly cold. You're radiating pure female menace right now, honey. There's not a man in sight who will have the guts to ask you to dance."

"Except you?" she challenged too sweetly.

Lucas shook his head in response to her question, the smile edging his mouth positively lethal. "Nope, not me, either. I'm not here to ask you to dance."

Jessica's eyes narrowed as her senses registered the danger she had known lay in the depths of this man. It was as if he'd kept it hidden for the past few days. Long enough for her to convince herself that such a degree of male menace couldn't exist in civilized society.

"Really?" she dared. "Afraid I might refuse?"

"Damn right," he grinned. "I don't handle rejection well."

But he could, she thought a little wildly. He could ignore it and go after what he wanted regardless of how much rejection a woman handed out. Jessica swallowed as the realization went home. Again she tried to right her suddenly disoriented world. "If you're not going to ask me to dance, would you mind vacating that barstool? As long as you're sitting there, it's a cinch no other man will ask me to dance, regardless of my frozen smile!"

"I know. That's why I'm sitting here," he explained as if she were a child. Lucas took another sip of his bourbon and water, watching comprehension dawn on her face.

"You mean you're deliberately going to chase off anyone who might want to introduce himself?"

"Simple but effective. Consider it close surveillance."

The red stained her cheeks. "Why you arrogant...ex-cop! You know damn good and well I won't dance with you, but you've got the nerve to make it impossible for me to have any fun with someone else!"

"Where are you going?" he inquired politely as she stood up.

"As if I'd tell you!" Jessica snapped over her shoulder as she walked away from him with long sinuous strides that carried her quickly out of earshot. But not quite quickly enough.

"A ship just isn't that big, Jessie. I'll find you." The words floated after her, dark and full of promise.

And he did exactly that, over and over again as the evening progressed. He was sitting beside her as she caught the late cabaret act. He was standing in line behind her when she went through the midnight buffet. He was near enough to warn off other men when she went into the nightclubs. He never touched her, never put a hand on her. He was always just there, watching her, urging her with his eyes to accept his presence because there was no alternative for her.

It was the way it had been out in the desert, Jessica thought despairingly. He'd never put a hand on her then, either, until the fateful night when he'd led her away from the others and made love to her. By then she'd been unable to shake off his grasp and what followed had seemed inevitable at the time.

She would not allow him to turn this ship into another hunting-ground, she swore to herself again and again. It was all a matter of psychology. She had to bring herself to totally ignore his presence. It was the only way to defeat him. The difficulty lay in summoning up the willpower to ignore a man whose mere presence in a room caused her nerves to vibrate in awareness.

At one o'clock in the morning, she knew she could take no more that night. She needed sleep and a plan, neither of which she was going to get by spending her energies in useless evasion tactics. Lucas was right about one thing. The ship just wasn't big enough to get lost in for long. The only safe refuge on board was her stateroom.

Grimly she set down the last of her unfinished caviar and rose. Lucas, who was lounging across the room, watching her eat, did the same. For a moment she faced him, unaware of the other passengers who filled the room, and then she turned on her heel and left.

She thought he probably followed her, at least as far as the corridor which led to her stateroom, but she didn't see him as she stood at the door, fumbling with her key. Nevertheless, it was with a sigh of relief that she let herself inside and locked the door behind her.

Walking across to the neatly made bed, she sank wearily down onto it and tried to think, her chin in her hand. What was she going to do? Let him push her into getting off the ship in Mazatlán? Would she be able to find a flight back to the States from there without too much trouble?

The realization that she was thinking of escape startled her. She didn't need to escape, she was supposed to be safe in her own world. Oh, God. What was it he had said? When she realized that what she felt here in "reality" was the same as what she had felt out in the desert, everything would be all right.

It was all such a jumble tonight, Jessica decided sadly, slowly undoing the fastening of her black dress. She had started out feeling contrite and he had turned the tables completely. Now she was undeniably on the defensive, nervous and wary. In a matter of hours he had made her realize he had the power to make her feel the same emotions she had felt after the plane crash.

And somehow, incredible as it seemed, Jessica had the horrifying impression it had been easier for him to put her on the defensive this time, because she had learned so much more about him. Lucas Kincaid was no longer a domineering, autocratic stranger. She knew both sides of his nature, the side which could offer a woman protection or hunt her down, and the side which found satisfaction in owning a pet shop. That last made her think about his previous career.

What had it been like for him, those years in the LAPD? Jessica shuddered at the thought. A world of violence and corruption. A man would have to be a little hard to do his job effectively in such an environment. He would have to be capable of blocking off his gentler emotions in order to get on with the rough and sometimes deadly work at hand. A man who felt too compassionate or overly responsible for others would be highly subject to job burnout.

Yes, she could see why Lucas had made the decision to leave the force.

And what the hell was she doing thinking about that when she should be worrying about how to get herself out of the snare he was tightening around her? Jessica demanded of herself as she slithered out of her dress and angrily went about the business of getting ready for bed.

Knowing both sides of a man made it difficult to hate him, she realized grimly. And in some strange way, perhaps she even envied him. Lucas Kincaid had proven that he understood and could deal with the various sides of his own nature. He had accepted himself.

But when she had been forced to recognize the aspects of her own personality, which she had repressed, Jessica had fled, wanting nothing more than to turn her back on that alien, somehow threatening side of herself.

Nine

The following afternoon Jessica sought refuge in the small ship's library. It wasn't fear of Lucas that drove her into the quiet room lined with bookshelves and filled with the style of library furniture that might have been found a century ago in a stately English home. It was simply that she needed time to think and Lucas had kept her nerves on edge since breakfast. It was impossible to think clearly around him.

He had been exasperating and mildly intimidating since the moment she had arrived, a bit defiantly, at the breakfast table to find he had already ordered for her. Short of causing an embarrassing scene in front of the Howards, there wasn't anything Jessica could do except eat the food he had selected for her.

"I would have preferred the Eggs Benedict," she muttered at one point as she surveyed the plain bacon and eggs the waiter was setting before her.

"You eat whatever your man can provide." Lucas grinned unabashedly, digging into his hash browns. "Women have been doing it for years. You did it very graciously not so long ago, yourself!"

"Only because there was no alternative," she reminded him sweetly, eyes glinting as she remembered the way she had quite greedily consumed the food he had made available after the plane had gone down.

He looked up and said simply, "This morning there is no alternative for you, either. Eat."

There was a poignant pause, during which two strong wills clashed silently over the breakfast table. In the end Jessica told herself she backed down solely because she didn't wish to embarrass herself or the Howards. Picking up her fork, she smiled very brightly at the man who had somehow managed to make it seem as if he had provided breakfast. "Women may have been eating whatever their men brought home for years, but I'll bet they've been complaining about some of the selections equally long!"

"But getting fat off what was provided, nonetheless," Ann Howard broke in to advise cheerfully. "It was just a little joke, dear," she added confidingly, with a quick glance at Lucas's bland expression. "Lucas said he thought it was time you tasted some *real* food, as he called it!"

Jessica refrained from saying she wasn't in a mood for jokes at that hour of the day and smiled to show she could appreciate the humor. The smile was more than a little forced, however, because both she and Lucas knew there had been no joke involved.

The maneuver was only the beginning to a day Lucas devoted to proving his point: Incredible as it seemed, he was quite capable of duplicating on board a luxury cruise liner the same sensual tension, the same sense of hunter and hunted, the same feeling of inevitability that had assailed Jessica in the remote desert canyon several days earlier.

He was there when she went swimming, his iron-hard gaze following every movement of her body in the water as if she were an exotic species of tropical fish he planned to net. He was there with iced tea when the sun became too warm, but when she drank it, Jessica felt as if she had somehow accepted one more link in the chain he was using to bind her. Actions that in another man would have shown gentlemanly courtesy, had another meaning, coming from Lucas. There was no way to refuse most of them without appearing churlish to onlookers, but every time she accepted the smallest act of politeness, Jessica knew she was only tightening her own bonds.

There was no question of using another man as protective cover. No other man even came near her now. Even if one had been inclined to brave the glittering, nervous look in her eyes, none wanted to brave the promise of iron in the gaze of the man who was always nearby. Lucas had trapped her in a primitive, isolated little world from which escape was as impossible as it had been in the desert.

They spoke little throughout the better part of the day. Lucas seemed willing enough to talk when Jessica began a conversation, but her words generally turned scathing within a few sentences and Lucas lapsed into silence, a knowing look in his eyes. He knew how trapped she was beginning to feel, Jessica realized. Every time she came close to losing her temper, he simply waited for the explosion. Perversely, she refused to oblige him.

By the time she had resorted to seeking out the solitude of the ship's library, Jessica was very much in need of its quiet atmosphere. She sank into one of the large, wingback chairs, propping her sandaled feet on a hassock. The full skirt of her yellow-and-blue patterned sundress added a decided splash of color to the subdued room.

What was happening to her, she asked herself, staring at the rows of books on the far wall. No, she ought to rephrase that question: What was she *allowing* to happen to her? A woman had to take responsibility for her own actions and reactions and there could be no denying that her mind and her body responded with vivid awareness to Lucas Kincaid. His quiet pursuit here on the ship wouldn't have worked if she had been able to ignore his effect on her senses. At most he would have constituted an annoyance.

She should have been able to laugh at him, tell him to go to hell and mean it. But she couldn't, just as she hadn't been able to do so during those five days after the plane crash. A woman was not a mindless, helpless quarry like a rabbit. Unless he resorted to violence, a man could not force her to step into his snare, much less remain there. And if there was one thing about Lucas of which Jessica was certain, it was that he would never resort to violence.

Yet there she was, struggling in his snare. Again.

The realization made her close her eyes briefly in dismay and confusion. When she opened them Lucas was coming through the library door, a tray in his hands.

"I didn't want you to miss afternoon tea," he drawled, placing the tray with its teapot, cups and a plate of scones beside her. "Will you pour?" he added with grave politeness as he sank easily into the chair across from her. "I believe it goes with the room."

"My pouring tea?" she murmured, glancing warily at the innocent pot.

"Umm. A feminine tradition or something."

There seemed no point in refusing and in any event she wanted a cup herself. It was only as she passed him his tea together with a scone that it struck Jessica how little the setting really mattered. She might as well have been handing him his chunk of roasted rabbit from the other side of the campfire. It felt exactly the same to her. She was serving him the food he had provided. Her hand shook a little as she acknowledged that Lucas could make the formality of afternoon tea a decidedly primitive exchange between a man and a woman.

"How did you find me?" she asked with a touch of flippancy to cover her uneasiness. Carefully she poured herself a cup of tea, using the action to avoid meeting his eyes.

"There aren't that many places on board that could afford a woman a quiet retreat." He smiled gently. "You weren't cowering in your stateroom so, by process of elimination, I tracked you here. Doing some thinking, Jessie?"

"Yes." She refused to be provoked into telling him what she had been thinking about. Besides, he undoubtedly already knew.

He did. "Jessie, neither of us could ever ignore or escape the other," Lucas said quietly. "Are you beginning to understand that?"

"I'll admit that in an artificially confined world such as this ship it's a bit tricky," she said crisply.

"It would be the same anywhere. That's the only point I'm trying to make."

"Lucas, what do you want from me? An affair? We've already had that!"

"I told you. I want you to come and live with me. I want to give you a home where you can let the gentle side of your nature flourish. I want to be the man on whom you lavish all your softness. Don't misunderstand me; I admire your strength, a part of me likes the challenge of it and another part of me likes the idea that it can be relied upon in a thousand different ways."

"What ways?" she bit out, unwilling to admit what his words were doing to her. "You've tried to crush the strong side of me from the beginning!"

"That's not true, honey," he denied gently. "The only time I ever tried to master the strength in you was that first day after the crash and then I had no choice. I did it for your own good as well as that of the others. But I certainly didn't set out to permanently crush your spirit and you know it. A man needs strength from his woman, just as he needs softness."

"Why?" she asked starkly.

"It's the strong side of your nature that assures me I can trust you implicitly," he surprised her by saying simply. "Once you've accepted me completely with your mind as well as your body, I'll know you will never turn to another man. I'll know you'll use your power to defend our relationship, not destroy it. You see?" he concluded whimsically, "your strength is as important to me as your softness. I'm a greedy man. I want both."

Jessica swallowed, fighting down the strange rush to give him everything he wanted. It would be so easy. All she had to do was put her hand in his and let him lead her into his world. For a long moment she sat very still, staring at him and then, with a deliberate effort of will, Jessica managed to shake off the dangerous urge to surrender. But, dear lord! Each time the task of collecting her straying senses was becoming more difficult. How much longer could she continue to fight the undermining feeling of inevitability? In only a few more days they would be back in Los Angeles. . . .

The next day in Mazatlán, Lucas arranged for Bill Howard to go out on one of the deep-sea fishing boats. The older man was overjoyed at the prospect of fishing for the big, sleek gamefish available in the Mexican waters. Jessica was, if not exactly overjoyed, definitely feeling a sense of relief as she and Ann watched the men prepare to leave on the boat they had chartered. Lucas had taken charge of renting the proper equipment and he had sought out a charter captain with whom he had worked previously. Lucas was going with Bill and therein lay the reason for Jessica's sense of relief. It was the first time she had known a sensation of freedom in days.

As if aware of her inner excitement, Lucas paused for a few minutes before joining Bill on the fishing boat. "Goodbye, Jessie. We'll be back in about four hours. In the meantime, stick with Ann like a good girl, hmmm? And both of you stay in the main tourist areas, understand?"

"Are you being patronizing, Lucas?" Jessica inquired interestedly. She wasn't certain, herself, exactly where this urge to tease him had come from.

"I'm going to be damn annoyed if you aren't waiting here on this dock in four hours," he retorted, noting the glint of laughter in her eyes. "Just remember what happened the last time you disobeyed orders, woman!"

"I do. You came gallantly to my rescue and then took me out to lunch."

He grinned, a slow, wicked promise of pure male menace. "This time it will be different."

He was teasing her, Jessica realized belatedly, precisely because he knew there was no real risk of her getting into trouble. She would stay with Ann Howard and the two of them would confine themselves to the crowded areas of town. Lucas must have had a sixth sense that told him exactly how much under his control she had slipped.

"Have fun!" Ann called out as he released Jessica to step on board the gently bobbing boat. Bill waved back at her a little absently, busy going over his rented equipment. A moment later, Lucas joined him and neither man did more than glance back once at the two women waving goodbye on the dock.

"I don't know what they think they're going to do if they do catch anything," Ann grumbled good-naturedly as she and Jessica caught a cab for the shopping district along the waterfront. "We can hardly take a marlin back on board the ship!"

Jessica laughed. "After they get their pictures taken with the creature they'll give the fish away for local consumption, I imagine. Come on, Ann, I've heard there is some fabulous leathercraft around this part of Mexico."

"You know, it was really very nice of Lucas to arrange this trip for Bill. I'm sure it's going to be the highlight of my husband's entire vacation, whether or not they catch any fish!" Ann confided sometime later, "Lucas is a very charming man, isn't he?" They stopped to peer into a shop window.

Jessica thought about that seriously for an instant. "He can be," she finally admitted cheerfully. "He can also be incredibly annoying. Oh, look! Do you like that purse, Ann? I found one similar to it in Acapulco, but Lucas more or less talked me out of it. He said I'd probably never wear it anywhere except on vacation in Mexico!"

"Well? Isn't that a good enough reason to buy it?" Ann countered with perfect logic.

"You're right. Why didn't I think of that?" Without further pause, Jessica entered the small shop and made the purchase.

At lunchtime they found a restaurant serving food in a pleasant, shaded courtyard. Later they toured the main plaza, took a horse-drawn carriage tour of the town, and finally, precisely four hours later, stood waiting on the docks for the return of the fishermen.

"Oh, my goodness," Ann exclaimed as the small boat eventually came into view. "I do believe they got something!"

It was a beautiful, blue monster of a fish and judging from the ear-to-ear grin on Bill Howard's face a few moments later, it was a good bet the older man had been the successful fisherman on board. Lucas jumped lightly ashore, and helped to tie up the boat, a pleased look of satisfaction on his face.

"Did you get anything?" Jessica asked as he stepped back and the work of unloading the fish began.

"I got a lot of fun out of watching Bill land this beauty," Lucas told her lightly. And she believed him. Lucas had set out to give his companion a good day and took his pleasure in having achieved his goal. He didn't seem the least depressed about his own lack of success. A nice man. She chewed her lip at the thought. Why was it that every time she turned around there was something else about Lucas Kincaid that appealed to her? It wasn't fair!

By the time the last night on board ship arrived, Jessica was feeling more high-strung than she had ever felt before in her life. The sense of an impending climax to Lucas's pursuit was mixed now with the first hopeful glimmer of a new possibility. This was her last night trapped with him on the vessel. If she got through tonight, she would be free.

Nothing had changed in his tactics. He was still there whenever she swam or ate or read in a deck chair. He concentrated on letting her feel his power through all the little, innocuous ways a man has of making himself known to a woman. For the first time in her life, Jessica had begun to wonder if there hadn't always been something more than simple courtesy behind the small things men traditionally did for women. When Lucas performed such tasks as opening a door or ordering her food, he managed to make her totally aware of him, totally aware that, instead of providing her with comfort, he could just as easily have been assaulting her, taking her.

The bizarre thought was one of many similar notions that had been flickering in and out of her head for days, Jessica realized as she dressed for their last dinner together. Just as he had in the desert, Lucas wanted her to acknowledge his ability to provide for her. Perhaps now his need to force her recognition of his strength was even stronger in some ways, because he knew of the role that Scanlon Hotels played in her life. His rival was not another man, whom he could easily have defeated, but a huge, monolithic corporation.

Jessica wasn't sure what made her choose the flirty red dress she had worn that first night, but even as she reached for it, the gown seemed appropriate. The beginning and the ending of a trip and possibly of one of the strangest affairs on record, she told herself with a wry curve of her lips. Would Lucas be moving in for the kill tonight? He had yet to pressure her back into bed, seeming content to settle for total awareness of his presence, instead.

But tonight was the last night they would be together. If he didn't try to consolidate his victory this evening, he would never have another chance, Jessica thought as she brushed her hair into its familiar sleek knot. Tomorrow they would be in L.A. and she would be safely out of his reach again, back under the protection of Scanlon.

Of course, that was what she had told herself the last time they parted! Jessica winced at the memory, a part of her shivering with excitement at the thought of having been unable to escape him.

Damn it! What did she want? Furiously she slipped into her high-heeled shoes and headed for the door. What was the matter with her? She had been ricocheting back and forth between two extremes of emotion for several hours, until she wasn't sure she had any idea of her true feelings in the matter.

All she had to do was get through the next few hours, Jessica decided grimly as she reached for the knob of her stateroom door. By tomorrow morning everything would be back to normal. All she had to do was make it through this last night.

And then she opened the door and found Lucas waiting on the other side. Quite suddenly the possibility of surviving the night seemed remote, indeed. Jessica froze, staring up at him with all her impending surrender in her eyes.

He smiled down at her with a politeness that didn't mask the desire in his own gaze. "Ready?"

Jessica scrambled for self-control, seizing it with a force she'd never had to use before in her life. But she managed to hide that momentary betrayal of emotion, which had been in her face when she'd found him unexpectedly at her door. Deliberately she summoned her most polished smile.

"I'm ready. I believe the Howards are expecting us for a farewell drink before we go in to dinner?" Bravely she left the security of her stateroom and shut the door behind her. Why did it seem as if she'd just slammed the door of her cage—from the outside?

"They're in the lounge on the upper deck," he said, taking her arm with a gentle firmness that sent tremors through her.

Jessica slanted a glance up at him as they walked along the corridor. His hair was neatly combed and the white shirt under the corduroy jacket was crisp and clean. She wondered idly if he'd had the cabin steward launder it. Another tip. This trip must be costing him a fortune, she thought guiltily. Well, it wasn't her fault he'd followed her, she told herself in the next breath. But perhaps he'd felt he hadn't any choice. Did she have any choice about the final outcome of this complex, deeply sensual dance? The sense of inevitability hung heavily about her.

They toasted the sunset with the Howards, sipping margaritas in the cocktail lounge and enjoying the panoramic view of sea and sky. The conversation was light and easy and Bill Howard thanked Lucas once more for the fishing trip.

"He'll be talking about it for months," his wife chuckled.

"He deserves to talk about it," Lucas said, grinning. "It was a hell of a good catch."

"It's too bad you didn't get anything," Ann observed regretfully.

"I took great satisfaction out of having Jessie stay out of trouble for the day," he laughed.

"Well, there wasn't much trouble to be gotten into that I could see!" Ann retorted.

"Jessie can get into trouble in the middle of nowhere," Lucas informed her. "That's why I stick so close, generally. She needs me around to keep her safe."

Jessica lifted beseeching eyes toward heaven and the others all laughed. But as they rose to go into dinner she shot him a withering glance. "I hope you're enjoying yourself, Lucas!"

"I am."

Having arrived at the table with the others, Jessica was able to make a beeline for her own menu and she had her order ready when the waiter appeared. Appalled at the small sense of triumph it gave her, she rattled off a request for raw oysters on the half shell with mignonette sauce, cucumber and dill soup, and chicken in walnut sauce. When she flashed a triumphant glance at Lucas from under her lashes, he merely laughed back at her with gleaming eyes.

The ridiculousness of her small victory brought a somewhat rueful smile to her own lips.

The last night on board. Jessica found herself wanting to enjoy it to the fullest. She felt alive and excited and rather reckless. It was a kind of high brought about by her sure and certain knowledge that Lucas wanted her and that she had only to put him off for one more night in order to be free.

At the end of dinner the Howards joined other friends, with whom they had played bridge on board, and Lucas smiled at Jessica a bit too politely. "Shall we go to the lounge?"

"So you can amuse yourself chasing off the few men who might work up the courage to ask me to dance?" she retorted.

"It passes the time," he responded calmly, taking her arm and leading her toward the door. "Besides, the band is pleasant to listen to, even if we don't dance."

"We don't dance because you haven't asked me lately!"

"I told you, I can't stand the thought of being rejected," he quipped.

They found one of the few remaining tables and ordered brandy. The band was warming up for a group of passengers determined to spend their last night on board enjoying themselves to the fullest extent. It was going to be a somewhat boisterous crowd this evening, Jessica thought, glancing around in amusement. Off to one side she saw her acquaintance from the first day, Kirk Randall, busy chatting with the redhead from the aerobics class. The woman had confided happily to Jessica that morning after class that she had been having the time of her life since she'd met Kirk. He was, it appeared, everything a woman could hope to find on a cruise ship. Jessica was forced to acknowledge privately that she, personally, hadn't missed Kirk in the least. Lucas had seen to it that there was no room in her thoughts for another man.

Couples, including the gay couple, crowded out onto the floor as soon as the music began. No one was going to waste a minute of the precious time left. Jessica sat with Lucas and watched, sipping slowly at her brandy. She wanted very much to be out there with the others and she would have given a great deal if one of the men in the room had approached her. But she knew by now that that was highly unlikely and even if one did get up the nerve, Lucas would quash the interloper in a hurry. On the other hand, she thought resentfully, he wasn't going to ask her, himself. She didn't for one moment believe his explanation about a fear of rejection. It was just another tactic, Jessica decided as she took another swallow of brandy. She wasn't sure of the purpose of this particular tactic, but Lucas never did anything without a purpose.

Under the table the toe of her sandal swung restlessly as she watched Lucas's profile. He was reclining in his chair with a catlike grace that somehow managed to stir her senses, his eyes on the dancers. What was he thinking? she wondered.

"Missing the bunnies and parakeets?" she asked, breaking the silence between them with taunting sweetness.

"They're in good hands." He shrugged. "My assistant is very reliable."

"How about Clarence? Will he rush to greet you when you walk through the door of the shop?" she persisted, unable to control her desire to provoke him tonight.

"The only time Clarence rushes anyplace is when his food is dropped into his cage. Snakes are basically lazy creatures."

"I didn't know."

He turned his head to look at her, a smile tugging at the corners of his mouth. "You'll have to come and meet him sometime."

"I'm not too fond of snakes," she said thoughtfully. She was suddenly conscious of an intense curiosity about Lucas's pet shop.

"What *are* you fond of, Jessie?" he asked quietly.

"Dancing," she returned without hesitation.

"Poor Jessie. You haven't done much of that for the past few evenings, have you?"

She shook her head, waiting for him to ask her. Surely he would tonight!

"I rather enjoy dancing, myself," he informed her in a husky, gravel-rough voice. The iron-gray eyes met hers, pinning her. "So why don't you ask me?"

Jessica blinked. "Ask you? You're supposed to ask me!" she breathed, her pulse quickening at the expression on his face. Then, before he could say anything further, she rushed on, "Lucas, will you dance with me, please?"

"Thank you," he responded politely, getting to his feet, "I'd be delighted."

Jessica allowed him to lead her out onto the floor and pull her firmly into his arms before she lifted questioning eyes to his unreadable face. "Why didn't you ask me? Why did you insist on waiting for me to ask you? And don't give me that line about rejection!"

He slid a hand along the length of her back to the base of her spine and forced her gently into the heat of his thighs. "I wanted you to realize that I'm the only man on board with whom you're free to dance," he muttered thickly, his lips in her hair.

Jessica felt the strength in his arms, knew the controlled grace of his body, and experienced a violent longing to give herself up to the power in him, if only for the course of the dance. Unable to speak for fear of revealing more than she wished, she rested her head on his shoulder and let herself be swept away on the sensual tide of the music.

Lucas made of the dance a deeply sensual, wholly compelling ritual that engaged all her senses. Heedless of the other couples on the floor, he circled her waist with both arms, leaving her no option but to entwine her hands around his neck. When her fingers found the thickness of his dark hair, he groaned almost inaudibly and used his palms to mold her intimately against him.

Jessica had no wish to fight the tightening strands of the silver snare; not just then; not while she was still relatively safe on the dance floor. The crowd around her served the same purpose as the other passengers from the plane had served as they sat grouped around the campfire. There was safety in numbers.

But if Lucas was aware of the protection she imagined around her, he didn't show it. His body seemed intent on tantalizing hers, beckoning her closer into a furnace from which there would be no escape. Deliberately he began to build the pressure, letting his fingers sear the areas of sensitive flesh bared by the red silk dress, making her aware of the hardness of his thighs, inviting her to toy with the slightly curling ends of the hair at the back of his neck.

Like a small creature tempted by the promise of pleasure just inside the trap, Jessica hesitated on the outside, willing herself to look but not touch. She was safe as long as she kept her head. She knew that much intellectually, but it didn't seem to have any influence over her emotions. Heaven help her, but tonight she wanted Lucas Kincaid.

And tonight she could not have him without surrendering.

It was that knowledge which made her lift shocked eyes to his as the music drew to a close. There in his own gaze she saw the same knowledge. She could have him but only if she gave herself completely. As his arms fell away from her, Lucas held her a moment longer with his gleaming glance.

"Go ahead, Jessie," he advised in a drawling whisper, "run one more time. I'll find you."

She stared up at him as all the conflicting emotions within her seemed to coalesce, and then she whirled and fled through the crowd of dancers, seeking a way out of the trap; searching one last time for the safety of her gilded cage.

What she found out on deck was the railing, which barred further flight even while it protected her from the depths of the sea. She came to a halt beside it, inhaling deeply of the salt-scented night air while she tried to regain her equilibrium. Her nails dug into the wood as she stared out to sea.

Why was she running? She belonged to him. Hadn't she known that from the beginning? It wasn't because he was the dominant male in the herd. Here on the ship he was only one of many men, several of whom, including the captain, surely were far more dominant in the accepted sense. It wasn't the same as it had been out in the desert, yet for her Lucas Kincaid was the only man who counted. He would always be the one man who could dominate her senses, the one man who could arouse this primitive response. He knew her in a way no other man ever would and, in turn, she knew him as thoroughly.

It was that last thought which gave her the courage to turn slowly as the tingling sense of awareness flickered to life within her. He was there in the shadows across the deck, waiting to claim her. Dark and lean and radiating a power which seemed tuned to her alone, he stood braced against the soft motion of the ship and waited.

She regarded him mutely for a timeless moment, the moonlight gleaming on her hair, the red silk whipped around her legs by the breeze.

"Jessie, I need you."

"I know," she whispered. "I know."

Wordlessly he put out his hand and Jessica stepped forward to let his fingers close around hers.

Ten

He led her down through the ship the way he had once led her out into the desert and Jessica followed willingly, drawn by the need in him and the warm lock he had on her wrist. Lucas said nothing until she turned a questioning glance up at him as they stepped from the elevator out into the corridor that led to his stateroom instead of hers.

"I don't particularly want Scanlon to be a part of this tonight," he growled softly, gray eyes caressing. "Tonight I'll provide your bed and anything else you need."

Jessica nodded, understanding, and then they were at his stateroom door. Lucas's hand shook a little as he fit the key into the lock and the sight sparked a wave of tenderness in her that made her reach out to touch his sleeve. Her aquamarine eyes were soft and gentle in the corridor light.

He glanced down at her as the door opened and Jessica thought she would melt beneath the need and the desire in his face. He was a thoroughly honest man and he deserved to know how completely she was coming to him tonight. As the door closed behind them, she moved into his waiting arms.

"I need you, Lucas. I didn't fully understand that the first time and I was too busy trying to manipulate you the second time to analyze my own feelings. But tonight I know the truth.'' She spoke the words wonderingly as they came alive in her mind, half-afraid to believe them yet knowing they were the right words. "I need you as much as you need me.''

"I'm not sure that's possible," he confessed hoarsely, gathering her close. "But I would go out of my head if I couldn't believe there's something important in this for you, Jessie. I don't want to just take.''

"You never just take," she whispered, pressing her face into the solid warmth of his shoulder. "You give and I . . . I guess I'm not accustomed to men who know how to give even when they're making a claim.''

"Jessie!" he breathed, his hand sliding into her hair to pull it down around her shoulders. "Jessie, you are everything I need tonight and I want you so.''

He buried his face in her hair as it came free at last and Jessica sighed with a longing that consumed her totally. Lucas felt the tremor go through her slender body and he forced her more closely against him, as if he would still the shiver with his own body heat. His hands tunneled under the tumbling fall of tawny hair and then began to move achingly down her back, burning through the red silk.

"Oh, Lucas, Lucas . . . I . . .'' Her jumbled cry was swallowed as his mouth came down on hers, making words unnecessary. Jessica's lips parted at once for the passionate invasion, welcoming him deep into the honeyed secret behind her teeth.

The kiss was a preliminary uniting that restaked a claim that could never again be denied. Lucas surged deeply into the intimate depths, hungrily retaking what had been his since that first time in the desert. His tongue sought out hers, coaxing, persuading, challenging until she could do nothing but respond in kind. The hot love-play fed their senses, invoking tremors of mounting excitement.

Unable to resist, Jessica's gilded fingertips slid inside the opening of the corduroy jacket, probing the strength of his shoulders. Somehow the jacket fell to the floor in a soft heap and then she was loosening the tie. So intent was she on finding once more the well-remembered warmth of his bronzed skin, Jessica was barely aware of her own red silk dress being gently slipped to her waist.

And then a thick, muffled groan trembled in the broad chest beneath her fingers and Lucas's hands moved to cup her small, curving breasts. The shock of the passionate touch stirred her deeply. He held the soft weight of her for a moment, savoring her, and then his thumbs began to rasp tantalizingly across the still-shy nipples. Under his gentle, exciting insistence, they began to bud forth eagerly, and Jessica moaned with longing as the tips of her breasts told him of her escalating desire.

With fingers that fumbled a little under the impetus of her own passion, Jessica managed to remove the white shirt, leaving the striped tie draped around his throat, the ends hanging down his chest. She pulled away from him as the shirt fell to the floor, picking up the ends of the tie and tugging gently.

Lucas's mouth tilted in lazy passion and he let her lead him toward the single, narrow berth. At the edge she halted, still retaining her hold on the leash and smiled up at him invitingly.

"Is this what they call being led astray?" he murmured, his eyes darkening in the soft light.

"Probably. Are you worried?" she asked throatily.

"No," he admitted thickly, "I'd follow you anywhere."

"You've got that backward, Lucas. I'd follow *you* anywhere," she told him with a sudden certainty that heightened the glow of her eyes.

"Would you?" The words sounded cryptic to her ears but, before Jessica could question them, Lucas was moving his hands to her waist, sliding his palms inside the folds of the red silk dress and pushing it over her hips. It fell into a crimson froth at her feet.

Then he went down on one knee in front of her, his lips searing the silky skin of her stomach as he slowly, deliberately, began to remove the scrap of lace and satin that was all that remained of her clothing.

He drew the panties down with exquisite, teasing slowness, exploring each new inch of flesh with his mouth as it was exposed. Jessica gasped and her fingers wrapped themselves deeply into the thick darkness of his hair. Her eyes closed tightly against the rush of passion invading her bloodstream. When the bit of lace and satin lay at her feet, she felt his teeth in the gentlest of stinging little kisses on her thigh. Simultaneously his hands shaped the full globes of her buttocks, holding her still for the flick of teeth and tongue.

"Lucas!" It was a cry and a plea and it only served to provoke him into more of the unbearably thrilling little kisses. His lips moved over the skin of thigh and hip, nipping, soothing, stinging, exciting until Jessica thought she would go mad.

Her nails slid down to his shoulders, digging into the hard flesh as her body arched to his touch; when she called his name again, this time in an agony of desire, he began to climb slowly to his feet. En route, his kisses were lavishly trailed across each breast and then along her throat until at last he rediscovered her mouth.

By then Jessica was trembling with the force of her need. When he had risen to his full height in front of her, she curved her arms around his neck and leaned into his strength. There her body found the unmistakable evidence of his own rising passion and the taut, uncompromising demand of his maleness made her moan once again.

"Finish undressing me, Jessie," he commanded softly. "Touch me, sweetheart. Please touch me."

She obeyed, her mouth pressed to his bare chest as she dealt awkwardly with the buckle of his belt. Then she found the zipper and at last he was stepping out of the remainder of his clothing, gloriously, unselfconsciously naked. Only the tie still dangled around the firm column of his throat, symbolic of the collar she had once sought to chain him with. When he removed it absently, as if only vaguely aware of its presence, Jessica smiled to herself. There was no need to chain this man. He could be trusted completely.

Jessica, pressed close against the demanding warmth of him, reveled in the power of his passion. Her fingers began to tease and toy with the curling hair of his chest, tracing it down to his waist and beyond. When her probing touch suddenly became excruciatingly intimate, Lucas growled with a fierce promise that took away her breath.

"Jessie, you've been mine since our first time together. Tonight I need to hear you admit it. Do you understand me, sweetheart?" He swung her off her feet and settled her on the narrow bed, his eyes full of the question he had just asked.

Jessica looked up at him as he towered over her in the muted light. He needed the assurance that this time she fully comprehended the extent of their relationship. "I understand, Lucas. You've been right all along. I should never have run from you. I was only running from myself."

"Jessie!"

He came down along the length of her, covering her with his heat and fierce need. She folded him close, giving way as he forced his legs urgently between her own. The roughness of his thighs was a further incitement to her spinning senses, deliciously contrasting with her softer contours. The male scent of him was a primitive fragrance she inhaled deeply. The teasing scrape of his chest hair on her aroused nipples caused her to twist sensuously against him. When she feathered his throat with her lips, Lucas rasped words of longing into her ear and his fingers stroked the skin of her shoulders as if he were stoking a delicate fire.

There in the small room Lucas concentrated on bringing all of her senses alive. This time, Jessica knew with sure, feminine instinct, there would be no doubt about the completeness of her surrender; but, by the same token there would be no doubt, either, about the totality of what he was giving in exchange. They needed each other. It was as simple and as unbelievably complex as that.

Without hesitation Lucas used his muscled weight to pin her to the bed, but the sensation was infinitely thrilling. Every time she moved, every time she arched against him or explored the length of his leg with her bare foot, he was there, enveloping her. When he raised his lower body slightly away from hers to explore the invitingly intimate area below her waist, Jessica sucked in her breath.

"Sweetheart," he breathed huskily, "I can feel the want in you. Tell me about it. Tell me of your need."

Her head shifted restlessly on the pillow, tawny hair fanning out around her. Her lashes veiled the brilliance of her sea-colored eyes. "Lucas, I would not be able to stand it tonight if you did not make love to me. I need you so desperately!" She lifted her hips against his hand, her body opening like a flower to him as he stroked the petals of her with erotic sensitivity. "Please, Lucas! Please!" she gasped, her breath catching in her throat.

He seemed to test himself against her, letting her know the readiness of his manhood. And then he was storming her body in a rush of power that brought his name to her lips in a silent cry.

Now the captivating tenderness of his earlier lovemaking gave way to an assault on her senses. To Jessica it seemed as if he filled her, surrounded her, chained her completely, and the heady mix of sensations made it impossible to do anything else except respond. She clung to him as if he were the only reliable thing in her world and he merged them into a single, trembling entity. The shivers that coursed through one, coursed through the other, and the damp film of perspiration generated by their bodies seemed to function as a source of electrical contact binding them together.

Again and again Jessica whispered Lucas's name as she wrapped herself around his surging body, absorbing him into her very being. In turn he grated short, incredibly arousing words against the skin of her throat. As it had the night she had set out to seduce him, the gentle pitch of the ship on the sea provided a strangely exciting counter-movement to their lovemaking, as basic and elemental as the human bonding taking place on board.

The intensity of their passion spiraled quickly, forcefully out of control. There was no attempt to tease or provoke or play. Tonight the final link was being forged in a chain that would bind her, Jessica knew instinctively, to Lucas for the rest of her life. She did not question the fact, content instead to allow it to happen. Her nails raked his back in ancient meaning and when he slid a palm beneath her buttocks to raise her more tightly against him, she felt his fingers sinking deeply into her softness.

The small pain acted as a stimulant to her already overheated senses.

"Lucas!" Her words were breathless, choked as her whole body went abruptly, exquisitely taut. "I don't...I can't..."

Instead of gentling the tension in her, he muttered her name and fed it further by finding a throbbing nipple with his lip-sheathed teeth.

"Oh!" She slipped over the edge of the precipice as he thrust into her with a final flash of power. The tension that had arched her feet and throat and coiled so tightly in the pit of her stomach suddenly exploded, ricocheting back along each individual nerve ending in a series of tiny, shivering convulsions that brought indescribable pleasure to every inch of her body.

Even as she succumbed to the riveting series of sensations, Jessica was conscious of Lucas arching himself simultaneously into her, pressing her far into the depths of the bunk with his weight and strength. The reaction of his own release rippled through the muscles under her hands and Jessica gloried in the knowledge that it had been as intense as her own.

For an unknown time there was only silence in the small room. Jessica lay sprawled beneath the relaxed strength of the man who had just claimed her so completely, languidly content to stay in such a position forever. It was where she belonged. They needed each other.

When he finally lifted his tousled head to search her love-softened features, Lucas said nothing for a long moment. His clear gray eyes roved over her as if he was examining a personal treasure. Then, wordlessly he bent his head to kiss her lips in a seal of promise and commitment.

"Go to sleep, sweetheart," he whispered, rolling onto his side and pulling her close against him. "Go to sleep." He stroked her hair tenderly back from her forehead and tucked her cheek down onto his shoulder. "It's almost over."

She wanted to ask him what was almost over, but the aftermath of their passion had left her limp and drifting. She welcomed the instructions to sleep and her body obeyed without hesitation.

It was the silence of the ship around her that awakened Jessica the next morning. For a few minutes she couldn't comprehend exactly what it indicated, and then she realized they must have docked in L.A. Out in the corridor there came the sounds of people rolling suitcases along the halls, preparing to leave the ship. Opening her eyes, she glanced around and found herself still swallowed in darkness. The drawback to an inside stateroom, she thought in amusement. No window.

And then she realized that the narrow berth was empty except for herself.

"Lucas!" Anxiously she called his name into the darkness and when there was no response she fumbled hastily for the light switch. Blinking in the abrupt glare she glanced around. The small cabin had been vacated. Had Lucas already left the ship? Surely not without her!

A curious sense of panic welled up inside, driving her out of the bed and sending her scrambling for the protection of her clothes. Where was he? Why had he left? He couldn't have done this to her!

She found the note propped against the cabin door where she could not fail to find it on her way out. Nervously she reached for it and slit open the envelope, which carried the cruise liner's crest on the outside. Jessica read the short message with her heart in her throat.

Sweetheart, there is one more step which must be taken to fill the space between us and you must be the one to take it. You have to be sure, Jessie. I want you to know your own mind. I don't want an affair with you, I want to make a home with you. That means Scanlon must become merely a career and not a substitute family for you. Come to me, Jessie, when you no longer want to live in a gilded cage. I was wrong, honey, I can't reach in and force you outside. I can only open the door and ask you to come out and join me.

In the lower left-hand corner was scrawled an address. Tears burned her eyes as Jessica carefully folded the note and stuffed it into the opening of her evening bag. Then, dressed in the crimson silk she had worn the night before, she walked out into the hall and up the stairs to her own stateroom. She would have to hurry. After all, Scanlon would have a car waiting for her outside on the docks.

It was several days later that Jessica halted on the sidewalk of a pleasant, palm-lined San Diego street and glanced again at the address on the card in her hand. It couldn't be much farther, she decided with a frown of concentration as she lifted her eyes to scan the signs of the various shops and businesses along the street. Then she saw what she was looking for, a colorful wooden sign with the store's name in red letters: THE PET CONNECTION.

For the first time since she had climbed into the Scanlon car at the docks, and been driven back to her hotel apartment, Jessica's nerve faltered. What if Lucas had been trying to back out of the relationship? What if he had left the note because he thought it was a simple way for both of them to end a shipboard romance?

Then Jessica shook her head and her mouth edged upward in a smile of returning certainty. Lucas Kincaid would never have chosen to end things with a note left propped against the door the morning after. Nor would he have said anything in that note that he didn't mean. Lucas, she knew very well, was an honest man; a man who could be trusted with her life or with her love. Chin lifted, the faint smile echoed in her eyes, Jessica strode briskly toward the door of the pet shop.

She opened it and stepped inside, her arrival announced by a bell which tinkled overhead. There she halted in her tracks, eyes widening with amused interest. Pandemonium reigned.

"What the hell?" It was Lucas's voice, coming from somewhere toward the rear of the shop near a row of cages. She couldn't see him, but she could hear him quite clearly. "Whoever just came in, for God's sake shut the door!"

Jessica did so at once and then stood there trying to make sense out of the confusion. On the left a huge parrot screeched, flapping his wings as he stalked up and down his perch. He was responding to the shouts of a little boy racing down the aisle toward him, waving a net.

"I think he went this way, Mr. Kincaid!" the boy shouted happily, diving under a counter with his net. The parrot, not yet convinced the net hadn't been aimed at him, squawked again.

Several puppies could be heard, adding their excited barking to the general din, and the large cage of parakeets was a flutter of screeching activity. Green, yellow, and blue wings filled the space available as the alarmed and angry birds reacted to the clamor around them.

A cat hissed furiously as another little boy rounded an aisle full of empty goldfish bowls. This one, too, was waving a net and industriously checking under every counter as he hurried along. "He's over here, Jeff! I saw him head this way!"

A stack of tropical fish food cascaded to the floor as the other boy responded to his friend's call. Jessica watched, fascinated, as animals yelped, meowed, screeched, or raced around their cages in agitation. The two boys were clearly enjoying themselves enormously as they threatened everything in sight with the nets.

Then something tiny and white raced across the open toe of her sandal. She looked down the length of her leg in time to see a small mouse dash for cover behind a package of dog food. Quite suddenly she knew what the nets were for.

"Over here, boys," she called cheerfully. "He went that-away."

"Where? Where?"

Mutely, Jessica pointed to the bag of dog food and the boys rushed forward. "We've got him, Mr. Kincaid!"

"Well, keep him cornered!" Lucas yelled back, starting up the aisle. "If the cats see him again there will be hell to pay!" He didn't see Jessica for a moment, his full attention on the two boys as they attempted to cage the scampering mouse with their feet while swinging the nets wildly.

Jessica took the opportunity to drink her fill of him, not bothering to hide the love in her eyes. He was wearing jeans and a white, long-sleeved shirt with the sleeves rolled up. The hard contours of his face and the lean strength of his body satisfied some of the hunger she had been feeling for the past few days. He glanced toward the door an instant later and Jessica did not try to hide the revealing expression on her face as his frowning gaze collided with hers.

"Jessie!" He came to an abrupt halt, mouse and children and general confusion clearly forgotten at the sight of her. "Jessie," he repeated in soft wonder. "You came."

"Didn't you think I would?" she returned with a tender, teasing smile.

"To tell you the truth, I was getting a little scared," he admitted starkly. "It's been several days."

"I had a lot of loose ends to tie up," she whispered.

"Jessie, I love you," he said very clearly above the general din. "I've loved you since that first day in the desert. I'll love you for the rest of my life."

"Oh, Lucas!" Aqua eyes glowing, she went toward him, throwing herself into the security of his arms with a force that was self-explanatory. "I love you, too. Why else do you think I'm here?"

"Jessie, my sweet Jessie." He held her fiercely as if he would never let her go.

"Got him, Mr. Kincaid! Here he is!"

Jessica glanced down, her cheek still pressed against Lucas's shoulder, to see one of the boys gleefully holding the hapless mouse by its tail. "Can we feed Clarence now? Can we?"

Lucas grimaced, not releasing Jessica. "You can. You know I can't bear to watch. Just be damn careful the mouse doesn't escape again, understood?"

"Yes, sir!" Together the boys raced back up the aisle toward the rear of the shop.

Jessica lifted her head to smile up at the man who held her so tightly. "Are you supposed to use language like that around children?"

"When one has been sufficiently provoked, it's unavoidable!" He gazed down at her with an urgency and a satisfaction that touched her heart. "Oh, God, Jessie, I've missed you so. I was going to give you another week and then I would have come after you."

"Again?" she teased lovingly, her arms resting happily around his neck.

"And again and again," he confided huskily. "Until you finally realized what you wanted."

"I want you, Lucas, and a home."

"And Scanlon?" he asked as if he had to.

"Scanlon is my company. It's a good company, Lucas. They even gave me a transfer down here to the San Diego office when I asked for it. But it's you I'll be living with. You're the only one who can give me a real home."

"Jessie, will you marry me?" he whispered.

"I was just about to ask you the same question." She grinned. "Of course, I'll marry you, Lucas Kincaid. I told you on the last night on ship that I would follow you anywhere."

"I wanted you to be sure, honey. I couldn't take it if you ever changed your mind." She saw the truth of his words in his eyes and she let her answer show in the way she pulled his head down to her own.

The two boys, returning from their snake-feeding, broke up the embrace. "It's all done, Mr. Kincaid," the taller one told Lucas helpfully, curious eyes on Jessica as she pulled herself a few inches away from Lucas. "Give Clarence about ten more minutes and there won't be any evidence left," he added proudly.

"Thank you," Lucas drawled wryly, his mouth curving in repressed amusement. "I'll see you again tomorrow. Remember to tell that new boy who moved in next door to you about Clarence."

"I sure will. Maybe his mom will see what a really terrific snake he is. My mom just didn't understand him," the boy sighed. "Come on, Jeff, let's get going. It's almost dinner time."

"Which reminds me," Lucas said softly as the shop door closed behind the two. "I've spotted the perfect restaurant for you. It's almost closing time. Give me a minute to lock up and I'll take you out to dinner."

A few minutes later, he locked the door on the now-quiet store and hooked a possessive arm around Jessica's shoulders, tugging her close against his side. "You're going to love this place, Jessie. Tailor-made for you."

"I can't wait," she chuckled, loving the proprietary feel of his arm and the warm grace of his body alongside hers. "Are you going to tell me exactly what sort of restaurant this is?"

"It's a sushi bar," he announced grandly. "Raw fish served in a thousand beautiful ways. Just your kind of place!"

She giggled. "Have you ever had sushi?"

"Nope. I've been saving the experience to share with you," he told her dryly.

"Don't worry, the Japanese have been enjoying it for years. You'll love it," she reassured him. "You know, you should be grateful I'm so fond of fish. After all, you're fond of catching them, aren't you? We make a good team."

"Precisely what I kept telling myself out there in the desert," he murmured.

"Don't give me that," she chided. "Teamwork was not exactly what you had in mind out there and you know it!"

He started her determinedly down the sidewalk. "Jessie, that's behind us," he declared firmly, "and you know it. Don't tease me about it any more. Please!"

"Okay," she agreed easily, eyes gleaming as she slanted him a sideways glance. "Whatever you say. Boss."

"Jessie!" He swung her to a halt, rueful frustration twisting his mouth and narrowing his gaze as he glared down at her. "If you don't let the subject drop, I swear, I'll...!"

"You'll what?"

"I'll change it," he retorted very smoothly, a wicked light flaring in the depths of his eyes.

"Change it to what?" Jessica prodded in amusement.

"To the little matter of your taste for raw fish."

"What about it?" she dared.

"Have you always loved raw fish? I don't recall your pining for it in the desert."

"I've enjoyed it off and on for years, why?"

"I mean, have you always made a habit of eating it with almost every evening meal?"

"Well, no, but it was especially well prepared on the boat and tonight it sounds very good again. What are you getting at, Lucas?"

He smiled with unabashed male anticipation and then gently pulled the snare taut. "Didn't your ex-family ever talk to you about the facts of life? About the significance of certain cravings, for example?"

As his meaning dawned, Jessica's eyes went wide. She did some hasty addition and came up with some answers. "Oh, my goodness. I hadn't realized how much time . . . I've had so much on my mind lately and I didn't stop to think. Lucas, you don't really suppose I might be pregnant, do you?"

"You're in a better position to judge that than I am," he answered, his eyes moving over her slender figure possessively as if he hoped very much to see some early sign. Then he sobered as she continued to stare at him, lips slightly parted in bemusement. "Honey, would you mind very much if you found out you were going to have a baby?" he asked anxiously.

"I think," Jessica stated slowly, "that you would make an excellent father. I'm not so sure about my mothering capabilities. Lucas, I know very little about children."

"Don't worry, I'll start bringing home some kittens and puppies and things," he assured her happily. "You can practice on them."

"You'd like to have a baby, wouldn't you?" she marveled.

"Yes," he told her unequivocally. "I would like very much for you to have my baby. I want a family as badly as you need one, sweetheart. Don't worry, I'll be there every step of the way. I told you once I'd never abandon you under any circumstances, remember?"

"I remember." Jessica smiled, relaxing as she accepted the idea. "I guess it would be the luckiest kid on the block. His choice of almost any pet from his father's pet shop!"

"And his mother will always be able to get him into the best hotels. What kid could ask for more?" Lucas concluded, pulling her close.

"I don't know about the kid, but I can state categorically that his mother has everything she wants," Jessica murmured as his lips found hers.

*　*　*　*　*

A Note from Patricia Gardner Evans

Flashpoint, my first published book, launched my writing career. The book also "launched," although it took me several more books to recognize it, my fondness for writing romantic suspense. I don't seem to be able, in fact, to write anything without suspense in it somewhere. That makes sense, considering that I grew up on a steady reading diet of Mary Stewart, Alistair MacLean, Helen MacInnes, Ed McBain and other assorted romantic suspense, thrillers and mysteries. I read all of Zane Grey, too, but that's another story. I hope you like this one—

Patricia Gardner Evans

P.S. The schoolhouse in *Flashpoint* actually exists. I had seen it, abandoned and for sale, and, of course, buying it was completely impractical, even if I could have afforded it. Instead, I let my heroine live in it so I got to "own" it that way.

FLASHPOINT

Patricia Gardner Evans

Prologue

"You're going down the tubes, Ryan Jones."

The russet-haired, green-eyed Irish pixie sitting across the kitchen table from him was, he reflected, the only person he'd have accepted that from. He picked at the remains of his lunch. The hell of it was, she was right.

Annoyance thickened her brogue noticeably. "No wife, no family, nothin' but self-indulgence and pushin' your luck as far as you can. Well, congratulations!" Her little hand slapped the tabletop in frustration. "You almost pushed it too far this time. Why don't you find yourself a good woman and stop wastin' your life?"

One corner of his beautiful, almost cruel mouth curled up in a cynical offer. "Well, Mother Eileen, why don't you find one for me? How about a beautiful virgin over the age of consent, if any still exist, and I'll make the ultimate sacrifice."

"A virgin?" One russet eyebrow crooked in sardonic amusement. "Tell me, Ryan, is the lucky bride goin' to get a virgin, too, on her weddin' night?" Her soft laughter chided him.

Eileen Jones studied the dark man slouched in the chair opposite her and wondered for the hundredth time how two brothers could be so unlike. Oh, physically they were quite similar, same features, same height, same lean build. Her husband's bright blue eyes and rusty-red hair turned his older brother's aloof, dark elegance into an open, friendly warmth, but one would still easily recognize them as brothers. But inside, in their hearts and souls, where it counted, the resemblance ended. She gave thanks that her husband was free of the devils that plagued his brother.

Ryan joined in the laughter, mocking his own chauvinism. Then he realized that he'd been more than half-serious. An oddly bleak look passed over his face. Unrealistic as it might be, he did want a woman who was untouched, his alone. Maybe her innocence could cleanse his soul.

Eileen Jones lay close to her husband in the wide bed. She was frowning absently at him. "I'm really worried about him this time, Rick. Watching himself slowly bleed to death out on that ocean made him take a long look at himself. I don't think he liked what he saw."

"I know, Eileen, but he sure as hell won't take any advice from me." His low voice was harshly bitter. "Not after what I cost him."

"Know what he told me when I said he should find a wife and settle down?"

"Geez, you have more nerve than I do, honey." He kissed his wife lovingly and settled her under his arm. "What'd he say?"

She told him. "I think he was half-serious. A virgin, indeed!" She sighed, disheartened. "He'll be well enough soon to go back to L.A. Then he'll have another chance to kill himself with one of his loony stunts."

"Oh, I don't know," Rick said slowly, idly playing with the short russet curls tickling his chest. "There just might be somebody for him. Exactly what he wants."

His wife pushed against his hard belly and sat up, catching the scheming glint in her husband's innocent blue eyes. Only she knew just how far from innocent they really were. "Oh, no. No, no, no, Rick," she moaned despairingly, giggling in spite of herself. "Surely you're not thinking what I think you're thinking. This isn't the Middle Ages, Richard," she reminded her husband tartly, stifling her laughter. "She isn't chattel to be given over to another man's protection. And besides, Ryan is hardly a white knight in shining armor."

"No," he admitted reluctantly, laughing, "he's definitely more like a black knight." He watched his wife's face grow thoughtful. The gleam in his eyes got brighter and craftier.

"You know, though," she said slowly, "they would make a very good pair. But how will you ever get them together? She can't leave, and you'll never," she declared flatly, "talk him into burying himself in some dinky town in Montana, even for a week."

With a slyly wicked chuckle, he pulled his wife back down firmly into his arms. "Oh, yes, I will," he growled into her ear with great anticipation. "In fact, I already know how I'm going to do it."

His wife caught an odd undertone in his voice, and she was suddenly stiff in his embrace. "You still think there's a possibility she's guilty, don't you, Rick? And your boss is convinced of it, isn't he?" Her small fist connecting with his solid shoulder was not gentle. "How can you think that after all she did for us while she stayed here? Caring for Erin, colic and all, and me, so sick with that infection I couldn't lift a finger to help myself? And she kept you together, too, Richard, in case you've conveniently forgotten."

Rick Jones sighed. He knew that deceptively soft tone in his wife's voice only too well. For the second time in one day she was about to lose her fine Irish temper with one of the Jones brothers. "The evidence, Eileen—"

"Evidence!" The rich disgust in her tone conveyed Eileen Jones's opinion of the evidence. "How you lawyers love evidence! You've said yourself that all the evidence against her is circumstantial. It could just as easily prove her innocence as her guilt."

Rick Jones placated his wife with his soothing voice and hands. "I know, Eileen, I know." He felt her relax, her temper cooling as quickly as it had flared. Then he glimpsed a flash of fear in her green eyes.

"You think she's in danger! That's why you're sending him."

"It's a possibility," he admitted reluctantly. "There have been some new developments in the case, and someone may decide to ensure her silence permanently."

His wife nodded slowly. "No one could protect her better than Ryan."

Rick Jones closed his eyes tiredly. Ryan would protect her, and she could settle a debt that had been outstanding far too long.

The woman closed her mailbox and began walking up the dirt track toward an old, red brick country schoolhouse. Her steps slowed and finally stopped as she read the open letter in her hands.

The September sun caught her golden hair, glinting around her bent head. The large brown dog by her side sat automatically, resting against a long, slim leg. Patiently she waited for her mistress to resume their walk.

The small smile on the woman's striking face spread into a large grin as she laughed softly at the color snapshot in her right hand. The blond, bearded giant in the picture looked like a Viking marauder. He actually managed to make nearly six-foot-tall Suzi, who stood beside him with his arm draped possessively over her shoulders, look petite. From their goofy, beautiful smiles and the way the camera had caught their eyes sneaking back to each other, they were clearly very pleased with themselves and each other. The love shining out of those joyous faces was so obvious that it almost hurt to see it.

She refolded the letter and slipped it back into the envelope with the photo. She glanced up at the blue mountain peaks guarding the small Montana valley. They looked so cold, so lonely in the Indian-summer sunshine. Her grin faded. Curling into the soft fur, her fingers unconsciously sought the heavy head leaning on her thigh. She was truly overjoyed for her best friend, and the love she had found, but the letter brought back the awful, restless impatience once again. A tear glittered as it fell unnoticed down her cheek. When would she be freed from this life . . . and maybe have a chance to find love, too?

She spoke to the dog in a low voice, and they continued their walk, heads down, plodding through the dark dust toward the empty house.

The parcel bin in the self-serve post office sighed shut, and the package fell inside with a solid thump. The man in the nondescript trench coat strode briskly back through the air terminal.

She would probably notice the San Francisco postmark, but the note inside should allay any suspicions. He had heard the young assistant D.A. she'd once lived with laughingly refer to himself as her "secret admirer." Even when the police discovered that the district attorney hadn't sent the package, there was no way it could be traced to him. The odds were against the package even being traced back to this particular mailbox. Even if it was and someone had seen him mail it, no one would remember the man with the lank blond hair and scraggly, drooping mustache who'd taken the red-eye flight up, then gone right back. Even the stewardesses had been half-asleep.

One had to take risks in business every day. The trick was to calculate the odds and make sure they were solidly in your favor. He was taking an infinitesimal risk in order to buy a lot of insurance.

He felt a small twinge of annoyance. It really was unfortunate that his "insurance agent" had only done the job halfway. It had been easy to get the "agent's" name one night when the old man was in his cups, reminiscing about the good old days. It was the same way he'd gotten other names, other information. He'd tracked the "agent" down. A lot of money and a little blackmail proved to be an irresistible offer for the small exterminating business the man had for sale. The blond man smiled unknowingly at that choice of career; the man's second profession wasn't far removed from his first. The absent smile was returned by a porter trundling a heavy trunk through the airport.

Even if the man hadn't died before the police could question him, he would have been able to tell them nothing about the man who'd hired him. His widow, if she'd known anything, had wisely kept her mouth shut, mentioning only her husband's nonexistent despondency over his retirement. Then she'd moved to Bakersfield to be near her grandchildren and quietly spend her sudden wealth. No, he was fully covered. He'd waited nine months, but, before the week was out, the last premium on the insurance policy should be taken care of.

The old man had been a fool to let the business go, he thought, but it hadn't been all that hard to start it up again. He'd had the money and a marketable name. He'd kept a few items from the old man's line and introduced a few new ones. Everything was going quite nicely. It just illustrated the classic law of supply and demand, and for what he supplied, there was a very profitable demand.

If only Dennis hadn't become so unreasonable about that woman, although he supposed, in a way, he should be grateful to her. It was her innocent suggestion that had solved their courier problem two years ago. Of course, she was also the reason he'd had to find the "insurance agent" and a new courier, since it was because of her that Dennis had wanted out.

And now he was having supply problems again, although in all fairness he couldn't blame her this time. Garza had been betrayed. By whom and for how much didn't matter; Garza's people *would take care of it, and Garza wouldn't talk. He was much too fond of his lovely teenage daughters. A new supply line had already been established, but the news of the arrest of the cocaine king of Guadalajara, as the papers had dubbed him, was still going to cause panic among all those with red, drippy noses, but no colds. It should be very good for business; he ought to be able to raise prices fifteen or twenty percent.*

Garza's picture had been plastered all over the West Coast papers. Her copy of the San Francisco Chronicle *would take a few days to reach Montana, but she'd see a picture sooner or later and remember a man who'd been someplace he shouldn't have been, talking to someone he shouldn't have known.*

And for that she had to die.

Chapter 1

There she was—every California girl the Beach Boys had ever fallen in love with and immortalized in song, the star of his adolescent fantasies, hundreds of miles from the nearest beach. She looked a little older, wiser, definitely sadder, but all the golden radiance was intact.

Her body was slender to the point of thinness, bent now to catch the giggled words of the little blond girl running up to her. The laughing smile on her face was an echo of the innocent smile beaming up at her. Ryan hadn't decided yet if it was a beautiful face, but it was certainly arresting. Her features were sharp angles softened by almost oversize blue eyes with long lids and a surprisingly full, soft-looking bottom lip. They gave her narrow, aristocratic face a startling touch of sultriness.

He watched the little girl skip away and the woman smile after her fondly. After all that had happened, how could she retain an illusion of innocence? Seeing her now, the sun gilding a halo around her summer-blond head, it seemed impossible that she could be guilty of murder.

As if she felt his intent gaze, she turned, her golden smile flickering over the crowd to him. The smile faded into a wary curiosity. Guarded eyes, as blue as the Indian summer sky over his head, stared directly into his. He stepped forward, crossing the few yards between them, and smiled.

"Ariel Spence? I'm Ryan Jones."

The low velvet voice brushed over her, and she felt lower than dirt. She had been furious when Chief Dye told her that he had sort of promised the empty half of her schoolhouse to Ryan Jones, the son of an old friend. He knew she wouldn't mind, really. The poor guy had had this terrible accident and needed a quiet place to recuperate, only for a month or so.

She did mind. Really. "The son of an old friend" was being sent to spy on her, he wouldn't have so much as a hangnail wrong with him. It wasn't enough that the whole town was watching her; now they wanted someone actually living in the house with her, to tell them when the big payoff came, or to snag the hit man when he finally showed up. It was all so absurd that she would have laughed it off if she hadn't been so furious. The chief had waited to tell her until it was too late to stop the "son" from coming, but she'd fixed him anyway, plotting her revenge with a fiendish glee.

But now he was here, and he very obviously *was* recovering from some awful trauma. He was at least a head taller than she, a little over six feet, and that long, rangy body was carrying too little weight for those broad shoulders and narrow hips. He was terribly thin, downright skinny, actually. Ariel was suddenly seized with the strange urge to cook hearty, fattening meals to put some meat on that malnourished, but nicely proportioned body. She laughed silently at the thought. Her cooking would undoubtedly make the poor man even skinnier.

She glanced back up to his face. The mouth was hard, yet it was curving now in a sweet, disarming smile. His skin was stretched too tightly over his cheekbones and it had an unhealthy, prisonlike pallor. His eyes were the color of bittersweet chocolate, bright, no sign of illness there. They were hooded, slightly mocking, as if he knew a secret she didn't. The straight, blue-black hair was healthy looking, too, parted on the left side and brushed back.

What was he going to say when he saw the condition of the place that was to be his home for the next month? Probably demand directions to the nearest motel, just as she had planned. A sickly ghost of her usual smile haunted her face, "Mr. Jones, I'm happy to meet you." She reached out a welcoming hand and a strong hard one clasped hers in return.

Ariel's eyes widened, a slight gasp slipping out between her abruptly parted lips. A sharp tingle had traveled from those long fingers up her arm. This man might not be what she'd been expecting, but he could be a problem just the same.

One winged black eyebrow arched. The wonder in his eyes was replaced by speculation before they became carefully blank. "I'm happy to meet you, Miss Spence," he returned gravely. There was just a hint of laughter in the smooth, dark voice.

She was definitely not happy. She looked very nervous about something, worrying her bottom lip, smoothing down her blue slacks and tugging on the hem of her navy pullover. It was a very nice little sweater, short sleeved, with tiny white flowers, but it fit too loosely, as if she'd lost weight. She probably hadn't been eating enough the past few months. He decided suddenly to do something about that.

Ariel realized that he still had her hand, and that his thumb was caressing slow circles over the too-rapid pulse in her wrist. She pulled free immediately. "How did you know who I was, and where to find me?"

"I stopped to see why all the cars were here, what was going on," he explained, then finished with a smooth lie. "Someone pointed you out to me when I asked for directions to your place."

"Oh. Probably you would like to go out to the house now." She wished she could sound more enthusiastic. "Why don't we—"

"Are you leaving, Ariel?" She was given a brief reprieve by the arrival of an older man with grizzled faded red hair. A large paunch spilled over his polished Sam Browne belt. He hitched it up, adjusting the holster more comfortably, and eyed the dark stranger with less than friendly pale blue eyes.

"Yes, Chief, I'm taking Mr. Jones out to the house." His hostile look finally registered. "Don't you know . . . ?"

"Chief Dye and I have never met," Ryan answered quickly. "I just heard about your place from my—"

"Right!" The chief picked up his cue immediately. "Ryan. Ted Dye." The two men shook hands. "How is . . . ?" He purposely didn't finish, and Ariel never noticed, because Ryan filled in with perfect timing.

"He's fine. He sends his regards." Ryan's right hand lightly gripped Ariel's elbow, and he began to guide her toward the jumble of vehicles parked in a dusty field. "Miss Spence was just going to show me where my new home is. I'll check in with you tomorrow and fill you in on the news from San Francisco."

The chief waved them away and walked back into the crowd gathering before a makeshift bandstand to hear the finalists in the fiddlers' contest.

Halfway to an older, orange Dodge power wagon parked off by itself, Ryan pulled Ariel to a stop. "I'm sorry; I never thought. Maybe you wanted to stay awhile longer?"

"Not really. Three hours of old-time banjo and flat-top guitar music is about my limit." Honey-colored eyebrows shades darker than her hair rose questioningly. "I thought you were from Los Angeles, but you mentioned San Francisco just now."

The sunlight playing through her loose, shoulder-length blond hair held his attention for a long moment. "My family lives in San Francisco. My law practice is in L.A. and, of course, I live there." He chose his words carefully. For reasons he didn't care to examine, he didn't want to tell her any outright lies. Tugging gently on her elbow, he started off again, but her feet were stubborn, rooted in the grassy field.

Cocking her head, her generous mouth pursed in consideration, she asked, "How did you know I didn't come with someone today, Mr. Jones?"

What would that soft mouth taste like? He would find out. It was just a question of when. "Because," he stated with utter conviction, "he would never have left you alone." His fingers slipped down the bare skin of her forearm to clasp her hand, and he led her away.

He followed her in his truck. Eventually Ariel signaled for a turn off the two-lane highway, glancing in the rearview mirror to be sure he was still with her. The wooden roadside sign by the cluster of mailboxes and newspaper tubes had been weathered gray by a half century of snow and rain and sun. Burnt Fork School, Ravalli County, Montana. Est. 1912, it read in fresh, brick-red letters. She drove automatically down the dirt road, her thoughts on her new tenant.

He'd favored his right leg, grimacing a bit every time he took a step on it. His half of the schoolhouse might be a mess right now, but he couldn't spend even a night at the Rustic Hut Motel. Only the upper level was open, and those steep slippery stairs would have him in agony before he was halfway up.

She'd noticed a lot more than his limp. She'd never before been so aware of a man's looks, so aware of a man, period. There was a peculiar air about him that made even his casual clothes seem elegant. When he moved, even with the limp, there was another kind of elegance, fluid, without wasted motion.

That too-handsome face belonged to a Regency rake, or his modern counterpart—the male model. Yet there was nothing dandified about Ryan Jones. Instead of a snowy, starched cravat tied in the complicated Mathematical knot, there was the open necked rust chamois shirt. Loose corduroy jeans were belted around his thin waist, not skintight pantaloons. He definitely wasn't modeling plastic masculinity and designer clothing on the pages of some slick magazine, either. His masculinity was all too real. She had sensed a very male, very primal sexuality, kept in control by smooth sophistication, yet undoubtedly still hazardous. Unleashed, she suspected it could quite possibly be lethal.

His clothes probably did have designer labels, though. They were well-made, obviously expensive, but they'd seen a lot of use, just like his truck. Clearly he didn't discard something simply because the newness had worn off and he could afford to replace it. Except women, she thought, one corner of her mouth tilting with wry amusement. A woman, she strongly suspected, would have a very short tenure with him.

She inventoried his truck as he drove up and parked next to her silver Blazer. The four-wheel drive pickup had at least two gas tanks, heavy-duty tires, a winch on the front bumper, an empty motorcycle carrier and a faded orange camper shell. It was hardly the kind of transportation she had imagined for a single thirty-four-year-old attorney of the caliber Chief Dye had intimated. Odd that he seemed to know so much about his friend's son, yet had never met him until today.

Gingerly Ryan eased himself out of the truck. His leg was killing him. He swung up the back of the camper shell and pulled down the heavy tailgate. Alongside three well-used leather suitcases on the truck bed were a hand-tooled leather gun case and a cardboard carton of law books and file folders.

Ariel joined him, and they each grabbed a suitcase. Ryan picked up the gun case in his free hand and started for the front door.

Ariel frowned at the oddly shaped case. "Do you hunt, Mr. Jones?"

A strange smile crossed his face. "I used to."

She started to ask him just what he used to hunt when a movement at the edge of her vision made her glance sideways. To her horror, she saw a large, brown, furry blur barreling around the corner of the house straight for her new tenant. "Murphy! No! *No!*"

Ryan swung the suitcase between the wicked-looking fangs and his leg. Just as he was bracing himself, praying that his leg wouldn't buckle, the vicious dog dropped, stopped dead and began a wriggling dance of demented delight. She yipped ecstatically, tail wagging, trying to worm her head under the hand with the gun case. He glanced dryly at Ariel, who was standing stock-still ahead of him.

"Great watchdog."

Ariel snapped her mouth shut. Now the darned dog was making calf's eyes at the man as he scratched behind her left ear. "I don't understand it," she muttered, shaking her head. "She's always very hostile toward men, even the ones she knows."

He slanted her a look from under sooty eyebrows. "Like her mistress?"

Ariel smiled sweetly. "I'm just careful, Mr. Jones."

"And one can't be too careful, can one, Miss Spence?"

He'd said it innocuously enough, but his eyes were laughing insolently at her. Ryan snapped his fingers and her dog trailed obediently at the heels of his old leather sneakers. What magic did this man possess? He'd been here less than two minutes, and already he'd seduced her man-hating dog. The only male Murphy had even shown that deranged affection for was Dennis.

"Why did you name her Murphy?"

"I didn't, actually. I inherited her from...a friend." Setting down his suitcase, she fished her keys from a suede shoulder bag. She wiggled the worn brass key in the lock until she heard a click, then pushed the door open with her shoulder.

Ryan noticed a new dead-bolt lock on the door, but she obviously didn't bother to use it. That would have to change immediately, he decided. She wasn't going to leave herself vulnerable to an attack, or come home to find that some burglar had... The thought brought him up short just inside the front door. He had no right to tell her how to lock her doors, no rights to her at all. Just the same, long dormant feelings of possession and protection began to stir.

Ryan pushed them aside, along with the door that he shoved open wider. Bright sunlight followed them inside, and he concentrated on his home for the next month. A long narrow hallway ran the length of the first floor of the schoolhouse, separating what had once been two large classrooms and were now two apartments.

Opening off the common hallway were two more doors, with pebbled-glass windows, one on each side for each apartment. The doors looked like the originals, unrefinished, and Ryan began to wonder just how rustic his accommodations were going to be.

Ariel threw open the left-hand door with a small flourish and an inward groan. Now she'd find out just how good a sport a high-priced, L.A. superlawyer could be. "Here you are," she said brightly. "I've, ah, been doing a bit of remodeling. I'm not quite done, but by next Thursday, at the latest . . ."

Her voice trailed off like a music box winding down as she watched him furtively from the corners of her eyes. His had widened slightly as he'd glanced into the half bath near the door. A neat black cap was over the floor drain instead of a commode. The sink was also missing. His eyes narrowed when he walked into the kitchen and saw the gaping hole in the yellow Formica countertop where that sink should have been, the vacant space for the non-existent stove and the floor only half tiled with yellow and blue squares. His eyes narrowed even more, and Ariel sighed resignedly, thinking of the surprises yet to be appreciated upstairs.

Ryan spared a brief glance for the dining area and living room, then began to climb a wrought-iron spiral staircase. Still lugging his suitcase, Ariel trailed after him, wincing and feeling smaller and meaner every time his right foot took another careful step on the stairs.

At least the two bedrooms were all right, if a little Spartan and small. Ariel had taken her half of the second floor and more in order to keep the bell tower for herself. Each of his bedrooms held only a double bed, rag rug, antique oak dresser and a straight-backed kitchen chair. The first also had a squat black wood stove tucked in one corner. He probably wasn't going to be too thrilled when he realized that all their heat came from wood stoves.

Ariel held her breath as he opened the bathroom door. She would bet he needed to take long, hot baths for his leg. That was going to be a bit difficult, with the tub missing. She heard him open the bathroom's other door, presumably to look around the second bedroom. No comment about the vanished tub, sink and toilet. The suspense was beginning to get to her.

Ryan walked slowly back into the bedroom, advancing silently with an unreadable expression on that wickedly handsome face. His dark eyes impaled her. Ariel backed up until the backs of her knees pressed against his bed. There was a vague feeling of menace in the sunny bedroom. Why didn't he *say* something. Complain? Yell, even? But yelling, she thought, wouldn't be his style. He wouldn't need loud words to be intimidating. Those blank eyes, the subtle cruelty hiding in that beautifully carved mouth, the way he moved, were adequately sinister.

She assumed a posture a Marine drill instructor would have praised and smiled sunnily. Stop being ridiculous, she scolded herself silently, and stop cringing! This is just a man, tired, in pain, who is being made to suffer unfairly the inconvenience of your childish spite.

"I know things look a little…rough, right now, Mr. Jones," she temporized, "but it's only for a few days, and in the meantime I'm sure we—"

"Weren't you expecting me?"

That low silky purr was definitely more intimidating than shouting. Ariel was suddenly, humiliatingly certain that he knew she had torn up his quarters out of maliciousness and that, somehow, he even knew why.

"Yes," she conceded in a helpless mutter. "Things just got a little…confused." She sidestepped neatly to escape being trapped between the bed and his body. "Let's go over to my side and … oh!"

With her usual devotion to duty, Murphy had positioned herself a few feet from her mistress. Ariel tripped over the dog and started to tumble. Her hand flailed through the air in her desperation to find something to stop her fall. As she fell, she clutched Ryan's leg with all her strength. His body, much heavier than it looked, landed squarely atop hers, squashing her into the bed.

An agonized groan echoed in the quiet room, followed by the jangling of Murphy's dog tags and her anxious whine. The dog's cold nose on Ariel's neck helped her jerk her face from its suffocating burial in the fine black hair at the open neck of his shirt. Ariel gulped in a shaky breath that brought in much-needed oxygen and a citrusy, musky scent.

Ryan groaned again, and Ariel was suddenly aware of her left knee—and her hand. Trapped as it was between them, she could only relax her fingers, but not move her palm from the growing warmth beneath it. She closed her eyes tighter in mortification. Her thigh was firmly snuggled between the tops of his. She wasn't sure if the groans were caused by her knee hurting his injured leg or her thigh and hand unintentionally pleasuring a little higher up, and she really couldn't give it any more thought. She was desperately fighting the urge to moan a bit herself. His hand had found a softness, too, but his touch was much gentler than hers, molding, stroking.... Her body, which had been so obedient for twenty-seven years, was abruptly defiant. It refused to move, preferring to enjoy the sensations short-circuiting through her.

Ariel finally opened her eyes. Ryan's face was turned toward hers on the bed. Immediately she straightened her knee and tried to slip out from under him as gently and rapidly as possible. His mouth showed fine white lines of strain and his eyes were shut tightly, as if in pain. Long black lashes curled against his cheeks. He hardly looked like a man copping a cheap feel, she berated herself.

As she started to push up off the bed, an amazingly strong hand shot out and clamped her wrist to the gold bedspread. "Wait!" he grated. "Don't move yet."

Ariel was appalled to see moisture at the corners of his still sealed eyes and a clammy sweat on his pasty forehead. She lay tensely, in an agony of embarrassment. Her free hand made a fist and hit the bed helplessly. "I am so sorry I hurt you, Mr. Jones," she whispered. "We just seem to have gotten off on the wrong foot entirely; I—"

"Literally," he gasped. He lifted his head and looked at her, a wicked gleam chasing the pain out of his eyes. His lashes curled even when his eyes were open, she noted absently. "Although I rather enjoyed your direct approach. If you wanted me on the bed, Miss Spence, all you had to do was ask. I never refuse a lady."

She'd just bet he didn't, she thought as he allowed her to stand. And few would refuse him. She sighed regretfully. "I *always* refuse, Mr. Jones." Her only annoyance, if she was honest, was at her body's traitorous reaction to his caressing hand, and not to his teasing. She joined in his groaning laughter from the safety at the top of the stairs.

"I really am sorry this degenerated into a slapstick routine." She saw his smile stiffen with pain as he tried shifting his leg to roll over. "If you want to rest for a while," she suggested gently, "I can explain later what I think we can do about the bathroom and cooking situation." She started down the spiral steps. Just before her head disappeared from view, she flashed him a quick grin. "I'll be around all afternoon; just come over whenever you're ready."

Ryan eased onto his back and inched up toward the pillows, stuffing one gingerly under the throbbing in his right thigh. The contemptuous smile on his face was solely for himself. He linked his hands behind his head and settled more comfortably onto the narrow bed. He stared up at a boring white plaster ceiling, seeing big blue eyes full of dismay at causing him pain. She would have been shocked if she'd known of the sweet aching in the middle of his body and the tingling he still felt in the center of his palm. And she would be outraged if she knew the ideas that ache and that tingle were giving him.

The file folder on the table spilled out photocopies of newspaper articles, police forms, grand-jury transcripts and IRS returns. Long fingers, dusted with fine dark hair, gathered the contents together. Meticulously they straightened the edges of the papers and laid the file gently on the trestle table. Ryan rocked onto the back legs of his chair and braced his good leg on the edge of another, stretching his right leg across the seat. A couple hours' rest had greatly eased the ache of two days of travel and Ariel's hard knee.

He knew virtually every word on the 173 pages in the file, and still he didn't know exactly what he was supposed to be doing here . . . or why he had agreed to come. He was here in no official capacity, just doing a favor for his brother and making a few decisions about his life.

Both his brother Rick and Rick's boss, the district attorney for the county of San Francisco, wanted the case closed. There had been an ongoing investigation into the murder for months, costing time, money and manpower, and turning up nothing. According to Rick, the investigation had stalled and would remain that way unless there was some kind of a break. After so many months, that didn't seem likely.

Ariel Spence was a murderess, guilty of the cold-blooded killing of her fiancé, Dennis DiSanto. The D.A. was convinced of it. She hadn't pulled the trigger, but she had been on the scene, orchestrating the event. Rick, the chief assistant district attorney, seemed less sure, but he wasn't ready to declare her totally innocent, either.

As the D.A. handling the investigation, Rick had been free to make copies of everything he had on the case. He had done so, then given them to his brother, ostensibly just to seek Ryan's opinion on the difficult case. Ryan had gotten hooked on the mystery, the too-many "coincidences," in the case, just as Rick had known he would. Then Rick had casually suggested a month's recuperation in Montana, where he just happened to know about half of a comfortable, converted schoolhouse for rent. Ryan could relax, fish the little mountain streams, let his leg finish healing—and ferret out a few of Miss Ariel Spence's guilty secrets. What else did he have to do for the next month?

Nothing. Ryan had admitted to himself that he wasn't ready to resume his law practice; he wasn't even sure he wanted to. So he had pretended not to see through his brother's transparent ploy and agreed to come to this town on the road to nowhere. The only problem was that Ariel Spence didn't look like she had any secrets, guilty or otherwise.

He picked up the file, tapping it absently on the table top. So just how was he going to occupy himself for a month? Maybe he would just catch his mental breath. The five days he had drifted on the Pacific under a scorching sun, watching his life ooze red drop by red drop into the salty green water, had brought on a crisis he'd thought to avoid forever.

Whenever he thought about his life, which was as seldom as possible, he always thought it would probably end in a glorious blaze of recklessness. He supposed he should be grateful to the anonymous powerboat that had run him down, leaving him to die off the coast of Kauai. There had been no glorious blaze, only a misty red agony and a grinding determination to survive just one more minute. As he had dangled beneath the rescue helicopter, his only lucid thought had been that he had made it; the fight to stay alive was over.

When he left the hospital, he discovered that the fight wasn't over, it was just moving to a more difficult battlefield. His law partner had informed him that he would handle Ryan's three pending cases, but no more. He was tired of defending guilty scum, no matter how much dirty money they could offer. Either they changed the type of client they took on or the partnership was dissolved. Ryan couldn't blame him. He was tired, too, tired of defending human trash he knew to be guilty as hell, but rich enough to pay his price. There had to be more to his life than that.

So, here he was, catching his breath, helping out his brother. He glanced at the file. He was going to satisfy his own curiosity about the woman, too.

Dennis DiSanto's murder had made headlines even down the coast in Los Angeles. The wealthy, handsome dentist had been one of the most sought-after bachelors in San Francisco. Yet he had successfully eluded every woman determined to snare him. Then, about two years ago, it appeared that the thirty-five-year-old DiSanto overcame his severe allergy to matrimony. He was seen constantly in the company of a young blond librarian turned his-

torical researcher, whom no one had ever heard of before. He made
no secret of the fact he was now the one determined to get married, while the lady seemed decidedly cool to the idea. Cynics had
predicted that his interest would soon flag, but it never did. On a
blustery December day in Golden Gate Park, nine months ago, it
was in the arms of the blonde that he had died. And suddenly everyone knew her name.

DiSanto's killer had suffered a heart attack immediately after
firing the silenced rifle. He died without ever revealing the moti-
vation for his murderous act. When his widow tearfully lamented
his depression over his recent retirement from the exterminating
business and publicly begged the forgiveness of the DiSanto family and Dennis's fiancée, the respectable newspapers let them all
rest in peace.

Not so the more scandal-minded tabloids. Ariel Spence's name
and face were smeared over their pages regularly. The story had all
the elements of a long-running epic designed to titillate readers.
Rich, handsome hero; beautiful, somewhat mysterious heroine;
hero's uncle reputed to be an old-time organized-crime boss. There
were whispers that the killing had been a gangland execution. There
were louder whispers that the hero, while supposedly besotted with
the heroine, had occasionally been seen picking up a one-nighter
in a singles' bar. Through it all, Ariel Spence repeated her contention that the killing was just a random shooting by a pathetic, crazy
old man.

The uncle had indeed had organized crime connections—twenty-
five years before and on the opposite coast. When Dennis Di-
Santo and his younger brother Robert were orphaned, the old man
had divested himself of his old friends and "businesses" and
moved cross-country to Bel Air. The real estate development
company he had recently turned over to his younger nephew was
totally legitimate.

Ariel Spence said she was a researcher for several best-selling
authors of historical romances. She politely declined to publicly
name them, saying it might hurt their reputations and credibility,
and her income. Rick hadn't seemed to think that income remark-
able; indeed, he'd been reluctant even to discuss it, but Ryan had
been astounded. He'd dryly observed to his brother that if she
could make that much from doing mere historical research, they'd
both wasted their years in law school. He would see, over the next
month, just how much research she did.

Dennis DiSanto had been more than a simple dentist, it seemed. After his death the police had discovered his very profitable, very illegal sideline of writing prescriptions for morphine and other controlled substances for addict "patients." He'd dabbled in some small-time drug smuggling, but he hadn't hit the big time until two years ago.

Two years ago Ariel Spence had met Dennis DiSanto when she was well into several months of on-site historical research in a remote area of Mexico, populated by Yaqui Indians, impoverished farmers and, coincidentally, drug smugglers. Dennis DiSanto had accompanied Ariel Spence on several of her trips, dispensing free dental care in as many villages as possible, making contacts all over the area, another coincidence. Suddenly DiSanto had become a very successful smuggler of whatever illegal drug was turning the most profit at the time. Coincidence?

DiSanto continued his charity missions, alone, one weekend a month, right up to his death, dispensing dentures, filling cavities—and taking delivery from an unknown middleman. A familiar sight to the U.S. border patrolmen, they'd waved him through each time, without even the most cursory search. Not one of them could believe that the good dentist who gave so generously of his time and skill could be guilty of smuggling in a fortune in high-grade cocaine and heroin in his pickup and camper.

Ariel Spence had certainly been shocked to learn about DiSanto's little prescription business. The D.A. had dismissed her surprise as an act, a much better one than her restrained, dry-eyed grief. They hadn't let her know they knew about the drug running, hoping she'd get careless and give herself away. So far, she hadn't.

It was obvious to the D.A. that DiSanto had been set up by someone close to him, someone who knew where he would be that Wednesday afternoon in December, someone who could even have suggested the outing herself, then been on hand to see that there were no mistakes. And no one seemed to have been closer to Dennis DiSanto than Ariel Spence—the most incriminating coincidence of all. She was guilty. She had to be.

Proving it was another matter. All the district attorney's office had were the sworn statements of informants who would sell their mothers for a dime bag of heroin, oblique references, and too many "coincidences" that strained belief in her contention that DiSanto's murder was just a random killing. Rick had been told to come up with solid proof, not circumstantial evidence, responsible witnesses to produce in court, and a motive.

In the D.A.'s mind Ariel Spence was an opportunist who had formed a partnership with Dennis DiSanto that would earn both of them far more than research or dentistry ever could. The most likely motive was that opportunity to make even more profit had presented itself, and Ariel had taken it. Most likely someone wanting to get rid of the competition had approached her with the deal to set DiSanto up.

Both DiSanto and Ariel Spence's profits remained well hidden. DiSanto's rather modest estate had gone not to his fiancée or to his uncle and brother, who hardly needed it, but to endow a dental-school scholarship in his name. Ariel Spence had inherited only his dog, his guns and all his photographic equipment.

Her tax returns had been scrutinized under a ten-power microscope: every penny in her checking and money-market accounts, the cash that had bought her house in San Francisco and the Burnt Fork School, even the $76.95 she'd splurged on an angora sweater last month, had been accounted for. Ryan knew it was easy to hide income, though, especially income you didn't want to have to explain. Several of his clients had shown him the tricks to establishing secret accounts that were virtually untraceable and purchasing holdings that could be lost in a labyrinth of dummy corporations.

The San Francisco District Attorney hadn't given up. When every lead had been followed diligently to a dead end, he'd declared Ariel Spence a material witness and put her in Rick's custody for her own "protection." For the first two months she had lived with Rick and Eileen, helping with their newborn daughter while Eileen recovered her strength. Then Rick had come up with the plan to isolate her in her Montana schoolhouse, where her contact with the outside world could be carefully monitored, and sold his boss on it. Ryan didn't imagine Rick had had to do much selling to Ariel. Even isolation in this tiny Montana town, under the watchful eye of Chief Dye and with a tap on her phone, had to be better than house arrest in San Francisco.

The D.A. was sure that a final payoff was coming, or that the insurance of her permanent silence would eventually be attempted. In nearly eight months neither had happened. She lived quietly, occasionally renting out half of her schoolhouse to vacationers. The rest of the time she was alone, except for the dog.

Page fifty-eight of the file had been a shocker, although it had nothing to do with the case. Ariel had exhibited symptoms of a miscarriage a few weeks after the murder. A copy of the doctor's treatment record revealed that a pregnancy would have made medical—and possibly religious history. In an age of free-and-easy sex, Ariel Spence was a virgin, an anachronism belonging to the age she specialized in researching.

Ryan knew his brother had been expecting some snide chauvinistic comment on that bit of information. He had only felt wonder as to how she had held off, yet still captivated the reputedly sexually voracious DiSanto. The only truth he was certain of in all the half lies, innuendos and impossible coincidences was that Dennis DiSanto had truly loved Ariel Spence.

He had also been oddly outraged that even this privacy, the most intimate of all, had been invaded, revealed for all the boys in the D.A.'s office to snigger at and lewdly speculate on. Rick had assured him that the report had never been in the open file, had never been seen by anyone but the two of them and the D.A. himself.

The quiet tapping on his door roused him. He grinned wryly as he went to answer it. Perhaps she'd come to tell him how to cope with the results of her mischief. He sincerely hoped she would take pity on him and not condemn him to the tumbled-down privy and rusty pump he'd seen outside.

She was smiling shyly and, he liked to think, a little hopefully as he opened the door. "Hi. I've fixed some supper and thought maybe you'd like to share it."

"Thank you." He was genuinely pleased by her offer, even though he knew it had been made only to atone for the unwelcome surprises she'd had for him.

Relaxing in one of the captain's chairs around a round oak dining table, he watched her ladle bean soup from a big pot on the stove top. Her half of the schoolhouse was a gem, but then his own place had surprised him. He had been expecting second hand store castoffs, not good solid antiques and comfortable, very masculine, leather couches and chairs. Ariel owned the schoolhouse, but DiSanto had obviously furnished the half Ryan had rented, making him wonder just how much time the man had spent here with her. Whatever else he might have been, DiSanto had liked comfort and had good taste. Ryan focused on Ariel's straight back and softly flaring hips as she worked at the stove. He'd already known DiSanto had good taste.

His eyes wandered around what was essentially one large L-shaped living room. Her place was softer, more feminine, with more of the touches necessary to make it a real home. Most of her furniture was antique, too, but lighter in color and smaller in size. The carpets were softly faded Orientals that showed as much character as age. Overstuffed, deep green plush chairs and a couch were drawn close to an elegant cast iron and brass wood stove with etched glass doors. His glance lingered on the sofa. It was long enough to accommodate his height and wide enough for two bodies, if one of them was rather slight.

Behind the sitting area was a wall of books. A narrow door exactly in the middle led, he guessed, to the garage. The shelves were crammed, but orderly. Reference books for her research, perhaps, but most likely, he decided, a lot of recreational reading. His private little smile was scornful. She and the dentist would have needed something to do on those long evenings.

A massive rolltop desk holding a word processor stood at right angles to the outside wall. Papers spilled out of the countless pigeonholes. Across the oak floor from the desk was the original staircase to the second floor, a half bath and closet tucked under it.

He looked back across the green tiled countertop separating the kitchen from the dining area. Ariel was swinging down the black glass door of the oven and pulling out a baking sheet. Two shiny, narrow loaves of French bread slid free onto a wire rack. The aroma of the fresh-baked bread brought a low, ravenous growling from his stomach, and Ryan realized how starved he was.

She brought their dinner to the table and sat down. "I'm sorry there's not more," she began, "but I'm not—"

His hand, already holding a slice of bread, waved her apology aside. He took a bite, swallowed and grinned appreciatively. "Don't apologize. This is really excellent."

She smiled back, then frowned at Murphy. The dog had seated herself next to Ryan's chair and was looking wistfully at the bread in his hand. "I can cook a few things very well, and everything else very badly. Murphy, go—"

"She's okay." He fed the dog the bit of bread. "What few things?"

"What . . ." She would tell him later that she never allowed the dog to beg at the table.

"What few things do you cook well?" he repeated patiently. The devilry in his eyes told her that he knew she didn't like him feeding the dog, and he was going to do it anyway.

"Soup and bread."

One black eyebrow went up. "Why only those?" He took a cautious sip of the cloudy liquid in a glass by his soup bowl. It was the best apple juice he had ever tasted. He enjoyed a long swallow, marvelling at the contentment he felt sharing a very simple, ordinary supper with her.

"Because you can make a lot of soup and bread at one time," she stated succinctly. "So I do, and freeze the leftovers. Then I just pop them in the microwave later." She sliced more bread, popped a sliver in her mouth and grinned at him.

"That's all you eat. Soup and bread?" No wonder she was so thin. He got up for a refill, silently gesturing toward her blue stoneware bowl with the ladle.

"Salads, fruit." She shrugged. She accepted her full soup bowl back from him, frowning at it doubtfully. "I didn't want this much."

"Eat it," he said blandly. "You need it." He considered the glass in her hand and not the look of consternation tightening her soft mouth. "That apple juice is good. You make it, too?" He reached across the table. With the tip of his finger he blotted a fleck of brown foam from the corner of her mouth. Holding her eyes, he slowly licked his finger clean.

Her glass frozen in midair, Ariel stared at him. She was thoroughly unnerved. His casually intimate gesture unsettled her, she supposed, because it was so completely unexpected. "Umm…this place…came with an old apple orchard." With an effort she broke her trance, noticing the glass still in her hand. With a quick, jerky movement she set it down, feeling completely foolish. This was undoubtedly his standard operating procedure with any reasonably attractive female. She certainly wouldn't be seduced as easily as her addled dog. "There was a very good crop this year, so I made juice and froze it. It's easier to make than soup," she finished briskly.

Realizing that he was probably close to eating up those leftovers she was counting on, he regretfully passed up another bowl of soup. A few minutes later, spooning up some of the golden cherries in the dessert bowl she set in front of him, he savored a taste that could never have come from a supermarket. "Did you freeze these, too?"

"No, I canned them." She twisted in her chair, indicating a quart canning jar on the counter, half filled with cherries. "One of my neighbors traded me for some apples."

He looked at her in surprise. "Home canning? I didn't think anybody did that anymore."

She looked back in equal surprise. "It would have been wrong to waste them."

Ryan bit back a laugh that threatened to choke him. The dangerous murderess spent her time canning cherries. "So what else do you do, besides make apple juice and tear out the plumbing?"

Ariel shot him a wary look. She didn't see anything more threatening than polite interest on his face. "Oh, I refinish antiques I pick up around here and," she glanced at him guiltily, "I'm about done with remodeling the house." Her hand gestured vaguely. "I do some research for a couple of historical romance writers. Right now I'm interviewing some of the residents at the rest home in town, trying to get a better perspective on life around here at the turn of the century." It had been so hard at first to find enough to occupy her long days and empty nights. Finally she had managed to establish a routine that kept her from going crazy at the waiting.

He nodded interestedly, then pushed himself back slightly from the table. Propping an elbow on the edge, he rested his cheek on his palm. His free hand reached across, idly brushing her hair behind her shoulders. "Now, Miss Spence," he said with deceptive mildness, "suppose you tell me what I'm going to do for a bathroom until Thursday."

What he was going to do was simple. He was going to use hers. She would leave her door unlocked, which he exasperatedly suspected she did anyway, so he could use the bath and shower whenever he wanted. She also offered him unlimited use of her kitchen. She was making it ridiculously easy for him. He would be free to poke around as much as he pleased until he found the evidence of her guilt.

Chapter 2

Ariel stared into the unblinking yellow eyes that had silently wakened her. Burying her head under the pillow, she groaned, "Darn it, Murphy, why didn't you think of this when I let you out before we went to bed?" Muttering under her breath, she climbed out of bed. Not bothering to put a robe over her short lavender nightshirt, she stumbled sleepily downstairs. She opened her door, traipsed down the short hall in her bare feet, and threw open the outside door to a chill, night breeze.

"Out!" she commanded fiercely. The dog scratched infuriatingly at the lawyer's door instead of going obediently outside.

"Murphy! What's gotten into you?" she scolded in an aggrieved whisper. Bracing her feet on the rough floor while the breeze whistled up her nightshirt, she tried dragging the stubborn dog by her leather collar. Murphy had passive resistance down to a fine art. She collapsed on the floor, curling her upper lip in a sly grin.

"Oh...phooey!" Ariel snapped. Mentally, she could swear with the best of them, but her oral vocabulary of four-letter words included only such hair-curlers as rats, nerd, snot and drat. It was all her mother's fault, with that toothbrush and that damned cake of soap.

"You are *not* going to bother that poor man," she informed the intractable dog sternly. "Now, come away from there and go... out... side!"

A low whining issued from Murphy's throat, and her eyes seemed suspiciously moist. Ariel knew what was coming next. The whine would become a loud whimper, then a full-fledged howl. Murphy was usually well-behaved, but she could be totally pig-headed on the rare occasions when she decided to challenge Ariel's authority. And Ariel always lost. She simply didn't have the heart to apply the discipline needed to win.

"All right!" she whispered furiously. "I'll let you in there, but, so help me, if you wake him up, I'll—"

Murphy never learned what her dire punishment would be. As soon as Ariel opened the door the sounds coming from the bedroom upstairs made her swallow the rest of her words. Murphy's nails clicked over the floorboards and up the spiral steps, finally galvanizing Ariel into scurrying after the dog.

She hesitated on the top step, uncertain of what to do. Should she intrude, or withdraw before she caused him any embarrassment? Dim moonlight seeped through the drawn curtains, and she could see Murphy's brown head resting on the man's pajama-clad knee. The dog gazed up sadly at his dark, bowed head.

Ryan sat on the edge of the bed, harsh sobbing breaths racking his body. His knuckles scrubbed dazedly at the tears still slipping from his tightly shut eyes. Suddenly his eyes opened wide, glazed by some inner horror. He locked his fists locked between his knees and shuddered violently.

The look in his unseeing eyes decided her. On bare feet she crossed the floor silently; then knelt beside him on the bed and gathered him into her arms.

"Ryan, it's all right." She spoke quietly, as if to reassure a frightened child. "You're safe here, Ryan."

Frighteningly strong arms wrapped around her, trapping her against him. Surprisingly she felt no fear, just deep compassion, a need to offer comfort, and another, unnameable emotion curling deep inside her. Her hands soothed over his bare back, warming the gooseflesh skin. Her fingers traveled over the too-sharp bones in the small of his back, the too-prominent ribs up his sides. Cords of hard muscle registered, too, and a long thin scar she wouldn't remember until later.

"Ryan. Wake up, Ry," she encouraged him gently. The darkness and his distress drew her into unconscious intimacy, and she unknowingly used the nickname again. "Wake up and talk to me, Ry."

He clung to the soft voice commanding him out of the shadow land he visited all too often. The voice called him back with a name out of his childhood. He eased his grip slightly, and his hands spread over her back and up into her soft, loose hair. Fingers like cool snowflakes were lifting the tangled hair from his clammy brow and combing it back. His harsh, uneven breath warmed her neck as he buried his face in silky, flower-scented hair.

God, he wished it were truly over. The dream was always the same. He was back on the surf ski, half crazy with pain and thirst. And the sharks were circling. A snow-white bird perched on the end of the board, looking at him with the dead eyes of the young girl he had found in the Cambodian hut. She had been one horror too many.

He had carefully moved the girl aside, then emptied the clip of his automatic rifle. The men he had surprised inside the hut had never had a chance to reach for their weapons.

He had left the silent girl with the dead brown eyes with the good French sisters in Bangkok. The nuns had sadly assured him that such cases were not uncommon, but with time and God's love the girl would forget and be healed. He had thought he had finally forgotten, but the ordeal on the ocean had brought the dreams back. He knew now that he had never forgotten, never been healed. God's love apparently didn't extend to him, but that wasn't surprising. He wasn't sure he believed in a God that allowed such atrocities to happen to innocents, then chose him as the instrument of His revenge. He wasn't even sure he believed in Ryan Jones sometimes.

Ryan hadn't heard his own hoarse whisper as he recounted aloud the nightmare he had been reliving in his memory. He didn't feel the warm tears soaking into his hair or hear the smothered sobs trembling through the body holding his. His rigid body relaxed, and he was suddenly freezing cold and too exhausted to sit up any longer. Collapsing back on the pillows, he pulled Ariel down with him. He was reluctant to lose the human contact, the comfort and warmth she offered. He felt her try to pull away, and he hugged her more tightly to him, patting her back with what he prayed was reassurance.

"Please don't go," he whispered raggedly against her cheek. The warm wetness on it didn't register. "Stay just a minute longer." Hold me, he begged silently; don't leave me.

He felt her relax at last, felt her arms hug him back. Her heat began to seep into his chilled body, and he fell asleep, his heart and mind curiously at peace.

Ryan started to put his razor and toothbrush back into his kit bag, then decided he liked the way his things looked, jumbled in with hers on the bathroom counter. After splashing on after-shave, he set the bottle next to her cologne. He picked up the black fili-greed atomizer and sniffed. It was the same warm-sunshine and spring-flowers scent that had lingered on the nightshirt he'd found in his bed this morning, after the best night's sleep he'd had in years. The name etched on the gold cap was Femme. He took an-other whiff. The name and the scent suited her perfectly.

He gathered up his clothes and bag, then stood in the bathroom doorway, looking around her bedroom. She'd left a note on her door, saying she would be back from church at about ten-thirty and that he should help himself to whatever he could find in the kitchen for breakfast. He would, in a minute, but first he wanted a quick look around, and her bedroom was as good a place as any to start.

An elegant royal-blue-and-orange-enameled French parlor stove stood in one corner. The highboy dresser was a meticulously re-finished antique. There was an antique pier mirror and an old church pew under the window.

Her bed was fascinating. He was absolutely certain there couldn't be another like it anywhere. The roof under the cupola housing the old school bell had been removed. A platform bed had been constructed there, with three steps leading up to it. A built-in bookcase, with reading lights and mirrored shelves, formed the headboard, a brass blanket rail made the footboard. The upper walls of the little bell tower were now glassed in. Someone lying in that bed at night could look out at the stars in the black sky and almost feel a part of it. The word processor downstairs might be-long to a practical researcher of dry history, but this bed belonged to a romantic who indulged in a bit of fantasy.

Downstairs Ryan prowled through the drawers and cubbyholes in her desk. Everything was trustingly unlocked. There were in-numerable sheets and scraps of paper covered with something that looked like the shorthand his secretary used. The word processor on the desk was the same model as his own. He switched on the machine and took a disk marked SA-I from the file box.

"Retrieve file SA-I," he commanded. The screen remained blank. He tried a couple of variations. Nothing. Apparently there was a code word. Maybe she did have secrets after all. He couldn't retrieve so much as a comma from any of the ten sets of disks in the file, all identified only by two initials and the Roman numerals I or II.

He supposed he should feel a bit guilty, but Rick had told him to nose around. He knew now that Rick and the D.A.'s suspicions were totally absurd. Murderesses did not hold virtual strangers in their succoring arms in the middle of the night. They didn't bake bread and worry about wasting fruit. There might be a problem about the inexplicable income, but he would stake his life that she'd had nothing to do with DiSanto's murder.

He moved over to the bookcase and gave the titles a cursory inspection. In fact, he was very suspicious of Rick's suspicions. Had Rick talked him into coming here hoping that he would find exactly nothing so the D.A. would finally be willing to close the case? There was another possibility, but he didn't think his brother was capable of such deviousness.

Hearing the sound of her returning Blazer, the tires crunching on the gravel outside, Ryan ambled into her kitchen and started the coffee. Murphy came in a couple of minutes later, ahead of her mistress. After nudging Ryan's hand she went to lie by the chair she had already decided was his. Ariel responded to the greeting he tossed over his shoulder and studied him while he finished making the coffee. This morning he was dressed in black chinos and a scarlet-and-black rugby shirt. Red was a good color for him; so was black. She fidgeted just a little. How would he deal with last night, especially when she'd had to leave her nightshirt in his bed? While she'd been searching for a spare blanket to wrap up in early this morning, she'd been in a panic that he would wake up and see her scampering naked around his bedroom.

Ryan knew she was waiting for him to turn around and talk, but he wasn't ready to, not yet. He wasn't too sure how she was going to react to the previous night. Oddly, he felt no embarrassment, but she might. He sliced some of last night's French bread and toasted it.

Ryan put the plate of toast on the table along with the coffeepot, while Ariel found apple jelly and butter in the refrigerator. Then, pulling out her chair, he seated her almost formally before pouring coffee into heavy mugs he'd found in a cupboard. She looked so fresh and pretty this morning. She'd wound her hair into a knot on top of her head, but it was refusing to stay there. He could have it down just by removing a couple of pins. Her dress was a soft peach, loose, but still clinging nicely here, floating there, and swirling around her knees when she walked.

"I didn't think to ask you if you wanted to go to church." There was a question in her soft words.

"I haven't been to church in years," he said almost wistfully. "Do you go every Sunday?"

"Usually."

His eyes followed the tip of her tongue as it darted out to lick a crumb of toast from the corner of her mouth. Forcibly he dragged them back to hers; she was watching him with a hint of unease. "I'm sorry if I frightened you last night," he said quietly.

The unease vanished. "You did, at first," she admitted, then smiled in understanding. "I've had a few nightmares myself and wished there had been someone—" the smile faded, and her eyes dropped "—to sit with me." Her eyes flickered up to his, then immediately back down. Someone to hold me, she added silently. To promise me that this limbo life would end soon, to tell me the bad dreams would go away and never return.

"I wish I had been here, Ariel." His fingers were as soft as his voice as he brushed a stray wisp of hair behind her ear. "I would have been happy to sit with you." To hold you, to keep the night demons away. "What happened?" he asked gently. His fingers drifted down the side of her neck and stroked lightly.

Ariel regarded him soberly for a few seconds. She felt the same curious feeling she had had last night in the darkness of his bedroom. She could only describe it as the fragile bonding of two souls. The brief moment passed, and she sighed, then shrugged tiredly. Chief Dye would no doubt give him all the dirt, anyway.

"I was involved in a murder," she said bluntly. "In San Francisco, where I live." She corrected herself with a sad little smile. "Used to live." The smile turned bitter. "My picture was in all the papers. Maybe you saw it; I understand it made headlines even down in L.A. Your landlady is quite a notorious woman, Mr. Jones."

She turned her head and stared hard out the window over the sink. His hand rested on her shoulder, kneading the tight muscle. "I was a material witness. Actually, I'm still in the custody of Richard Jones, an assistant district attorney in San Francisco.

"He arranged for me to live here so I could move without two policemen constantly at my heels, but there's still not much freedom. I can't leave town, and there's so little to do here." She grimaced with barely contained frustration. "Give me bag ladies and winos, dirty fog and cheap tinsel any day."

She drew a deep, settling breath and faced him. Ryan's hand fell away. "That's why I was so tacky and tore up your place. I thought you had been sent to snoop, and I was furious."

With maximum effort he kept the guilt off his face.

"I'd been meaning to do it all summer, and now seemed like a better time than any what with the opportunity to make life miserable for the 'spy.'" She met his unreadable gaze levelly. "I am truly sorry about the mess. I've just let myself get paranoid the past few months."

"I'm sorry, too." His eyes, dark and full of secrets, locked with hers. "This can't be much of a life for you."

She was grateful that he didn't seem interested enough to ask for any of the details. Gradually his eyes resumed their usual blankness. Silently he reached over to the chair next to him and picked up her ruffled nightshirt. He bunched the soft lavender material in his hand and slid it across the tabletop to her.

"I guess I should explain that." She laughed sheepishly.

"I was hoping you would," he said conversationally. "I'd hate to think something special had happened last night, since I could remember absolutely nothing this morning." Something special *had* happened last night, he knew and the memory was precious.

Her eyes widened on the word "special"; then her soft mouth tightened primly. "Nothing happened, Mr. Jones," she stressed. "You were simply sleeping on part of my nightshirt. I couldn't move you, and I didn't want to wake you, so I just... unbuttoned..." She faltered, swallowing to wet her stubbornly dry throat. One long, dark finger had been rubbing the soft fabric of her nightshirt. Now his hand was fiddling with the buttons. She could feel skittering tingles under her skin, as if she was wearing the nightshirt while he was touching it, feeling the brush of those graceful fingers as they unbuttoned... "Unbuttoned it, slipped it off and left," she finished in a rush. A curious warmth flooded her body. She tore her eyes away from his hand and snuck a peak at his face.

He wasn't grinning, or looking smug, just staring at her with a vacant, dreamy little smile. His eyes suddenly focused. "It's Ryan, not Mr. Jones, Ariel. I think we got past the formalities last night." He paused, looking at her speculatively. "Why *did* you come in last night?"

"Murphy," she explained hastily. The dog raised her head languidly at the sound of her name. "She wanted to check on you, sleep in your room. I used to share the schoolhouse with . . . someone else sometimes. We left our doors open at night so she could go back and forth. Now, for some reason, she wants to resume the practice."

"I'll leave my door open, then," he promised with an odd little smile. He pushed himself back from the table, sweeping his clothes and bag off the chair, and stood up. "Maybe later you'll tell me where to buy groceries. I can't keep eating yours." After the fantasy he'd just had with her nightshirt, it might be best if she was out of his sight for a while. He would still think about her, of course. He had decided what he wanted from her, but already he was wondering if it would be enough.

Murphy got up to follow him across the hall, and Ariel called her back sharply. Reluctantly the dog returned to sit at her mistress's feet, gazing lovingly at the door.

Ariel aimed a disgusted look at the animal's head. "Traitor!" she muttered. "Really, Murphy, you're supposed to be protecting me." Yellow eyes granted her a brief, puzzled look. "The first handsome stranger who shows up, you nuzzle up to him like the worst kind of floozie!" Ariel wadded up the nightshirt in her fist and went upstairs to throw it in the hamper.

The sweat was running down into his eyes, blinding him. Ryan tore of the saturated sweatband and wiped the perspiration out of his eyes. He lay back down on the living room rug, his knees bent, and gasped air into his burning lungs. He really should have done the exercises before his shower, but his leg had just been too tight without the hot, pounding water to loosen it up. The sit-ups and push-ups were nothing, but the right leg lifts with a five-pound weight strapped to his ankle left him as drenched in sweat as if he'd run a ten-mile road race.

His door suddenly swung open, and Ariel stepped inside. "Ryan," she called, not seeing him on the floor at first. Then her sweeping glance found him. Quickly she crossed the room to him, her face paling noticeably. Falling to her knees beside him, she reached a hesitant hand toward the dimpled mass of white scar tissue and purpled flesh that was his right thigh.

"Oh, Ry," she breathed softly, her eyes clouded with distress. "Whatever did you do to yourself?"

She used the nickname she'd used last night naturally now, he noticed, as her cool fingers caressed his leg, sending fiery shivers up his groin to his belly. "It was more like what the propeller of a boat did to me."

His voice was hoarse, and she snatched her hand back, afraid she'd hurt him. "What happened?"

"I'm a little fuzzy on the details," he admitted with a harsh laugh. He sat up slowly, wishing she would touch his leg again. Her fingers seemed to drain away the pain. "All I remember is hearing an engine, seeing a light. When I came to, I was hanging on to what was left of my surf ski."

Her shocked eyes were still on his wound. "Did it take them long to get you to a hospital?"

"Five days."

Her head snapped up in disbelief. That explained part of his nightmare last night, the part about drifting on the ocean. "Five days?" Outrage sparked in her sky-blue eyes. "The person who ran you down didn't even stop? My God, you might have died!" Her anguished gasp was healing music to his soul.

"I almost did." He shrugged it off lightly. She'd taken down her hair when she'd changed into the tan slacks and green crew-neck shirt she had on now. As she bent closer to trace the scar with her eyes, her hair feathered over his belly, bared by his hiked-up sweatshirt. Involuntarily he sucked in his breath and held it. Finally she sat back on her heels, and he could breathe again.

"They even had to graft some muscle," she said slowly. She remembered something from the night before, and her hand went unconsciously to his back, unerringly following the long, thin scar it had found last night. "From your back." Her eyes returned to his, compassionate, but not pitying. "Are you all finished with surgery now?"

He nodded. "I just have to strengthen it now."

She glanced at the weight on his ankle. "It may not look too wonderful," she admitted with a rueful smile, "but the important thing is you still have it, and it still works." She patted the leg gently with approval.

Oh, love, he thought, where were you two months ago when I needed you? His hand threaded through her spun gold hair to bring her closer. I'm glad you're here now, he added silently, because I think I need you even more.

She was being drawn irresistibly toward him.

"Ariel? Where are you?" The deep, masculine shout came just before the door was thrown open.

Ariel was scrambling up off the floor as a curly-brown haired giant stalked in. Ryan stood up slowly behind her, measuring the man who was frowning at him through wire-rimmed glasses. Murphy sat beside Ryan growling quietly.

The giant was some four inches taller than he was and a good sixty pounds heavier. Ariel looked like a little girl standing next to him. Ryan shifted his legs slightly apart and tucked his thumbs in the waistband of his raggedy gym shorts. So, he had competition. He stared back at the man, who was also younger and darkly tanned, as if he spent most of his time outdoors. To fit the outdoor image, he wore worn Levis, scuffed boots and a khaki field shirt.

Ariel stood between the two unsmiling men. She knew they were sizing each other up like circling tomcats, and she sighed in vexation. Really, this was ridiculous.

"Sam Bass," she said a little sharply, "Ryan Jones, my new tenant. He's a lawyer from Los Angeles." Her hand gestured toward Sam, and he caught it before she could pull it back. "Sam is a fish biologist. He's working on a project on the Bitterroot River."

"Bass." Straight-faced, Ryan extended his hand. So Bass's life's work was studying his fishy cousins. The fish biologist had to drop Ariel's hand and step forward to take Ryan's. There was the briefest of handshakes.

"Jones." Sam Bass's deep voice rumbled. He turned to Ariel, effectively blocking her view of Ryan. "Ariel, I'm going up to the bridge to check my fish traps. Want to come along for the ride?"

"Okay. I just need to tell Ryan where to get groceries and—"

"I'm sure he can find the store by himself." Sam's soft brown eyes shot Ryan a hard look. "There's only the one, and it's right on the highway. He can't miss it."

"Go ahead, Ariel," Ryan allowed generously. "I'll see you when you come home." He let the giant digest the fact that he was living there, and the giant wasn't. "Will you be back for lunch?"

"No. She won't," Sam answered pleasantly, and wrapped a bear paw around her shoulder to take her away.

Ariel opened her mouth to protest, then decided it would be wiser to keep it shut. Later she would make it clear to them both that she wasn't an old chicken neck for them to fight over.

The fish biologist's voice rumbled in through the open window minutes later. "I thought all the plumbing fixtures were out of there, Ariel. What's he doing for a bathroom?"

Ryan heard her blithe answer. "He's using mine." He bent down to unstrap the weight and smiled to himself.

He wasn't smiling hours later as he slouched in one of her armchairs, his right leg stretched over the hassock, nursing a nearly empty glass of dark rum. He was watching Humphrey Bogart bid goodbye to a tearful Ingrid Bergman at a snowy airport. It wasn't snowing in Casablanca; it was snowing inside Ariel's television. Her reception was lousy. He supposed he was going to have to do something about *that*, too, along with his competition, the unused door locks and her skinniness. She hadn't been back for dinner, either. He'd finally given the extra spaghetti to a most appreciative Murphy.

Tilting his head against the chair back, he watched the credits roll and drained the glass. He didn't particularly care for movies with "noble" endings, where the hero gave up the girl to the "better" man. He'd always been more than a little skeptical of this one in particular. He had a sneaky hunch that ol' Rick would look Ilsa up after the war. That's what *he* would have done—if he had let her go in the first place.

A car drove up outside. He stayed where he was. One door slammed. If two slammed, he was staying right where he was all night, if necessary. The engine revved and the car left. Fish biologists were apparently a little short on manners. Sam hadn't even walked her to the door and seen her safely inside, Ryan thought perversely. Dr. Bass wasn't going to make any points that way. Ryan silently saluted his departing competitor with his empty glass.

Ariel closed her door quietly, started toward the stairs, then abruptly halted. "What? You're still up? It must be after midnight!"

"Twelve thirty-seven," he supplied obligingly, and turned his head to see her face. "What happened? Did he run out of gas? Have a flat?"

"No, he didn't run out of gas or have a flat," she denied with syrupy annoyance. "I didn't know he meant the bridge down by Darby. It was after five before he finished his count, so we just decided to have dinner in Darby and go to the movie there."

"Mmm." He turned back to the snowy test pattern. "I hope you had a nice time." Sam the Bass was a wilier fish than he'd given him credit for.

Ariel scowled at the back of his head. Why had she felt obligated to explain her lateness. As if she was back in high school and he was her father? "I've got a headache," she announced. "I'm going to bed. Please—"

"Wait." He was out of the chair and between her and the stairs before she had taken two steps. "We leave our doors open tonight, right?" The corners of his mouth quirked up in a strange anticipatory smile. He took a step forward, trailing his thumb down her smooth cheek to her jaw.

"For Murphy." The words were a little breathless. She felt timeless longings stirring at long last to life, coiling their first, shyly eager tendrils deep inside her. She stepped back.

He closed the distance between them again, in the oldest of dances. His thumb followed the line of her jaw, stopping in the soft hollow beneath her chin. It took only the slightest pressure to tilt her mouth to his. "I just wanted to make sure," he whispered. His breath, rum scented, cooled her suddenly flushed face.

The kiss wasn't what she'd been subconsciously expecting for the past twenty-four hours. His mouth was surprisingly soft, incredibly gentle and unscrupulously experienced. His lips nibbled and sucked at hers, subtly coaxing her to respond. She would have resisted a rough demand, but she was utterly defenseless against this insidiously smooth persuasion. Only the top of his right thumb and his lips were touching her, and she felt melded to him, unable and unwilling to move.

Her warmed lips parted on a sigh, and his right hand dropped to her throat, long fingers circling it lightly. His left hand came up to comb through the hair at the back of her head. As he held her with a magician's light touch, his tongue delicately stroked over her moist lips, beguiling her mouth with magic. Her tongue met his with a shy sorcery of its own. As her arms rose to bring his body closer to satisfy a sudden craving, he pulled back and the illusion ended. She didn't hear her quiet moan of protest as her hands fell, frustratingly empty, to her sides.

His dark gaze searched her flushed face and smoky eyes. There was a hint of satisfaction in his velvet voice when he spoke. "You're very responsive," he murmured. His fingers traced her lips. "I wasn't expecting that." He brushed a whisper soft kiss over her forehead. "Goodnight, Ariel Spence. Sweet dreams."

He silently disappeared across the hall, leaving her thoroughly confused and not a little panicked by the unfamiliar hungers slowly winding through her. She'd wondered what sort of magic he possessed that had worked so well on Murphy. It seemed it worked just as well on her.

Chapter 3

Ariel, I don't think your heart is in this today, dear."

Ariel started guiltily. She looked back at the elderly woman sitting across from her in the sunny bedroom at the Valley View Rest Home. The woman's face was seamed, a line for every hardship and tragedy in her long life. Yet they gave her a timeless beauty, reflecting her triumphs and the defeats she'd had to accept with quiet dignity and unflagging spirit. Despite the near uselessness of her body, she sat erect in her wheelchair. Bessie Ruff dealt with infirmity with the same fortitude that had seen her through being widowed, left penniless with five small children sixty years before.

Flipping off the tiny recorder, Ariel replayed the past few minutes through her memory. It was no use; she had no idea what Bessie might have been telling her. Ever since that first galvanic handshake with Ryan Jones, she had been slightly out of kilter. It was not an uncomfortable feeling, though, more like the anticipation of some unknown delight that would soon be hers.

She sighed contritely. "I'm sorry, Bessie; I'm just wasting your time. I have . . . other things on my mind today."

"Don't apologize. I always tried to think of something else myself," the old lady confided dryly, "when I had to help my mother make soap. Are you still going to try it?"

"As soon as the butcher gets me the fat. I already have the lye."

"Well, you're certainly going to extremes for a little authenticity. You must remember what I said, and don't inhale any lye dust or splash the stuff on you. Lye burns are more reality than you need."

"I will." Ariel gently patted the arthritis-gnarled hand curled on the table between them. The age-spotted skin looked so fragile.

"I hear you've got a new tenant." Her ninety-six years and a stroke might have slowed Bessie's body, but her bright brown eyes still saw very clearly through her trifocals. Something, or someone, had finally put a sparkle in those sad blue eyes.

It had ceased to amaze Ariel that Bessie, without leaving the rest home, could know everything about everybody in the valley. "He's a lawyer from Los Angeles, recuperating from an accident. He has this terrible scar on his right thigh." Bessie's sparse white eyebrows rose just a bit. "He's awfully thin, but—" Ariel cleared her throat "—he's rather good-looking."

The little nurse's aide had seen him at the fiddlers' contest and said he was a "hunk." Maybe there was hope for the girl yet. The big-city lawyer might be the one to dig her out of her piles of research books and convince her that there were better ways to waste time than making lye soap. "How long's he staying?" Bessie asked interestedly.

Murphy's cheerful yipping and Ariel's oddly out-of-breath voice trying to hush her had nudged him awake that morning. After climbing a little stiffly out of bed, Ryan had stood at the side of his open bedroom window. He'd watched her pound across the last few yards from the orchard through a withered garden in an all-out race with the galloping brown dog. The golden wash of early-morning sunlight rinsed through the blond hair flowing behind her as her long legs gracefully lifted her over a pile of frost-blackened tomato vines. She'd looked like a carefree twelve-year-old out playing with her dog.

Her green nylon running shorts pulled over the tight curve of her bottom as she bent over, hands on her knees, gulping air. Even under the sexless, white UCLA sweatshirt, he had seen her breasts heaving with effort. Murphy had shoved her cold nose into the small of Ariel's back, and she had straightened with a shriek, then glanced up guiltily to his window. He knew she couldn't see him. Severely admonishing the dog again, though with a wonderfully silly giggle, she had led the way through the back door of the house. During his exercises the diesel rumble of her Blazer had announced her departure, and Murphy had come to see what was keeping him.

Taking a second mug of coffee with him, Ryan wandered to the wall of books. He looked much more closely today, pulling out the contents at random. There were albums of faded photos, yellowed newspapers, tattered diaries and bundles of letters with exquisite Spencerian script, as well as crudely bound little volumes from long-defunct local presses. He decided that she must have grubbed through endless dusty boxes at estate sales and in junk shops to acquire a literary collection of early Western Americana most museums would covet.

There was also an eclectic range of recreational reading, just as he had figured: science fiction, novels, poetry, mysteries and Westerns, of course. His eyes were drawn to a nearly empty shelf. All the others were full, the books crowding each other, yet this one held only ten thick paperbacks by the same author. Why were these ten segregated to themselves, and what was she saving the much-needed space for?

Choosing the first, he scanned the cover. A beautiful blond girl, her old-fashioned dress artfully revealing, clung to the massive, mostly bared chest of a copper-haired cowboy. He was cradling her lovingly, if a bit lasciviously, in one arm, while the other cracked a bull whip.

Ryan grinned knowingly to himself. So Ariel was fond of the romances she did the research for, except . . . His brow creased in puzzlement. The book looked like it had never been opened, much less read. He idly flipped through it, then stopped to skim a page. He read with greater attention, going back a few pages to get the background.

The hero and heroine were out in the open wilderness. Blinding snow devils from an imminent blizzard were swirling around them. They stumbled on, practically into a river, where the hero saw steam rising. A hot spring! They were saved! They could wait out the storm in warmth and relative comfort.

The hero, obviously a quick thinker and ever resourceful, convinced the doubtful heroine to take off her clothes and stash them with his in a tiny cave so they would have dry clothes when the storm ended. They sank to their necks in the steaming water. One thing led to another and they ended up making love in the lifesaving water in the middle of a snowstorm. The heroine melted in the hero's arms as satisfyingly and completely as the snowflakes in the hot water.

Ryan felt a little steamy himself as he finished the scene. He would love to try it sometime; a hot tub would pale by comparison. The author, Felicia Fury—the name had to be a pseudonym—had either really done it or had a fantastic imagination. Either way he would like to meet her. Then he grimaced at his foolishness. "She" was probably a he, or a frustrated, fat, fiftyish old maid.

His eyes drifted back to the open book in his hands. The passage was undeniably erotic, but beautifully written. He could feel the heated water lapping his own body with every thrust, while the steam and storm mingled around their naked bodies. The same shivers of delight raced through him as the heroine's hot, slick tongue licked icy crystals of snow from the hero's chest, curling around his hardened nipples.

Ryan shut the book with a snap and reshelved it. The fantasy was becoming a little too real; Ariel's face had replaced that of the girl's on the cover. Maybe later he would find out what other fantasies Felicia Fury had. As he strolled out to the backyard, the coincidence of the characters' names struck him; Spence Tucker and Ariel March.

Ariel was following the measured thunk of an ax. She stopped short at the back corner of her schoolhouse. Sunlight flashed off the newly sharpened and cleaned ax as it rose and fell solidly into the chunk of dry apple wood. Ryan's back was to her, the fabric of his chambray shirt straining across it as the ax swung again. It paused for a pulse beat at the top of its arc as those strong, elegant hands slid along the smooth handle to a new grip. His slim hips shifted in old khakis, his thighs tensing as the ax arced down and neatly split the log.

Unconscious of his audience, he set another log on the block. He rested the hickory ax handle along his long leg, unbuttoned his shirt and shrugged out of it, then he tossed it carelessly aside into the scattered, fragrant wood chips. Ariel's fingers remembered the feel of his back. The muscles in his arms and shoulders bunched and slid smoothly as the ax flashed again. They pulled tight under the sweat-shined skin, and her palms began to itch oddly. The metal drove into the wood, and she felt the impact herself, the sense of something cleaving through her.

Murphy's welcoming woof broke his rhythm on the next piece. He turned to find her watching him. A soft warmth lit his dark eyes. "Hi. Been home long?"

He reached down for his shirt and slowly slid into it, flexing his shoulders to find a comfortable fit. He left it hanging free, unbuttoned, and took a couple of steps toward her.

"Ah...no." Her answer had a curiously wistful sigh in it. Pulling herself out of a languorous fog, she added, avoiding the glint in his chocolate-brown eyes, "Thank you for chopping the wood, but you don't—"

"Did you cut this all yourself?" he interrupted. The sweep of his arm indicated the cord of neatly stacked logs and the stumps of dead apple trees in the orchard.

Her thin shoulders lifted carelessly. "It takes a lot of wood to heat the house, and it's good exercise."

He suppressed a smile, raking her slender body. He couldn't think of any other woman he knew who would consider using the heavy chainsaw he'd found next to the ax "good exercise." "What's that in your hand?"

"The mail. You've already got a couple of letters." She handed over the envelopes and frowned puzzledly at a package in her hands.

After scanning his mail quickly, Ryan stuffed the letters in his back pocket. "What's that?" He pointed to the box under the brown wrapping paper she'd already torn through.

Ariel shook her head. "I don't know. There's no return address, and the postmark is smeared." Suddenly her face lighted with a golden smile as she read the enclosed note, and she laughed delightedly. "Oh, I think I know who this is from!" Ryan bent down and idly picked up the paper she'd discarded. "There are these two high school boys, Billy Greef and Davey Severson, who always want to help whenever I substitute for the school librarian. I think," she confided with a shy smile, "they have a crush on me."

He squinted at the postmark, trying to make it out. The city and the date were hopelessly smeared, but he could decipher, barely, the two-letter abbreviation for the state at the bottom of the circle: CA—not MT for Montana. He seriously doubted that Billy and Davey had made a quick trip to California to mail a surprise to their teacher. That sixth sense he'd learned to trust in jungle shadows years ago raised the hair on the back of his neck.

Ariel lifted the yellow lid of the three-pound box of candy and offered it to him. "Here, would you like a piece?"

Being deliberately clumsy was not easy, he discovered. He acquired new respect for clowns and their seemingly effortless pratfalls. His foot apparently tripped on the uneven ground as he reached for a piece of candy, and his hand hit the box and sent it sailing. Chocolate rained down on the white woodchips.

"Uh—oh. I'm afraid I owe you a new box of candy." His tone was deeply apologetic.

Ariel looked from him to the empty yellow box to the sawdust-covered candy on the ground, then finally back to his chagrined face. An odd expression crossed hers. "That's all right," she answered shortly. "Actually, I don't really care for chocolate. I probably would have taken it to the rest home anyway." Her eyes narrowed, closely studying his face. "Are you okay?" she asked softly.

One shoulder lifted negligently. "Sure. My leg just buckled."

She gave him another close look, then stooped to gather up the candy. His left leg?

As he bent to help her, Ryan gave Murphy's nose a surreptitious swat when it came sneaking under his arm to snitch a piece of chocolate. He took the box from Ariel's hand when he was sure every piece was back in it, then picked up the wrapping and the note by their edges. He tucked the box under his arm, careful not to smear his sleeve over it.

Brushing a loose curl off her cheek, he pulled Ariel up with him. "I'll treat you to lunch in town to make up for the candy you didn't really want." His fingers guided the errant curl behind her ear again. "Anyway, it's the thought that counts." He almost laughed at his macabre joke.

She finally smiled at him. "Thank you, but I should warn you—it's going to cost you a cheeseburger with everything on it, fries and a strawberry shake."

"Even onions?" he groaned, laughing.

She grinned evilly. "Piles of onions."

Detouring to his kitchen, Ryan placed the papers and candy box in an empty grocery sack. Nearly every drugstore in the United States sold this brand of candy. The cheap white paper and wrapping paper were even more readily available. The note was a single line of handwritten block letters—"FROM YOUR SECRET ADMIRER." The attempt was rather crude and definitely amateurish, and Ryan was absolutely certain the candy had been meant as a deadly, not sweet, surprise.

But why? He refused to believe that the district attorney was right, that she'd had anything to do with DiSanto's death beyond being unfortunate enough to witness it. Yet the D.A. would seize upon this incident as further proof of her guilt. He would say that her partner was getting worried that she could become a liability and had decided to ensure her silence. The D.A. would still see her as a suspect, not a victim.

And just how did Ryan Jones see her? As a puzzle, a fascinating puzzle with a few key pieces missing that, inexplicably, he felt compelled to find. She had a sweetness, almost an innocence, about her that was startling combined with her sly wit. The prospect of sharing greasy French fries with her at a seedy drive-in was more exciting than taking the most beautiful, experienced woman in Los Angeles to an elegant restaurant and then home for a long dessert, and he couldn't explain that, either. The thought that someone was trying to harm her filled him with cold-blooded rage.

Ariel sat on the worn seat of Ryan's power wagon, watching him lock first the old schoolhouse lock, then the new dead bolt. Chief Dye had installed it personally, but she never took the time to bother with it. That's what comes from living in Los Angeles and having only criminals for clients, she decided self-righteously. You don't trust anyone.

Then she sighed. And you, Ariel, you chump, you trust everyone. Will you never learn? This is how it started with Dennis, and look how *that* turned out. Just a snack, he'd said, as if they were simply going to the drive-in after school. The next thing she knew, she was planning to marry him. And she would have, never knowing how he'd lied to her. He had let her believe him to be nothing more than a handsome, charming, successful dentist. Never had she suspected the even more successful career he'd had writing very proper, very aboveboard—and very illegal—prescriptions for dope. The police had told her the truth, and she suspected there was more truth that they hadn't told her.

Yet she must have suspected, unconsciously, that Dennis wasn't quite what he appeared to be. That must have been what had kept her from making the ultimate commitment to him.

She followed Ryan's progress toward his truck. His easy stroll all but hid the limp. And this one is even more handsome and charming than Dennis, she realized, and even less what he appears to be.

* * *

After lunch Ariel vanished into her half of the house. When Ryan stuck his head in her door an hour later, he found her kneeling on the floor. Gold-rimmed half-specs had slid halfway down her straight nose as she busily sorted through the indecipherable scraps he'd found in her desk. Whispering to herself, she seemed to be arranging them in some order only she could ever hope to understand. Despite the absentminded wave of her hand, he knew that she hadn't heard his promise to fix dinner.

He had to use the pay phone at a gas station. There were no phone jacks in his apartment, and he could hardly use Ariel's phone for this call. After half an hour and a pocketful of quarters, he found a private lab in Missoula that assured him that they could test for the more common poisons in a couple of hours. He glanced at his watch as he hung up. It was too late to make the two-hour trip today, but he'd be there when they opened their door in the morning.

Stopping next at the Forest Service barracks, he got a map of the hiking trails in the area. The doctor in San Francisco had prescribed walks or easy hiking as part of his therapy. A few more stops and he realized his brother's wisdom in sending Ariel here. There was no one he had met, from the gas-station attendant to the grocery clerk to the retired schoolteacher chattily pointing out the treasures in the little town museum, who didn't know who he was and what he was doing in town.

He got back to the schoolhouse in time to fix most of their dinner. Ariel defrosted and warmed a loaf of cracked-wheat bread and a jar of broccoli-cheese soup. Ryan made cottage fries and grilled two thick pork chops. They made a salad together while he told her about his house on the beach in Malibu, and she wistfully described her restored row house, almost on the bay in San Francisco.

Ryan probed delicately into her life in San Francisco and her acquisition of the Burnt Fork School. He wanted her to mention DiSanto, to see what, if any, feeling she still had for him. She'd been engaged to marry the man. One could reasonably assume she'd been in love with him, yet she hadn't even mentioned his name yesterday when she said she'd been involved in a murder. She certainly didn't seem to be grieving for a lost love. Nor was she exhibiting anger over a love betrayed when she found out that Dennis DiSanto wasn't quite the hero she'd thought. She'd obviously been genuinely saddened by his death, but just as obviously she had had no great passion for the man. Of course love and passion didn't necessarily go hand in hand, he reminded himself cynically, yet he still felt curiously pleased.

Adroitly Ariel avoided the subject completely, saying little about San Francisco and nothing about Dennis DiSanto. She did mention that she had fallen in love with the vacant schoolhouse two summers before when she was in the area doing research and had bought it for a vacation home.

Ryan's hand dropped casually below the edge of the table, and there was a gulping noise. "Ryan," Ariel began hesitantly. He had supplied and cooked most of the dinner, but rules were rules. "We don't feed Murphy at the table. That's the first rule I made for her when she came to live with me."

"I noticed *we* don't," he agreed easily. "Only *I* do." He leaned toward the dog and advised in a stage whisper, "Chew with your mouth closed, Murph." Yellow eyes gazed up at him adoringly. "It's okay, girl. Stick by me; I'll see you don't starve."

There was an unladylike snort of disgust from across the table. Ariel glowered at the both of them. "Starve? Look at her! She's overweight!" Picking up her fork, Ariel stabbed determinedly at a piece of pork chop, her eyes fixed on her plate and not his impertinent grin. "Don't feed her at the table," she ordered firmly. "She'll just become a drooling mooch." A drooling mooch pooch. A giggle almost escaped, and she clamped her teeth together. Her lamentably irrepressible silliness insisted on surfacing at the worst time. This man was definitely a bad influence on her and Murphy both. Increasing the severity of her scowl, she glanced up at him. He was looking at her oddly. "What's wrong? Is there something wrong with the food?" She hadn't tasted the bread yet and hastily took a bite.

He continued to regard her thoughtfully for a moment longer, then resumed chewing. After swallowing, he finally spoke. "She's not overweight, Ariel. She's with puppy."

It took her a second to fully absorb the deadpan joke. "She can't be pregnant," she denied flatly. "I was *very* careful."

"I imagine you always are," he said blandly, "but Murphy definitely wasn't."

Giving him an exasperated glare, she went on doggedly. "But I never saw..." He laughed, and she groaned. "How soon?"

"When was she in heat?"

"Toward the end of July."

"And this is the end of September. I'd say about anytime."

Ariel turned on the dog and wailed woefully. "Oh, Murphy, how could you? Your father and I raised you to be a good girl."

"Father?"

"Well, you have to say that," she explained. "It's traditional."

"I see. You've had this discussion with her before, then?" His lips were twitching.

"No." Ariel shook her head mournfully. "She was a virgin." Addressing the dog once more, she scolded sadly. "Oh, Murphy, I warned you about smooth-talking strangers." Her desperate straight face finally dissolved into laughter, as she patted the bewildered dog.

Ryan laughed with her, a trifle uneasy. He might well be described as a smooth-talking stranger, and she was definitely a virgin.

Shortly before midnight, he lounged in her open doorway, his hands in the pockets of his black pants, a yellow sweatshirt pulled hastily over his tousled hair. He'd looked over a case and polished off the last of his rum. Then he'd gone to bed, tossed for an hour and gotten up. The soft light diffusing through the pebbled glass in her door had drawn him like a moth.

The funny little glasses were sliding a little farther down her nose every time she wrinkled it at the letters on the screen of the word processor. She shoved them up impatiently, hardly breaking the rhythm of her fingers flitting over the keys. He sighed to himself. He was having fantasies about historical researchers lately.

Ariel dragged a hand through her hair. Suddenly she looked up, catching the almost hungry look on his face. It vanished as soon as he met her eyes, a slow smile taking its place.

"I see you couldn't sleep, either." He eased away from the jamb and came to lean over the top of her desk. "I thought—" he glanced toward the bookshelves "—I'd come over and get a boring book to put me to sleep."

Ariel switched the machine off. Casually she crossed her arms over her chest, wishing she had broken this bad habit she had of going to bed and then getting back up to empty her overactive mind without putting her clothes back on. No telling how long he'd been watching her with that absolute stillness he had, like a predator choosing the moment for the kill. The long sleeves and high neck of her sturdy nightshirt more than adequately covered her, but his lazy, appreciative look up and down her body had made her feel stripped.

She eyed him over the lenses of her glasses. It wasn't a book he was after. She suspected that hotshot L.A. lawyers had a very low boredom threshold, and she'd known right where he would come looking for entertainment first. Maybe she was bored, too, though, because she didn't feel as irritated as she knew she should. She stared at his feet, not seeing them. No, it couldn't be boredom, because there was gentle, oh-so-willing Sam, and she had never felt the slightest urge to take him up on his unspoken offer. Urges...this man aroused urges, sweet, confusing, dangerous urges.

"Do you have a foot fetish?" The polite, velvety voice disturbed her musings.

"What?" Finally she saw what she had been staring at, and then saw that he was staring at her feet just as hard. "No, do you?" she responded just as politely.

"I haven't decided yet," he murmured. "Are those your typing clothes?"

She didn't need his barely contained laughter to tell her that she looked ridiculous. Most people did not wear red-striped nightshirts, mismatched fuzzy knee socks and seedy slippers to type in. Most people wouldn't be caught dead in an outfit like that. Well, it ought to at least induce him to take his boredom elsewhere. "The dryer, or Murphy, ate a couple of my socks," she mumbled inanely. "Besides," she looked at him pointedly, "I wasn't expecting company."

He did laugh then, and went over to the bookshelves. Behind him he heard noises from the direction of the stereo system on the opposite wall.

Ariel was riffling through plastic cassette cases looking for something noisy. She fed a tape into the machine and set the volume up a bit too high. A raucous voice rasped out a song about "Hot Legs." Maybe he'd take the hint that she'd gotten out of a warm bed to work, not to talk.

Apparently he did, departing through the door with a book and without a word. Resolutely she ignored a niggle of disappointment and squinted at the little green blurs on the screen. Entertaining Malibu beach boys in your nightgown at midnight was not particularly wise anyway.

An hour later Ryan shut his book and let it drop to the floor. Kicking off his shoes, he stretched his legs over the hassock and slid down in the chair. He watched her through slit eyes, listening to a sexy saxophone and the lazy rhythm of a snare drum coming through the stereo speakers. He'd never realized that historical research was so riveting. She'd never even noticed him come back or lower the volume on the stereo. Occasionally her hand would dart out and seize one of the bits of paper tacked across the front of the desk with Scotch tape. She would study it intently for a few seconds, crumple it, then toss it in the general direction of an old pickle crock she used for a wastebasket. Then she'd type furiously again for long minutes.

The words of the song on the tape insinuated themselves into his subconscious. Sung in a rusty-hinge voice by a jaded rock star was the blueprint for a sweetly tender seduction. The tape continued to wind unnoticed through both the cassette player and his subconscious.

She was frowning again, worrying that soft lower lip. Her slender hands were clenched together, as if she was praying fiercely for divine inspiration. Somehow he didn't think she needed it.

Gradually he became aware of the silence after the tape ended. He roused himself and silently padded across the carpet. Ignoring her tapes, he pulled one from his back pocket.

Ariel shut off the computer and pushed the swivel chair back from the desk with a satisfied sigh. She cocked her head at the unfamiliar tape. Quizzically she stared at the chair across the room. He'd come back, and with his own music. The Beach Boys—how appropriate.

His long body was sprawled over the chair and hassock, his thin fingers laced peacefully across his chest. His eyes were almost shut against the orange firelight flaring through the glass doors of the wood stove. The glow played over a hazy smile softening his hard face. She waited quietly until the tape clicked off. He deserved to listen to reminders of a simpler, happier time undisturbed.

"'Be True to Your School'?" Her soft laughter filled the sudden silence.

"'Hot Legs'?" He rose from the chair with a slow, fluid motion, rather like a sleepy cat that didn't particularly want to move. A luxurious stretch pulled his sweatshirt up, exposing his taut, concave belly. Her eyes lingered on a silky black swirl and pale skin, and then dropped, reluctantly, when his arms did.

Ryan walked leisurely across the room to her, took off the glasses carefully, then pulled her unresisting body out of the chair and into his arms. The action seemed peculiarly natural, comfortably familiar. Bemused, Ariel let herself rest against his hard chest. The soft sweatshirt under her cheek was still toasty from the fire, and she snuggled unconsciously into its warmth, shutting her eyes with a contented sigh. The fire's heat seemed to have intensified his scent of soap, citrus and warm male.

"If you didn't sleep alone," he breathed into her hair, "You wouldn't need socks." His long, bare foot slid down the back of her smooth leg, catching the top of her knee sock and dragging it down her calf to her ankle.

Ariel's eyes flew open as the erotic tickling moved back up her leg to the top of her thigh, and she jerked back. Ryan let her move only a few inches, his hands tightening just enough to remind her that she wasn't free.

"Let me go." Neither the words nor the fists pushing on his chest were as determined as they were supposed to be.

"No. I don't think I will." He rocked her gently in his arms, his soft eyes teasing her. "Look, but don't touch. Is that another of your rules, Miss Spence? You seem to have quite a few of them."

"It shouldn't bother you, Mr. Jones." Her husky voice was sweetly scathing. "Rules appeal to you lawyer types, don't they?"

He laughed and hooked a finger in a loop of the red bow tied at the neck of her nightshirt. A gentle tug and the ribbon pulled loose, opening the throat of her gown. "We lawyer types are always looking for ways around the rules. Didn't you know that? It's ninety percent of our business, especially us criminal-defense types." His soft lips whispered against her prim mouth, "And your defense of your many charms is truly criminal, Ariel Spence."

It was supposed to be a light kiss, a hint of things to come, but her response caught him off guard. With a moan Ariel's mouth softened and clung to his, relishing the subtle flavor of dark rum. The mellow taste seemed to burn through her as if she'd swallowed the liquor herself, making her drunk on the kiss. Her fingers laced through his blue-black hair to hold his head so she could enjoy the taste again. The hunger that had been awakened the night before made her suddenly ravenous for the feel of his mouth nourishing hers.

Before he could consider the wisdom of it, Ryan's right hand clamped over the back of her skull. His mouth crushed down on hers, driving her deeper into passion. His left hand moved up to the four white buttons of her nightshirt. Her mind was too tangled in the onslaught of sensations swirling through her to appreciate how deftly his fingers freed the tiny buttons. Her body appreciated it, knew that its hunger to be touched was about to be satisfied. It throbbed, even before his hand slipped under the chaste flannel and covered her heart, hard calloused flesh over soft.

She clutched at his shoulders desperately, as if she was on a sinking ship and he were the only lifeline. She was sinking into a dark pool of sensuality. She couldn't swim out of it; she could only hold on and let him save her—or pull her deeper into the whirlpool.

Ryan took her softness into his rough palm, ignoring the inner voice reminding him that he had decided to move slowly with this woman. He gave in to a pounding impulse too ancient and too fundamental to be ignored.

The ruthlessly skilled hand on her breast stroked, shaped, maddened. His other hand slid down her spine to the base of her naked back. He pressed her firm flesh, and her knees turned liquid.

"No." Ariel's voice was a breathless whisper in the midnight stillness of the room. She arched against him helplessly as drowning waves of unbelievable pleasure washed over her. "Oh, don't."

His mouth was greedy against hers, silencing her weak protest before he sought satisfaction at her bared throat. Ariel breathed his name in a thin, tremulous groan.

Ryan's head came up. He shook it, as if surfacing from deep underwater, and gazed into the vulnerable face below him. Eyes closed, lips trembling as her breath stuttered over them, Ariel waited. He could take her now; on that wide sofa. And she would hate him for it in the morning. It was much too soon. His smoky eyes cleared, and his hands moved to the safety of her shoulders. He could wait. It would be just that much sweeter when he satisfied his hunger...and hers.

Her blue eyes opened, clouded, questioning. "I..."

"Should go to bed," he said completing her sentence. He pulled her back for the light teasing kiss he'd originally intended, then released her.

Swaying slightly, she grabbed at her desk for balance. She glanced around the familiar room, as if seeing it for the first time. "Yes, it's late." She pushed a trembling hand through her disheveled hair. "I should go to bed," she echoed faintly.

Clutching her open nightshirt closed, she turned toward the stairs, still half-dazed. "Good-night, Ryan."

He switched off the lamp on her desk and moved to the door. "By the way, Miss Spence." His dark eyes glittered in the firelight as he grinned back at her over his shoulder. She stopped halfway up the steps, watching him uncertainly. "You have *very* hot legs."

Chapter 4

Damnit, Dye, she has to be told!"

"The odorless, almost tasteless poison on the report you keep shoving under my nose, Jones, is used by half the exterminators in the U.S. Isn't it just possible that the candy got sprayed along with the cockroaches in some warehouse?"

Ryan spun away from the chief's desk, jamming his hands in his pockets so he wouldn't break something. The chief played devil's advocate with maddening reasonableness. Ryan stood for a long time at the station window, looking at nothing.

"All right," he conceded grudgingly, his back still to the police chief. "It's possible, but pretty damned unlikely. I still say Ariel should know."

"Know what? That someone, we don't know who, *might* have sent her a box of poisoned candy? Anyway, your brother's boss doesn't want her upset."

Ryan's opinion of the San Francisco D.A. was short and obscene. "He doesn't want her upset," he repeated tonelessly, his mouth curled in a sneer. "He's using her to draw out the real murderer. If she just happens to get killed in the process, that wouldn't bother *him*."

"The guy's tipped his hand. If he tries again, we'll be ready for him," the chief said noncommittally.

When, not if. Ryan lit another of the cigarettes he thought he had given up three years ago. He inhaled deeply, trying to settle himself. This conversation was infuriatingly similar to one he'd had from a phone booth in Missoula two hours ago. His brother must have called Ted Dye as soon as Ryan had slammed the phone back on its hook.

He found himself in a position he should have been used to by now, defending someone everyone else seemed convinced was guilty. Only this time, the person he was defending was innocent.

He knew he was rationalizing his excuse for not telling her for purely selfish motives. The San Francisco D.A. be damned; he should tell her. But then he would have to tell her who he really was and why he was there.

Chief Dye swiped a hand down his well-worn face and heaved himself out of his chair. He was too old for this. That was why he had retired to this nice little town in the boondocks, where the biggest crimes he had to worry about were stolen chain saws and the Geilenfeldt brothers tearing up a bar on Saturday night. He laid a heavy hand on the younger man's shoulder.

"Rick told me a little about your military experience. If anybody can keep her alive, you can."

Ryan wished he shared the chief's confidence.

Arriving back at the schoolhouse at dusk, he parked his truck next to her Blazer. Telling himself that it wasn't cold fear he felt, just the autumn chill in the air, he shouted Ariel's name when he couldn't find her. At last he located her, crouched in a corner of his kitchen, calmly laying the last of the blue and yellow floor tiles. Her shocked look and stiff reply told him that she neither understood nor appreciated his growled curse or the snarled demand that she yell louder next time.

He came downstairs from using her shower an hour later to find her staring disconsolately at the smoking skillet in her hand. "What happened?"

"I tried to cook something that wasn't soup or bread," Ariel muttered. She dropped the skillet in the sink and switched on the exhaust fan.

Leaning over the sink, Ryan examined the brown mess in the pan. "What was it?" he inquired politely.

She sighed and resisted the bizarre urge to smooth back the lock of damp hair falling over his forehead. "Two rainbow trout. They'd been in the freezer about a year; I guess they dried out."

"Hmm. Did you catch them?"

She was silent for a moment. Dennis had caught them on his last fishing trip. "A friend did."

Opening the freezer section of the refrigerator, Ryan pulled out a white package he'd put in yesterday. He put it in the microwave and punched the defrost button, then lounged back against the tiled counter. "Do you like to fish?"

Her nose wrinkled as she leaned against the opposite counter, facing him. "Not very much. I never catch anything, so I get frustrated." Apparently her rather shameless behavior last night was not going to be a topic for discussion, for which she was most grateful. It made it much easier to convince herself it had been just a temporary lapse of sanity.

Ryan laughed, a deep, cheerful sound, very pleasant in her too often quiet kitchen. "Look," she began firmly, "I can't let you fix my dinner again. I—"

His hand dismissed her objections. "I don't like eating alone." His smile was a genuinely friendly invitation, with none of the coolly sardonic amusement he usually treated her to.

Ariel looked at him doubtfully. He didn't look like the kind of man who minded eating alone. In fact, he looked like one who often preferred it. Self-sufficient...a loner...a solitary man, but by choice. She was quite sure he could fit comfortably into, or more likely control, almost any situation. A cool tingle shivered up her back. Who was he really? Not just some fancy lawyer. Several times his carefully civilized veneer had peeled back a little, allowing her a glimpse of a ruthless, cunning, rather dangerous man. She'd seen it during the retelling of his nightmare, as well as on the day he'd knocked the candy out of her hand in the accident that wasn't, and again this afternoon, when he was so peculiarly angry at her for not yelling loudly enough.

Three minutes later she was laughing at her absurd imaginings. The sinister Ryan Jones was standing in his bare feet, a blue-and-white checked dish towel tucked in the waist of his green rugby pants, expertly slicing steak into thin strips and pounding it with the edge of a heavy plate. Browsing in her refrigerator, he'd found two green peppers, and had plopped them in front of her. "Slice," he had commanded, and she sliced. They were going to have pepper steak, he had calmly announced.

Half an hour later Ariel savored her first forkful. His rice was moist and fluffy, not stuck together in gluey clumps as hers always was. The steak practically melted in her mouth. And he hadn't even used a recipe book. "Where did you learn to cook like this?"

"I learned while I was in law school." He refilled his plate and added more to hers. "I got tired of TV dinners and cheap restaurants."

"That's fortunate for the women you date and fix dinner for." She said it sincerely, ignoring a silly twinge of jealousy.

The sardonic smile was back in place. "The women I 'date' aren't into home cooking."

"Then maybe you date the wrong women," she said lightly.

The smile turned speculative. "Do you like home cooking, Ariel?"

"Of course." She smiled breezily. "Especially if it's my home and someone else is doing the cooking." She changed the subject abruptly. "Do you like to fish?"

Ryan had to think for a minute to remember the conversation before dinner. "When I get the chance." He looked at her curiously. "Why?"

"There's a lot of fishing stuff in the garage. I'll get it out for you," she offered ingenuously. "I noticed you got some maps, and there are lots of places around here to fish. Maybe you can catch me another trout." She grinned. "And maybe I can manage to cook it without incinerating it."

"I'll do my best," he promised gravely.

The television was on, but Ariel had turned the sound down. Curled up in her fattest armchair, she was making unkind faces at the sheaf of computer paper in her hand. Her glasses were sliding down her nose, but not far enough for her to bother to do anything about them. As she slashed through several lines of type with the red pen in her hand, she clucked her tongue in disgust. The paper was beginning to look like it was bleeding. Felicia wasn't doing well at all with this one. At this stage she should be fine-tuning, doing a little cosmetic work, not major surgery.

The heroes were usually the easiest, always rounders and rakes who were reformed, barely, on the last page by the love of a good woman. She had lost control of this one, though; he was suddenly behaving quite dreadfully. He was as much of a rogue as the rest, but he was arrogant to boot, full of insufferable male smugness.

As if that weren't enough, there was an inexplicable cloud of menace settling over the characters. Ariel heaved a huge sigh and shook her head resignedly. The glasses slipped to the end of her nose. As usual, she was the only one who could save the patient.

A shadow fell over her. She looked up and barely stiffled a small shriek. Pressing her papers to her chest, she finally squeaked out, "Ryan! You scared the stuffing out of me!" He had crossed the old floorboards without one betraying creak. Since he'd left as soon as they cleaned up after dinner, she hadn't expected to see him again tonight.

He slid the glasses back up her nose. "What are you working on?"

"A mess," she muttered, trying to get to her feet and put the papers safely away in case he was planning on spending the evening. Grasping her hand, Ryan hauled her to her feet, and Ariel sidestepped quickly to her desk.

"You know," he said observing the silent TV, "the picture on that set is atrocious."

"Yeah, I know," she admitted, cramming the papers in the first half-empty drawer she could find. "There's a movie I want to see, though, so I guess I'll have to put up with it." She shoved hard on the overstuffed drawer, trying to close it.

"Why haven't you gotten a satellite dish?" He'd already checked; they were available even in this tiny town.

"Oh, I was afraid, with so little to do here, that I might get hooked on soap operas or something," she answered absently. Finally she gave up fighting with the stubborn drawer and went back to her chair, tucking her feet under her as she sat. "This way I only watch it when there's something I really want to see."

Ryan suppressed a grin; he couldn't imagine her avidly following the bed-hoppings on a soap opera.

"Are you going out?" Seeing the canvas jacket hooked over his shoulder, she hoped, and didn't hope, that he was.

As he sat on the arm of her chair, Ryan tried stifling the urge to see if her hair was as soft and silky as he remembered. "Yes." He wound one loose curl around his finger, then released it slowly. It was. Bending, he dropped a quick kiss on her startled mouth, then rose lithely from the chair arm. "I'll be back in a couple of hours."

From the doorway he added, in that damnable irritating velvet purr, "Keep the doors locked, including the dead bolts."

"I don't use the dead bolts." She gave him a cool look.

"Starting tonight you do." The outside door closed solidly, emphasizing his order.

Ariel blinked in astonishment and stared after him. Muttering to herself, she retrieved her crumpled papers and red pen and went back to operating.

Several hours later Ryan let himself back into the darkened schoolhouse. She had locked the dead bolt, he noted with satisfaction, then sighed heavily. It wasn't going to be that easy; no doubt he would have to remind her a few more times.

Murphy met him just inside the door. "Hi, girl," he whispered, scratching behind her ears. "Your mistress in bed already?" He started down the short hallway to his door.

Maybe his phone calls would produce a few leads. He would have liked to have taken Chief Dye up on his offer of the police-station phone again but the deputy had been a little too interested in the long numbers he was dialing. He'd had to use the pay phone at the gas station again, his conversations punctuated with dings from the service bell every time a car rolled over the hose.

There was a faint thump from the garage. Murphy cocked her ears and growled, then sniffed the air and relaxed. Ryan debated going for the .45 in his kitchen drawer and decided against it. Moving soundlessly through Ariel's living room, he reached the door in the wall of books. It opened on silent hinges.

The garage was lit by one dangling bulb. There was a jumble of cardboard cartons, a tall metal cabinet with a heavy padlock, and little else. Sitting on her heels in the midst of the boxes was Ariel, her golden head bent over the framed photograph in her hands. A dented, rusty tackle box and a fishing rod lay on the concrete floor next to her. Murphy padded over to sniff at the khaki fishing vest lying across Ariel's knees. Whining softly, the dog lay down, her head resting on the grimy vest.

Mindful of the start he'd given her earlier, Ryan spoke her name quietly to warn her of his presence.

One hand flew up to her eyes and brushed over them quickly. Keeping her face averted as he crossed the floor, she said in a thin voice, "I . . . I was just getting the fishing tackle."

He knelt in front of her, staying her hand as it tried to put the photograph back into a carton. He recognized the curling dark hair and handsome, sensual features of Dennis DiSanto. His arm was slung across the shoulders of a younger, slighter man. Both of them were displaying large fish with the exuberant pride of small boys. It was time, for several reasons, that the subject of Dennis Di-

Santo came out in the open. "Who are the men in the photograph, Ariel?"

The harsh light overhead caught the wet sheen in her eyes. "The man I'm supposed to have murdered and his brother," she whispered, then burst into tears.

"So many tears, love." Ryan's low murmur in Ariel's ear was as comforting as the strong arms that held her. They relaxed a little and let her shift slightly on his lap. She only nestled closer; his warmth and gentle strength were assuaging a pain that had been gnawing inside her for months.

Rubbing the backs of her hands across her tear-clotted eyes, she thought reluctantly about sitting up. A larger hand brushed hers aside and gently wiped with a clean handkerchief. The soft cloth wrapped around the end of her nose. "Blow."

With a self-conscious giggle she obeyed, working up the courage to look at him. His smile was warm and gentle. She smiled back damply, then looked down at her lap, trying to think of some way to explain her bizarre behavior. The soft orangy glow and heat from the wood stove made her realize that they were no longer in the garage, but sitting together in her favorite chair. "How did we get here?" she asked huskily.

He laughed quietly, lifting her to a new position on his right thigh. "I carried you," he said simply. "That cement floor was hardly the spot for a good cry."

She plucked a piece of invisible lint from her pants. "I'm sorry," she mumbled. "I'm not generally so...hysterical."

Strong fingers raised her chin, and his serious eyes held her embarrassed ones. "You were hardly hysterical, Ariel. I think you've been saving those tears for too long. I'm just glad I was here. Your answer about the men in the picture," he added with an encouraging grin, "could use a little explanation, though."

"I'll bet it could," she agreed softly.

He released her chin, and her head seemed to fall automatically onto his shoulder as his arm closed loosely around her. Her low voice floated with the firelight in the warm, peaceful room.

"You might remember some of the story. Like I said, it even made the papers in L.A. almost a year ago." Her small laugh was harsh. "The older man in the photograph was Dennis DiSanto. He was a dentist, came from a wealthy family, knew everybody who was anybody in San Francisco. I was just a nobody, and perfectly happy that way." He felt her small sigh, then a deeply in-drawn breath. "I met him down in Mexico where I was doing research. We saw a lot of each other down there, and then, the next I knew, all my spare time was spent with him."

His hand stroked slowly over her soft hair. "Were you in love with him?" His tone was casual. His hand paused as he waited for her answer.

"No. I loved him, but I wasn't in love with him."

Ryan's hand resumed its slow play. "Was he in love with you?"

"Yes. He would ask me to marry him about once a month. I would say no; we'd laugh, and he'd say he'd wear me down sooner or later." She laughed ruefully. "Finally I guess he did. I decided I was never going to find any knight in shining armor, and having someone love me the way Dennis did was very special. I knew I could make him a good wife. The next time he asked me, I surprised him and said yes."

Her voice fell to an almost inaudible whisper, and unconsciously she settled deeper into his arms. "Only we never had the chance to get married. Dennis liked to take pictures of little kids and old people; it was quite a hobby with him. He was even thinking of trying to put together a book of his pictures. One day we were in Golden Gate Park, taking photos, and he was shot—killed by a crazy old man."

The last memory of Dennis filled her. She saw again the small ring of shocked and ghoulishly curious faces staring down at them as he lay in her arms. She felt again his warm, red life seeping through her frantic fingers, swallowed up by the thirsty ground. Once more she heard, dimly, the shouts echoing off the serene slopes of the park. She heard clearly Dennis' final, rattling whisper—her name.

Ryan felt her shudder, and folded her closer. Her tortured whisper seemed a shout in the quiet room. "At first I wished I'd said yes sooner, so I could have made him happy, at least for a little while. Then I found out he wasn't quite the man I'd thought he was."

She pulled free to look intently into Ryan's face. He could see the bitter tears glistening again. "Between the guilt and the disillusionment I felt, I couldn't even cry for him, not even at his funeral."

The overwhelming sadness ravaging her beautiful face tore at his heart, and he felt an irrational hatred for the dead man who'd loved her. It made his words harsh. "You shouldn't feel guilty about having doubts and being honest about them, Ariel. Would you rather have married him and then learned he wasn't what you thought?"

She shook her head, answering softly. "No, I think I finally came to terms with it tonight, when I saw the picture."

She was silent, and he enjoyed the quiet pleasure of just holding her. He heard her smothered yawn and knew the storm of weeping and its emotional release had exhausted her. "I remember an article now," he lied. He knew every one by heart. "Wasn't his uncle supposed to have organized-crime connections? Didn't the police think maybe it had something to do with that?"

"That's what the district attorney still thinks." She was too tired to give the words much of her usual acid. "He also seems to think I was involved somehow. I think he thinks I set Dennis up to be shot." She pressed her hands flat on his chest and sat up to see his face. "I think that's really why I'm here, so he can have Ted Dye and probably half the town spy on me and let him know when they either send me the big payoff or come to shoot me."

Tears filled her eyes again, and she began shaking her head in anguished bewilderment. "I lived with Rick Jones, the assistant D.A., and his wife for two months before I came here. They told me it was protective custody, but it was really so they could keep me under constant surveillance. I took care of their baby as if it were my own when Eileen was sick, yet even Rick still seems to think I'm guilty. How can he?" she cried. Her fingers curled into the soft fabric of his shirt, and she shook him unconsciously to make him see the truth.

Ryan hardened his heart to her pain and resisted the almost overpowering desire to wrap her in his arms and simply tell her the truth. He needed to hear this, to hear her side. Unknowingly she might give him the clue he needed to prove her innocence.

Suddenly she seemed to realize how hard she was shaking him and dropped her hands to her lap. She struggled visibly for control and went on in a calmer voice that trembled only slightly. "The worst of it is, they've never been open about it, never charged me with anything, so I don't even know what evidence they think they have against me. It's like they're playing some horrible game, waiting for something to happen to me, and—" her voice broke in a sob "—I don't even know why."

Ryan's left hand moved strongly up her back. His fingers spread through the hair on the back of her head, and he gently forced her body to relax against his. For a moment she resisted; then he felt her snuggle sleepily against his chest.

"If it didn't make me so crazy, it would be funny. There was no cold-blooded murder plot; it was just a random incident, a terrible, senseless killing." Her voice trailed off as she drifted into sleep.

He wished that ass of a district attorney could have heard this and then tried to tell him that she had anything to do with DiSanto's murder. He sat there long after the fire had burned low, sifting her hair through his fingers, thinking of random killers and sinister plots and evidence that could be seen two ways, and the golden California girl asleep so trustingly in his arms. His hand slid down unconsciously and curled possessively around her soft breast as he wondered exactly when she had become so important to him.

Apparently his sweet gift had not done its work; he should have heard something by now. Maybe the poison hadn't been strong enough, or she hadn't eaten enough. Whatever. Some business problems demanded one's presence to be solved.

Fortunately he had anticipated just such a situation months ago, when he'd bought the isolated cabin above Tahoe. He prided himself on his ability to foresee problems and solve them before they could cause trouble. That was one of the reasons he was so successful and others weren't. They simply didn't give enough attention to all the variables that could adversely affect business then take care of them ahead of time.

Everyone was used to his occasional absences now, assuming he used the cabin as an escape from his tremendous pressures and his grief. No one knew how easy it was to hike through the wilderness for a few hours and be on the highway, waiting for the bus to take him to the nearest airport.

With his filthy knapsack, grubby patched clothes and too-long dirty-blond hair, he would be just another of the aging hippies come down out of the hills. The local cops paid them no attention, letting them cultivate their little patches of marijuana and live their useless lives undisturbed.

He would have to do something about that damned dog. He'd never get close enough to take care of the problem otherwise. That dog hated him. He had never understood Dennis's absurd fondness for her. She should be easy enough to dispose of, though.

Chapter 5

The extra mile she'd added to her run this morning hadn't helped. Standing here in her bright kitchen, grinding coffee beans in the antique delft mill as she had done every morning for months, listening to Murphy's snore in a patch of sunshine, did absolutely nothing to solve her problem, either. Had she finally met a man whose mere touch could produce that fabled tingle, that little sexual shock of instant attraction? She knew it existed—between the pages of romances. She had ten and a half books in the other room to prove it. But that it existed in reality she had not believed—until she'd felt those eyes on her back last Saturday.

That he knew she was attracted to him annoyed her no end. "No doubt," she muttered fiercely to her disinterested coffee maker, "like every other female he subjects to that ruthless charm." Yet his tender caring last night, his refusal to take advantage of her vulnerability, had her defenses in a shambles this morning. Under that devastating sex appeal was a decent, even tender, man, something she suspected he didn't even know and would ignore if he did. Leaning her head against a cupboard, she moaned and silenced the tiny imp at the back of her brain that was telling her to quit fighting and find out if the other things described in those romances might be true, also.

"What's the matter with Murphy?"

She jumped. That was another thing! He was always sneaking up on his cat feet, scaring her to death. Ariel turned around and sighed, disgusted with herself. Murphy had heaved her heavy body off the kitchen floor and was trying to wrap it around his legs in their worn black jeans. Even in the jeans, scuffed hiking boots and a ragged flannel shirt open over a faded black T-shirt he was, as Bessie would say, "drop-dead handsome." She glanced up to his black-and-silver baseball cap announcing the Los Angeles Raiders' victory in Super Bowl XVIII. "She sees your hat and thinks you're going to take her for a r-i-d-e. Dennis always seemed to wear one when he took her out."

He gave her a dry look. "Ariel, you don't have to spell in front of a dog." He squatted down and patted the furry head pushing into his hand. "Want to go for a ride, girl?"

Murphy went berserk, racing circles between him and the door, sliding on the slick floor, barking small ecstatic woofs. Leaping on Ryan's chest, she knocked him flat on his back. In the eye of the canine cyclone, Ariel stood calmly, her arms folded across her chest.

"I warned you," she murmured in a smug singsong.

Glaring exasperatedly at her as he sprawled gracelessly on the floor, Ryan fended off Murphy's frantic tugs on his arm. "What else do we have to spell?"

"C-o-o-k-i-e, or y if you're in a hurry." Reaching down, she gave him her hand to help him up. Ryan's wrist twisted, and suddenly she was sprawled on his lap.

As she struggled to sit up he tugged a strand of her unruly hair to bring her closer. His eyes fell to her mouth, lips parted, breath suspended between them.

"Kiss me good-morning, Miss Spence."

That damned, rakish charm in his smile got her every time. Ariel sighed, closed her eyes and obeyed. His mouth was sweet and tender, undemanding. As his arms closed gently around her she felt calmer, warm and . . . curiously safe.

He drew back, his sober eyes searching her face. "Are you all right this morning?"

"I'm fine," she said softly. "Thank you for putting up with me last night." She cleared her dry throat. "I was a tad surprised to wake up minus my clothes, though." Mortified was more like it, thinking of his hands on her, undressing her. Maybe just the tiniest bit disappointed, too, that she'd been asleep and unable to enjoy it.

Murphy finally settled down, barricading the door with her body, worry wrinkling her forehead at the man's unwarranted delay.

The slow smile reappeared. "I've found that women are generally more comfortable in bed without their clothes." He laughed delightedly at her scarlet face, and his voice dropped to a husky whisper. "Don't worry, I wasn't ogling your luscious, naked body. I didn't turn the light on; I took your clothes off by touch alone." He hadn't dared turn on the light; he never would have left if he had.

"Undoubtedly because you've had so much practice undressing women in the dark," she sniffed. She scrambled out of his arms and stood up rapidly. She had a mug of coffee ready to thrust into Ryan's hands by the time he was standing.

He added enough milk from the carton on the counter to cool it and drained the mug in one long swallow. "Mind if I take Murphy hiking today? I don't think it will be too hard on her, in her condition."

She agreed readily. "No. I'm sure she would love it." Having him out of the house was an excellent idea.

Settling the baseball cap more firmly on his head, Ryan gave her an innocuous smile while his knowing eyes gently mocked her. Murphy, with a long-suffering air followed him out.

Ariel spent the day doing everything but what she was supposed to be doing. Mr. Severson, the town plumber, electrician and whatever else was needed, showed up right after Ryan left, with the new plumbing fixtures and stove. Pressed into service as his apprentice, Ariel learned more than she'd ever cared to know about the intimate details of sewer drains, flexible gas pipe and plumber's putty. After waving him off, she had stood in Ryan's kitchen looking a little forlornly at the new stove. She was going to miss their meals together, miss his toothbrush hanging in the rack next to hers, and . . . she reminded herself sternly that the meals he cooked were too fattening, and he always made her eat too much and, anyway, he kept leaving the cap off the toothpaste. She marched across the hall and gathered up all his toiletries from her bathroom and his food from her refrigerator, then put them where they belonged.

When Ryan returned late in the afternoon he saw Ariel standing in the doorway of the schoolhouse wearing a soft green dress. She looked as if she was trying desperately hard not to laugh. He knew the reason only too well. Murphy, he had discovered, did not ride in the back of a pickup like a normal dog; she rode in the cab, on the seat next to him. She'd jumped in when he'd opened the door, and no amount of halfhearted cursing and tugging would budge her. On the way home the dog had sidled over and casually draped a paw over his shoulder. He'd received several startled looks on the highway, the other drivers no doubt convulsed by his girlfriend.

Ariel smothered another laugh at his look of saintly suffering while he patiently held the truck door open for Murphy's careful descent. "You know, I used to tease Dennis that Murphy was the reincarnation of one of his old girlfriends. But now—" one golden honey eyebrow arched as elegantly as his "—I think she's just a reincarnated nymphomaniac."

"You said she doesn't generally like men," he retorted.

"Well, perhaps, a discriminating nymphomaniac."

He laughed. "I suspect the terms are mutually exclusive, but since it's the first compliment you've paid me, I'll accept it—left handed though it may be." His gently reproachful tone made her realize just how easily he managed to put her on the defensive.

He added disinterestedly, as he unloaded the tackle box, fishing rod and stringer of trout, "Going out for dinner again with the fish biologist?" The significance of the dress had finally struck him. He was sure it wasn't for his benefit.

"Yes." She eyed the fat fish and wished she weren't.

"Hmm. You seem to see a fair amount of him." He tried, but he couldn't quite keep the hint of censure out of his voice.

Ariel cast a sidelong glance at Murphy, who was leaning lovingly against Ryan's leg. With his free hand, he was absently fondling the dog's ear. Her murmur was sweetly snide. "At least I stick to my own species."

She held the door open for him. As he started to turn into her apartment, she threw open his door and announced, "Your kitchen arrived while you were fishing. It's all set up. The bathrooms, too."

Ryan gave her a wordless look and passed through his door. Ariel felt a perverse tickle of satisfaction at the brief flicker of disappointment she'd seen before his eyes had blanked over.

He tossed the stringer in the spotless white sink and set the tackle down on the new lemon-yellow countertop. "Got any newspaper so I can clean my fish?" His tone was cool. If he'd had any choice in the matter, the plumbing would never have been installed.

Ariel disappeared across the hall and returned in a couple of minutes with the past Sunday's issue of the *San Francisco Chronicle.* She slapped the fat newspaper on the counter.

"This is all I've got. It came today, but I've already glanced through it. Sunday's paper is mostly ads, anyway."

Ryan spread several sheets over the counter. He pulled open a drawer holding a jumble of old silverware and utensils and fished out a razor-sharp filleting knife. The flexible blade began whisking silvery scales from the iridescent skin.

Ariel leaned against the counter and watched as the fish were efficiently shorn of their scales. When Ryan moved to a clean area of the newspaper and began to gut them, she swallowed and looked away. Her gaze fell on the section of the newspaper he'd already used.

Out of the corner of his eye Ryan saw her lean closer to the paper, staring at something intently. "Careful," he murmured. "You'll get this mess all over that pretty dress."

She didn't hear him. With the tip of her finger she brushed several sequins of fish scales from the cheek of the man in the newspaper photo. Delicately she dabbed at the fish slime covering the lower half of his face and the caption. The small, precise mustache over his thin mouth showed briefly on the damp paper, and then it began to dissolve. The caption and the article underneath it were gone, too.

"I know this man," she muttered to herself. "I wonder why his picture is in the paper? He's not from San Francisco."

She felt Ryan leaning over her shoulder for a look. "Who is he?" His warm breath tickled the nape of her neck and wisps of hair that had escaped from the pins.

Her forehead wrinkled as she looked up at him. "I don't think they ever introduced me," she said wonderingly. "One afternoon I dropped by Dennis's office. He wasn't expecting me, and this man—" her finger touched the photo "—was with him, and somebody else." She frowned harder, trying to see the third man's face. "Dennis's brother, Robert? Their uncle?" She shook her head impatiently. "I can't remember. I do remember this man in the paper had a heavy accent. Spanish. Dennis mentioned that I'd been the one who told him about the Mexican villages that were so desperate for dental care, and that I was going down with him to help with the clinics."

She glanced at him hastily, sure that now he would have some question or comment about her relationship with Dennis. But Ryan seemed to be staring at the photo as hard as she had been. Ariel breathed a tiny sigh of relief. Ryan Jones was a very private person who clearly meant to respect her privacy... or maybe he just wasn't interested. She saw him glance up to the top of the page—for the date? page number?—and then farther up, to her. He was silent, as if waiting for her to finish the story.

"He was very angry with Dennis about it, said it was too dangerous. That man—" she gestured again toward the soggy paper "—was from Mexico, I'm sure." Her eyes shifted away to stare vacantly at the wall over Ryan's shoulder, and she smiled. "I'd forgotten that. It was sweet of him to be worried about me. I left right after that, so we never got around to introductions. And Dennis never took me with him to Mexico again."

The smile faded as she bent to study the photo again. She shook her head slowly. "I wish I could remember who else was in the office that day, but—" she straightened, dismissing the thought "—it doesn't matter anyway."

Ryan turned back to his trout, apparently losing interest in the whole matter. "If you don't think about it," he advised, "maybe it'll come back to you."

Minutes later Ryan watched from his living room window as the woman he was trying so hard to protect drove off with another man. He broke the seal on a new bottle of rum and poured a tumbler full. What the hell was the matter with him? It wasn't that he consciously sought to avoid romantic entanglements, he just never found any. The women he did find knew the score as well as he did—good sex, good times, no involvement.

Now, suddenly, he wanted involvement with a woman who didn't even know the game, much less the score. A virgin, for God's sake! It was just the knight-in-shining-armor syndrome. Every man suffered from it at least once in his life. He imagined himself the protector of some pure and fair maiden, prepared to slay a dragon to save her.

Then he remembered the flippant comment he'd made to Eileen, his sister-in-law, the comment that had been more serious than he cared to admit. Maybe he'd found his untouched woman at last, one who could be his alone. Perhaps her innocence could give him back what he'd lost so long ago.

His armor wasn't shiny; it was dented and tarnished, like his soul. And the dragon only had two legs, but the maiden was certainly fair, and he was more than willing to do battle. His laugh was short and harsh. The black knight rescuing the golden maiden. Who was really saving whom?

He slammed the empty glass down on the table. At least he didn't have to go to that damned gas station again; he could use her phone. It was precious little consolation.

"Were you able to find anything out yet?"

Rick Jones heard the impatience in his brother's clipped voice. "You were right on three so far. I haven't gotten answers on the others yet. The exterminator—" Rick allowed himself a grim chuckle at the black humor in the chosen profession of DiSanto's killer "—sold his business three months before the murder for twice what it was worth. The purchaser was a dummy corporation. We're trying to ferret out the real buyer."

"What happened to the equipment, the poisons?"

"The equipment, building, trucks, everything was bought from the new owner by a young guy at a bargain-basement price. He never met the actual seller; everything was handled by an agent who sent all the paperwork to a P.O. box in San Francisco. Both of them are clean. The box was rented for just a month. Nobody remembers what the guy looked like who rented it, of course, or if it even was a guy. False name, false address, dead end there."

Ryan swore pungently. "What else?"

"As you expected, no fingerprints on the candy box; it was wiped clean. Also, you were right about the levels. The concentration of poison was higher on the inside of the box than the outside, indicating that it was open when it was sprayed. Nobody else thought of checking that, by the way."

"So we know it wasn't accidently contaminated sitting around in some storeroom." The satisfaction of being right brought no pleasure, just a greater gnawing of tension in his gut.

"Know who Felicia Fury is yet?" There was suppressed laughter in Rick Jones's voice.

For the first time in several hours Ryan felt like smiling. "I know. Why didn't you just tell me how she really makes her money?"

"Because I know your opinion of love and romance," his brother retorted dryly. "I wanted you to be surprised."

Surprised? Ryan's smile abruptly vanished. He had been surprised, all right. Just what game was Rick playing? Did he think Ariel was guilty or not? His boss sure as hell did. He changed the subject curtly. "Nothing on the DiSantos' various enterprises yet?"

"I told you, we checked them out before," Rick said patiently. "Since the old man moved out here with the boys, he's been so clean you could eat off him."

"I'm convinced there's something there, buried deep, and maybe not to do with the old man, either. Keep digging," Ryan insisted stubbornly, and heard his brother's weary sigh. "What about the exterminator?"

"We've gone back about twenty-five years, to before he opened his business. Nothing so far. His wife is no help. That's when she met him, and she says he was very close-mouthed about his earlier life."

"She could be lying," Ryan considered, rubbing the bridge of his nose tiredly, "but I doubt it. Reilly was probably too smart to tell her anything."

"We'll keep working on it, Ryan," Rick promised. He restrained himself from asking his brother how he and his landlady were getting along. "Anything else?"

"Yeah. Find out whose picture was on page A-4 of last Sunday's *Chronicle*."

The sound of a car's leaving woke Ryan. He had tried to stay awake until Ariel came home, but he'd had too much fresh air, too much exercise and too much rum, and he'd had to go to bed. He focused blearily on the luminous face of the travel alarm by his bed. He decided dispassionately that if it was the green government-issue pickup of Sam the Bass leaving, he would shoot him.

Ryan pulled aside the curtain on his bedroom window. Moonlight frosted the silver Blazer, its headlights aiming down the dirt road to the highway. Murphy nudged his thigh aside for a look. He stared again at the clock in disbelief. Where the hell was Ariel going at four forty-five in the morning? Alone, without even her dog. He and Murphy exchanged a worried frown.

The sun was already high when Ariel returned. She was met at the door by two reproachful faces. She walked inside and slumped wearily on her couch, letting it support as much of her body as possible without actually lying down.

Tossing another chunk of apple wood onto the fire he'd kept going in her stove, Ryan took the wing chair opposite the sofa. While he'd waited for her to return he'd discovered several new meanings for the word patience. "You were up early this morning," he commented mildly.

"Research," Ariel yawned, eyeing the sofa pillows.

"At four forty-five in the morning?"

His sharp, almost accusatory tone was puzzling, but Ariel was too tired and too cold to worry about it. "It was the only time I could do it. Have you had breakfast?" she asked hopefully, momentarily forgetting that they weren't sharing meals any longer and she'd have to fix something for herself.

"About three hours ago. Going to leave your boots and coat on all day?"

Her jaw almost popped with a second yawn. "Probably." She closed her eyes and savored the fire's heat on her wind-chapped cheeks, contemplating this morning's fiasco. It ranked right up there with the night she'd camped on a southern New Mexico desert during what the locals referred to as the "breezy" season—a period of gale force winds that lasted only three-hundred-sixty days a year, she'd learned later.

Whenever she did the research for a new book she tried a couple of the everyday activities of the period she was working on. Often she was guided or inspired by one of her local sources. It gave her a feel for the setting and characters that she couldn't seem to get otherwise. At the moment she was truly doubtful that she would ever feel anything again with her cold-numbed fingers.

Old Mr. Applebury at the rest home had been very inspiring when he had lyrically described the idyllic goose hunts of his youth. He'd even solemnly given her his handmade goose-call to use. And she was giving it back. She'd honked herself silly and gotten only one scornful hoot from a scruffy owl in response, and that wasn't the worst of it.

She'd thought to incorporate an equally idyllic hunt into Felicia's latest book. The hero could enjoy a peaceful day's hunting as a respite from vigilantes and hired guns, ambushes and murders. She suspected now that he'd probably have welcomed an ambush or two to avoid such "respite." Mr. Applebury's memories had been rather selective. He'd forgotten to mention freezing to death on a muddy riverbank while a frigid wind whistled down his neck and up his pant legs.

Her left leg was suddenly pulled out straight. Reluctantly she sat up and opened her eyes. Ryan was crouched before her, sliding up the cuff of her stiff field pants and very efficiently unlacing her heavy boot. Balefully she regarded the drying mud she'd dropped on her clean floor. One boot came off, then the other.

Pulling her forward onto his chest, Ryan eased her out of her fleece-lined coat. Her arms fell naturally around his waist. Ariel closed her eyes again and relaxed against him. It would be so nice to go to sleep this way. She felt his warm fingers lingering on her chilled throat.

"What were you researching this morning?" he murmured.

"Goose-hunting," she whispered into his sweater.

"You didn't bring in a gun."

Ariel sat up quickly and looked at him, shocked. "Oh, I didn't want to shoot one! I was just . . . capturing the atmosphere." She shivered. "It was miserable."

His brow lifted. "Seems like a lot of work just for a little atmosphere."

"One of my greatest strengths as a . . . researcher is the thoroughness with which I do it," she lectured him loftily. "It adds immeasurably to the authenticity of the finished product."

The rest of Thursday and the next day passed quietly. Ariel deserted her computer long enough to drag the carton from Ryan's new stove back inside. After cutting down one side, she lined the box with old blankets to make a nursery. When Ryan returned with another stringer of trout he paused in the hall, admiring her efforts with a small smile. He was sure Ariel had impressed upon the dog the importance of using the box. He was just as sure that Murphy would ignore her.

An hour later he brought over dinner. The sound of the shower overhead detoured him from the dining table to the microwave to keep the fish warm.

The rolltop desk was festooned more fully than usual with little notes in that hen-scratch code. Out of habit he switched on her computer, absently playing with the command keys. The sudden whirring of the drive arrested his head, and he gazed at the screen, transfixed.

Ariel hadn't remembered to code access to what she'd been working on for the past few hours. The water was still running upstairs; he hoped she was fond of long showers. Settling in her swivel chair, he began to read.

Luke Tanner rocked back on the heels of his worn boots. His long legs, still in dusty bat-wing chaps, were spread arrogantly on the Persian carpet. He tilted his flat-brimmed hat with a careless thumb, letting it hang down his back from a knotted rawhide cord. Despite his rough clothes and the long black hair curling over his collar, he looked strangely at home in the elegant parlor.

Drucilla Sloan resolutely faced him. Her soft white shirt, streaked with dust was only half tucked into a black serge riding skirt. Her red-gold hair was a glorious tangle of flames around her beautiful, dirt-smudged face. She was exhausted—from the frantic ride, the choking dust, the frenzied shouting and shooting. The stampede had been diverted, only just, from the rim of a steep canyon. And now she had to fight another battle, worse than any range war, one she was far less sure of winning, not even sure she wanted to.

She squared her fragile shoulders. "I don't love you, Luke." She looked steadily into the farseeing gray eyes, lying through her teeth.

"Sure you don't, Drucilla," he drawled with a cynical curl to the black-bandit mustache.

Sapphire eyes flashing, she shrugged indifferently and turned to leave him. Amazed at her own acting ability, she prayed she wouldn't dissolve in heartbroken sobs until she was safely locked behind her bedroom door.

Steel fingers closed over her shoulders, digging in gently. His spurs jingled as he took another step forward. Her traitorous body betrayed her, yielding to the hard body behind hers. He widened his stance, easing her back full-length, trapping her between his leather-clad legs. The scent of cold wind and horse and musky male made her giddy, and her knees threatened to buckle.

Cupping her shoulders in his hard hands, Luke bent, trailing his hungry, open mouth up her neck. She felt a sharp nip on her earlobe that sent a gleeful shiver down her spine. Then his hot tongue bathed the tiny hurt before it dipped and swirled in her ear, freeing more delightful sensations. "Tell me again," his warm, moist whisper tickled deliciously through the sunset wisps escaping from her hairpins, "that you don't love me."

She shook her head frantically, unable to speak. Her arms rose and crossed over her full breasts in an instinctive gesture of protection. The silky mustache caressed her warming skin as he strung a line of softly stinging kisses down her neck.

Helplessly she arched her head into his shoulder, tilting it to bare more of her throat to his pleasuring mouth.

"Uncross your arms, Cilla."

"I mustn't. It would be bad of me," she moaned like a small child. Trying to twist away from those insolent hands and glorious mouth, her body burrowed deeper against his hardening warmth.

"Be bad for me, Cilla." The seductive whisper came as his tongue grazed in the pulsing hollow of her throat. "Uncross your arms."

"Nooo." Her groan dissolved in an ecstatic sigh as her arms, with a will of their own, fell to her sides. His calloused hands slid over her shoulders and down the chaste, thin blouse to cradle the breasts that were aching for his touch. His long brown fingers teased exquisitely the taut peaks swelling under the fine white linen.

"Tell me you love me, Cilla." His mouth was busy again at her ear, while one of his hands began gliding slowly down, over her chest, her flat belly, lower, hovering, teasing. They brushed lightly over the damp heat of her femininity.

"Tell me, Cilla!" he demanded huskily, his mouth closing hotly over the heavy pulse throbbing below her jaw.

"Damn you, Luke Tanner! I love you!" she groaned, barely able to speak. "Now take me, dammit!"

"I will," he promised fiercely, sweeping her up triumphantly in his arms and striding into her bedroom. He kicked the door shut behind them. "You're mine, Drucilla Sloan! And when I get through loving you tonight, you'll never doubt it again."

Ryan's mouth crooked in reluctant admiration. The shower overhead had stopped and, filled with the images the words on the screen had evoked, he tried to shut his inner eye to another one, of her getting out of the shower, toweling off the glittering beads of water trickling down the curve of her thighs, the slope of her breasts, the rough terry-cloth caressing smooth...

His half-cocked ear and a squeaky hinge told him that she was dressing. He glanced at the empty diskette jacket lying next to the machine. LD-1 was neatly printed on the cover. He considered it thoughtfully. Surely it couldn't be that simple, but then, the obvious was often the hardest to see.

"Retrieve file Luke Drucilla I," his long fingers rapidly tapped out. There was a note of victory in his quiet laugh when "Range-fire by Felicia Fury appeared in green letters. There was a brief synopsis, then the first chapter followed.

The time was 1892, and the setting was Johnson County, Wyoming. The heroine found herself caught in the middle of the Johnson County War. Her father having been killed in an ambush, she was trying to hang on to her thousands of acres of prime grazing land, beleaguered on one side by the ranchmen and their hired gunmen, and by the alleged rustlers and their friends on the other. The hero rode in on his horse Lucky one day. His only allegiance was to money, and for a price he agreed to help the heroine. In true romance style they fell in love, fighting it all the way, of course.

Ariel's light, almost skipping step sounded on the stairs. Ryan cleared the screen. He was setting her table as she hit the bottom step and swung around the corner into the living room.

"You forgot lunch," Ryan murmured twenty minutes later. Ariel had just polished off her third trout, easily half of the hash browns, and was now reaching for the last of the salad.

Her hand froze on the salad bowl. She gave her plate, empty save for three bare skeletons, a somewhat shocked look. Slanting him a sheepish grin, she forked the remaining salad onto her plate. "I tend to lose track of time when I'm working."

"I never realized historical research was so absorbing."

Ariel cocked her head, puzzled by the strange smile curving his mouth. "It can be," she answered with an odd, secret smile of her own. "I had a satellite dish installed out back today," she added casually. "If you'd, ah, care to watch something tonight . . ." Ariel wondered a little despairingly where this sudden urge to play with fire had come from.

His quick, surprised grin was a definite yes.

Frosted moonlight flowed through the windows under the cupola and over the sleeping woman burrowed under the quilts. He really hated to wake her up. A far better idea would be to slip into that cocoon of quilts with her. Her body warm and pliant and her mind hazy with dreams, it would be so easy to arouse her and realize a few of his own dreams. But she deserved better than that. Her first time should be special, unforgettable. It could be that the man who wakened all that latent sensuality, expressed only in print, would be unforgettable, too.

"Ariel, wake up, love." He shook her shoulder firmly. "Time to play midwife."

"I don't know anything about this," she said doubtfully, trailing down the steps after him. Why did babies always choose such uncivilized hours to come into the world? Pulling the belt of her old fleece robe tighter, she stepped into the cold hall and her toes curled. She should have taken the time to at least find her slippers. Ryan had gotten completely dressed. She envied him his warm-looking blue sweatshirt and navy cords.

Ariel stopped in the hall, frowning at the empty stove box. Ryan reached back and pulled her along after him, through his door and up the spiral staircase. "Ry?" There was sleepy bewilderment in her husky voice. "Where is . . . oh, no!"

His bedroom was lit by the small lamp on the dresser. By its dim glow she could see that one of the rag rugs and Ryan's velour robe had been scratched into a comfortable birthing bed; and it was too late to do anything about it. Murphy was placidly licking a squirming, wet body so tiny it seemed her rough tongue would surely crush the fragile bones.

"I'm sorry, Ryan; I really thought she would use the bed I made."

"Don't even worry about it." He sat at the dog's side and pulled Ariel down beside him, carefully arranging the robe over her crossed legs. Murphy rose unsteadily, whimpering, and Ariel grabbed Ryan's hand anxiously. "Maybe we should call the vet."

"Relax." He put his arms around her, drawing her closer. "Murph knows what to do. We're just here for moral support."

As the second puppy made its appearance, with its flattened ears, zippered eyes and mashed-in face, Ariel clasped his hand delightedly and whispered, "Oh, Ry, how beautiful. He's so precious."

In the cool, dim room her hair smelled like sweet, warm sunshine. His long fingers separated hers, sliding between them and bringing their palms together warmly. "You've never seen puppies born?"

"I've never seen anything born. My mom is allergic to animal fur, and we kids could never have any pets." She gave him a dazzling smile that brightened the dark room. "Did you and your brother have a dog when you were growing up?"

They'd exchanged the usual family information over dinner one night. Ryan had left out one or two significant details about his brother, along with the fact that his father had died when he was thirteen. Ariel had mentioned her twin sisters, still in high school, one brother who had recently graduated as an engineer and another in college. As she had talked Ryan had seen clearly the strong bonds of love and easy affection that held her large family together.

"Mmm, we had a dog." He laughed. "She was a mutt with the very original name of Lady, but she wasn't one. She had puppies with great regularity until my mother had the vet put an end to her wanton ways."

They laughed together softly. Murphy whined again, and Ryan stroked a soothing hand along her flank, murmuring gentle encouragement as more puppies entered the world. Ariel sat on the cold, drafty floorboards, watching silently. She shivered suddenly and snuggled unconsciously closer to him.

"Hey!" He looked at her in concern, his fingers rubbing her cold cheek. "You're freezing!" She couldn't argue; her bare feet had passed freezing five minutes ago. Drawing her up, he pulled back the bedspread and blankets, commanding, "Get under the covers. There's no sense in you catching pneumonia."

Amazed at her lack of maidenly reluctance to climb into his bed, Ariel sat in the middle, wrapping the blankets around her shoulders. She imagined that she could feel the heat from his body still trapped in the covers. She buried her cold nose in them, smelling his citrusy, musky scent. "Does it usually take very long?" Her voice was muffled by the covers.

"Not too much longer, I think. First litters are usually small, and she's already got five." He paused for a moment. "She was DiSanto's dog, wasn't she?"

"Yes. When Robert couldn't take her, I did."

"Why didn't he want her? If they were as close as you say, I would think . . ."

"She never liked him, almost seemed to hate him, in fact." Her face in the shadowy light became reflective. "Dennis and Robert were very close, but so different. The three of us spent quite a bit of time together. Dennis was basically an uncomplicated man, easy-going, with simple wants and needs."

And one of those wants was you, he added silently. How had DiSanto kept his hands off her for a year and a half, when his own fingers were itching right now, after only a week, to rip off that prim little nightshirt and show her the reality of those love scenes she wrote so imaginatively.

"Robert is very intense, very complex. He was two years younger than Dennis, but Dennis always deferred to him, just to avoid conflict, I think. Dennis didn't like arguments, any kind of a fuss. He'd always give in to keep the peace."

She smiled at a happy memory. "Robert's a terrific actor, does a lot of amateur productions around L.A. With just a little make-up, some clothes, maybe a wig, he can become completely unrecognizable. He came to Dennis's Halloween party dressed as a bag lady. He stood right next to me, talking for ten minutes, and I never recognized him."

"Is he married?"

"To his business, the one he took over from their uncle. He's the quintessential businessman, fascinated with figuring all the angles, profit margins, risks. No mere woman," she said, laughing "could ever hold his interest very long."

She scooted closer to the edge of the bed. The five damp fur balls were rooting around for breakfast already. The unruly lock of Ryan's hair had fallen over his forehead again, and she brushed it back without thinking. "You're not an easy simple man, either, are you, Ryan Jones?" she murmured.

He caught her hand and held it for a moment to his cheek. She had startled him. Just the light touch of her fingers had aroused him. He laid her hand back on the spread. "And just what do you think you know about me, Miss Spence?" he bantered lightly.

"I know you and your brother don't have a comfortable relationship. There's a strain in your voice whenever you mention him."

What was it about the dark that made confession so easy, he wondered. Maybe it wasn't the dark. Maybe it was the woman, instead, with her gentle, compassionate voice inviting the burden of his sins.

"We used to be close, like you say the DiSantos were. But we lost it a long time ago."

"What happened?"

"I was supposed to go straight on to law school after I graduated from Annapolis. Just before I graduated my brother wrote me that he was going to drop out of college and join the army so he could go to Vietnam. I guess he thought he was missing out on the fun or something." Ryan's cold smile was twisted with bitterness. "He looked just like our dad, and I knew it would kill my mother if anything happened to him. So I requested immediate active duty in the same area. I knew Rick would never be allowed to serve in a combat zone when his mother was widowed and his brother was already there."

Ryan held his breath, wondering if Ariel would catch the slip he'd made, revealing that his father, Chief Dye's "old friend," had been dead for years.

She didn't.

"And something happened to you instead."

It wasn't a question. How did she know? Was it so obvious? "Yeah, something happened to me. I really wasn't trained for anything, but I'm a natural marksman, so they put me in command of a company of snipers. We were very good." His low voice dripped gall. "We did ourselves out of a job after a few weeks."

"I know. The first night you were here, when you had the nightmare, you talked about some of what you were remembering." Her hand rested hesitantly on his shoulder. He looked down at the slim, strong hand, realizing suddenly that he hadn't had the nightmare again since that night. He slid her hand down and held it over his heart.

"I killed so many men I lost count. I stopped counting intentionally," he corrected himself. "Some were men whose faces I never saw. Others were men whose faces I sometimes think I'll never forget." He leaned his head back on the edge of the bed, his eyes tightly squeezed to shut out the memories. "After the fall of Saigon my men and I stayed in Southeast Asia. We were given new training; each man became an expert in infiltration, assassination, intelligence or weapons and demolition. Since I was the leader, I had to master all four."

Ariel's heart ached for the man who had showed such kindness and gentleness to her and her dog as he described the horror in a flat, unemotional voice. "You quit after the girl in the hut."

He nodded, swallowing back the bitter taste in his mouth, "I thought, I'd learned to handle the fact that you could buy anything you wanted there—drugs, of course, a man's murder, a woman, a child. Every unspeakable desire could be gratified and—" his harsh laugh sounded like it came from a raw throat "—the prices were amazingly low. The Navy gave us medals and sent us home. But they couldn't—" his soft voice was unbearably sad "—send back the naive innocent boys we'd been, or give us back even one of our illusions."

"What happened to your brother?" she asked quietly.

"Oh, he lost the supersoldier urge, finished school and feels guilty as hell, trying to figure out how to pay the debt he thinks he owes me. And I feel guilty because I can't figure out how to convince him that he doesn't owe me anything. I made my choice freely."

He shook his head tiredly. He opened his eyes and with his free arm, gestured with mock grandeur. "Now I brilliantly defend guilty clients who pay me exorbitant amounts of money when I get them off." He laughed mirthlessly.

"Why?"

He turned to smile sadly at her, her hand still clamped to his heart. "Because I just didn't care anymore, Ariel."

He sat for a moment longer, watching her quietly, then stood wearily and sat on the edge of the bed, his hip nudging hers under the covers. Obligingly she moved over and pulled the covers back automatically.

"I think Murphy's all right, but—" he muffled a yawn "—we ought to keep an eye on her just a little longer, okay?"

His yawn was contagious, and she collapsed back on the pillows, feeling totally exhausted. "Okay, I'll stay a little while longer. But don't," she admonished sleepily in the midst of another yawn, "let me fall asleep here."

Chapter 6

Ariel wriggled blissfully deeper into the lean, hard warmth at her back. Blinking at the sunlight burning through the crack between the curtains, she tried to turn away from it, then realized that the heavy weight across her chest wouldn't allow her to. The weight flexed and tightened. She recognized drowsily that the weight was a long, muscular arm with a hand attached that was—every cell in her body snapped wide awake—gently kneading her breast.

Every muscle as tight as a piano wire, she could scarcely draw even a shallow breath. What the hell had happened last night? After she had recklessly invited Ryan to watch TV, they had sprawled comfortably in her armchairs and viewed a grade-C Western. They had munched the popcorn Ryan made during a commercial and drunk the two bottles of beer Ariel had unearthed at the bottom of her refrigerator. When the movie ended they had solemnly agreed that the sidekick's mule should not only have gotten top billing, but also been the script writer, too. Then Ryan had taken his leave with one of those electrifyingly enthralling kisses that sent restless longings stirring crazily through her. Just when she'd finally fallen asleep, he'd gotten her back up to help Murphy.

Ariel let her breath out carefully. Nothing had happened. But she'd better get out of this bed immediately, because those feelings were clamoring for attention more insistently than ever, and if he woke up she would be terribly tempted to do something about them.

Furtively she tried to inch out from under his arm. His hand was reluctant to give up its hold. She shut her eyes in consternation. Now what? She felt the mattress shifting next to her. Opening one eye, cautiously, she stared up into dark chocolate eyes with a look of distilled wickedness.

"Oh dear," she whispered, trying to fight the giggle at the back of her throat.

Propped above her on one elbow, Ryan smiled down lazily. "Good morning, Miss Spence. It seems you fell asleep in my bed once again."

He'd moved his hand, but still having his arm stretched all the way across her wasn't any improvement. His arms and chest were bare, but her investigative toes told her that he was still wearing the soft cords. With a lightning move Ariel caught his arm with both hands and wrenched it away, scrambling out of bed without a shred of dignity. "And I've escaped again, Mr. Jones," she crowed.

Not quite. Her nightshirt was caught under his hip. Ryan reached out almost carelessly, seized it and hauled her back down on the bed. Rolling over swiftly, he trapped her under him. Her eyes grew impossibly wide and dark as his mouth descended. He watched the color draining from her face as he brushed his mouth teasingly over hers.

"Are you afraid, Ariel?" he murmured, tracing her lips lightly with the tip of his tongue.

Her breath drew in sharply; then he felt the warm, ragged explosion on his cheek. "Not of you," she whispered. "Me."

Ryan smiled briefly; then his eyes closed, and his mouth took hers stunningly, thoroughly.

Ariel could sense the barely restrained hunger in him. Her nightgown crept up with the aid of his nimble fingers as his warm palm slid over her thigh and hip, past the curve of her waist to rest on the underside of her breast. She felt his other hand pulling the quilt back over them. His tongue was probing, tasting, coaxing a response. Ariel sighed and gave in. Her legs tangled languidly with his, while their bodies began to nestle into each other's. Her fingers climbed up the taut cords in his neck, plunging into his thick blue-black hair. The strands of rough silk slid between her fingers as she pulled his mouth closer.

The soft warmth of the bed produced a drowsy coziness, and the feel of a hard male body against hers no longer seemed so unfamiliar. It seemed natural...and comfortable. His lips nibbled across her mouth with a slow thoroughness. When he reached the opposite corner he rose on one elbow to lean over her, his other hand still radiating heat on her breast. He seemed content for the moment just to look at her and to touch—slow, delicate, hypnotic caresses circling her breast, but never quite touching the ultrasensitive tip. His other hand reached up languidly to brush her hair away from her face and back onto the pillow. His palm and long fingers smoothed the hair back with long soothing strokes that matched the motions of his other hand.

Where only moments before every muscle in her body had been tight, ready to leap off his bed, now Ariel felt a languor seeping into her, relaxing those tight muscles one by one. She didn't know if it came from the warm quilts, or his body covering hers, or the heat his hands were spreading. Maybe it was the glow warming, softening, his hard dark eyes. She didn't particularly care; she didn't really want to think about it at all, just enjoy it and hope this delicious, weightless sensation didn't end too soon.

She brought her hand up as she studied his face. Her eyes followed her finger tracing over his winged, black eyebrows. Down it went over the sharp bones in his cheek and across his hard mouth, relaxed now in a soft smile. It ended in the hollow between his too-prominent collarbones. His pulse was fast and steady under the light touch of her fingertip.

"You're so thin," she murmured, her eyes too innocent to hide her concern and awakening passion.

Ryan's hand brushed lightly down her ribs and back up to the startlingly full undercurve of her breast. "So are you."

He rolled onto his back, pulling her on top of him.

She whispered a kiss over the sharp bones at the base of his throat. The tip of her tongue delicately traced around his strong pulse before she sealed a warm kiss over it. "The first time I saw you, I wanted to fatten you up, fix you all sorts of hearty, nourishing meals." She laughed, the tip of her tongue now tracing over the bones. "If I had tried, you'd be even thinner."

One dark brow lifted, and her finger returned to follow it. "I only inspire your maternal instincts?"

"A few others."

"Which ones?" His voice and smile were deep and lazy as he tipped her chin up to read the expression in her eyes. He was en-

joying simply letting her play with him, getting used to the feel of
a man in bed with her, as long as he was that man. The celibate
habits of twenty-seven years wouldn't be overcome in a single
morning, but he wanted to show her what it could be like to wake
up every morning like this, to learn the fun of teasing banter in a
warm cozy bed wrapped in each other's arms. "Which ones?" he
repeated.

She laughed lightly, tossing her head. "Oh . . . passion, desire . . . to name two."

"Those are pretty good ones—for a start," he acknowledged
with a lingering kiss. "Are you flirting with me, Miss Spence?"

"I'm trying to," she admitted honestly, laughing a little self-
consciously. "But I'm not any good at it."

"Oh, no," he assured her, "you're *very* good. A little more
practice and you'll be irresistible." He guided her mouth down to
his.

Ariel linked her arms around his neck. My Lord, she realized
absently, I didn't even know how to kiss before. Her virginal mouth
was rapidly losing its innocence as his tongue thrust and explored
and danced with hers. With a small moan she melted completely,
her hips unconsciously settling into the cradle of his.

Ryan's other hand slipped down her back and under her nightshirt, skating across her hip to the small of her back. He held her
tight against him as he rolled them to their sides. He tightened his
thighs, tangling their legs tighter as his hand moved up her bare
skin to her shoulder. His mouth smiled against hers as he felt the
little shivers under her cool skin.

Ariel felt Ryan push gently against her shoulder. Her body as
fluid as liquid gold, she leaned away until his hand closed over the
sharp bones, caressing, stopping her. The hand that had been idling
at her breast moved up to untie the satin ribbon at the neck of her
shirt. It spread the soft flannel, and his mouth left hers. It cruised
down, trailing a ribbon of smoldering heat. Ariel closed her eyes,
her fingers tightening in the hair brushing the back of Ryan's neck,
waiting. She felt the unruly lock of his hair that insisted on falling
over his forehead brush against her throat, and her head arched
back slowly. His head moved lower, brushing the rough silk of his
hair across her chest. His mouth was warm on the upper curve of
her breast. The hand on her breast drifted lower, pausing at her
waist, drifting again, seemingly aimlessly, across her belly to her
thigh. The long fingers stroked over the lean muscle on the out-

side down to her knee, then back up the softer silken flesh on the inside.

As Ryan's hand slipped up languidly, Ariel's hand dropped to his chest and pushed unconsciously. "Ariel." Her eyes opened slowly when his soft whisper called her.

Suddenly she was standing unsteadily on shaky legs, his arms around her for support. Uncomprehendingly she looked up at him.

To the unasked question in her dazed eyes, he answered with a crooked smile, "Not an escape, Ariel, a rain check, until you're not afraid of either one of us." When he had felt her push him away and she had opened her eyes, he had seen lingering traces of fear. He gave her a proprietary kiss and turned her firmly in the direction of the stairs, sending her down them with a friendly swat on the fanny.

Ariel drifted slowly across the hall and up her own stairs. Bemusedly she sat on the edge of her bed, hands folded in her lap. She'd been right to think him dangerous. She shook her head, trying to clear the confusion. Oh, yes, he was dangerous, even more than she'd imagined, but she no longer cared in the least.

This was definitely the man, the one she'd risk her heart and the beliefs of a lifetime for. Her hands clenched achingly on each other. Now the question was, did she have the courage to do it? Especially when she had no guarantee that she wasn't just a little vacation fling?

As she stared across the room the clock finally came into focus. It was past time to stop daydreaming and get dressed. Bessie was expecting her very soon, and she still had Murphy and her puppies to move, and Ryan Jones to avoid.

After a hurried breakfast Ariel stepped into the hall. She found Ryan had already moved Murphy into her nursery. Kneeling by the box, she laughed softly at the puppies wriggling around blindly on the old blankets like fat, furry grubs.

"You going to be a good mama, Murphy?" she crooned, scratching the velvety head. Murphy opened her yellow eyes for a moment, then closed them tiredly. "Poor girl, you didn't know the price you'd pay for a few minutes of fun," Ariel commiserated with a giggle and patted the dog's deflated abdomen. "That rat didn't stick around when you told him you were pregnant, did he? Was it that sneaky ol' Chester from down the road?" The dog opened one eye and moaned quietly. "I thought so. Don't worry, girl, we'll sue him for puppy support."

"I'll represent her for free." Ryan hunkered down at Ariel's side, reaching out a finger to gently stroke a mewling puppy back to sleep. He shot her a sidelong look. "What are you going to do today?"

She returned the look from under thick lashes. "Oh, just go to the Apple Fair in town. You wouldn't be interested."

"I like apples." He dragged her up with him as he stood.

She tried to sound as boring and discouraging as she could. "I'm taking Bessie Ruff from the nursing home."

"I'd like to meet her." He truly did want to meet the ancient woman with whom Ariel had forged such a strong bond.

Silent, Ariel picked up the shotgun leaning against the wall, cradling it in her elbow.

"Is there going to be an apple shoot?" He lounged in the doorway, blocking her exit.

"No, a turkey shoot." A crafty little smile lit her face. On second thought, she did want him to come with her. "Skeet shooting, actually," she added. "With a twenty-five-pound turkey for the prize."

"Alive or dead?" That explained the gray sweater she was wearing with her red slacks. The sweater, which made her blue eyes bluer, had a leather patch sewn on the front of the left shoulder, a shooting patch.

"Already plucked and dressed. Want to come? I'll even lend you a gun."

He followed her out into the garage to the tall, locked metal cabinet. He wanted to be sure he got the Browning Magnum he had seen when he had picked the lock one afternoon while she was out. She undid the padlock and threw the door open wide, silently indicating that he could have his choice. Without hesitation he took out the Browning twelve-gauge and a box of shells.

He stowed both guns behind the seat of his truck. "Yours is old, almost an antique."

"It was my grandfather's. He taught me to shoot."

She was sitting next to the door, too far away. He wanted to slide her across the seat hard against his side. "But you don't hunt. Why not?"

"I never liked the thought of killing anything." She grimaced. "I'm too soft-hearted, I guess." She said it as if it were a defect in her character.

"Don't apologize for it," he said harshly, then consciously softened his voice. "What will you do with the turkey if you win it? Make gallons of turkey soup?"

"*When* I win it," she corrected him gently.

"Care to make a side bet?" One raised black brow challenged her.

"Oh, I couldn't take your money," she said kindly. "I would be taking unfair advantage of you."

A small smile tugged at his lips as he stared straight ahead through the windshield. "I wasn't thinking of money. And you can take advantage of me anytime."

He was too sure of himself. He deserved to be taken down a peg or two; it would be good for his rascally soul, she decided self-lessly. "When I win, you have to fix dinner for me. Whatever I want."

"I hope I don't win the same," he said in mock alarm, laughing at the horrible face she pulled at him. "Well, don't worry." He gave her a slow grin. "I'll think of something."

"I'm not worried," she advised him sweetly, shaking the hand he offered to seal their bet.

Bessie Ruff was waiting for them on the sidewalk outside the nursing home. She didn't seem to be surprised to see Ryan. Ariel made the introductions, and then Ryan carefully lifted the elderly woman while Ariel collapsed the wheelchair and hoisted it into the back of the truck.

Ryan was hardly aware of any weight in his arms. It was as if the fragile bones were no more than air, and the only substance Bessie Ruff had was the indomitable will that refused to let go of life just yet. He glanced at her sharply, an unconscious question in his dark eyes. Bessie met his gaze unflinchingly. Then her eyes shifted to Ariel at the back of the truck, and her head shook almost imperceptibly. Ryan smiled sadly at her, nodding once, and then his eyes rested on Ariel. There was tenderness on his usually unreadable face. Ariel was soon to lose someone else she loved. He was only grateful that he would be present this time to try to ease the pain. Bessie Ruff studied his unguarded expression, then looked back to the young woman she regarded as more of a granddaughter than those of her own blood. Her crinkled face softened in a contented smile.

The October day was as crisp as the red apples shining in the slatted bushel baskets filling the backs of the trucks parked along Main Street. Overhead the cobalt sky was unmarred by a single cloud and the sun glowed like a molten gold coin. It was as if Mother Nature had decided to grant one last perfect day before she allowed the long, cold winter to close down on the valley.

The still air was quintessentially autumn: a faint drift of burning leaves, a subtle taste of high-country snow, the warmth of pure sunlight on cool cheeks and the scent of apples everywhere. Ripe apples, cinnamony apple pies and apple butter, and freshly pressed apple cider tempted the noses of locals and tourists alike as the crowd browsed at the booths scattered over the lawn surrounding the county museum.

Ryan, Bessie and Ariel detoured to the baseball park across the street, where the turkey shoot would be held later. Already a number of men and a few women were practicing with the targets stapled to hay bales. Ariel handed over Ryan's gun and took the handles of the wheelchair. His hand curved around the walnut stock of the gun as naturally as a wino's around the neck of a bottle. Her stomach tightened as she remembered how that same hand had closed around her breast only a few hours before. She shook her head to banish the unsettling memory and offered some friendly advice. "That gun shoots high and a little to the left."

He nodded and took the box of shells out of his jacket pocket. His first shot was low and to the right of the bull's-eye. Resting the gun on his shoulder, Ryan turned to give Ariel a calculating stare. She responded with a gesture of exaggerated innocence. Grinning, he turned back, swung the gun down firmly against his shoulder, hardly taking aim and shot the center out of the target. Ariel rolled Bessie back across the street, wondering if maybe she should have practiced just a bit more.

The Mountain Fiddle Band was tuning up. Ariel parked Bessie so she could enjoy the sunshine and folded herself gracefully down onto the grass at the old woman's side so they could listen. She held a palsied, weightless hand in hers.

"He's a scoundrel, isn't he?" Bessie's strong voice was full of humor.

"Who?" Ariel looked up artlessly.

Bessie gave her a dry look.

Caught out, Ariel laughed. "Yes, I expect he is. Also arrogant, complicated and much too good-looking. But..." Her glance strayed across the street, where she could see his red shaker-knit sweater and wheat jeans standing out among the blue denim and cowboy shirts. "He definitely has style." Her expression turned wistful. "I've fallen in love with him." The words slipped out so easily that for a moment she didn't realize how naturally she accepted the knowledge. She examined the words, savored them and knew they were true.

Bessie's knobby hand tightened convulsively on Ariel's. She stared at the girl in rueful astonishment. She'd figured it would take Ariel longer to figure it out, and she'd never expected her to accept it so blithely.

Ariel didn't notice Bessie's reaction as she softly voiced her thoughts aloud. "I've only known him a week; it hardly seems possible. Isn't love supposed to come slowly, comfortably, after knowing someone a long time?" She sighed lightly. "Maybe it's just lust, and it will pass."

"Don't discount lust, girl; every marriage can benefit from a healthy dose of it." She smiled down fondly. "But you don't think it's lust, do you, Ariel?"

Ariel smiled back wryly. "No, Bessie, I don't." She gazed off into the distance again, her eyes automatically seeking out a flash of red. "And I think he may well break my heart," she added softly. She grinned up hopefully. "Any words of grandmotherly wisdom would be gratefully accepted."

"I knew John Ruff all of ten minutes before I decided I was going to marry him," Bessie said reflectively. "The only reason our first son wasn't born shamelessly soon after the wedding was because I talked John into getting married just two weeks after we met."

Ariel laughed in delight. "Why, Bessie! You impetuous, scandalous woman!" Her joyful face gradually sobered. "I don't think I could be that convincing."

"If you want him badly enough, you can be."

Did she want him badly enough? Was she willing to trade her solitary, placid, rather selfish life for excitement, passion, shared joy and sorrow... and the very real possibility of being terribly hurt? Ariel sighed in frustration. If only she could know how Ryan really felt. But that was part of the adventure, the excitement of falling in love, the not knowing, the risk of offering yourself with no guarantee of winning, gambling with the highest stakes of all—your heart. And she had never been much of a gambler.

"I've wondered why you never remarried, Bessie."

"Widows with five young children don't get that many offers," Bessie informed her dryly. "Especially with no farm or business to sweeten the pot."

"Still," Ariel searched the old face which still held traces of the beauty she had once had, "I know you must have been asked."

"If I had an offer soon after John died, I would have accepted. I was so frightened and alone." Remembered grief and fears sixty years old shadowed her eyes. "But after a while I got to enjoying my independence, hard as it was. I decided I wouldn't settle for less than what I'd had with John. And," she finished matter-of-factly, "I never found it."

"Well, I think I have." Ariel laughed dismally, burying her head in her hands. "But I'm not sure what I'm going to do with it."

Bessie's worn eyes spotted a blur of red moving toward them. "You'll figure it out soon, dear," she predicted reassuringly.

They did the grand tour of the booths. Ryan bought a jug of hard cider and five dollars' worth of chances, though on what he wasn't quite sure. Ariel bought a quilted pillow, and then she and Bessie spelled the women at one of the pie booths for a time.

After reclaiming his ladies Ryan bought lunch, and they settled on the rustling carpet of red and gold under a maple tree to eat it. Ariel watched Bessie closely, not liking her color or the increasing tremor in her hands.

"Bessie, would you like us to take you back before the shoot? There are so many people; maybe you'd like to get away from the crowd." Ariel always tried to phrase her suggestions that Bessie rest as innocuously as possible, but she was never able to fool her.

"I'm not ready to be put down for my nap yet," Bessie told her tartly. "And I certainly don't want to miss the shooting contest between you two." Her bright eyes fixed on Ryan guilelessly. "Did you know Ariel won the last two shoots, even beating the man who'd been the valley champion for four years?"

"So more than several people took great pains to tell me," Ryan confirmed dryly. He also knew it was one of her lesser accomplishments. Ariel Spence, with Dennis DiSanto as her partner, had won the mixed doubles and trapshooting championship for the entire state of California two years ago. He anticipated an interesting contest. He anticipated what he would get if he won their bet even more.

The shoot quickly developed into a three-person contest. Only Ariel, Ryan and a surly man with almost no neck and the build of a football tackling dummy progressed past the third shooting station.

The competitors had to hold their shotguns waist high, standing at each of eight stations. Without warning bright orange clay disks were released by the trap machine to whiz across in front of them at ninety miles an hour. Since there were two machines, one on each end of the firing line, the contestants never knew from which direction the flying saucers would come. Their guns had to be whipped up against their shoulders, aim taken and a shot fired in a little less than two seconds. Two consecutive misses and a contestant was out.

The former valley champion missed two in a row and had to stand with the rest of the crowd. He took up a position with his two brothers, near a tallish, slight stranger with lank blond hair. The stranger was watching the duel with great interest.

The acrid smell of burned gunpowder and blue smoke drifted over the field as Ariel and Ryan moved to the sixth station. They'd both had misses, but within a second had managed to fire again and shatter the target before it was too low to be safely hit.

At the seventh station the trap released the disk and Ariel threw up her gun in a smooth, almost careless motion. The target exploded. She moved aside, gesturing graciously to Ryan. He shifted his hips a few times, settling into an easy stance. The orange blur flew across in front of him and he missed. He fired a second shot immediately, and the blur blew up.

The eighth and final station was by far the most difficult, with the targets passing almost directly overhead. The avid crowd pushed forward, offering encouragement, and a few more bets were made.

Ryan decided it was time to shift the odds in his favor. As Ariel sank into a half crouch with her gun, he pulled her back up and planted a long, leisurely kiss on her startled mouth. Her free hand came up immediately to push him away, but it ended up lying limply on his shoulder. He tilted her face to a new angle, drinking a deeper kiss from her softening mouth, then set her firmly away from him, smiling down into her wide eyes. "For luck, Miss Spence."

"Yours, I think," she whispered back. Trying vainly to gather her scattered wits, she kept her back to the laughing crowd. Nodding to the trap operators that she was ready any time—though she wouldn't be for at least an hour—she tensed. She missed both shots.

There was a roar of male approval and feminine groans. She faced the crowd with a shrug and a sheepish smile. Ryan took her place, and she moved just inside his peripheral vision. Twice he looked at her suspiciously, obviously expecting some outrageous distraction. She smiled at him cheerfully each time. He was glancing at her once more when he heard the trap. He barely had time for two shots and both went wide.

Ryan and Ariel saluted each other gravely with a perfect Regency bow and curtsy, and then burst out laughing along with the people who had enjoyed their performance. After accepting joint custody of the turkey they began to make their way back through the crowd to Bessie.

The voice on the loudspeaker caught Ryan's attention, and he stopped Ariel with a touch on her arm. He pulled a handful of raffle tickets out of his pocket and listened more closely. "Hey," he said wonderingly, "I think I won the raffle!"

"What did you win?" Ariel asked, laughing at the boyish excitement on his face.

"Damned if I know." He grinned at her. Slinging his arm across her shoulders, he headed them back toward the bandstand. "Let's go find out."

Ariel and Bessie struggled to keep their giggles at bay. "Oh, no, Ry! What are you going to do with *that*?" The look of total consternation on Ryan's face was too much for them, and they gave up. The cool, unflappable Ryan Jones was at a loss for words.

"Uh, Mr. Jones." The foreman of the lumber mill that had donated the prize stepped forward. "We kinda have to deliver it today; we need the truck. We can let you keep the trailer for a week or so, though," he allowed generously.

Ryan looked at him in greater disbelief, if possible, and then back at his prize: a low trailer with a pyramid of logs, each about twenty to thirty feet long.

"Gee, there must be twelve to fifteen cords of wood there," a bystander said interestedly. "Hope you have a good chain saw, Jones." The man slapped his congratulations on Ryan's back and walked away. Ryan's mouth tightened fractionally.

A prudent woman would have kept her mouth shut, but Ariel was apparently not a prudent woman. "Let's see, you could ship them back to Los Angeles and build a log cabin," she contributed thoughtfully. "No, that might look out of place on Malibu beach. Oh! I know," she said brightly, giving him her best cheerleader smile. "You can give each one of your friends a log as a Christmas present; I understand firewood is *very* expensive in L.A. Be sure you buy plenty of ribbon," she instructed. "Red, I think."

His black look sent her off into another convulsion of laughter. Both of them nearly missed the foreman's comment that the lumber company had used the low flatbed instead of a standard logging trailer to make unloading easier. By releasing one particular chain in the metal web holding the logs in place, he explained, they would be able to tumble the whole load off the truck.

"Come on, Ryan," Ariel said plopping the fresh turkey into his arms, "let's take our prizes home." Pushing Bessie's chair, she led the way to his truck, muffled giggles escaping her every few steps.

"What do they usually do for fun on Saturday nights in this town?"

Ariel stuck the last dish in her dishwasher and kept her head down, not offering any suggestions. After delivering Bessie to her room at Valley View, she and Ryan had come home and eaten the leftovers out of both their refrigerators for supper.

Ryan stretched his long legs across the floor as he leaned back against the counter beside her. "What about that place just down the highway?"

Ariel straightened slowly and faced him, hoping he wasn't going to suggest what she was afraid he would, because she would go. "It's kind of a rough place, especially on Saturday nights," she said dismissively.

"The sign says they have a live band and dancing. It can't be too rough."

"It's all stomp dancing, and the band is two guitars and a fiddle."

"Let's go." He had grabbed her hand and was leading her out the door in one of those smooth, lightning moves before she could think of one good reason why they shouldn't.

Two happy loggers reeled out as he opened the scarred plank door of the Stumble Inn for her. "This place should be called the Stumble Out," Ariel muttered to herself. One look around the smoky, barebones saloon, and she knew it had been a mistake to come here tonight. There were few women, and those few looked as hard and tough as the men. She'd forgotten that the lumber company had brought in roughhousers to do the particularly nasty and dirty job of harvesting the timber burned in a forest fire last month. The usual neighborhood crowd had wisely stayed away tonight.

Ryan stopped just inside the door. Rocking back on his heels, he braced his legs slightly apart, elbows cocked, hands in the pockets of an old leather bomber jacket. He surveyed the rough interior and its even rougher occupants and checked to see where the fire exit was. He felt that old recklessness stirring. The bar reminded him of his favorite hangout in Bangkok years ago. The dress was a little different and the men a little bigger, but the atmosphere of good-natured belligerence was the same. He glanced at Ariel and suppressed a smile at the worried pull of her eyebrows. He was confident he could get her out before the inevitable fight got too rowdy.

They started toward an empty table, and Ariel's stomach hit the floor. It hadn't been a mistake to come here; it had been insanity. The slightly slurred voice caught them in the act of sitting down and directed all eyes to them.

"Well, well, if it ain't Annie Oakley and the big-shot lawyer from California." The word "California" sounded like an obscenity.

Ariel occupied herself with removing her jacket, keeping her head down. She could feel the hostility from the back of the room. A chair scraped on the wooden plank floor, and she knew their adversary was coming closer, like a foul-smelling cloud. She looked up and caught Ryan's eye. He smiled benignly, seemingly unaware of the menace in the air.

"I think we should leave, Ryan," she whispered hurriedly. She reached for her jacket and started to put it back on. "That's Shirley Geilenfeldt, the one we beat today. And he's got his brothers with him. We don't want—"

"Shirley?" Ryan checked a laugh. "What are his brothers' names?" Calmly he removed her suede jacket and arranged it neatly over the back of her chair.

"Beverly and Gus." Ryan's head went back, and he laughed freely. Ariel looked at him, incredulous. "Listen!" she scolded in a low, fierce voice, shaking his arm to wake him up to the situation. "The three of them collectively have the personality of a wounded rhino, and Shirley's the meanest. And the fact that he was beaten today by a woman *and* a city slicker won't have improved it. Now, let's go!" she hissed, trying to stand up before the walking tackling dummy with the nasty smirk on his face made it to their table.

Ryan's hand closed over her arm and held her in her seat. "Sit down, Ariel. We haven't even had a drink yet," he reminded her reasonably. He lounged back in the wooden chair, legs crossed, one ankle resting on the opposite knee.

Ariel caught the suppressed excitement and anticipation lurking in Ryan's eyes and glared at him. "You're enjoying this, Ryan Jones!" she accused in a disbelieving whisper. "We're probably going to get killed by those three apes and you . . . oh, no . . ." She moaned and hid her face in her hands.

"Where'd you learn to shoot like that, boy?" Shirley Geilenfeldt sneered. Good manners dictated that he exchange a few pleasantries before he rearranged the pansy's pretty face.

"Potshotting at the ducks in MacArthur Park." Ryan leaned farther back in his chair, balancing it on the back legs, his hands in his front pockets. He stared blandly into Shirley's washed-out green eyes. "Shot a few skunks, too."

A lanky man with stringy blond hair and worn Levis stopped by the front door, as if reluctant to miss what would undeniably be the best show in town that evening. The door opened and Chief Dye ambled in. The blond man and a couple of others decided that discretion was the better part of valor, slipping out the door before it closed. The chief's sousaphone voice reached even into the back room, where the poker game was going strong. Shirley squinted at him glumly, grunted one last opinion of city boys and rejoined his disappointed brothers.

The band began to play, and three couples got up to dance. Ariel watched Ryan stroll over to the bar and order two beers. The limp was gone. The hours he was spending in the mountains had strengthened his leg rapidly. He'd even gained some weight. He leaned an elbow on the bar, relaxed and totally comfortable, laughing with two burly loggers. His red sweater and Calvin Klein jeans and topsiders certainly weren't de rigueur dress for a Montana bar, but he was accepted here as easily as he would be at the poshest lounge on Nob Hill in San Francisco.

Women found him incredibly attractive, of course; she hadn't needed to see their appraising looks at the fair today to tell her that. Yet men instinctively liked him, too, sensing, she guessed, the cool toughness under the suave charm. Only a Shirley Geilenfeldt, full of drunken bravado, would be stupid enough to challenge him.

Chief Dye made the rounds, carrying a mug of beer that never lowered appreciably from table to table. He offered his congratulations when he reached their table, asked Ryan to stop in and see him on Monday, then moved on. The band swung into "Cotton-Eyed Joe," and Ryan pulled Ariel up to dance. He danced, she discovered, as he seemed to do everything else, with a consummate, easy skill. The band downshifted into a slow Texas two-step.

Ryan closed his arms over her back, holding her body against his so closely that she had no choice but to rest her head on his shoulder and wind her arms around his waist. She let her body indulge itself in the deeply pleasuring sensations generated by his hips and thighs and chest sliding lazily against hers. They swayed to the languid beat of the bass guitar, and Ariel nestled her head closer into his sweater, catching the tang of his cologne and a wisp of crisp apples and clean fall air through the smoky, stale beer smell of the bar.

The band decided to take a break. Dropping a light kiss on Ariel's forehead, Ryan went to investigate the possibilities of the jukebox.

Ariel looked around for the ladies' room. On her way back to their table she passed a table full of loggers. An arm as hard and thick as a middle-aged pine tree shot out and clamped around her waist, dragging her onto the lap of the biggest man. Her startled gasp was cut short by a low drawl from over her head.

"The lady is with me."

Ariel looked up warily. The mood in the bar was suddenly very primitive. Ryan stood less than two feet away, balancing easily on the balls of his feet, his hands relaxed and loose at his sides. He reached out and jerked her up to his side, his arm around her unmistakably possessive.

"If she's your woman, you should keep a better hold on her," the logger grumbled.

"I will," Ryan agreed with a slow smile.

"I am *not*—" Ariel started in a clear voice.

"Shut up, Ariel," Ryan said pleasantly as he began to guide her back to their table. "Unless you want to be fair game for every man in here, including Shirley."

She gave him a disgusted glare and turned to give one to the logger, too. Instead she reached down to the table they were passing and grabbed the first thing her fingers touched—a full heavy mug of foamy beer. The Geilenfeldts had seen Ted Dye leave and apparently decided they had waited long enough to avenge Shirley's honor. All three of them were closing in on Ryan from his blind side. She yelled a warning and swung the sloshing mug at Beverly Geilenfeldt's head at the same time.

Chapter 7

Oh, Ry, brawling—making a public spectacle of myself!" Ariel was desperately trying to look both ashamed and disapproving and to avoid Ryan's eyes. They caught hers, and she cracked up. He had managed to drag her out through the fire exit, almost unscathed, just as Chief Dye and two of his men had charged through the front door of the Stumble Inn.

Her stern mouth widened in a huge grin, her blue eyes filled with unholy glee, and she collapsed on her sofa in gales of helpless laughter. Ryan caught her contagious insanity and stumbled to the couch, too. Just as they began to regain control of themselves, they made the mistake of looking at each other, setting them off again.

Finally, hugging her aching sides and groaning, Ariel bent over, trying to catch her breath. She controlled hiccuping giggles long enough to gasp, "Did you see the big one's face," she wiped her teary eyes and caught another jagged breath, "when you hit him over the head with the spittoon?" She dissolved again.

"Dammit, Ariel, they were all big! Why the hell did you have to start a fight with every damn one of them?" He rested his head on the back of the sofa, his streaming eyes wide, trying to stifle his giggles.

"Me?" she squeaked indignantly. *"Me?"* She fell on his chest, too weak with laughter to sit up. Ryan's left arm automatically came around her, his hand threading through her disheveled hair to hold her. "You were the one," she felt constrained to point out, "who kicked the chair out from under the one with the red beard and then called him a—"

"I know, I know," he admitted, chuckling again. "But you didn't have to dump the other one's pitcher of beer over his head and then call him a fat twit." He heaved in a huge breath, trying for control again until the air exploded in another gusty burst of laughter. "A twit!" he groaned. "My Lord. I've got to teach you some better words if you're going to hang out with me. I've got a reputation to maintain."

"It's all my mother's fault. Every time I start to say what I'm thinking, I taste soap and I choke." She lay half sprawled over him, relaxed, an occasional giggle still vibrating through her body. At last she realized exactly where she was and struggled to sit up, pushing on his hard chest and thigh.

Ryan let her up, but tightened his fingers around the back of her neck. "Well! I, ah, guess I should see to your eye," she said in a small voice, refusing to look at him. She stared at her hands, folded prissily on her lap.

Ryan hardly felt the abrasion from somebody's fist. "Forget my eye," he commanded huskily. He flexed his wrist and gently forced her face to tilt up to his. "You swing a mean beer mug, Ariel Spence. I'm glad you were on my side."

Almost against her will her eyes, wide and uncertain lifted and were instantly trapped by his, half-lidded and sultry. "Y—you were?" She was unable to move. His free hand was opening the top button of her shirt and sliding under the fabric, his thumb feathering over the satiny skin at the base of her throat.

"Uh-hmm, I was," he reaffirmed softly. His warm breath fanned over her parted lips, making silky wisps of her hair tickle her cheeks and neck. "I like to raise hell every now and then. I think you have a secret desire to do it, too." His mouth touched hers briefly. "What other secret desires do you have, Ariel?"

His eyes slid shut, and his lips closed over hers, taking possession as his hand slipped up her throat to her chin, keeping her mouth where he wanted it.

She moaned regretfully, her eyes closing, too. "I can't tell you." Her arms stole around his waist as he bore her back slowly on the couch. One of her legs bent; the other stretched straight on the sofa, trapped between his. The kiss deepened, sweetened, his tongue curling leisurely in her mouth. Hers joined in, hesitantly at first, then gliding slickly along his to taste him, dark, tangy, male. His knee bent, sliding up her thigh to rest snugly at the apex of her legs nudging gently with a slow, seductive rhythm.

A husky sigh purred deep in her throat, and her eyes, hazy with rising passion, opened to look into his. "I really shouldn't be doing this. I don't know you well enough."

"Miss Spence, the librarian, might feel obligated to say that, but the woman who coldcocks bullies in barroom brawls knows it isn't true, doesn't she, Ariel?" he asked quietly, rubbing his moist mouth lightly over hers. "I think we knew each other before I ever got here," he added whimsically. "We just hadn't met yet."

For an answer her arms tightened around him, her fingers slipping unconsciously under his belt with a will of their own. They tugged up his sweater and trailed down the groove of his spine to the cool hollow at the base. They rubbed, pressed, urging his hips and knee tighter against her, sliding, straining to relieve that deep, sweet ache.

With a deep groan, Ryan moved his hand rapidly down, freeing the buttons of her silky cream shirt. Leaving the hungry softness of her mouth, he rose above her and spread the shirt wide. His head bent again, his mouth nibbling at the hollow in her throat. His hands swept slowly across her shoulders and down her chest. He was learning her, savoring the taste and texture of her skin with his lips and tongue and teeth and rough fingertips.

Her hand clenched on his sides as his fingers brushed the hollow between her breasts and freed the catch on her bra. His warm tongue touched the spot where his fingers had been, then slid wetly over her cool skin to a puckered tip. He drew it into his mouth and suckled gently. Ariel arched into him strongly with a sharp cry.

Ryan pulled back, his face full of tender concern. "Did I hurt you, love?" His hands moved up to frame her face, his thumbs brushing the soft hair off her flushed cheeks. His body was urging him to take her, but he forced himself to be patient as he waited for her answer.

"No," she whispered, her face flushing more deeply at her unsophisticated reaction. The women he was used to probably considered this casual petting. The trickles of liquid fire that his gentle mouth had sent through her were anything but casual, and she'd been totally unable to control her response. She desperately hoped he wouldn't guess just how little experience she really had. Yet she didn't know how she was going to hide it if his every touch sensitized nerves she hadn't known she had and made them stridently demand more.

She wouldn't meet his eyes, and he felt her embarrassment radiating in palpable waves. He slipped his arms behind her and rolled them to their sides. She buried her face in his shoulder.

"Ariel. Look at me." His hand prodded her chin up firmly. "Didn't Dennis ever make love to you?" He knew DiSanto hadn't introduced her to the ultimate act, but surely...?

"Not much more than this," she whispered miserably. She felt like such a baby, but she might as well tell him the rest of it so he could have a really good laugh. "And I, ah, never had this... reaction."

He stared at her, trying to hide his astonishment. Despite those steamy books of hers, she was almost a complete innocent. She didn't even realize the power she had given him over her by what she had just admitted. "You two had a rather unusual relationship, didn't you?" he mused aloud. "You weren't lovers, yet you traveled together, shared this house."

Talking about a woman's lovemaking experience with another man, especially when he'd been in the middle of making love to her himself was out of character, to say the least. But suddenly, he wanted to know all about their relationship. He sensed that there were still a few ghosts for her to lay to rest. And perhaps, without that exorcism, his relationship with her could never be all that he wanted—and he found he was wanting more with each passing hour.

He could feel her still-aroused nipples teasing his chest even through his sweater, and it was too distracting at the moment. Deftly he redressed her and sat her up, his arm firmly around her waist to keep her close to him and the subject.

They had left off most of the lights when they had come in. The warm room, softly lit by firelight, was just right for telling secrets, and Ariel felt an odd compulsion to go on telling hers.

"It *was* a strange relationship." She leaned her head on his shoulder and smiled up sadly at him. "I've had months with little else to think about. I loved him, but that spark, the little tingle all the heroes and heroines in romance novels feel, was missing." She turned her head and stared into the fire. "I finally decided that was just another part of the fantasy. That's when I decided I would marry him."

"Did he feel the same way about you?" He knew DiSanto hadn't; everything he'd read pointed to a man crazily in love.

"You mean, no tingle, no spark?" Her head tilted on his shoulder, and she gave him a quick smile. She shook her head almost sadly and went back to studying the fire. "He had a very strong desire for me, but a lot of patience, too." Her low laugh was self-mocking. "Obviously. Then, too, he was nine years older than I am; perhaps he had some rather fatherly feelings, too."

Ryan grinned wryly at the top of the golden head resting on his shoulder. He was seven years older than she was, but his feelings for her were anything but fatherly.

"He used to build up a lot of frustration," she admitted softly, "and then he would find someone for the evening."

"He told you that?"

"No. But I always knew...somehow. I'm sure the police and Rick Jones did, too, but they were kind enough never to mention it." Ariel began to pleat the tail of her shirt into precise folds. "I used to worry that after we were married, he would be... disappointed with me, that he wouldn't want to give up those other women."

Ryan stilled her nervous hand and held it warmly against the strong heartbeat in his chest. He rested his cheek against her soft hair. "No, Ariel, he wouldn't have been disappointed, just very happy that you were finally his," he reassured her quietly. He was beginning to feel an odd kinship with the dead man who had unknowingly bequeathed him this woman. "But you would have been, eventually, knowing there should be more."

"No. I would have been perfectly content," she began without thinking, "as long as I never met..." She finished in a reluctant whisper, "You." She clucked her tongue and drew away. Throwing him a swift look, she whispered huskily, "Ah, yes. Well, now you know all my secrets."

Weaving his long fingers through her sun-rinsed hair, he brought their mouths together. "You have others, but I'd already guessed this one. We have far more than a mere spark between us." He took her mouth gently, rapidly fanned the spark to a full flame. He wouldn't let things go too far tonight. He had another plan for her seduction at the back of his mind, one that was a little foolish, romantic. But he did want something for himself now, and he wanted to make her a little hungrier.

His arms urged her closer; his impatient tongue opened her willing mouth and was welcomed. Vaguely they were both aware of an odd sound, like the collapse of a heavy body on the floor. There was a faint, sighing moan.

"Ry?"

"Hmm?" He was more interested in undoing the buttons of her shirt again than in conversation.

Suddenly she jerked away, her face white, her eyes on the floor. "I think something is wrong with Murphy!"

Ariel hated fluorescent lights. The fragile glass tubes seemed to be filled with the lifeless light from a cold, dead planet. They didn't glow like an incandescent bulb; they gave off no warmth, no comfort. Instead they seemed to suck the heat and color and life out of everything they shone on. They were, to Ariel, the lights of death.

Once upon a time she had never even noticed them, but now she never walked into a room without being immediately aware of them. Dennis's death and the mandatory visit to the morgue, the grand jury room and hours in an interrogation cubicle under that harsh sterile light had assured it.

She sat huddled motionlessly on the vinyl couch in the vet's cold waiting room. The only sound was the faint hum from a faulty ballast in the fluorescent panel above her head. Ryan had set her there with terse instructions to stay put. Coward that she was, she was obeying. She'd watched him disappear behind the closed door with Murphy. She had had to watch Dennis die; she couldn't watch his dog die, too.

She stirred, drawing in on herself more, shiveringly cold. The chilly plastic slipcovers, protection against the vet's nervous patients, cracked stiffly. Ariel wrapped Ryan's bomber jacket more closely around her body, like a small girl with her security blanket. She nuzzled her cheek against the worn fur collar, inhaling the comforting smell—aftershave, old musky sweat, Ryan. Her fingers twisted in the butter-soft leather, rubbing it between them.

Ariel had panicked when she had seen Murphy lying at their feet in convulsions. Ryan's calm, swift efficiency had infused itself into her. While he had wrapped the dog in a blanket and laid her in the back of his truck, Ariel had called the vet. He had even thought to load the puppies, too, box and all. During the endless ride to the vet's office she had cradled Murphy's wretching, convulsing body with her own.

The white door opened and both Ryan and Dr. Hughes, the lanky, sandy-haired vet, emerged. Ariel's eyes strained past them. Murphy was lying on the stainless-steel table, a silvery space blanket covering all but her brown head. A green plastic tube dangled from her slack mouth into a glass jar. A slow bellows on the jar pumped soundlessly. Another tube, darkly red, led out from under the silver blanket and up to an IV stand.

Not daring to hope yet, Ariel finally fixed her gaze on the two weary men, their grim faces seemingly drained of blood by the humming lights. Ryan's expression was a black study: eyebrows fiercely lowered in a slashing line, dark eyes narrowed dangerously, mouth turned down. Seeing Ariel's impossibly pale face grow even more wan every time her eyes snuck back to the motionless dog, he reached behind him and pulled the door shut.

Shoving his hands into his pockets, the young vet came over to her. "I think she's going to be all right. You go on home now; I'm going to stay with her just a little longer."

Ariel swallowed hard, forcing down the tears burning at the back of her throat. They settled in her chest, almost robbing her voice of any sound. "I know I should have called you to check her after the puppies were born. This is all my fault."

Dr. Hughes shook his head and started to speak. A sharp glance from Ryan silenced him. Ryan moved to the couch. Gently freeing her hand from its death grip on his jacket, he let her fingers wrap bruisingly around his. His other arm went around her thin, hunched shoulders. "It wasn't your fault. The vet couldn't have predicted this," he said with grim conviction.

Ariel looked to the vet for confirmation, and he nodded, clearing his throat. "What do you want to do about the puppies?" he asked gruffly.

Her eyes widened in horrified comprehension. Ryan felt the convulsive shiver jerk through her and pulled her more strongly to him. "Murphy can't feed them, of course," she whispered hollowly. "Could we . . ." Her voice trailed off as the vet's basset-hound eyes grew even sadder.

Sniffling loudly, Ariel scrubbed her free hand fiercely over her eyes. Her voice was congested by unshed tears. "I guess it's silly to feel sorry over a bunch of mutt puppies you really didn't want in the first place." She took a deep, shuddering breath that ended in a sob, knowing what she had to say.

Ryan's low, calm voice saved her again. "What about your dog?" He addressed his question to the slumped vet who was raking his hand through his thin hair.

His hand stopped. "If she'll accept them, it would work out great." He looked to Ariel to explain. "My old Lab had pups last night; only two of them made it. She still has plenty of milk. If we can get her to take Murph's pups, they'll make it fine." His sudden grin was boyish and carefree. "Let's go see."

The golden Labrador retriever lay in a back room with her two glutted black puppies. She raised her head, gave her master and the two strangers with the big cardboard box a bored glance, and went back to sleep. Carefully the vet lifted out the pups one by one and laid them with their noses on his dog's swollen teats. Their tiny toothless mouths clamped on and began suckling greedily. They slurped and grunted like satisfied piglets. The old dog's head snapped up, and the three humans held their breath. She frowned at the tiny strangers pulling so familiarly at her, a hint of consternation in her cocked ears. After sniffing at their little bodies, she looked at Dr. Hughes with an obvious question in her eyes.

"It's okay, old girl," he murmured affectionately, patting her smooth head. He continued his reassuring motions until the dog laid her head back down with a resigned sigh, apparently accepting her role of wet nurse. The humans slipped out quietly, and Ryan took Ariel home.

She fell asleep on his shoulder during the short ride. When they arrived, he shook her awake gently. "Ariel, wake up. We're home." He eased her out of the truck and inside supporting most of her weight as she tried to go back to sleep under his arm.

"In you go. Watch the step, Ariel, dammit!" he scolded, laughing softly. Trying to maneuver her boneless body was like trying to manhandle a drunk. He wanted to carry her, but he didn't think his leg, after the fight tonight, would support both of them.

Ariel blinked open sleepy eyes to find herself half standing, half collapsed on Ryan, on the second step of her stairs. Grabbing the banister, she pulled herself a little farther upright.

"Can you make it upstairs by yourself, Ariel?" His concerned gaze flickered over her eyes which were smudged with exhaustion, and down the drooping line of her body. He sincerely hoped she could get herself to bed on her own. If he had to go up those stairs and help her, he wouldn't be crossing the hall to his own bed tonight.

"I can," she assured him in a drowsy whisper. She brushed a kiss over his unsmiling mouth. "Thank you, Ryan. Murphy and I would never had made it without you." He captured her soft mouth in a brief, intimate kiss, that ended before he awakened her too much. Firm hands on her waist turned her around and started her up the stairs with a little push. He stood below, watching until her shuffling feet disappeared around the bend in the staircase.

Rapidly he crossed the room, grabbed the flashlight on the shelf beside her door and went outside. There was one more thing he had to do before he, too, could go to bed.

He followed the white beam of light, searching slowly across the darkened ground. Murphy had been fine when they had let her out after coming home from the bar. Less than fifteen minutes later she had been dying. His sharp eyes and the flashlight found what he was looking for by Ariel's Blazer. He bent and picked up the half-gnawed chunk of raw, red meat.

Before storing it in his refrigerator he rechecked the dead bolts on both outside doors and climbed Ariel's stairs noiselessly. She had managed to get her shoes off, but nothing else, before she had crawled under the quilt. He pulled it back long enough to loosen her jeans and reach under her shirt to unhook her bra. She smiled in her sleep, mumbling something incomprehensible and nuzzled into the pillow. He grinned down on her ruefully, tucked the quilt around her and left for his own lonely bed.

Ariel rolled over, glanced at the clock radio on her dresser and groaned. They had already sung the last hymn, Reverend Todd would have given the benediction, and the congregation would be filing out of the beautiful little church in town. She shambled into the bathroom. Her brain still drugged from her exhausted sleep, she didn't immediately remember the reason for Murphy's absence from the foot of her bed. Over the past week she had gotten used to finding the dog gone in the morning. Although Murphy went to bed with her, at some point she always awoke and finished the night with Ryan.

Ariel yawned hugely and turned on the shower. Frowning down at her clothes, she stepped out of them. Why was she still wearing... Then she remembered Murphy's agony of the night before, and she was suddenly wide awake. She caught her hair with a rubber band, then stood under the shower only long enough to wash down her body, hardly rinsing off before she was reaching for a towel.

Tearing a comb through her hair, she raced down the stairs. She tossed the comb on the kitchen counter, then grabbed the phone.

"I've already called him. She made it through the night just fine."

Ariel sagged against the wall for a moment before straightening to face Ryan. With her total concentration and headlong rush down the steps she hadn't even noticed him standing by the wood stove, absorbing the warmth of the fire he had built.

He left the stove and stopped a few feet away from her across the counter. Tucking his lean fingers in the front pockets of his tan slacks, he shoved the sides of his black windbreaker back with his elbows. Her eyes followed the action that tightened the navy sweater over his chest and pulled his slacks taut across his hips and flat belly.

"Why don't you eat some breakfast and I'll take you in to see her?"

Ariel finally noticed the cup of steaming coffee, already creamed and sugared the way she liked it, and the plate of toasted muffins on the counter in front of her. Absently she spread jelly on a muffin and bit into it. "Thank you for this, Ry, and for last night," she said quietly. "I wouldn't have Murphy anymore if you hadn't been here."

One hand came out of his pocket to wave away her gratitude. "I'm just glad I was here to help you."

This time. The words, unspoken, echoed through the room as if they had been shouted. Last night had brought back the memories of Dennis's death too vividly; the lights, the panic, the hideous sense of helplessness had all been there. But last night Ryan had been there, lending his silent, calm strength. She had wanted only one thing more, but she had fallen asleep before she could ask him. She had wanted him to hold her while she slept, just for a little while. She had tried to tell him when he'd come back up to check on her, but he hadn't understood.

As she was putting jelly on another muffin her hand suddenly froze. "I forgot to ask the vet what made her so ill!"

"She was poisoned." Ryan heard her gasp. His hands knotted in his pockets, and he stared at the floor beneath his spread feet. If she saw his face, she might guess the truth. "Three other dogs along this road were poisoned, too. They weren't found until this morning."

"They..." She had to swallow to control the tremor in her voice. "They didn't make it?" She saw the shake of his downcast head. "How were they poisoned?" Even she hardly heard her croaky whisper, yet somehow Ryan did and answered in a neutral voice.

"Chunks of raw meat. Chief Dye says it was just a random incident; it happens every once in a while." He himself thought differently, but the lab in Missoula wouldn't open until eight-thirty tomorrow morning.

Ariel's stomach clenched, and she felt the clammy sweat of nausea. Mechanically she put away the jelly and carried her dishes and the remaining toast to the sink. She couldn't let herself dwell on this; it would be too easy to slip back into self-destructive memories. Her thin voice barely sounded over the sound of running water and the garbage disposal. "Whoever did it didn't know about Murphy's sweet tooth. S-she doesn't care much for meat. If they'd used a bag of chocolate-chip cookies they'd have had better luck."

Her macabre attempt at a joke failed wretchedly. Ryan heard her liquid sob and was pulling her into his arms before she could take another breath.

"Oh, Ry, who would do such a rotten thing?" Her despairing moan was muffled in his soft wool sweater. He shut his eyes tiredly and rested his chin on the top of her head.

"I don't know, Ariel; I just don't know." He heard the note of frustration in his voice. The only thing he did know was that the poisonings hadn't been just another "random incident."

They visited the vet's office and found that the puppies and their new family had adjusted well to each other. Murphy was still unconscious, but out of danger. Dr. Hughes wanted to keep her a few more days before he let her go. Ariel went home feeling oddly bereft.

As she and Ryan drove back to the schoolhouse, Sam Bass was just turning away from the door. Ariel climbed down out of Ryan's truck and hurried over. Ryan followed more slowly, but when he stopped next to Ariel, he draped an arm around her shoulders. She tried to ease away nonchalantly. The arm tightened.

Sam's kind brown eyes were filled with concern. "I just heard about Murphy. Is she okay?" he asked hesitantly. There was nothing hesitant in his eyes as they shifted from Ariel's upraised face to Ryan's arm.

"She's going to be all right," Ariel replied softly. "Thank you for coming by to ask about her." Whatever Ryan Jones's game was, she wasn't going to play. She would ignore both him and the hot spark skipping down her spine.

Sam's warm eyes grew perceptibly colder. "Perhaps you'd rather I didn't come for dinner tonight, what with the upset . . . and all." He stared pointedly at Ryan's hand as it closed over her shoulder.

Ariel hoped that her shock didn't show on her face. Unobtrusively she tried to shrug off Ryan's hand while scrambling for an answer that wouldn't let Sam know she had completely forgotten the invitation she had extended Wednesday night. She smiled warmly at him. "I want you to come tonight. Is six-thirty still okay?" Two long fingers began rubbing lazy circles through the red and blue flannel of her shirt. Ariel discovered that the back of her right shoulder possessed a previously unknown, tremendous erogenous potential.

Sam returned her smile. "Six-thirty it is." He glanced back to Ryan, his friendly face hardening again.

Ryan shifted his stance slightly. His feet moved a little wider apart, his thigh brushing Ariel's lightly, his body straighter, his head thrown back a fraction more. The stance, the faintly wolfish smile, the cold eyes staring directly into Sam Bass's, delivered a primitive male message far clearer than the arm around Ariel's shoulders.

She could see that Sam understood the agressive challenge only too well. Tonight she was going to gently tell him that there wasn't much point in seeing each other anymore. She'd planned to tell him a week ago, but had delayed, unconsciously using him as a buffer against the bewildering attraction she had felt for Ryan Jones from the very first.

Sam would believe her, but for all the wrong reasons now. He would never believe that it was because Ryan Jones or not, she could never offer anything more than the easy friendship they'd enjoyed all summer. Sam would think it was because of this dark stranger who had moved into her house only eight days ago and already staked his claim.

Her body tensed with the struggle to control her rising temper and her reaction to that secretly caressing hand. Ryan's eyes never wavered from the bigger man, but his fingers tightened warningly on her shoulder. He needn't have worried; she wouldn't give him the satisfaction of a scene.

"Good," she said firmly. "I'll see you at six-thirty."

Sam turned away with a nod and climbed into his battered pickup. Ariel wrenched her shoulders strongly, throwing off Ryan's arm. After unlocking her front door, she stalked into her kitchen. Ryan, she knew, was right behind her.

He propped himself against the kitchen wall, following her quick, stiff movements with hooded eyes. "What are you going to fix him for dinner? Soup and bread?" His voice was mildly bored. "He'd probably like some of that apple juice."

Ignoring him, she took a package of T-bones out of the freezer and jerked open the door of the microwave.

"I'm glad you're not planning to fix our turkey," he said conversationally. "It would never defrost and cook in time."

She slammed the door shut and jabbed viciously at the buttons. She had hated the hurt, defeated look in gentle Sam's eyes, something she had been trying so hard to avoid. Regardless of her feelings for Ryan, Sam Bass deserved better than that.

She turned on Ryan. "You're very good, aren't you? It's quite a trick, intimidating a man who's so much bigger than you." She advanced on him, her blue eyes like glittering ice chips, her voice as frigid as an arctic wind. "Was it an inborn talent, or did you work long and hard to cultivate it?"

Ryan moved away from the wall, seemingly relaxed. He had curled his hands into fists in his jacket pockets to keep them from curling around her stiff, fragile neck. The hunger to sample again her sweet, mysterious taste turned his thin smile cruel. "And just what else," he sneered suggestively, "will you be sharing with the good doctor tonight, Ariel, besides a meal?" He knew she was making him lose control, and he hated it, yet was helpless to stop himself.

"That's none of your damn affair!" she exploded. She turned her back to him, gripping the counteredge until her fingers were numb. The emotional elevator she'd been riding for the past two days had left her ragged, and she knew she was dangerously close to falling down the empty shaft. "I am sick to death," she gritted between clenched teeth, "of people poking their noses into my business."

Ryan paled, remembering the nastily insinuative news clippings in the file in his kitchen drawer. "You're absolutely correct," he agreed expressionlessly. "I have no right to ask." He turned away and took a few aimless steps into her living room. Frustration tightened his lips into a thin, bloodless line. "It's just hard to be right across the hall, knowing he's over here with you, wondering what he's doing with you." Ryan rammed his hands deeper into his pockets, feeling completely frustrated and murderously jealous. They were new emotions to him; and he found he despised them.

It was only then that she understood how truly furious he was. The taut empty face, the even, emotionless voice, were the usual careful sham. His naked eyes betrayed the truth: cold rage warred with hot passion in them, and something else—entreaty? A vein jumped in his temple, near the tumbled lock of hair that her fingers habitually itched to brush back. Despite the explosiveness of the situation an exultant thrill surged through her.

"There's nothing between us, Ryan."

"He wants it, Ariel." Bitter chocolate eyes pinned her remorselessly.

She met his gaze unflinchingly. "But *I* don't." She turned on her heel, then looked back over her shoulder at him. "And as far as rights are concerned, counselor," she advised shortly, "perhaps you ought to think about establishing a few."

There was a low hiss of indrawn breath behind her, and suddenly she was spun around. Fingers locked bruisingly on her shoulders. "I believe I will. Right now."

His hard, punishing mouth swooped down. Her avid lips melted under his, enticing him deeper. His mouth softened over hers after the first stinging nip of his sharp teeth. He saw her blue eyes beginning to heat before they slid slowly shut. Her hands pressed against his back to bring him closer. He resisted, not allowing full contact.

"Ryan, please." Was that breathless voice really hers? Ariel couldn't be sure. The room was suddenly much too warm, muddling her brain as his mouth wandered along her throat, blazing a trail of soft kisses.

"Ryan, please, what?" he mocked gently, his warm breath whispering across her moist skin. "Please kiss me?" His lips moved back over hers, which were parted and swollen from his rough kiss, her breath hurrying raggedly between them. The tip of his tongue lightly teased hers.

"Please, Ryan, touch me?" His hands roamed down her back and over her hips, loitering to span her waist before one glided up her ribs. His fingertips traced and counted the fragile bones under the soft flannel. His hand came to rest on her breast, cupping its weight, molding its softness to his palm. "Please love me, Ryan?"

"Is that what you want, Ariel?"

His husky voice whispering in her ear, his gently demanding touches on her body, his mouth, all were cajoling and leading her further into passion. They promised so much more gratification if she would only surrender to him.

"No, no," she lied, moaning against the mouth that was now biting softly at hers. "I don't want it." She forced her hands to drop from his back. Empty, desperate to touch him again, they balled into fists and hit weakly at his shoulders.

"Yes, Ariel, yes," he countered in a lulling whisper. "You do." His palm moved up, rotating hypnotically over her hardened aching nipple that begged for release from his delicious torture.

"No, I can't." The moan became a mournful sob. "Not now." Desperately she pushed herself away from him, staggering a little. He steadied her with a hand on her elbow, then let go. Gasping air into her starved lungs, she stared at him, striving to regain her tattered composure.

He caught the wild excitement in her eyes before it began to fade. As he lit a cigarette with hands that shook only slightly, his eyes narrowed and he watched her over the yellow flame and curling smoke.

"I've, ah, got to start dinner now." Ariel willed her jellied legs to walk into the kitchen, silently cursing the faint undertone of hysteria in her voice.

Ryan nodded once, the habitual sardonic smile back in place, and strolled toward her door. "Enjoy your meal," he said blandly. His goal was more than accomplished. She wouldn't be thinking about the fish biologist tonight.

The poison hadn't been necessary after all; the dog didn't seem to be around anymore. The expense for the meat had been negligible, however, against the anticipated reward. Besides, the local police chief and his force of three would be too busy investigating the rash of poisonings by the dog hater to worry overmuch about any accidents befalling the owner of the Burnt Fork School until it was too late.

Who was the guy living with her? Bodyguard? Lover? Obviously not just a temporary tenant, not from that kiss. He wouldn't have minded being her lover himself, but smart women and business didn't mix. Dennis had shown remarkably poor business sense, becoming infatuated with a smart woman. They asked questions, and sooner or later they got the wrong answer. In his business, he couldn't afford risks like that.

He'd gotten the man's name from someone in the crowd at the fair, and it nudged at the back of his mind. He frowned puzzledly for a moment, and a stewardess stared in his direction. He dismissed the subject. Whoever Ryan Jones was, he shouldn't be any problem.

He waved off the hovering stewardess and leaned his head tiredly on the high back of the airline seat. It was going to be nice to have his weekends free again. And he could sell that damned cabin. He'd always hated roughing it.

Chapter 8

She was up earlier than usual this morning. When the back door had creaked open, Ryan had wakened instantly. He was at his window in time to watch Ariel running toward the river. It hadn't seemed right to see her without a big brown dog at her heels.

Nearly an hour later he was at the same window again, dressed now, with his second cup of coffee, waiting for her to return. He saw the flash of gold and pink at the far end of the orchard. Her hair was loose, floating, catching the first rays of the sun rising over the valley. As a concession to the cooler weather a pair of hot-pink sweatpants hid her long, driving legs. She flitted through the long shadows and bare twisted trees in the old orchard like an exotic gazelle. Effortlessly she cleared the only portion of the split-rail fence still standing, guarding the ancient apple trees.

Ryan made it down his staircase and across the hall just as she came in the back door, wiping the light sweat off her forehead with the sleeve of her white sweatshirt. He followed her into the kitchen and leaned over the counter, sipping his coffee and watching her hop around on one leg like a wounded flamingo as she tried to get the sweatpants off over her running shoes.

"Here." He pulled out a chair and pushed her into it. "Sit down before you fall on your butt." She collapsed on the chair, still huffing from her run. Obligingly she lifted herself off the seat as he squatted down and grabbed the soft pants. He pulled them impersonally down her legs and over her shoes, letting his palm slide back up over the smooth, warmed muscle of her calf.

"You're up early. Are you doing something special today?" Ryan stood back up and tossed the pants carelessly over a chair.

"I have to play librarian at the school for the next three days." Her voice was still slightly breathless. From the run, he thought. From his hand, she knew. She scooted back on the chair seat, tugging down the legs of the old purple running shorts she'd worn under her sweats. She watched him set down his mug of coffee and dig a brownie out of the pan on top of the stove.

"You make these for the fish biologist?" he asked around a mouthful of rich chocolate and pecans. He chewed thoughtfully and swallowed, a look of frank surprise on his face.

Ariel wrinkled her nose in complaint. "He was too full to eat very many, and now I'm stuck with them. Brownies are my one weakness," she moaned. "I'll probably eat every one." She tossed him an upward glance as he snitched another from the pan. "You can have them, if you want," she said offhandedly.

His eyes danced with secret mischief. "Only one weakness, Miss Spence?"

Ariel laughed, her head down.

"Brownies are one of my weaknesses, too." He licked crumbs delicately from his fingers. "And these are the best I've ever eaten." He slanted her a look. "I thought you could only cook soup and bread?"

She gave him a pained look. "I spent an entire summer when I was in high school learning how to make brownies. Lord only knows how many pans I threw out before I finally succeeded."

He held a brownie in front of her mouth. "You're only going to be working through Wednesday?" he asked casually.

"Mmm-hmm." She opened her mouth and he stuffed in a huge bite.

"So you won't have to get up early on Thursday?" he persisted.

Ariel was sneaking a sip from his mug, grimacing at the sugarless coffee scalding her tongue, and missed the speculative look that went with his question. "Not if I don't want to."

"I'll fix dinner Wednesday night," he mentioned carelessly. *And I'll guarantee you won't want to get up early Thursday, Ariel Spence,* he thought grinning to himself.

"That would be very nice." Her surprised, pleased smile warmed him more than the sunniest California day. Ariel glanced at the clock and leaped up. "I better get moving. I want to stop and check on Murph before school starts."

Thirty minutes later she stuck her arm out the window of her Blazer and waved goodbye. He was in his truck close behind her. She turned left onto the highway, toward town. Watching in her rearview mirror, she saw Ryan turn right, toward Missoula.

"That's the most common, over-the-counter rat poison sold in the United States." Ted Dye's voice was infuriatingly calm, almost bored. "Hell, they have it next door for $1.98 a box. I bought some last week...."

Ryan tuned him out. He'd had this conversation before, six days ago, to be exact. He had been totally frustrated then; now he was incensed—and, even more, frightened. He stood at the chief's office window, shoulders hunched, knotted hands cramping in his jacket pockets, staring out. Same cars out on the street, too. Well, he'd done what the technician in the Missoula testing lab had hinted at so pointedly. He had talked to the police. But the police weren't listening. He tuned out the disembodied voice of his brother asking a question from the phone speaker on the desk, too.

Chief Dye watched gilded dust motes drifting lazily in the afternoon sun rays burning through the front window of his office. The role of apologist had been assigned to him. "Look, Jones, these random poisonings happen every once in a while. There is *nothing* indicating that Ariel's dog was the real target and the others were just a smoke screen."

The dark, oddly menacing silhouette at the sunny window finally spoke. "I'm going to tell her. She's got to be aware of the danger so she'll be more careful."

"No!" Even after traveling a thousand miles, Rick Jones's voice was sharply forceful. "What if she gets scared and runs, Ryan? We'll lose her."

"She won't run."

"Can you be sure of that? You've known her little more than a week. I've known her nearly a year, and I can't predict what she'll do."

"I'm sure," Ryan said evenly, turning away from the window to stare at the black speaker on the chief's desk. It was just one more frustration to have to talk to that box instead of his brother, face-to-face.

Rick offered a sop. "You know that newspaper photo you asked about? It was Antonio Garza, the so-called cocaine king of Guadalajara." There was a brief pause. "Why *did* you ask?"

"Ariel saw the picture, but the caption was missing. She remembered seeing him in DiSanto's office one day and wondered why his picture was in the paper. Why was it?"

"He was just arrested by the Mexican authorities for drug smuggling. She pretended not to know him?"

"She wasn't pretending. If she'd known him, if she was guilty as you and your boss Davidson are so sure she is, she'd never have mentioned it at all."

"Maybe she just wanted you to think she didn't know him?" Rick ventured.

"Now why in the hell would she do that, Rick?" Ryan asked with exaggerated patience, trying to hang on to his temper. "She doesn't know who I am, remember?"

Rick's sigh was audible over the phone speaker. "Davidson doesn't want anything to alert her that we know about DiSanto's smuggling. If you tell her about the poisonings you'll have to tell her everything. Give us another week. I have a gut feeling we're getting close to that hidden truth you have me digging for."

"Jesus Christ!" Ryan didn't know if he was blaspheming or praying, probably both. One fist came out of his pocket and slammed down impotently on the glass-topped desk, making everything on the surface, and the chief, jump. "One week, Rick, and that's only if nothing else happens."

Ryan felt a little sicker, knowing only too well how easy it was for a determined man to kill. And whoever this man was, he was not only determined, but clever. Murphy's poisoning had obviously been intended to get her out of the way so the killer could set up some sort of deadly "accident." He'd spent most of Sunday afternoon and evening unobtrusively checking out the Blazer, the propane tanks outside, the well house and anything else he could think of, for signs of sabotage.

Rick had hung up, and Ryan, with a scarcely civil goodbye for the police chief, reached for the doorknob.

"Jones." The chief's voice stopped him. Ted Dye had found it hard to equate the tall, dark man across the room from him with the stories Rick Jones had told him about his brother Ryan until he'd looked at his eyes. The idle thought that he would never want

to be the cause of that deadly look in those flat, cold eyes crossed
the chief's mind. He believed Rick's stories now. And who better
to catch a killer than another?

Chief Dye cleared his throat. "I've had the patrols increased on
Ariel's road. All the strangers in the area have been checked out;
they're okay. The neighbors who can see the course she runs along
the river are watching for her every morning."

Ryan silently acknowledged that the chief was truly doing all he
could.

"And you," the chief shot Ryan a mild look from under eyebrows like rusty Brillo pads, "try to keep her out of bar fights, will
you?"

Ryan's mouth quirked into a small, reluctant grin as he shut the
door quietly behind him.

He drove back to the schoolhouse slowly. He could tell her, and
there wouldn't be one damned thing Rick or Davidson could do
about it. But he wasn't going to.

The foul taste of self-disgust was in his mouth. He was going to
continue his deceit, knowing full well that Ariel trusted him, that
she was no longer fighting the tremendous attraction between
them. Maybe she was even falling a little bit in love with him. How
long would she trust him, love him, if she knew how he'd lied to her
right from the first?

Ryan felt a terrifying vulnerability, worse than anything he'd ever
felt in the jungle, when he'd known invisible eyes were on him. His
skin would shrink, his gut shrivel as he waited for the next instant
to bring death. That had been a Boy Scout camp out compared to
this.

He couldn't lose her now, not when he hadn't even believed she
existed two weeks ago. She was all the dreams he'd lost or given up.
They'd been given back to him, were just within his grasp, and they
could be snatched away from him so easily. He almost wished he
hadn't found her, because knowing that he could lose her was the
worst fear he'd ever known.

Ariel got home a little after four o'clock. Ryan seemed to have
been watching for her and handed over her mail as she entered the
house. She looked it over, giving only half an ear to Ryan's desul-
tory questions about Murphy, her day, who had she seen, had she
ever remembered who'd been in the office with Dennis that day?
She went into her living room, absently dropping her purse on the

dining table. She was anxious to set down the pages she'd plotted out in between stamping and shelving books and teaching fourth graders the basics of the Dewey decimal system.

Ryan stood for a moment in her doorway, watching with wry exasperation as she bent over her desk, reading a couple of the rat-track notes stuck to it, then left. When he checked the outside doors at midnight the faint hum and tap of her word processor and a yellow glow still came through the frosted window of her door.

Leaning against the front fender the next morning, he watched her climb the high step into her Blazer. He supposed, as a gentleman, he should offer assistance, but then, he'd never been much of a gentleman. Besides, he was enjoying the long length of graceful leg she had to show too much. She was definitely Miss Spence, the librarian, this morning. The proper little navy wool suit and low-heeled shoes were exactly right for the role. Her wavy, shoulder-length hair had been disciplined into a severe bun at the base of her neck. The gold-rimmed little glasses, he was sure, were tucked somewhere in the navy clutch that matched her shoes.

Her suit jacket fell open as she reached to pull the door shut. One black eyebrow rose. The apricot silk blouse was quite unlibrarianish. The high-necked Gibson-girl blouse had interesting lace-filled cutouts. He lifted his eyes and met her look of wide-eyed innocence. It couldn't quite mask the sly laughter underneath. Whatever her reason for concealing her true profession, he suddenly knew she derived a great deal of innocently wicked enjoyment from her deception.

Ariel slammed the door hastily and fumbled for her keys. She should have known those impertinent dark eyes would see through her Marian-the-librarian disguise. She drove down the dirt road, sending up only cottontail puffs of brown dust instead of the usual rooster tails. Her sedate speed was a futile attempt to control the rowdy exhilaration singing through her that came just from seeing him and receiving a measly peck goodbye on the cheek. I will not make a fool of myself over you, Ryan Jones, she vowed, steadfastly ignoring the imp inside her laughing uproariously.

When she got home after school, Ryan was hard at work in her half of the house. Law books, papers and manila file folders were scattered over her round dining table. Ever since he'd arrived he had been working on a very involved case, when he wasn't hiking in the mountains or distracting her. There had been several long discussions with his partner Jack Smith on her phone, and twice he had used her computer to transmit information over the phone line to his L.A. office. She had enjoyed a private laugh when she'd learned his partner's name—Smith and Jones. It sounded as if they used aliases, just like their shifty clients.

"Hi," Ariel said brightly.

"Mmm," he answered absently, not even looking up from the file in his hand. His lips moved silently as he read over the pages, making rapid notes in the margin.

Ariel went over to her desk. There was a package that Ryan had signed for waiting for her. She gave him a peculiar look that he didn't see. The package had been opened, the contents disturbed, as if it had been . . . searched.

She shook her head, dismissing the crazy notion. The package just hadn't survived its rough handling by the postal service; there was no reason for him to be searching her mail. She pulled out photocopies of local newspapers from the time of the Johnson County War. She'd ordered them from the Buffalo, Wyoming museum over three months ago and given up on ever seeing them. At the moment she couldn't seem to work up much enthusiasm for them.

Ryan snapped the file shut and closed his eyes. He let his head roll back, working the kinks out of his neck.

Ariel sat in her old swivel chair, idly rocking it a little, back and forth. "Is that the case you've been working on all along?"

He didn't open his eyes. "Mmm-hmm."

"From what you've told me this client is actually innocent. Can you get him off?"

He finally opened his eyes and favored her with a perturbed look. Then he grinned wryly at the mischief in her oh-so-innocent big blue eyes. "After getting so many guilty ones off, it would be a hell of a note if an innocent client went to jail, wouldn't it?" Ryan sighed, rubbing the back of his neck tiredly. "His ex-partner really has him framed, though. The whole tax-evasion scheme looks like my client's work, while the partner plays the outraged innocent. Unfortunately for him, however," he shrugged modestly, "I know the setup from the inside out." He gave her an ingenuous grin. "I've had one or two of these cases before."

"They were all framed, too, no doubt," Ariel murmured dryly.

Ryan merely laughed and started to gather up his papers.

"Want to stay for dinner?" Ariel tried not to sound too hopeful. "I have curried potato soup and fresh sourdough—"

"I've got other plans tonight."

"Oh." She managed to keep most of the disappointed surprise out of her voice.

The comically startled look on her face almost made him laugh. He knew what she was thinking. What would she say if she knew his "date" was with his favorite pay phone at the gas station? Working on the tax-evasion scam had made him think of another angle on the DiSanto case Rick could check out. A whisper of suspicion in the right ear would be enough. More than one criminal had gotten away with murder, only to be tripped up by a dogged IRS agent.

"See you later," Ryan waved breezily and was gone.

Ariel wandered aimlessly around the house. Murphy wasn't even around to keep her company with her crazy romping gyrations. The vet had said today when she'd visited that he wanted to keep her a few more days. She really missed that dumb dog. That was undoubtedly why she suddenly felt so lonely and cold.

Building up the smoldering fire in the wood stove took only a little of the lonesome chill out of the air. She went upstairs and changed into a wool sweater, blue wool pants and her floppy fleece slippers, but she still felt chilly.

She spread the papers from the Buffalo museum over the living room carpet, then put on her spectacles and plopped cross-legged on the floor. She read through the papers, taking notes, until a supper break at eight o'clock. Sipping the curried potato soup, she wondered somewhat wistfully what Ryan had had for dinner…and where…and with whom. It wouldn't take an old beach boy like him long to find a warm and willing body or two.

It was after eleven when she heard his power wagon pull up outside. The outer door slammed; then he tapped on her door and stuck his head inside. His black hair was damp, fitting his well-shaped skull as sleekly as a seal's. With a small start, Ariel realized that it was raining; she hadn't even heard the soft pattering of raindrops on the windowpanes.

"Remember—dinner, tomorrow night," Ryan instructed. "Don't bring anything but yourself."

Before she could think of a subtle way to find out what he'd been doing half the night, the door was shutting on his cheerful, slightly off-key whistling of an old Beach Boys tune. Grumpily she gathered up the papers she'd been squinting at for hours and put her notes in order.

Well! she humphed to herself. He might have stayed to talk a bit. No "Hi, Ariel, guess where I was?" Not even a "What are you working on?" No . . . nothing!

She caught herself remembering those treacherous, calculating, consummate good-night kisses. She would do better to remember, she reminded herself severely, that regardless of her feelings for him, he no doubt thought he'd acquired her with the month's rent he'd paid—stove, refrigerator, bed warmer.

The next morning the weather was still damp and dreary. Yet the dripping clouds, layered like sodden, dirty fleece over the valley all day, couldn't drown her inexplicable happiness and the persistent, peculiar sense that some special surprise was about to delight her. Giggling at her foolishness, Ariel shooed the last of her faithful, male high school helpers out the library door and locked up.

She swung by Dr. Hughes's veterinary clinic. Murphy was much livelier, the dull, death-shadowed look out of her eyes. Assured that she would be able to take her dog home the next day, she left the vet's office. She had one more stop to make before going home.

She had expected to find Bessie in the large lounge of the rest home, her wheelchair pulled close to the fire in the stone fireplace. Instead she found her already tucked in bed, her body only a faint mound under the wedding-ring quilt she'd brought from her home.

"Bessie? Are you all right?" Alarmed, Ariel chafed a hand that seemed to be nothing more than one layer of thin, age-spotted skin stretched over glass bones.

"I'm fine, girl." The fragile fingers gripped Ariel's with surprising strength. "This blasted gloomy weather just gave me a chill, and I got into bed to warm up." Her faded brown eyes were shadowed, as Murphy's had been. "You get your soap made yet?"

Ariel shook her head. "Mr. Hankins, the butcher, say's he'll have the fat I'll need to melt down Friday."

The chitchat dispensed with, Bessie got down to what she really wanted to know. "How's that handsome devil, Ryan Jones? You two cooked your turkey yet?"

Ariel flashed her a bright smile. "As handsome and devilish as ever, Bessie. We haven't cooked the turkey yet; maybe we'll have to find a special occasion." No, the turkey wasn't cooked yet, but she had the sinking feeling her goose was. Suddenly restless, Ariel got up to wander around Bessie's tiny bedroom.

Her back was to Bessie, but the old woman saw the unguarded expression on Ariel's face in the mirror over the dressing table. It showed the mixed longing and fear she felt about making a one-sided commitment to a man she was so unsure of. Bessie ached for her, yet felt a sentimental envy. She remembered the sweet joy and desperate agonizing that came with gambling your heart on a risky love.

"You know, you remind me of myself in many ways, Ariel. Be careful that you don't let your independence become a habit you can't break," she warned softly. "Be willing to take a chance, my dear. You can get to like living alone too much. After a while, you become too selfish to share your life with anyone else."

Ariel toyed with the delicate petals of a yellow spider mum. When she turned back, Bessie's eyes were closed. She seemed to have drifted into a nap. Ariel patted the covers around her friend and tiptoed from the room.

Ryan grinned happily to himself, looking over his equipment. It had been years since he'd planned a seduction. It had become disgustingly easy over the past few years to get a woman into bed. But then, maybe he'd had the wrong kind of women . . . and the wrong word. Seduction implied that the woman was tricked or otherwise led astray. He didn't want Ariel that way. Although he expected to lead the way, he wanted her following willingly, joyfully, cooperating fully in what they would share.

The sound of the outside door closing snapped him out of his anticipation of the evening ahead. He met Ariel as she was hanging her wet trench coat on a hook in the hall.

"Hi. I'm sorry if I'm a little late." Her smile was a ray of pure sunlight brightening the rain-gloomed hallway. Shaking the raindrops from her hair, she started to go in her door. "I'll just go change and be right over."

"No," he said quickly, staying her with a hand on her arm. The plum dress under his fingertips seemed to have been spun from the fur of the softest kittens. His gaze swept the sweater dress with its row of tiny pearl buttons running from the collar diagonally down across her breast. "You look fine; I don't want you to change." His hand rested against the middle of her back, lightly urging her through his door.

He guided her to the leather sofa by the old potbelly stove. "Dinner will be ready in a few minutes."

"Can't I help?"

"Not tonight. I'll do it all."

Ariel sank back against the sofa's fat arm and pried off her gray pumps, wiggling her cramped, chilled toes appreciatively. Tucking her feet under her, she smoothed her dress over her knees and rested her head in the corner of the sofa. She soaked up the dry warmth of the potbelly stove that had heated two and a half generations of little bodies. Heated a little too much. Absently Ariel loosened the first four buttons of her dress.

She could hear Ryan's quiet movements in the kitchen and the occasional hiss of rain falling down the stovepipe to boil on the crackling apple wood. The sweet scent of the burning wood and the rain and the smell of hot cast iron masked the odor of whatever he was fixing for dinner. She watched fat raindrops leave wet trails along the smooth, dark glass of the living room window.

Ryan came silently across the oak floor and handed her a glass of wine. Ariel's mouth crooked wryly when she saw the glass holding the clear, pale gold liquid. He'd filched two dime-store wineglasses from her kitchen cupboard. It wasn't class, but it was definitely a step above the gas-station-giveaway plastic tumblers stocking his own cupboard. Without tasting the wine, she looked at him, bending down to adjust the damper on the stove. She realized with surprise that this was the first time she'd seen him in anything but the most casual clothes. Now that he'd gained some weight the charcoal wool slacks were perfectly tailored to his slim hips and strong thighs. His black shirt had a dull sheen, like silk, and was formfitting, pulling tight over his broad shoulders as he stood up. His days outdoors had darkened the sickly pallor of his face to a healthy bronze. He looked more rakish and impossibly handsome than ever.

Ryan sat in the leather armchair across from her and picked up his wine.

"Are you planning on seducing me tonight, Ryan Jones?" she inquired watching the tiny bubbles fizzing slowly to the top of the glass in her hand.

"The thought had crossed my mind."

"It's also crossed mine a time or two," she admitted softly with a small smile. Raising her wineglass and smoky, fathomless blue eyes, she toasted him soberly. "Here's to the success of your plan."

He touched his glass to hers with equal solemnity, his mouth twitching. Damn you, Ariel Spence, he demanded with silent laughter, are you going to let me do this right or not?

Ariel met his eyes over the rim of her glass. She drank the contents in one long swallow. Perhaps the wine would drown the butterflies in her stomach.

Ryan took the empty glass from her unresisting hand and pulled her to her feet. Wrapping an easy arm around her waist, he walked her to the table. "Dinner is served," he announced with a charmingly crooked smile. "Then we'll see if my plan's going to work."

The table wasn't set with fine crystal and china, or spotless linen and sterling. The ordinary white wine was poured into her cheap wineglasses; the plates were chipped blue spatterware; the utensils were mismatched and worn stainless; and the placemats were faded brown calico with frayed ruffles. No tall, elegant tapers lighted the polished old table, just the stubby candle she'd stocked in a kitchen drawer for the occasional power outage.

Ariel enjoyed every mouthful of crisp salad with tangy homemade dressing and trout stuffed with wild rice. He had really outdone himself on the meal, and maybe the setting wasn't the most glamorous and expensive, but it couldn't have been any more romantic or perfect. Her nervousness vanished along with the food on her plate. For this night, at least, she was giving herself over into his care, implicitly trusting him with her body and her heart.

Ryan drained the last few inches of wine into their glasses, then led Ariel back into his living room. He settled easily on the couch beside her, his arm around her. He played with her hair, winding silky wisps around his fingers and freeing them. He raked his hand slowly through her heavy hair, letting it slide between his fingers as if trying to free the golden sunlight trapped in its depths. "You have the softest, silkiest hair," he murmured, tilting his head to watch his hand play. "It's just like a baby's."

Her mouth curved in a teasing smile. "Maybe that's to make up for being totally bald as a baby."

"Shh, don't make jokes. You'll ruin my plan." His grin was slow and sexy, his eyes half closed as they focused on her mouth. His arm tightened, and he leaned over, kissing her wide eyes shut before brushing her lips with his. His mouth closed over hers, his flicking tongue demanding an entrance. Her lips parted, and he rapidly deepened the kiss. His hand slid around her throat, the thumb measuring her pulse. It had jumped when his mouth first touched hers, then settled into an accelerated, slightly ragged beat, like his own.

Ariel felt as if she was spinning, slower and slower, sinking down smoothly at last to rest. Somewhere in the endless spiral she had lost her wineglass. Her arms opened and closed around a hard, male body, her palms sliding up over silk warmed by the heat of the long, tight muscles shifting underneath. She lifted heavy eyelids and stared into the depthless, dark eyes above, softer and warmer than she'd ever seen them.

She was lying back on the wide leather sofa, Ryan's body a satisfying weight on hers. He raised himself on his elbows, watching his thumbs brushing her hair back from her cheeks and temples, watching the sharp, aristocratic angles of her face softening into the sultriness he'd glimpsed the first day.

"You are so lovely, Ariel Spence." His smile was a little blurred as he bent to string a long necklace of kisses around her throat, following his hand as it undid the rest of the pearl buttons on her dress.

"I'm not," she murmured in a little sigh. "But it pleases me that you think so."

His head snapped up, and his suddenly fierce eyes burned into hers. "You are. And before the night is over you'll believe it." He took her mouth a little roughly, as if impatient to prove to her the truth of his statement.

She breathed in sharply as his right hand moved down to her straining breast. She released her breath in a long sigh of pleasure as his thumb and finger began to shape her flesh gently. "I don't know all that much about this, Ryan," she whispered.

His mouth began nibbling its way down her arched throat, and she bit her lip. "In fact, I may have been the only twenty-seven-year-old virgin left in San—"

"I know," he muttered against the heavy pulse in the hollow of her throat. His tongue tickled back up her neck. "In just a few minutes it will be my very great pleasure," he whispered gravely in her ear, the tip of his tongue circling the delicate rim, "to correct that serious flaw in your education."

He pulled back to see her face, full of shyly hesitant excitement. Desire burned hotly in his bright eyes, yet sympathetic understanding and an oddly tender humor were in his smile.

He spread the edges of the soft, clinging dress wide. Moving down her body, his lips and teeth and tongue worried a hardening, dusky-rose nipple through misty lace.

Each tug of his mouth was a hot wire uncoiling deep in her belly. Her hands skimmed over his shoulders, down his chest and even lower, impatient with buttons and zippers that kept her from feel-

ing skin gliding on skin, smooth muscle working under her quest-
ing hands, a hard fullness to fill that aching emptiness inside her.

She found herself at the foot of Ryan's bed with no clear memory of how she'd gotten there. The small lamp on the dresser filled
the room with soft shadows and softer light. "The light," she
mumbled. She felt the resurrection of the butterflies in her stomach.

"No hiding in the dark," he admonished softly, holding her
anxious eyes, his strong hands gentle on her tense shoulders.
"From the first, Ariel, I want no secrets, no shame between us. I
want to see you and you to see me, to see us together and know how
right it is."

Wordlessly he undressed her, her clothes falling away under his
hands. He stood relaxed before her, his arms and legs spread
slightly, silently indicating that she should return the favor. His
shirt and belt joined her clothing, but he had to finish his own dis-
robing when her faltering fingers could go no further.

He tipped up her chin until she opened her miserably embarrassed eyes. He kissed her again, slow, drugging kisses, bringing
their bodies together gradually, letting her get used to the feel of
naked, male flesh on hers. She shivered once as he brought them
into full contact, and she felt his body's heavy desire for hers.

When he ended the kiss he just held her tightly to him until he
could feel her begin to relax, her softness filling his hard empty
hollows. Turning, he drew back the spread and sheet on the double bed. He sat her on the edge of the bed, then sat beside her,
carefully pressing her down until she lay on the virginal white sheet.
Her hands were clasped primly over her chest as her trusting eyes
locked on his.

Linking his hands with hers, he stretched her arms above her
head. He let his frank gaze wander over her slim body, over its
gentle curves and high, firm breasts. "You are beautiful, Ariel,"
he whispered. At the melting heat in his chocolate eyes, she began
to believe it.

Raising her right hand, he kissed the palm; then, starting at her
wrist, his tongue traced the blue veins under her creamy skin. Past
her elbow, over the sensitive flesh of her inner arm, his mouth
whispered across her shoulder and down her chest to the pale
softness of her breast. He spiraled closer and closer to the swelling, dusky aureole and nipple. His tongue flickered and tasted
delicately until she was whimpering with need. Finally his hot
mouth fastened over the hard nub, his teeth scraping with a tiny

pleasure-pain before he began to suckle and soothe. She cried out, desire pooling between her thighs. Her hands dragged at him desperately, urging him up, closer.

"Please," she begged. "Please now, Ry."

"No." He captured her grasping hands, imprisoning them on the sheet by her restless thighs. "Not yet." He watched her flushed, writhing body, held her pleading, passion-heavy eyes with his. "There's more."

"I don't think I can take any more." Her throat was already so tight with wanting that she could hardly speak.

"Yes, you can." His beautiful, chiseled mouth was almost stern. "I'm going to give you much more."

"No. No," she moaned, shaking her head slowly in sweet agony. "I'll go crazy."

"I know," he agreed with a slow, satisfied smile.

Still shackling her straining wrists, he moved to her ankles and began the sensual assault once more. He lavished attention behind her knee, to the top of her thigh. He went back to her other ankle. Lingeringly he finished the wet mapping of her body, testing the outer limits of his control.

Shivers raced through her. To be so totally in his thrall should have terrified her, she understood dimly, but it didn't. She felt only an incredible excitement and the expectancy that the impossible was going to get even better.

When Ryan reached the top of her thigh he paused, looking up at her. Her eyes were squeezed shut, as if in pain, and her small perfect breasts heaved, her fingers twisting into the bottom sheet. Tears of frustration were seeping from under her dark lashes. "Ry, *please!*"

Her hoarse cry exulted him. She was more responsive than he had dared dream and completely in his power, his power to please and satisfy her totally.

Her eyes slit open, glittering down at him. "Ryan Jones," she gasped raggedly, "you're driving me out of my mind."

His fingers slid into her, and she arched violently, moaning. She was so tight and warm and so ready for him.

Her hand wrenched free, and she dragged him up her body with a strength that astonished him. "Now!" she demanded fiercely.

"Now," he agreed hoarsely. Before I go out of my mind, he thought in abandon. He surged strongly into her, and then was still.

She hardly felt the small, stretching pain as her body adjusted and accepted the newness of his.

Stretching out flat over her, he imprinted the soft surface of her body with the hard, male feel of his. His hair-roughened skin slowly rubbed against her smoothness. After tonight her body would never forget his; never would she be able to let another man touch her without remembering Ryan and what he was doing to her. He knew his action was unforgivably chauvinistic, but he felt the overwhelming, primitive need to make her his in the most basic, undeniable way possible.

He moved inside her, steadily building the rhythm. "Tell me you want me," he rasped. Her physical surrender wasn't enough. He wanted all of her.

"I want you, Ryan." He could barely hear her choked whisper. "Oh, God, I want you." She flexed against him. She'd learned the rhythm, and suddenly he knew he had surrendered himself, as well. His body would never forget hers, either, never be satisfied with any other woman's.

She was losing track of time and space, lost in exquisite torment. Slowly, torturously, her body was being stretched with a tension that must break soon or she would surely fly apart.

"No," she groaned desperately, her nails raking urgently down Ryan's back, her teeth sinking into his shoulder. "No, I can't!"

"Don't fight it, Ariel. I'll take care of you." His mouth moved over her face, down her throat. "Just go with it. Let it take you. It'll be so good, Ariel," he crooned. "So good for you." His lips softened on hers, coaxing, his hands encouraging.

Her voice high and thin, she began shaking her head frantically, tears slipping faster and faster from her closed eyes. "Nooo, I-I—"

He was laughing! Laughing triumphantly as he controlled her wild body to his rhythm. His hard hands dug into her hips, holding her tightly to him to meet his demands...and hers. Behind her closed eyelids every color imaginable whirled faster and faster. Her body was tautening, tautening, too tight. She splintered in a sweet, glorious explosion, the snapping tension flinging pieces of her into a consuming fire.

The flames died down. Her body had somehow managed to put itself back together. She lay trembling with a delicious weakness. Gradually she became aware that he was still lying over her, his body a wonderful, warm weight on her.

Tenderly he caressed the damp wisps of hair off her forehead, his eyes searching hers deeply. "Are you all right?"

"I'm more than all right." She smiled. "I'm deliriously happy. Your plan was an unqualified success."

He laughed quietly, as if well pleased. The motion made her aware that he was still inside her, full and pulsing.

He nodded slowly at the wondering realization he saw in her face. "The first time was for you, love." He inhaled deeply as his hands began moving in a languid exploration of her body. His body picked up the rhythm of his hands and began stroking, too, leisurely, long. "This time—" he bent his open mouth to catch hers "—is for me."

Minutes later, recovering from a galvanic implosion that left her feeling gloriously fulfilled, she decided that it had been for both of them. He held her still beneath him, soothing wordless sounds in her ear, stroking her hair, gently kissing her stunned eyes shut, absorbing the tremors still pulsing through her body.

Finally he rolled to his side and stretched out next to her, dropping a kiss on her nose. "I wish I hadn't had to hurt you," he murmured, continuing on to her mouth. "It will never be like that again."

Her vastly disappointed voice froze him. "It won't ever be like that again?"

Slowly he raised his head and examined her sad face. Finally he asked carefully, "What exactly do you mean, Ariel?"

Her blue eyes glinted up at him as a slow, provocative grin spread over her face. "I want it to be like that again. Every time." One of her hands came up lazily, and her fingers brushed back the lock of hair that had fallen over his forehead, staying to weave through the heavy silk strands.

"You didn't hurt me, Ry," she assured him softly. "It was . . ." She shrugged helplessly. "Indescribable."

Her face was suffused with a glowing, inner light that took his breath away and filled him with an incredible surge of power and love. She started to reach up for his mouth, but he turned her on her side, clasping her possessively to him. Burying his face in her rain-scented hair, he whispered achingly, "Oh, my virgin girl, you are truly in my heart and soul." Smoothing back her tumbled hair, he kissed her forehead. "Sleep now."

She relaxed against him, her breathing slowing gradually. "I love you, Ariel Spence." He whispered the words he had never spoken to another woman into the quiet of the bedroom. He wasn't sure if she were awake to hear him or not.

He lay awake for a long time afterward, listening to the rain on the tin roof over his head and her soft breathing as she slept. He reveled quietly in the simple joy of holding her. He knew he could never let her go now. When he had recovered from that mindless, shattering ecstasy, he had felt pure and new again, his soul cleansed. Her totally unselfish gift of innocence had given him that.

He had thought that knowing he was the first was what was important. Perhaps it was, but now it was knowing, being absolutely certain, that he would be the last was what really mattered. His arms tightened around her pliant, sleeping body. Mine, he thought fiercely, my woman. He fell asleep before his happiness could be dimmed by the thought that she was his only if he could keep her alive . . . and only if she chose to be.

Ariel awoke by degrees, absorbing the marvelously right feel of Ryan in bed with her. She lay very quietly, not wanting to disturb the man sleeping beside her, or that feeling. The weight of his arm, thrown over her waist and fitting the curve so naturally, told her that if ever she woke up again without him, she would be incomplete.

The heavy curtains at the window blocked most of the early-morning light, but there was enough to see him clearly. He lay sprawled on his stomach, his head turned toward hers, sharing the same pillow. Easing carefully away, she studied his face. With his hair sleep-rumpled and his firm mouth not quite so hard, he looked younger, almost . . . vulnerable. The sharp bones seemed to have softened in sleep, the cynical curl of his mouth gentled. The long, curling eyelashes, so unfairly wasted on a man, shuttered the eyes that usually showed the world nothing, or only sardonic amusement at the goings-on around him. They had shown her many things last night. She just wished she knew if one of them had been love.

Rolling onto her back, she studied the patterns of light and shadow on the white ceiling. If anyone was vulnerable this morning, it was she, frighteningly so. Falling in love was a heady, magnificent feeling, but she was discovering that it was also rather terrifying. It took great courage to speak your love when you didn't know if the other person returned it, or ever would. Had Ryan really whispered those five words as she was falling asleep. And if he had had they been anything more than a meaningless cliché said to every woman he slept with? She'd heard that practically everyone said those words, words that once were so special and private, to the "love" of the evening. Did they say them because it was expected, or because they had to reassure themselves and their partner that casual sex with strangers really made them feel pleasured and socially sophisticated, and not empty and just a little sleezy?

She really shouldn't condemn anyone for saying "I love you" when he didn't. After all, she *did* love Ryan, but she hadn't said so. She just wasn't brave enough yet to risk the pitying rejection in his eyes if he refused the gift of her love, or the heartache she would feel if he accepted and gave nothing in exchange. She knew one should not give a gift, especially love, expecting, or even hoping, to receive anything in return. But she was too selfishly human to be able to do that.

Closing her eyes, she sighed dejectedly. She had another problem, too, though much more minor. Those books on the sixth shelf of her bookcase, full of heroines rapturously rhapsodizing about love and their lovers, were laughably poor and lacking. She was embarrassed to realize just how inadequate they were, but then, she'd had no way of knowing before. Two-dimensional black letters on white paper that could be appreciated by only one sense couldn't possibly convey an experience that involved at least three dimensions, all five senses and every conceivable color. She could certainly improve her heroines' future experiences, but she already knew with depressing certainty that never could they equal the love she felt for Ryan and the wonder of their physical response to each other. "Felicia" simply didn't have the words.

Turning back on her side, she tucked an elbow under her head and watched him sleep. Slowly she realized that her nose was turning numb. The room was frigid. Neither of them had stoked the little stove and banked it to burn lowly through the night. Her mouth curved into a satisfied smile as she reviewed the reason why. She buried her nose in the covers. There was a lingering trace of her cologne and his, and the musky earthiness of love.

The spread and top sheet had slid down to the middle of Ryan's back, and his bare skin was exposed to the chilly air. Ariel's gaze drifted over his relaxed muscles. Her palms itched slightly as she remembered the feel of those muscles, rippling in straining ridges and ropes under her hands last night.

Her hand snaked out of the warmth of the covers and pulled them up over his shoulders, her fingers lingering in the hair at the nape of his neck. The raw silk texture was so different from her own hair. She had never been aware of the differences in texture between a man's and a woman's body. They were as obvious as the visual differences, and they fascinated her. She'd been careful to let him sleep before; now, perversely, she wished he'd wake up.

Her hand stroked around his neck, and her leg inched closer to his. She was like a greedy child sneaking into a cookie jar. She wanted to experience everything she had last night, but with the time to savor those fascinating differences: the feel of a hair-roughened thigh sliding up between silky smooth ones, a sandpapery cheek brushing over a satiny one, a hard muscled chest easing over soft cushioning, nipples tickled by wiry hair and the best—hot, sleek strength gliding into a snug moist welcoming.

Ryan moved suddenly, and Ariel found herself trapped in the two strong arms that had lashed around her under the sheet. After a hard hug and harder good-morning kiss, he levered himself up on one elbow to peer over her shoulder at the clock on the dresser. She saw his sleepy eyes widen in horror at the time. He flopped down, groaning and twisting onto his back at the same time, pulling her over him.

Nuzzling fiercely into her neck, he growled, "Ariel Spence, you are a heartless woman. I thought this morning, of all mornings, you would sleep late."

"Why?" Her innocent tone was ruined by a giggle as her fingers scaled his ribs. "Did something unusual happen last night?"

Ryan nipped warningly at her throat while his hands roamed down her back. "Brat," he muttered, shoving her tousled hair back to get at her ear. "I'll show you unusual."

His shoulders, bared to the cold air by the slipping covers, flinched, and he looked up at her blankly. "It's freezing in here!"

"Mmm." Ariel rubbed her cold nose against his, her hair a golden curtain around their heads. "Maybe that something unusual you're going to show me will warm it up," she said hopefully.

Ryan let his head fall back weakly onto the pillow and moaned disconsolately. "Good Lord, I've created a monster." His eyes rolled wearily upward, and he addressed the ceiling. "The woman's insatiable already."

His eyes slid back to hers, filled with a satanic anticipation. "Lucky for you, so am I." He leered evilly while Ariel laughed in delight. Then, in a lightning move, he slid out from under her and stood up. He shivered convulsively. "Unfortunately, even that wouldn't be enough to warm this place up."

Wincing every time his bare feet had to touch the icy floor, he grabbed a paper and kindling and relit the stove.

Ariel buried herself in the warm bed, laughing heartlessly. As Ryan crouched before the open door of the wood stove, the flames spread a glow over his face and bare chest. They reflected in his eyes as he turned to give her a happy grin. Ariel was a little shocked at herself. She was feeling decidedly insatiable and rather uninhibited. She felt no shyness at all, looking at him as he came back to bed. Maybe, she mused, it hadn't been inhibition at all that had kept her from looking at naked men before but simple lack of interest.

The gleam in his eye should have warned her. Ryan ripped away the covers, and Ariel scrambled up with a shriek. "You are completely vicious, Ryan Jones! It's like an icebox in here!"

"We'll take a shower and warm up." As he dragged her up off the bed, he let his eyes wander appreciatively. Holding her in a loose embrace, he saw her eyes flick down and around. He grinned over the top of her head. Miss Spence was still just a little shocked by casual nudity. Rocking her bare body against his, he watched her blue eyes widen a little more and begin to turn smoky.

Ariel felt herself color. Well, perhaps there was an inhibition or two left, after all, but she doubted they would last much longer.

Ryan gave her an exuberant kiss and released her. He tossed her his black shirt from the night before as he shrugged into the brown corduroy jeans he had draped over the chair. "Put that on until the shower's ready. You're turning an interesting color." His eyes teased her unmercifully.

"From the cold," she sniffed primly, then gasped. The silk shirt was like putting on a layer of frost. "You have a lot to learn, Mr. Jones," Ariel told him severely, "about hospitality. It is *not* hospitable to let your guests freeze to death."

"Actually, I'm the guest," he informed her, disappearing into the bathroom. "*You* own the place."

"Then I'm going to get a fire going downstairs and warm my place up a little faster," she called, skipping down the circular staircase.

Ryan smiled to himself and leaned into the shower to turn on the spray. He felt so fantastically good this morning, better than he could ever remember waking up feeling before. There were one or two things he did need to tell her, but he would pick the time and the place. He was confident that he could explain his deception without getting her too upset.

She was yelling something at him from downstairs. Sticking his head out into the bedroom, he heard her call again.

"Where are your matches?"

"In the kitchen drawer by the stove," he yelled back. He went back into the bathroom to check the water. Abruptly, with an explosive curse, he turned off the shower so violently that he nearly tore the handle out of the wall. Desperately he ran for the stairs. He had just remembered what else was in that drawer.

Chapter 9

Ariel was standing in the middle of the kitchen, heedless of the cold tile under her feet, or the chill creeping up her bare legs beneath the tail of his shirt. The horror and profound pain in her huge eyes and bloodless face froze Ryan in the doorway. The box of matches was open on the floor. The little blue-tipped sticks were scattered like bits of the happiness they'd shared just moments before. His .45 dangled, ready to fall, from the fingers of her left hand. Ryan thought furiously, trying to remember if he'd left the safety on.

Her right hand clutched the damning file, the blood-red letters of her name on the cover screaming an accusation at him. "Who are you? Where did you get this?" Her voice was that of a little girl trying to understand some incomprehensible tragedy. Her hand jerked, and the file fell, spilling its Judas contents over the cheerful blue and yellow tiles. "You knew all about me before you ever came. Dennis, the murder, everything. You even knew I was a virgin."

The agonized guilt on his face brought a hideous suspicion to reality. "My God!" she breathed, the horrifying indictment glazing her eyes. "You *were* sent to spy on me!" Rationality fled.

She brought the gun up in slow motion, frowning at it puzzledly, as if trying to remember how it had gotten into her hand.

Every cell in Ryan's body tensed. If she shot him, perhaps it would be no less than he deserved. Suddenly she flung the gun away with an inarticulate cry, as if it were indescribably evil and filthy. It skittered across the floor and came to rest with a small thump against the baseboard.

Ryan went limp, as the breath he didn't know he'd been holding burst out. Then the look of helpless panic on her stark face shocked him immobile again.

In a soundless whisper that seemed like a scream in the quiet kitchen she demanded, "Were you sent to kill me? Have you been toying with me, playing some perverted cat-and-mouse game?" Her head began to shake slowly from side to side as she tried to deny the truth. Her thin, disbelieving wail echoed loudly in Ryan's ears.

Her sense of betrayal was complete and totally devastating. She had opened herself physically and emotionally to the dark man standing across the room from her, so silent, denying nothing. The only man, ever. She had joyously shared her body and her love, freely offering it in the most exquisite, soul-satisfying experience in her life. He had profaned it, turning it into a brutal, vicious rape, violating her in the most fundamental, soul-destroying way possible. The recognition of her own all-too-willing, ecstatic complicity physically sickened her.

The realization that Ariel's knees were buckling thawed Ryan's frozen body. He sprinted across the kitchen and caught her just before she hit the floor. "No!" he roared in helpless rage. She recoiled from him in abject terror, and he forced himself under control. "No!" he repeated strongly as he compelled her cringing body into his arms. Heaving sobs racked it against him.

"No, no, no, Ariel." His rough voice gentled into a deep soothing litany. "It's not what you think. It's not what it seems."

Over and over he crooned the words as he rocked her gently against him, like a mother cradling a hurt child. Her bitter tears warmed his bare chest. His hand tangled in her hair, pushing her head tightly into his shoulder as he tilted his own head back, swallowing the tears burning his throat and blurring his eyes. He felt a deep, angry despair at the possibility that Ariel would twist the most beautiful night of his life, the only shared fulfillment he'd ever experienced, into something sordid, another selfish emptiness. He couldn't allow that.

Slowly her sobbing eased. A shudder passed through her as she drew a deep breath and then, too weakened to resist, sagged completely against him. Ryan's wet cheek rested on the top of her head, his arms tight around her.

"That's the only trouble with this place, not enough drawer space," he muttered inanely. Easing her away so he could look into her face, he gripped her shoulders. Shell-shocked blue eyes finally focused on his grim face.

"Ariel, I'm going to explain that damned file to you, and a hell of a lot more. Please, please believe," he shook her roughly for emphasis, "that I am telling you the truth." The lost, hopeless look on her face would haunt him to the end of his days. He sensed that she had retreated from him completely, like a mortally hurt animal that crawled into the deepest corner of its den to lick its wounds.

Her robot body obeyed his hand on her arm. She walked across the room. She sat when he pushed her gently down into one of the hard, wooden chairs at the table. She stayed, staring at nothing, as he lit the fire she'd never had a chance to start.

He waited until the kindling was well caught, then placed two logs on the fire and shut the small door. He was readying himself for the most important defense of his life, with himself as the defendant, knowing she had probably already convicted him on the evidence in that damned drawer.

Taking the chair opposite her, with the narrow table between them, he reached for her frigid fingers. He held them tightly, warming them in his. Maybe she would feel the truth if her ears refused to hear it. In a quiet voice he began answering her first two questions.

"I am Rick Jones's brother. He gave me the file and sent me to watch over you."

He was drained, emotionally and physically. He wanted nothing more than to take her back upstairs to bed and prove the truth of his feelings in the most irrefutable way possible. His wish wasn't going to be granted; he knew it all too well. Shock still haunted her blue eyes, and there was a wariness about her, as if she were ready to bolt at the first wrong word.

Ariel withdrew her hand from Ryan's. "You lied to me, Ryan." Her voice was deadly calm.

"I never told you a single word that was untrue," he denied quietly, each word slow and clear, looking for an acquittal on a technicality.

"There are silent lies as well as spoken ones," she reminded him neutrally. "They're the cruelest ones of all. You had numerous opportunities to tell me who you really were."

Her tone took on an exaggerated carelessness. "Oh, by the way, Ariel, Rick Jones is my brother. He sent me to keep an eye on you, snoop around, find out what dirt I can on you." Her voice lost the carelessness, lowered, throbbing with the intensity of her anger. "That was the plan, wasn't it, Ryan? What a sweet little setup! Cozy up to the suspect, entice her with the oldest lure in the book—sex. She'll spill everything. And it worked, didn't it?" Ryan saw that the tears were back, bitter tears at her own gullibility and his betrayal. "I fell right into your bed and loved every second of it."

His heart made a cautious leap at her unconscious confession. "But it was for nothing, because I don't know anything!" Ariel's fists bunched against the edge of the table as she strained across it, fairly screaming the words at him.

She slumped back in her chair, defeated. "I didn't even know about Dennis's prescription racket until the police told me."

Ryan looked at her for a long, silent moment, seeing his dreams fading like the illusions they were. "I'm sorry, Ariel," he whispered softly. And she didn't even know the worst of it yet.

"I'm sorry, too." She could barely get the whisper past the tears clogging her throat. Hugging her arms around herself, she dragged in a deep, trembling breath. Gradually she became aware that the room was still uncomfortably cool, and that he was wearing only a pair of pants, while she had on only his shirt. "You ought to get a shirt on," she remarked absently, her voice husky from crying. "You'll catch cold."

His mouth quirked with the ghost of his usual sardonic smile. "You're wearing my shirt."

Her eyes thawed slightly. "Then we may both catch cold." But she made no move to get up and find something warmer, and neither did he.

Her voice even huskier than before, she asked almost diffidently, "Why did you come?" Her eyes stayed on his fingers toying with the wooden salt and pepper shakers on the table.

He knew what she was really asking. Why had he gone along with Rick's harebrained suggestion? "I was bored, not ready to go back to work." He gestured toward the papers still littering the floor. "Rick gave me the file, and I read it. You intrigued me. He knew you would."

He watched her eyes follow his hand and saw her mouth tighten. That file really disturbed her, as well it should. It was an obscene invasion of her privacy, but the motive behind it had been pure. "No one but the D.A., Rick and I know what's in that file, Ariel," he reassured her quietly. "We're the only people who have ever seen it." It was obvious she hadn't had enough time to see the reports on DiSanto's smuggling. He made an instant decision.

Ariel finally looked up at him and nodded briefly. Her eyes remained on his, the oddly pleading defiance in them a sharp contrast to her flat emotionless voice. "Did you think I was guilty of Dennis's murder?"

His hand sought hers and tightened gently before he answered her just as flatly. "Yes." Her eyes closed as if in pain, and she tried to jerk her hand away. He wouldn't let it go. "I thought you might well be implicated; the evidence could be interpreted that way." He tugged on her fingers until she opened her eyes to glare at him. He grinned back, "By the morning after I met you, I was convinced you weren't guilty of anything."

"What changed your mind?" The curiosity in her voice overrode the cold stiffness.

"Cold-blooded murderesses don't make homemade soup, and they don't hold strange men in their arms in the middle of the night and tell then not to be afraid," he responded softly, his dark eyes even softer.

She searched his face, finally nodding slowly. This at least wasn't a lie. "What is the evidence against me?" Her voice was amazingly matter-of-fact. "Why do your brother and Davidson think I murdered Dennis?"

Ryan understood now how her tremendous self-control had worked against her. Her seeming lack of emotion after Dennis's death had been taken as yet another sign of her guilt.

He followed through on the decision he'd made moments before. "Dennis was involved in more than writing a few illegal prescriptions for painkillers, Ariel." Her pale face grew whiter as she instinctively prepared herself to even more pain. There was no easy way to tell her. "He was smuggling in cocaine and heroin every time he came back from one of his mercy missions to Mexico. One of those little villages was his supply point."

Ariel sat very still. The numbness settling over her had nothing to do with the coolness of the house. "My God," she whispered, "and I actually used to accompany him down there." Staring

sightlessly past Ryan's shoulder, she understood immediately part
of the evidence against her. "How could I have been that blind?"

"You saw only what he wanted you to see, Ariel."

Her eyes came back to his. "And I thought he wanted to help
those people. He was just using them, like he did me."

"He did help them, Ariel," Ryan reminded her quietly. His
thumb stroked soothingly over the pulse in her wrist. It was still
much too fast.

"I don't think he ever intended to use you. On the contrary, I
think he tried to keep you from being tainted by his 'business.' The
one thing he never lied to you about was that he truly loved you."

Why was he defending a man who didn't deserve it? Because, Ryan
thought bitterly, he was defending himself, too, subtly justifying
his lies because of his own selfless concern for her. He ought to be
honest with himself, at least. His concern was purely selfish. He
didn't want what they'd had together for so brief a time to be ir-
retrievably lost.

"Does your brother really believe I'm guilty, Ry?"

Ryan shook his head wearily. "I honestly don't know, Ariel."
The cautious hope in her eyes died, and they were filled with a
bleak despair.

He rose from the table and picked up the scattered pages of her
file. He offered it to her, and after a moment's hesitation she took
it.

"Read it, Ariel. You can see the facts of the case and how Davidson sees them as evidence against you."

Ariel opened the file reluctantly. Seeing all the tabloid articles
again made her feel physically ill, yet she couldn't bring herself to
shut the folder. She skipped over them to the lengthy report on
Dennis's smuggling. She read every word with a morbid thoroughness.

She was unaware of the quilt Ryan tucked around her. She absently drained the mug of coffee he placed near her hand, never
noticing as it was refilled. Ryan moved around the kitchen quietly, preparing breakfast. As Ariel closed the file she felt the
warmth of the old quilt around her and smelled the mundane,
somehow comforting scents of coffee and bacon and toasting
bread.

She stared vacantly at the closed cover of the file; her name in
red letters seemed like the name of a stranger. The evidence the
police and the district attorney's investigators had unearthed after
Dennis's murder was very convincing. All circumstantial, of

course, nothing that could be presented in court without more solid substantiation, but still convincing. It all pointed very clearly to her. Anyone reading the file would at the very least wonder if Ariel Spence had not been Dennis DiSanto's accomplice.

A couple of motives for her part in setting him up for the killing were advanced, but the one the district attorney seemed to favor was the classic one; greed. Ariel had seen a chance to increase her share of the profits by murdering her partner and taking it. Davidson expected that she would eventually disappear, so she could spend her ill-gotten wealth. He had it all worked out. The only flaw in his reasoning was that he was wrong, but how could she prove it? She was guilty until proven innocent, and she began to understand that she might have to live with that supposed guilt haunting her for the rest of her life.

Ryan set a plate with crisp bacon, two fried eggs and toast in front of her. She glanced over to him; he was already back at the stove, his back to her, dishing up his own plate. She wasn't up on the new etiquette for lovers, but she suspected it dictated that he should provide the breakfast, since he had provided the bed.

Lovers. Ariel salted the eggs absently and began to eat automatically. The numbness that had frozen her emotions was beginning to wear off. Ryan sat down across from her silently.

Lovers. This meal should have been a very intimate special celebration of the night before, their eyes making promises of more such nights. But she had been cheated out of that, the promises broken before they were even made. Here they sat, only the narrow trestle table between them, but they might as well have been light years apart, so perfect was their isolation from each other.

With a violent motion Ariel shoved her half-eaten breakfast away. She rose abruptly from the table, her usual grace gone as she tripped over a leg of her chair. She could no longer bear to be in the same room with him.

She was suddenly mad, gloriously, furiously *mad*. Mad at closed-minded district attorneys with tunnel vision, mad at liars, cheats and sneaking spies, all of them with the name Ryan Jones. She reveled in her anger, wallowed in it, stoked it to a white-hot fury—to keep at bay the soul-wrenching hurt, the emptiness threatening to destroy her.

Ryan half rose from his seat, starting to call after her as she rushed from his apartment. He sagged back in the chair without speaking a word and stared after her bleakly. Nothing he could say would bring her back. The only words that might have done it stuck in his throat. They'd been so easy, so natural, in the warm aftermath of loving last night, but now, when he desperately needed them, they wouldn't come.

Ariel took her shower alone. No matter how hard she scrubbed, how scalding the water, she couldn't seem to wash away the feel of his body on hers, the lingering warmth of him, his scent.

She stepped out of the bathroom to find her clothes from the night before neatly folded in the middle of her bed. She ignored them; she would not wear that dress again. She pulled a neon-pink sweatshirt and baggy carpenter's pants from the closet, dressing automatically.

She dried her hair with even less attention. She turned her head in the hot stream of air, her fingers automatically lifting the wet, heavy hair. He would leave immediately, of course. Let him explain it to his brother. She switched off the dryer, combed through her almost dry hair and went downstairs.

She couldn't shake the feeling that something had been missing from the file, something she sensed between the lines, something talked around, but never clearly stated. Yet what more could there be?

Pausing by her front door, she shrugged into her blue ski jacket. Before she told him to get out, she wanted Murphy back. The house would be too quiet, too lonely, without . . . her.

She fastened her seatbelt and started the Blazer. As she turned the truck around she glimpsed the tall dark man standing on the front step. He was watching her over the rim of his mug. The steam from the hot coffee framed his sober face, those dark hooded eyes following her.

She started off down the muddy track to the highway. They hadn't spoken since he'd handed her the file. The road in front of her was suddenly blurred by fresh tears. The conflict inside her was so strong that she felt she was tearing apart.

He'd betrayed her trust, her love. This morning's revelations had destroyed the trust, but the love was still there, insidious, like a weed pulled out of the garden. The top was gone, but the deep taproot remained, the plant waiting to spring up again.

The memory of the night before stubbornly refused to die. He had orchestrated the evening to provide her with a memory that was not of a disappointing loss, but of a special gift full of joy. She might not have had much experience with passion, but she knew that he'd exerted tremendous control over himself to ensure her pleasure before he took his own. How could he have been so sensitive to her needs...and yet so full of deceit? Had last night been the ultimate deception?

Ryan meandered aimlessly across the muddy yard. A stiff breeze was chasing the tattered tail end of the storm over the western mountains. His shoulders automatically hunched at the chill wind whipping through his plaid flannel shirt, but it cleared the dull ache from his head. The sun was shining brilliantly from a rain-washed, azure sky. The air was invigoratingly brisk, freshly cleaned by the storm and scented by the damp prairie surrounding the schoolhouse.

He would take it one day, one hour, at a time. Little by little he would coax her back to him. She would retreat again, when he told her the one detail the file hadn't contained. He hadn't thought she could bear any more bad news this morning. His hand clenched on the stoneware mug in his hand. He *would* have her back.

He frowned at the ground where Ariel's Blazer had been parked, vaguely disturbed by something out of place. The coffee-colored dirt underneath the truck had dried out overnight. Suddenly Ryan bit off a violent curse, flinging the coffee cup aside as he raced for the house and his keys. The significance of the four identical wet spots on the ground where the wheels of the Blazer had rested had finally dawned on him.

Ryan leaped into his truck, grinding the reluctant engine into sputtering life. Ruthlessly he jammed the cold transmission into gear and floored the accelerator. The wet mud sucking at the deep treads on his tires made his progress hideously slow. He had a clear view of the silver Blazer following the straight fence line to the highway. The heel of his hand slammed on the horn, but even he could hardly hear it over the noise of his truck.

He watched her approach the intersection with the highway in agonized desperation. If there was no oncoming traffic he knew just what she would do; he'd watched her often enough the past thirteen days. His subconscious recognition of the superstitious number bypassed his rational mind and sent a chill down his spine. With no traffic to worry about, Ariel would ignore the stop sign, let the truck slow down on its own, gear down, lightly tap the brake pedal and pull out onto the highway. With the mud dragging at her tires, slowing her more than usual, she'd never notice that her brakes weren't working.

Then she would climb the steep hill, top it and start down the long twisting road leading into town. There was a solid granite wall on one side of the road and a drop-off of two hundred feet to the river below on the other. Either would provide an adequate, if fatal, brake for a runaway vehicle.

Through the stinging mist clouding his vision he saw the brake lights ahead of him flash briefly, then stay lit, the blood-red light seeming to mock his useless attempt to stop her. Angrily Ryan swiped a hand across his eyes to clear them, just in time to see a fully loaded logging truck barreling down the hill toward her. The Blazer slewed wildly as Ariel, obviously trying to avoid a collision, wrenched the wheel hard to the right.

Slippery mud had been tracked onto the highway by other cars before hers, and Ryan watched in oddly detached horror as the silver truck slid inexorably closer to the logging truck. The action seemed to be taking place in slow motion, each detail of the deadly scene before him brilliantly clear. In petrified fascination he saw her coolheadedly turn the wheels into the skid, still fighting for control.

The truck driver, too, was trying to take evasive action, but the pavement was slick and he ended up jackknifing his rig across the highway.

Without being aware of it, Ryan had stopped his power wagon a scant hundred feet from the intersection. His white knuckles locked around the steering wheel, and the bitter taste of panic mixed in his dry mouth with the salty, metallic flavor of blood from his bitten-through lip.

At the last possible second before impact Ariel gunned the engine, twisted the wheel again and prayed that just one tire might grab enough to send her past the wall of logs looming inches from the front bumper.

The right rear tire hit a dry patch of asphalt. The vehicle spun just enough to slide past the tail of the logging truck with the screeching sound of tearing metal. The additional acceleration destroyed the precarious balance of the Blazer, and Ariel began a crazy roller-coaster ride as the truck rolled. Hanging on to the steering wheel grimly, she watched through the bursting windshield as the trees in front of her swung insanely upside down and the sky changed places with the ground.

Ryan was shocked out of his terrified trance. He nearly tore the door off its hinges as he slammed out of his truck and began running toward the tree-lined shoulder of the highway. The Blazer rolled onto its roof and rocked there for a few heart-stopping seconds; then its momentum carried it over onto its side. It trembled to a shuddering halt with a metallic sigh like a dying mechanical elephant. The only sounds were Ryan's harsh breathing as he reached the overturned truck and the last, quiet tinkle of glass from a smashed window.

He paused by one rear wheel that was still spinning lazily. Diesel fumes were burning his eyes; the fuel was less volatile than gasoline, but an explosion was still very possible, and even the fastest way to get her out might be too slow. He bypassed doors that might be warped shut by the wreck and crashed through thigh-high cockleburs to reach the open windshield.

"Ariel!"

"What?" A strong voice that sounded more exasperated than scared answered him. A moment later a white face with a smear of bright blood on the left cheek appeared in the opening formerly occupied by the windshield. A body that seemed none the worse for wear, judging by the speed with which it was crawling through the window, immediately followed.

"I think we'd better get away before it blows," Ariel advised calmly, albeit somewhat breathlessly, as she scrambled across the crumpled hood. "I can smell—"

Steel fingers hooked into the sweatshirt under her gaping jacket and dragged her down off the hood to a hard, heaving chest. Before Ariel's sneakers could touch the ground she was being hauled and shoved through the brambles.

There was a soft whoosh behind them, then a deafening roar. The force and heat of the explosion hit them in the back, sending them sprawling over the wet prairie grass.

Ryan and Ariel staggered to their feet, their arms unconsciously seeking each other, holding on as if to reassure themselves that they were truly all right. Silently they watched the truck driver try to battle the inferno with a puny fire extinguisher. He gave up after a few minutes and came to stand with them, his hands brushing absently over his face. Wordlessly, all three of them saw the ravenous flames consume the Blazer, their faces grimly sober. Pungent smoke and fine ash drifted over them like a dirty snowstorm.

The scream of sirens announced both Chief Dye and the county sheriff's deputy. Although technically out of the village police chief's jurisdiction, the deputy deferred the investigation to him. Ted Dye stood by himself, considering the already dying fire and twisted metal. Then he trudged over and called the stunned truck driver aside.

Ryan felt a strong shiver run through Ariel's body. He looked down at her, his face darkening with concern. Underneath the grime and blood her face was pale and composed. The eyes looking up at him were smoke-reddened, but sharp. The trembling under his hands said she wasn't as calm as she appeared.

"The brakes failed, Ry." Her voice and face expressed her bafflement. "Completely. If they were only wet, they should have grabbed at least a little, shouldn't they? I don't under—"

"They weren't wet," Ryan said tersely. Out of the corner of his eye he had seen the chief pat the truck driver on the shoulder, dismissing him.

"And you were right behind me," Ariel said slowly. His comment deepened her puzzlement to disturbing suspicion. "Why were—you...?"

"Ariel, can you tell me what happened?" the chief asked as he lumbered up. His grizzled eyebrow lifted as he noted Ryan's arms linked possessively around Ariel's shoulders, her body drawn protectively into his side.

Ariel answered the chief with a distracted air that he put down to shock over the accident. When she mentioned the failed brakes he glanced sharply at Ryan, who nodded almost imperceptibly. The chief's questioning ended abruptly. He seemed to lose interest in her and wandered back to the dying fire.

Ryan took Ariel's hand and led her toward his power wagon. As if it were an afterthought, Ted Dye called him back.

"Wait for me in the truck, Ariel, I'll be back in a minute, and then we'll go get Murph." Ryan's smile was easy as he shut the door firmly after she'd climbed up. It vanished immediately as he headed back to the police chief.

"You're sure?" the chief asked after a few minutes' discussion. He glanced sideways from where his boot toe was destroying the ash skeleton of a weed to the stern man smoldering, blackened framework that had been a shiny silver truck. Greasy black smoke still coiled around the wreckage and the two men.

"As sure as I can be without any proof." Ryan sighed tiredly and scuffed through a pile of ash with a frustrated kick of his hiking boot. "Luck still seems to be with our unknown 'friend.' The proof burned up with Ariel's Blazer." He swore bitterly as he turned to leave. As a bodyguard he was a joke. If Ariel hadn't been as lucky as her would-be killer, she would be part of that smoking pile of metal right now. Impotently he thrust his hands into his pants pockets. He hoped the gods were enjoying their obscene little chess game. Which mortal pawns would be sacrificed to gain a win?

Ariel accepted the vet's concern over her accident with a lack of concern that raised Ryan's eyebrows and detoured the vet back to his usual cheerfulness. She responded to his instructions for Murphy's convalescence with polite monosyllables. Before letting her leave, he sat her on his examining table to wash her filthy face and examine the cut on her cheek.

Leaning in the doorway, Ryan watched Dr. Hughes's stubby, clumsy-looking fingers clean away the soot and dirt and blood. The veterinarian kept up a constant stream of soothing nonsense. Ryan's impassive face showed neither the irrational jealousy burning in him as the vet's impersonal hands touched Ariel, nor the acute self-disgust that jealousy was causing him. He had wanted to be the one to care for her, but she was undeniably better off in Dr. Hughes's care—and that galled him.

"I hope the local doctors don't find out I've been treating two-legged patients as well as four-legged ones." Dr. Hughes grinned at her as he swabbed disinfectant on Ariel's cheek. He called Ryan over and showed him the hairline slice from a stray sliver of glass. A single drop of bright red blood oozed onto her pale cheek.

"She certainly doesn't need stitches, but I'm going to put two butterfly Band-Aids on it, just to be sure the edges stay together. There won't be a scar," he murmured to Ryan. Both of them ignored the fidgetings of the patient. "Be sure she doesn't get any dirt in it."

"Perhaps *I* could see it?" Ariel suggested caustically.

Dr. Hughes blinked and looked at her in confusion for a moment; then a sheepish grin split his good-natured, homely face. "I'm sorry, Ariel. I'm used to patients who bite, not talk, and to anxious owners who are worried about their precious pets." He handed her a small mirror.

"Ariel wouldn't make a very good pet," Ryan murmured blandly, his dark eyes laughing slyly. "She's not very obedient." But she was infinitely precious.

Ariel sent him a sugary, withering glance, then solemnly accepted a giant dog biscuit from the vet for being a good patient.

Murphy jumped into the back of Ryan's pickup, content to cede the cab to Ariel, and Ryan slammed the tailgate. Despite her brief show of spirit in Dr. Hughes's office, Ariel was still far too quiet and self-controlled. Ryan knew that she'd already had more than enough shocks for one day, yet the worst one of all was going to have to be faced in a very little while. He'd hoped to spare her for a few more days, until her strength and defenses were not so weak, but that was no longer possible.

The ride home was silent. Murphy leaped out of the truck and tore around the yard, obviously fully recuperated. She took off after a pair of imprudent ground squirrels that had decided to take up residence under the front step during her absence. Ryan escorted Ariel into the house with an unobtrusive hand at her back.

He sat her in her favorite armchair, put a log in the stove and sat on the couch across from her. He waited. She looked at him for a long minute, her face closed, her eyes as cold and empty as ice. When she finally spoke her question was so quiet Ryan had to strain to hear it over the popping of the wood in the stove.

"My accident wasn't an accident, was it, Ryan?"

"No, Ariel."

She considered his toneless confirmation. Her voice was as expressionless as his. "How was it done?"

"Probably with Xylene, or any of several other solvents, replacing the brake fluid. Xylene is the easiest to obtain. You drain the master brake cylinder and refill it with the xylene. It eats away at the rubber seals for a few days until the fluid leaks out all at once. The brake failure is total." His smile was faint and humorless, his eyes far away for a moment. "It's an especially successful tactic in hilly terrain."

He answered the stark question that pierced the blankness in her eyes. "Vehicle sabotage was a specialty of mine once. Doing the brakes is particularly effective. There's a fatal crash, and no proof that it was anything but ordinary brake failure. No one suspects a thing."

Her hands were gripping her upper arms so tightly that he knew she would have bruises tomorrow. She breathed in suddenly, deeply, and consciously relaxed, unlocking her fingers and taking hold of the fat arms of her chair. She dug into the green plush viciously.

"And Murphy?" She took another quick breath and conquered the slight waver in her voice. "The other poisonings were simply camouflage. Someone needed to get Murphy out of the way to work on my Blazer.''

"Yes."

"That candy you knocked out of my hand that day...was that...?" Her lips worked but were unable to form the awful word again.

"Poisoned?" he finished for her. "Yes, it was." His voice was quiet and steady, his heart aching as he read the emotions she could no longer mask flitting across her face; stunned disbelief, anger, then recognition of her terrifying vulnerability to an unknown killer.

"This is what you left out this morning," she whispered. Her eyes closed again to shut out the horrible truth. "I knew there was something you weren't telling me, but I thought it was that you had guessed..." A hysterical giggle bubbled up in her throat, and Ryan started off the couch. She swallowed it down, her body rigid as she battled to control her fear. Ryan sat back, seeing her fingers whiten on the chair arms. He wanted so badly to hold her, but she'd shown no sign of wanting him. She didn't trust him enough any longer to seek his comfort.

"Who is it?" she demanded in a fierce whisper.

"I don't know, Ariel." All his frustration and unacknowledged fear were in his answer.

The tension went out of her body, and she slumped in the chair. Two tears seeped out from under the dark fringe of the lashes resting on her white cheeks. With a soft curse Ryan rose in one furious, fluid motion and scooped her out of the chair. The hell with what she wanted; he knew what she needed. Her eyes flew open, and she stared warily at his set jaw as he took her place in the chair. He settled her on his lap, surrounding her with his protection. There were no more tears. He wished there were; she needed the release.

"Why does someone want me dead, Ry?" Her poignant whisper expressed the total incomprehension that he himself had known the first time he'd been shot at and realized, to his astonishment, that someone was actually trying to kill him. At least he had had a glimpse of his enemy.

"We think it might have something to do with Dennis's death," Ryan said hedging a little.

Ariel sat up, almost clipping Ryan's chin with the top of her head. He loosened his arms only enough to let her lean away to see his face.

"That was only a random incident, Ryan," she argued forcefully. "Your brother tried to prove otherwise, but even he couldn't turn up anything concrete. He even searched through all of Dennis's photographs, looking for someone in a picture who shouldn't have been there, or something suspicious happening in the background." Something in the look on Ryan's face made her eyes narrow suddenly. "You've looked at them, too, haven't you," she realized quietly. "You picked the lock on the cabinet."

"It was an easy one," he said neutrally, shrugging off the heat from her gaze. "I didn't see anything, either."

"Is there anything of mine you haven't snooped into, Ryan Jones?" Her tone was a little too silky. "Is there *anything* you haven't lied about?"

Yes. There were the five words he'd whispered in the warm darkness last night, five words he couldn't repeat in the cold, bright daylight. He knew she thought they were the biggest lie of all.

Actually, he preferred her anger. It would counteract the effects of the accident and keep her out of the dangerous apathy that fear could produce. And it was putting some color back into her chalky face.

Ariel tried to stand, outrage stiffening her body. Ryan held her easily, hauling her up against his chest. One implacable hand caught the back of her skull, holding her face so close to his that she felt his breath cooling her hot cheeks. A struggle would be undignified, and she would lose, anyway. She had to content herself with staring coldly into those eyes that caressed her pursed lips as effectively as teasing kisses. At least, she recognized dimly, when she was angry with him, she couldn't be afraid.

Ryan spoke quietly. "I was looking for anything that would give me a clue to the killer's identity. Compared to saving your life, violating your privacy didn't seem like much of a crime."

The sudden tears that flooded her eyes startled both of them. She tried to turn her head away, and he released it immediately. Raising her chin, she sat stiffly on his lap. She sniffed, vainly trying to blink back the tears. "I'm sorry," she said thickly. Her fingers were twisting the hem of her sooty pink sweatshirt hopelessly out of shape. Ryan stilled them and kept them captive gently in his own. She whispered so softly that he had to lean closer to catch the words. "You've lied to me, yet you saved my life, and Murphy's, too." She turned back to him, her eyes achingly vulnerable. "I-I can't..." She was unable to put her conflicting emotions into words.

"Oh, Ariel," he murmured helplessly as he kissed her cheek tenderly. He tasted the salty moisture on her skin then drew her head down to his shoulder. He laughed grimly. "All that's happened to you in less than twenty-four hours is that you've lost your virginity and thought the man who took it was sent to kill you, but he only turned out to be a liar instead. You've survived a near-fatal accident and then discovered someone really is trying to kill you. I suppose—" he rubbed his cheek over her smoky, silky hair "—you're entitled to a few tears."

Ariel nestled against the smoke-soured flannel of his shirt and closed her eyes in sudden exhaustion. It was despicably weak of her to lean on him, she knew, but those strong arms around her felt so good, and she was so alone, so frightened. She sighed sadly, "If you have any more little surprises for me, Ry, maybe you could save them for tomorrow." Within seconds she was asleep.

Ryan held her for a while longer, her softness melting slowly over his hard angles. Finally he stood and laid her on the sofa, then removed her sneakers and covered her with a rainbow afghan. Sighing heavily, he kissed her sleep-soft mouth. Her mouth curved in a dream smile, and he echoed it unconsciously. Reluctantly he straightened and went to her desk; then dialed the eleven digits of his brother's phone number.

Ariel moved slowly through murky dreams to fuzzy awareness. She blinked her eyes open and stared around her living room dazedly. The sunbeams slanting through the side window were nearly horizontal. It had been a little before noon when Ryan had brought her home; now it was nearly sundown. She must have slept for hours. She listened; everything was quiet. Where was Ryan?

The crash of wood against metal only a few feet from her head made her start violently with a small scream. A growled curse came through the cast-iron door of the the wood box built into the wall near the stove. She rose stiffly from the couch and padded over to the small square door.

Bending down, she swung it open and peered through the square tunnel in the brick wall. The corresponding door in the outside wall was open. Ryan was squatting in front of it.

"Hi."

Ryan's head snapped up from the log he was carefully laying inside. He grinned ruefully at the woman shoving the tangled blond hair out of her sleep-flushed face. "I was trying to be quiet so you could sleep."

"You blew it with the first log." Against her will her eyes pleasured themselves on the man framed by the hole in the wall. The last rays of the dying sun picked out the blue highlights in the black hair ruffled by the cold breeze. Apparently he had been chopping more wood, because wood chips clung to his black jeans, and his flannel shirt hung open over a white T-shirt despite the chill. The exercise had given his face a healthy flush and his eyes a dark sparkle. He looked like a man who'd simply been spending a quiet afternoon around the house, enjoying ordinary, everyday chores. The traumatic events of the morning and his duplicity receded to the back of her mind for the moment.

Without thinking about it, she reached through to flick back the stubborn cowlick over his forehead. He caught her hand in his and brought it to his cold lips, warming them with a kiss on her palm.

He felt her shiver and released her hand. "Shut the door before you get a chill. I'll be in in a few minutes."

Ariel shut the door with a small clang. The cold draught of air that had come through the wood box had cleared the sleep from her brain, but one last, jaw-stretching yawn snuck up on her as she went into the kitchen. There she saw two thick steaks marinating on the counter and a loaf of her Italian bread defrosting beside them. Her stomach reminded her that she'd slept through lunch.

She pulled open the refrigerator to see what she might throw together for a salad and found one all ready in a wooden bowl on the glass shelf. He had been busy this afternoon.

She leaned over the door of the refrigerator, staring vacantly at the crisp green lettuce and red tomatoes. There was no possibility of his leaving now. She would have to accept his preparation of dinner tonight as the first gesture of the uneasy truce that was going to have to exist between them. She suspected that Rick Jones could, through some fancy legal finagling, force her into letting his brother remain in her house, but that wasn't why she would allow him to stay. She couldn't accept his deceit; she couldn't forgive him, but the sense of how truly alone she was against this unknown terror threatening her was overwhelming. She needed him.

The cold air pouring out of the refrigerator onto her stocking feet finally roused her from her daze. The door slammed shut with a little more force than was necessary.

Hunkering down before the cabinet under the sink, she looked inside. She could at least make the gesture of baking a couple of potatoes for their dinner. Her eyes skimmed over her pants, pulled tight over her left knee. A long, nasty scratch she hadn't even felt showed through a wide rent in the cloth. She must have acquired it during the wreck, or more likely in the mad scramble after it. At the same time she caught the nauseating smell of burnt upholstery and melted plastic trapped in her sweatshirt. Her nose pinched involuntarily to shut out the odor, but it was too late. Her brain registered both the sight and the smell, and her memory all to easily supplied the details.

Was it only this morning that her safe little world had been so ruthlessly destroyed along with her Blazer? But then, she had been living an illusion all along, for twenty-seven years. She'd been lucky to enjoy her illusions about life longer than most people did, certainly longer than Ryan Jones had. And his lessons had been much more painfully learned, and not at the hands of a tender lover.

It was past time she came out from between the covers of her books and acknowledged that life wasn't always neat and tidy with a "And they lived happily ever after" ending. It was messy, unpredictable and even ugly at times. Sometimes people disappointed you, especially the ones you loved the most.

She knew she was spending an inordinate amount of time sorting through the potatoes. Irrationally, she felt safe, crouched here on the floor, hiding where no one could see her. If only she could crawl into the little cupboard and pull the door shut after her. No one would find her. She could huddle in the dark like a little girl pulling the covers over her head until the bogeyman went away.

Strong, gentle hands closed around her arms, pulling her up against a warm, solid body. Ryan had come looking for her. She felt no surprise; her subconscious now recognized him automatically. Wordlessly he turned her, shutting her in the safety of his arms. She stood passively, letting him support her, her head pressed against the strong, even heartbeat under her ear. He nuzzled his chin into the silky hair at her temple, rocking her slowly in his arms. She shut her eyes, her brain registering and savoring the ordinary scents of fresh-cut wood, cold autumn air, Ryan.

At last he put her from him and stopped to pick two potatoes out of the sack. "If you're through playing with these," he commented lightly, "maybe we can bake a couple for dinner."

After dinner they each took books from her bookcase and kept up the pretense of reading for nearly two hours. Ryan felt her eyes on him, looking at him covertly, anxiously, many times. He had a pretty good idea what was worrying her. He raised his eyes from the twelfth page of the mystery he wasn't reading. She managed to shift her gaze back to her own book just before he caught her watching him.

"I think I'll go to bed," he announced, rising from the chair.

Ariel said nothing, merely nodding, keeping her head down, apparently too absorbed in her book to spare him even a glance. How on earth could she be wanting him to stay? The words to ask him were already in her throat. She swallowed them back.

She was still completely off balance, teetering between despair and disaster. Her anger with him was abiding and deep, smoldering inside her, but so was the desire she felt for him. She didn't have to try to recall last night; the memories came unbidden—those lean dark fingers on her virgin skin, stroking with unforgettable pleasure, his mouth hot and demanding, her mouth, her body, meeting his demands.

Her chin lifted, and she looked at him squarely. Maybe she couldn't help the desire, but she *could* control what she did about it, which would be nothing.

Ryan paused by her chair, looking briefly at the thin stern face meeting his gaze unflinchingly. He leaned down and brushed a light kiss over her set, beautiful mouth. He tasted a trace of desperation and felt the tiny quiver of her lips. He almost stayed.

If he could have honestly believed that they would share her bed in sleep only, he would have. Danger, as he well knew, was a powerful aphrodisiac, and the physical spark between them generated a desire that was incredibly strong. The near loss of her life today would only have distilled that desire, making it more potent and pure. Despite what she thought of him, her body was craving the release of his. He didn't want them to use each other for that kind of release and temporary gratification. She would wake up tomorrow despising herself and hating him even more.

"Good night, Miss Spence," he said softly.

She smiled back crookedly. "Good night, Mr. Jones."

Chapter 10

"W hat are you doing this morning?" Ryan leaned against the schoolhouse and watched Ariel feed kindling to a small fire fighting the wind for its life. It was trying to heat a cast-iron pot hanging from a rusty tripod. His nose wrinkled at the evil odor wafting in his direction. The rig looked and smelled exactly like a witch's cauldron.

"Making soap," she answered blandly. She glanced at him and sighed. The wind was teasing his hair into a black halo around his head. A fallen angel. She laughed grimly to herself. His eyes were squinted against the smoke, his hands stuffed into the pockets of the old bomber jacket. His tan pants were almost as scruffy as hers. As usual, he looked fantastic.

Shouldering himself away from the brick wall, he sauntered over to her. Holding his breath, he peered into the pot, though not too closely. He arched a black eyebrow and slanted her a look. "Of course. I should have guessed." A corner of his mouth kicked up in a sly offering. "I'll share mine if you're that desperate."

She gave him a long look before turning back to her pot. "I'm doing research."

The wind rolled an empty can with a large skull and crossbones and large red letters spelling out "LYE" under the log trailer. Ariel reached for the stout stick leaning against the trailer. Planting one fist on the hip of her paint-splattered jeans, she leaned as close as she dared to the kettle and stirred.

Ryan observed her stirring and scowling at the struggling fire, as if daring it to go out. Another gust of wind whipped her hair into her face and flapped the tails of the faded denim shirt she wore. He grinned to himself. She looked like a beautiful, down-and-out witch, with her hobo clothes and wild hair, trying to conjure up a powerful spell to change her luck. His smile dimmed. Maybe she could conjure one up for both of them.

After reading two of Felicia Fury's books, he could testify to the skill of her research and writing. Just as she had with the more interesting scene involving Ariel and Spence in the hot spring during the snowstorm, she infused even mundane happenings with extraordinarily vivid life. The love scene, naturally had come mainly from her imagination, but much of the rest was obviously the result of painstaking research and actual experience.

In one book the reader shared with the characters a pot of beans flavored with mesquite smoke and blowing gypsum grit. Ryan had tasted the smoky beans, felt his eyes grow red and scratchy, and chewed the sand in his teeth. The readers of *RangeFire* were apparently going to know the reality of having the linings of their noses cauterized by lye fumes.

Absently Ariel brushed the hair out of her eyes. Ryan tugged out the bandanna he'd shoved in his pants pockets earlier. He stood in front of her, taming her windblown hair with the red-and-black cloth. Reaching his arms over her shoulders, he knotted the scarf at the nape of her neck. His hands subtly cajoled her closer in a loose embrace.

"You look a bit tired this morning," he murmured, scanning her upturned face critically. Before she could respond his hands tightened across her back as his mouth covered hers.

Ariel froze; then the stirring stick dropped unnoticed as her arms locked around his slim hips. After the miserable night she'd spent, her coldly rational mind warring with her hotly unreasonable body, she needed this kiss. Perhaps it would be enough to satisfy the irrational cravings she was still trying to ignore.

When it ended she leaned on him, breathing deeply. "I didn't sleep very well last night," she muttered.

His chuckle was rich with rueful understanding. His decision to leave her last night hadn't been made out of any sense of chivalrous nobility. It had been purely selfish, as had been most of his decisions concerning her. He had wanted nothing, not even tem-

porary pleasure, to ruin his chances for the permanent right to that
soul-satisfying joy he'd found two nights ago . . . and the right to
the woman he'd shared it with.

"Did you sleep well?" Ariel murmured. She used the excuse of
needing a windbreaker to burrow under the open edges of his
leather jacket and snuggle against his soft chamois shirt. The
warmth of his body and his familiar scent dulled her resolve to stay
out of his reach. It was so easy to believe she could do it when he
wasn't around, and so hard to do when he was.

"Mmm." He bent his head, his warm mouth finding the wind-
chilled skin under the collar of her old shirt and heating it.

He laughed soundlessly. He had slept lousily. At first light he had
given sleep up as a lost cause and left his lonely bed to drink too
much coffee and try to straighten out the convoluted case he was
helping his partner with. Not long after he'd gotten up, he'd heard
Ariel whistle softly for Murphy, who had been stretched out under the table with her nose on his foot. The dog had nudged the
door open and trotted across the hall to accompany her mistress on
her run. He became so absorbed in the case that he was only pe-
ripherally aware of their return an hour later. When he'd crossed
the hall to use her phone, he'd been surprised to find her house
empty. Looking through the back window, he'd seen her doing her
"research."

With a deep sigh she began to untangle herself from his jacket
and his arms. It was time to get back to work.

Ryan tucked an escaped strand of gold back under the bandanna and squeezed his arms around her in an exuberant bear hug
before he released her.

Ariel started to stir yellowish lumps in the cauldron.

Ryan looked in warily at the foul-smelling mess. "What's that?"

"Fat. The butcher gave it to me. I melted it down and strained
it last night." She leaned a little closer to check the consistency of
the seething, dirty-white mess. Bessie had said it should be the
consistency of butterscotch, whatever that meant. She'd never
made butterscotch, either. "If I was really going to do this right, I
should have made my own lye water by dripping rainwater through
wood ashes," she commented absently. "This should be enough
for authenticity, though."

"I should hope so," Ryan murmured dryly. He wondered if her
readers appreciated what she went through to provide them with
realism. The wind shifted. "It certainly smells authentic."

"I know," she agreed with a small laugh, her nose wrinkling. "Proctor and Gamble doesn't have to worry about competition from me."

Ariel kept stirring with her makeshift paddle, her face averted to avoid breathing the fumes. Suddenly the pot belched rudely and the boiling soap splattered over her hand. Ariel snatched it back, uttering a curse that would have guaranteed her a mouthful of soap as a child. She caught herself just before her scalded hand clapped itself over her astonished mouth.

Ryan threw back his head, roaring with appreciative laughter as he groped for the hose. He doused her hand with icy water. "You're learning, Ariel. Maybe I won't have to teach you too many words after all. That's a pretty good, all-purpose one." He chuckled approvingly.

Pulling her numbed hand out of the hose's spray, she tried to look both contrite and vexed, but only succeeded in laughing. "Oh, Lord," she groaned helplessly. "My mother would faint dead away if she ever heard me say that."

"Really?" Ryan asked interestedly, taking her hand to examine the reddened skin. "Why? Surely she'd heard it before."

"Not from any of her children," Ariel mumbled. "I have to finish making the soap. And you—" she gave him a stern look "—have to come up with an idea for all the firewood you won. They're coming for their trailer on Monday."

He gave her hand a final pet and released it. "You're okay, no burns." He turned and regarded his raffle prize balefully.

Ariel gingerly stirred her soap one last time and began setting out foil-lined cardboard flats. Very carefully she ladled out the liquid soap with a long-handled, blue enamel spoon. It had been Bessie's.

With the last of the soap cooling in the improvised molds, Ariel filled the kettle with clean water and drowned the fire. Glancing around to make sure she hadn't forgotten anything, she dusted off her hands in satisfaction, then looked over at Ryan. With his hands on his hips and his feet braced apart, he was still frowning at his logs.

What game was he playing this morning? He was acting as if everything was normal, maintaining the easy relationship that had been growing between them until she'd found him out yesterday morning. Did he honestly think she was going to go along with that?

He'd *lied* to her, for God's sake! Just like Dennis had, only Ryan's lies had been much crueller, because she hadn't been in love with Dennis. She hadn't felt this pain, hadn't realized with such humiliation what a fool she'd been. He must have been secretly laughing at her as she'd tearfully poured out the whole sordid little tale he already knew by heart.

She watched him rake his hand through his wind-tousled black hair, and her fingers unconsciously mirrored the motions, remembering the feel of those rough-silk strands. He shook his head at the wood and shifted his stance, his hands shoved now in the back pockets of his tan pants.

Her fury vanished as suddenly as it had come. No, he hadn't laughed at her; she knew that instinctively. And the lies had been gently not cruelly meant, intended not to harm her, but to keep her safe. If he had told her the truth when he'd come, she would have refunded his rent and cheerfully kicked him out. And she would have taken the candy to the rest home, then eaten a piece or two with Bessie and the other old people she loved. She would never have known the fearful, glorious wonder of falling in love with him.

But still he had lied.

Finally she stepped forward, slapped her palm on the butt of one of the lower logs and offered her suggestion. "Why don't you—"

There was an odd sound, like the distant rumbling of an avalanche. The next thing Ariel knew a body had slammed into her, tackling her and rolling them both under the log trailer.

With the sounds of wood splintering and smashing echoing and reechoing in her ears, she raised her head. The sight of Ryan's white, too-tight face above hers choked off her words. His mouth had thinned to a straight slash across his face, and his jaw was clenched. Ariel stopped struggling against the unintentionally cruel hands biting into her arms. She turned her head, following the direction of his cold, empty eyes.

The wind was already clearing the air of the dirt and wood dust that had been stirred up when the full load of logs had rolled off the trailer. Ariel felt the blood drain from her face and her body turn frigid. Anyone standing by the trailer would have been crushed, every bone in his—or her—body smashed.

Her voice startled her as she spoke at last. It was amazingly calm and matter-of-fact. "Another accident-that-wasn't?"

Ryan's head turned sluggishly, as if he was awakening from a drugged sleep. He looked down at her. She'd been wrong about his eyes; they weren't cold and empty at all. They were burning with an out-of-control rage.

The hands on her arms tightened until she thought the bones would splinter. She couldn't stop her small cry of pain. Anguish replaced the fury as his black eyes slowly traveled down her body, looking for the cause of her distress and stopping at his own white-knuckled hands.

A choked cry broke free from deep in Ryan's throat. It ended in a strangled laugh as he instantly relaxed his grip and rolled them onto their sides in the dirt. One hand slipped up to the back of her head, his long fingers sliding through her tangled hair to cradle her face against his shoulder.

"Oh, Ariel, I'm sorry." His harsh voice was unsteady. "I'm not much of a bodyguard if I save you from disaster, only to break both your arms." He buried his face in her throat, and Ariel could feel his warm, stuttering breath playing a ragged counterpoint to her skipping heart.

He shuddered once, and she wrapped her arms strongly around his body. She was strangely clearheaded and composed. It was as if, during the miserable night she'd spent, she had reached a silent understanding with her unknown killer. She accepted that he was going to continue his deadly game of attempted assassination, but he would have to accept that she was determined to survive until she succeeded in outwitting him and learned his identity. She was, admittedly, depending heavily on Ryan Jones's help.

"Ryan." There was a trace of unlikely laughter in her raspy voice. "I can't breathe."

Ryan's head lifted and he stared down at her, frowning. His eyes narrowed warily. He suspected she had slipped over the edge into hysteria. Not that he blamed her; he felt a little hysterical himself. Her wobbly smile was marginally reassuring as she pushed against him, silently asking for release. He let her go reluctantly. She began crawling on her belly toward the front of the trailer. He was right behind her when she stood up and brushed the dirt and wood chips from her clothes.

"How did he do it, do you think?" she asked, absently fending off Murphy, who had come over to sniff curiously at the fallen logs.

Ryan bent, groped under the trailer for a moment and pulled out a heavy chain. "Did you unhook this chain?" he asked almost idly. Mutely Ariel shook her head. "Neither did I."

Wordlessly they stared at the chain in his hand. It was the chain that the lumber man had shown them last Saturday. Simply open the spring hook, he had said, and the carefully balanced load would come tumbling down at a touch. Neither of them had unhooked it, and it couldn't have come unhooked accidently, yet the logs had come tumbling down at her touch.

"Very likely he was standing just a few feet away from us last Saturday, listening to everything the guy from the mill told us," Ryan said grimly. He tossed the chain down in frustration. It whipped into the rusty side of the trailer with an angry clank.

Ariel wrapped her arms around her chest to ward off the cold wind. "Well, at least this solved part of our problem about what to do with the wood."

He responded to her black humor with an obscenity hissed between his teeth. Then he turned at the light touch on his arm and looked down into her huge blue eyes.

"Ryan, thank you," she whispered.

He closed her carefully in his embrace. "That one was too close," he breathed into her ear, staring sightlessly across the orchard, seeing instead the slow shift of the logs and feeling again the terrifyingly leaden motion of his body as he tried to reach her before they did.

"Do you think he booby-trapped anything else?" Her words were whispered, but steady.

She really astounded him. The stricken look on her face when she'd first seen the avalanche of logs had told him that she understood the lethal reality of her situation quite well. Then her body had stiffened and her chin had lifted, and he had known that she had no intention of dissolving into a puddle of helpless hysteria. There had been resolution, not resignation, on her grim face. She was every bit as strong and courageous as the heroines she created.

Turning her in his arms, her back against his chest, he rested his chin on her head. His arms were crossed tightly over her breasts as he surveyed the yard.

"I don't think so," he said slowly. "He didn't have that much time, and the brake job would have used most of it."

"Then I guess we wait until he pays another visit," Ariel answered tiredly after a minute.

"Maybe not. Rick had some interesting information yesterday afternoon when I called him." She let his arm curl loosely around her waist as they ambled toward the back door of the schoolhouse. "I called him while you were sleeping, but I didn't tell you, because I thought you'd had enough for one day."

"Yeah," she agreed softly as the door swung shut behind them.

A little while later Ariel pushed Ryan onto her sofa and sat on the edge of the chair opposite him. She looked at him with barely disguised impatience. "So what did Rick say yesterday?" They had cleaned up, eaten lunch, stuffed their turkey and put it in the oven to roast, but Ryan had yet to utter a word about his conversation with his brother.

"It bothered me from the beginning that a retired Los Angeles exterminator would go all the way to San Francisco just to shoot somebody at random. If that's all he'd had in mind, he'd have stayed home to do it."

Ariel prayed for patience. The Perry Mason in him was finally coming out. She'd suspected all along that beneath that controlled, cynical exterior there was a secret love of courtroom theatrics and playing to an audience. She'd had many glimpses already of his mischievous humor and carefully hidden almost boyish delight in pulling surprises. He was going to make her suffer through the opening statement and the presentation of exhibits *A*, *B*, etc as he built up to the surprise witness.

"Dennis's killer worked for his uncle back in New Jersey. Reilly was his enforcer, only his name wasn't Reilly then: it was O'Fallon. Rick did some checking on old man DiSanto's background in Newark and found the connection." He saw Ariel pale and tense, but she said nothing.

"Reilly, or O'Fallon, was an ex-cop who apparently decided that enforcing DiSanto's law was more lucrative than enforcing the city of Newark's. An old desk sergeant who's just about to retire remembered him, even had a picture. They were in the same police-training class. Rick says it may be thirty years old, but there's no doubt that Reilly and O'Fallon were the same man.

"DiSanto set him up in the exterminating business and then, as far as Rick can find out, there was little or no contact between the two men for the next twenty-five years."

Ariel understood the implication immediately, and she shook her head emphatically. "No, Ryan. Whatever else Mr. DiSanto may be guilty of, he did not have his old hitman kill his nephew. He loved Dennis very much."

"From what I've read of the reports, I'm inclined to agree with you, Ariel. I doubt that Reilly even knew who Dennis was. There was an almost obsessive loyalty between him and his old boss. He was the only one of his men that DiSanto brought out with him. I don't think Reilly would have knowingly harmed anyone DiSanto cared about.''

Ryan shrugged. ''Why Reilly took the job, I don't suppose we'll ever know. Maybe he was being blackmailed; maybe the offer was too good to refuse.'' He was silent, letting Ariel puzzle through this unexpected information.

Her dark gold eyebrows lifted as she stared at him distractedly. ''Whoever hired Reilly obviously knew about his old life and connections. That almost guarantees he knew Mr. DiSanto, probably very well.'' Her hands chopped the air in helpless frustration. ''But who is he? That report in my file showed that they've investigated everyone close to Dennis. Not just me, but Mr. DiSanto, Robert, his friends. There just weren't any leads, except—'' her mouth twisted bitterly ''—all that circumstantial evidence they're using against me.''

''There's been a new lead,'' Ryan revealed quietly. ''Do you ever remember hearing Dennis mention an Antonio Garza?''

Ariel thought hard, finally shaking her head. ''Never. Who is he?''

''The man in the newspaper photo you wondered about, the man you saw in his office. Until his arrest two weeks ago he was the main distributor of cocaine in western Mexico. Apparently Dennis was his best customer, but Garza's not talking.''

Ariel passed a hand over her eyes tiredly. ''My God. No wonder he was so angry with Dennis for taking me with him on his trips to Mexico.'' She laughed mirthlessly. ''And I thought he was worried about my safety.''

''Have you ever been able to remember who the third man in the office that day was?''

She rubbed her forehead, shaking her head in frustration. ''No. I've replayed that scene in my mind a hundred times.'' From the vacant look in her eyes he knew she was replaying the scene for the one hundred and first time. ''I can see Dennis sitting behind his desk, Garza on his left, but the other man . . . ?'' She sighed wearily. ''Nothing.'' She stared at Ryan helplessly. ''I can't even remember that he said anything.''

''Maybe you won't let yourself remember,'' Ryan said thoughtfully. At the angry frown threatening to darken her face he explained himself quickly. ''It might be too painful a shock if you remembered right now. Perhaps it was someone close to Dennis, someone you liked.''

"I don't think there can be many more painful shocks for me after yesterday, do you, Ryan?" She laughed harshly.

Ryan returned her accusing gaze, his face revealing nothing of his thoughts. Ariel looked away first. No, love, I don't, he agreed silently. His elbows resting on his widespread knees, he bowed his head. He studied his clasped hands, which hung loosely between his knees. If only we'd met under different circumstances, he thought.

Ryan raised his head and stared at her, his eyes empty and bleak. If only I could start fresh with you, love, no lies between us. If only—the two most useless words in the English language.

Ariel was grimacing at the floor. She hadn't seen the look that had passed across Ryan's face. Consciously she relaxed and whispered to herself. "Whoever he is, maybe he's the one who's hired another killer for me."

Ryan's cool answer startled her. "I don't think he's hired anyone. A professional killing is generally very straightforward, something none of the attempts on you has been. They've been very amateurish, although fairly clever. I think he's after you himself."

Ariel's gaze sharpened on Ryan until he could almost feel it cutting through him. "You have a suspect, don't you?" she deduced, her voice devoid of emotion. "Who?"

Ryan matched her impassivity and raised it. "I don't want to tell you yet. It's someone you know rather well." He watched anger flush her cheeks, and her eyes acquired a hard glitter. His smooth words cut through her first, hot burst of anger. "If I do tell you, and I'm wrong, you'll have lowered your guard against the wrong person. I want you suspicious of everyone, it's your best chance of staying alive."

He hated telling the facts to her so cruelly, but he would hate losing her a thousand times more.

The cold brutality of his words shocked her into silence. The realization that the killer stalking her was someone she knew, most likely someone she trusted and liked, was devastating. A faceless, nameless murderer was hard enough to cope with, but the idea that it was probably someone she considered a friend made the situation all the more unbearable. She understood what Ryan was doing, but she almost wished he'd left her in ignorance. At least she could wrap ignorance around herself like a warm old sweater. Ryan had stripped it away, leaving her to face the cold, hard reality with no protection at all.

Her heart suddenly started racing, pumping icy blood through her body. Her courage faltered. Was he also warning her against himself, warning her not to trust him, either, not to expect too much? Maybe all he had to offer her was a few nights of passion.

Too agitated to sit still any longer, she leaped to her feet and began pacing the small area in front of the sofa. "This is such a tangle of mystery men, hidden motives . . ." She wheeled and faced him. "I feel as if when it's unraveled, all the loose ends will be neatly knotted into an obvious answer everyone's missed." She shivered suddenly in the toasty room. "I just hope I'm around to know the answer," she whispered softly, staring into the orange flames in the stove.

Ryan rose and gathered her carefully into his arms, ready for her resistance. There wasn't any. "You'll know the answer, Ariel, I guarantee it." He felt sick at heart. It was the first outright lie he had told her. He couldn't guarantee anything. He could only try with every skill learned in the old days and every ounce of intelligence he possessed to keep her alive.

She believed in him, though. At last she lifted her head from his shoulder and looked up into his hard face, her hand tightening on the back of his soft shirt. Her eyes were even more vulnerable than they'd been the morning when she'd found the file.

What then, Ryan? she wanted to ask. What about us? She felt a giggle bubbling up in her throat. Maybe she was getting hysterical. Why else would she be wanting to ask such an insane question? Hadn't she had enough misery over the past two days? Why would she intentionally lay herself wide open for more?

Certainly she was due the luxury of a little hysteria after all she'd been through. What a release it would be to scream, rant, cry, totally lose control. But she couldn't risk it. If she ever lost control she might never find it again.

Ariel gave herself a mental shake. She wasn't really close to hysteria. Last night she had been in her cold bed in the dark, alone, but not now. She was asking about her future with Ryan because the answer was as important to her as the identity of the killer.

The bitter pain growing inside her was becoming unbearable. What did they really have between them besides one night of passion and lies? Ariel cringed inside when she imagined just how many such nights Ryan had enjoyed. No doubt many, most of them much more enjoyable with much more practiced lovers. Only she had believed it had meant to him what it had to her. Certainly he hadn't had any foolish dreams based on one romp in the sack.

Maybe, when it was over and he left her, she would be lucky. Perhaps the memory of his lies would leave her enough self-righteous anger and pride to forget that night.

Ryan saw the questions in her eyes, but he wasn't ready to answer them. Instead he offered a curiously sexless kiss rife with boundless love and affection. He held her against him for a moment longer before he set her free.

"I'll carve the turkey if you'll get the rest of the dinner on the table," he said. The rest of the evening passed as had the night before, the wary truce continuing.

Something had obviously gone wrong—twice. There had been a wreck; she'd mentioned it when he'd called her on the phone for their monthly visit. But she'd walked away with only a scratch. Then she'd made a brief comment about a "peculiar" accident with a load of logs.

He'd finally remembered why the name and face of the man living with her had seemed familiar. Ryan Jones. He'd filed the name away in his memory a couple of years ago; in case he ever had need of a good defense attorney. Jones was reputedly one of the best. He laughed humorously to himself. Jones would hardly be willing to defend the man who deprived him of his lover, although he'd heard, if the price was right . . . and everyone had a price.

He toyed with the rolled playbill on his desk. It had seemed too much of a coincidence that the assistant D.A. and her new "tenant" had the same last name, no matter how common. They had been too careful with her, allowed too few people close to her. Still, it had been a bit of a jolt to have it confirmed that they were indeed brothers.

Had Richard Jones sent his brother to watch over her? Was that the reason his "accidents" hadn't worked? Could they be suspicious—of him?

He killed the thought as soon as it came. Not possible. He was utterly confident that there was no way they could tie him to anything suspicious.

It was a pity the candy hadn't worked. The mail was so convenient. Too bad he knew nothing about letter bombs. Unconsciously his nervous fingers unrolled the playbill and smoothed it over the desk top. He wasn't free this weekend, but he was the next. And, coincidentally, it was the start of the deer-hunting season in western Montana. He knew about that the same way he'd known about

*the apple festival and the old biddy in the nursing home who she
was fond of, from the occasional, chatty letters she sent him.*

*The annual fall rite would bring out plenty of hunters who would
be only too eager to shoot at anything that moved. They would be
along the river, waiting, where the deer liked to come for water in
the early morning, where she liked to run in the early mornings. He
would also be waiting. Who could know where a stray bullet had
come from.*

Chapter 11

W**hat** are you going to do for transportation?'' Ryan sat at Ariel's dining table, looking on as she attempted French toast. In a minute he was going to have to get up and save it from cremation.

''I guess I'll have to go dicker with the car dealers in Hamilton on Monday.'' She wrinkled her nose disgustedly, whether at the French toast or the unpleasant prospect of haggling with car salesmen, he wasn't sure. ''The insurance adjuster says I should have a check within a week.''

''Why not go today?'' He rose from his chair and sauntered across the floor to stand by her. She had on a blue heather tweed suit with a navy silk shirt. It was obvious that she was going somewhere. He reached around her, his arm brushing the swell of her breast, to flip the toast. Unconsciously she leaned back into him. Even if he hadn't seen her wearing her running clothes earlier, he would have known she'd been out. Her cheeks had a healthy, outdoor rosiness, and he could smell the cold, crisp morning in the silky hair grazing his chin.

Abruptly she stiffened and stepped from between him and the stove. ''I have to go to the monthly birthday luncheon at Bessie's rest home.'' She gave him a sidelong glance. ''I was hoping I could borrow your truck.'' She left the sentence dangling.

"Will there be enough cake for one more at the party?" he inquired idly, concentrating on the French toast on the griddle.

"If not, you can have mine. The Valley View ladies would run me out of town if I didn't bring you," she informed him dryly. "My 'drop-dead handsome' boarder has been the main topic of conversation for two weeks." That too-rare, boyish grin lit his face, and her heart contracted.

Ariel was placing the last dirty plate in the dishwasher when Ryan walked back into her kitchen. She smiled approvingly at the gray herringbone sports coat, charcoal slacks and soft yellow open-necked shirt he'd changed into. The ladies would certainly be enthralled. She had seen him every day for two weeks, and she still was. But then, she sighed hopelessly, she would be even if she saw him every day until she was as old as Bessie.

She opened the refrigerator and pulled out a two-and-a-half gallon kerosene can. The fractional lift of his left eyebrow was his only comment.

"Research," she explained.

"Naturally."

"Also our contribution to the party," she added, laughing at the skeptical look he threw the blue metal can. He took the heavy container from her, noting the roughly cut circle that had been cut near the spout. The patch covering it had been sealed with a shiny ribbon of dribbled lead.

"Bessie and I made it a couple of months ago." Ariel whistled up Murphy and let her inside as they went out. Ryan shot her a despairing glare she didn't see and turned back to lock the dead bolt.

Ariel slid onto the truck's worn upholstery. She raised her voice over the growl of the engine. "When Bessie was a girl, her mother used to preserve fruit in empty kerosene cans. Every wash day they'd fill up the cans with the used wash water and rinse them until the kerosene smell was gone." She caught Ryan's faint look of distaste directed toward the can on the floor mat. "Don't worry," she reassured him in a grave aside, "this can never had dirty washwater in it.

"Anyway," she continued the history lesson, "in late summer they'd gather whatever wild fruit was around and pick any that was left on their trees and boil it together in a sugar syrup. Next, they'd pour it into the cans and seal them with lead. Then, if the cans didn't swell they'd have fruit all winter. Bessie said whenever they opened one, it was like opening a can full of summer."

"Why did the cans swell?"

Ariel shrugged blithely. "Boiling didn't always kill all the bacteria, and sometimes the fruit spoiled."

"Did this can swell?"

Ariel laughed at the slightly ill look on his face. "No," she assured him sweetly, "it didn't. Bessie and I decided we'd open it this winter and do just like her family and their neighbors did—share it around with everyone." Her forehead wrinkled. "I wonder why she decided not to wait for winter?"

"What kind of fruit did you use?" he asked quickly. He didn't want her thinking about Bessie's reason. "Apples?"

"Hmm? Oh—peaches, wild plums, pears. No apples." She grinned at him, then made a face. "The pears were horrible. I had to peel them, and sticky juice ran down my arms. Ugh. And Bessie made me do all of them, too."

"You love Bessie very much, don't you?" He glanced away from the road to her, his eyes soft and a little sad.

"Yes, I do," she answered quietly. "Most people grow up knowing their grandmothers, maybe even one of their great-grandmothers. Mine were all gone before I was old enough to remember them." She smiled back at him a little mistily. "Bessie is like all my grandmothers and great-grandmothers in one."

His arm came around her hard, dragging her close for a quick hug before she could pull away.

As soon as they entered the gathering room at the rest home Ariel had to choke back a laugh. As if they were all connected to the same radar, Valley View's residents materialized as one. The ladies fluttered like elderly butterflies around the young, handsome *man*. The old men looked on, disgusted, until they could pull him aside to talk about really important things, like the memories of youth only another man could appreciate.

"He's a fine man." Bessie's voice behind her was like dry, dead leaves caught in a winter whirlwind.

"Yes, he is." Ariel knew Bessie was seeing more than the good-looking face and lean, graceful body. She wheeled her friend closer to the fire, lit at midday for this special occasion. Bessie had looked cold, huddled under the daffodil-yellow afghan the two of them had crocheted together this spring. Her usually neat hair was a wispy cloud around her head, and her eyes were dull and rheumy.

Ariel threw another of the home's carefully hoarded logs on the fire and suddenly knew what Ryan could do with his raffle prize. She looked across the room. Ryan was lounging on the sofa, apparently quite content to be Mr. Applebury's new audience for his long-winded rhapsodies about goose-hunting. Ryan had, of course, charmed all the old ladies and gentlemen in less than ten minutes.

The preserved fruit brought back so many childhood memories as it was spooned over angel-food cake that Ariel wished desperately for her tape recorder. She sat on the carpeted floor of the gathering room, surrounded by a dozen surrogate grandparents. All were intent upon sharing their reminiscenses with her, to be sure someone would carry them on to the next generation. Absently she noted Ryan taking Bessie back to her room.

It was another hour before she wandered down the east hallway to say goodbye. Bessie was already asleep, both her exquisite wedding-ring quilt and the yellow afghan covering her withered body. Ariel sat by her bed for a few minutes anyway, trying to organize the priceless memories her elderly friends had stored in her mind. Finally she rose, tucked the covers more firmly around Bessie and tiptoed out.

She went two doors down to visit with Mrs. Donner, who was recuperating from a broken hip. It had kept her from the party today, and Ariel knew she would be dying to hear whatever gossip Ariel might be able to spread.

Enid Donner was Bessie's first cousin and only a decade younger, but there was no family resemblance. Where Bessie was spare and tall, Enid was short and as plump as a comfortable, overstuffed chair. She dyed her hair a brilliant red that Bessie had confided tartly one day had *not* been her natural color when she was younger, even if she did tell everyone that. It was curled in an elaborate style popular thirty years before, but, curiously, it went with her remarkably smooth rose milk skin and sharp black eyes. Despite the impression she gave of being a vain and silly old lady, Ariel knew her to be as true an example of a real pioneer as Bessie. She also possessed an incredible motherlode of memories, one Ariel had mined for fascinating bits of treasure many times.

Ariel recounted the highlights of the party. Glancing down at Mrs. Donner's bedside table, she picked up an open paperback. "Mrs. Donner, I'm surprised at you! Reading books like this." She laughed a bit uneasily. She'd never dreamed Mrs. Donner would read this book.

"Like what, dear?" Mrs. Donner seemed fascinated with something over Ariel's left shoulder.

Ariel held up the book, *StarFire*. The cover depicted a half-fainting, raven-haired woman in danger of losing her blouse. She was clasped in the muscled arm of a Western hero, his black Stetson pushed back on his curly, golden hair, his shirt unbuttoned halfway down his impossibly virile chest. His perfect white teeth flashed under a luxuriant mustache as he blazed away with a sixgun.

Mrs. Donner tore her gaze away from whatever she was finding so captivating and spared a glance for the book. "Oh, I just love Felicia Fury's books," she enthused. "They're so..."

"Trashy?" Ariel supplied.

Mrs. Donner flushed a delicate shade of rose. She reproved Ariel gently. "They may be a bit naughty, dear," Ariel barely kept a straight face at the eighty-six-year-old lady's choice of adjective, "but they are like a very exciting history book, too, full of so much detail, and very accurate." She sighed appreciatively. "The stories are really so good, full of action. The hero is always so handsome and always gets the beautiful girl."

"Yes," Ariel said knowing nearly deaf Mrs. Donner couldn't hear her dry murmur, "numerous times." Old ladies, she decided, had their dreams, too, or memories. There was an odd sound behind her, like a strangled snort, and she turned to look over her shoulder. Ryan was standing in the doorway, his hands in his pockets, enjoying her verbal footwork. He gave her a pleasantly innocuous smile, and she was instantly wary. She barely heard Mrs. Donner's next comment.

"But then, I don't have to tell you about her books, do I, dear? You must know her very well."

Ariel's head snapped around. "Why would you think I know Felicia Fury, Enid?" she asked, aghast. How was she going to get Ryan out of here within the next five seconds?

Mrs. Donner indicated the book Ariel still held in her hand. "Because in her newest book, the same thing happens to the heroine as happened to my sister on her wedding night." Ariel tossed *StarFire* back on the nightstand as if it had suddenly burst into flame. "She hears a pack mule braying and is sure it's a cougar. The hero has a hard time convincing her it isn't until he thinks of a way to make her forget about it entirely." The elderly lady's sly giggle was surprisingly girlish. "I know I'm the only one alive who remembers it, and I haven't told that story to anyone in years—

except you." She gave Ariel a sharp look. "I hope she appreciates all the research you do for her, dear." She added hopefully, "Do you suppose you could get her autograph? She *is* my favorite author."

"I don't know her, Enid." She could feel the heat of dark eyes on her back. "I just do general research, and then the editor gives it to whoever needs it." Ariel scuttled to the door. She relented a little when she saw Enid Donner's profound disappointment. "If I ever meet her, though, I'll get it for you."

Mrs. Donner's happy smile returned. "Oh, would you, dear? I would be so pleased!"

Ariel smiled goodbye stiffly, then grabbed Ryan's arm and began dragging him down the hall. He hung back long enough to wave to Mrs. Donner, then let her lead him on. Casually he looped his arm around Ariel's shoulders, glancing down at her innocently. "I wonder if Felicia does appreciate all the hard work you do for her, dear."

"I wouldn't know, Ry," she said irritably. "Oh, look!" She skidded to a stop, grateful for anything to change the subject, even a terminal bore. "There's Mr. Caldwell! I need—"

"Another time, Ariel." His arm tightened implacably as he led her through a side exit to his truck.

They drove in silence for several minutes. His offhand question broke it. "Are you going to give her the autograph, Felicia?"

Ariel waited until she could breathe evenly again. "You think *I* write those . . . ?" She struggled for an adequate word.

"Louis L'Amours with sex?" he offered.

Pretty good, she silently congratulated him. She sounded properly affronted. "How could you think I—"

"I know, my dear Miss Fury." He parked the power wagon in the grocery-store lot. Draping his long arms over the steering wheel, he turned and grinned at her. "There was a mystery of your astoundingly large income for doing mere historical research." At her look of surprise, he confided, "My brother didn't see fit to tell me how you really made your money. I had to find out for myself."

She remained silent, waiting for the rest of his evidence.

"First there were those ten sexy books on the sixth shelf of your bookcase. Then—" he got out and walked around to open the door "—there's the matter of your name, your real name, which you just happened to use for the hero and heroine of your first book, *WildFire.*" He headed her toward the store with a firm hand on her back. "You also left your computer on one day. I figured out the code on those sets of discs you have and . . ." He let his insufferably smug smile finish for him.

"Damn!" Ariel's fist bounced off the fender of the car they were passing. "I *knew* you'd be sneaking around someday when I left it on accidently." She sighed disgustedly, gave him a black look, then sighed again.

"How should I sign the autograph, do you think?" A grin flirted with her mouth. "Just 'All my love, Felicia'? Or 'To my dear friend, Enid, love from Felicia'?"

He pushed open the heavy glass door, and Ariel grabbed a cart, one with a wobbly, noisy wheel. He calmly took it away from her and exchanged it for a better one. "Oh, I think she deserves the full treatment, don't you?" He leaned over and whispered in her ear as they reached the frozen-food cases, "Don't worry. I won't betray your secret, Felicia." He turned her mouth to his and kissed it gently.

When they got back to the schoolhouse they unloaded their groceries, then parted company in the hall to put things away and change clothes. Ryan had agreed that Bessie and her friends should have some of his raffle prize, even suggesting that he and Ariel cut it up and deliver it.

The sky was a watery blue, partly overcast, and the pale sun gave little warmth. By the time Ariel got out to the backyard Ryan had already parked his pickup by the pile of logs and gotten her chain saw and ax out of the storage closet in the back hall. She slapped an old pair of gloves she'd scrounged up into his hand, pulled on her own and they got to work.

It was one of the happiest afternoons Ariel could remember, and she spent it doing nothing more exciting and exotic than cutting and stacking firewood. With a great deal of wonderful silliness as she tried to follow Ryan's contradictory directions, they managed to wrest the awkward, lightweight camper shell off his truck. Both of them had to put on heavy flannel shirts with their jeans and sneakers against the chill of the day, but as soon as they'd staggered over to the orchard fence to prop the shell against it, they stripped down to T-shirts.

Muscles that had been tight with tension for several days warmed and loosened. They traded off on the chain saw and ax several times, and the pile of split pine grew steadily. Despite the hard, physical work Ariel felt oddly relaxed. There were long silences between them, broken only by an impersonal word or two commenting on the work, but the silences were companionable, filled with quick, flashing grins and shared smiles when their eyes happened to meet. They made, she realized, a good team.

Turning the twenty-foot logs into fireplace-size chunks demanded strong muscles, but not much thought. The monotonous drone of the saw, the metronomelike thud of the ax and the smooth steady rhythm of her body as Ryan swung up chunk after chunk of wood, which she caught before turning to stack it neatly in the bed of his truck, seemed to clear the clutter in her mind.

Life is hard, Bessie was fond of saying, and then you die. Ariel had found she was giving a good deal more thought lately to dying than was usual. There was so much of life that she hadn't even experienced until Ryan Jones had come to rent her schoolhouse and spy on her, and then the experience had been much too brief to be satisfying. Even though she didn't plan on obliging her unknown killer by dying anytime soon, she didn't want to waste time, either.

She sat down on the roof of the cab, waiting for Ryan to split the last few logs to top off the load of firewood. He'd really seemed to enjoy the afternoon, maybe because it was such a novel way for him to pass a Saturday. She doubted that he spent many weekends in Malibu chopping wood, yet he'd been relaxed, his attitude carefree and happy. Ariel unknowingly echoed the grin he flashed up to her. It faded slowly as her expression grew thoughtful and a little sad.

The novelty of a small backwater town would soon wear off, though, or the mystery would be solved, and then he'd leave. Before he did Ariel wanted some more of that life she'd experienced all too briefly. The love that had been quietly growing for him, impossible as it seemed, refused to die, even though she knew she couldn't trust him any longer. Indeed, it still seemed to be growing.

There was a chemistry between them that was very rare; even she, with her paltry experience, knew that. Whether it was good or bad chemistry she couldn't predict, but she couldn't resist experimenting to find out. The reaction might produce a brilliant blinding flash, like Fourth of July fireworks that burst gloriously across the night sky, then died all too quickly, leaving her with a broken heart. Or it might produce what the ancient alchemists had dreamed of, solid gold, a love that would last.

Whatever the final result, Ariel was willing to risk it. She had no way of knowing how long they had together; she wanted all the experience, all the memories, she could have.

Ryan's imperious whistle brought her down to her feet just in time to catch the log he'd tossed her. The last few were piled on, and then he reached a hand to swing her down to the ground.

"I'm going to take this on over to the rest home. I'm sure I can find someone to help unload it and be back pretty quick. Why don't you—" he flicked a speck of sawdust off her nose "—take your shower and heat up some of that turkey chowder you made yesterday for dinner?"

Ariel nodded, and he bent to pluck the flannel shirt out of the wood chips, where she'd carelessly thrown it. He shook off most of the chips and held it out to her, but he didn't let go when she reached for it. Ariel looked at him questioningly.

"Build a fire in your bedroom, too," he suggested quietly. He'd seen the answer to his unasked question in her eyes. Tonight he was staying.

They lay close together in her bed in the bell tower, the first, impatient demands of passion satisfied. They were reluctant to sleep, wanting instead to savor for as long as possible the joy they'd found in the sanctuary of the tower. Here, for a few precious hours, the specters of death and suspicion and distrust were forbidden.

Ryan's hand tangled in her hair, weaving moonbeams through the gold, letting it fall over his chest like a silken blanket. "How did a virgin manage to write such good love scenes?"

She twisted over onto her stomach to give him an innocent look. "My mother always said I had an excellent imagination." Her finger traced lazy circles through the silky black hair around his navel.

He detained her wandering hand. "Why did you remain a virgin so long?" he asked curiously. "I'm not complaining, you understand—" he gave her a quick kiss "—but you certainly bucked the trend and, as beautiful as you are—" she was starting to shake her head when his mouth stopped her again, longer this time "—you must have had countless opportunities." He rolled them onto their sides, and an easy arm around her waist kept her close.

She shrugged off the question with a studied casualness. "My parents impressed on all us kids that sex wasn't a form of aerobic exercise, but a part of a very strong commitment to another person—a commitment to build a life together, maybe raise a family—and I just never wanted that with anyone."

"Marriage," Ryan murmured, watching her closely.

She gave him a quick glance, then looked away. "Yes." She was silent for a long moment; then he felt her release a long, quiet sigh. She continued in a matter-of-fact voice, "Then, too, I'm the oldest, so I had the responsibility of setting an example for my brothers and sisters.

"But maybe—" her hand unconsciously sought his as she smiled softly "—the greatest reason was seeing my parents' marriage, how devoted they still are to each other. Yet they've allowed each other to develop as individuals, too. I want that."

"So you planned to save yourself for your husband?"

"Certainly a ridiculously outdated notion." She dismissed it with a flip of her hand.

"No." He looked deep into her shadowed blue eyes. "A lovely notion."

Ariel swallowed, her throat suddenly dry, then managed to send him a look of pure devilment. "Of course," she added thoughtfully, "being the daughter of a minister in a very small town also might have helped."

He laughed in delighted surprise. "A preacher's kid. No wonder you didn't know how to cuss." He looked at her suspiciously. "But I thought the preacher's kids were always the wildest ones in town."

"I didn't know how to do a lot of things, Ryan Jones, until I met you," she retorted wryly. "And I was the most disgustingly sedate preacher's kid you ever saw until a little-old-lady writing professor convinced me that my future lay in racy novels." Ariel's grin was irresistible. "Even if she didn't think my first book was sexy enough."

Ryan's hand smoothed the bright fall of her hair. "Maybe they're too romantic for most men," he said resting her head on his shoulder as she laughed in rueful agreement, "but they are everything Mrs. Donner said. I can see why you've been so successful."

His lips brushed over the top of her head. "Your family doesn't know who you are, do they? That's why you give out that story about being a historical researcher."

She grimaced, picking at the white piping on her navy sheets. "I've always been afraid it would embarrass my parents if people knew their number-one daughter wrote sexy—" Ryan nipped her shoulder warningly "Okay, *historical* romances," she conceded.

"Part of my college education was paid for by a scholarship from my father's church. The members raised the money with bake sales, church suppers, raffles. I never wanted them to know what I did with the education they helped pay for."

"You have nothing to be ashamed of, Ariel." A long forefinger trailed up her bare arm and across her milky shoulder to the hollow in her throat. "And I doubt your parents would be as embarrassed as you seem to think. Their values come through in your books quite clearly." He knew they were her values for all her blithe talk. Marriage, a man's and a woman's affirmation of faith in each other and a future together, was what all her heroines believed in. She did, too. He just wished he had her faith.

He nibbled up her throat to her ear. "Did Dennis know?"

She shied a little from the exquisite tickle of his warm breath. "Mmm-hmm. I had to tell him." She giggled. "He had this crazy idea I was somebody's mistress."

Ryan didn't laugh. He would have had the same crazy idea and hated it at least as much as DiSanto undoubtedly had. Sliding down in her bed, he pressed his arms around her to bring their bare bodies together. In the dead quiet of the house, they drifted off to sleep at last.

A hand had slipped between her knees and was sliding inexorably upward. "What are you doing?" she murmured sleepily. Sable lashes fluttered open, then closed again as she rubbed her cheek over the silky-crisp hair and warm flesh of his chest.

The dark velvet voice drawling in her ear sent shivers up her back. "I would think it's obvious."

Her body was soft and warm with sleep. With languorous deep kisses and slow hands he brought her to full wakefulness.

Ariel sat up and leaned over him, the sheet caught over her left shoulder. Ryan lay quietly, his hands still, to see what she would do. The midnight moon shone through the glass walls of the bell tower, silvering her blond hair and turning her skin to translucent white porcelain. The figure bending over him might have been a beautiful, cold and lifeless statue, but the fingers brushing through the hair down to the smooth skin of his chest were warmly alive. They hesitated, then caressed lightly over his nipples, making his breath catch in his chest. He looked into her face, illuminated by the pearly cataract of light.

Her expression was intent as he allowed her to satisfy her curiosity about his body. His right hand reached up and idly brushed aside the sheet. It floated to her waist, revealing her breasts, moon frosted white skin and dark, mysterious centers. A slow, seductive smile curved her mouth. She trailed one set of fingertips over the sensitive skin of his abdomen.

"What are *you* doing?" He grinned lazily. His hand slid around the back of her neck to bring that giving, wonderfully sensual mouth closer.

She resisted, one raised eyebrow expressing her sly surprise. "Exploring. I would have thought it was obvious." Her instinctively clever fingers teased his navel, then moved lower over his twitching skin.

He inhaled sharply and felt the sharp claws of desire deep in his belly. "Two," he breathed, "can cover more territory." His free hand glided up her back, bending her to him as he arched up. The top of his tongue touched her breast.

Ariel felt her stomach clench with anticipation as her body began to change, heating, softening, opening. Her breathing deepened and slowed, as did the movements of her hand.

Ryan's lips closed around her nipple. He suckled gently, letting her unique taste seep slowly through him. Her wordless murmur of pleasure was echoed by his, as his lips and tongue and her hand fell into the same rhythm, languid and soul deep. Her head lolled back as Ariel arched nearer to his delight-giving mouth. His hips shifted, telegraphing his need for more of her touch.

But their caresses became too exquisite, crossing the line between excruciating pleasure and pain. The bed shifted as Ryan pulled himself up. The iron grasp of his hand on her wrist stopped her poignant torture of him. She felt the stroking of his strong fingers through her hair as he cradled her head a breath away from his. "Ah, witch, I want this to last," he whispered hoarsely as he took her mouth.

She wanted it to last, too, but with the first delicate probing of his tongue, she knew it was too late for leisurely pleasuring. Her hand captured his jaw, and she returned his kiss with a furious urgency, telling him how great was her hunger, her need, her love.

Ryan groaned deep in his chest, rising above her. Ariel's head fell back deepening their kiss. Her hand was freed as his other arm slid around her waist. His hard body and avid mouth forced her slow, backward fall onto the tangled sheets. His hand explored her hip and thigh, back up the soft inner flesh, teasing at the top, then moving to clamp her arching hips to the bed, holding her still as his mouth worked down deliciously from her breast. He could feel the headlong race of her heart falter, then pound even faster. His tongue flicked over the quivering skin of her stomach like a liquid flame, burning intricate patterns, lower and lower.

The anticipation of its ultimate destination became a maddening torment. When his searching mouth at last touched the heated core of her, madness overcame her.

Ariel's hands clawed at his back, digging into his tight muscles urging him over her. Ryan heard her incoherent cry, then his name on the breath that shuddered from her body as he drove her to the first peak. He thrilled to that cry, determined to drive her higher yet. He was greedy for the dark, sweet taste of her, high on the power he felt as he relentlessly controlled her mindless body with his.

Ariel was beyond pleading with him to take her. Speech was no longer possible. The most primitive need to fill the sweetly aching void inside her ruled her. With a sudden surge of impossible energy, her slender hands locked over his shoulders and wrenched his heavier, stronger body up hers. Her trembling thighs tightened around his hips, demanding that he satisfy the need he had created.

Ryan's ruthless command over his own need was destroyed. "Next time," he groaned against her arched throat. "We'll make it last next time." He thrust into the moist heat that was so ready for him. Gritting his teeth, he held himself still above her, denying his body's insistent demands that he enjoy the deep, pulsing pleasures immediately. "Ariel, look at me," he rasped.

Midnight-blue eyes, hazed with passion, opened to see his own eyes glowing fiercely above her.

"We belong together now," he said almost violently. "Do you understand, Ariel? Nothing," his voice was harsh with passion as his body began to move, emphasizing the truth of each word, "nothing is going to take you away from me."

"Or you from me." Her eyes closed as she began to move with him.

The fierce exhilaration that surged through him at her words swept away his control. He joined her straining reach for the apex of perfect pleasure. They found it together with a brilliant burst of heart-shattering joy that banished, for a time, the dark shadow lengthening over them.

* * *

Ryan lay on his back, utterly relaxed, totally sated. He could, he thought, happily spend the rest of his life here, like this. He tried to fight off the sleep that had claimed Ariel almost immediately. What greater contentment could there possibly be, he wondered, than to lie in this fantastically comfortable bed, holding your woman, soft and warmed from loving, asleep in your arms as you gazed up at the beautiful diamond stars glittering in the black velvet sky? His eyes closed on a sigh of pure pleasure as one of the beautiful stars fell to its death across the inky night.

Chapter 12

Ariel was dreaming that the telephone was ringing. She hoped someone would answer it soon, because she certainly wasn't about to, not when it meant leaving a warm bed and the even warmer body curled around hers. She dreamed on, not hearing softly growled curses when bare feet hit a cold floor and colder air hit a bare body. She woke up only when she realized that, while the bed was still warm, the body was gone.

She threw off the quilt and danced naked over the icy floorboards until she found her fleece slippers behind the mirror. Her teeth were chattering by the time she shivered into the pink nightshirt she grabbed off the back of the closet door and tried to button up the countless tiny buttons with stiff fingers.

She reached the bottom step in time to hear Ryan's quietly despairing curse. He was leaning against her desk, running a hand through his rumpled black hair distractedly as he listened to whoever was on the other end of the phone. His eyes had closed in an angry scowl before he could see her, and he rubbed the bridge of his nose absently. He'd slipped on only his jeans, zipping but not buttoning them. His ankles were crossed, his long bare toes curled against the cold floor. The skin on his belly and shoulders was roughed into gooseflesh, yet he seemed oblivious to the cold, concentrating only on the obviously bad news coming from the other end of the phone line. Ariel felt a chill that had nothing to do with the lack of heat in the house.

To give him privacy she slipped out into the hall and opened the front door a crack. Sometimes the neighbor at the end of the lane brought by the Sunday paper from Missoula and left it on her doorstep. Ariel stooped down and picked up the paper and a package that had apparently been left in his mailbox by mistake.

Ryan was still on the phone when she came back in. With his back to her, he didn't see her as she set the paper and package on her desk and moved toward the kitchen. When she turned on the water to fill her coffee maker he heard her and turned, his eyes tracking her automatically as she moved quietly around the room.

"No!" he shouted forcefully. "Don't worry about that, I said. There's no way in hell he can do that. I'll file a writ of endangerment so fast it'll make his head spin." He paused. "No, I'll come up with something and leave as soon as I can." He spoke for another minute or two, then hung up.

He shivered violently. "God, it's cold in here!" Ariel was in the living room kneeling before the stove, laying in kindling. As he crossed to her, he gathered up the rainbow afghan she had thrown over the back of the couch. He crouched behind her, draping the afghan over his shoulders and then wrapping it around her as his arms crossed over her breasts.

"What did we do, forget to stoke the stoves again when we went to bed?" He chuckled, burrowing his cold nose into the warm curve of her shoulder.

There was no humor in the tension she felt radiating into her back from his taut body, and there had been none in that phone call. "Yes," she murmured, striking a match and swinging the door shut. She turned in his arms, and her fingers whisked the tousled black hair off his forehead. "Who was on the phone, Ry?"

"You can keep this nightshirt," he murmured, his gaze wandering down the front of the soft pink material to the shirttail brushing the carpet behind her. His darkening eyes ticked off the Victorian ruching high around her neck, the fuzzy smocking over her breasts and the tiny shell buttons marching primly from her neck to her knees. "I can have such fantasies while I'm undoing all these buttons," he growled against her throat.

He arched her tightly to him under the afghan, his hands rubbing leisurely up her back. Ariel was caught between his thighs as his hands ran back to her hips, securing her warmly in the saddle of his. His strong fingers flexed, and an involuntary moan escaped her as he pressed her closer to his hard warmth. One hand slipped around and up to the first button of her shirt.

Ariel caught the hand at her throat. She kissed his fingers quickly, then cradled them to her breast. As she sat back on her heels the afghan slid off their shoulders. With the fire's heat, neither noticed. "What's wrong, Ry? Please tell me." Her worried blue eyes, huge in her pale face, searched his. They were shuttered once again, revealing nothing.

A muscle in Ryan's cheek twitched; then he sagged back on his heels. He brought up his other hand and laced their fingers together tightly. Was there no end to the lies he had to keep telling her? When would things finally be open and honest between them?

"There's trouble with that case I've been helping my partner with. He wants me to come back right away and help him out."

Ariel controlled her voice carefully to keep the ridiculous panic she was beginning to feel out of it. "You have to leave? Today?"

He nodded. "The trial resumes tomorrow." His tone became very casual. "Too bad you can't come with me, but you'll be safer here, of course."

Ariel's shock was showing clearly in her face, and he felt it in her suddenly icy hands. Unconsciously he began to chafe some warmth into her freezing fingers.

"I would be safe with you. Whoever's after me wouldn't know where I was," she suggested hesitantly in a whisper he could barely hear.

"If you change the routine you've had for so long, he's liable to be scared off. It may be months before he thinks it's safe to try again." His voice was so damned reasonable that she wanted to scream. "And you'll have to wait those months." *And so will I,* he added silently. "Don't you want it over with, so you can get on with your life?" *A life we might share.*

She said nothing, just stared at him as if not really seeing him.

"Don't worry; you'll be fine here. I'll let the chief know I'm leaving. There won't be any problems while I'm gone, I'm sure." Who was he trying to convince, he wondered, Ariel or himself? "Just keep the home fires burning till I get back."

As soon as the flip words left his mouth, he knew it had been the wrong time for a lousy joke. She was stiff and cold in his arms.

"This isn't your home, Ryan," she pointed out expressionlessly, "and I'm not your wife."

He answered her very softly. "I know where my home is, Ariel, and what you aren't." He dropped her hands and stood up slowly, like a tired old man. "I have to call the airline."

Ryan walked back to the phone, and Ariel went back into the kitchen as if she were sleepwalking through a bad dream. Automatically she poured two mugs of coffee, adding exactly the amount of milk Ryan liked to one. So, the novelty had worn off sooner than she'd thought it would. Her harsh laugh turned into a sob, and she almost choked on the gulp of coffee she took.

The case was just a flimsy excuse to leave. She could see through his lie as clearly as if it were glass. He just didn't care about her as much as she did about him. How could he? If he did, he couldn't leave now, when she needed him so badly. Didn't he understand that even with a whole army division surrounding the school-house to keep her safe, she wouldn't *feel* safe unless he was inside it with her?

She glanced at him as he hung up the phone without speaking and walked toward her, his face unreadable. Maybe he did understand; he just didn't care.

"The line was busy," he said as he picked up his coffee.

"That's too bad. I'm sure you'll get through in a minute," she said tonelessly, calmly sipping her coffee.

She didn't notice how badly her hand was shaking, he realized. The scalding coffee sloshed onto her wrist, and she didn't even seem to feel it. God, what an impossible position his brother had put him in. Did he leave her in ignorance, sure he was lying to her again and hating him for it, or did he tell her the truth? Davidson wanted her back in San Francisco to make the bait more accessible...and to ask her why a Bahamian bank had sent a letter to her house telling her that she was now the owner of an account with over half a million dollars in it.

Rick felt they were close to the real murderer now; there was no need to expose Ariel to any more danger. If someone could just hold off Davidson for a week or so... And who better than Ariel's new attorney, Ryan Jones—who just happened to have an appointment at nine-thirty tomorrow morning to discuss his client's not very-protective custody? Rick's machinations were peculiar indeed for a man who had professed to believe Ariel was as guilty as his boss did.

The hard bitter lines Ariel hadn't seen for days were back in Ryan's face. "It shouldn't take more than a few days to wrap everything up, and then I'll be back."

Her face lit with a curiously wistful smile for a moment before the mask of utter impassivity slid back into place. "Of course you will."

Ryan's mug slammed down onto the table. Ariel jumped at the sudden violence in his action. Milky coffee began seeping from the crack in the bottom of the mug. His temper was at the flashpoint. The quiet desperation in her eyes and the frigidly dignified words were threatening to crack his control like angry screaming never could have.

He turned his back to her and stared sightlessly through the window over the sink. If he had to look at her, his control would break completely.

The heavy silence in the kitchen was darkening the sunlit room. Ariel sighed shudderingly, and fierce arms closed roughly around her. She turned, giving herself up to the temporary luxury of his protective embrace.

His words whispered over the bare skin of her neck, melting a little of the fear icing her heart. "Please try to understand, Ariel. It just isn't safe for you to go."

His arms cradled her tenderly, when what he wanted was to crush her to him and hold her forever where he knew she would be safe. His fear at leaving her alone, unprotected, was ripping him apart. They stood in each other's arms for a long, silent moment.

The phone lines into the Missoula airport seemed to be permanently busy, and Ryan finally went across the hall to dress and pack. He reappeared in a navy pin-stripe suit, the jacket hooked over his shoulder, carrying one suitcase. Ariel was just putting their breakfast on the table. She had managed bacon and toast and a perfect omelet that Murphy ended up eating. They made careful small talk that completely avoided what was uppermost in each of their minds.

Unable to sit still any longer, Ariel shoved back her chair and left the table. Remembering the package she'd found on her doorstep, she sat again, this time in the swivel chair at her desk. She pulled the package onto her lap and glanced at the postmark, then began to tear off the brown wrapping paper.

The package was jerked rudely out of her hands. "Where the hell did this come from?" Ryan demanded furiously. He turned the parcel over gingerly, examining all sides carefully.

"It was on the front step this morning. It must have been delivered to Mr. Hanson by mistake, and he brought it by with the paper." She calmly grabbed it away from Ryan and proceeded with her unwrapping.

Ryan jerked it away again and held it up over his head, out of her reach. "Who's it from?"

"My mother," she said evenly. "Ryan, I am not going to wrestle you for it. Now hand it over."

He lowered the box, but didn't give it to her. He walked into the kitchen very carefully, set the box on the counter gently and began filling the kitchen sink with water. Out of the corner of his eye he saw Ariel reaching for the package.

"Do not touch that package, Ariel." His voice was low and dangerous.

"Ryan, I don't know what you think you're doing, but this is from my mother and—"

"Uh-huh, and you thought the poisoned candy was from two lovesick high school boys, too," he reminded her.

He started to lower the parcel toward the water-filled sink with one hand.

Ariel hissed in frustration, her eyes widening with disbelief. With both hands she seized his wrist, staying the package inches above the water. She forced herself to speak calmly. "Ryan, the postmark on the package is Weaverville, where my parents live. That's why you were suspicious of the candy, wasn't it—the postmark wasn't from anywhere in Montana?"

Ryan nodded, but didn't release the package.

Ariel nodded in return. "That's what I finally figured out. John, the postmaster, knows everyone in Weaverville, and he knows me. No stranger could mail a package to me without him remembering it. I don't think the killer would be that stupid."

Ryan stared hard at the box in his hand, as if trying to see through the brown paper, and finally handed it over.

Ariel sat down at her desk and returned to her unwrapping. "Why were you going to put it in the water?" she asked curiously.

"I thought it might be a bomb," he answered matter-of-factly. "Water would ruin the detonating mechanism, but not any fingerprints. I'd have called the state police to disarm it."

Ariel blanched. The funny incident was suddenly not so funny. The last bit of wrapping paper tore free and out tumbled eight copies of *RimFire*, Felicia Fury's latest romance, available in bookstores and supermarkets everywhere.

With numb fingers and a feeling of dread, Ariel reached reluctantly for the note on her mother's blue stationery that had fallen out with the paperbacks.

"What does she say?" Ryan asked interestedly, trying to read the note over her shoulder. It was a short one.

Ariel looked at him dazedly over her shoulder. "She says..." Her voice came out in a squeak, and she tried again. "She says she would like me to autograph these, one for her and the rest for her friends." Ariel had to stop to clear her throat. "She mentions that she was suspicious about Felicia Fury's identity with the last two books, but knew for sure with this one. She recognized the heroine's two little boys as my brothers. She wants to borrow my copies of the other books to read; she can't find any in the used bookstore." Ariel looked at him, shaking her head slowly. "I didn't even know my mother read books like mine," she whispered, shocked.

Ryan threw back his head, laughing at her astonishment. Sheepishly, Ariel joined in, and for a few moments the room was filled with laughter. Then their eyes met, and their laughter abruptly died. Ryan's suspicions about the very real possibility of a bomb and his imminent departure killed it very effectively. A pall of depression settled over her.

Wearily she bent to gather up the books. She supposed she was really very lucky. For some reason she was sure that the idea of a bomb had occurred to the killer. Fortunately for her, he apparently lacked the knowledge to make one.

The phone rang once more, and Ryan answered it. Ariel could tell by Ryan's end of the conversation that it was Chief Dye. Too upset to wonder how he'd known Ryan was leaving, she climbed the stairs to dress while he and Ryan discussed the least useless ways of keeping her safe.

She came out of her bathroom, still in her nightshirt, to find him standing by the bed, unbuttoning the cuff of his ivory, satin striped shirt. It was already hanging open, pulled free of his slacks.

"My plane doesn't leave until two o'clock," he said huskily. His fingers reached for the first small button at the neck of her nightshirt.

The fresh fire she'd built in the blue enamel stove was already heating the room. The curtains filtering the midmorning sunshine gave it a dusky gold light. The air was warm and thick with an almost tangible sensuality.

Ariel had been disconcerted by her body's sudden addiction to Ryan's, even a little embarrassed. Suddenly it became even more pervasive, as if her body realized that the fix it needed to get through the long days and longer nights was about to be provided.

They took the time to savor each nuance of taste and texture and response. Hands and mouths that could have been rough and demanding were gentle and coaxing. Pleasure that could have been rushed and desperate was unhurried and relaxed, drawn out to the fullest before a new pleasure was discovered and totally explored.

Ryan undid the tiny pink buttons, lingering over each new bit of soft flesh that was exposed to his fingers and eager mouth. As he sank to his knees her finger twined through the heavy blue-black silk of his hair. Her head fell back, and her stance unconsciously widened. When the pleasure of his agile, searching tongue became too delicious, she urged him up. His trip back up her body was leisurely. As he straightened fully, her nightshirt floated to the floor like a pink cloud.

Ariel took her turn to undress him. His shoes and socks were gone already. She took off his shirt and draped it carefully over a chair. The silky-crisp hair of his chest and belly slid between her cool, slender fingers as they followed the dark path narrowing down to his belt. Her body drifted down along his until her knees touched the worn rag rug. Her nimble hands unbuckled his belt, drawing it slowly from around his waist. She savored the little quiver of pleasure rippling through his muscles as she unhooked his slacks and slid them down his lean flanks. A touch on the back of his ankles and he stepped out of them gracefully. She folded them precisely and laid them across the seat of the chair.

She reached back up, and her hands slipped inside his briefs, dragging them free. She let her palms glide first down the warm satin skin of his hips, then enjoying the change as they caressed the hair roughened skin of his thighs and calves. He kicked his briefs free, and her fingertips brushed back up his legs.

Ryan breathed her name into the still, warm air. "Ariel. Oh, sweet, love." His hands seized her shoulders tenderly and she slithered up his body. He twisted unexpectedly and guided her gentle fall to the bed.

The room was peaceful, filled with the quiet sounds of their accelerating breathing, small sighs, bodies subtly shifting on crisp sheets, the faint hiss and crackle of the fire. The light fragrance of his citrus after-shave and her spring flowers-summer sunshine cologne mingled with earthier, natural scents.

His stroking hands wove an invisible web of desire over her body. His mouth grazed, licked and tugged, breathed hot whispers over her skin. The slow, delicious slide of his calloused palm over her hip and down her smooth leg sent cool shivers through her that melted into a shimmering pool between her thighs.

She wanted to give pleasure as well as take it. Rising up on one elbow, she splayed her hand across his chest and slowly pressed him back on the bed. The balance of power shifted to her as she leaned down to kiss him. Her lips traveled across his mouth, her teeth nibbling delicately at his bottom lip, inviting that beautiful, hard mouth to play. His lips softened and bonded to hers in a kiss that scintillated through her blood like burning gunpowder. Lazily they took turns taking the kiss deeper. Her lips wandered to the sensitive hollow of his shoulder, and a hot spark skidded down his spine. Then her mouth journeyed lower, following her adept hands. Her tongue tarried at the hardened brown nub of his nipple, then dipped into his navel. He tangled his hands into the sheet to allow her freedom to pleasure him . . . and herself.

The top of her silky head brushed the twitching flesh of his belly as she shifted between his thighs. Her warm tongue rasped languorously, sampling forbidden flavors, salty-sweet, tangy. His body slowly arched off the bed like a bow drawn back by a powerful archer, his head twisting sinuously on the pillow.

Her low laugh whispered over him. His fingers buried themselves in the golden floss of her hair and dragged her head up to his. Her smile was primitively satisfied as she watched him lose control.

Suddenly she was on her back, pinned by the muscled thigh pushing imperiously between hers. The raw hunger in his face and the ruthlessness in his movements might have frightened her. Instead they exhilarated her, filling her with an exultant power that she could make this cool, self-contained man burn for her as he made her burn for him. She absorbed the shock of the primal joining of his body with hers, touched with a trace of savagery. Then the long, silken friction began, and she could think no more.

Their bodies flushed and totally spent, they drifted together in a golden haze. At last they were forced to rise reluctantly and dress, interrupting each other a time or two to wordlessly caress and kiss.

The two-hour drive to Missoula was quiet, each of them busy with private thoughts. In the parking lot of the airport Ryan showed Ariel how to lock the front wheel hubs and shift the balky transmission into four-wheel drive. It had been decided that Ariel would use his power wagon while he was gone.

At the boarding gate he prayed that she could control the tears that had filled her eyes and were threatening to spill over. If she cried, no force on earth would get him to leave her behind. Deliberately he riled her out of her tears.

"Four things," he said imperiously. His long fingers ticked them off in front of her nose. "One—keep the dead bolt locked at all times, even when you're home. Two—keep the pickup locked in the garage when you're not using it. Three—keep your lead foot off the gas pedal of my truck."

Ariel made a rude face and the tears receded. When he paused, she asked dutifully. "What's number four?"

His voice was low and fierce. "I'm coming back!" He wished he could be sure she believed him.

They exchanged a brief kiss as he held at bay his heartsickening fear and worry at leaving her. There was so much he wanted, needed, to say, but this wasn't the place, and the time wasn't right. Would it ever be? Gently disengaging the hands clinging around his neck, he held them bruisingly for a moment. When her hands were free Ariel clasped them tightly behind her back to keep her arms from winding around him again.

"I'll call you every day," he whispered. "Here are a couple of numbers where you can reach me if you need me." He stuffed a scrap of paper into her jacket pocket.

His thumb lingered over her cheek, as if trying to memorize it softness one last time. Then he was striding away from the frost-pitted concrete toward a red-and-white jet.

The trip up to the airport hadn't seemed as long as the one home. She dashed the foolish tears from her eyes as the feeling of abandonment finally swamped her. Of course he was coming back. Her grim laugh echoed in the truck cab. He had to get his precious truck, didn't he?

Watching him cross the runway had made her realize what an illusion their life together during the past two weeks had really been. He was going back to his real life, where beautiful navy blue silk and wool pin-striped suits, perfect tone-on-tone ivory shirts and burgundy satin ties were the standard dress, not old jeans and flannel shirts. Reality wasn't scuffed leather sneakers, a ninety-year-old schoolhouse in the boondocks of Montana, sitting around at night watching old movies on TV, fishing, splitting firewood or messing around in the kitchen fixing dinner.

Reality was scuffless black Italian shoes with elegantly smooth wing-tips, a house on the beach in Malibu, fancy restaurants, beautiful women, and the excitement of the courtroom. *That,* she reminded herself viciously, was his real world, a world in which he might decide she had no place.

She pulled down the garage door and let herself into her cold house. Murphy looked past her expectantly, then whined questioningly when she saw that Ariel was alone. "He'll be back soon, girl," Ariel assured the dog with a cheerfulness she didn't feel.

She awoke much too early the next morning with a familiar ache in the small of her back and the sudden awareness that she had been appallingly irresponsible. Unaccountably, the ache also made her a little sad. She forced aside the unbidden mental vision of a small scamp with a rascally grin and blue-black hair.

Ryan was accustomed, of course, to women who handled the modern little social niceties like pregnancy prevention themselves. Yet he had certainly known she was neither sophisticated enough nor experienced enough not to have committed the ultimate faux pas by becoming accidently pregnant. She'd never even given it a thought. And she knew quite well that he had done nothing to prevent it, either. It seemed a very odd oversight; Ryan Jones was hardly the sort of man to have "accidents" like that.

The trip to the doctor's office and the little town pharmacy wasn't as mortifying as she had feared. Despite her flawless impersonation of a red-faced, mumbling teenager, the prescription was written out routinely and filled without comment. There were no knowing smirks or raised eyebrows, no pointing fingers or outraged whispers.

Congratulations, Ariel she told herself dryly. At last you're a part of the sexual revolution. A three-months' supply of white dots assuring worry-free, socially acceptable and responsible *fun* is tucked in your purse.

Suddenly her free, helpless laughter filled the cab of the truck. Listen to you! she chided herself. You sound like a self-righteous old maid eating sour grapes.

She was irrevocably in love with this man. He was the one she had waited twenty-seven years to share herself with. And she had enjoyed every glorious minute of it. Whatever happened, she knew she would never regret her decision.

Maybe it wasn't particularly rational to fall in love with a stranger, but she really hadn't been given any choice in the matter. She *had* a choice of whether she would act on that love, and she had made her choice freely, joyfully. She wasn't naively confident that they would live happily ever after together. Her choice could have a very high price, but she was willing to pay it. She suspected that even if she lived as long as Bessie, loving Ryan Jones would be the greatest adventure of her life.

The second greatest was going to be staying alive. She wasn't naive about that, either. She was all too aware of her vulnerability. She was inclined to agree with what Ryan had told her and Ted Dye believed: that whoever wanted her dead had made only one lightning personal appearance so far. He'd set up his delayed strikes then left as suddenly as he had come. Strangers in the valley were always noticed. Only during some event that drew an out-of-town crowd, like the apple festival, would he be able to enjoy anonymity. The next logical time for him to strike was the coming weekend, when deer-hunting season opened and the town would again be full of strangers, drawn by the valley's large deer population. Still, she would take no unnecessary chances.

By Monday evening, only one day after Ryan's departure, she was already a little stir-crazy, Following one of Ryan's forceful "suggestions," she had locked herself inside the schoolhouse after coming home from town. She had baked pumpernickle and made turkey noodle soup that she wasn't hungry enough to eat, then worked on *RangeFire*. As the day had worn on the ache in her back had disappeared, but its vague echo seemed to be lingering near her heart. And Murphy kept looking at her accusingly, as if asking her what nastiness she had done to make Ryan leave.

She found herself reaching again into the tissue box on top of her desk. It was dumb to cry over a book, especially one of your own. And she was about to commit the unpardonable sin of writing a romance with an unhappy ending. No matter how she tried, she couldn't seem to get Luke and Drucilla to resolve their differences. Luke was about to ride off into the sunset—alone. James, her editor, would have heart failure, and she wouldn't make a dime.

She switched off the word processor, not bothering to save what she'd just spent two and a half hours writing. She stood, hugging her arms around herself. Damn, why was she still cold? Maybe she was coming down with something. She'd put on the green wool pants and cream fisherman's knit sweater she wore on the most frigid winter days and built up the fire an hour ago. Now she was sweating, for heaven's sake—and still freezing. Perhaps a hot shower would help.

Ariel kept twisting the hot-water faucet just a little farther as she stood under the steaming water until her scalded skin protested vehemently. After drying off she redressed in her mismatched fuzzy knee socks and a green-sprigged flannel granny gown that would really have made Ryan laugh. After locating her slippers which had migrated under the bed, she strayed over to Ryan's half of the house.

She told herself that she had to keep the stove going to keep the pipes from freezing, but she knew she wouldn't have to worry about that for at least another month. She just wanted to be someplace where she could still sense him. A trace of his after-shave lingered in the cool air, and he had left some books and papers scattered over the maple table. Murphy had bounded up the spiral stairs, sure he had to be around somewhere. Ariel trudged up after her when the dog refused to come when she was called.

Prowling around his bedroom, Ariel poked listlessly through the jumble on the oak dresser, some loose change, the bandanna he'd tied around her hair the morning she'd made the soap, the watch she'd seen on his arm every day for two weeks. A discreet gold watch had nestled in the dark hair of his wrist under his suit cuff when he'd left. She picked up the old skin-diver's watch and wound it carefully. The brass-and-chrome case was worn on the corners, and the crystal was scratched, but the steady ticking in her ear was oddly comforting.

He'd left clothes scattered around, too. She picked up an inside-out gray sweatshirt and rubbed the soft fleece over her cheek. It smelled of him, the clean scent of his ordinary soap and the musky sweat he worked up exercising his leg. She slipped the shirt over her head and felt suddenly warm and very tired. She went back to her own room to sleep, the brown dog trailing dejectedly behind her.

Lamplight gleamed dully on the long barrel of his hunting rifle. There was a brighter flash as the light caught briefly on the lens of the powerful scope mounted on the barrel as he slid the gun carefully into a custom-made, tooled leather case.

The rifle hadn't been dirty, he reflected, fitting the cleaning supplies precisely into their place in the kit box. Still, it was best to leave as little to chance as possible. He couldn't afford a misfire because of a speck of dirt.

He wiped the cleaning oil from his fingers on a clean rag. He would certainly have liked to have a silencer, but acquiring one would draw attention to himself. He would just have to do without.

He set the rifle case in an olive-drab, army-issue duffle bag, the type favored by the seedy hitchhikers he often saw along the highway. The bag gave the appearance of being full of all his worldly possessions. In fact, it held only the rifle and a quantity of crumpled newspapers. He would have to check it in as luggage at the airport; he'd never get it past the scanners as carryon baggage.

He stored it in his bedroom closet. Pity he wasn't the shot Dennis had been, but his skill was . . . adequate.

Chapter 13

Most people would never receive a letter from the Grand Bahama Bank of Nassau telling them that there was an account in their name with a balance of $622,300.48. Ariel had never received her letter, but the money was waiting for her just the same. Ryan tossed the letter back onto the kitchen table, the same kitchen table, he reflected, where he'd sat less than a month ago and told his sister-in-law to find him a beautiful virgin over the age of consent, if any still existed. His hard mouth softened in a smile; one *had* existed.

Rick had wisely never sent the letter on to its rightful owner, guessing that Ariel would be so shocked she would do something dangerous and foolhardy, like rushing back to San Francisco to find out what the hell was going on. His brother had guessed correctly, Ryan thought; that was exactly what she would have done, and Davidson would have been ecstatic. She would have been right where he wanted her.

Instead he was here, pretending to be her attorney, coming to negotiate her release from custody so she could spend her money. He stared at his brother, who was seated across the table, bouncing his tiny daughter on his knee and laughing at her squeals of delight. Would Ariel's daughters have their mother's blond hair, he thought absently.

He wasn't pretending, however. He was going to be fighting for Ariel's best interests tomorrow morning, harder than he had fought for any paying client he'd ever had.

He sighed and picked the letter back up. It wasn't going to be easy. This straightforward, innocuous letter was the most damning piece of evidence against her yet. It concerned the account of one Dennis Michael DiSanto. There had been no activity in the account for the past ten months so, pursuant to Mr. DiSanto's instructions, it was being transferred to Miss Ariel Spence. The bank extended a cordial welcome to its new customer and wanted her to know that it would be very happy to serve her in any way possible. Ryan had laughed cynically to himself when he'd come to that line. Any bank would welcome a customer with over six hundred thousand dollars.

Had DiSanto had some disturbing premonition, or had he simply been doing the equivalent of making out a will? The latter, Ryan suspected.

Davidson was convinced that the bank had already performed an invaluable service for Miss Ariel Maria Spence. Long a haven for tax-dodging Americans and a laundry for dirty money, Bahamian banks took in sacks full of soiled dollars and returned them squeaky clean. Ariel's new wealth would be untraceable, the chances of the Internal Revenue Service laying claim to any of it slim at best.

No wonder, Davidson had gloated, she'd put up so little resistance to moving to Montana. She'd known she had only to be patient for a time and the money would be hers. DiSanto had undoubtedly told her about it. She was being compensated twice for setting him up for the hit. The one thing she couldn't have known was that she would be double-crossed and set up for a hit herself.

The hell of it was that Davidson's theories had merit. They were plausible; they fit the evidence and a Grand Jury might well find them convincing.

Another piece of evidence against her, one Ryan knew the district attorney would never present to a Grand Jury but would consider almost as damning, was the fact that she'd retained Ryan Jones to represent her. Even in San Francisco everyone knew you only hired Ryan Jones when you were guilty and only a slick lawyer who knew all the dirty tricks could get you off. And for Ariel he would use every one of them and learn a few new ones besides.

His niece was reclaimed by her mother for the nightly bath, and Rick Jones turned to his brother across the kitchen table.

Ryan gave his brother a long, speculative look. "You're walking a very thin line, you know."

Rick rubbed both hands down his face. "Don't I know it!" he groaned feelingly. "But I didn't know what else to do. I've been sure she wasn't guilty since she lived with us, but Davidson is so sure he's right. I'd thought to let it just ride, that sooner or later he'd give up and she could come home. Then we got word that Garza was about to be arrested. We already knew his connection with DiSanto, and I got a bad feeling." He sent his brother a sidelong look. "That's when I thought of you. A hunch couldn't get her any official protection, but I was sure she was going to need it. You're better than a police bodyguard anyway."

Ryan gave his brother's flattery a dry look.

Rick leaned his head tiredly on his hands. "It turned out to be just as I'd suspected. She knew something somebody else was afraid of, something that seemed so insignificant at the time that she forgot about it." He glanced up hopefully at his brother. "Has she remembered who the third man in the office was yet?"

Ryan shook his head. "No," he replied shortly, "but I'll lay you a thousand to one it was our man."

"Ryan . . ." Rick reached hesitantly across the table and laid his hand on his brother's arm. "You realize that unless we can find some way to prove he acted alone, Ariel's still going to be under suspicion?"

Ryan shut his eyes wearily. "I know, Rick."

Ariel's nemesis was right on time for his nine-thirty appointment the next morning. Edward James Davidson, district attorney for the county of San Francisco, was a small man, slight, with a thin pointed nose that twitched occasionally, a wispy soft-brown mustache that matched his hair and bright button eyes the color of black coffee. If he'd been an animal, he would have been an innocuous field mouse. However, Ryan knew that this field mouse had the soul of a wolverine. Ferociously tenacious, Davidson would sink his teeth into his victim, worrying it and shaking it until he made his kill. And his next victim was going to be Ariel Spence, unless he could be tempted to attack a juicier one.

"How long have you been Miss Spence's attorney, Mr. Jones?" The district attorney smiled, showing sharp white teeth.

"Since she's gotten tired of people trying to kill her," Ryan replied blandly.

Davidson merely smiled again. He would be an interesting man to play poker with, Ryan thought.

He smiled genially at the D.A. and the other man in the office, Rick. "Suppose we talk about how you're going to keep my client alive, gentlemen?"

Edward Davidson explained his plan slowly and carefully. If Ariel came back to her town house in San Francisco she would be much safer with round-the-clock police protection and his personal guarantee of her safety. But Ryan read the silences between the careful words.

It would be leaked that she was home, to the tabloids, most likely. The waters surrounding the murders would be stirred up again with more salacious headlines and speculation. The killer would have to be blind not to know she was back when the headlines would be flaunting her presence from every supermarket checkout stand. The killer would make his move; the police would make theirs—and Ariel would be caught in the cross fire.

They argued it back and forth politely and then, at the properly orchestrated moment, Rick produced a confidential report from an IRS agent grateful for the tip Ryan, through his brother, had supplied. Suddenly the little D.A. saw a fatter victim to sink his teeth into.

Ryan stared out at the foggy drizzle while he waited for his brother to finish plotting new strategy with his boss. Davidson wouldn't forget about Ariel; he was just going to leave her be until he could prove that his new suspect and his old one were in league. Ryan knew the district attorney didn't expect it to take long; Ariel Spence and the man knew each other very well. But at least he'd bought her a little time.

Ariel had gotten up with the cool, mid-October sun. After dressing in a chrome-yellow sweater and bright blue pants to try to cheer herself up, she rambled downstairs. She turned away from the waiting word processor with marked distaste. Gazing longingly out the window over the kitchen sink, sipping coffee, she watched the weak yellow light grow stronger. It gilded the tops of the trees along the river, seeping slowly down through the shadows to sparkle off the silvery water. Long, lonely runs along the river bank weren't very sensible anymore, but she was dying to go outside. Why hadn't she ever noticed before how big and quiet this house really was?

After sharing her breakfast with Murphy, she gassed up the heavy chain saw and marched determinedly to the remains of Ryan's raffle prize. Gingerly she heaved and rolled a log off the haphazard pile. Four strong tugs on the saw's starter rope produced an ear-numbing drone, and the mechanical beaver began gnawing into the wood.

Several hours later she sat on the back step and lolled back on her elbow under the noontime sun. A slight breeze from the river dried the wisps of hair that had escaped from her ponytail and stuck to her damp neck. The strong clean scent of fresh pine was the smell of satisfaction. The pile of logs didn't look appreciably smaller, but there was a respectable stack of firewood beside it.

Ariel flexed her sore shoulders and rose from the steps. Hefting the saw and ax, she went inside to store them away until her next attack of cabin fever. She took the empty gas can and walked through the house into the garage to put it in the back of Ryan's truck. She left the garage door open so she would be sure to hear the phone if Ryan called.

He had been faithful to his promise so far, calling at least once each day. And, he'd only been gone two and a half days, she reminded herself. She'd spent those two and a half days trying to solve the puzzle of Ryan Jones. With his disturbing, distracting influence gone from the house, she found she could think about him a little more objectively.

She was in love with a man who, she suspected, didn't believe in love or in trust. For several years his very survival had depended on his superior talent for deception. Lies and mistrust had been a way of life, and those habits would die hard. She doubted that Ryan Jones had trusted anyone—man or woman—in years.

Did she trust him? She had examined her innermost feelings, the secret ones she seldom chose to confront except under duress. She'd found that she didn't know if she trusted him or not. She wanted to, desperately, because love without trust had little chance of succeeding.

Ariel believed staunchly in love. She didn't just write about it and deposit those healthy checks in the bank, laughing all the while. She knew she was as big a sucker for romance and love and happy endings as her avid readers—probably more so, because she created the illusion, yet still believed every word of it, every heated glance, every heartthrob, every tender vow. It was like a magician being taken in by his own tricks. He'd lied to her, and she knew it, and she loved him anyway.

As she lifted the gas can over the side of the truck she stubbed her toe on one of the cardboard boxes she'd shoved against the brick wall. They contained Dennis's darkroom equipment, cameras and photo files.

Kneeling on the concrete floor, she dragged over one of the three cardboard files and pulled open the drawer. Inside were hundreds of eight-by-ten black-and-white glossies. She and Dennis's brother, Robert, had packed up all the equipment and photos one afternoon and delivered the file boxes to the police. She remembered Robert patiently thumbing through the pictures one by one, seemingly fascinated by them. The boxes hadn't been opened since the police had returned them.

What she really ought to do was sort through this stuff. The chemicals probably weren't fresh anymore and should be disposed of. The expensive equipment wasn't doing anyone any good, either. She pulled a photo out at random, marking its place with her finger.

The picture was of her old neighbor, George Lu and his five-year old great-granddaughter, Amy. They were feeding peanuts to the park squirrels. The pair could be found somewhere in Golden Gate Park almost every Wednesday afternoon. She and Dennis had spent a lot of his Wednesday afternoons off there, too. Dennis had taken countless shots of the spare man who smiled only for his effervescent China doll, Amy.

Ariel smiled softly, remembering the prints in the file. She had persuaded Dennis to make some of them into a little album. Mr. Lu had thanked them gravely in his impeccable Hong Kong English that had always made Ariel's tongue feel clumsy. Then he had sat on a peeling green park bench with Amy, counting the visual treasury of their very special relationship, tears in his old almond eyes. Amy would be in school all day now. Grandpa George would be spending Wednesday afternoon alone.

She replaced the glossy and pulled out one of the last shots. It was of her. The files were full of pictures of her, too. She had been wading in the surf off Point Lobos, her jeans rolled to her knees, but soaked anyway, her hair in pigtails.... Dennis had delighted in taking pictures of her in all her "best" moments—hair flying away on a windy day, face fog-washed and utterly devoid of makeup or hanging upside down on the park jungle gym with Amy.

She kept waiting for the pain these black-and-white memories should evoke. It never came. She had Ryan to thank for that, she realized. He had helped her lay the past to rest at last. There was no pain anymore, only a bittersweet remembrance of all the good times she and Dennis had shared.

She slipped the photo back, but it wouldn't quite go down. She felt around on the bottom of the box and fished out a glassine envelope of negatives. They must have gotten mixed up with the prints when she and Robert had packed things up that day. There on the bottom of the box, they had probably been overlooked by the police, too.

She held a strip of celluloid up to a bright sunbeam burning through the dusty garage window. The picture was of her again, leaning over the arched bridge in the Japanese Tea Garden. It had been drizzling that day, the last time they had been to the park before the afternoon Dennis was shot. Her hair was plastered to her somber face. What had she been thinking?

She glanced rapidly over the remaining strips, light and dark reversed in the negatives. Dennis must never have printed them, because she had never seen the glossies. She scanned the last strip, then stopped at one in the middle, her forehead puckering.

It was a long shot of a grassy slope. Dennis had taken several shots of an elderly woman carefully matching her patient steps to those of a teetering toddler. In this one, something...someone...else was in the upper left corner, partially screened by a bush.

After tearing up the taped lids of three boxes, she finally found the cases with Dennis's cameras and lenses. She held an 80 mm lens over the upper corner of the picture like a magnifying glass, revealing two men. Their heads and chests, along with the pointing arm of the taller man, were magnified into sharp focus. Dennis probably hadn't even noticed them, but the camera's sharper eye had caught the figures hidden behind the shrub. The clothing and hair colors weren't accurate of course, but there was no mistaking the shorter, older man: Patrick Reilly; the man with him, she didn't recognize.

Squinting at the tiny negative, she mentally extended the line of the unknown man's upraised arm. What had he been pointing out to Reilly? Dennis? No, the angle was wrong, he should have been pointing directly at the camera, and he wasn't—he was pointing a little to the left. The left. She had always stood to Dennis's left, and a little behind, so she could pass his film or a lens . . . With a sickening certainty Ariel suddenly knew that she too, had been supposed to die that raw December day in the park. Only an opportune heart attack had saved her.

She blinked away the sudden tears blurring her vision and focused fiercely on the face of her killer. There *was* something familiar about him, about the eyes and the bone structure of his face, half-concealed under a drooping dark mustache and lank, dark hair. Blond, she mentally corrected; it only appeared dark because this was a negative. She ignored that. She did know this man, but she knew him with dark hair, not blond, and without the mustache.

When the name came to her, the blood in her veins crystallized into ice. "No!" she whispered in agonized denial while the name ricocheted in a scream inside her head. As the scream died she remembered at last the face of the third man who had been in Dennis's office with Garza that day. This was the same man.

She scrambled up off the floor and ran inside for Ryan's keys. Less than a minute later she was forcing the power wagon to bolt down the rain-rutted dirt road, ignoring the bone-jarring bucks of the vehicle and the stop sign at the highway.

Minutes later she screeched to a halt in the high school parking lot. "Billy! Billy Greef!" she shouted as she flung open the truck door.

A lanky, dark-headed boy paused in the act of climbing into his red pickup. He looked across the lot for his summoner. A look of shy delight and wonder brightened his homely face when he saw who was running toward him.

"Miss Spence!" His voice was amazingly deep for such a thin body. He shoved the heavy glasses back up on his hawk nose with a nervous gesture.

Ariel clutched his thin arm with steel fingers. "You don't have football practice or anything today, do you?" she demanded shaking his arm fiercely.

His Adam's apple slid up and down several times before he managed a bullfrog croak. "N-no, ma'am. Coach cut me from the team; said I was too sk—"

She cut him off impatiently. "Good! I've got a negative that needs printing. Can you do it right now?"

Billy felt the red flush creeping up to his ears growing hotter. His hazel eyes flicked around the rain-puddled parking lot, seeing a group of his buddies eyeing the interchange between him and the wonderful, so out-of-reach Miss Spence with great interest. He straightened his skinny shoulders and quit slouching. "Sure," he said easily. "I just got a new enlarger last week; I can—"

"Great!" She shoved the strip into his hand. "The third one from the top. Just as soon as you can."

He spared a glance down at the strip of celluloid in his bony hands. "I'll do 'em all," he promised eagerly. "It'll only take a few more minutes, and I've got plenty of—"

"No! Just that one. That's the only one I'm interested in."

"But I can do it easy," Billy persisted persuasively. "There might be something you want to see in one of the others, too."

Ariel felt a hysterical giggle of desperation rising. "No, no. Next time. You can do a whole roll if you want next time," she promised recklessly. "Today I just want the third one, and print it on the largest paper you have."

"Well, okay," he agreed reluctantly. "But I—"

"Thank you, Billy. You just don't know how grateful to you I am." Ariel kissed his cheek quickly and headed back across the parking lot. She called back over her shoulder, "I've got to see Bessie Ruff, and then I'll drop by your house about—" she glanced at the old skin diver's watch pushed halfway up her forearm "—four-thirty. All right?"

"All right," he answered dazedly. Then, catching the eye of his best friend, who was starting determinedly toward him, he shrugged his thin shoulders carelessly under his letter jacket and sauntered nonchalantly back to his pickup. He drove off with a cool flick of his hand to his openmouthed buddies, the spot Miss Spence had kissed burning like fire.

Two hours later Ariel was staring at the glossy prints spread over her round oak dining table. Billy had printed the negative in every size from three by five to eleven by fourteen. Any one would have been all the proof she needed. She would have to let him take whatever of Dennis's darkroom equipment he wanted, she thought absently. Even in the biggest, grainiest print there was no doubt about the identity of the second man.

She opened the closet under the staircase and pulled out the jacket she'd worn the day she'd taken Ryan to the airport. She found the crumpled scrap of paper with the phone numbers that Ryan had stuffed in one of the pockets.

Glancing at the clock in the kitchen as she crossed to the phone, she debated which number to call first. Given the one-hour time difference between Montana and the West Coast, she might be able to catch him at his office, if he wasn't in court. His secretary should certainly be able to get a message to him if he was.

As she smoothed the piece of paper, the better to read the numbers, it occurred to her that she had decided to call Ryan without consciously thinking about it. He, not Rick Jones, and certainly not Edward Davidson, had been the automatic choice to share her news and help her decide what to do about it.

The first number was probably his office. As she read the neatly printed numerals the hair on the back of her neck rose. She didn't know the area code for Los Angeles offhand, but 415 wasn't it. Four one five was the area code for her phone number . . . in San Francisco. Ryan was supposed to be in Los Angeles. Both of these phone numbers were in San Francisco. With numb fingers she dialed the eleven digits of the first number.

After one and a half rings a man answered. It was odd that she hadn't noticed the similarity between Ryan's and Rick Jones's voices before, even though she had known they were brothers. Ryan's was perhaps a touch deeper and smoother, but Rick's had that same tight note of impatience that she'd heard in Ryan's voice a few times. She hung up the phone gently without saying anything.

Sitting down carefully on the edge of the sofa, she took a deep, calming breath. Well, now she knew the answer to one question she'd been puzzling over. She did not trust Ryan Jones. Bleak, heart-destroying desolation turned into a fierce all-consuming anger.

She slammed one fist down on the coffee table by her knees, making Murphy leap up with a startled yelp. Dammit! He had lied to her again! And this time it was worse, much, much worse. All his protestations that she would be safer here than with him in Los Angeles had been lies. She saw immediately what he and his brother, no doubt with Davidson's blessing, had done. They had withdrawn her protection, leaving her alone and vulnerable. If they had sent the killer an engraved invitation they couldn't have made their intention any clearer. They were inviting him to take a clear shot at her. Of course, they were no doubt planning to nab him as soon as he did, but that would be small consolation to her.

Ariel leaped to her feet and snatched up the jacket, shrugging into it as she hunted up her purse and Ryan's keys. Well, she wasn't going to sit around here, moaning and wringing her hands like some helpless, terrified ninny. She was too furious to be terrified and the only thing she planned on wringing was Ryan Jones's neck!

How could he *do* this to her? Twice! And how could she have been so stupidly trusting as to have let him? She knew the answer to that one already. She'd known he was lying the morning he'd left; she just hadn't wanted to admit it to herself. Because you didn't want to miss one last chance at him in bed, she reminded herself viciously, ignoring a wave of shame and fresh despair.

Ariel took a medium-sized print off the table and slid it carefully into her purse. She was going to stuff this damned photograph down their throats after they'd had a good look at it. Then, whether the Jones brothers and Davidson deigned to accompany her or not, she was going to confront the subject of the photo and ask him why he was trying so hard to kill her. Then... But she couldn't think beyond then. It was too painful.

Ariel backed the power wagon out of the garage and forced herself to drive slowly down the dirt road to the highway. She came to a full stop at the sign. She wanted to do nothing to draw attention to herself. Once she was clear of town, beyond Ted Dye's sharp eyes, she would have no trouble getting to Missoula and catching a flight out. She should be in San Francisco by early morning.

As she crested the long hill that led into town she glanced to the left at the steep canyon and the ribbon of river below. It was a pity she needed his truck. It would be so satisfying emotionally to simply let it roll over the edge and watch it crash onto the rocks below. She drove through town with a small prayer of thanks that the chief's patrol car was nowhere in sight.

Dusk was just deepening into true darkness when she drove onto the bridge that crossed over the Bitterroot River on the far side of town. The lights of the truck flickered down the length of the narrow span, shining off a white car parked across the other end, blocking it. Ariel moaned despairingly. Now she knew why she hadn't seen the chief's car.

She abandoned the idea of simply ramming his car and continuing on. She had no desire to have the state police scouring the highway for her between here and Missoula. She parked the orange truck a few feet from the white patrol car, lights on, motor running. She climbed down from the cab and strolled across the where the chief was lounging against the front fender of his car.

"Evening, Ariel."

"Chief."

"Out for a little drive?"

"Yes. It's a-a nice night for one." Ariel stifled a nervous giggle. Surely the chief wasn't buying this? She couldn't be so lucky.

Chief Dye pulled the toothpick he'd been sucking on from the corner of his mouth and examined it. "Thinking of going up to Missoula?" he asked idly.

No, she couldn't be that lucky. The chief might have perfected his hick-sheriff routine, but the "hick" had been a detective lieutenant with the S.F.P.D. and hadn't been fooled for a second. "I found some evidence I think the San Francisco district attorney should see. I'm going to fly out there with it tonight," she stated boldly.

"Let's see it." His hand was in front of her, the toothpick flipped away faster than she would have thought a man twenty years younger could move.

Ariel pulled out her photograph and gave it to the chief. He frowned at it a long time in the headlights of the truck.

"What's it supposed to prove?"

Ariel explained.

Ted Dye nodded, still considering the photo. He didn't point out to her that the picture could also prove that the taller man was pointing out to the shorter, older one the person he was *not* to shoot.

"I'll take it into Missoula and send it off on the state police wire-photo machine."

"No!" Ariel made to grab the picture back. "I have to take it myself, to explain it. Otherwise the D.A. won't believe it's the same man."

Dye's burly body easily blocked Ariel's arm. He reached through the open window of his patrol car and laid the photo on the dash. Privately he was certain Davidson wouldn't believe it whether she went or not.

"I'll send your explanation with it, Ariel," he promised. "Now go on home."

She stood toe-to-toe with him. "And if I don't? What are you going to do. Shoot me?" she demanded sarcastically.

"No. I'll arrest you for being disorderly and refusing to obey an officer, and throw you in jail," he answered calmly. "Jones told you to stay put. You can either stay at home or stay in jail. I imagine he'd bail you out when he gets back," he added as an afterthought.

If she had to wait for Ryan to come back she would rot in jail. Ariel blinked back tears of frustrated fury, she would *not* cry. She glared at the chief defiantly.

He stared back implacably. "Ariel, I can't go to Missoula until you climb back in that truck and go home," he explained patiently. "I promise you, as soon as you do I will drive up to Missoula and send the picture off. You can call Davidson first thing in the morning to confirm it."

Ariel gave him one last belligerent glare, then climbed back into the truck. If she wanted the photo to reach San Francisco, she would have to do it his way.

She slammed the door shut and started to put the truck in gear. The chief held up his hand and walked toward her. She rolled down the window, and he stuck his head in. A notebook and pencil materialized in his hands.

"Okay now. Tell me again, exactly, what this picture proves."

Ariel was curled into the comforting arms of an overstuffed chair, staring at her phone. Murphy's head on her knee spread a little warmth through her cold body. The dog gazed at her mistress, whining softly. Absently Ariel patted the brown head.

Should she swallow her pride and call the second number Ryan had given her? She'd checked her address book and her suspicions had been confirmed. The first number was Rick Jones's home phone. Ryan had probably never dreamed she'd use the numbers and had felt perfectly safe in giving them to her, to reinforce his image as the concerned lover, no doubt.

She roused herself from the chair, scrubbing away a half-dried tear with the back of her hand. No, she wouldn't call; she wasn't that desperate—yet.

Come on, Ariel, she chided herself as she paced the living room, Murphy pacing with her. You've plotted at least a dozen hairbreadth escapes from vengeful posses and irate Indians. Surely you can come up with something to get away from a middle-aged police chief.

She would not meekly wait around here for somebody's target practice. She would confirm the photo's arrival tomorrow morning, all right—in person. And she would be there with the police to see the look on the killer's face when he opened his door.

She paused in the middle of the floor, tapping her finger absently on her cheek as a plan took form. Ryan's orange pickup wasn't exactly inconspicuous, but Mr. Hanson's pickup was. Battered, rust-eaten, it looked like half the pickup trucks in the valley. Ever since he'd bought his new car, Mr. Hanson rarely drove

the truck. If she told the right story of automotive woes he would
be more than willing to lend it to her.

She could cut across his hay field to the levee road along the
river. The road went close to the county line, well past Ted Dye's
jurisdiction. If she called Mr. Hanson now she could still catch a
late flight out of Missoula and be in San Francisco by morning.

Her hand was on the phone when it rang. She lifted the receiver
expecting to hear Chief Dye's gruff voice making sure she was at
home. It wasn't Chief Dye.

The bell on the wire-photo machine rang shortly after midnight, waking the police aide from his daydream of apprehending
four dangerous bank robbers single-handedly and receiving sergeant's stripes on the spot. He waited by the machine, yawning
until the photo and the message accompanying it were complete.
Carefully he tore the paper free, scanning it briefly. Vaguely disappointed to see no mention of a bank robbery, he placed the
photograph and message in a folder, dropped it in the basket for
the district attorney's office and went back to daydreaming.

The folder was picked up by a courier promptly at eight o'clock
the next morning. By eight forty-five it was in the hands of a secretary in the D.A.'s office. She was just about to carry it into her
boss's office to lay it on his desk when the phone rang. She laid the
file temporarily on the stack of files to be returned to the record
room in the basement to be refiled.

A runner from records stopped by her desk, nodded at the stack
of files questioningly, and the secretary, busy taking a message,
nodded back absently. The runner scooped up the files and continued on his rounds. At ten, just in time for his break, he dumped
the load of records in the refiling bin. The empty chair nearby was
usually occupied by the pretty young clerk in charge of refiling.
He'd hoped to buy her a doughnut and a cup of coffee and try
again for a date, but she was still out with the flu. He sighed di-
sappointedly; she would probably be out all week.

Chapter 14

The headlights of the rented Firebird cut a misty swath through the fog swirling over the highway. It was very late. Actually, Ryan corrected mentally, it was very early Saturday morning. He'd been extremely lucky; his had been the last plane to land before the fog had closed down the Missoula airport. But then, he'd been very lucky all day.

He guided the responsive car around a curve and was suddenly out of the fog. This was so much more fun to drive than his cumbersome truck. Maybe he could talk Ariel into replacing her Blazer with a sports car they could both enjoy. They weren't going to need two four-wheel-drive vehicles when they went back to California. And they'd be going back very soon.

Her would-be murderer would have been taken into custody about two hours ago, while Ryan was thirty thousand feet in the air over Oregon. He would have liked to have been there, but the shock was going to be hard for Ariel when she learned who it was. She was going to need him with her.

The man was in custody, but not for murder. The carryon suitcase of a tourist boarding a plane in L.A. bound for a little fun and sun in the Bahamas had suffered an unfortunate accident when it mysteriously fell from the overhead luggage compartment. The other passengers were rather startled to see, not swim trunks and

Island shirts and tubes of sunscreen, but neat green-and-white bundles spilling from the broken bag. The money wasn't the courier's and he hadn't been about to go to jail for it. The IRS agents had offered a deal and he had taken it, giving them the name of the man Ryan had already pegged for Dennis's death.

Ariel wasn't above suspicion yet, but Ryan was confident he could find the evidence to convince even Davidson of her innocence eventually. And when he did, he knew the discovery would bring a soul-satisfying sense of rightness that had always been lacking when a guilty client was found innocent on a technicality.

He turned onto the narrow two-lane road that dead-ended in the valley. It was finally over. He would clear the air between them, then tell her what he wanted from her. She was probably going to be a little shocked. He'd been rather startled himself when he finally realized that he had the decidedly old-fashioned intention of carrying her off to keep forever, to bear him a brood of lively little California girls and dark-eyed little boys. Well, one of each, anyway, for starters. No sense in getting carried away. He didn't see his silly grin in the rearview mirror.

The low Firebird bounced cautiously over the ruts in her road. What had happened during the past three days? The first time he had called when she wasn't home, he had called Dye immediately. The chief had said that his truck had been parked all day in the Valley View Rest Home parking lot.

Ariel had given him her promise that she wouldn't leave the house unless it was absolutely necessary. If Bessie Ruff had needed her, he knew Ariel would consider it absolutely necessary to go to her.

She was still gone at midnight the next night, but this time Dye told him that his truck was at the small valley hospital. Yesterday, with every call, he had known with the first ring that the phone was ringing in an empty house.

Dye kept assuring him that she was fine, just staying with Bessie at the little hospital in Hamilton. If Bessie were that ill, why hadn't she called him? He knew she would need him, need somebody.

She didn't even know he was coming back tonight. Not only had he been unable to reach her today, but the chief, too, had been unavailable. At least he didn't have to worry about her safety anymore.

The L.A. police had had their man under surveillance for several days. When he was packing his car for what appeared to be a short weekend trip the L.A. police had checked to see if he should be picked up. After a brief council that Ryan had been privy to, it was decided to tail him instead, and to use a search warrant to legally ransack his house while he was away. He'd arrived at his cabin near Tahoe in midafternoon and, Rick had assured Ryan before he left, would be picked up by the county sheriff.

The schoolhouse was dark. He'd seen his truck through the garage window when the car lights flashed over it. At least she was finally home. The front door was unlocked and he felt the touch of an icy finger on his spine. He cursed quietly, fear making him choose words that were uncharacteristically vile. If he shouted for her and someone else was in the house...

He opened his door and moved soundlessly to the kitchen to get the .45. He stepped back across the hall just as silently, then paused outside her door and listened. It was half open. There was no sound. He pushed the door wide and stepped into the room; flattening himself against the wall. The fire in the stove was dead. The house was as cold as a tomb.

Weak moonlight barely illuminated the living room. There was a huddled figure at the end of the sofa, and a darker shape on the floor.

"Ariel?" he called softly. Fear formed a choking lump in his throat, and there was an obscene taste in his mouth.

For long breathless moments there was no answer. Then the figure on the couch stirred. The white light of the dying moon glimmered briefly on blond hair. The dark head resting on the daffodil-yellow afghan that was wrapped around the figure lifted with a welcoming whimper.

"Bessie died while you were gone, Ry," Ariel said dully. "Her funeral was this afternoon."

The gun fell soundlessly on the carpet as he dropped next to her. He crushed his arms around her, his voice gentle. "Oh, baby, I'm sorry, so sorry." He cursed again, silently. "And I wasn't even here for you." He rocked her gently as she lay passively against him. "Why didn't you call me, darling?"

A long shiver trembled through her. She closed her dry eyes, trying to keep the tears locked inside. It was no use. They began to seep silently down her cold cheeks, glittering in the even colder moonlight. He shifted her to his lap, wrapping the folds of the warm afghan more tightly around her chilled body.

Ariel's voice was a poignant whisper. "I've known she was dying for months, but I wouldn't let myself think about it. I tried to call you yesterday. There was no answer at your brother's house, and his secretary said she'd take a m-message for you when I called his office. I left the message, but I-I needed you r-right then." The thin, pitiful cry of a lost child filled the cold, quiet room. "I w-wanted you to come back so b-badly!"

Ryan closed his eyes, resting his cheek on top of her head. So she knew where he'd really been. When she heard his reason for lying to her, surely she would forgive him.

Ariel sniffled and tried for control. It was beyond her. "When you didn't call back, I knew you w-weren't ever coming back." With a broken sound she turned her face into the soft sweater under her cheek and gave into her grief.

Ryan gathered her closer, his body a shield against any more pain and hurt. "Oh, love, no. No, no. I'd have come back right away if I'd known. I love you." Silently he swore every obscenity he could remember. He'd never gotten the message.

Dennis's death, the long months here alone, Murphy's poisoning, the murder attempts that she'd barely survived—none of them had broken her spirit. But Bessie's death and then the thought that he'd betrayed her once again had shattered her.

Ryan's voice was a lulling wordless purr. His cheek soothed over the soft wisps of hair at her temple. With a strong gentle rhythm he slowly stroked her back. After a long while her last tear was spent, brushed from her cheek by his tender thumb. Her convulsive shivers eased as she absorbed his warmth, and her breathing evened. She lay still across his lap within the shelter of his arms. He brushed a kiss over her forehead, heard her quiet sigh and he was sure she had slipped into healing sleep. She was broken, and he would put her back together, restore her, tonight—and whenever else she might need him.

The grandfather clock on the opposite wall played its Westminster chimes and struck twice. "Ryan." He thought she was calling to him in a dream and drew her still closer.

"Ryan."

He felt the butterfly wing flutter of her lashes on his throat.

"Please make love with me."

Please comfort me, she was asking; please heal me. He answered with gentle fingertips raising her mouth to his. His lips, warm and unbelievably soft, held hers in a passionless, loving kiss. Then, silently, he rose with her in his arms and climbed the stairs, praying he would have the gentleness she would need tonight.

He laid her on the bed in a patch of gauzy moonlight. His hands, delicate as moonbeams, undressed her. She closed her tear-ravaged eyes against the pale light. The bed shifted, and he was naked beside her. As he drew the quilt over them, he reached out to bring her close to him.

For a long time he only kissed her, those incredibly gentle patient hands whispering over her, asking for nothing and giving solace, peace, tender care. Then his mouth followed the path of his hands, never arousing, never urgent, never demanding. He offered only sweetness to neutralize the bitter pain. His lips came back up to hers, the sweetness distilled to an absolute purity that seeped through her, dissolving the bitter ache.

He let the kiss deepen with the softest coercion, and her pain poured into him. As her body relaxed, she knew dimly that she was selfishly taking, returning nothing. Her boneless arms lifted toward him.

"No, love." He caught her hands, holding them loosely as he kissed the slow, steady pulse inside each of her wrists. Then, rolling her over onto her stomach, he eased her arms above her head and stretched them over the pillow. She felt the slight pressure of his knees at her hips as his strong hands began a tranquil massage up her back, across her shoulders, down her sides. Lean, sure fingers kneaded her waist, eased the last knot of tension in the small of her back.

Ryan's voice stroked over her, too, like velvet, telling her how much he loved her, how much he had missed her, how precious she was to him. She drifted, serene and wonderfully slothful, in his loving care. His breath warmed the nape of her neck a fraction of a moment before his light kiss. Ariel felt the first mild sting of passion as he continued the trail of soft kisses down to the base of her spine.

Time seemed to cease its flow and began to swirl and eddy around them. His sensitive fingertips noted the quickening of her body. He turned her back to face him again, his mouth and his hands treasuring her body. They were still unselfish, giving subtle pleasure, cosseting her. Ariel luxuriated in the feel of his hands. She felt as if she was something exquisite to be appreciated at his leisure, lingered over.

The clock downstairs chimed again. Three deep tones reverberated through the quiet house. The moon floated from behind a thin cloud, its light washing her body in white translucence. Ryan saw clearly how slight, how perfect, she was, like a fragile, priceless statue of the rarest porcelain. Eyes closed, the statue barely moved, save for the shallow rise and fall of her breasts.

He lowered his mouth to one nipple and felt, rather than heard, her low moan. As he inhaled her familiar, bewitching flower scent, his lips dawdled. She moaned again, her body beginning to shift, inviting him to take more. Ryan's tempo never varied, still easy, still unrushed.

He wanted her; the flames licking deep in his belly were ravenous, but love damped them down. Tonight was solely for her, her pleasure, her needs. He would find his pleasure in hers.

Ariel basked in the warmth of his hands and mouth. When his tongue laving her breast changed mere warmth into heat, her body began to thrum, stronger with each soft touch. All the pain was gone; even the sweet pain of desire was absent. He permitted only succoring pleasure. She concentrated on the gift of exquisite bliss he was giving her body.

His mouth pressed to hers, and she met him mindlessly, lost in his flavor and scent and feel. He reminded himself of her fragility and took her with infinite tenderness and care and love. She wept again—with joy.

The coppery October sun rose and hung high overhead. Only a few mares' tails, the leading edge of a storm front, swished over the northern horizon, marring the empty perfection of a pure azure day. They slept on in each other's arms like exhausted children. Finally Murphy's apologetic whimper woke Ryan. He shook his sleep-fuzzed head and laughed into Murphy's yellow eyes. His hand left its warm hold on Ariel's breast and reached out to scratch the dog's ears.

"Glad to see me, girl?" he whispered.

Murphy's eyes rolled ecstatically.

Easing his angular body away from Ariel's soft heat, he swung his legs over the side of the bed and stood. He stretched sinuously and then, not bothering with his clothes, bounded down the stairs.

He swore feelingly under his breath. Energy conservation was all very well, but they were going to have to get some reliable heat in this place. He was tired of freezing to death every morning. But even the shivering gooseflesh covering his bare body couldn't lower his spirits. He hadn't had a chance to tell her last night that the killer had been apprehended. She was finally free, and they were going home. First he had to get dressed, though, and get some coffee in her to be sure she would understand what he was going to say to her.

He let Murphy out, then picked up his suitcase which was still standing by the door. As soon as he got a fire started in the wood stove he went back upstairs. He built one more fire in the little French parlor stove, watching the top of the tousled blond head showing above an old wedding-ring quilt for any sign of life. He went into the bathroom, shutting the door quietly. When he came back out twenty minutes later she was peering owlishly at him from her nest of quilts.

Ariel blinked the sleep out of her eyes. It hadn't been a dream; he really was here. His hair was damp; it must have been the sound of the shower that had woken her up. He was wearing a smile and an old pair of jeans, one of the first ever made, from the looks of them. They were faded gray-blue at the knees and blue-white at the fly, the cuffs and pockets frayed. The waistband was a little loose. Whatever he'd been doing the past week, he'd lost weight.

Ariel stared at him silently as he crossed the bare floorboards.

"Going to stay in bed forever, lazybones?" He reached out to ruffle her hair affectionately. He glanced significantly at the little clock on the dresser. "You've already been there most of the day."

"I may." Ariel closed her eyes again. She wasn't ready to deal with this. She'd convinced herself that he wouldn't be coming back, and now here he was, calmly walking out of her bathroom as if he'd never been away, never lied to her again. Had he left her in the hopes of drawing out the murderer or not? And what smooth lie did he have all prepared for her this time?

His hand caressed over her temple, smoothing back the tangled hair. "Are you feeling better this morning, love?" His chocolate-colored eyes were loving and kind.

"I'm better," she answered softly, with a bittersweet smile. She pulled his hand down and for a moment held it to her cheek. "I should never sit on your lap. I always end up crying."

He bent down to give her a gentle kiss. "I wish I could have been here sooner." His dark eyes were shadowed with regret.

Ariel laid his hand carefully on the bed and sat up, drawing Bessie's quilt protectively around her. She wished she had on one of her nightshirts instead of being naked. Her nakedness under the soft quilt was too sharp a reminder of his tender, selfless loving of the night before.

Ryan sensed her withdrawal even before she had released his hand. He waited, tension slowly tightening his stomach.

She looked at him for a long time, saying nothing. When she finally spoke, her question was quiet and very clear. "Why did you lie to me again, Ryan?"

"Davidson was going to bring you back to San Francisco to make you an easier target for the killer." His tone was neutral. "He was sure you would draw him out, and Davidson would be able to catch him. I went back to talk him out of it."

"Why didn't you tell me the truth?"

Ryan answered honestly. "Because I was afraid you would go."

Ariel felt suddenly cold. She would have gone. "Why now, all of a sudden, did he want to do that?"

"Because of the money Dennis left you, Ariel," he told her gently.

She started to shake her head uncomprehendingly. "Dennis didn't leave—"

Ryan explained. As he spoke he watched her eyes widen in disbelief at the amount. She shook her head violently. "I don't want it!"

"We'll figure out what to do with it," he assured her quietly. "Ariel, it's over. We can go home now. The man who was after you was arrested last night."

She looked at him, dazed. "It's over?" she whispered. Why didn't she feel something? Joy? Jubilation? Even just relief? She felt . . . nothing, nothing but incredible weariness.

Ryan nodded. "Ariel, love, I'm sorry; this is going to hurt. It was—"

They said the name together. Ryan looked at her, stunned. "You knew? For how long?"

"I realized it a couple of days after you left." His puzzlement didn't dawn on her for a few moments. "I was poking through Dennis's picture file when I found a bunch of negatives that he'd never printed, and I saw Robert in one with Reilly. One of the high school boys printed the negative for me and—" His deepening frown finally registered. "Wait a minute! Didn't you see the photograph Chief Dye sent Davidson?"

"No."

Ariel laughed bitterly. "He never sent it! I was going to take it to Davidson myself, but I never got out of town."

"Thank God," Ryan murmured.

"The chief took the photo and said he'd take it to Missoula and send it on the state-police wire-photo machine. Obviously he didn't. I was going to call Davidson to confirm it, but then Bessie . . ." Her eyes dimmed; then something else occurred to her. "Then what was he arrested for?"

"Tax evasion, for starters," he said tightly. "Ariel, why the hell didn't you call me when you found it?"

She looked at him bleakly. "I was going to. That was when I realized you were in San Francisco, when I saw the numbers. I thought you'd left me unprotected to lure the killer," she finished softly. "I didn't think you'd be back."

"I'm so sorry, Ariel." He pulled her into his arms. "Of course you'd think that." He laughed mirthlessly. "What else could you think?"

He rocked her gently in his arms until he felt her begin to relax. Nuzzling his mouth through her silky hair to her ear, he whispered with gentle humor, "You should have known I would come back. I had to get my truck and the rest of my clothes." He felt her flinch. "And you," he breathed. He looked down into eyes filling with a hesitant hope and kissed her softly. He took another kiss, longer, infinitely sweeter.

When he at last relinquished possession of her mouth, her face was luminous with the overpowering happiness suffusing her body, but her husky voice was cautious. "What exactly are you saying, Ryan?"

His smile was tender and oddly uncertain. "I'm saying I love you, Ariel." His hot, insistent mouth reiterated his vow.

For a few precious moments Ariel allowed herself to wallow in the glorious feeling of being loved and desired, ignoring the niggle of doubt that still persisted at the edge of her mind. She pulled back, and he held her loosely in his arms, a question in his eyes.

"It was hard to be sure," she admitted softly. Her eyes didn't meet his.

Ryan felt a jab of heartache. What she was saying was that she found it hard to believe him. He couldn't blame her; he'd hardly given her much reason to.

"The first night we made love, you told me you loved me, but I thought you were just saying it because everybody says it in those circumstances."

He bit back his laugh at her attempt to be casual and sophisticated. "You didn't," he pointed out solemnly.

She shrugged slightly, her voice nonchalant. "Umm, well, I'm a novice. When I have more experience I'll undoubtedly say it, too." Her eyes flickered up to his, then quickly back down. She was leading him shamelessly, but she desperately needed more reassurance.

His arms shifted, his hold a little rougher. His voice was nearly as careless as hers, but with an underlying warning. "Then you'll be saying it to me, because you're going to be getting all your experience with me."

Ariel felt her heart stop, then restart with a rapid jerk. She still couldn't let herself quite believe what he was implying about their relationship. "I'd been thinking...maybe you were attracted to me out of boredom—you know, something to do while you were stuck in a small town." Her anxious eyes belied her complaining banter.

Ryan finally exploded in helpless, disbelieving laughter. "Boredom? Ariel Spence, if you can't tell the difference between recreational sex to pass the time—now *that*'s boredom—and a man making love to you because he's crazy about you and can't keep his hands off you, you do need experience." He started to nuzzle her neck ferociously. "A *lot* more," he warned ominously, taking tender love bites up to her ear lobe.

Though she was laughing delightedly, she reluctantly pushed him away. "I should get that photograph to show you." Oddly, it didn't seem so urgent anymore.

His eyes searched her face, a faint frown replacing his smile. She was thin, almost gaunt. She probably hadn't eaten a decent meal in days. The violent shadows under her eyes bespoke too much grief and too little sleep. "It can wait, Ariel," he said gently. "He's not going anywhere."

He stood and pulled her up after him. The quilt caught and she was suddenly shivering, naked, in the middle of the cold room. A low fire burned in his belly. He tamped it down. They had a few things to settle first.

He spotted his old sweatshirt under the quilt. Wordlessly he held it up, one black brow arching.

"I was...cold," she explained.

"Of course." He nodded with an arrogant grin. He pulled the shirt over her head, kissing the top of her cold nose as her head popped through. "Get dressed," he ordered. "I'll scrounge us up some lunch, and then we'll decide when we're going home."

She nodded solemnly and turned away. She took a few steps toward the bathroom, then suddenly whirled. She ran back, flung her arms around his neck and gave him a jubilant kiss. "It's over, Ry!"

"Yes, love," he affirmed softly, smiling into her eyes. "It's finally over."

Half an hour later he watched her devour the second plateful of scrambled eggs he had fixed. She fed the last bite of her bacon to Murphy, laughing for the sheer joy of it. The sadness that had shadowed her face ever since he'd met her was gone, her golden radiance shining brightly.

She got up for more coffee and refilled his cup, flashing him a brilliant smile.

Why wouldn't she say it? he wondered. He knew she loved him. After twenty-seven years of chastity she hadn't surrendered for casual sex or out of curiosity. She had given him her heart as well as her body, so why wouldn't she say it, dammit? He wanted, *needed*, to hear the words; actions weren't enough.

The left corner of his mouth curled in self-derision. Hell, he knew why. A bittersweet pain settled near his heart. He had betrayed her trust twice. She was just protecting herself, making sure she had a little pride and self-respect left in case he did it again. He sighed in resignation. He could wait until he had her complete trust again; he had nothing but time.

They cleaned up the few lunch dishes; then Ariel took Ryan by the hand and led him to her desk. "I want to show you the photograph, Ryan. I'm sure it would be enough proof to convince Davidson that Robert was the one who hired Reilly." She pulled a large manilla envelope from the bottom drawer of her desk and undid the clasp. "He was wearing a disguise, and I don't think even I would have recognized him from the photo, but I saw the negative first." She lifted the flap and began to ease out the largest print. "With light and dark reversed, the blond hair was dark like his really is, and he used to wear a mustache a couple of years ago."

The photograph lay on the desk. Ariel stared at it sadly. "As soon as I saw it I remembered who the third man was in Dennis's office that day; he and Dennis must have been doing the smuggling together." There was agonized bewilderment in her voice as she raised her haunted eyes back to Ryan. "But why would he kill his—"

The rest of the question froze in her throat. Ryan had lost his color, and a look of sick certainty had tautened his features. He bit off a savage, impotent curse halfway through, staring at her starkly. "That man—" his lean finger stabbed the blond man in the photo "—sat across the aisle from me on the flight to Missoula last night."

* * *

So the last act in this deadly drama hasn't been played out after all, Ariel decided wearily. She sat on a rickety folding chair in a corner, ignored by the rest of the crowd in Chief Dye's small office. The chief had called his three men back to duty, and the county sheriff had arrived with one of his deputies.

Ryan stood at center stage, listening to the others deliver their lines about roadblocks and bloodhounds, awaiting his cue. Or maybe now he was the director. Occasionally he would ask a question or make an even quieter suggestion.

The chief had been vindicated. As Ryan and Ariel had been leaving the schoolhouse to confront him, the phone had rung. Rick Jones had been on the other end. The photo had apparently been languishing at the bottom of a file basket for most of the week. It had finally made its way to the district attorney's office after Robert had been fingered by the courier—and after they realized that he had given his tail the slip and was probably already on his way to Montana. Ryan had told him that Robert had already arrived.

Ted Dye hung up the phone and slumped back in a tired swivel chair. The chief's faded blue eyes looked worriedly to Ryan, who was now sitting, seemingly totally at ease, on a corner of his desk. "He rented a car about ten minutes after you did, false name on the credit card, of course." Dye tore a sheet off a notepad and tossed it across the desk. "Here's the make on the rental car and the license number." Ryan flicked a glance over the sheet. The other men pulled out pocket notebooks and pens and dutifully wrote down the information. They each had a photograph of the suspect already.

Ryan ambled over to the large map of the county mounted on the back wall. He stood before it, rocking a little on his heels. His right hand was shoved loosely in his jeans pocket, jingling his keys and change. The men who had served under him years before and numerous prosecuting attorneys who had faced him since could have testified that now Ryan Jones was at his most dangerous.

His dark eyes narrowed and traveled over the relief map. His left hand reached out and curled around Ariel's neck, his thumb fondling her cool satin skin almost absently. He found he had the wholly understandable compulsion to keep her in sight, preferably within reach. He took his right hand out of his pocket, his forefinger pinpointing exactly the location of her schoolhouse on the map. Then it traced idly over the nearby river. The banks, he remembered, were thick with concealing brush and trees. A man could easily keep watch on the schoolhouse and its owner with binoculars—or a rifle scope—and never be seen himself.

Ryan's left hand slipped across to her shoulder and prompted her to rise. "I think we'll go now." He said it as if they were leaving a rather boring cocktail party after putting in a polite appearance. "If anything develops, you know where to find us."

Ariel murmured her thanks and goodbyes, Ryan's arm solidly around her.

Since he had discovered earlier that her refrigerator was almost empty, Ryan made a quick stop at the grocery. He was sure she had lost the few pounds he had managed to put on her and a couple more besides.

Later Ariel choked down enough of her dinner to loosen the tight lines around Ryan's mouth. He slid a large slice of cheesecake in front of her and gave her a hard look. Murphy enjoyed most of it while Ryan was occupied with clearing the table. They finished putting her kitchen to rights in a silence that communicated more than hours of conversation could have.

The oddly telepathic silence continued as they sat on her sofa, paying little attention to the television. Ariel curled up against his side, under the arm that had seemed to be around her all day. Eventually they went up to bed. There they made love with hands and mouths that were greedy and a little rough, their movements driven by an almost desperate urgency neither wanted to acknowledge.

Ariel jolted awake violently. She lay in the dark, her heart racing. The sheet beneath her was clammy with perspiration. Left with only the vague dread of some horror she found the nightmare that had awakened her all the more terrifying than if she could remember the details. Carefully she eased from under the heavy arm that tried to hold her. She wanted no more of dream-riddled sleep tonight.

She found her woolen robe in the closet and went downstairs. In the dark bathroom she turned on a faucet and waited for the icy water to heat. A sense of calm finally settled over her. Somehow she knew that whatever was going to happen would do so before nightfall.

With a warm wet washcloth she wiped the clammy sweat from her body. She wondered if this was the way someone felt after making her tragic choice to take her own life. She was not choosing death, however, but life. She hung the rough towel on the rack and pulled the rose wool robe tightly around her as she walked into the kitchen.

Ryan came in silently a few minutes later. "Do you always eat everything in the refrigerator at—" he squinted blearily at the clock "—three forty-seven in the morning?"

The tiny grin that had been tugging at the corner of her mouth gave up. "Only when I'm scared and can't sleep." The entire contents of her refrigerator was scattered haphazardly over the oak table. She considered the bowl of leftover salad, then shoved it aside. Finally she looked at him.

He'd pulled on the old jeans and his gray sweatshirt. After dragging out the chair opposite her, he straddled it, his arms crossed over the back. He buried a yawn in his arms, then raised his head.

The look of compassionate understanding and love in his sleepy eyes nearly undid her. Ariel got up and began putting the food away.

"What would you like to do?" he asked softly. He knew she wouldn't be able to bear going back to bed.

Pausing before the open door of the refrigerator, she thought for a moment. "You know what I'd really like to do? I'd like to be outside, maybe along the river. I am so *tired* of being cooped up."

Going down to the river might not be a wise move, but Ryan understood what she was feeling. She couldn't stand waiting like a small animal caught in a trap, helplessly anticipating the hunter's return. Besides, four o'clock in the morning should be safe enough.

"Okay." Rising from the chair, he held a hand out to her. "Let's go get dressed."

She had dressed in her warmest clothes, olive wool pants, a heavy tan sweater and hiking boots, and was just shrugging into a fleece-lined brown corduroy coat when Ryan returned from across the hall. He was dressed as warmly as she was. He'd exchanged his jeans for khaki field pants and added a thick gray sweater and a worn cowhide ranch coat. Ariel's eyes widened, but she didn't speak. In his left hand, as if it were a natural extension of his arm, was an automatic rifle she knew you couldn't buy over the counter of the local sporting goods store.

They went into the garage. Ryan turned the dancing Murphy back firmly at the door. "No, girl, no rides today."

Ryan used the keys he had lifted from Ariel's purse and opened the metal cabinet along the side wall. He took out her ancient shotgun and wordlessly handed it over as she was climbing into the truck. Her eyes widened further, and she balked at taking the gun. His quiet tone had a finality that wouldn't brook argument.

"Take it, Ariel."

He would much rather have given her the hunting rifle with the high-powered scope, but she had mentioned once that she had never fired anything but a shotgun. Now was no time to start lessons.

Ryan backed out of the garage and left the truck idling to warm up the engine while he shut the garage door. He stepped out into an eerie scene that was all shades of the same color—gray. The peculiar half light promised that the sun was rising, but it was still too far below the eastern horizon to add any color to the world.

Ashen pines blurred into the massed pewter clouds crawling over the charcoal mountains guarding the shadowy valley below. He could barely distinguish the silvered walls of the schoolhouse against the slate backdrop of the sky. Even his truck had lost its bright orange and looked like tarnished silver in the strange light. His hand on the door handle had a ghoulishly bloodless tint. A chill ran down his spine that had nothing to do with the wind. It was, he remembered, the favored hour for executions.

The wind eddied around the schoolhouse. Despite the heavy frost it was only crispy cool outside. His dark head thrown back, he sniffed the air like a wild animal. It carried reminders of snow-covered granite peaks and bottomless, ice-rimmed high-country lakes. The impossibly clean air began to stir his sluggish blood with a curious, restless excitement.

Ariel sat on the fraying seat, oblivious to the way the truck was bouncing over the washboard river road. Numbly she gazed at the shotgun, as familiar to her as her own body, securely upright between her knees. For the first time since her grandfather had placed it in her eager hands seventeen years ago and she had brought its wobbly weight to her shoulder, she was forced to recognize the gun's true purpose. The dully gleaming steel and aged walnut had not been fashioned into a game piece for her to use in a harmless sport. They had been made to be a lethal weapon, an instrument of death. Never had she aimed it at any living thing. Even in defense of her own life, could she now?

Ryan quietly asked for directions.

"Turn here." Ariel indicated the high, narrow levee road. It bordered a field of random haystacks that looked like giant loaves of pale bread iced with frost. They took the road for a few minutes into a wilder stretch along the river. Here the river turned back toward the steep walls of the valley. There were no farms or any other sign of man's attempt to domesticate this wilderness, except the winding road cut into the foot of the mountain. Ryan parked the truck at a wide spot in the road.

Frozen mud crunched under their boots as they tramped across a wide flat toward the river. The wooden trestle of the Burlington Northern railroad bridge loomed out of the river mist like the fossilized skeleton of some prehistoric beast. Ariel carried her shotgun, unloaded, over her shoulder. Ryan's rifle, with a full clip, was resting with deceptive casualness in the crook of his elbow.

He scanned the shadowed valley wall behind them, then the brushlined riverbanks. He saw nothing unusual, yet the short hairs on the back of his neck had risen as soon as they had left the truck. He listened. There were several scattered shots, comfortably distant, probably deer hunters. From nearby came the lazy sounds of the geese resting on the quiet water, and the whisper of the rising wind at their backs.

They stood downwind of the geese, behind a chest-high screen of young willows. The geese had neither seen nor heard their stealthy approach. Because of the hour and the ghostly light they automatically hushed their voices.

They were making it so easy for him. The woods were full of hunters, but they had neglected to put on orange clothing. Who would be surprised if dressed as she was in drab brown, she was mistaken for a deer by an overeager hunter without the courage to step forward and admit what he had done?

He slipped three shiny brass bullets with lethal copper rocket tips into the breech of the rifle. The bolt slid home. He sighted through the scope, centering the cross hairs on the back of her head. Satisfied, he lowered the rifle and melted into the underbrush.

Ariel dug around in her coat pocket for the gloves that should have been under the buckshot shells Ryan had given her. Without taking his eyes from the river, he reached for her cold hand and tucked it with his into the fleece-lined warmth of his jacket pocket.

The scene before them was reminiscent of a busy day at the Los Angeles airport. The big Canadian geese were unusually restless, using the slow water for endless takeoffs and landings. A new squad flew in low, buzzing the trestle and alighting with hardly a splash.

The geese sensed the approach of the winter storm that had built a week ago high above the Arctic Circle. It had moved like a ponderous, invading army down across Canada. Now the first outriders of wind were infiltrating across the U.S. border fanning across the valley, rippling the water and ruffling the geese's feathers. Ariel's hair lifted in the fitful breeze, blond strands tangling with the blue-black of Ryan's.

Engrossed in the geese, Ariel paid no attention to the strong, swift breeze that passed by her cheek, or the two puffs of dirt kicked up a few feet in front of her. Suddenly she was facedown in the mud and cockleburs, a pitiless hand on her head keeping her there. It took all her strength to twist her head out of the dirt so she could breathe. Squirming onto her side, she started to demand furiously what the hell Ryan thought he was doing when she realized he was crouched protectively over her, paying absolutely no attention to her. Blood was welling slowly from a peculiar slash on his neck, just above the collar of his coat.

The deadly looking rifle was ready at his waist as his hooded eyes searched the steep hill behind them, inch by torturous inch. A harsh sound in his throat and a twisted smile said he had found what he was looking for. Halfway up he'd caught a clumsy movement through the trees.

Ryan watched for a few more seconds, then seized Ariel's arm, dragging her up into a half crouch. "Stay down," he commanded, pulling her after him. The limber branches of the tamarisks whipped back as he pushed through them, stinging her cold cheeks and bringing tears to her eyes. Ariel bit her lip, determined not to cry, either from the flogging branches or the paralyzing fear. In the shelter of a massive fir, safe from the eyes of anyone on the mountainside, he halted, his hand still bruising her upper arm.

"Is he here?"

Ryan broke off his continual scanning of the area behind them to spare her a glance. She was tense, yet trembling like a frightened fawn, and her eyes were three times too big for her face, but her whisper had been steady. "Yes, he's here." Ryan looked back to the hillside. His arm rose cautiously, and she followed the direction of his pointing finger. "He was there when he shot, but he's moved off to the right and down now." His arm tracked the killer's progress. "He's probably sure he hit us and is coming to check.

As long as he thinks we're dead or wounded, we have the advantage.''

Ryan began moving again, and she followed, still tethered to him by that viselike hand. They moved through a thin wall of brush into a tiny glade carpeted with frost-crisped grass. Two more sides were walled by impenetrable brush. The fourth side was the levee, where Ariel could see the top of the orange shell on Ryan's truck. A quick scramble up the sandy slope and they would be safe.

Ryan dropped her arm finally to dig his keys out of his pants pockets. "I want you to take the truck, go back to town and bring back Dye and his men." He said the words casually as if he was sending her out for pizza.

Her chin tilted, and she answered calmly. "No, Ryan."

He began to curse her, driven by the fear and desperation wrenching his gut. His words were all the more terrible because they were delivered in a flat, passionless tone instead of the satisfying shouts of anger he wanted. He didn't dare lose enough control to shout, because if he did, he would touch her. And one touch would be too much. He would shake her until that beautiful stiff neck snapped. Or he would hit her, a solid right on that stubborn chin she was leading with so temptingly. Actually it wouldn't be such a bad idea at that, if he could remember to pull his punch at the last second. He could throw her in the back of the pickup and lock her in, where she would be safe. But he knew he couldn't trust himself. She would probably end up hating him forever.

Her face starkly white, Ariel stood silently letting his words roll over her harmlessly. He truly loved her, she knew. He could never say such awful things if he weren't scared to death of losing her. However, his hot rage was no match for the icy fury consuming her.

Scenes from the past ten months played before her eyes: Dennis in her arms, his bright red blood staining her gray slacks; Murphy's limp brown body on a cold, polished steel table; the charred black bulk of her Blazer; Ryan, the sun finding blue fire in his black hair, as he reached for a piece of poisoned candy. Ryan, standing before her now, the black hair mussed, the beautiful mouth that could smile at her with such love and tenderness hard and cruel as the blood oozed into his sodden, red coat collar. Ryan, who would risk his life once more because he loved her. And the man up on the hill had tried to kill him.

"No, Ryan," she repeated tonelessly. "He's taken a year of my life. He's tried to kill me five times." She looked at him steadily, unaware of the silent tears slipping down her cheeks. "He's even tried to kill you. No one deserves to go after him more than I do.'' She pumped a shell into the shotgun with cold efficiency. ''Coming?''

The iron fingers shackling her upper arm would probably shatter both bones any moment, she thought dispassionately. No matter, she could always shoot with the other. Then the brutal hand slipped up to her cheek in the tenderest of caresses.

Ryan felt the madness drain out of him as he responded to the love her shuttered eyes couldn't quite hide. His hand lightly brushed away the tears she still wasn't aware of, smearing their muddy tracks. ''I guess you do deserve it, love. But—'' he pulled the collar of her coat up around her ears ''—I want you to promise to do exactly as I tell you.''

''But—''

''Promise me!''

The searing intensity that blazed in his suddenly gaunt face burned away her protest. ''I promise,'' she whispered.

The flame died as quickly as it flared. The warm, chocolate eyes that melted when they were loving her were now opaque mirrors, showing nothing. They were the eyes of a man who had killed before, and would again—for her. A tiny corner of her brain screamed, frightened at how easily she accepted this side of him. Ruthlessly she strangled the voice into silence.

''You stay here and watch the truck.'' Ryan delivered his orders in a detached, lifeless voice, so different from the velvet purr that could lick over her skin like a warm, living being. ''If he comes, shoot to wound him only. I want him alive.''

Holding her eyes, he took her mouth in a harsh, thorough kiss. Without a word he turned and crossed the clearing. Her hesitant voice, calling as loudly as she dared, stopped him.

''You be careful, Ryan Jones! I love you.''

There was a quick flash of that rascally, rakish grin. ''I know.'' He turned and faded into the brush.

Ariel discovered that she was a miserable failure as the one who had to stand and wait. Belatedly she realized Ryan's ploy. The killer would never bother with the truck until he determined the success of his ambush. Ryan, of course, planned to intercept him, with her safely out of the way. She paced the clearing, torn by indecision. Should she go after him, risking his wrath and possibly spoiling his plan? Or should she keep her promise and remain here, feeling utterly useless and worried almost out of her mind. She finally decided that she would wait, unless she heard gunfire. Then no promise on earth could be strong enough to keep her from going to him. She was listening so intently for a gunshot that she never heard the small snap of a broken twig behind her.

"Set the shotgun down very carefully, Ariel."

The blood in her veins congealed. She hesitated, gauging her chances, but she knew that even she could never turn and fire fast enough to beat a bullet in the back. Like a sleepwalker, she laid the gun on the frozen grass.

Odd, she could hear the infinitesimal breakage of each blade, but she hadn't heard him approach. Her senses had become acutely sensitive. Was she suddenly so aware because she might have little time left to be aware of anything? She smelled a whiff of a familiar cloying cologne on the ragged breeze and heard the small sigh of relief behind her.

"Good girl. I'd hoped you would be sensible. Now kick it away." Her toe nudged the shotgun away. "You can turn around now," he added, almost as a polite afterthought.

She asked the question as she slowly turned. "Why, Robert?"

Robert DiSanto's red-rimmed green eyes narrowed sharply. "Ah, I see you're not surprised. That may change things a bit. Does anyone else know?"

"The IRS, the D.A. in San Francisco, the L.A. police, to name a few. There are roadblocks up here in the valley," she informed him with quiet satisfaction, then repeated her question. "Why did you kill your own brother, Robert?"

Robert DiSanto pulled away the wig of lank blond hair and gingerly peeled off the scraggly mustache and eyebrows, revealing thick, curly auburn hair. The rifle aimed at her heart wavered only a fraction. "Dennis and I were in business together, cocaine, some other things." His free hand gestured vaguely; then he shrugged. "But you probably already know all that."

"He got cold feet." Robert's low laugh was obscene. "He was afraid you would find out he wasn't as lilly-white as you thought he was. I told him—" his sigh indicated his forbearance "—he shouldn't choose a woman over business, but he wouldn't listen."

"But why kill him, Robert? He never would have told me."

Robert explained with the patience necessary for a backward toddler. "Because he might have decided to bare his soul to you after all, or let something slip. I couldn't take the risk. And then, you'd seen Garza that day in his office with us. Once he was arrested, I knew, if you saw his picture in the paper you'd remember. He saw the flicker of recognition when he mentioned Garza's name. "There, you see?" He'd proved his point. He shrugged eloquently. "You can understand my position. It was nothing personal, Ariel, just business. Just as you must understand—" he sounded confident that she did "—why I can't let you go now, you or your lover."

"They'll catch you, Robert." Ariel edged almost imperceptibly toward the closest thicket. If she could get within five or six feet she could dive for cover. "You'll never even get out of the valley."

"But they're looking for me in this, aren't they?" he said, his hand flicking contemptuously at the wig he had stuffed in the pocket of his scruffy jeans. He saw by the twinge of dismay crossing her face that he was right. "I can leave here easily, as myself, driving the car Jones rented. Nobody's looking—"

"It won't work, Robert," Ariel interrupted, her voice reasonable. "You may get past the roadblocks, but you won't be able to go back to Los Angeles. You'll be on the run, penniless, no one to turn to." She had decided to go not for the brush but for her shotgun when the time came. Just another few inches . . . "Why don't you just—"

"I think not." The barrel of the rifle gestured warningly, and Ariel froze. He began turning gradually, the rifle leading her in a slow, macabre dance around the clearing, until his unprotected back was to the levee. "I have quite a bit of money in a Bahamian bank," his smile was pleased, "for just such a contingency." His eyes looked past her for a moment, thoughtful. He caught her subtle move toward her gun, and they snapped back to her. "A little plastic surgery, and everything will work out fine." His tone indicated that he forgave her all the trouble she had caused him. "How did they find out?" he asked curiously.

"You weren't quite as clever with your money as you thought, Robert. And then I found a negative Dennis hadn't printed. You were in it, with Reilly, at the park. It was just an accident that you were caught by the camera." She felt a perverse flicker of satisfaction. "I recognized you, even through your disguise." He was holding the gun loosely; maybe if she rushed him, he would be so surprised he would drop it. She tensed, readying her body.

Robert nodded ruefully, his hands tightening their hold on the rifle. "Call your lover, Ariel; tell him you need him. Call him; he'll come."

Ariel's throat was achingly dry. She would get down on her knees and beg, throw herself on his gun, anything, but she wouldn't call

Ryan. She tried to swallow, her voice coming out a harsh rasp. "No, Robert."

Robert raised the rifle, and she couldn't keep from cringing. Then she stiffened her quaking body, using every ounce of willpower that she possessed. "I won't call him. You'll have to shoot me first."

Robert's finger moved to the trigger of the rifle. "Call him, Ariel. Now."

"He's already here, DiSanto." The feral growl came from behind him. "Drop the gun."

Ariel saw the shock blanch Robert's face as she dived for her shotgun. She rolled twice, then scrambled to her feet the gun leveled at his chest.

Robert DiSanto considered his options, then dropped his rifle.

"Back away from it," Ryan ordered. "And turn around."

DiSanto took three steps backward and turned. Slowly he raised his hands. "Pity," he reflected. "I'd thought about hiring you, Jones, if I ever needed a good criminal attorney. I don't suppose you'd be interested now." There was a hint of question in his voice.

Ryan held his gun almost carelessly. Reaching into his jacket pocket, he pulled out the last cigarette in the pack. He lit it, inhaling deeply, and breathed out a long stream of smoke. "No."

DiSanto made a small, indecisive move toward the gun lying on the ground in front of him.

"Go ahead, bastard," Ryan encouraged softly. "I've had you in my sights for the past five minutes. It wouldn't bother me in the least to pull the trigger, and *I*—" Ryan's cruel smile was self-mocking "—would certainly never be found guilty of murder."

"Why didn't you shoot?" The words were torn from DiSanto involuntarily.

Ryan didn't answer immediately. Now there was a question. Why hadn't he? He'd wasted precious minutes before he'd realized that the killer had done the unexpected and was not going to the riverbank. He'd had to waste more time circling back. When he'd topped the levee and seen Robert pointing his gun at Ariel, it was as if he were suddenly back in that Cambodian hut. He'd raised his rifle and sighted through the dull red mist clouding his vision. A small, sane inner voice had struggled to be heard over the bloodthirsty clamor in his brain. Then he'd heard her voice, rigidly controlled, low and rational. He could see she was terrified, her face was bloodless, her eyes enormous, but she'd held her trembling body straight and faced her murderer. And he knew she would never have called him. He'd felt such pride in her...and such love, and he had lowered the rifle.

"Because, as much as you deserve it, the woman you've tried so hard to kill saved you. I don't think she could take another death right now—not even yours. Besides," he added conversationally, "you probably won't be around much longer anyway. Your business associates won't be too happy with you. They're going to be afraid that you might develop a sudden urge to talk to the wrong people. Even in prison you'll have to look over your shoulder all the time."

Ryan watched as fear turned the man's handsome face ugly.

The woman Ryan thought couldn't take another death spoke at last. Ariel had almost fainted at the wild surge of relief and joy she had felt when Robert dropped the gun. She had been ready to fling herself into Ryan's arms. Then an ice-cold aftershock of lingering fury had numbed her emotions and her body. "Turn around, Robert," she said now. "Unlike you, I'm averse to shooting a man in the back."

The hunter turned on his quarry, but now he was the frightened animal at bay. He looked halfway across the little clearing into empty blue eyes. There was no hate in them, no remorse, no mercy for him.

The dark man behind them was forgotten. Only he seemed to hear the approaching sirens. Ryan thought furiously. He saw her eyes, too. She was going to shoot, and there wasn't the slightest hope that she'd miss. If he shot first, just to wound... It was too late. She had raised the gun to her shoulder and taken aim.

Robert DiSanto stood frozen, his green eyes widening in growing horror.

"No, Ariel. Oh, love, no." Ryan's despairing whisper was barely audible, his agile brain already planning her defense.

Her finger stroked the trigger in a lover's caress and tightened. The shotgun blast shattered the breathless quiet.

Chapter 15

Robert DiSanto screamed and fell. Two more shots echoed across the river. The startled geese milled frantically. They climbed high overhead, honking querulously.

Nothing in the clearing moved. Then, cautiously, Robert DiSanto uncurled his arms from around his head and rose up on his hands and knees, looking incredulously at the woman with the smoking gun.

"No, Robert," Ariel told him, her voice and smile oddly gentle, almost kind. "I couldn't kill you. Ryan was right. I couldn't bear another death, not even yours."

An avalanche of sand and dirt poured down the face of the levee. The men who had been stricken motionless by the tableau below them were piling out of their vehicles and sliding down the slope. Ariel, feeling strangely detached, saw the chief jerk Robert to his feet, snapping on handcuffs as he read him his rights. Ryan started toward her. He seemed to be moving in peculiarly slow motion. She ejected the last spent shell and handed her shotgun to the sheriff's deputy beside her. Then she quietly fainted.

When Ariel revived she found herself in what seemed to be becoming a common position for her. She was lying cradled in Ryan's arms across his lap. She kept her eyes closed, listening to the words flying over her light head. A game warden had evidently spotted Robert's rental car and called it in. Chief Dye and the sheriff had converged on the area. Coincidentally, Rick Jones and a federal marshall had arrived to take charge of their prisoner.

Ryan felt her relaxed body tighten with the return of consciousness and grinned up at his brother. His brother grinned back happily, then withdrew unobtrusively.

Ryan shifted a little on the cold ground. "Think you can stand up, love?" he murmured near her ear.

Ariel nodded and opened her eyes. The first thing she saw was the bloody collar of Ryan's coat. The bullet graze no longer oozed.

Ryan hauled her to her feet and was immediately called over by the federal marshal. Ted Dye put a stabilizing arm around her shoulders, and Ariel leaned against him gratefully. When he was sure she could stand by herself, he reclaimed his prisoner and marched him up the levee to a police car. Ariel watched as Ryan and his brother moved to the edge of the clearing to speak privately.

"I imagine Davidson will admit he may have been a little narrow-minded when he gets DiSanto's statement," Rick Jones predicted dryly. He watched Ryan's eyes drift back to the woman standing alone in the middle of the glade. His wickedly knowing grin was the identical twin of his older brother's. "I knew you'd like her."

"Yeah." Suddenly Ryan wrapped his brother in a crushing bear hug. Rick hesitated for only a heartbeat, then returned it, clapping Ryan on the back enthusiastically. They broke apart, hands clasping once. "I'll call you as soon as we're home," Ryan promised.

As suddenly as they had appeared, the men and their assorted cars and pickups vanished. Rick, the last man to leave, paused on the top of the levee. He watched as his brother put his arms around the woman he loved and folded her close. Her arms wound around his waist, pulling him closer. Wearily, they leaned on each other. The bloodied but victorious black knight was claiming his lady. With a soft, satisfied smile Rick walked away. The debt was paid at last.

The sun was only minutes below the rim of the valley. The dingy gray clouds were tinted with infinite shades of gold and rose. A few stray feathers of snow drifted down on their heads.

Gently disengaging herself from Ryan's arms, Ariel retrieved her shotgun. Her back to Ryan, she squared her drooping shoulders and drew a deep breath of the chilled air. She feared it was going to take far more courage to face the man she loved than it had taken to face a killer.

Trust, she'd discovered, required a small leap of faith. She'd made the leap and landed safely on her feet. Now she was about to take an even more desperate, sweeter gamble—her happiness on one verbal toss of the dice. "No"—two letters, snake eyes—and her life was going to be as bitter as venom. "Yes" and it was happily-ever-after-time.

"There's something that still has to be settled."

Ryan started toward her. "What's that?"

"Marriage," she said calmly. She leveled the shotgun at his belt buckle, and he halted abruptly.

Ryan eyed the shotgun. It was wobbling just a bit. He knew the gun was empty. He relit the dead cigarette and puffed leisurely. One elegant black brow arched. "Is it going to be a shotgun wedding, then?" He looked totally unconcerned, almost bored, and Ariel felt a shaft of killing pain. "Are we pregnant?"

The shotgun wavered badly. "Not—" her voice cracked "—yet."

He nodded disinterestedly, then moved without warning. The shotgun was jerked from her hands, and she was dragged into his arms. Clamping a ruthless hand on the back of her head, he tilted her face up to his.

"Say it!" he rasped. "It sure as hell took you long enough to admit it the first time, and I want to hear it again."

"I don't know if I will now." She sniffed petulantly. "I think you're trying to evade the issue here, counselor."

"Brat!" he growled in her right ear. "Say it, dammit!"

Two bright tears rolled down her cheeks as she gave him a dazzling smile. "I love you, Ryan Jones. Will you—"

His hand over her mouth silenced her question. "I love you, Ariel Spence." His dark eyes softened with a sweet poignancy. "And I want to be the one to ask. Will you marry me?"

Her yes was lost in an endless kiss. The sun finally broke through the clouds and flooded the little glade with brilliant sunlight.

Swirling snow devils hid the landscape outside the schoolhouse. Ryan stood behind Ariel at the window, his arms loosely around her.

"Isn't there a hot spring on the river, not far from here?"

Ariel watched the silent snow fall for a moment longer. "Mmm. It's supposed to be like a natural jacuzzi."

"The snow's supposed to last all night," he murmured. He tilted his head to look down at her, a sly smile flirting with his mouth. "I've always wondered how accurate certain details of your first book were, Felicia."

Her answering smile was wickedly innocent.

A short while later the steaming water was lapping at their bodies. Huge snowflakes fluttered down like white butterflies, landing on the smooth black rock. They tasted sweet and cool when caught on the tongue, but they tasted even better when they were licked from heated skin, icy hot and tangy.

"Ryan, I'm sinking," Ariel murmured, unconcerned.

"Hold your breath," he counseled. His lips melted a snowflake on her breast.

With a laughing gasp she clutched at his shoulders as she slid precariously lower. His hands were gentle on her hips as he lifted her over him. Delicately her tongue flicked another icy crystal from the black hair on his chest. "I love you." The words were whispered over his wet, warm skin.

"I love you," he echoed, burying his mouth in her throat.

As they sank deeper into the warm water, soft murmurs became even softer sighs of pleasure.

Reality, they discovered, was so much better than fiction.

*   *   *   *   *

A Note from Kathleen Korbel

I love to tell the story of *A Stranger's Smile*. It was the first book I ever wrote, the romance I wanted to read. When I sent it around to every publisher in the industry in the early eighties, I was told, and I quote, "You have suspense, a dead body and a Vietnam vet for a hero. What romance reader is going to want to read this?"

I can't tell you how glad I am that not only Silhouette but you, my readers, agreed with me about what kind of romances you like to read. I still love a good suspense, and a mysterious hero who has old scars and a week or two isolated in a cabin in the mountains to stir things up to a nice pitch—with the lady he is sure he doesn't want to fall in love with. And I still, and always will, love a happy ending. So, I hope you enjoy my very first fictitious hero, Jonathan Bradshaw Harris, and the lady he's sure he's not supposed to fall in love with, Anne Jackson.

Kathleen Korbel

A STRANGER'S SMILE

Kathleen Korbel

Chapter 1

"**Y**a know, it's been a long time since I've had the chance to
undress a handsome man." Anne pushed an errant strand of blond
hair out of her eyes and returned to fumbling with buttons.

A masculine voice answered from behind her. "Don't you think
you should wait till you get someplace warmer?"

"I will," she said, grimacing toward where Jim Thompson
waited for her in the darkness. "I'm just checking him over to see
whether he's worth taking home."

It was pitch of night. Anne and Jim crouched together at the
bottom of a steep ravine trying to assess the injuries of a man
who'd been discovered there. They found themselves working in
typically bad conditions. It was pitch-black and cold, the wind wet
with promised snow. Bare-limbed trees set up a thrashing that
drowned out the voices of the rest of the rescue party who waited
above, and flashlights flickered back and forth like agitated spirits. The narrow gulley echoed with the turbulence of a gathering
storm.

There was no ambulance or helicopter waiting to whisk Anne's
patient away to the safety of a trauma center. He'd fallen on the
wrong end of the Appalachians for that. Anne Jackson was a rural nurse; her helpers were farmers and storekeepers. Their transportation back down seven miles of negligible path to where they
could reach a helicopter was horseback and travois.

Anne rubbed her hands against her pant legs to warm them up. The temperature was dropping so fast that her gloves offered little protection for numbing fingers. For a brief moment she even courted the idea of trying to finish the examination with her hands in her pockets. Then she picked up her flashlight and went back to work.

Her patient was a stranger, a tall man with darkly handsome features, probably a few years older than her. It was hard to tell much more from the brief glimpses she could manage with the flashlight. She could tell for certain that he wasn't from anywhere nearby. His outerwear was too expensive, his hiking boots spotless and too frivolous for daily use. Then there was the matter of what Anne discovered when she finally did get his jacket unbuttoned. She started to laugh. The man was wearing a custom-tailored, three-piece, pin-striped suit.

"Well, that does it," she announced with a grin as she showed Jim her discovery. "I'm going to have to take him home just so I can find out how he got here. It ought to be one hell of a story."

Jim chuckled with a shake of his head. "Who do you think he is?"

"I don't know," she said, her flashlight again sweeping the strong features and glinting against the warm-brown hair. "But I hope this isn't one of his favorite suits. I'm going to have to ruin it."

"You about ready to move him?" It was getting harder to hear Jim's voice above the wind. "I still need to have Silas and Ed send down the basket."

Anne straightened from where the injured man lay crumpled against a tree and jammed her hands back into her pockets. "Yeah, I think so. I'm going to need a little help splinting his leg first."

While Jim retrieved equipment, Anne took a moment to stretch out the kinks earned from an already long day of rounds. She felt as if there were sand in her eyes and wool in her mouth. And she was freezing. In the two years she'd lived back on the mountain she'd grown accustomed to people showing up unexpectedly at her door for help, but she'd never really gotten used to the long hours. She'd already been up since four that morning and was looking at at least another five hours before her patient was in the helicopter and she was back in bed.

Anne lifted her face to the harsh, swirling wind and took a breath of the biting air. The wild darkness made her shiver. On a night like this she could almost wish that she'd never given up the comforts of Boston.

Almost.

She took another look down at her patient with his expensive clothes and well-groomed good looks and recognized the familiar tug of antipathy. No, she decided with a scowl. On second thought, even the prospect of warm toes and a good brandy wasn't worth the thought of going back to Boston.

Ten minutes later it started to snow. They never made it to the helicopter. They never got farther than the two miles down to Anne's house, still high in the backwoods, still beyond the reach of conventional vehicles. Blinded by driving snow and wind, it had been almost more than Anne and Jim could manage to get the injured man to the horses. The rise from the gulley was steep and loose, good finger holds rare, and the footing treacherous enough to twice send Anne sliding almost to the bottom before finally reaching safe arms at the top. It took forty-five minutes to maneuver her patient that far.

By the time they deposited the man in Anne's spare bedroom, the snow was battering incessantly at the windows, and covered the ground in a thick, white blanket. A fire was stoked in the living room, and in the bright red-and-white kitchen three men huddled over cups of steaming coffee. Anne spent two hours in the bedroom before she had the chance to get hers.

She took her stethoscope from her ears for the final time to hear the clock strike midnight. The wind had eased to a dull whine, and the conversation in the kitchen had degenerated to sporadic monosyllables. The air was close with the heat of the fire and the smell of drying wool.

Anne admitted the first feeling of relief. It looked as though her patient would be all right. Even though he was still unconscious, his vital signs were finally as stable as a rock. His injuries appeared to be manageable now that his temperature had reached a safe range. And he was beginning to show signs of coming to, which meant that she might just get some sleep herself. Now all she had to do was get the rest of the rescue party out of her kitchen and on home.

Anne wondered again just who her patient was. She could almost have mistaken him for a rancher of some kind if she didn't know better. Even with the pallor and bruising from his injuries, he was deeply tanned, his angular face rugged and windburned. His hands were work roughened and strong, the fingers almost gracefully long, and there wasn't an ounce of city-bred fat to be found on his long frame. Probably six foot one or two, he was tightly muscled, with the almost hungry, lean look of a backwoods man.

But this man was not from any backwoods. From years of all-too-unhappy experience, Anne recognized all the hallmarks of social privilege. Above and beyond the beautiful suit she'd had to cut off, he showed evidence of a lot of high-priced pampering. Someone from a top salon in New York had recently had his hands in that thick chestnut hair, and a manicurist had been at those nails. The cologne he wore was exclusive, and the down outer layer that had helped save him was L. L. Bean's best.

All of which meant that the outdoor labor he performed hadn't been herding cattle or felling trees. More likely mountaineering in Switzerland or skiing the Dolomites. Anne could easily visualize him in the rigging of his sailboat as he sped up the Atlantic coast in the America's Cup race, trading dares with the other contestants. The perfect fantasy man. A brunette version of her ex-husband, Tom.

She scowled irritably, suddenly sorry that her handsome patient wasn't a farmer or miner from nearby. She had a feeling that she knew just what kind of person he'd turn out to be, and that she'd end up hating him for it—a painful reminder of what she'd escaped by running home to the mountain.

As if aware that he was being scrutinized, Anne's patient began to stir. She took hold of his restless hands and leaned toward him.

"C'mon," she coaxed gently, "talk to me, mister. I want to know who you are. Open your eyes and talk to me."

He responded, though his words were jumbled and meaningless. Only the name Charlie stood out clearly. When he began to speak in French, she answered until she realized that she was responding to a very smooth proposition.

"Not tonight," she said, smiling wryly, wondering just what memory she'd tapped. "I have the feeling you're going to have a headache."

When he did come to, he did it with a start. His eyes snapped open and he bolted upright.

"Take it easy," Anne said soothingly, pushing him back down. She stopped suddenly, the rest of her words lost within the unexpected jolt of contact. She was stunned, thrown off center by the clear lake-blue of his eyes. Bottomless, sunlit blue. When those eyes opened, features that had been handsome became mesmerizing, magnetic. There was power there, a vitality that compelled. This was a man people watched and listened to and followed. A shudder of recognition rocked through her for a man she'd never met.

Anne realized that she was staring, unable to control the surge of lightning his touch suddenly sent through her. She caught herself just short of bolting from the room.

"You're fine," she said, struggling to keep her voice level and professional even as the ground fell away. "You had a little accident."

He stared at her, his eyes unfocused and frightened. Anne found herself wanting to touch his face, to gently guide him back to lucidity. She didn't.

"It's okay," she said, smiling, trying to keep his attention focused. "My name's Anne. Can you tell me yours?"

"I..." It seemed to surprise him that he didn't have the strength to express himself. His eyes wandered again. "What...happened?"

"You fell, but you're okay. How do you feel?"

"I hurt...everywhere."

"I know. You were pretty banged up. You're okay, though." It was a good idea to keep repeating pertinent facts. People who had suffered concussions tended to have short, disjointed memories. Besides, Anne couldn't seem to think of anything else to say. "Can you tell me your name?"

"Was anyone else...?" He moved to ease some discomfort and discovered an even greater one. His face tightened with the surprise of it.

"No one else was hurt. You were alone." She was losing him again, his eyes blurring with confusion and pain. Again she fought the urge to reach out to him. She had never in her life reacted like this to a man—not even Tom—and it unnerved her.

His eyes drifted closed again, and Anne straightened, still shaken by her reaction. Now that his eyes were shut he seemed no more than another good-looking man, slightly worse for wear, who had the misfortune of reminding Anne of the people she'd once courted as her right.

She stood abruptly. The thought of her life in Boston hadn't really bothered her in a long time. The last thing she needed on this dark, snowy night was to find herself rehashing a painful past. Yet that seemed to be what she was about to do. Anne took one last look at her sleeping patient, her eyes unconsciously accusing, and turned to leave.

She met Jim heading in from the kitchen.

"He okay?" At five foot ten, he stood a few inches taller than Anne, his rust ponytail haloed in the hall light.

Anne took a minute to hang her stethoscope on the door before answering. "As far as I can tell. He's stitched and splinted and warm as toast. It would sure be nice to have some diagnostic equipment up here to make sure, though."

He grinned. "It'll make a difference when the clinic's open."

"I know," she said on a sigh, automatically checking the cracked face of her watch. "But we couldn't have even gotten him that far tonight. There has to be a better way."

"We'll get you a heliport for Christmas."

Anne finally grinned back and linked arms with her friend. "Don't make promises you have no intentions of keeping. C'mon, let's see if you guys can get home."

"Don't hold your breath. Silas is planning to camp out on your couch until we find out just who your mystery guest is."

She scowled playfully. "One of these days it's going to dawn on him that I'm not ten years old anymore."

Jim guided her back down the short hallway with a laugh. "Like I said, don't hold your breath."

When Anne walked into the kitchen the other two men stood to greet her. Wearily waving them back down, she disengaged herself from Jim and headed for the stove.

"There isn't any more we can do tonight," she said simply. "Better get on home while you can."

There wasn't an immediate answer to her offer. She filled a mug and brought it back to the big oak table. The oldest of the men who sat there scrutinized her as she eased herself into the chair across from him. She was already beginning to stiffen from the evening's exertions, but it wouldn't do at all to let him know. Taking a good sip of the hot brew, she fought the urge to confront the challenge in those watery blue eyes and be done with it. That was not the way to handle Silas, though. He defused more easily with patience and control.

"He should be okay," she said evenly, eyes back to her coffee. "I'll just keep an eye on him for a while to be sure."

"He sure was lucky Ef found him," Silas offered laconically, his own gaze retrieved. "One night like tonight woulda killed him for sure."

"He's just lucky that the fall didn't do it first. Six inches one way or the other and we wouldn't have needed to bother going after him until spring."

"I imagine his family'd be up here before that," Silas said, his eyes still as carefully averted as Anne's. "He sure ain't from around here."

Anne couldn't help but laugh. "I'll drink to that. Nobody around here's dumb enough to walk off a mountain."

"Not in a suit, anyway." Jim said with a grin. That elicited a round of chuckles and bemused head shaking.

"I don't suppose you found a name in those fancy duds?" Anne asked.

Silas laughed with a short, wry bark. "Not likely, seein' as how it was Ef that found him first."

"Yeah, I did notice that he disappeared awfully fast," she said and nodded with a rueful grin, thinking more of how the mug in her hands felt almost unbearably hot. She'd taken a good part of the slides up and down the ravine on her now-tender palms. Without thinking, she blew on the chafed skin to ease the stinging.

Jim reached out and pulled her hand over for inspection. "That looks awful," he scolded. "You'd better see to taking care of yourself."

"It doesn't really bother me." She shrugged, smiling at his concern even as she railed at his bad timing. She might never get Silas home now. "All in a day's work."

Silas frowned down at her in his patriarchal way. "Not a lady's work to go traipsin' down a mountain like that in the middle of the night."

"I told you, Silas," she chided, unable to prevent a playful grin from crinkling her gray eyes. "I'm not a lady. I'm a nurse."

He scowled, the deep creases on his weather-beaten face growing with disapproval. Anne had a good deal of trouble refraining from another grin. Silas had considered her as one of his own children since her mother had died years ago. He'd been with her on that day. He'd always been there when Anne had needed him, his gentle strength a fulcrum against which the rest of the world could balance. And he always treated her as if she were still the small girl who used to beg him for piggyback rides and make thrones from his huge, handcrafted chairs.

With what little energy she had left, Anne lurched to her feet, coffee still in hand, and turned to the silent third of the trio. John Edward had watched the preceding exchange with quiet amusement. He looked up at Anne with carefully passive eyes.

"John," she said, "I'll just go in and see if your things are dry for the trip back. Would you like to bring the horses out?"

"Sure thing, Annie."

When he stood, so did Jim and Silas. Silas took up a position next to Anne, still none too pleased.

"You can't take care of that man by yourself," he protested, as much from moral as practical considerations. Anne confronted the tall, scarecrowlike old man who all but dwarfed her.

"I can take care of him and ten others like him," she said gently. "The real work's been done. All I have to do now is baby-sit. You don't need brains or brawn for that so I'm the perfect candidate." She hurried on with the clincher before Silas had the chanced to protest. "Silas, I don't want Sarah to worry about you.

You know her. This very minute she's standing by the front door watching the snow, and she won't move till you get home.''

Jim and John had already edged toward the front door. Anne followed without again challenging Silas eye-to-eye and helped pick drying coats and hats from the quilt rack in front of the couch. Silas kept his silence as a matter of principle, but he began to dress along with the others.

John had just shut the door behind him when Jim poked into his jacket for gloves and came up with a surprised look on his face.

"Oh, Annie, I almost forgot. I have something for you."

Anne looked over to see him pulling a long envelope from his pocket.

"This came for you this afternoon, and when John stopped by for me, I figured I'd bring it along. Special delivery letter."

He waited for Anne to take the envelope, but she hesitated, having already seen the return address. For the second time in an hour, Anne felt her foundation slipping away, this time for an entirely different reason. Anger knifed through her stomach and brought bile to her throat.

The corner of the envelope bore the ostentatious logo of a distinguished Boston law firm. The best legal minds in Massachusetts, especially if you had corporate piracy in mind. Anne should have known. It was the law firm that Tom and her brother Brad had always used.

She'd told them to leave her alone. That she'd come home to Cedar Ridge to get as far away from him as she could, to save what was left of her sanity. She'd never wanted to hear from Tom or Brad again. It seemed that they couldn't leave well enough alone.

She accepted the letter from Jim and immediately folded it into her pocket. Silas, standing next to her, watched in growing astonishment. He'd never had a special delivery letter in his life, and considered them second only to divine revelation in importance. He simply could not understand her cavalier disregard for this one.

"Annie," he objected as tactfully as he knew how. "It must be important if they went to all the trouble of sendin' it special delivery."

She smiled, trying to keep her tone light. "Silas, it's from Brad. He sends birthday cards special delivery. But just in case it is bad news, I'm not about to read it until I've had a good night's sleep. Maybe I'll open it tomorrow after I've had my coffee." Maybe never.

Anne knew that Jim would understand. Silas did not. Wide-eyed and silent, he glared at her even after Jim had passed him his big coat. Anne was saved from another lecture by John's timely reappearance. Silas merely shrugged, as if he'd once again given up on comprehending her, and followed John back out into the night. Anne watched his angular frame bend into the white wind and wished again that she could tell the old man how much she loved him.

Jim paused beside Anne before stepping out the door. "Are you all right?" he asked quietly, motioning vaguely in the direction of the envelope.

She grinned ruefully. "Sure. It just galls me that I can still react like that to them after all this time."

His brown eyes softened with empathy. "Cassie'd say you have every right. Put that thing away until the morning and get some sleep. You won't be much good to you or your patient if you don't. The Thompson kitchens will take care of dinner tomorrow."

"Thanks, Jim." She smiled at her friend. "Give those babies a kiss for me."

He shook his head slowly, admiration in his eyes. "You know something? You're quite a lady."

"Go on and get out of here," she ordered with mock severity as she pushed him toward the door. "You keep talking like that, and I'm going to ask for a raise."

Anne stood at the window for a few long moments watching the men disappear into the darkness. Then, turning away, she pulled the crumpled envelope from her pocket and deliberately dropped it into the trash.

It took Anne another hour before she had time to relax and dry her hair in front of the great crackling fire in the living room. The lights were out in the cabin, with only the molten glow of the fire washing over the rough wooden walls. Anne eased herself down to sit cross-legged on the giant hooked rug in front of the couch, her old hairbrush in hand, another cup of coffee beside her. She'd finally taken the time to peel off her soggy clothes and slip into the comfortable warmth of her flannel nightgown and robe. The salve she'd spread on her hands was beginning to ease the tenderness even as her other joints set up a chorus of protest.

She knew that she should have been in the extra bedroom waiting for her patient to wake up. Somehow she couldn't bring herself to do it just yet. Before she walked headfirst into a new problem, she needed the time to sit and unwind from the demands the day had already put on her.

She hoped that she could relax without slipping into a coma. When she'd climbed up earlier to the loft where she slept to change clothes, her big old four-poster had almost beckoned to her. If she chanced going up there again, that old bed might just reach out and catch her.

Anne smiled wryly and leaned a little to the side, catching the braid of her hair in one hand and slowly unknotting it. When her hair fell free, cascading over her shoulders, she took the brush to it and shivered at the heady sensation. The straw-gold curtain shimmered richly in the firelight, lush and full. It had always been Anne's outstanding feature, a treasure that had transformed her patrician features into a singular beauty. Tom had always loved to touch it, running his hands through it as if it were a magical gold. He had encouraged her to wear it up, sleekly styled so that it complimented the cool gray of her eyes and classic lines of her face.

She had to admit that she'd always turned heads when she'd walked into a room of the social and political elite. She was the essence of sophistication, one of the ten best-dressed boss's daughters on the Eastern Seaboard. Now when she had finally gained the self-esteem to match the picture she'd once presented, it seemed that she was much better suited to braids: easy to take care of and practical. The way her life had become.

Anne sighed and straightened, her hair swinging behind her to brush at the small of her back. The coffee was the last of the pot Silas had brewed, and it tasted bitter and hot, helping to wake her from the comfort of warm clothes and a fireplace. Maybe enough for her to stay awake through a book. She hated it when she found herself rehashing the follies of her life, and she resented emotions that had never been properly put in their place at the conclusion of relationships. The well-groomed stranger in her bedroom and a special delivery letter were quite successfully dredging up regrets that she thought she'd given up long ago.

For some reason, she thought of Jim and how he reflected the changes in her own life. Once she would have considered him an anachronism, the kind of man one heard about in *National Geographic* or *Mother Earth News*. Who could imagine, after all, an ad exec from Chicago who pulled in seventy-five to a hundred thousand a year giving it all up for a life like the Waltons'? But Jim Thompson had done just that.

Tom would have savagely dissected Jim's manhood with the precision of a surgeon. Sipping at his vodka martini, he would have wondered how any man could survive the ignominy of running away from the real world to hide in, of all places, the Appalachians. His laughter would have been cruel and unforgiving.

Even her father would have been bitterly disappointed if she'd brought Jim home from college instead of Tom. Tom had had what her father had called an inborn knack for big business. Anne, in a rare moment of insight during her first year of marriage, had correctly labeled it the jugular instinct, an instinct that Jim simply didn't have.

Her reflections were interrupted by the first sounds of a man struggling for consciousness. As quickly as her aching limbs would let her, she got to her feet and headed for the bedroom.

Only a small night-light was on by the bed. Within its soft pool of light she saw her patient moving a bit, as if caught in a bad dream. His brow, swathed in a bandage, puckered momentarily before his whole face took on a frown. He looked as if he were trying to remember something. His hands lifted aimlessly from the bed, seeking the air and then dropping again. The pain even touched his subconscious, and he made little moans as he moved.

Anne reclaimed her seat and resumed trying to talk her stranger back to consciousness, this time with more caution and not a small amount of trepidation. It didn't take him as long this time. Within a minute or two, his eyes opened and focused on her.

Anne decided that it was definitely too late for her to still be up. Her reaction was even stronger this time. She had to restrain herself from looking away from him, afraid all of a sudden that with just his eyes he would pierce the innermost corners of her soul. Again she felt herself go rigid in response to the heat he stirred in her.

The minute his eyes locked into hers she felt that jolt, as if the chair wouldn't hold her. His eyes were clear now, not so fogged with confusion. Anne saw in them the winter sky above the pines. Alive, kinetic.

Her smile was unconsciously stiff. "How are you feeling?"

He let his gaze wander over the shadowy room for a minute and then return to rest on Anne's face. "Pretty bad. What happened?"

"You must have been hiking in the park and gotten lost. We found you just beyond it, in a ravine." She didn't think to mention the suit.

"The park?"

She nodded. "Great Smoky Mountain National Park. Do you remember being there?"

It took him a moment to answer. "I...I guess so. Is this... a...hospital?"

"Oh, Lord, no." She grinned, genuinely amused. "I'm a rural nurse. You're at my house on the backside of Bennett's Mountain. We couldn't get you any farther than this. It's snowing outside."

"Snowing." He rolled the sound of the word around as if considering a new phenomenon. "I wouldn't have...gone back...in the snow."

Anne was enough of a mind to appreciate the distinction he made. He would go in his best suit, but not if it were snowing. Real city logic.

"I'm sure you wouldn't have," she said, nodding. "It didn't start until after you fell. Can we notify anyone?"

He nodded slowly to himself as if his actions had been justified. When he winced with the discomfort of the action, Anne found herself leaning toward him, almost sensing his pain.

"What's your...name?"

"Anne," she said quietly, suddenly wanting to hold him, to rock him to an easy sleep, and just as suddenly realizing how ridiculous the idea was. "What's yours?"

His face softened into a smile, but the light was fading in his eyes. Anne bent closer as if to follow the flight of his attention.

"You're..."

"A nurse," she repeated.

"Beautiful." She could hardly hear his voice, but he managed a more wry smile before letting his eyes close. "I feel so...tired."

"Best thing for you," she agreed, realizing with a start that she'd again taken hold of his hand. "Can you tell me your name first?"

She was too late. Surprised, she watched him as he slept. He looked like a tousled little boy, making her want to reach over and brush the dark hair back from where it tumbled over his forehead. It occurred to her then that his voice matched his eyes, clear and quiet.

She sat where she was for a moment, willing the fire to die in her, listening to the silence around her as she marveled at the spark that attracted her to a stranger. Spark! Hell, it was more like bonfire. She spent all of her time wishing for the Jims of the world and still became caught in the allure of another Tom.

Maybe she'd be wrong. Maybe when he woke up in the morning he would still be as quiet and genuine as he was tonight. She found that she wanted that very much.

No matter what, she thought as she looked down at him, the mysterious electricity once again dimmed, she was going to get him back out of her house as fast as she could and get on with her life. Blue eyes or not, she was a big enough girl to be able to keep her professional distance. And that would be that.

Chapter 2

"So, you weren't a dream after all."

Anne's eyes shot open. For a moment, she couldn't remember where she was. The sight of her patient brought her abruptly back to reality. She'd ended up crawling into an overstuffed chair in the corner of the guest room sometime the night before, and had evidently not made it back to her own bed. Every muscle in her let her know what a smart idea that had been.

Wondering what time it was, she took a minute to rub at the sleep in her eyes before attempting to launch herself from the soft cushions. She was not looking forward to testing her morning-after muscles. Pain was not her favorite wake-up call.

When she finally did lurch up, there was no choice but to quickly admit to a temporary setback. She mouthed a surprised little "Ooh," and sank right back down. Her patient watched every move in silence.

Anne couldn't help but notice that his eyes were even more uncannily bright in the daylight. Only a surrounding ring of darker blue seemed to delineate the iris at all. This morning they were more alert, more in control. And even more mesmerizing.

"I'll be up in a minute," she said grinning sheepishly, her eyes only briefly meeting his as she tried to quell the sudden staccato of her heart. It was too early for this. "I'm a little stiff this morning from a bit of surprise mountain climbing last night. How are you feeling?"

"Like I tried to share a small seat with a truck," he said, his voice very quiet as if its proper use would cause discomfort. He was smiling, though. "I started to feel better the minute I woke up and saw you.... You were here last night?"

"You remember?" Foolishly, Anne felt dread, waiting for his pleasant demeanor to change, waiting to be disillusioned.

He shook his head slightly. "Your face, not much more."

She nodded to herself as she once again tried to launch herself from the chair. Every joint protested vigorously, and her knees were tender from where they'd made contact with every rock on the slope, but everything was in working order. She made it over to stand by the bed without too much difficulty.

"You were found last night at the bottom of a nearby ravine."

"And you sat up all night with me?" He snapped off a perfect, flashing smile that sent Anne's stomach plummeting. She recognized the look with sick fatalism. Barracuda teeth, she called it. Tom had a similar look. She saw the control grow on the stranger's face, the facade take shape before her eyes, and she knew without a doubt that her instincts had been right. She was going to hate this man, regardless of his magnetism.

She had wanted so much for him to be different.

"I wasn't sure how badly you were hurt," she answered, realizing with some regret that her voice had automatically taken on the smooth, icy tones she'd cultivated on the cocktail party circuit. Suddenly Boston wasn't nearly as far away as she would have liked.

"How badly am I hurt?"

"Well, I know for sure that you broke your leg, you have a dandy cut on your forehead and you're scraped up just about everyplace else." As she talked Anne took out her medical equipment and began to check the injuries she'd listed. It occurred to her that he must have had a similar conversation sometime in the past. The night before she'd discovered a number of scars that wrapped around his left side. Fine lines now from very good plastic surgery, they represented a once-severe injury. "Where else do you hurt?"

"Besides everywhere?"

"Besides everywhere."

"My back, down low. And my chest, right about here." He motioned to an area of bad abrasions.

She nodded, gently palpating the point midway across the right side of his chest. "You probably cracked a couple of ribs when you landed. You wound up wedged against a tree. I'd imagine that your backache's from a muscle strain, judging by where you say it hurts."

"Aren't you going to feel it to make sure?"

Again she froze. Why couldn't he keep that suggestive gleam out of his eyes, or come up with a half-human response? Just the tone of his voice was so much like Tom's that Anne found herself bracing for the hurt and humiliation that had to follow. It was all she could do to remain still.

"No," she told him, straightening, "I'm going to make breakfast. Do you feel like some soup and toast, or would you rather just rest awhile?"

"I'd rather get to know you better."

Her smile was rigid. "That wasn't one of the choices."

He wasn't in the least fazed. "In that case, I'll rest up so that I can have the strength later—when it is."

She ignored that. "As soon as we can get you down the mountain we'll transport you to a hospital. Right now it's a little difficult to travel. We had our first snowfall of the season while we were picking you off the mountain, and I'm afraid it was a beaut. Until we can get you to civilization, is there anyone who should be notified?"

His expression remained nonchalant, but Anne could see that he was tiring. "Oh, I'm sure there is, but don't bother. I don't think I'm going to feel like putting up with them for a few days."

"You're on the wrong side of the mountain for visitors," she said. "Phone lines are down from the snow, and nobody can get up here unless it's on horseback."

He looked astounded, eyeing the room about him as if expecting to see kerosene lamps and chamber pots.

"The peace and quiet can be deafening," she said, turning for the door. A parting thought kept her there for a moment. "If you need anything, yell. My name's Anne. I'm afraid that since we didn't find any identification on you, I don't know yours."

"My wallet? My briefcase?"

"If you had them when you fell, you didn't by the time we got to you."

"What do you mean?" he demanded, his voice imperious and condescending. "I have some important papers in that briefcase. Somebody'd damn well better find it."

"Actually," she retorted dryly, "I have it. And I'm splitting the credit cards in your wallet with my cohorts. We're going on a shopping spree in town tomorrow."

He wasn't amused. A cold disdain lit his eyes. "I doubt that any of the hicks in that two-horse town would know what to do with a credit card if they had one."

That did it. If only he could have kept his mouth shut, Anne would have gladly drowned in the tides of his eyes. She could have at least dreamed that there were still, in fact, some decent people in the society she'd left behind. This guy was making her more and more glad that she'd gotten out when she did.

"And may I say for all the hicks who had the questionable sense to pull you up a ravine in a snowstorm," she said, trying very hard to keep her voice even, "you're welcome."

For a moment he glared at her as if at a not-too-bright salesperson. Then, with a suddenness that left Anne confused, he sighed, and the emotion drained from his face as if the effort were too great. "I'm sorry, Anne. I seem to have forgotten my manners. Jonathan Bradshaw Harris. And I think I'll get a nap now and try to eat something later."

Anne walked out quickly to prevent staring openmouthed at him. He wouldn't have noticed. His eyes were closed by the time she reached the hallway.

Anne had been mistaken. Her patient wasn't going anywhere. There was a good foot and a half of snow on the ground. She saw it the minute she stepped into the kitchen and looked out the windows. The wind had eased during the night so that the snow wasn't blowing hard, but it still fell heavily and steadily, making visibility limited. The hills looked like vague watercolors painted in shades of gray, the firs by the barn spearing black and sudden into the light morning sky. If the snow kept up, they wouldn't be able to get Mr. Harris down the mountain for days, and after Anne's initial conversation with him, that prospect didn't appeal to her at all.

Dressing quickly in an old flannel shirt and jeans and shoving a heavy knit cap on her head, she threw on her jacket and headed out to tend the animals.

Her big bay gelding, Andy, greeted her by stamping impatiently against the side of his stall. He wasn't a fan of the cold weather, especially when he had to saddle him up on frigid winter mornings to make rounds. He never balked from her touch, but let her know nonetheless exactly how he felt. Anne smiled at his call and protest, knowing that he would be far friendlier when he realized that this day was to be spent lounging in the protection of the barn.

Pulling on the heavy door, she shut out the white morning and enveloped herself in the warmer, damp smells of hay and animals and leather. Her father had often said that she should have been born in his grandmother's time when the farm had been a working one. She had always loved taking care of the animals, and had spent some of her most contented moments grooming the horses or milking the cow.

Today, though, her private demons wouldn't leave her alone long enough to enjoy the peace the physical work usually afforded. The chores she did were by now so rote that she ended up with even more time to think and remember.

Maybe if she'd only gotten the letter from Brad, or just had the unexpected visit by a handsome stranger in wolf's clothing she could handle everything with more composure. But one arriving right on top of the other had proven too much. Suddenly the old pain gnawed at her like fresh fire.

For the past two years, Anne had done everything in her power to wipe out the events that had driven her back to the mountains. She'd severed her ties with the city and reestablished relationships made during the years her family had used the cabin as a summer home away from the pressures of her father's position. Leaving the power and wealth behind her, she'd resurrected the simple customs of the generations of Jacksons who had lived on the land before her. She had carefully structured her life to include only the present and those selected memories that could no longer hurt her.

She'd become so involved with life on the mountain that if it weren't for the few keepsakes she'd brought with her from Boston, she could have almost thought that there had never been a life there at all. The wealth and the crowded existence of the socially elite might not have ever existed. She could have almost thought that there had never been a business.

She frowned, hating even the sound of the word that had so shaped her life.

Business.

Jackson Corporations Limited had not been just a business, but a living thing. Her father had created it with equal parts dream, ambition and obsession. JCL had in turn bestowed her family with more status than even status-hungry Boston had demanded and given power beyond even educated imaginations. It had transformed old family names into a dynasty, a dynasty that should by rights be handed over to the oldest child. Or, in the case of Peter Jackson, who held fast to the belief that women had no place in the crucibles of power, to the oldest son.

What had been unfortunate was the fact that the oldest son, the only son, was an unworthy heir. Bradley Jackson had been blessed with none of the natural leadership, organization and charisma that had served his father so well. A weak, resentful child, he had never earned his father's respect or trust. After waiting longer than Brad had thought reasonable for the authority he equated with his birthright, and which his father, for fear of his business refused to give, he resorted to the natural talents he did have. He schemed with a willing brother-in-law to rob his father of the very empire he had created.

In the end Brad and Tom won. Peter Jackson died, a man broken in spirit, and Anne, caught between father and husband, lost everything in a fight she wanted no part of. She had come home to bury her father and stayed, too distraught by what had been done to ever consider going back.

Anne stopped a minute, the memories beginning to suffocate her. Her eyes rose, drawn to a small yellow glint in the barn's soft gloom. It was still there, above her head on a nail she'd driven into the stall post, the small plain gold band she'd hung up two years ago, the symbol of why she'd vowed never to leave the mountain again.

Unbidden, the picture of Tom taunted her. Handsome, electric, intelligent, overachiever Tom McCarthy had thrown her away in his lust for the power he saw in her father. She looked at the ring and knew that it had been Jonathan Harris, with his electric blue eyes and power-modulated voice, who had blown this particular ill wind back into her life. He was so much like Tom that it was like being forced to face her ex-husband again here where she'd finally left him and where she still sought to exorcise the memory of that last meeting.

It had been November, a clear bright day when the mountain had been brilliant with autumn. Anne had brought her father home to the cabin when the fight for control of the company had become too vicious. He'd looked sickly and so suddenly old. She'd thought that maybe the isolation would help.

Then Tom had appeared, tall and blond, well-groomed and controlled. She'd known why he'd come and instinctively tried to hide from it. She remembered it now coldly, as if it were part of a bad movie she'd seen instead of the final dissolution of a marriage she'd so long cherished.

He came up behind her, his sleek cap of blond hair glowing like a halo in the afternoon light. It was then that he finally admitted to her what he and Brad were doing, as if she hadn't already known. They were about to take final control of the company away from the man who'd given his life to it.

He reached down to touch her hair as it hung freely down her back.

"Anne, come home." His tone was smooth, well modulated, prepared. She heard no pain or grief to make the words sound honest.

She steeled herself against this. For as much as she hated him, she still, even after what he'd become, loved him desperately.

"What for, Tom?" she asked, her eyes away on the peaceful hills. "What is there to come home to?"

"Come home to me, Anne." It didn't seem to occur to him to mention love or need. "I'll take care of you."

Was that why she'd married him? Had she needed someone to take care of her?

"Like you took care of my father? He trusted you, Tom. He couldn't have given you more opportunity in that company if you'd been his real son."

"Don't be stupid, Anne. I'm giving you another chance. All that old man ever gave you was the money to mingle with the right crowd."

She'd turned on him then, the anger rising. "He is my father. And he's never in his life deliberately hurt me. You, on the other hand, seem to have made a career of it. I think you'd better go."

He'd allowed an eyebrow to arch, as he gave one parting shot. "Your father and I are the same person," he said with some satisfaction. "If we weren't, you'd never have married me. You're dependent on men like us, my love."

He had turned back to the road before she finally said it, sealing their future. "You'll hear from my lawyer on Monday."

It had been the last time she'd cried.

Anne was collecting the eggs when she heard the muffled sounds of hoofbeats. More than one horse was approaching the cabin. She picked up her basket and walked over to give a much more amiable Andy a parting pat on the nose before opening the door.

The snow hadn't stopped while she had been inside. She had to lean heavily on the door to get it open, and the tracks she'd made two hours earlier were almost obliterated. She was beginning to despair of ever getting Jonathan Harris down the mountain.

"Annie, there you are."

Silas strode quickly over from the porch, followed closely by Jim.

Anne grinned at the look on Silas's face. "What are you doing back up here so soon?" she asked. Silas took the basket and pail from her just as he always did.

"Sheriff's busy," Jim offered with a slow grin, "and since we were coming up this way anyway, we told him we'd check up on your patient for him."

"I'm not harboring a notorious criminal, am I?" she asked mischievously in Silas's direction.

"Don't know." The old man shrugged, opening the door for her. "Never did come up with any identification."

"His name's Jonathan Something-or-other Harris," she said obligingly as she pulled off her jacket and gloves to hang before the fire. The men followed her lead, stamping the snow from their boots on the throw rug by the door.

"He awake?" Silas asked.

"He was. Coffee, anyone?" She didn't wait for an answer but headed out to the kitchen and the coffeepot. She wanted some even if they didn't.

"Can we talk to him?"

"Sure, if he's awake," she said with a nod. "He doesn't have much stamina right now, but you can find him in the guest room if you want to grill him."

"Silas," Anne asked quietly a moment later, "is there any way we can get him down the mountain?"

"Is he hurt bad?" he said frowning.

"Not really," she admitted, pulling out some coffee cake she'd baked a few days earlier. "I'm afraid there's a personality conflict. He's beginning to remind me of Tom, and I don't want to end up pitching him back over a cliff in a couple of days."

Silas nodded, suppressing a half grin. "Can he go on horseback?"

"No."

"Then we can't. Snow's already too deep for a wagon, and the radio's callin' for another foot or so before it stops."

"Another foot?" she immediately protested, turning on him. He was pouring coffee into mugs for her and shaking his head in disbelief.

"Annie," he admonished, "you've got the fanciest stereo in the county up here. Why don't you at least listen to the weather once in a while? You wouldn't keep gettin' surprised like that."

It was no use trying to explain her little quirk to Silas. She'd tried once and ended up sounding paranoid even to herself. But at first even hearing the sound of a professional radio announcer had brought her too close to the city. After a while she had truly begun to prefer the comfort of silence over the repetitious babble of a radio—even the best one in the county.

"We won't even be able to get him down on horseback for much longer," he continued, evidently not expecting an answer. "That's why we came now, so we could get a name and notify kin."

Anne almost made the mistake of letting Silas know how his news affected her. She nearly screamed. But he was looking at her closely, his eyes suspiciously noncommittal, and Anne realized that he was only inches from staying for the next few days. That would have been even worse than just having Mr. Harris on her hands. She smiled without a word and handed him a cup of coffee.

After Silas went off to join the one-man posse in the bedroom Anne realized that she needed a dish towel. The extras were in the hall closet across from the guest room where Silas and Jim were interrogating her patient. She stood alone in the kitchen for a minute listening to the sounds of conversation that came from the down the hall, the compulsion pulling at her. Like an itch, she thought absently, that needs to be scratched.

It didn't take her more than a minute to give in to temptation.

By the time she reached the hallway she knew Silas had heard Mr. Harris's opinion on the notification of relatives. He was asking if there were any reason Mr. Harris didn't want his family called. To someone like Silas that was as unthinkable as it was suspicious. Anne had to repress a grin. Jim would appreciate her reaction, but neither Silas nor Jonathan Harris would.

The impulse died when Jonathan answered Silas's question. Suddenly Anne felt as if she'd missed something.

It wasn't so much what he said, which was something about avoiding company hassles, but how he said it that baffled her. Smiling ruefully, he spoke with the same quiet respect most of the people in the area expressed when talking to the old man. No condescension, none of the smug patronization Tom or Brad had always shown for someone from the mountains.

Anne was impressed. If nothing else, he was certainly a crafty animal. She imagined that whatever it was he did, that he did it very well. And if he wanted something in that rarefied atmosphere in which he traveled, he usually got it.

At that moment Jonathan caught her staring at him. Without missing a beat he flashed a knowing grin at her that knocked into her like a kick. Those damn white, perfect teeth. Why didn't they seem to bother anybody else as much as they did her?

When her first reaction died, something else dawned on Anne. Jonathan was giving her a message. In his eyes she saw the admission that he was a different person than the men he faced. His initial reaction to being caught up here outside his universe would never do, and he proposed to change his attitude when he dealt with these people. She also had the very unsettling feeling that he considered her as much an outsider as him, which made her fair game.

She felt totally confused. Jonathan Harris seemed to be going out of his way to keep her off balance. He caught her this time with her mouth open.

"Don't worry about me," he was saying to Jim and Silas even as his eyes held Anne's. "I'll behave. My nurse trusts me even less than you do. She won't let me get away with anything."

Silas and Jim turned to see her standing across from the doorway. Anne allowed herself a slow, controlled smile just for Mr. Harris.

"He's right, Silas. I'll probably end up bringing in the shotgun from the barn. Just in case Mr. Harris tries to steal the chickens."

Jim couldn't quite control the corners of his mouth. Anne decided that if he thought it was so funny, he could stay up here instead of her. She'd much rather run a general store than tap-dance with Mr. Harris for a week. Come to think of it, she thought as she swung the towel over her shoulder, maybe she should let Silas stay up here. Then she could just ride off and not have to worry about Jonathan at all.

By the time Jim and Silas finished the interrogation Anne had the table set and fresh bread out. Silas appeared in the kitchen doorway, a suspicious frown clouding his features. Anne knew that it had everything to do with the fact that Jonathan was playing the mysterious stranger. Knowing Silas, she was sure that he would ride straight down to the station to have the sheriff run Jonathan's name for wants and warrants. She couldn't help the grin this time as she invited him to sit for another cup of coffee.

"We'll try and have somebody up here every day to check on you, Annie," Jim offered as he sat. "And I'm sure I can get the boys at the phone company busy on your lines."

Anne sat across from him. "If you're worried about my virtue, Jim, don't. Even the best mashers I've known would have trouble making time on a broken leg. I can move a lot faster than he can."

Silas didn't take to her levity. "It won't hurt any to accept the help, Annie." He frowned his admonition. "You don't know who that man is. For all we know, that fancy name of his ain't even real."

"That just shows he has a classy imagination." She grinned. "If he's a burglar, he must be a good one. That was a five-hundred-dollar suit we cut off him. As for his true identity, get ahold of Ef Tate. I'll bet he's sporting a brand new Gucci wallet that has all of Mr. Harris's ID."

"We tried him already," Jim said grinning dryly as he finished his coffee in a gulp. "He's the soul of innocence. I'm afraid Mr. Harris isn't going to see his wallet again."

"Another cup?" Anne asked automatically.

"No, thanks, Annie," he apologized. "I think we'd better get going."

She smiled, knowing that Silas had undoubtedly been pressing to at least get as far as the nearest working phone to check out Mr. Jonathan Harris. In the perverse humor she was in, she hoped something would show up, just to see not only Silas's reaction, but Jonathan's.

Taking his cue from Jim, Silas quickly finished his coffee and followed him to his feet, the old chairs scraping noisily on the red tile floor.

Jim turned to Anne as they walked into the living room. "I could probably arrange for someone to stay up here with you if you want."

Anne shook her head. "Only if they can cook and clean windows."

"Annie," Silas admonished.

Anne waved aside the objection and stood by the front door as the men donned their coats. "I promise I'll be fine," she assured them with a gentle smile. "Unless he's a great healer or a lot more determined than he looks, Mr. Harris won't be out of bed for at least a few days. He'll be no trouble or inconvenience. Besides, if the snow doesn't stop, I don't want to have to end up feeding all kinds of people. Two's more than enough."

Anne's word sparked a reaction from Jim. "I forgot. That dinner I promised is out on the mare."

"Let me get my coat," Anne offered, reaching for her down jacket. "No sense you having to traipse in and out when I have to go out and see you off anyway."

A few minutes later, Jim handed her five large plastic containers that all but filled her arms.

"Jim," she accused, surveying them. "This isn't dinner. It's a week's rations for Fort Benning."

He answered after he'd mounted the large dappled mare he used for deliveries to the homes on the mountain. "You know Cassie. Product of an Italian mother. She just wanted to make sure you'd be okay if we didn't get up here for a few days."

"I think this should probably take me through Labor Day," she said, smiling. "Thanks."

"Is there anything else you need?" Silas persisted.

Anne shook her head. "If you can figure out a way for it to stop snowing so that I can be free of Mr. Harris's stellar company, all my troubles will be solved, and I promise I'll be a happy woman again."

She waited as long as it took for her riders to disappear into the snowy fog before turning to go back inside. Out of habit, she checked the indoor-outdoor thermometer by the door as she stamped her boots. Fourteen wet, blowing degrees. She certainly hoped Mr. Harris realized how lucky he was not to be lying out under a couple of feet of snow tonight.

There wasn't any sound from his room as she passed, so she assumed he was asleep again. She wasn't surprised. Besides the fact that his injuries had sapped his strength, he was probably bored to death already. She wondered if he had ever eaten from a vegetarian menu, as he would if he had an appetite tonight. Cassie was one of the best vegetarian cooks Anne knew. Opening the refrigerator door with three fingers, Anne piled the containers inside, unaware that the anticipatory grin on her features was almost malicious in its glee. If he were indeed like Tom, he'd choke. Anne couldn't wait for dinner.

Once the food was put away, Anne made a beeline back through the living room to work on the fire, her mind consumed with the truth of the words she'd said to Silas. If only she could get her unwelcome houseguest back to wherever he came from, she could get back to the soothing peace of her routine. Then her life would be what she'd waited two years for it to become.

As Anne bent to gather more wood from the stack by the door, she bumped into the trash can. It briefly occurred to her that it was getting full and needed to be emptied. Especially with that fancy envelope from Boston in it.

Then she turned to stoke the fire, all thoughts of her past once again deliberately shoved aside.

Chapter 3

By six o'clock the next evening the snow had topped thirty inches and still fell steadily. Anne sat in a wing-back chair by the front window looking morosely outside. She'd finally turned on the radio as Silas had suggested, only to hear that the state was under hazardous weather warnings. Most secondary roads had been closed, especially at higher elevations. The airport was shut down and every piece of snow-removal equipment had been on the major highways since early morning. And more snow was to come.

That explained why no one had ventured up to see her that day. She was glad they hadn't, really. There was probably more than enough for them to do everywhere else. The meteorologist came on the air again to give an updated report that sounded depressingly like all the others. His voice frazzled and apologetic, he assured the public that weather of this severity in this area was a freak of nature. More like one of the plagues of Egypt, Anne amended for him, able to picture him repeatedly loosening his tie and running his hands through his hair as the snow continued to pile up without his permission.

She could have told him why the state was suffering the first October blizzard in memory. It had everything to do with the fact that she had Mr. Harris as her surprise houseguest. She was snowed in with him because, with the exception of Tom or Brad, Jonathan Harris was the last person on earth with whom she wanted to be stuck in an isolated cabin.

It's Murphy's Law, she thought. When she'd worked in the emergency room, it had moved from the eleventh to her first commandment, neatly displacing all the others. If anything could possibly go wrong it would, and at the worst possible moment. Here she sat, once again living proof of that axiom.

It wasn't that Jonathan didn't need her help. He most certainly did. The concussion he'd suffered would have had him on breathing support for at least the first twelve hours. He'd slept away the vast majority of the day, not able to keep any kind of solid food down until lunch. He wouldn't be going anywhere for a while on that leg, and she'd have to guess that at least three of his ribs were broken. All that added to low back strain and exposure made him a pretty sorry sight.

It was just that she felt he had the personality of a snake. Peppering his speech with cute little clichés culled from the *Cruising Corporate Head's Guide to New York*, Jonathan seemed to believe that given enough time, any woman would melt for his hundred-watt smile and religiously unoriginal turn of phrase. And that soon that same woman would ask for no more than to serve his every whim. Anne expected to see the venom appear when it finally got through to him that she would want no part of it. Just like it had happened some three years ago with Tom.

What truly galled Anne was the fact that beneath all that gloss and party-game atmosphere, she sensed another person entirely, someone she could like and respect. Maybe it was just a newfound optimism, but she thought she might have seen a little of his true self the first night when his eyes had been so very vulnerable. She wanted to think that the word games were just a protection, maybe a habit.

Face it, she thought dourly as she watched the snow steadily pile up outside her bay window, you don't want to think that you could be attracted to that kind of personality again. You don't want Tom to have been right about needing that kind of man.

There was no question that she found Jonathan handsome. She'd caught herself peeking in at him much more than was necessary and had to admit that even with the ravages of his fall, he still stood right up there in the unforgettable-looks category. But she'd known and worked with a host of handsome men before. On more than one occasion she'd found herself in stressful and emotionally charged situations with them and had handled it with levelheaded common sense every time. It bothered her very much that she was in danger of losing that precious objectivity with the one man she most needed it for.

So engrossed was she by the increasingly depressing cant of her thoughts that it took her a moment to hear her patient's voice. When she did, she scowled, wishing that she could tape his mouth shut. She imagined that he considered himself original by calling her Florence Nightingale. Heaving a sigh of capitulation, she uncurled her feet from beneath her and got up to answer the call.

"Ah," he said, smiling as she walked through the door, "if it isn't the light of my dark days."

"How are you feeling?" she asked, pulling the chair over again and sitting down. She took note of the fact that only a small amount of blood had seeped through the bandage on his head, and that the inevitable bruising had begun under his eyes. She also noticed for the first time how small crow's feet creased the corners of his eyes when he smiled, somewhat easing the ruggedness of his features.

"Better now that you're here." He grinned, showing her all his teeth and ruining that impression of familiarity. "Hold my hand and I'll feel like dancing."

She ignored him, pulling the cover back from his feet to check his injured leg for color and pulse. It, too, was swollen and bruised, but the circulation was unimpaired.

"Does your leg hurt?" She examined the wrappings, but they hadn't slipped or kinked and didn't really need the check.

"Only when I laugh."

"Does your foot feel tingly and cold at all?"

"No more than the rest of me."

Anne replaced the covers and straightened up, wondering how she could get around rewrapping his head.

"Aren't you going to check my chest?" he demanded, reaching for the sheet.

Her smile was a bit chilly. "Not unless you stop breathing and turn blue. Do you feel like eating some dinner?"

"What's on the menu?"

"Lentil and cheese casserole, cucumber salad, nut bread and peaches."

"Of course." He nodded with mock severity. "It all fits. The communal period, right?"

"Pardon?"

He motioned vaguely with one hand to signify her environment. "The communal period. Vegetarianism, *Foxfire Manuals* and homesteading. Are you preparing for the end of the world?"

"No. Just dinner." She got to her feet.

"I'll eat on one condition," he decided, reaching for her hand. She deftly avoided it with a move she'd perfected at Mass General. He pulled what was meant to be a handsome frown of disappointment. "You come in and share dinner with me."

"I prefer to eat alone," she replied evenly. "Besides, I have to tend the animals, so I won't be eating for a while anyway."

"You can't mean that you'd prefer to spend your time with the cows rather than me."

She offered a dry smile. "I can."

His eyes narrowed as if he were gauging her, his smile almost sly. The look of a man who was sure he had the upper hand. "What if I told you that I could take you away from all this if you wanted?"

"I'd say take yourself away. I like it here."

His smiled widened. Anne could see the challenge in his eyes. What she did not see was warmth. "I could give you everything you ever wanted."

Anne actually had to close her eyes when she heard that, the sense of déjà vu too painful. "I'll give you everything you'll ever want, Anne. Everything," Tom had promised. In the end, he had taken it instead.

She took a slow breath to quell the urge to scream and opened her eyes again. "This may come as an unpleasant surprise to you, Mr. Harris," she said quietly, "but I had everything I wanted before you fell down my cliff. And after you're gone, I'll have it again."

This time when Jonathan smiled, Anne could actually see the challenge die and be replaced by what she could have sworn was sincerity. She found herself staring.

"Please," he said, his voice sounding earnest. "I really hate to eat alone. And I'd like to have the chance to know more about my benefactor. If I ease up a little, will you stay?"

Anne had the irrational impulse to applaud the performance she was witnessing. Somehow, she couldn't. She gave him another chance to surprise her.

"It'll take me an hour or so before I can get to dinner."

"That's okay," he said, the veneer already solidly back in place. "It'll be worth the wait."

When Anne did get back with dinner, she found that he'd fallen asleep again, his face peaceful and quiet. That angered her anew. It annoyed her that the mind inhabiting that handsome, rugged face could spoil the image by constantly bartering on the sincerity and honesty suggested there. She hadn't seen a chin so square and strong since Gary Cooper; the cheeks were solid as granite ledges, as if etched by wind and water. Even his nose perfectly suited his face, straight enough to have been drawn. It was just that none of his features fit the personality. It was like watching a movie with the sound track out of sync.

He stopped her as her hand touched the door, about to leave him to his sleep.

"You're not going to back out of our dinner date at the last minute, are you?"

Anne turned to see his eyes open and gently mocking. Their light seared her enough to make her answer abrupt. "I thought you were asleep."

"As good an excuse as any," he said with a shrug. "But I don't let beautiful women shirk their commitments, especially to me. Is that the vegetarian delight I smell? It awakens gustatory anticipation."

Anne got out a small folding table as she thought how, even on his back, Jonathan Harris remained able to command control of a situation. It also occurred to her how typical it was of his kind—not the ability to do it, the need. There had never been any problems in her own marriage until she realized that she no longer wanted to delegate every decision in her life to Tom.

She set everything out on the table and then reached into the closet for more pillows to prop up Mr. Harris for dinner. He was reaching over very carefully to nibble at the salad while he waited, allowing that he was, indeed, hungry. Again Anne wondered how hungry he'd be after tasting something as alien as cheese and lentil casserole.

She walked around to the head of the bed to help him get to a sitting position to eat.

"No thanks," he told her agreeably. "I'm going to sit in that old chair you slept in."

She balked a minute. "I'm not really sure you're ready for it."

"Nevertheless," he said with a smile, "that's where I'm going to eat. With your help or not."

"Were you this stubborn the other time you were hurt?"

Jonathan stared at her, the humor dying in his eyes. Anne wasn't quite sure what she saw there instead, but it made her uneasy.

Finally, he offered a short nod. "Yes. Now, how 'bout a hand?"

Anne acquiesced with a shrug. After getting the chair situated next to the bed, she bent to pull him up into sitting position.

"This will be uncomfortable," she warned, still not sure it was a good idea, "so I'll take it slowly. Let me know if you need to stop."

"I know the routine," he snapped a little sharply. "Let's get going."

Anne moved as quickly and efficiently as possible until he was sitting on the side of the bed. Even as easy as the movement had been, she saw Jonathan's jaw clench with pain and perspiration break out on his forehead.

"C'mon," he gasped, seeing her hesitate. "The chair."

She stooped again to get him to his feet. Her arms around his chest, she felt the iron-hard tension of his muscles and the power of the arms that encircled her for support. Jonathan had been successfully seated in the chair a good few minutes before Anne could get her pulse to slow down.

Then she caught the tension in his suddenly pale face, and remembered that he'd neither asked for nor received anything for pain since he'd arrived. There was no question but that he was in pain.

"Are you okay?" she asked quickly, her fingers trapping the bounding pulse at his wrist. "Maybe you should lie back down."

"Don't you move me an inch," he chided with a grin that was a shade tighter than he'd wanted. "I can see four of you, and they all have the most beautiful frown of concern. I'm flattered."

"Do you need anything for the pain? I don't have much, but..."

"What pain?" He was quickly regaining control. "That's hunger you see. All I need is some of that lentil and cheese casserole you promised."

"Are you sure?" She couldn't understand him. There was no reason for him to play John Wayne. That wasn't the way his kind of man handled a situation like this. They were more apt to become demanding and loud. Yet she could see, only because she was used to looking for it, that he was still fighting against the pain and dizziness the exertion had brought on. He controlled it with a fierce concentration that amazed her. He wouldn't accept her help.

Guided by instincts her profession had long ago taught her, Anne turned for the door, leaving him the privacy he seemed to need.

"Coffee or tea for dinner?" she asked, not bothering to look around.

"Coffee's fine."

She took a little extra time in the kitchen, hoping it would be enough. Harris had spent the whole afternoon running true to form, when suddenly he had thrown her a complete curve. There it was again, that anomaly, the small bit of information that didn't fit. Realizing that if she weren't careful she could easily grow to respect Jonathan Harris, Anne found herself hoping yet again that he wasn't only what he would appear to be.

The high, shrill whistle of her grandmother's teakettle broke Anne's reverie. She reached for it, turning off the flame. Steam had filmed the window over the stove, disguising the faint white of the snow. The roof creaked a little beneath the ponderous weight, and Anne could hear the low, sad moan of the wind as it probed the windows and doors. The sounds of the cabin in the snowstorm gave her comfort, the feel of a familiar place crowded with happy memories. The house on Beacon Hill had never evoked that kind of feeling and never would. Anne assembled the things for the tray and thought yet again how thankful she was that she had this little cabin to wear around her like a warm cloak to protect her from the madness of life. She also wondered if Jonathan Harris had a place like this where he was safe.

Jonathan's attitude during dinner angered and unsettled her even more. When she first reentered the room, he was totally at ease and in control, as if the moment of weakness had never happened. Everything was a target for his caustic tongue, from the snow to her choice of attire. She did notice, however, that he made short order of the food before him. Anne only wished that her own appetite could hold up to his sense of humor.

"You're not from around here," he said suddenly as he refilled his plate from the table. Anne couldn't help but stare at him. Her Boston accent had certainly softened since she'd been in the mountains, but no fool could have possibly missed it.

"Your powers of observation, Mr. Harris—"

"Jonathan," he interrupted with a stern wave of the fork.

She ignored him. "—are overwhelming."

"Thank you." He smiled with satisfaction. "Why did you leave Boston?"

"I became tired of living there."

An eyebrow rose. Anne recognized the reaction. How could anyone give up all that, et cetera, et cetera. Maybe that was why he so delighted in baiting her. Perhaps he felt the same disdain—the sense of smug superiority that bred condescension and intolerance—that Tom had when he'd discovered that Anne wasn't returning from the mountain to the real world. Anne decided not to enlighten Mr. Harris further on the subject. He chose not to take the hint.

"Beacon Hill?"

Her startled reaction gave her away.

"I thought so," he said, nodding and returning to his food. "Most people don't have the money to run away from home in such style. What happened? Was your grandfather a robber baron, and you couldn't stand the shame of it anymore?"

"No," she answered pointedly, her eyes flashing at his attitude of smug superiority, "I got tired of swimming in the same waters as the barracudas."

Anne stood to leave, unable to remain for any more and not even bothering to take her half-finished dinner with her. She didn't even get to the door before he called out.

"Anne, I'm sorry. Don't leave." That strange note of sincerity had once again found its way into his voice. Anne stopped with her hand on the door, trying her best to understand why she hadn't already walked out, or better yet, heaved the casserole into his lap.

"I promised to behave." He spoke up again. "I guess I haven't."

She didn't answer, struggling with her indecision and angered by it.

"Anne," he said quietly, "I was out of line. Don't go."

She faced him then, even more irritated and confused by the contradictions in his words and actions, and wondered what capitulation would cost her. The strength of his eyes ate at her resistance.

"This isn't New York," she said with very careful control. "If you insist on playing New York word games, no one will talk to you. Especially me."

The bravado in his smile dimmed a little. "Ah, but you're such a worthy opponent."

"Worthy perhaps, but not interested. Unless some kind of truce is called, I'll be more inhospitable than a cold north wind to a bare backside. Your choice, Mr. Harris."

"You'll sit back down?"

After a small hesitation, she nodded.

"Good. I'll try to stay on neutral subjects." He motioned her to her chair and resumed his dinner. "I already have a question."

Anne looked up warily as she sat down. He immediately grinned at her reticence.

"It's only about your reading material," he defended himself, hand raised.

"You want to read something?"

He nodded, still grinning, his face disarmingly boyish. "I'm sure I will. You don't offer much up here in the way of diversion."

"You're right," she countered evenly, going back to her dinner. "The ballet left last week, our museum collection's out on loan and baseball season doesn't start for another five months."

"Touché." He bowed stiffly, his eyes almost as clear as the first time Anne had seen them. "That wasn't my point, though. Right now, I'm more interested in a far more existential question having to do with the choice of reading material available at this library. It's really... unique."

He motioned to the floor-to-ceiling bookcases that lined the wall opposite his bed and held her collection of paperbacks, old nursing manuals, magazines and a variety of keepsakes she'd never had the heart to remove from what had for years been her room. Anne's eyes were immediately drawn to the top shelf where her old dolls sat in a tumbled and comfortable row. The largest of them were her Raggedy Ann and Andy dolls her mother had made the year before she had died. They were perched on either end and watched the room with timeless eyes and sewn mouths.

"I don't throw anything away," Anne said. "It all ends up here at one time or another. The good books are in the living room."

"Then I'll have to get in there soon if this is any indication." His eyes roved among the hundreds of titles. "I must say that I'm astounded by it."

Again she followed his gaze. "Why?"

"Oh," he began, his hand up for elaboration, "the disparity. The contradictions." He pointed. "The *Foxfire Manuals*, and *Mother Earth News*, those fit. *Nursing, Guide to Medicinal Plants*, even Kahlil Gibran. Those all go with the vegetarian stew and braids. Very communal." His hand moved again, discovering more. "The classics... I imagine there are more in the living room...."

She nodded automatically.

"Those are marginal; a bit frivolous. But *Time, Wall Street Journal*, William F. Buckley? No self-respecting homesteader would be caught dead with those. And *Tax Shelters*? Richard Nixon's autobiography? Unheard of. Simply unheard of. Are you an imposter, *madame*?"

His tone was so easy and light, without a trace of condescension, that Anne knew he meant no offense. She found herself grinning.

"You're a victim of preconceived ideas," she accused, pointing her fork at him. "Where does it say that a modern homesteader isn't allowed to read *Time*? Just because one is isolated doesn't mean she wants to be caught unprepared." She was reminded of Silas's admonition on that very subject and couldn't help but grin again. "And who says I'm not allowed to read anything I want? I happen to belong to three book clubs and subscribe to magazines that also make the community circuit."

He shook his head with a mischievous grin. "You should be putting money into the crops and time on the chores. Sunup to sundown."

"I'm a nurse," she countered, "not Grandma Walton. I raise enough to feed myself and do enough chores to keep from tripping over hungry animals."

"What about the *Tax Shelters*?" He demanded. "The last time I heard, nursing didn't exactly rank among the most lucrative professions."

"It doesn't even rank that low," she assured him. "The book was my father's. That, Nixon and the subscription to the *Wall Street Journal*. He also had the finest paperback collection of murder mysteries in seven states."

She didn't realize that as she scanned the titles, she lost her smile.

"Past tense?"

She nodded. "He died about two years ago. You can tell what a pack rat I am if I can't even throw out a book on tax shelters." The truth was that she hadn't managed to work up the nerve to go through any of her father's things. Silas had carried most of them up to the attic for her but the books had been left here.

"You brought them here from Boston?"

She turned back to him, trying to lose the past's hold on her. "No. We used to come here during the summer. It was the only way father could escape the business. I took the house over and worked it again after he died."

She didn't notice that at her words Jonathan's eyes snapped open. "Well, that explains the Nancy Drew mysteries, I guess." He was watching her, as if expecting to find something in her face. After a moment he let his eyes wander over the room and then settle back on Anne, the color fading oddly as he squinted in examination.

Anne had gone back to her dinner. She nodded with a smile. "I kept every one. I figured that I'd give them to my little girl to read someday."

"If you'll pardon my asking, how did you come to spend summers here? It's a little off the beaten track, you know."

"My father was born here." Anne looked up and found a sudden frost in his eyes. It confused her. "This house has been in my family for about seven generations. My grandfather was the first to leave it during the Depression. When you're up and about, you'll see the quilts that are hung on the living-room wall. The oldest belonged to my great-great-great-great-great grandmother Sarah from before the War of 1812."

"The house looks pretty sturdy for being so old." Jonathan met Anne's eyes and spoke with quiet interest, but it was as if the life in his voice were dying. Anne could hardly manage an answer.

"The, uh, living-room walls are all that's left of the original stucture, and those have been refinished. The second story, kitchen and bedrooms are all new. And, of course, there's the modern plumbing. This homesteader does admit to enjoying her conveniences now and then."

"I can well imagine." His smile sprang on her like a trap. She saw his eyes sweep the room hungrily before landing with wolfish glee on her startled face. "Especially since you were the baby girl of one of the scions of Boston industry." He wagged his finger at her in an almost accusatory manner. "I've finally placed you," he announced triumphantly, the last of his easy-going manner disappearing in a chilling flash. "Pete Jackson's daughter, heiress to two separate fortunes, toast of Boston social society, patroness of the arts, marital catch of the decade . . . you were caught, weren't you? And you made quite a name for yourself by making a career of sorts well below your allotted station in life. Not exactly what daddy would have wanted you to do, was it?"

Anne didn't even bother to wait for him to finish before getting to her feet. Barely able to keep her silence, she began to gather together the dishes, the line of her jaw rigid with the struggle for control. It was all she could do to keep from hurling something at him. Not for the questions, which she had expected sooner or later, but for the attitude. With deadly, unerring aim, he had used his voice and eyes like lethal knives to humiliate her. She had spent the last two years recovering from that kind of pain, and she trembled with the familiar feel of it.

Jonathan didn't seem the least distressed by her reaction, evidently still too pleased with his coup to care.

"Not willing to answer the charges?" he finally asked.

She stopped briefly and turned on him, her eyes like steel. "Are you always this predatory, or do I just bring out the best in you?"

"An opportunity I simply couldn't pass up." His teeth gleamed almost maliciously now. "I thought you'd at least fill me in on how you arrived at this most interesting crossroads in life. It is, after all, a long way from Debutante of the Year."

"It's where I choose to be. That's the only information you're entitled to."

He shrugged nonchalantly. "I'm a bit disappointed. I at least expected some of that world famous breeding to peek through. A well-placed sneer, a haughty stamp of the foot."

"I'm sure it would make you feel right at home. These days, though, I find that I prefer a much more direct method of communication." She paused a moment, her eyes delivering the full promise of her next words. "A twelve-gauge shotgun, for instance."

And then she walked from the room.

The dishes were washed with great vigor and staccato rhythm that evening. Color flaring high in her cheeks, Anne seethed over the conversation she'd been roped into. She was furious with Harris for lulling her into a false sense of security only to spring his verbal trap with all the cheap theatrics found in a bad movie.

What was worse, she couldn't understand how she'd let him get away with it. She knew better. It was, after all, a carbon copy of the trick Tom had perfected on her with such destructive precision, especially toward the end. When she'd tried to fight his takeover of the business, he had taken to dissecting her in public with brutal delight. The feeling, she realized, was as painful and infuriating as it had always been. Mr. Harris was successfully resurrecting an ambivalence that Anne hadn't had to deal with in a long time, and she hated him for it.

She knew she should go and get Jonathan back into bed, but the thought of having to be that close to him kept her in the kitchen even as it unaccountably attacked her pulse rate again. Damn, it just wasn't fair.

By the time she did get in, however, he was so worn out that it was all he could do to carry out his part of the maneuver. Anne covered him up and wiped the perspiration from his drawn face, her mind consumed all the while with the picture of Tom as he'd told her what kind of man she needed.

"I'm going to head upstairs now, Mr. Harris," she finally said, putting her equipment back on the closet shelf. He hadn't made any comments when she'd changed the dressing around his head. "If you need anything for pain you'd better let me know now."

"I don't get a little bell to ring?"

She didn't realize how deathly tired her own voice sounded when she answered. "Not unless you brought along your own butler to answer it. I'm going to bed now."

"I'll let you go on one condition." This time he didn't even make an attempt at her hand. "You might as well call me Jonathan."

"It doesn't make any difference to me," she said with a shrug, not bothering to face him.

"Then Jonathan it is." She wondered if he'd meant that to sound hearty. He sounded almost as disinterested as she. "I mean, it's only fair since I don't know which last name to call you by if you insist on remaining formal."

She faced him then, stonelike. "I told you already that you were right. My name is Jackson."

"No. I mean your name now."

"Jackson," she repeated and left.

Chapter 4

Wednesday was traditionally Anne's baking day. Whenever she wasn't out on rounds, she spent the better part of the day baking loaves of grain, sourdough and vegetable breads, coffee cakes for breakfast and any number of muffins and rolls. Many of the proceeds were passed out among her needier neighbors, but Anne was glad that she worked hard enough to keep off the calories from what she kept and ate each week. It was a weakness she'd given in to early and often, deciding that honey and cinnamon were certainly a healthier addiction than tobacco or alcohol.

She finished tending the animals early, trudging heavily through snow that still fell and flew in fits and starts. Then, after retrieving last night's teacup from the little Hepplewhite table by the couch and patting distractedly at the cushions, she gathered breakfast together for her patient.

When Anne knocked on the bedroom door, she was invited in with a monosyllable. She thought it just as well. She wanted to get through this and on to her baking. If Jonathan were uncommunicative, she wouldn't have to waste valuable time and energy on his games.

"I thought you might like to get around a little today," she suggested without making eye contact. She kept her mind on the day ahead as she set out the food. If only she could make it through this quickly. Damn Jonathan Harris. He'd cost her sleep and peace of mind, and still the sight of morning sunlight striking the hard planes of his face threatened to steal her breath.

"You won't walk me out the front door and shut it behind me?" he asked without emotion.

"Not unless you sorely tempt me." She busied herself moving the easy chair over to the window where he could see outside. "The only thing you have to remember when you get up is to not put any weight on your injured leg. You can put your arm around my shoulder to steady yourself until you can use crutches."

"And when will that be?"

Anne positioned herself by the bed. "When your broken ribs let you." She helped him pull himself up to a sitting position and swing his feet over the side again. She worked in silence, wanting to avoid watching his face. She didn't want to see the struggle that he waged to move this far, the stoic concentration reflected in the steel-tight muscles of his jaw. It would only make her want to reach out to him again. After last night, she knew how impossible that would be.

She gave him a few moments to gather his strength before going on.

"The game plan's the same as yesterday. Put your arm around my shoulder, and when I straighten, get to your feet."

She bent at the knees, the correct physiological position, and prepared to help him stand. Jonathan slid his arm around her neck as before. Then he stopped. Anne was forced to finally make eye contact, discovering a controlled half smile that held no humor.

"Quite the professional," he taunted quietly. "I have to admit that I miss the beatific smile you bestowed on me the first night I was here. I'm afraid you've changed."

The look Anne gave him in response left him in no doubt as to whose fault she considered that to be. "Haven't we all?" was all she said.

She should have looked away again. Better yet, she should have straightened back up and walked away. Her chance for escape passed even as she glared at Jonathan, the challenge in both of them inexplicably dying.

With the devastating speed and shock of lightning, Anne suddenly found herself trapped, unable to move, unable to defend herself from the pain of contact. It was as if for that brief moment she and Jonathan were fused, united. Only his touch and the contact of their eyes held them, but it was enough to set Anne to trembling.

There was a physical reaction, she couldn't deny that. Her skin suddenly felt as if it had bumped against dry ice: burning and freezing, curling her toes and crawling along her scalp like a premonition. Her knees lost their rigidity, and she had to lock them straight to keep them from buckling altogether. Her lungs couldn't hold enough oxygen, and her heart found an entirely new rhythm. It was without a doubt a physical reaction, but if it had only been that she could have handled it, no matter how powerful.

What threatened to overwhelm her was what she found in Jonathan's eyes. Without warning, and for only the barest of moments, the veneer disintegrated over those fathomless pools of blue, and Anne became certain that she would fall in and become lost.

Like currents that shifted at different depths of the sea, Jonathan's eyes bared emotions that both bewildered and compelled Anne. She saw a vulnerability, a feeling of open space and invitation there. Beyond that, pain existed someplace she wasn't allowed to pry, a bare wound that still festered. She could see memories that she wouldn't be allowed to touch and the vacillation of a man who wasn't as completely in control as this one pretended.

But what left her more shaken than even those places in him she suddenly wanted to explore was the discovery of a deepest, primal place that stunned her. She briefly caught a flash of anger—almost hatred—that was directed exclusively at her. This was not the cool disdain of a man who simply thought her beneath his consideration, but an active, seething cauldron of hot animosity.

Just as quickly as it appeared, it was gone. Before Anne had the chance to react to the revelation in those potent eyes, the veneer was back up, the smooth patina of civilization concealing the anger. Once again Jonathan watched her with the cold, hard eyes of tolerant amusement.

Anne took a breath, struggling to regain her own composure. The last thing she could afford to do with this man was to lose control. If she did, he'd leave her in pieces scattered in the snow.

"Straighten when I do," she said very quietly, her face a careful mask.

Jonathan challenged her with a smile of smug superiority. "Are you really that cool?"

Anne faced him deliberately as she fought for the upper hand. "I really am."

Anne wasn't sure whether Jonathan's body shook from exertion or the perilously close confrontation. She knew that she was trembling too, and that made her angry. The weight of his rock-hard body against her as she helped him to his feet sent a jolt through her that threatened her heart rate again. She didn't have to look up to feel the electricity of his eyes on her. Her skin tingled with the power of it.

Of all the times for her to react like this to a man. It made her want to do rash things like confront his anger and hostility to defuse the glare he leveled at her. If he'd been anyone else in the world, she would have wanted very much to make love to him.

But he wasn't anyone else. The facade was too familiar, and she'd seen the inconsistencies that lay beneath. There was too much lightning in him, too much frost. After all the time Anne had spent constructing her fragile peace of mind, she didn't need this man to come along and shatter it with his volatile eyes and callused hands.

She'd intended to let Jonathan try walking out to the front room. She ended up only being able to make it twice around the bedroom before steering Jonathan toward the easy chair.

If she hadn't been so caught up in her own confusion as she lowered him into it, he would never have surprised her. He had both arms around her neck to ease his descent. Anne bent her knees to let him down and then leaned forward to scoot him comfortably back into the chair. At that moment, he pulled her over.

Badly off balance, she fell against him, her reaction a startled cry. He moved more quickly than she'd given him credit for, lacing his fingers into her hair and pulling her face to his for a kiss. She couldn't avoid the deliciously salty taste of his lips.

Anne's first instinct was to succumb, to match the bruising power of his mouth with her own. The heat that had been building in her exploded like a nova with the contact of his lips. His taunting caress lit fires she'd thought were dead long ago. She felt his breath catch in surprise and knew that he was as aroused as she. Their meeting could have been cataclysmic, but if there was one thing Anne prided herself on, it was control.

Jerking upright, she glared coldly at the triumph in Jonathan's eyes. "Don't expect outrage or hysterics," she suggested with frozen restraint, the taste of humiliation beginning to rise again with the look in his eyes. It was all she could do to keep from wiping at her mouth. "I don't play those games."

"You want me," he accused with great satisfaction.

Her eyes never wavered, never surrendered. "About as much as I want the flu. Listen, I don't know what it is about me that sets you off, but I won't stand for it."

"What sets me off," he countered with cold displeasure, "are spoiled little rich girls who think they're the light of the world because they packed away the designer dresses for a season. Lady, you're a phony."

"And you," she snapped back, "are a conceited, self-centered bastard who'd better enjoy his privacy. Because if you keep this up, that's what you're going to get."

Without another word she turned on her heel and walked out.

The pattern of baking day had become a comfortable ritual since Anne's first return to her mountain home. Today, she observed the custom as if it were a rite of cleansing. Concentrating on the immediate tasks at hand, Anne worked very hard to block out the escalating friction in her very small cabin.

First organizing her ingredients across the long butcher-block counter, she pulled the sourdough starter from the icebox and set the oven. Once that was done, she donned her official baking apron, an old blue gingham that had been in the house as long as she could remember. The apron was a formality, really. By the end of the day her face, hair and hands would be liberally dusted with flour, and there would be white smudges on either side of the seat of her pants where she would unconsciously wipe her hands. She pinned her braids around her head to keep them out of the way and set to work.

Anne mixed the yeast breads first and let them rise while she mixed and baked the vegetable breads. As the yeast breads cooked, she would begin to mix the rolls and coffee cakes. It didn't occur to her that the noise of her movements was a little louder today, or that when she kneaded the dough for her breads it looked as if she were punishing it. She did notice that it only took about half an hour for her to begin to feel better. The cathartic effect of baking day had been documented well enough two years earlier.

Anne had just pulled her first two loaves of bread from the oven and set them on the counter to cool when she heard a knock at the front door. She looked up, startled from her preoccupation, and found herself staring across the cabin to the door as if it would offer explanation. Then she remembered that Jim had promised to stop by. Maybe he'd also found out something about the not-so-mysterious Jonathan Harris.

"Coming!" she yelled as the knock sounded again. Shedding bread and oven mitts, she headed in for the living room.

"You sure have a lot of company," Jonathan offered as Anne walked by the hallway.

"That's because they don't trust you," she couldn't help but retort. His answering chuckle unaccountably surprised her.

When Anne opened the front door, she was taken completely by surprise. It wasn't Jim who stood before her, but Jim's wife Cassie, donned in fur-lined parka and snowshoes. Almost as tall as Anne, she was in her mid-twenties and looked for all the world like the proverbial Indian princess. Her skin was a beautiful olive color, her eyes as black as her hair. And every one of her ancestors hailed from central Europe.

"Cassie, are you crazy?" Anne demanded.

"Just frozen." Her friend grinned. "Let me in before my nose falls off."

Anne made way for Cassie to enter and closed the door behind her, all the while shaking her head.

"It's five miles to your place," she protested again. "You shouldn't have walked up here."

Cassie grinned, shedding parka and boots. "I'd rather be here than housebound with three kids. The silence was soul saving; the cold I wasn't as fond of. If I'd wanted that, I would have stayed in Chicago. Got any tea?"

"Sure I do. C'mon in."

Anne brewed up some tea and sliced into the warm zucchini bread. Then popping two more loaves into the oven, she sat down to join Cassie.

Cassie accepted her tea and sat in one of the cane-back chairs Silas had made for Anne's father. "From what Jim says about your patient, I thought you might need a chaperone." Cassie had never been known for beating around the bush.

Anne's answering scowl was more thunderous than she realized. "More like a referee."

Cassie's eyebrows lifted. "Sure didn't take him long to get on your bad side. What did he do? Make some passes?"

Anne shrugged uncomfortably. "Any number of them. All indiscriminate and well rehearsed." Until the last one. She felt the heat rise again in her cheeks.

"I see you were impressed."

"I lived with a man like that for three years, which was plenty long enough to learn the style intimately."

Cassie nodded. "What I want to know is if we're going to find that poor man down a cliff again."

Anne had to laugh, her indignation easing a little under Cassie's easy humor. "No," she admitted as she pulled the kettle off the stove and poured the steaming water into earthenware mugs. "My parents raised me to be a Christian. The worst I'd do is hang him by his feet from the loft. I'd only do that if he really provoked me."

"It got close, huh?"

Anne looked up to see the empathy in those dancing eyes. Cassie took a long sip from her mug and set it back down. "Well, I'm gonna have to go in and properly chastise him before I leave. Besides, I want to see if he's really as handsome as I hear."

"More so," Anne had to admit, her eyes on the honey she was dolloping into her tea. "But please don't say that to him. I'm the one who'd suffer."

Anne was grateful that Cassie had come. She had the knack to defuse Anne's housebound anger and restore her perspective. As always, Anne asked about Cassie's three children. She enjoyed that topic of conversation much more, having always used Cassie's brood as a substitute for the children she'd never have now she was divorced. Cassie was the kind of person who made everyone want to be a mother. Anne fed on her glow when she recounted in graphic detail the antics and tribulations of motherhood.

Anne hadn't realized how long they had been talking. When the timer went off she jumped, surprised by it. She hadn't prepared anything to follow the loaves that were in now. She hopped up, grabbing the oven mitts. Cassie followed her to her feet and started rummaging through drawers.

"What are you looking for?" Anne asked over her shoulder, the air from the wall oven hot on her cheek.

"Apron. I want to help. I haven't been able to bake bread in ages."

Anne pulled out the last loaf and shoved the door closed. "There's probably an extra one in the hall closet."

Cassie was already on her way out. "That makes sense. . . ."

Anne busied herself with the next batch of bread and didn't discover for a good few minutes just how long Cassie was taking to return. She looked over in the direction of the hall and heard voices. Cassie was in checking out Jonathan Harris for herself. Anne grinned as she leaned back and forth, kneading the bread dough with a bit less enthusiasm. Cassie was fearless and forthright, cursed with an insatiable curiosity and blessed with the courage to salve it. There were more than a few times that Anne envied her that.

Cassie didn't reappear for a good twenty minutes or so. When Anne saw her, she had a privately amused look on her face.

"Is he really so much like your ex?" she asked, dropping Anne's apron over her head and tying it in the back.

"Every inch of him, down to the cute green alligator he probably has on his pajamas back in New York."

"He doesn't wear any."

"Cassie!"

"It happened to come up in the conversation," Cassie defended herself without bothering to look over as she started measuring out flour into a bowl. Anne decided not to ask just how it had come up. "And he's not really from New York. He was born in Wyoming. But you're right. He is awfully handsome."

"He is that," Anne conceded as she worked her own bowl. "It's too bad he has to open his mouth and spoil it."

"He sure seems fascinated by you," Cassie countered casually.

"That's because there's nothing else up here to keep him occupied," Anne retorted dryly, her quiet answer contrasting with the color that flared along the ridges of her cheeks again. It made her angry that she was flattered by what Cassie had said. After what had happened that morning, she should have no room for that kind of reaction. It was just that he was a handsome man, and small vanities like that were hard to leave behind.

Cassie nodded, as if to herself. "Could be, could be."

Anne looked over to the secret smile in Cassie's eyes and straightened from her work. "What's that supposed to mean?"

Cassie shrugged. "Oh, nothing. You know me, always reading more into something than really exists."

"Out with it."

The smile broadened. Cassie still didn't bother to look up. "Oh, I don't know. He strikes me as...all bark. Kind of like the fourth-grade boy who hits the girl he likes the most."

"You've been on this mountain too long."

Cassie grinned and went on mixing. The two of them worked in a companionable silence for a time, both enjoying the quiet comfort of the Jackson kitchen. The timer buzzed, and Anne moved to the oven to pull out the latest batch of bread. She hummed tunelessly under her breath as she brushed stray hair from her forehead with the back of her arm and left another smudge of white there.

When they finally broke for lunch, Cassie insisted that they set up the table in the guest room and visit with Jonathan. Anne knew that it would be easier to survive a meal with Cassie present, but still couldn't manage to get in there soon enough to help her set up. Cassie didn't seem to mind in the least.

When Anne finally brought in the food, Jonathan was smiling and politely polished, commenting generally on the wonderful aromas that filled the house and the decaying state of the weather. He was nothing if not the perfect gentleman, which made Anne furious. She knew that he was pulling out all of his best manners for Cassie, and she couldn't understand why. Maybe the problem wasn't just Jonathan after all, but Jonathan and herself.

Anne answered when she had to with studied politeness as she helped ready for lunch, but she never quite faced Jonathan. It didn't seem to matter since Cassie was happy handling the majority of the conversation anyway.

By the time he was ready to eat, Jonathan had been sitting up in the chair for quite a while. Anne could see that he was beginning to wear thin, but it seemed that he refused to let it get in his way.

"This keeps getting better and better," he announced. "If I would have known there was so much to see outside New York, I would have left a long time ago."

Anne ignored him. She was sure that Cassie would have laughed at her reaction had Jonathan not been in the room. "Quiche?" she asked instead.

His answering smile, as he held out his plate to be served, reminded Anne of the wolf as he spotted Red Riding Hood's grandmother. If only it had happened five years ago, Anne would have found it all amusing and tolerated the leering with good-natured amusement. The wounds were still too new, though, and Jonathan seemed too much like Tom to let them heal. He'd managed to break right through the armor of isolation she'd so carefully built and instinctively attacked her most vulnerable spots.

Anne realized suddenly that Cassie and Jonathan had been talking, and that she'd been staring directly at Jonathan with undisguised anger. He couldn't have missed it, and yet he was blithely conversing with Cassie as if Anne weren't even in the room. She quickly lowered her eyes to her plate, embarrassed by her own bad manners. She'd have to try to be more civil.

"Where do you live in New York?" Cassie was saying, ignoring Anne's sudden lapse in courtesy.

"Upper Sixties, near Central Park," Jonathan answered.

Cassie nodded. "Nice. We have some friends there. Do you work nearby?"

Anne looked up in time to see a delighted, knowing smile light Jonathan's eyes as he waved his fork in Cassie's direction. "I really work in Philadelphia. I commute."

Cassie grinned right back. "We'll find out sooner or later."

"Well then, let it be a surprise. I love surprises."

"Will it be?"

"A surprise?" He shrugged. "I guess not really unless you're back in New York. But allow me my little game anyway." He took a drink of coffee and smiled ruefully. "The truth of the matter is that I don't want to be bothered with any of it right now. I'd like to consider this as my vacation in the mountains. When people know who you are, they expect certain things from you. This way there's no pressure."

Cassie persisted, quite undaunted. "Won't somebody miss you?"

"I imagine so."

"But you don't want to notify them."

"I don't think so." He went back to eating, the same irreverent smile still playing across his face. Cassie laughed and went back to her own meal. Anne stared at them both and stopped eating hers.

"You're giving up awfully fast, Cassie."

Cassie took the accusation with aplomb. "It's all in the timing, Annie."

"Yes, but you don't have to stay here with him. He could be the vicious criminal Silas thinks he is. I'm not sure I'd want to talk to him then." She caught herself wanting to grin. "Maybe we shouldn't even call him Jonathan."

"You could find something to talk about," Cassie responded as if Jonathan weren't there. "We've already discussed his sleeping attire and Wyoming. Neither of those has anything to do with his criminal career."

"You don't know that."

"She wants to know if my name's real," Jonathan said. "Tell your spies that, yes, my name is real. I don't have the energy to invent a name like that. I use all my energy just being vicious."

"I've never met a criminal with a middle name of Bradshaw," Cassie obliged as she picked lurking anchovies from her salad. "Most of them are something like Bubba or Billy."

"Bradshaw is my grandmother's maiden name." He reached over to steal the anchovies Cassie was piling at the side of her plate. "That's Emily Baldwin Bradshaw. Baldwin was her mother's maiden name . . . should I go on?"

"I don't think so." Anne shook her head. "That wouldn't leave us anything to talk about tomorrow."

Jonathan looked up from the fish he was popping into his mouth. "We could talk about you."

Even though Anne saw that his eyes were gentle in their teasing, she stiffened. "No, we won't."

Cassie stopped in the middle of dishing up seconds. "Her grandmother's name was Ellen Josephine McLaughlin. She was born over on the next ridge."

Anne shot Cassie a warning glance, afraid that the conversation would get around to Boston after all, and that Jonathan would attack like he had before. She had begun to relax for the first time since Jonathan had woken up, and she didn't want to jeopardize it.

Cassie chose to ignore her. "Anne was born here in the cabin, but she was raised in Boston. Somewhere near the bay."

"Boston's one of my favorite cities," Jonathan offered.

"I hate it," Anne retorted evenly, returning to her food.

His eyebrows raised. Cassie grinned, enjoying the sparks.

"Well, you've been to New York, haven't you?" he coaxed.

"I hate New York."

Cassie laughed over at Jonathan. "And you call this a vacation?"

"Don't worry," he retorted, "I'll get to her. I can be very persuasive."

Anne looked up, trying to keep her voice light. His eyes carried no further than this conversation, but she couldn't help but think of the aggression in them earlier. "Well, she isn't very impressed," she said. "She's spent better meals in the barn."

Cassie saluted with a fork. "Touché."

"I'm an injured man," Jonathan defended himself. "I should at least be recognized for making the effort."

Cassie turned for Anne's reaction. Anne shrugged easily, permitting a smile she didn't feel. "I guess I feel pretty generous today. I'll give you points for remaining an enigma in the face of Cassie's persistence."

He grinned brightly. "I'll take that as a compliment."

"Was that so difficult?" Cassie asked as she helped dry dishes after lunch.

"Was what so difficult?"

"Talking to Jonathan."

Anne flashed her a sour look. "It's so important?"

"I'm not the one stuck in the same cabin with him," Cassie shrugged. "I can go home."

"And I can put him out into the snow. No jury in their right mind would convict me."

"Ease up, Annie. You were being entirely sociable in there after the first few minutes. Why the sudden change of attitude?"

Anne thought of his kiss and the unwanted fire it had ignited. And then she thought of Jonathan's eyes when he'd done it. She finished putting away the cups before answering. "Because I'll lay odds that the minute you walk out of here, he reverts to form."

"I think you're making all this up to protect your sense of self-righteous indignation."

"And I think he's putting on a show for you. The charming, witty, much-maligned rich boy from New York. I get the picture."

Cassie shrugged her resignation. "Okay, be that way. I was just trying to help. Since you won't accept it, I might as well go on home."

Anne took a look at the clock and nodded in agreement. It would be about dark by the time Cassie got home. Anne had to admit that she would sorely miss the enjoyment of her unpredictable company.

"Well, at least take some bread with you," she offered, reaching to pull some out.

"Caramel rolls, maybe," Cassie said, nodding. She hung her towel over the white pig's head that protruded from the wall by the sink and turned to Anne. "But there's something else I want more."

Anne looked over to see that Cassie had something important she wanted to say. "Well, spit it out."

Cassie grinned broadly. "The whole darn mountain wants to know what's in that letter."

Anne found herself staring suspiciously at Cassie. "What letter?"

Now it was Cassie's turn to stare. "Come on, Annie. The special delivery letter. Except for Mr. Harris, it's the most interesting thing to happen up here in months."

"Your sense of priority is beginning to atrophy," Anne said dryly. "In Boston the snow would have at least made honorable mention."

Cassie was not to be put off. "The letter, Annie."

Anne tried to shrug offhandedly as she walked Cassie over to her coat. "It was nothing. A bit of business about my mother's trust."

Cassie might have been satisfied with the explanation if she hadn't pulled her coat off the hall tree and sent the whole thing crashing onto its side.

"Oh, I'm sorry..."

Anne bent with her to pick up the various articles of clothes now scattered over the floor. "Don't worry about it, Cass. Next time I'm over for lunch, I'll dump out your silver drawer."

"Annie..."

Anne turned to see Cassie stand up beside the waste basket, unopened legal envelope in hand. "I knew I should have dumped that thing out," she muttered to herself.

"You didn't even open it."

Anne shrugged with forced nonchalance. "I make it a point not to correspond with people I don't like."

Cassie walked over and took Anne's hand, placing the envelope firmly in her grasp. "You can't ignore it, honey. It might be important. Just read it through once. While I'm in saying goodbye to Jonathan." She smiled with friendly warning. "Or, I'll read it myself." She waited until Anne had ripped open the envelope before heading for the guest room.

When Cassie returned to a few minutes later, it was to find Anne standing before the fireplace, letter in hand, her eyes staring and empty. Cassie's heart lurched. Something terrible had happened.

Chapter 5

"Annie? Annie, what's the matter?"

Anne couldn't bring herself to answer. She could only stare at and past Cassie as if she weren't there, shaking her head slowly. Cassie led her to the sofa and sat her down.

"I have to get to Boston," Anne finally managed to say, turning to her friend. "I have to go now before he closes."

"Closes what? Honey, what's in that letter?"

Anne took a breath to steady herself against the panic that threatened to choke her. "Cassie, he lost it. He's lost Cedar Ridge."

"What do you mean he lost it? Who lost it?"

"Brad. He put up the deed to Cedar Ridge to finance a futures deal . . . and he . . . he lost it." Her hands were at her mouth as if to stifle the enormous, overwhelming fear. It was too much to comprehend.

All she had asked was to be left alone. She hadn't wanted their money or their power or their madness. All she had wanted for the first time in her life was some peace. She had asked them for no more than the only home she had ever known and enough of her mother's estate to survive. No more. Now they'd taken even that from her.

"Anne, how could he do that?"

Again Anne shook her head, still trying to understand what her husband and brother had done to her. "Oh God, Cassie, I have to get up there and save it. I have to get to Boston."

"Annie, you can't. Nobody's going anywhere in this weather. I'm not even sure I can get a telegram out yet."

Anne stood, giving motion to the anger that was beginning to curl in her stomach, an anger that threatened to drown even the fear. She walked to the window, watching the snow as it drifted lazily across the yard. The sky was heavy with it, the wind picking up a little. The storm wasn't over, and she was trapped by it, impotent to stop her brother from selling her home out from under her to a resort developer. The snow, so benign and soft and white, whose quiet beauty she'd always loved, was stifling her and she wanted to scream. She wanted her hands, literally or figuratively, around her brother's neck. Better yet, Tom's. After all this time, she knew well enough who had orchestrated this deal.

"He can't really do it, can he?" Cassie asked. "It belongs to you both."

"It belongs to him. My father left me very little. Father was of the school that felt that money matters were better left to the men. That way Brad and Tom could take care of me." Anne turned from the window to find that Cassie had followed her over, anxiety creasing her forehead.

"You could contest it," her friend offered. "Maybe buy it outright. You have your mother's inheritance."

Anne shook her head, crowded again by the real fear that she would lose her cabin, her home. "That money is sunk in the clinic. I don't have enough to buy Cedar Ridge back." She found herself staring into the colors of the fire. The wood smoke lent a warmth to the air, a familiar comfort. The fireplace had been built by her father with stones from the mountain.

When Anne spoke again her voice was so quiet that Cassie could hardly hear it. "Cassie, what am I going to do?"

It was dark by the time Cassie finally left to go home. She tried to stay longer, insisting that Anne needed her there, but Anne was adamant. She didn't want Jim and the kids worrying about Cassie trying to get home, especially when more snow was threatening. Even though Cassie could see right through her and Anne knew it, she gave it one of the game-trooper routines as she saddled up Andy for Cassie's ride home.

"I'll be back up in the morning," Cassie promised.

"No you won't," Anne retorted evenly. "You have babies to take care of. Just set Andy loose tomorrow. He'll come home."

"Annie, you can't face this alone."

Anne's answering smile was genuine. "I won't, Cass. You can help most by keeping an eye out for the first flight to Boston. And by sending a telegram as soon as you can, telling them that I'm on my way."

"Do you want me to get ahold of your lawyer?"

For a moment, Anne blanked. "I don't have a lawyer."

Cassie stared at her. "You're kidding."

"No. I found out too late that the family friend I used for my divorce was a better friend of Tom's."

"You must know somebody."

"I'll find someone."

Cassie threw up her hands in frustration and turned to mount Andy. After knowing Anne for as long as she had, she knew better than to pursue the matter. Anne would, indeed, find someone. Cassie just hoped that whoever he was would be smart enough to save Anne's home. Cassie had a bad feeling about the whole thing.

Anne didn't go back inside for quite a while after Cassie had gone. The hard work she was able to do in the barn helped keep the terror at bay. Every time she paused, the words of her brother's terse letter returned to taunt her until she thought that the only thing left that would save her sanity would be for her to take a long hike into the woods for a good scream.

She had no idea how she would ever get any sleep until she made it to Boston. She wasn't even sure that she could stand to spend any time in the house. There were too many memories there for it to be comfortable tonight.

Surely it was a mistake or Brad's idea of a bad joke. She'd wake up tomorrow to find Jim at the door with another letter that said to disregard the previous one. Even Brad couldn't be cruel enough to pull her feet out from under her like that. Even Brad couldn't sell the land where he and seven other generations of Jacksons before him were born. It wasn't just home; it was a legacy.

Anne stopped a moment and leaned on the pitchfork she'd been using. Brad certainly would be stupid enough to let Tom do it all. And once done, Brad wouldn't give it a second thought. He had never been comfortable on the mountain, claiming that there were the spirits of too many ancestors wandering the place who probably didn't like him any more than his father did. He would never even know that the cabin was gone. Anne stared blankly ahead and fought back tears for the first time in two years.

"Have you been avoiding me again?" Jonathan demanded from his room as she walked past. She gritted her teeth, not at all sure she would be able to remain civil. She could tell that he had already discarded the gentlemanly demeanor he'd proffered to Cassie, and she was really afraid that his nasty personality would drive her beyond control this time.

"Do you need something?" she asked, going on through to the kitchen.

"A bit of beautiful company would be nice."

Anne reached the kitchen with its aroma of baking bread and suddenly wished that Cassie hadn't gone home. It was going to be difficult to even be in this room tonight where the memory of Anne's mother still lived in the warm aromas and frayed comfort of the furniture. The teakettle her grandmother had used sat on the stove, and the old kitchen witch that had hung in the sink window for as long as Anne could remember still kept the room safe. Even the old Depression dishes and glassware and the red gingham curtains that matched the tablecloth, familiar sights that had comforted her when she was first alone, now tore unbearably at her. How could she get through the night surrounded by what she would lose? How could she sleep with the memories whirling madly in her mind?

For the first time since she'd moved to the mountains Anne seriously considered getting drunk. She still had her father's old stock of liquor, so supply was no problem. Jonathan wouldn't care. Except for his leg, he was doing pretty well. Maybe if she were drunk, she could stand the additional strain of his company.

"Annie, you're ignoring me again."

She stalked to the door of his room. "The name," she said slowly, suddenly losing her temper, "is Anne. A-N-N-E. Now, what is it that you need?"

He feigned a hurt look. "What happened to noblesse oblige? We were doing so well when Cassie was here. I thought you were beginning to like me. She did."

"Cassie's a generous person."

"And I'm a tough one. You'll find that I don't intimidate easily." His smile was hard.

"More's the pity."

With her words the look in his eyes melted into the more familiar smugness. "I'll find a way, Anne Jackson. You're attracted to me. I consider your coolness a challenge. And I love challenges."

She refrained from comment. "Do you want dinner?"

"I want you." Again it seemed that his eyes didn't agree.

"That wasn't a choice."

His smile broadened. "It will be."

He ate alone. Finding that she needed most of her energy to cope with the news she'd received, Anne served dinner and cleaned up in near silence.

For Jonathan's part, even the momentary lapses he'd allowed into a gentler personality disappeared. He spent all his time true to form, goading and challenging, as if pushing Anne to react to his outrageous behavior. At any other time Anne wouldn't have given him the satisfaction. Tonight, it didn't seem to make any difference.

At nine, she found herself standing in the living room with nothing left to do to keep her occupied. The animals were bedded down, the house was sparkling clean for a change, enough baking had been done to last a month and Jonathan was quietly reading in his room. Anne sat alone with nothing to do but think about the letter.

She remained rooted in one spot searching desperately for something to do to keep her busy. It had to be involved enough that she'd have to pay attention to what she was doing. The needlepoint that sat on the sofa wasn't enough, and any of the books that lined the walls on either side of the fireplace were too much. She walked back into the kitchen and brewed some coffee, although she wasn't thirsty, and pulled out some cookies she didn't feel like eating.

"I was heating up some coffee and thought you might like some." She stood in the doorway of Jonathan's room with tray in hand. He looked up from his book, even more startled than Anne by her actions.

"What's this?" he asked. "A second chance?"

"Just coffee," she replied evenly.

"Will you sit with me?"

"For a moment." She heard herself say it and still couldn't believe it. His eyes were like aquamarines tonight, like faceted gems that flashed surface sarcasm and hid the deeper levels. She almost thought that if she moved a little she could find something else there. Well, at least sparring with him would keep her mind from Brad's idiocy.

"What shall we talk about," he asked, "your grandparents or mine?"

"Yours."

She set down the tray and stood to evaluate the condition of her patient. He'd been sitting up since morning and now looked stretched. "Would you like to get back to bed first?"

"I do that and I may not get around to the coffee."

She sat across from him in the straight-backed chair. "How are you feeling?"

He smiled, his eyes inexplicably softening. She didn't know why he seemed to be making an effort to be nice, but she was grateful. "Pretty good. When do I get to scale the living room?"

"In a couple of days if you're still feeling like it. By tomorrow I imagine you can be up and around your room more."

"Child's play."

She had to laugh. "Only with a pair of sound legs and a full set of working ribs."

"I've made it with less."

She raised an eyebrow, believing him. "In that case, let's take a turn around the block now."

He met her gaze with a challenge of his own. "All right. I've been wanting to see what the living room looks like anyway."

Anne blinked. "You're serious."

His answer was given with a wry grin. "Best way I know of getting back on my feet is getting back on my feet."

The procedure for helping Jonathan to his feet was the same; the walk was not really that far. And the spark between them just as potent when they got close. Anne felt the tension ignite in her like a stifling pressure, threatening her breath and attacking her pulse.

Jonathan stood unsteadily and leaned against her, his chest heaving. Anne closed her eyes for a moment against the urge to hold him. To find those places she could share and cherish. For these fleeting moments of contact, she felt as if she had tapped a primal energy source, and that at the core of that energy lay the secret to Jonathan Harris. For those brief seconds, Anne found herself wishing that that core was made up of the blue of his eyes rather than the venom of his words.

"How long ago did you have that injury?" she asked as they made their way toward the door, Jonathan's arm tightly around her shoulders. Her arm circled his waist, and her hand spanned the scars.

"A long time ago."

"Fall off another cliff?" She couldn't believe how well he was doing. The lines of his face were etched with a fierce concentration that awed her. He never took his eyes from the far wall of the living room.

"Something like that."

"Why do you push yourself so hard?" The question came out before Anne realized: but she had to know. What drove him? What fires fueled that will?

For a moment he took his gaze from his objective and turned to her. Anne could almost see the flames deep in that blue, and a flash of vulnerability that tore at her.

"Twice in my life I was helpless to keep people I cared for safe from being hurt," he said turning back to the wall. "The second time it happened, I vowed never to be helpless again." They walked farther, his posture rigid. "Never."

They had made it back to the room before Anne spoke again.

"I think you can use the crutches tomorrow."

He nodded. "You didn't ask any questions about what I told you."

Anne gently swung him into bed, bending to support his injured leg as he brought it up. He looked so strained, so very tired for the effort he'd made.

"You aren't ready to tell me about it yet," she answered, sinking wearily into the chair.

Jonathan looked over in surprise. Anne knew she'd read him right when she saw the confusion. The vulnerability made a brief return to his eyes.

"Will you tell me what had you so upset earlier when your friend Cassie was here?"

Anne avoided his direct gaze, her hand picking at the lint on her jeans. "Oh, I, uh . . . find myself helpless to save something I care about."

When she finally lifted her eyes to him, they were rueful, the pain carefully hidden. It didn't seem to matter. Anne had the feeling that Jonathan found it anyway.

"Can I help?"

She shrugged uncomfortably, wondering where the enmity had gone. In the time it had taken to help Jonathan walk through the rooms of her house, they seemed to have gained an unexpected bond. The bond of unspoken understanding and respect.

"I don't know. I'm waiting for the phone to come back up, and for Cassie to get a telegram out."

His eyes were the gentlest she'd seen them. "Do you want to tell me about it?"

She shook her head, confused tears threatening. "No. Not now. I think both of us need a good night's sleep."

For a moment Jonathan's eyes melted, the blue a sweet, warm light in response to her pain. Then, before Anne could react to the change, a wall went up, a brittle, cynical edge that forced her away again. Once more Jonathan hid away where it was safe. He rolled over on his back and addressed the ceiling.

"Would you like another kiss?"

Anne stared, not as surprised as she should have been. It occurred to her how lonely his battles must be for him. "One per patient is my limit."

He turned to her with a slick smile. "Does that mean we're progressing to bigger and better things?"

Anne stood up suddenly and glared down at him. "I'm progressing to bed. Upstairs. Alone." She couldn't account for the unexpectedly shrill pitch of her voice. "If I hear one more ridiculous proposition out of you, you'll progress outside. In the snow. Alone!"

By the time she got up to the loft, she was wondering what had so abruptly set her off like that. She hadn't really been that taken aback by Jonathan's sudden mood swing. He'd done it before, and chances were, he'd do it again, even if he had begun to trust her with a glimpse behind his facade.

Anne looked back down toward where the guest room door was, as if to better divine an answer to a question that bothered her more than she wanted to admit. Without warning she was struck by the image of Jonathan's eyes as he'd talked about helplessness. The moment when they'd been so vulnerable, when Anne had wanted to reach out and ease the struggle there. Her mouth opened silently, her chest rising a little faster.

She had been so close to him at that moment, so close to whatever the real Jonathan Harris was, that it had frightened her. She didn't want to be close to him or any man; but especially to him. And yet she had begun to succumb to that translucent fire of his eyes, the electricity of his touch. When he'd turned on her again, betraying the moment of fragile contact with barbs tipped in malice, she had protected herself by biting at him like a shrew.

The same way he seemed to respond to her.

Anne stood where she was for a while longer, unable to go on. Something Cassie had said nagged at her about the little boy who hit the girl he liked the most. Oh Lord, she thought with sick dread, what if Cassie were right? What if Jonathan were as drawn to her as she was to him and reacted with the same defense mechanism? Anne thought of the abrupt personality changes, the jibes and directed attacks, and felt worse. It made more sense than she liked.

Please God, she prayed, not now. I can't handle this. I can't even handle the fact that I'm becoming more and more drawn to this man. His quiet strength and hidden pain, the brief flashes of empathy that give so much promise all compel me. A matched set of ambivalences is more than any person can handle in a small cabin in the snow. How can I be expected to deal with it now when my life is on the line? Thanks all the same, but if you have a new love interest in mind for me, it'll have to be some other time or place. Or person. I can't afford this one.

Yet even as she consciously turned away from the thought of Jonathan, Anne couldn't avoid the fact that her heart still hammered oddly in her chest, or that she could feel his powerful arms around her as vividly as if he were actually there with her.

She knew it was futile, but she went about getting ready for bed, brushing her long hair, slipping into a long flannel nightgown and climbing in under her big down comforter before turning off the small light by her bed. Downstairs, the fire in the fireplace was slowly dying, its soft red light licking up the chimney opposite the loft. The house was quiet, the wind gently brushing through the pines outside. Somewhere an owl called, a low, mournful sound of night. It was chilly enough that the comforter felt like the embrace of familiar arms. A wonderful night to fall asleep. Only Anne couldn't.

She lay still in the pleasant warmth of her bed, trying her best to relax, and knowing that she wouldn't. She stared at the flickering shadow patterns on the ceiling without relief, the demons chasing her in the dark of midnight. First Jonathan's, and then the ones her brother and husband had unleashed.

As the night passed with agonizing slowness, the loss of her home drove everything else before it with a vengeance. Fears and ideas and plans raced madly in her head, each a desperate attempt to deal with the unbearable reality of what had happened. The irrational became plausible in the dark and the impossible possible.

It would be simple. She would confront Brad and force his hand, contest the will and buy the land back. She would walk up to Tom and laugh in his face when he told her it was all only a ploy to win her back. She'd laugh at both of them when they told her she'd never get the land back again. She could be in control. She'd worked two long years to repair the damage done to her self-esteem, and except for one incredibly handsome stranger with piercing eyes and Tom's mannerisms, she'd managed to maintain a respectable amount of independence.

All she had to do to save her home was get far enough away from Jonathan to escape his turbulent magnetism. She needed to travel to Boston where she could find some breathing room and hire a reputable, firebrand lawyer who wasn't already in her husband's pocket.

For hours she tossed and turned, her brain feverish with plans of confrontation, her body exhausted from the strain of the past three days. If only she had someone to talk to, someone she could call up and burden with the dread that refused to ease. If only there were a friend in Boston who could recommend the proper channels to take to save Cedar Ridge.

Again, she thought of the fact that she had left no friends in Boston. She'd left no friends anywhere in her former life. The relationships she'd formed when in nurses' training had died of neglect when she'd become taken up with the world her marriage to Tom had created, the world she'd been born to and groomed for her entire life.

The people she'd known in her hospital days had been the most similar to the ones she knew here on the mountain. They were a rare and good group of friends she would always regret having lost. The people she'd known during her marriage had never really been more than acquaintances, a supporting chorus to the choreography of her life as daughter to the chairman of the board. These people were only faces that filled out the background, no one she considered worth the effort of friendship. To a person, they had considered an important discussion one that debated how to best maximize the social season. She couldn't remember any one person who stood out. They had all been the same. And they were all useless.

She had no one left now to turn to for the help she needed.

For a moment, she considered asking Jonathan for help. It seemed only reasonable that after all she'd done for him he could find her someone to help her fight her way through the legal maze her ex-husband had constructed. She could go down to him and tell him how she was about to lose the only thing that meant anything to her in the world, and that he had to help her if only out of gratitude.

Then with a startling clarity she saw the look in his eyes when he'd found out who she was and what she'd done with her life. She knew how he'd react to this new twist to the story, gratitude or not.

It was with a feeling of desperation she hadn't known in two years that Anne finally fell into a tiring, fitful sleep some hours later.

By the next night Anne felt like a zombie. She'd still had to do the heavy work, and had even managed an hour-long trek into the white silence of the woods above the house, restoring some of the internal silence stolen by Jonathan's intrusion into her life.

He had been another matter altogether. Hovering precariously on crutches, Jonathan had, with her help, begun to make his way more comfortably around the rooms of the small house. In between treks, he spent his time in the chair by the window. He communicated a minimal amount, much to Anne's relief, but the time in the room with him further solidified the conclusions she had begun to form about him the night before.

Jonathan spoke little, but when he did he was again politely distant but distant, exerting the majority of his energy on recovering his mobility. He worked hard, never giving himself a break. In his silence, Anne saw the quiet, sweating determination of a man driven. Then, every once in a while, he would throw off a few biting retorts, as if making up for an oversight of some kind.

It probably would have been easier for Anne to handle just the sarcasm. That way she could have decided that her observations about a more vulnerable side to this man were nothing more than the product of wishful thinking. But she couldn't deny his courage in those moments when he tested his own will the way no city-pampered, egocentric executive would have. She knew that those times somehow connected with the brilliant smile he'd saved for Cassie. He was bitter only with Anne.

She was still worrying as she got ready for bed, her exhausted mind ricocheting from the dilemma of Jonathan to the impending confrontation with Tom.

No word had come from Cassie, and there was no letup in the snow. Anne couldn't last much longer. As hard as she tried, the terror returned, especially in the dark, when the dread grew exacerbated by the crowded night shadows. Anne knew that sleep would again be a long time coming.

When she first heard it, she thought it was her own dream. The sounds were garbled and frantic, rising and falling as if heard through a faulty speaker. Names, cries for help, more names. One name. A name she'd heard before, that teased at her memory. Anne's eyes shot open into the dark, a strange chill of prescience filling her.

Silence.

Only the soft ticking of her alarm clock broke the thickness of the early-morning hours. Even the wind had died, leaving her in a frightening void, unable to remember exactly what had awakened her.

Then, faintly she heard it again. A voice strange yet immediately recognizable, floated ghostlike from downstairs.

"Charlie... It's Charlie... He's got me...."

She held her breath, waiting, suddenly cold. The voice was haunted, belonging to a place of nightmares and pain, and she didn't want to approach it.

"Carson...get down...you've gotta... No, move back!" His voice rose to a cry, urgent and frightened. Anne tumbled out of bed. Grabbing her robe she headed for the stairs. She was afraid he'd be thrashing around and would hurt himself, the instinct of action propelling her before the plan of action had a chance to crystallize.

Anne flipped on a small light in the short hallway and stepped to the door, the light falling at an angle across the small bed. The bedclothes were snarled, and the spread was bunched tightly in Jonathan's hands. A fine sheen of perspiration reflected on his face.

"I can't get out... can't get out of his line here...." He was struggling, fighting to get free of something. Anne could see him sweating and shaking, his hands opening and closing spasmodically around the blankets. She stood motionless in the doorway, mesmerized by a stranger's dream. She knew she should go and stop it before he hurt himself, and shouldn't let him go through the terror of whatever hell awaited him in his sleep, but his strange words held her rooted to the spot. She couldn't imagine what could possibly have such a terrible grip on his subconscious. The man Jonathan Harris seemed to be would have no room for nightmares.

His next words seared straight through her.

"Eddie, I can't get to you.... I'm...I'm hit...ah, God... Corpsman..."

He was grabbing at his side, where Anne had found the scars, and writhing in the bed whimpering. "Corpsman, let him... No, I'll...I can...Eddie."

Vietnam.

Anne's hand found her gaping mouth. Oh, dear God, she thought, her stomach knotting up and unbidden tears clouding her vision as she watched Jonathan flounder in his private hell. He'd been in Nam. The Charlie he'd rambled on about wasn't a specific person as she'd assumed. It had been the Vietcong.

She couldn't take her eyes from him, couldn't move to help him. What she saw left her confused and shaken. She wanted to back out the door and escape the pain that echoed in this room. She had enough of her own to consider courting his.

He was quiet a moment, and Anne saw his hand reach out to something, as if to touch it. He made a small blind stroking motion, the way a mother might touch the face of a child.

"Eddie," he whispered. "I'm sorry, Eddie...I...I tried...."

She didn't even realize that she'd moved until she found herself beside his bed. He still writhed, the sounds in his throat rising from an anguish that cut through Anne like a hot knife. She didn't feel the tears on her cheeks as she moved to gather him into her arms.

For a few long moments all Anne could do was hold him to her, rocking him and stroking his wet, tangled hair, her murmurs meant to comfort them both. He held onto her like a lifeline, his choked sobs released with the comfort of her touch. His hands found the rich fall of her hair and wound into it. Anne eased into his touch, bringing him closer.

She never saw his eyes open, and didn't realize that he'd turned his face to hers. When she felt his lips find hers, she responded out of instinct, out of the turmoil she'd brought to this room and the anguish she'd found there. Bending to him, she met his lips with her own and became lost within him.

Anne never had the chance to question what was happening. When Jonathan pulled her down to him, she followed blindly. His embrace was desperate, his hands searching her with almost frantic need. She clung to him, absorbing the fierce possession of his mouth with her own and purging her own pain with the feel of him. Her gown was no barrier to his callused, seeking fingers. He discovered the taut nipples that strained beneath him and consumed them with chafing discovery. Anne heard a small sobbing sound and realized it was her own. Her mind was a maelstrom and her body was on fire. From the moment he'd kissed her there had been no turning away. She felt herself drowning, pulled under by the ferocious pain that had been unleashed by a nightmare and trapped there by her own need to share and salve it. She stroked the planes of his face and the rigid line of his throat, comforting, seeking, the explosion building in both of them driving her beyond reason. Jonathan bruised her mouth with his explorations and savaged her skin with his fire.

His hands trembled when he found her thighs. Anne gasped at their strength. She turned her head to the side, somehow to be free, but Jonathan found her there and brought his mouth down again on hers, harsh with his need. His lips searched her face, her eyes, her forehead, their taste reckless. She arched against him, against the fire that swept her, an agony that was hard to distinguish from the pain. Her own hands sought, roaming along muscle and sinew that stretched in unyielding lines over chest and shoulder, hips and steely thighs.

It was only when his hand forced her thighs apart that she felt any fear. He was desperate with the need for release, for union. She was afraid she'd be hurt. Instinct brought her hands up to him, to find the rock-hard surface of his chest. He was panting against her, his body slick with sweat. She wanted to beg caution and care, but couldn't manage the words. Couldn't even bear to question what fires lit those coalescent eyes. The unbearable heat built in her as his fingers found her and silenced her protest.

Their joining was cataclysmic, as if by uniting they could purge their ghosts. Anne thought she would be crushed by him, engulfed by the white hot light he ignited in her. Her arms came up, her legs circled him, pulling him even closer as he drove into her. His face was buried in her throat, his hands grinding her against him. She arched to meet him. The agony in her belly was unbearable, the sweet torment of his gasping cry, torture. They rocketed faster, their passion soaring beyond need or pain.

Jonathan lifted his head then, his eyes trapping Anne's with their wild, piercing light. She threw her head back to keep those eyes before her, but he took her mouth again, his tongue hot and searching, his breath ragged against her. He brought his hands down to trap her body against his, his pelvis sharp against her soft skin, and thrust into her with a force that made her cry out. What hunger drove her she didn't know but it matched his bruising strength. She brought her hands to his buttocks and forced him back to her again. And the explosion came, rocking them both and tearing gasps from them as they shuddered and clung desperately and spent themselves in each other.

The old clock in the living room struck three, and Anne could hear the wind outside rise a little. In this room the stillness slowly returned, and peace crept back from the dim, shadowed corners where a terrifying dream had chased it. She felt Jonathan's breathing ease, felt his hold on her relax toward sleep. Her own body refused her the release.

Her life in this house had changed tonight. Jonathan had brought out something in her that she had long hidden away. She had been compelled by more than compassion to go to him, by more than empathy for a lonely, hurt person caught in the throes of terror. She had been drawn to him because his pain had seared through her in a way that had never happened before. And she had stayed, she realized now, because her need to give to Jonathan had been greater than his need to lose himself in her. There was nothing she would not do to keep him from having to face that kind of desolation again.

The clock struck again before Anne turned from the sight of Jonathan's soft, sleeping face toward the door, her steps carrying another burden as great as her own. She had to get out of this cabin before she lost her mind. Had to get away and come back, and then maybe she could understand everything that was going on.

"Anne..."

She turned to see that he was awake, his eyes sleep-clouded and unsure. There was no guile there to confront, and Anne suddenly wished there were.

"I...was just going...." she stammered, trying to turn again. "It's pretty late."

"Anne."

His voice was strained. Anne turned again and managed to face him. But they had no more words. Their walls had gone back up, the pain of contact too great. They were already far apart, and she didn't think they'd let each other close again.

Chapter 6

It wasn't until the next afternoon, after more long hours of near-silent work with Jonathan, the tedious, mind-numbing waiting alternating with spurts of fierce work, that Anne finally heard from Cassie.

Cassie's call was the first to make it over the repaired lines. By the time the phone rang Anne was pacing around the living room.

"Annie, are you all right?"

"What did they say, Cass?"

There was a pause, a gathering of tact. "I got a telegram. And a phone call."

"A call?"

"Yeah. Hon, it doesn't sound good."

Anne stared out the front window as Cassie explained. The snow was so brilliant, so peaceful. The pine trees she'd watched grow since childhood strained under the weight of it.

The telegram had been brutally curt. If Anne wished to interfere, she would have to do so when Brad and Tom met the new owners in New York. But there was really nothing she could do. The land was sold and Anne had no say in the matter. The accompanying phone call from Tom had contained a threat, thinly veiled as a bribe: if Anne would come home, all would be well.

"Now I know why you left. Tom has all the charm of a pet cobra."

Anne looked up distractedly. "I can get to New York in time?"

Cassie nodded. "Tomorrow. I have it all set. But who are you going to get in New York to help?"

"I don't know. I'll find someone. I still know some people in New York." Couturiers and maître d's, she thought.

"Honey, you'd better get somebody really good. I've heard hardball players flex their muscles before, and your ex-husband made all the right noises."

Anne couldn't answer.

"Annie? Honey, are you okay? Do you want me to come up?"

"Uh, no." Anne wondered if she should tell Cassie about what had happened during the night but decided not to. She still wasn't at all sure herself about what had happened. She just knew that she could hardly bear to be near Jonathan anymore, especially when both of them were held so rigidly by their uncomfortable silence. Anne knew that whatever it was she had discovered in herself when she'd been in his arms was interfering with her ability to handle Tom's threat to her with composure and common sense. She was afraid that she was beginning to lose control.

The sound of Cassie's voice brought her abruptly back from her thoughts. "It'll be okay, Annie. You'll see."

Anne's eyes burned. The snow was too bright, the future too frightening. "I hope so, Cass. I'll see you tomorrow."

Anne hung up the phone and stood for a long few minutes without being able to move. She stared abjectly out at the scenery she had so come to cherish.

"Do you want to tell me about it now?"

Startled, she jerked around. Jonathan was standing by the hallway arch, his eyes understanding. The very sight of him, so strong and determined, brought the tears back. Anne stood silently before him, her hand on the phone, and shook her head helplessly, completely at a loss.

Before she could gather the composure to speak, he'd hobbled up to her and put his hand out. "Come on. Let's sit down here so you can tell me what's going on."

Still she balked, even as he guided her to the couch. Trust was difficult to give in her world. "You don't need this kind of headache."

"You need to talk," he retorted, easing her into the cushions and then gingerly taking a seat next to her. "And who knows? I might be able to help."

"Why should you help me?"

His smile was rueful. "After last night that's kind of a stupid question."

She gave no quarter. "It would be a stupid question if you hadn't already done several one-eighties already. How do I know you're not looking for another excuse to bare your claws?"

For a moment Jonathan looked down at his hands, as if marshalling his thoughts. When he looked back up, Anne thought she had never seen eyes so empathetic. It was as if he had looked away to allow his defenses to fall a little.

"You only have my word, I guess," he admitted, taking her hand. She felt the strength there and longed to be able to rely on it. It had been so long since she'd been able to share any of her burdens.

"But you're right," he went on. "I have been an ass. There's an explanation for it, but it's too involved. I'm sorry, Anne."

"Well," she conceded, "you do have a point." She managed a grin. "You were an ass."

He grinned back, and Anne found herself wondering how long this truce would last. It was all beginning to hurt too much.

"I'm going to lose my home," she finally said, feeling vulnerable and terrified by it. "I have two weeks to prevent it from happening."

"You'll let me help?"

It was hard to meet his eyes. She kept seeing the savage light in them the night before. "I don't know yet. What do you think you can do?"

He shrugged, wincing as his ribs rubbed uncomfortably. "I don't know. It depends on what's going on. I'm a lawyer."

Anne found herself smiling again, the light in her eyes wary. "Of course you are."

"You don't believe me."

It was her turn to shrug. "Maybe if you had some identification."

"I'm serious, Anne. I am a lawyer. I got my law degree from NYU."

"Corporate law, no doubt."

A brief twinkle touched his eyes. "This time, it might be what the doctor ordered."

She couldn't help but flash a big smile at that. "Are lawyers always so original?"

"I can only think fast on my feet when I'm on my feet. Now, are you going to take me up on my offer?"

She was weakening beneath the bright candor of his handsome eyes, and it made her furious. She knew better than to trust an attractive smile. It had taken her months to begin to trust even Cassie and Jim, months she'd spent alone in the cabin, often without venturing out for days on end. Her faith in others had been shattered because she'd once trusted a man with a handsome smile.

But she'd never seen in Tom the emotion she'd found in Jonathan's eyes. Tom had been pure predator: first, last and always. He would never have had room in his character for the compassion she'd discovered in Jonathan. He didn't have the strength, the courage or the vulnerability. Tom had never reached out to another human being in his life, unless it was to further the career and material fortunes of Tom McCarthy. In one harrowing hour before dawn, Anne had realized that the same couldn't be said about Jonathan.

But could the aftermath of the nightmare make all the difference, when every other time she'd allowed him close he'd hurt her?

Before she knew it, she was telling him the whole story. She spoke of Tom's duplicity, her father's death and the deal she'd made with her husband and brother to set her free of their obsession with the company, and how Brad had now managed to throw away her home on a speculation.

When she looked up at the story's finish, she was surprised to see that Jonathan listened quietly, his eyes analyzing and alert. He'd assumed a professional demeanor, as if he were sitting behind a mahogany desk in a three-piece suit rather than propped stiffly on her living-room couch and clothed in Brad's old pajamas. Although his background was still a mystery, Anne was satisfied that he was a lawyer just as he'd said.

"Do you remember any agreements you might have signed?" he asked.

She had to shrug. "Divorce papers relinquishing alimony and the promise not to contest my father's will. I don't know. At that point in my life I wasn't thinking too clearly."

"That's understandable," he nodded. "Who was your lawyer?"

"Frank Wilson. Wilson, Talmadge, Pierce & Franklin of Boston."

"And you think he was in your husband's pocket?"

"I didn't have to think it. Brad finally told me so. He has the need to gloat."

Jonathan shook his head slowly, absently staring at the far wall as he contemplated what she had said. Finally his attention returned to her, his manner all business. Again, Anne had the passing feeling that she was really sitting in an office. "Could they have done anything illegal?"

"Why do you say that?"

"I don't know," he said with a shrug. "Maybe the overkill when you finally got in touch with them about this. Something's making them nervous."

Anne offered a dry smile. "You don't think my ex-husband wants me back because he can't live without me?"

Jonathan was polite enough not to answer.

Because he had no more questions, Anne knew she had to find out. The effort alone brought the fear back; an iron band tightened around her chest and closed her throat.

"Am I going to lose it?" she asked, her voice sounding very small.

Jonathan turned to her, his eyes troubled. "I don't know, Anne. You might. But you're a strong woman. Even if you do..."

Anne straightened abruptly, her eyes glittering with unshed tears. "You don't understand. This," she said, opening her arms to take in her surroundings, "is all I have. It's all I have left to remind me that I once had a family and was happy. It's the only place where there's anything left of my mother and father. I may get a new house, but I'd have no past. No memories to keep what I went through with Tom and Brad in its place." To keep what she was beginning to feel for Jonathan in its place. Her sense of stability was floundering and only the permanency of the cabin kept her upright sometimes. "This is my anchor, my sanity. Without it I would have lost my mind."

Holding her hand even more tightly, Jonathan captured her eyes with his own, offering her his strength and support, an understanding she knew to be genuine. He nodded to her and brought his other hand to her cheek.

"Then we'll have to fight like hell, won't we?"

Anne managed a small smile, fighting for some composure. "Sounds like a good game plan to me."

He gave her another nod and a smile, the winter light from the window clean and bright against him. Anne took a deep breath and surrendered her trust.

"All right then," he decided. "Let me make a call to someone I know in New York. I can give him the basics now, and you can fill in the details when you get there. He's the best you can get."

"My husband and brother don't own him?"

Jonathan's face lit with an almost piratical smile, teeth gleaming unnaturally. "That," he assured her with finality, "I can guarantee."

She finally nodded back, unaccustomed to the feeling of relief that struggled to take shape in her. "In that case, I'll get dinner while you call."

As she headed into the kitchen, she heard Jonathan dial. "Judson Fredericks, please. Tell him it's Jonathan Harris."

Jonathan finally allowed Anne to steer him to bed when she told him she wasn't staying up any longer to baby-sit him. She saw the weariness escape into his eyes as he let her cover him. He had paled a little, the lines along his mouth etched more deeply. She wanted so much to tell him to ease up on himself, to acknowledge his pain and let her help as he'd helped her. But she knew that this was a place severely guarded in him. He had to let her in first.

Anne stood next to his bed, caught between the image of the man who'd woken up in her house and the one who had offered to help save it.

"Jonathan, thank you," she said quietly. "I have to admit that until you gave me the name of your friend, I didn't know what I was going to do."

He smiled up at her, reaching over to take her hand. "Like I said, it's my way of saying I'm sorry. Besides . . ." His voice faded as he sought words that didn't seem familiar. "I had to thank you, too." His eyes searched hers. Something deliberate was happening and she wasn't sure she was ready yet.

"It's been a long time since someone's been that . . . unselfish." The struggle grew on his features, revealing the need for protection, the yearning for communication.

Anne sat gently on the edge of the bed, her hand still in his. She held his eyes just as surely. "I have nightmares, too," she said gently. "Would you like to talk about it?"

Jonathan had to look away. The ghosts were there, so close, and their pain was infecting him anew. Anne felt him stiffen and held her breath.

"You said that there were two times you were helpless to save someone else from being hurt." God, she wanted to hold him again. That dying light in his eyes couldn't possibly hurt more if it were her own. "Was that one of the times?"

For a long moment he remained very still, his eyes looking into hers. Anne waited. She heard the clock again, its rhythm the slow, steady pacing of time. The house muttered around her, and the fire popped in the living room. Her eyes were only on Jonathan as he fought his own battles of trust.

Finally, he nodded. "I was a platoon leader in Nam. Dong Ha. We were searching out VC hideouts when we ran across a whole network of tunnels." Anne felt the pressure build in her as he talked, his cadence as carefully measured as the clock's. "It was an ambush. Out of twenty men, only three of us survived. Ten were blown to hell in the middle of those tunnels." He stopped again, the images so vivid to him that even Anne imagined she could see them. The friends, the kids, the men who'd depended on him dying around him when he couldn't stop it. "We never even saw them. My best friend died right in front of me. He was supposed to be rotated out the next week."

Eddie. Anne felt the tears catch in her throat, a pain of frustration and futility welling in her. Jonathan finally looked up at her, only weariness left in his beautiful eyes, and offered a last shrug. "We never even saw 'em."

"Have you ever gone to see his family?"

"I haven't even been to the Vietnam Memorial." He found something in his hand to study. "I keep telling myself I'll go one of these days. Who knows?" he said with a shrug. "Maybe I will."

"Would it be easier if someone went with you?"

He showed his surprise. That was evidently not a question he'd often been asked. "I don't know. Mind if I think about it?"

"Not at all," she said smiling hesitantly, as surprised as he was that she'd made the offer. "I think I have to do the same."

They allowed each other tentative smiles. Things had changed a lot in a few days.

For a long moment Anne looked down at the handsome, magnetic, lonely man who had exploded into her life like a thunderclap. Unable to express herself in any other way, she bent forward and gently kissed him.

The lips she met were surprisingly tender, the feel of his cheek rough and strong. Instinctively her free hand reached for the curve of his jaw, as if it were a magnetic source of balance. Her fingers found it and tingled with the contact. Her own lips grew pliant, opening to the questioning probe of his tongue.

The brief meeting electrified her. It was as if she had found a wellspring, and the cold, clear waters that surged from it now suffused her body with a giddy effervescence that shocked her. She could hear her breath catch in a sob, deep in her throat, and her eyes closed against the delicious pain of it.

As if it were a natural progression, Jonathan reached up with his own hand and sought the warmth of her breast. Abruptly Anne straightened, his touch still searing her, her nipples stiff against the material of her shirt. Yearning leaped through her like lightning. Looking down at the message in Jonathan's eyes, she knew that she'd come perilously close to losing herself in him.

"You're a beautiful woman, Anne."

The blue of his eyes was suddenly intense, seething. For the first time in two years, Anne remembered what it was to feel beautiful in a man's eyes, to be regarded as desirable rather than capable. She caught her breath, arrested by the feeling, overwhelmingly frightened. For a long moment she could do no more than hold Jonathan's gaze, her hand still lost in his.

"I'm going to have to be able to get out of the mess I'm in before I can deal with new..." She didn't know what to call what was flaring hotly between them. She was afraid it was born of need rather than desire. All she could see was the light chilling once again in his eyes. "We have to be careful, Jonathan. Please understand."

A distance grew between them. Anne stood to a stiff kind of attention. This sudden fear was as powerful as the longing Jonathan had kindled in her. She had been betrayed by her own feelings, and now she knew that she wouldn't be able to untangle herself from this without at best involvement, at worst the kind of pain she loathed. And Anne had a feeling that it had already gone past the point of painless resolution.

She fled to her room without another word, unable to bear anything else Jonathan might admit. He never challenged her, but as the sun finally struggled up the next morning, Anne wasn't the only one who still hadn't fallen asleep.

She left in the morning without ever really talking to him. They passed social amenities as she brought in his breakfast and changed his dressings, but the air was charged and uncomfortable. It wasn't until Mary Dickey—the woman Anne had asked to take care of Jonathan in her absence—arrived with her two children that Anne finally went in to say goodbye.

When Jonathan caught sight of the preschoolers and considered their combined decibel level with a pained eye, Anne couldn't help but flash him a smug grin. He returned it with one of his own and invited the four-year-old to sit next to him. For a minute, it was as if the night before had never happened.

Anne got on the plane to New York with a sense of unease, unable to keep what had happened out of her mind. In the light of day, it almost seemed a delusion to think that Jonathan really cared for her. She'd probably read too much into the situation.

They had offered each other friendship, understanding and help. He had admitted as much when he'd thanked her for understanding what had happened after the nightmare. Unfortunately, as they became dependent on each other in the isolation of that little cabin, they could easily find themselves in a relationship neither of them wanted or could afford. Their combined emotions were fuses that ignited a pretty powerful powder keg.

Damn it, Anne thought, I'd just made it to the point of equilibrium. Maybe she wasn't ecstatically happy, but she'd been content. After all the years spent in the role of Pete Jackson's daughter and Tom McCarthy's wife she had finally forged the true cast of Anne Jackson, and she liked it. She was happy with herself. Jonathan Harris was a strong-willed, dominant personality, one who considered being in charge of his birthright. Anne wasn't at all sure that he was the kind of man who would encourage a wife to be independent.

He couldn't possibly understand what had gone into the building of Anne's self-determination. Or what it had cost. She couldn't let him tamper with it and possibly do it irreparable harm. Somehow, she'd have to hold on to her objectivity.

An awfully easy thing to decide in daylight. Especially three hundred miles away from the spell of his eyes.

Chapter 7

Anne had lied about disliking New York. She loved it. She could go there to just sit in one place for days and watch it, soaking in its kinetic energy as if recharging her batteries. Even when she'd lived in Boston, coming to New York had been like an electric shock. The amassed energy of twelve million people trapped within the high, skyscrapered canyons radiated like heat shimmering off streets in summer, charging the atmosphere like a thunderstorm. Her adrenaline shot up just by stepping onto the street.

Now, returning to the city after her isolation in the ageless mountains, Anne felt as if she'd just been thrown into a pool of cold water. She couldn't help smiling to herself as she walked along the crowded streets.

She found herself strolling down Sixth Avenue. The day was brisk, the sky, briefly seen near the break of Central Park, an almost bright blue above the smog. There had been no snow in the city and the streets were clear. Buses, cabs and limos chased along in fox and hound fashion, threatening the crazier pedestrians who stepped onto the street and challenged oncoming traffic like mad toreadors.

Dodging traffic was a game in New York. Anne refrained from trying her hand at it. It had been too long since she had competed, and she was afraid that her timing might be off. Besides, she had an armful of packages to protect.

It would be important to show a good face when she finally met up with Tom and Brad, so she'd stopped off at a few of the designer salons that were scattered along the upper Sixties. The salespeople she'd once known well had greeted her like a ghost returned from the grave. When she'd told them where she'd been the past few years, the reaction had been a universal pause and polite embarrassment for want of something to say.

Typical of these had been Madelyn, a tall, handsome woman who ruled over one of the most prestigious salons with rigid attention to suave style and judicious subservience. She had come to the door personally, hands outstretched as if greeting the proverbial prodigal child.

"Anne, my dear," she'd almost gushed. "We thought . . . well, of course we heard about the divorce. I'm so sorry." Feeling Anne out, she carefully cast for clues to the appropriate direction for the conversation. "We thought you'd simply gone on vacation."

Anne smiled, realizing this was like roller-skating. She'd need to work on her balance a bit more before really hitting the streets, but it was all coming back to her pretty quickly. "No," she admitted with a smile, "I've just moved."

The woman paused again, her eyes careful. "To the coast?" Those three words sounded more like, "We thought better of you." She'd probably never seen the other bank of the Hudson in her life. Anne couldn't wait to see how she'd react to the truth.

"No. I'm living in the mountains."

A nod, the same momentary confusion. "The Catskills?"

"The Appalachians." She let the woman founder only a moment, still holding both of her hands, before saving her. "My father had a retreat there. I needed the . . . well, the quiet. You understand."

"Of course," Madelyn nodded quickly, now on safe ground as she let Anne's hands go with a squeeze in preparation for getting down to business. "It's most understandable. And you look wonderful. The fresh air, I imagine. You positively glow, my dear."

And so Anne spent the first part of the day in New York readying herself to deal with its people again, getting her rhythm back for the games of the civilized animal. She had to worry about facing not only her brother and husband, but the lawyer Jonathan had recommended to her. After her years of experience she knew only too well how important it would be to make the correct first impression with this man, because she'd have to depend on him. There was truthfully no one else she had to turn to.

In one handshake, she would have to let the lawyer know that she was a woman to respect, not just the former arm ornament of Tom

McCarthy. There could be no mistaking her intentions or commitment. And if this lawyer were anything at all like Jonathan, she would have her work cut out for her.

Now, as Anne approached the Café de la Paix on the southeast corner of the park, its striped awning rolled up, she was still smiling. It had been a good day for getting her legs back. She only wished she could have the time to sit by the window and eat a leisurely lunch, watching the human traffic pass along the park. But time was at a premium. She had an appointment to keep.

She settled for a long walk around the fountain at Fifty-Ninth where street musicians played a strange jazz piece for tuba and guitar before she turned into the Plaza Hotel. Anne always stayed there when she was in town, never quite wanting to move away from Central Park, even to the clean geometric lines of some of the newer hotels farther south. There had even been a town house Tom had kept closer to Greenwich Village when he'd found that that was the thing to do, but Anne had always returned to the old-world grandeur along the park where she could enjoy what was to her the only green in the city.

Room service supplied a light lunch while Anne painstakingly dressed and groomed herself for her appointment with Jonathan's friend, sweeping her hair once more up into the simple chignon that Tom had preferred. She wore a two-piece red wool suit with short bolero jacket whose lines fell crisp and clean over her trim figure.

She had carefully chosen her small wardrobe for its simple, classic lines, because these best suited her and her mission. Today, she wore no more ornamentation than alligator pumps and pearl stud earrings. The effect was cool and professional. Anne looked more like a high-powered executive than a rural nurse. There was no doubt in her mind as she stepped into the cab taking her to the lawyer's office that she would need every bit of control she could muster to match the picture she presented. She couldn't get out of her mind the image of Jonathan as he delivered his well-placed barbs born of this city's cannibalism. It was all she could hope that his friend had a little more class than that.

When Anne walked into the office of Judson Fredericks, she was stunned. Walking toward her with an outstretched hand and warm smile was not another Manhattan flash, but a gentleman with the air of a Southern plantation owner. Judson was a handsome, tall, ramrod-straight, old-school lawyer who oozed confidentiality and trustworthiness. His handshake was firm and his smile brimming with the essence of cordiality. He led her into his office and sat her in a comfortable leather chair across from his desk before moving around to seat himself.

The office was decorated in dark paneling and leather, the perfect background to Judson's soft voice, distinguished head of silver hair and deceptively lazy eyes. His attitude toward her was almost openly paternal. It made her want to smile.

The first few minutes of polite observation of formal rules of office etiquette served them both to gain the other's respect. The call from Jonathan provided an easy introduction to business.

"Jonathan said he'd had an accident near your home," Judson said, frowning. "But he refused to illuminate me beyond the usual platitudes. Is he all right?"

"He's fine." Anne smiled. "He injured himself in a fall near where I live, and we were forced to keep him there due to snow and road conditions."

"There isn't any way to get him to a hospital?"

"I live in an isolated area behind the Great Smoky Mountain National Park, and it's a long, hard way to the hospital from there. Especially for a man with a broken leg and a couple of broken ribs."

He nodded, appeased. "Well, I'll certainly take your word for it. But please do tell me if there is anything he needs, and I will be more than happy to make the necessary arrangements." With this, he settled into his chair, as if to signal a change in the direction of the conversation. "In the meantime, let's look into what brings such a beautiful lady to my office. I've been able to begin gathering information on what Jonathan has told me, but I would like to hear the story again in your words."

Anne took a moment to gather her thoughts together, thinking that she already felt she couldn't have brought her problems to a better man.

She told him everything, slowly and in detail, and Judson listened attentively, not even making notes until she had finished. The window behind him suffused the room in soft gray light from the sky high above lower Manhattan. The office itself was silent but for the measured cadence of Anne's words, her manner as carefully composed as her appearance.

The silence, as comfortable as the dark overstuffed furniture, closed in again as Anne finished. Mr. Fredericks finally broke her gaze to contemplate what she'd told him, nodding quietly to himself and tapping on the mahogany desk with manicured fingers.

After a few long moments, he looked up thoughtfully. "Would you like your inheritance back?"

She wondered for a moment if he'd really heard what she'd just said. "I want my land. Nothing more."

"I ask because I'm not sure we can go only that far. You must challenge your brother's right to use that land as collateral for a personal loan. If we go so far as contesting your father's original will, you could end up with more than you bargained for."

She sighed. "All I'm saying, Mr. Fredericks, is that I don't care what they do anymore. I want none of it. I only want my home. But I will do whatever is necessary to keep it."

Again, he considered. Anne kept very still, her hands folded precisely over her bright red skirt. The rich smell of leather and thick carpeting should have soothed but somehow stifled a little.

"I'll have to do some work on it and that will take a little time," Mr. Fredericks finally said, looking back up with studious eyes. "Will you be in New York long?"

"No." She shook her head slightly. "I have to get back. I'll be back next week for the meeting with Amplex Corporation."

"Yes. Fine. And how should I contact you if I need to?"

"I'll leave you an address and a number."

He studied her a moment, considering her features and bearing, her sleek, rich hair, Gucci shoes, the well-manicured nails and faultless bearing. Then he afforded himself a warm smile of wonder. "I, of course, know of your family, Miss Jackson. And I have heard of Peter Jackson's home in the Smokies. But seeing you now, I simply cannot imagine your living there alone."

Anne returned his smile, content that she had made the impression she had sought. "Everyone has his own paradise, Mr. Fredericks. Some day you must allow me to show you mine."

His smile broadened, and again he nodded. "I think it must be a special place. I would consider the invitation a privilege. Hopefully, I'll get the chance to accept."

Anne stood to go, longing to ask about Jonathan's connection with this man, but for some reason hesitated to bring it up. She extended her hand to wish the distinguished lawyer goodbye. When he clasped it with genuine enthusiasm Anne's spirits rose. This man would indeed help her. And again she marveled at the enigma of Jonathan Harris, this man's friend.

The meeting with Judson so encouraged her that she decided to take things a step further and chance facing Tom. There would be nothing to be gained by putting it off, and she thought that he needed to be unsettled a little. It might be good to let him know that Anne wasn't the same person she was when she'd left Boston.

She was quickly surprised by a good portent. When she called to make her accommodations for the visit to Boston before heading home, she found out that both Tom and Brad were in New York on business. She could drop in on them, and without having to overcome the disadvantage of facing them on their home field. She'd have no trouble finding them: she knew exactly where they'd be.

Late in the afternoon Anne stood in her hotel room, readied for the meeting. Turning a careful circle before the mirror, she performed a final inspection. All was perfect. It was as if she'd never left. The vermilion suit highlighted the sun whiteness of her blond hair, the simple style of it offsetting her lithe legs. She had added the diamond-and-sapphire earrings her mother had left her to round out the effect.

Simple and smashing, Tom had always said. Well, he was about to get the full dose of both. Anne hoped that she was still good enough to hide the weakness in her knees and the nest of butterflies that had nested in her stomach. Standing tall and self-assured before the mirror, she smiled. She seemed smooth and cool. She could do it. She hoped.

Anne pulled on the fur jacket that would complete the picture and reached for her purse. A cab was waiting downstairs that would take her to the restaurant where Tom and Brad would be finishing their dinner. When she stepped into the taxi, the wide-eyed admiration of the cabbie was not lost on her. She wished her stomach would settle down a little.

The restaurant was small and elegant. The decor dramatically simple in chrome and burgundy. Anne had known the maître d' for years and found it embarrassingly simple to find out from him that, true to form, Tom and Brad would be dining there before flying back to Boston. She approached the desk precisely at six, knowing how well she had timed her arrival. Louis looked up from his book, his eyes widening in delight.

"Mrs. . . ." he faltered, embarrassed.

Anne quickly saved him from discomfort. "Louis, when are you going to call me Anne?" she said, smiling.

He melted visibly. "It has been too long since we have seen you. Will you be having dinner tonight?"

"After I've taken care of some disagreeable business, Louis. Where are they?"

"The same." He shrugged. "Always the same. Would you like me to take you?"

"No, thank you, Louis," she said, smiling. "I think I'll pop in on my own."

His smile didn't quite match hers, but he nodded her on with some enthusiasm. She walked back into the darkened restaurant, knowing that she wouldn't see them until she was almost upon them. They always ate at the same table in the back, shielded by Plexiglas and muted lighting. A rush of nostalgia threatened her composure as she remembered the times she, too, had been included in the meals here.

Ever since she'd been twelve, when her father had first set up his friend Louis in a business that was now one of the top five restaurants in New York, the Jacksons dined at Chez Louis. Once a week, without fail, they'd be seated at booth fifteen.

"Tom, Brad. I see that you don't break tradition easily."

She stood by the table, praying that she could hold out, wondering what the hell she was doing here. One look at Tom had almost been her downfall. With his blond, well-groomed good looks and smoky-green eyes he couldn't possibly be more handsome or magnetic if he tried. His face was intelligent and controlled, his nose straight, his mouth sensual and his chin perfectly firm. She knew that she was still mesmerized by him and hated herself for it.

In her confusion she almost lost the satisfaction of seeing the shock on their faces. They had just finished dinner. Coffee had been poured and Tom was just about to light up a cigarillo. The match burned out in his fingers.

Abruptly, they stood. Anne smiled with cool eyes.

"What are you doing in New York?" Brad asked sharply.

She eyed him without flinching. "It's nice to see you, too, Brad dear."

It struck her again how truly unremarkable Brad was. He had the kind of face that radiated weakness. His eyes were brown and his lips thin. The only kind thing Anne could say about him was that he had grown a moustache since she'd last seen him, and that it made him seem to blend more easily into a crowd.

Anne had not always disliked Brad. In fact, at one time in their lives, they'd been rather close. That had been when her mother had been alive. Her mother had been able to bring out the best in him. When she had died, so had any spark of decency in Brad. He had become isolated and resentful, developing the facial tics that still plagued him, and blaming his lack of achievement on his father's failure to show him favor. Most of the time Brad was merely annoying, but when he felt he was about to fail he tended to strike out blindly. He hadn't really become insufferable, though, until Tom had joined the business and begun to personally groom him for usurping what Brad had always sarcastically called the "Jackson throne." From that moment, he had never again taken Anne into his confidence. Now, after five years in Tom's shadow, Brad didn't have any recognizable traces of humanity left in him.

She watched him now as he began to sweat and twitch at the sight of her and she could only feel disdain. He didn't have any class.

"Of course it's wonderful to see you," Tom said, an almost imperceptible hesitation in his voice giving away his shock. He had the class in the company. "You're as beautiful as ever, Anne. More beautiful."

"Thank you, Tom. May I join you?"

"Please."

He moved to allow her room. She ignored him and sat next to Brad, knowing that Tom was regaining his balance quickly. She didn't think it wise to push her luck too far.

"What are you doing in New York?" he repeated more conversationally.

Francis, the waiter who'd always taken care of their table, now appeared silently with Anne's coffee and Frangelica. She shot him a dazzling smile, and he bowed a bit lower than was customary. After taking a sip of liqueur, Anne turned back to her family.

"I'm here to see my lawyer," she finally answered evenly, taking note of the quick, surreptitious glance that passed between the two of them and feeling more stable for their need of it. "You?"

"Business."

She nodded absently, sipping at her coffee.

"You haven't been in the city in a while. How did you happen to find a lawyer?" Brad asked, his eye pulling oddly at the words as if he were winking at her.

"Recommendation of a friend. Don't worry, Brad, it's no one you know. And no one you own."

"Anne . . ." Tom reached for her hand. Anne deftly avoided it, not wanting him to feel the calluses that one manicure couldn't erase. He hesitated only a moment. "Did you get my message?"

"The one about not having any choice about what happened to my home, or the one offering new lodgings?"

"You always have a home in Boston."

"Thank you, Tom. The invitation was eloquent, but I'm going back to Cedar Ridge."

"How long will you be here?"

"I leave tonight."

He frowned handsomely, the perfect modicum of concerned disappointment. "That's too bad. I thought maybe we could spend more time together."

She smiled again, the light in her eyes dry. "See the town? I've seen it, thank you. I really have to be getting back."

"Animals need tending?" Brad's voice was quiet, his insult implicit.

Anne's answering smile, delivered over the rim of the coffee cup, was unruffled at the impotent attack. "I guess I'm a creature of habit, too, Brad. I suppose it's a matter of what one gets used to."

Tom leaned back and lit the cigarillo he'd earlier forgotten. "You know, Anne," he said, his voice soft and dark, the music that had haunted her dreams, "sitting here with you, it seems hard to believe you've been away."

It was time for her to make her exit. She knew where his line was heading and didn't particularly want to be around when it got there. She was still afraid after all this time that she wouldn't be able to walk away from it.

"But I have," she assured him, finishing the last of her coffee and gathering her purse to go. "It's been good to see you two. I'm glad I could get the chance to stop in before my flight left. I'll give Silas and Sarah your love, Brad. My best to Ellie." Ellie was the thin-blooded heiress Brad had managed to marry. Anne turned to Tom. "Anyone I can pass on salutations to for you, Tom?"

His answer was a silent smile that lit his eyes with amusement. Anne was beginning to doubt whether she'd have the nerve to sneak back into the restaurant for their delicious bouillabaisse. Tom and Brad stood with her, Tom taking her by the hands before she could escape. His movements were too smooth to avoid.

"Why don't you come back to the city?" he coaxed, his voice hypnotizing the thoughts of bouillabaisse away. "You belong here."

Anne's answer was cool, even as she wondered whether he could feel the trembling his touch had given birth to. "I'm perfectly happy where I am, thank you. It's been wonderful, but I do have to go."

Retrieving her hands from him, she turned and left. Tom and Brad stood where she'd left them, knowing why she'd come, and, she dearly hoped, more unsettled for her performance. God knew it had taken enough out of her.

Contrary to what she'd said, Anne didn't leave that night. She managed to slip back into the restaurant for some of that promised dinner and the most shameless pampering she'd enjoyed in two years, and then spent a night savoring the luxury of the hotel. Bright and early the next morning she headed home.

It was just about lunchtime when she walked into Thompson's General Store wearing the same suit she'd worn to Chez Louis. She had been coming and going from the mountain for so many years that most of her neighbors had gotten used to the disparity in her appearance. It didn't occur to her that Jim had never seen her like this until she caught the look on his face.

At first it was blank, as if a stranger had walked in. Then it slackened into an openmouthed gape. Jim and Cassie hadn't come to the mountain until Anne's last case of clothing had long since been packed up and given away. They had never seen the transition before or, for that matter, the celebrated city side of Anne Jackson.

For the first time since she'd been coming home from the city, she felt out of place and slightly uncomfortable.

Two hours later she climbed off her horse to find Jonathan comfortably seated in the front porch rocker. By the smile that lit his eyes when he saw her, it seemed that he was glad to see her. She wondered how loud the kids had been.

"Well," she offered with an appraising grin. "I suppose you're pretty proud of yourself."

"It only took me twenty minutes to get out here," he answered nonchalantly. "I was beginning to get stir-crazy."

She could well imagine that it only took him twenty minutes. There was still a fine sheen of perspiration on his forehead from the exertion, but he looked like a kid rounding third for home. His enthusiasm sharpened her pleasure at seeing him.

"A long way from mountain climbing, aren't we?" she said, laughing.

"Annie, you're back." Cassie appeared in the cabin doorway, hands on hips.

Anne faced her with an identical pose. "So, I'm away for two days and the community takes over my patient, huh?"

"We barely got started," she retorted happily. "If it had taken you a couple of more days to get home, we could have had him tending the animals by the time you got back."

Jonathan scowled. "I hardly think so."

Cassie laughed and led everybody back in, Jonathan bringing up the rear. He closed the door as Anne shrugged out of her coat and hat.

"Oh, Annie, your hair," Cass breathed. "I love it."

Anne's hand went instinctively to the tightly coiled chignon, her voice unaccountably embarrassed, her eyes straying to Jonathan's passive face. "Oh. I'd forgotten about it."

"You're going to show me what you got in New York, aren't you?" Cassie demanded, bearing down on her. "I have the feeling that you have wonderful taste when it comes to designer rags."

Before Anne could move to protest, Cassie had one hand on the suitcase and the other on Anne. Anne had the choice of going up with her to the loft to do some modeling or trying to dupe her way to the kitchen for some tea. She gave up with a heartfelt sigh and followed upstairs as Jonathan settled himself onto the couch.

Fifteen minutes later Cassie stood before her, her reaction a momentary stunned silence. "My God. I wouldn't have recognized you."

Anne hadn't realized that when she'd slipped back into the suit, she had also unconsciously slipped into the city veneer that had barely protected her from Tom.

"Oh, stop it," she objected. "You act like Eliza Doolittle just walked in."

"I feel like it," Cassie assured her with an awed shake of the head. "Do you know how... formidable you look?"

Anne stared at her, unsure how to react. Jonathan's voice interrupted.

"Don't I get a show, too?"

His reaction was even more startled than Cassie's. The minute he saw her, the teasing humor in her eyes died hard. It was as if he'd just met her for the first time, and that he didn't like what he saw.

"Not you, too," she protested, not realizing that even her posture was more suited to her clothes than her surroundings, and the sophistication of it more alien than the sight of Jonathan's three-piece suit.

"Impressive," he said, his voice barely warm.

Anne was confused. "It keeps me from being taken advantage of," she answered, trying to keep the tone of her voice light, but failing.

"Seems a bit superfluous" was all he would say, a distant look in his eyes.

"I'm changing," she decided, turning impulsively on her heel. "This outfit is definitely not the dress of the day."

Before anyone could voice protest, she slipped out of the designer suit and pulled her hair down from the sleek hairstyle into the braids that more suited the surroundings.

As she put the suit away, Anne realized that she had enjoyed donning fashionable clothes again, dusting off the old social skills and seeing how well they'd held up. It disturbed her a little.

She had come to consider that part of her life without merit, had begun to resent its waste. In the end, all she'd been given, been privilege to, had come down around her like a house of cards. It had taken a divorce and her father's death to come to grips with all the years of her life when material luxuries had been only a substitute for a father's attention and a husband's love.

Maybe, she decided, there was some truth to the adage that absence made the heart grow fonder. Or maybe she had just been able to face the old life on different terms. Her terms. For the first time in her life, she had been the one in control.

It was a true pleasure to remember the confusion she'd unleashed by pouncing unannounced on Brad and Tom. It had been only the second time she'd won any sort of victory over them, and this time she'd been in a clear enough frame of mind to enjoy it. But, looking at the clean, expensive lines of her new clothes, she wondered if maybe there wasn't more to it than that.

"Better?" she asked a few minutes later as she reappeared in work shirt and jeans.

Cassie cocked her head to one side in appraisal. "I'm not sure if better is the right word, but I think I'm more comfortable with you like this."

Jonathan was more to the point, driving home his message with the brittleness of his eyes. He spoke with as much rancor as awe. "I'd heard the legend of Peter Jackson's little girl, but I'd never had the chance to see you in action. You must have been some rich bitch, lady."

Chapter 8

Anne was more surprised than she should have been by the sudden change of attitude. Cassie was astounded—she seemed to stop breathing for a moment she was so still.

"Don't you want to know how Mr. Fredericks is?" Anne asked instead, her manner measured and even, her control spread thin over her mounting confusion. Why couldn't he just once not swing back to the attack when she least suspected it?

Jonathan's quick smile at her words was amazingly tender, considering his last words. "Judson is always the same," he said quietly. "Quite a gentleman, isn't he?"

"A refreshing change, I must admit," Anne allowed. "I'm amazed that he'd consort with the likes of you. He seems to be such an upstanding sort."

Jonathan laughed. "He doesn't. He's an old family friend. Judson was born and raised in the wilds of Wyoming, too."

"In that case, I feel better. For a while there I was wondering what the catch was."

He raised an eyebrow. "With Judson? Unthinkable."

Anne took a minute to describe the older man to Cassie, who still stood slightly openmouthed at the exchange she'd witnessed. Anne said nothing about that, just glad that Cassie had finally seen that Anne wasn't making up Jonathan's knack for lightning mood changes. Now if someone could explain them to her, she'd feel even better.

"When will I be able to get back to civilization?" Jonathan asked.

Anne raised her own eyebrow. "I thought you relished the rustic atmosphere."

"I didn't think it was much a matter of choice."

"Can you ride a horse?"

His response was in the form of a pained silence.

"Come to me when you can. Or when the snow melts."

"Why can't I go in a cart or something?" he persisted. "Surely, you at least have wagons or something like that up here."

"We do, but we can't get one up or down the mountain right now. And why are you suddenly so antsy? One foray outside does not a recovery make."

"I'm not used to being so passive."

She grinned dryly. "A real take-charge kind of guy, huh?"

"You could say that. It's been a long time since I haven't been in control." In her preoccupation with making a snappy comeback, Anne almost missed the momentary light in Jonathan's eyes that suddenly made her think of other conversations they'd had. And she stopped, suddenly unsure of what to say. The brief glimpses of vulnerability still unnerved her.

"You confuse me almost as much as he does," Cassie said as she and Anne sat in the kitchen a little while later, voices hushed with secrecy. Jonathan still sat with his book not much more than a dining-room table away.

"Me?" Anne countered with a quizzical look.

"I think I would have hit him." Cassie paused a moment in consideration. "As a matter of fact, I almost did."

Anne laughed, sipping at her coffee and wishing that she could have stolen Louis's pot. Maybe next time she was in New York. "I'm glad you saw it. Now at least you know that I haven't been making it all up to dump a load of misplaced revenge on an innocent bystander."

"But you took it so well." Cassie looked up furtively as her voice got a little too loud. Jonathan didn't react.

Anne shrugged, her attention still purposefully on the hot coffee that was warming the travel chills from her. "I'm getting used to it." A lie, but more immediately acceptable than the truth of what that little confrontation was still doing to her stomach. "He seems to defuse a bit easily if you change the subject."

Cassie shook her head in frustration. "I still can't figure why he would pick on you. He's been nothing but a gentleman with me."

Anne refrained from shooting Cassie a look of surprise. She, after all, had proposed the schoolboy theory in the first place.

Anne had seen a part of Jonathan that she thought very few people had been permitted to see. And now Jonathan didn't know how to react to her anymore. Maybe he considered her to have some kind of unpalatable hold over him.

Formidable, Cassie had called her. Why would that have made such an impact on him?

"Uh, I don't know," she finally answered, careful to keep her voice as quiet as Cassie's. "Maybe I threaten him somehow. Maybe he has a wife somewhere he hates who looks like me."

"Well, I have to say that you both have the same dueling styles, that's for sure."

Anne looked over at her friend, recognizing the accuracy of her statement. Maybe she hadn't gotten as far away from the city as she'd thought.

For a few moments they sat in silence, eyes contemplative, the aroma of wood smoke and coffee comfortably filling the kitchen. Then Cassie spoke up again.

"How do your chances look for keeping the Ridge?"

"I honestly don't know," she admitted. "But it was certainly worth the trip just to throw Tom and Brad off balance. I saw them, you know."

Cassie's eyes widened appreciably. "You seem awfully calm about it."

"Sure, now that I'm far enough away. I have to admit, though, I sure confounded them with my footwork."

Cassie was still wide-eyed, studying Anne's face as she talked. "Annie, I'm really proud of you. I've never seen you this rational when you talked about those two before."

Anne smiled happily. "Maybe I'm finally getting my feet under me."

"You've done something, honey."

"Hey, I'm being ignored again! I can smell the coffee out here."

Cassie and Anne exchanged meaningful looks at the sound of Jonathan's voice.

"Ya know," Cassie said, "I think the saying for this occasion is that little boys don't grow up; their toys just get more expensive."

Jonathan ate dinner in the kitchen, but Anne begged off on the excuse that she was tired from traveling. Again, their dialogue was exceedingly polite and carefully distant, as if afraid to accidentally wander too near a weak point in their armor. Anne knew darn well that she should have walked in and demanded an explanation for his previous name-calling, but she didn't have the courage. He just might tell her. She only wanted to get herself to bed and her patient one day closer to being able to leave her to her silence and peace.

She was all too aware, as she stepped carefully around the stranger who sat in her living room, that as much as she'd breached his wall of security, he had done the same with her. He had drawn out emotions more intense than she'd allowed to surface in a long time. He had moved her. He had made her want to reach out to him, and she couldn't afford to do that. Tom had been reminder enough for any one of the risks involved, and the scene today had only served to emphasize that little lesson in life.

Yet she found herself watching him surreptitiously. There was something about the way the firelight softened his face, the way he ran his fingers through his hair as if to force it into some semblance of order as he pored through a thick volume of Flaubert. His features had lost some of their sharpness since he'd been there, until it seemed that they belonged to someone else who was comfortable in a rural setting.

Anne could imagine him on horseback now, or set in rhythmic motion as he chopped firewood, muscles straining against flannel and denim. She found herself fantasizing about Jonathan, Silas and the rest of the men in the community as they worked together in companionable humor to raise a new church or barn.

Flipping off the kitchen light, she deliberately set those mental pictures aside with the work she'd finished and walked into the living room to face the real Jonathan Harris. He looked up at her with weary question.

"Unless you're planning to spend the night out here, I'd suggest we start heading in," she suggested. "I'm ready for bed."

He simply nodded, closing the book and putting it on the table. Anne reached for the crutches, but he took them from her hands.

"Thanks, I'll get there by myself," he said a bit stiffly. "It's about time I started getting around on my own."

Anne said nothing as she watched him struggle to his feet. He was purposefully pushing her away. Anne, the nurse, was frustrated, knowing damn well that he was working himself too hard again. She could see it in the tight set of his jaw and the creases in his forehead. She was certain that Cassie had helped him earlier, probably with liberal doses of adventure and humor. Now, though, he fought in determined silence as if the whole thing were a grim battle to be faced alone.

Anne, the woman, realized that it angered her. Why was it that she got the feeling that she was such a threat to him? And why on earth did it make her feel so damn ambivalent?

She hated that feeling, always balancing on a razor's edge, wanting more and wanting less at the same time. She thought that she'd been finished with that kind of torment two years ago. After facing what her life had become the last time she'd gotten herself into a relationship with a man very much like the one she faced, she certainly didn't think she should have any trouble about handling her attraction to Jonathan. But she did, and it kept getting worse.

Not five minutes later as she followed him into his room, she discovered just how much worse.

He was trying to maneuver the corner, his progress slowing. Anne said nothing. She merely walked alongside him, watching the effort that once again brought a shine of sweat to his face and carved cruel lines on either side of his mouth. She was angry that he should put himself through this. She was also awed by the store of willpower he seemed to be able to call upon. No one she'd ever known would have put himself through this. At least not without the benefit of a generous amount of painkillers or alcohol. Jonathan had had neither since he'd arrived.

Anne found herself shaking her head, watching the broad back that strained against her brother's old pajama shirt and noting the signs that Jonathan was wearing out. Without warning, he lost his balance.

He had been trying to turn the corner to his room when he caught a crutch against the door frame, throwing him forward. He toppled quickly. Anne wasn't really as alert as she should have been, but her instincts were accurate. Her reaction saved them both from going down.

Jonathan fell to his right as he tried to catch hold of the wall, but his bad leg gave way. Without thinking, Anne clasped her arms around his waist. He gasped at the pressure against his injured ribs. Anne managed to get around and lean back against the wall, her face pressed into his chest as he fought to regain control of the crutches.

"Take your time," she told him, her voice muffled. "I'm not going anywhere." Except down, she thought as she braced her knees against his and fought to keep them both upright. Beneath the flannel shirt Jonathan's heart pounded heavily and his breathing was labored, but he stopped struggling for a minute. Taking some slow breaths, he rested his weight against her.

"We've got to stop meeting like this," he gasped above Anne's head.

Unaccountably, she giggled, adrenaline coursing through her like a heady liquor. "If Silas walked in right now," she managed, "he'd shoot you for trying to molest me."

Or maybe vice versa. She was having more trouble breathing, and it wasn't all exertion. It seemed like every nerve in her was on fire and that her heart was readying for battle. If only his muscles weren't so rock-hard, or his back so lean. Caution, or was it fear, made an attempt to break through the illogical exhilaration but failed. Her early-warning system had been thrown into shutdown.

"Wait...I...have it...." He was moving, straightening very slowly as he once again got the crutches securely under his arm. Anne straightened with him, giving him added support as he went.

"Should I pull the chair over here," she asked up to him, "or do you think you can make it the rest of the way without doing that again? I only have the energy reserves for one rescue a day."

He still leaned against her, wedging her against the door frame so that she couldn't move. "Maybe we could...just stand here for a...couple of...minutes so I can...get my breath." He caught her in his gaze, and Anne knew that she wasn't the only one having more trouble breathing than she should. A chill shot her spine like fire, another warning that she couldn't seem to heed.

"I'm not going anywhere until you do," she answered, her voice sounding breathless. She still had her arms around him and didn't seem to realize it, as if it were a natural thing. His eyes, looking down at her from the shadow-strewn hallway, glowed uncannily as if lit by a pale blue flame. The hottest fire is blue, Anne thought absently. She could feel the heat of his eyes as if it penetrated every pore. She wanted to reach up and test it, to run her fingers by that fire and challenge it, because it seemed to grow hotter even as they stood in silence.

Anne wanted to say something, to break the spell that seemed to be weaving its way around the two of them. She wanted to suddenly pull away, but knew that she wouldn't. And there in the depths of Jonathan's eyes she saw the same conflict: he was weakening just as surely as she.

They needed this; even against their wills, wanted it. Physically they needed it as if it were only to obey laws of attraction. Emotionally, neither could think of one logical reason to be attracted, one sane excuse that would explain the fact that they were so inexorably drawn to each other. Anne couldn't be certain of the reasons for Jonathan's distrust of and disdain for her. She had to assume it had something to do with the person she was, or maybe it was from his fear of dependency. She certainly knew why she loathed the idea of attraction to Jonathan, but right now that didn't seem to make any difference.

"I think I should be out getting the animals down for the night," she whispered, still unable to take her eyes from his.

He didn't move. "If you leave, I'll fall over."

Anne was having even more trouble getting her thoughts straight. "Maybe I should let you."

Jonathan didn't smile or reply. He bent to her, where her up-turned face waited helplessly, and caught her between his hand and his lips. Without thinking, Anne closed her eyes against the thrill his touch unleashed in her. Her lips softened against his assault, her arms tightening instinctively around him. This is insane, she thought even as she pulled him against her to steady his balance. Nobody in her right mind would be caught in an unwieldy situation like this. She felt the hammering of his heart against hers and thought no more.

He forced her lips open gently, his own softer than Anne could have ever imagined. With the hand he maneuvered away from a crutch he explored her back, sliding it purposefully up beneath her shirt to test the softness of her skin. Anne recognized the feel of his fingers against her spine like a brand. Arching against him, she sought the heat he seemed to radiate. She met his tongue with her own and searched the depths of his mouth, the soft warmth of his lips. She'd read that women melted when aroused by the man they loved, but she'd never believed such exaggeration. But suddenly she felt as if her skin had become molten, as if she had been poured into place and that Jonathan could mold her any way he wanted if only he tried. Her knees were having trouble staying locked, even when pressed against his, and she seemed to fit his contours better than her own.

His hand found her bra and unsnapped it. She allowed his hand to progress unheeded around her side to her breast where it un-leashed sparks like fireworks.

It had been a long time since she'd realized what mayhem a set of fingers could wreak when set loose against the sensitive skin of her breast. Not since Tom had she even anticipated the feel of a man's hand against the soft swelling, or ached for a slightly roughened thumb to chafe her nipples to exhilarating stiffness. Anne pressed against his hand, against the hypnotic strength of his touch. She straightened a little more so that his lips could find her neck and send her to gasping. At the same time she felt him against her, his arousal powerful.

She didn't want this moment to pass, didn't want to forfeit the headiness of his touch, the exhilaration of his nearness. But suddenly she saw the impasse and saw what she'd been ignoring. The fear she'd so far eluded suffused her with its chill until Jonathan's caresses froze her. Anne wished more than anything right then that she were the kind of person who could give in to her needs and wants without thought to repercussions. A handsome man held her in his arms, a man she was drawn to, and she wished she could let him make love to her.

She suddenly felt as if she were smothering.

"I don't know . . . about you," she gasped even as Jonathan's hands found another sensitive area, "but I'm beginning to lose my balance. We can't stay here indefinitely."

"Any suggestions?" he mumbled into her throat. He didn't seem to notice yet that her posture had stiffened.

"There are any number of obvious ones," she answered, her head against his heaving chest, her eyes squeezed shut against what she had to say. "But I'm afraid I can't think of one that would work right now."

He straightened at that, his eyes trapping hers mercilessly. "What's that supposed to mean?"

Anne took a deep breath to steady her racing pulse. "It means that maybe we shouldn't start something we can't finish."

"I'm not that much of a cripple," he said with a rakish grin.

She faced him with more purpose now, drawing herself up in defense of the lightning even his soft voice was unleashing in her. "But maybe I am. I'm not the type of person who can enjoy this particular recreation so erratically."

"Erratically?"

Both of them were still breathing quickly as if they'd just completed a race. Or were about to begin one.

"Maybe a better word is arbitrarily," she retorted with more force, even though the constriction in her chest threatened to suffocate her. She was too close to him to protect herself properly. She'd never been able to win with Tom, and she was suddenly very afraid that she couldn't win against this man who depended on her to even make it around the house. "It seems to me that you're the one who just finished calling me a rich bitch. That's not exactly my idea of sweet nothings."

"You were a rich bitch."

Anne was nonplussed enough to almost knock him over. "And that's all you have to say about it?"

"Anne," he said in his best conciliatory manner, the set of his shoulders softening, "we want each other. Isn't that all that matters?"

She shook her head. "No. That's not all that matters. I don't consider making love a passing sport." Her eyes flashed now and the intoxication of his touch died. "Do you?"

"No—Yes." He shook his head impatiently, easing his hold on her. "Oh, I don't know. I don't understand myself. I just know that no matter how I feel about you, you have the ability to drive me crazy. And I can't exactly take any cold showers." When his smile appeared, it was self-deprecating. "At least not without help."

His abrupt honesty threw her off again. This man who looked and spoke so much like Tom McCarthy, who showed flashes of the same bloodthirsty instincts, still had the knack of completely contradicting his image by almost grudgingly allowing his defenses to lag enough to be recognized as just that. Tom had never had defenses. He had been predatory to his toes.

Anne felt as if she were going to explode. She was literally and figuratively against the wall. Maybe if Jonathan had come along a few months later in her life she could have handled him with more aplomb. She could have dealt objectively with his confusing, compelling personality and been able to make a decision with the presence of mind she'd so desperately sought when she'd returned to the mountains.

But he hadn't waited to fall into her life, and Anne wasn't sure she wouldn't crumble beneath the pressure of his blue eyes and offhand sarcasm. She didn't yet know how to demand honesty from him. She didn't know whether to expect a commitment. She didn't know that she ever wanted one again.

"I can't, Jonathan...." Anne was beginning to have trouble breathing again. She knew what happening: she was hyperventilating. Some detached voice deep inside her commented dryly on hysterical females, but she couldn't seem to pay any attention. She knew that she had to get away, maybe out to the cool, clean air and moon-painted snow. She couldn't even bring herself to explain to Jonathan the reason she suddenly looked like a rabbit caught in the headlights of an oncoming car. She couldn't seem to pull the whirling memories and pain into a semblance of order to paint the picture necessary to make him understand. She had to escape.

"You're just going to walk away?" he asked quietly, not understanding.

"I have to." Anne felt tears threaten and was unnerved by the unfamiliar pain of them. "I have to go out and get the animals settled for the night. Can you get the rest of the way with some help?"

Her abrupt change sealed her words. Jonathan straightened, supported by the crutches so that Anne could let go.

"I told you before. I'll get there on my own."

When he turned away from her, Anne saw the frost in his eyes and realized that instead of feeling relief at the resolution of the dilemma, she felt worse.

Chapter 9

Anne and Jonathan seemed to have little to say to each other for the next few days. He was making enough physical progress to have free reign of the house. His attitude, however, had regressed. Anne knew what had caused this, but couldn't bring herself to bring it to issue with him.

She'd rejected him, had once again seemed to him in complete control of a situation that he couldn't master. She still didn't know for sure how he felt about her, but she did know now that the tensions in the little cabin had escalated sharply because of that moment of mutual weakness.

He was certainly chafing more and more at being restricted, even though it was his own injuries and not Anne imposing the restrictions. Even so, she was the one who received the weight of his impatience, his silences even more electric than his brief verbalizations. Meals were served and eaten in almost total silence. The only time Jonathan really talked to her was when she asked about his progress. He still experienced quite a lot of pain when he stretched his limits, but that wasn't something he would admit to. It seemed to make no difference that Anne couldn't help but see.

What troubled Anne was the fact that his present attitude bothered her so much. She didn't want his animosity. She wanted to tell him that she hadn't ever felt so alive as when she'd been in his arms, that she was awed by his courage and strength. More than anything, she wanted to go to him when she saw pain suddenly crease his face and invade his eyes. She wanted to hold him the way she had the night of his horrible dream, soothing away the strain, easing the frustration.

More than once she caught herself just short of reaching out to help. Each time the look in Jonathan's eyes had frozen her. Seeing that same struggle in his eyes, she wondered if he was having as much trouble sleeping as she. She wanted to have a chance to talk out the misconceptions they'd built up about each other and understand their limitations. But neither of them seemed to be able to allow the proper doors to open. Neither was able to bend and meet the other halfway. Until the day Mary Lou Sullins' baby was born.

Mary Lou's oldest girl, Emily, arrived on horseback at four in the morning to get Anne. Emily was sixteen and going to be married before the year was out, but she'd decided to wait to help her mother with the baby who would be born six months after the death of Will, Mary Lou's husband. Mary Lou was not in good health herself. She was too worn by her other seven children, Will's long illness and their crushing poverty to bear this baby easily.

It wasn't until well past midnight that Anne found herself back before her fire, a cup of coffee in her tired, aching hands. Staring into the fire, she thought of the people she helped. They were people like the Sullinses who had the babies they couldn't afford, who had more misery than should have been their share and who plodded on day after day just to survive. She thought of the baby, the joy she always felt at the new life she held, and how quickly it had been quenched when she saw the vacant look with which his mother greeted him. He deserved so much, and he would only get poverty and hunger and maybe later the chance to kill himself in a coal mine like his father or scrabble at the dirt they called a farm.

Anne turned to stare absently out the window and watched the fitful moonlight glitter on new-fallen snow like a shower of mystical sparks. She never felt the new tears that traced her cheeks.

"Hey! What's the news from the front?"

Anne lurched to her feet. Unaccountably irritated by the flippant tone of Jonathan's voice, she stalked to his room. He looked as if he'd just awakened, the night-light softening his features and sending up an unwanted aching in Anne's chest.

The sight of her stopped him short. "What's wrong?" he asked suddenly. "Is the baby all right?"

She deflated, dragged down by the bone weariness that had taken hold. "The baby's fine," she told him from where she stood in the doorway, resenting the wealth in this room, hers as much as his. "I guess that means that he has a one in three chance of making it past childhood. His father's dead, his mother's dirt-poor with eight kids and no skills. I had to send them a goat so that the baby would have milk. Other than that, he's fine.''

Jonathan's eyes seemed to melt with her words until he was left with an uncomfortable silence to fill. ''Have you eaten dinner?''

''No, I'm not hungry.''

Before Anne's exhausted brain could comprehend what he was doing, Jonathan swung his feet over the side of the bed and grabbed for his crutches.

''What are you doing?'' she demanded.

He grinned. ''Fixing you some dinner. Come on.''

She watched him hobble out and still stood where she was watching the empty door.

''Get out here or I come in to get you!''

An unwanted grin tugged at her lips and she shrugged, finally following him out the door.

By the time Jonathan served up a meal of leftovers and too-strong coffee in the bright, warm kitchen, Anne had recovered some of her energy, but not much of her spirit. Mary Lou's situation gnawed at her, for it was representative of all the people she helped care for. The disparity between this world and the one she'd left only a few days ago was simply too great, too ludicrous to comprehend. And Jonathan Bradshaw Harris was the very epitome of that disparity.

They had been eating for a few minutes in companionable silence when Jonathan suddenly stopped to consider her with a very appraising eye.

''Why you?''

Anne looked up to face him. ''Why me what?''

He motioned with his hands as if to take in everything around him. ''Why are you the one to minister to all this? Pioneer nurse and all that.''

''What would you suggest I do, start a Junior League?''

''You have to admit that it's a long way from Beacon Hill.''

''Yes,'' she answered definitely. ''It is. What's wrong with that?''

''Don't the two hats get a little heavy after a while?''

Within the span of his words Anne's listlessness disappeared, and her eyes flashed with warning. ''I don't think I have any difficulty. Neither do the people I live with here. Why should you?''

His face crinkled as if he had witnessed an advertisement for a two-headed man. ''The toast of Boston society setting bones and delivering babies?''

"I'm a certified midwife and an emergency room nurse practitioner. Money, after all, does come in handy for some things."

His eyes widened noticeably. "When did you accomplish all of that?"

Her eyes widened correspondingly in mock innocence. "Why, in between cocktail parties, of course."

He grinned without offense and then cocked his head to the side to consider her anew before speaking again.

"Paying the price for daddy's money?"

Anne took her time with the question. It wasn't that it surprised her particularly. She'd asked it often herself and had not always come up with a comfortable answer. She needed to make sure that she could give Jonathan the truth.

"No. I like it here. I have neighbors I can count on and something to do that's worthwhile, and that's more than I've had before. It's my home now."

"You enjoy it, don't you?"

Anne had the feeling that he wasn't referring to her work. "Enjoy what?"

"Belonging in two worlds. Famous socialite and rural nurse. It's real Walter Mitty stuff. You can indulge your expensive whims and then do penance in the mountains."

Color flared briefly high on her cheeks and she straightened, expecting to see the smug smile appear any minute. "Look around you," she snapped. "This is where I live. Do you see any designer touches? How about some calling cards from the jet set? There's not even a box from Bloomingdale's. I haven't been off this mountain two years!"

"The outrage seems sincere," he retorted evenly. "But I don't think you saw the gleam in your eyes when you slipped into those New York rags. If you won't be offended by the comparison, it reminded me of the stories of fire horses and the smell of smoke."

"Do you really think I'm going to be stupid enough to tell you that New York isn't stimulating?"

"You said you hated it."

"I lied. I can't abide smug, self-satisfied people who live their lives by a set of preconceived ideas."

"Me."

"I didn't say that. I merely admitted that I lied."

His eyes opened up a little, the sky there a little wider and warmer with honest amazement. "You really do like it here."

Anne was equally amazed. "Do you like Wyoming?"

Jonathan was fractionally taken aback. Then he shrugged, a bit too complacently. "I was born there."

"That's not what I asked." Suddenly, somehow, she was on the attack.

Again, he shrugged. "It's sometimes nice to see after I've been in New York too long."

"And you enjoy it, don't you?"

He stared, unsettled by her reversal. "Enjoy Wyoming? Sure. There's a sky in Wyoming."

"I'm talking about the double life you undoubtedly lead," she insisted relentlessly. "Maybe you're not a rural nurse, but I bet you're more the adventurer type, the sporting man. 'This executive names mountain climbing and conservation among his hobbies.' Which do you prefer?"

His smile was enigmatic. "There's no contest."

"That's no answer."

"What if I told you I prefer New York? Would you be disappointed?"

Her answering smile was just as cryptic. "I'd have a hunch that you weren't being entirely truthful."

An eyebrow went up. "Why?"

"Let's call it intuition." She leaned back in her chair a little and accused him with a small wave of the hand. "I think that you're an awful lot like me. We're able to exist comfortably in two completely different worlds, and that's hard to understand, isn't it? After living in some place like Wyoming, how do you come to grips with the other life of all the plastic, polished people you deal with? How do you rationalize living in a place where fashion is dictated by the outlandish and the rest of life is dictated by fashion? After having grown up with a moral system that taught the value of basic living, can you really define your life by who you were seen with at the Russian Tea Room or which table you get at Maxim's?"

"And if I do?"

"Then you wouldn't have said anything about Wyoming's sky, or being in New York too long. A true New Yorker would rather not bother with what's above the buildings. It's what's inside them that's attractive."

Now he caught the fire. They sat across from each other, their eyes bright with the contest. "You mean the power plays, the deals. Having lunch with half a dozen well-connected people and changing the course of history. The stock market jumping at your bidding. Politicians currying your favor because of the power you wield." He paused in friendly challenge, the adrenaline of battle warming the light on his features. "What's wrong with that?"

"You forget yourself," she answered evenly. "I may have been born here, but I was raised in Boston and nurtured in the very arms

of JCL. I cut my teeth on power plays, Jonathan. It's wise to remember while you're up there lunching with the powerful that in
that world the old are quickly cannibalized by the young. Don't
anticipate a very long life."

"I expect to be around for a while yet. Why do you mind so
much?"

Anne shrugged. "Maybe because I wonder how, after growing
up in Wyoming, you could be so attracted to the kind of life I threw
away." She stared hard at him, allowing an admission that she'd
hardly made to herself. "The kind of life I guess I'm still attracted
to. The same way you can't really abide by my decision to give up
the bright lights for life in the hills. Even though you're as attracted to them both as I am. We're both social chameleons, I
guess."

"Is this what comes of all that time alone to think?"

She had to grin. "Yes. Tell me about Wyoming."

Her sudden change of tack threw him off balance again.
"Wyoming? What about it?"

She shrugged. "I've never been there. What's it like?"

"Have you been west at all?"

Anne thought a moment. "Does Chicago count?"

His facial reaction alone was enough to tell her. "Hardly."

"Well, then, tell me so I'll want to go. Does your family live
there?"

"Chicago? No, they live in Wyoming."

She proffered a dry grimace. "Is that what you call a sense of
humor?" The easing of relations was not lost on her. The constant strain of waiting for the next barb had begun to disappear
with their comfortable banter. Anne looked at the handsome
crow's feet that gave Jonathan's smile such character and decided
that she was glad. She was very glad.

"I'm not at my best here," he was saying.

"That's good to know. I was afraid you were surly all the time."

Another raised eyebrow. This time his eyes were mischievous.
"Wyoming is called big sky country, you know."

"So I've heard."

"It also has the Rockies and the Tetons. Mountains."

"Yes."

"I'm from around Jackson Hole. My family first settled there
in the 1870s. Indian wars and all."

"Fascinating. Why, that's real *Roots* stuff."

"You wanted to know."

"Do you mountain climb?"

Jonathan winced. "Yes. So don't tell anyone I know how I got here."

At that she waved a finger at him. "Now that's something I would like to know. How did you get here?"

He looked deliberately confused. "You brought me."

Anne scowled. "I'm talking about how you came to do your swan dive off the Great Smokies in a five-hundred-dollar suit. That's the greatest story the locals have had since a training bomber mistook the lights on the ridge for a control tower and tried to land on Wallace Simson's front yard. And that was in 1945."

It was his turn to scowl. "I'd just finished some business with the TVA and was sort of in the neighborhood. I'd never been to the Smokies. Thought I'd take a look."

She nodded passively. "If that's just taking a look, I'd hate to see you after a climb."

His answering smile was almost brittle. "I'd had a few drinks. I'd made quite a successful deal at lunch. I'm afraid my judgment was a little off."

"Well, there's something you can certainly pass along to your friends. Don't drink and climb in the cold. It almost cost you some fingers."

"I'd only intended to look. It seems that the back of the park falls off a lot more sharply than I'd thought."

"But that's five miles off the road," she protested.

He shrugged. "In Wyoming that's no more than a couple of blocks."

"Why did you leave?"

This time he was ready for her. "I had other places to go, other things to do."

She nodded absently. "Is the rest of your family like you?"

"No, they're much more like Judson, whom I spoke with today, by the way."

Anne's head went up.

Jonathan's grin broadened. "He wanted to know if I was remaining on my very best behavior for the very lovely lady who saved my life." He tilted his head a little, taking a sip of coffee. "You seem to have made a conquest."

Anne had to smile. "Judson has very good taste."

Jonathan's expression never changed. "I know."

When Anne came in to say a final good-night before going upstairs, Jonathan motioned for her to sit a moment. She settled herself onto the edge of the bed and let him take her hand. His eyes had softened like the light before dawn.

"I think I should apologize," he started out. His fingers were tracing slow patterns against the palm of Anne's hand as he talked. She noticed how quiet the late night was, how intimate. And how warm Jonathan's touch was. "It seems that I've been behaving like a six-year-old again. I realized it when I saw the look on your face after you came back from delivering the baby." He took a breath that sounded more like a sigh. "There are some things that you're right about. New York makes a person very selfish. It's been a long time since I've known anything else."

"I don't think you're exactly a lost cause," Anne challenged with a gentle smile.

A fleeting brightness lit his eyes. "I can handle you much better when I make you mad. All this tolerance makes me nervous."

"All right," she said nonchalantly, the smile still lightening the gray of her eyes. "Have it your way. You were a jerk. Again. You were such a jerk this time that even Cassie began to lose faith in you, and Cassie would try to save the soul of Hitler."

"Better. Thank you."

"Can I ask a question?"

"Sure."

Anne considered the work-roughened texture of his hands and saw him again setting that ax into motion. "What did I do this time to warrant all the venom?"

Jonathan looked uncomfortable, as if he'd just been caught. "You surprised me. Every time I think I have a peg on you, you're not anything like what I thought." The sun neared the surface of his eyes. "I can't seem to keep up with who you really are."

"Now isn't that a coincidence? I seem to be having the same problem. Just goes to show you the worth of those preconceived ideas."

For the briefest of moments his eyes glinted oddly, as if she'd tripped over a secret of some kind. But just as quickly they softened again. An almost grudging empathy surfaced. "You know what? Your problem is that for a socialite, you care too much."

Anne saw the gentling of his smile and returned it to him. "Not at all," she disagreed evenly. "I'm only here to make the money to keep myself in designer clothes."

They sat together in silence for a few more minutes, the comfortable sounds of the house enveloping them, and then Anne stood to leave. Later as she lay in the darkness, alone in the big double bed, she finally admitted to herself how much she had missed the company of a man: the familiar warmth of him beside her as she slept, the quiet support of shared silence. She'd never realized how cold and quiet the cabin had been until it had once again been filled with companionship.

The snow continued to fall for the next three days until it became difficult to get down the mountain even on horseback. Poor Andy labored his way up and down as Anne made the few necessary trips out to settle her patients before she made her next visit to New York. On the Thursday before she left she tried to make rounds, leaving the cabin and its delicious bread-scented warmth well before dawn to haul a grievously protesting Andy out into the black cold.

The entire community knew about her plight, which didn't surprise her in the least. Everyone was pitching in to free her for the business in New York. The little Red Cross group was going to keep tabs on her patients, and the four families who lived closest to the house would take turns checking in on Jonathan.

By the time Anne once again approached the cabin it was the wee hours of Friday and she was cold and cramped. The ride back up had taken six hours beneath the brittle stars and waning moon. The scene was bewitching, a fairy tale in snow and shadows, the air clear with ringing silence. Only the occasional trill of a night bird broke in on her secluded world. Somewhere near Preacher's Seat a bobcat darted out in front of Andy, but the big bay just snorted and plodded on, anxious to be back in his barn.

It made Anne wonder as she proceeded up the sleeping mountain how she could so enjoy the pulsating racket of the New York nights where the noise and action weren't even stilled by the hush of dawn. But she did. She could easily thrive on both, living a completely schizophrenic life if given half the chance. She'd relished her time working the emergency room at Mass General, where organized chaos reigned and shouting was the only audible form of communication. But she cherished just as much her life on horseback in the primitive backwoods of the mountains. If only there were a way to combine the two painlessly.

Admitting that, Anne realized without qualification that she was really glad Jonathan Bradshaw Harris had fallen from her cliff. No matter the confusion and tension he'd created for her, his unspoken similarities had given credibility to the puzzling contrasts in her own life. The more she knew him, the more she felt their special kinship.

Much to her amazement, she found him awake when she got home. She saw his light on as she stamped her feet back into circulation on the way to the kitchen.

"Anne? Is that you?"

"In all my glory!" she called back, pulling off her gloves to put water on for tea. She was exhausted, shivering and uncomfortably aware of the pins and needles spreading through fingers and toes as the circulation made a first attempt to return after the long cold ride.

"Why are you so late?"

She couldn't help but laugh. "The last person who asked me that question in that particular tone of voice was my father," she retorted. "And if memory serves me, I was seventeen years old at the time. Want some tea?"

"Sure."

While the water was heating, Anne climbed the stairs to change into her flannel nightgown and robe, pulling heavy knee socks on to soothe her chilly feet. The rush of warmth the heavy clothes brought suddenly reminded her of the night she'd helped rescue Jonathan. It wasn't that long ago, and yet it seemed that he'd been in her house for months.

Anne absently unwound her braid as she thought of that time and how much things had since changed in her little house. She didn't see the soft glow reach her eyes or realize that she'd begun to smile. With her hair brushed out into soft waves that fell over her shoulders, she looked like a different woman than the one who had sat up with Jonathan that first night.

"Is this the woman who took New York by storm?" Jonathan demanded when Anne walked in with the tea. The lines of his face had softened, the weathered lines around his eyes crinkling comfortably with his smile. He was sitting up with another book in his lap, but his hair was sleep-tousled, and he rubbed at his eyes like a little boy.

"This is the woman who took Elder's Crossing by storm," she answered as she set the tray down.

"You look exhausted."

Sitting heavily in her chair, she offered him his mug. "You still have an admirable grasp of the obvious. I've probably ridden thirty miles, visited ten households, drunk gallons of tea and two cups of moonshine, bounced innumerable babies, argued with old ladies and been proposed to—again—by a seventy-nine-year-old widower. It has been a full day." Unconsciously, she rubbed at her frozen feet. There was a huge blister on her heel that hadn't been there yesterday. She'd need to get new boots.

"Give me your feet," Jonathan said abruptly.

She stared at him. "Pardon?"

"Give me your feet. I'll massage them for you."

She didn't move, not sure how to react.

He grinned smugly at her. "Afraid I'll try to take advantage of you? You already set down the ground rules there. Besides, feet aren't my fetish. They hurt, don't they?"

"They're killing me."

"Then don't argue. Hand 'em over. I happen to be a great masseur."

She did and was immediately glad. Having her feet off the floor was pleasure enough, but when he started to slowly work out the kinks, one foot at a time between his solid, capable hands, she thought she'd died and gone to heaven.

Jonathan kneaded the muscles slowly and carefully, almost, but not quite, hurting. Energy surged into Anne's overworked legs, making her want to stretch them. She even forgot the teacup she held in her lap. It felt so good to lean back, close her eyes and enjoy Jonathan's ministrations.

"You act like nobody's ever done this for you before," he observed.

"If they did, I can't remember when."

"Society nobility and never had a massage?" His words remained light and teasing rather than sarcastic.

She thought about it for a minute without bothering to open her eyes. "I don't think so. I can't remember ever having had time. Don't forget, I had a dual identity to support."

"In that case, you'll be happy to know that I also give world famous back rubs."

Anne opened her eyes in time to see him pat a spot next to himself on the bed.

"You should be asleep."

"I'm not the one who's been taking the light of medicine to the backwoods for the last twenty-four hours." Giving the bed another pat for encouragement, he grinned. "Go ahead and be passive for a change. You already know that I have great hands."

She studied him through half-open eyes. "You won't take advantage of me?"

He laughed, once again working on her feet. "I can't imagine anyone taking advantage of you."

"My family certainly seems to have done that," she retorted as she gave up and shifted around to the spot he'd indicated, feet now propped on her chair. Jonathan took her mass of hair in one hand and lifted it over one shoulder and out of the way. Then, gently, his fingers took hold of her neck. A delicious shiver raced down her back at his light touch.

"If you'll pardon my saying so, I can't imagine how. You hardly seem to be an easy target. Woman of steel and all." His fingers were moving slowly, working the muscles thoroughly up and down her neck, their pressure progressively more intense. Anne found herself relaxing against his hands, the pleasure of the massage as sharp as pain.

"I have not always been the confident, self-fulfilled woman you see before you." She could feel his breath on her neck and it tickled. More shivers. She wiggled her toes inside their wool socks. The pins and needles had been replaced by a kind of sweet fire that made her want to rub them against something. She could understand how a cat felt when its back was scratched. That fire was beginning to spread. "In Boston I was my father's daughter. My big act of rebellion was running off to be a nurse, but that was all right because nursing was an acceptable profession for a female. I didn't want to be a rock star or anything. And I neatly balanced the defiance by marrying Tom."

Jonathan's hands had found her spine. Subconsciously she could name the vertabrae as he passed over them. Up and down, thoracic, cervical, thoracic, lumbar, the movements slow enough to be hypnotic. She found herself stretching again as he found some particularly sore spots and began to work them out. A curious warmth radiated from his fingertips that was starting to wake Anne up again. She opened her eyes to see the hall light reflecting from the tips of her still-wiggling toes.

"Tom was your father's choice?"

"His dream. Genetically perfect for the big business. You'd love him. He's like you only blond."

It took Jonathan a moment to answer, and in that time a new tension had crept into his fingers. They moved a bit faster. "I'd be flattered if I didn't think that you just gave me your greatest insult."

Anne cocked her head at the words, wondering that Jonathan might have picked up on that. "No, I don't think so. I meant that Tom was the best at what he did."

"Sounds to me like he was a fool."

His statement surprised her. She wanted very much to turn around and find the meaning of his words in his eyes. She wasn't at all sure that she had that kind of nerve. Unaccountably she began to feel the same tension that infected Jonathan's movements, like electric wire that danced on the ground after a storm. It was more than physical proximity or the feel of strong hands searching out her weariness like potent salves. It was Jonathan.

"He's many things, but Tom is no fool," she disagreed carefully. "You remember your description of power? That's Tom. My father was the best, and Tom ground him beneath his feet."

"He threw a lot away in the bargain." Jonathan's voice was softer, surprised. Anne found herself holding her breath. He'd made a discovery, one that his touch transmitted. One that Anne already had come to know.

Her skin was beginning to ache with an addictive need for his touch. The wire jumped in her, its raw ends skittering over the deepest recesses of her belly. She knew that she should get bolt upright and get the hell out of this bedroom before she couldn't. She was too tired to resist and that was dangerous. She was much too close to falling in love, and she couldn't afford it.

"I guess that wasn't what he wanted." Her own voice was beginning to sound a little breathless.

"That's why he's a fool."

It was there in his voice. Anne turned her head to it, and his hands stopped, trapping her by the shoulders. It was in his eyes, too. The truth he hadn't been able to commit to before. For the first time Anne saw that Jonathan loved her. It was as if he'd opened a path for her to the depths of his soul, and all she could see there was a reflection of the yearning in her own eyes. She saw the imminent commitment there and was quite suddenly terrified.

She wasn't ready and might never be. Her footing wasn't solid enough on its own yet. Convulsively, she tried to jerk free, but he never moved. His grip remained strong. Anne tried to give voice, but couldn't. It was all she could do to hold his gaze.

"I'm sorry, Anne," Jonathan said very softly, his hands inexorably drawing her to him. "I lied. I'm not going to abide by the rules." His eyes were so close, his attraction smothering her. Anne dragged in a breath as if it were the most difficult thing she had ever done.

"Jonathan, please . . ."

He trapped the rest of her protest with his lips, gathering in her doubts with the strength and safety of his arms. Don't, she wanted to cry. Don't open that door. It holds back too much pain. I can't afford this. But there was no way out. The current arced between them, the longing to belong, the yearning for each other. It rose as sharply in her as fire and made her gasp at its fury. There was no turning back now, if there had ever been a time to turn back. Jonathan's hold on her was gentle, but Anne couldn't break free. She felt his hands hesitate, holding her at the waist, and she wanted to cry out for them to find her.

Then Jonathan pulled back, the taste of his last kiss still on Anne's lips. For a long moment he looked down at her, all of the questions he needed to ask there in his eyes. Without a word, Anne answered.

Her heart set a new record, trying to jump free of its mooring like the beating of a captive bird's wings against a cage. Her hands were like ice and she couldn't seem to breathe, but when she saw the tender invitation in Jonathan's eyes, she found herself smiling. With a deliberation that she had never known before and would certainly shock her later, she took hold of his hand and placed it against the throbbing of her heart.

"You're sure?" he asked, and she thought she'd never heard such a sweet question before.

"Not at all," she managed. And then she kissed him.

Later she would think that making love on a single bed with a man in a leg splint should have been awkward. But she couldn't remember anything at all that had been awkward. In fact, in that old brass bed that had held her childhood dreams and memories, Jonathan gave her a gift greater than any she could ever have imagined. He gave her himself. He lavished her with such an attentiveness that she would wonder how she had ever made love before.

When she stood to slip out of her nightgown, the soft durable flannel that had seen her through so many solitary winter nights, he took her hand and drew her down next to him, forbidding her the right to deny either of them any small pleasure they could share together. Jonathan unbuttoned her gown as he leaned over her, his eyes devouring hers with their bright flame. At each button he bent to kiss her throat, her chest, following the progress of the buttons with lips that tasted every part of her.

He never removed the gown but only draped it aside, as if to frame her body for him. After a last, lingering kiss that Anne shared in silent wonder, he turned to enjoy the sight of her creamy skin in the soft light. The tiniest of currents brushed across Anne with delicious warmth. She shivered, unable to stay still, yet unable to move. She could feel the heat of Jonathan's eyes wash over her as if they made contact with her. And when he bent to taste her strong body, he chose her stomach, the slightly rounded abdomen that should have held her children. The touch of his lips and the cool teasing of his tongue ignited a new ache there where he searched her hot skin with his hungry mouth, and Anne moaned with its delight.

Jonathan's hands traced the strong muscles of her thighs, the sleek calves that woolen socks hid, even as his mouth explored the ridges of her ribs. Long before his lips reached them, her breasts were taut with anticipation, the nipples waiting for his fingers to find them. He waited, though, torturing her with his deliberate patience. Sitting above her, he waited as she unbuttoned his shirt, mimicking his actions.

Anne slid her hands around his back and pulled him to her, the sensation of his skin against her like a narcotic. The hair on his chest chafed her breasts and nestled against her cheek. She could feel the taut pull of his back, the muscles there like strong rope. But again, just as she began to gather in the comfort of him, he pulled away, taking his turn.

"You're doing this on purpose," she accused, barely recognizing the anguished sound that was her voice.

"Yes, I am," he murmured back. "I want you to know what it feels like to be cherished."

He sought out her breasts then, first with his hands, which explored with maddening caution, and then with his lips. Anne could see him in the half light as he took her breast in his mouth, a gesture of giving and taking that measured a man's admission of vulnerability. When, a moment later he lifted his head to meet her eyes, she took his beautiful face in her hands and drew him down to her again. And there she held him to her, as if this would bind him to her, even as she tasted the new tears that cleansed her.

He took her with a gentle possession that made her cry out. She lay on her back beneath him, trapped by his power, bound by his commitment. Anne had never realized the breadth of her own passion until Jonathan met her mouth with his own and carefully rocked her to a shuddering peak. It was like a dark flower blooming inside, spreading its intoxicating petals so wide that it would not be bound within her. She began to move against him, wrapping herself around him as if to draw him even closer than he was. His arms encompassed her; his words united them. He vowed to make her whole again and she believed him.

Tears clouded Anne's vision, but she couldn't take her eyes from his face. He smiled at her, his eyes so close that Anne wondered that they didn't singe her. Even as the sweet pain engulfed her and she cried out Jonathan's name as if he could save her, she never lost sight of those eyes. They were the lifeline that had held and guided her. She saw them as they realized her satisfaction and kissed them as Jonathan followed her.

And when Anne and Jonathan were exhausted, their breathing ragged and worn from the gift they had shared, she took his damp, tousled head and lay it against her to rest. There he lay in sleep, nestled against the softness of her breasts, the slow rhythm of his breathing soothing.

For a long while Anne lay staring at the soft play of light against the ceiling, the chill of the late night never touching her. She knew that with the cold of daylight, though, reality would invade the sweet dream set free tonight.

Without realizing it, she gave voice to her dilemma. "What am I going to do when you leave and I'm alone again?"

There was a long silence, punctuated only by the sound of the incessant living room clock.

"What am I going to do?"

Chapter 10

Anne reached Judson Fredericks's office still in a state of anxiety over Jonathan's threat to her fragile independence. When they had awakened that morning each had dealt with the other warily, as if afraid to make too much of what had happened the night before, yet not wanting to treat it too lightly. They had ended up parting without even really talking about it. Now Anne was left with trying to distance herself enough from that crisis to deal successfully with the one Tom and Brad posed.

The office was, as ever, like an oasis of serenity hidden amid the chaos of the city. Judson stood up as she entered and smiled warmly. His sincere compliments pleased her; the dark wood and hushed lighting helped settle her. Anne held out her hand and returned his greeting.

"I've looked forward to seeing you again, Anne," he said graciously, as he guided her once more to the plush green leather chair across from his own. "I hope you don't have plans for dinner tonight. I took the liberty of making reservations in the hopes that you would dine with me."

She smiled at the almost quaint manners Judson displayed. He seemed such an anachronism in this city. He acted more like an old-style southern gentleman than a high-powered New York lawyer. "I would be delighted, Mr. Fredericks."

"Please, you must call me Judson."

Anne nodded her acquiescence and allowed the lawyer to get down to the business at hand. Judson pulled a file toward him and opened it.

"Now, I have been doing some research here," he began, picking up a pair of glasses and carefully adjusting them onto the bridge of his nose with a finger as he studied the papers before him. Perfect, Anne thought with delight. The glasses only made him look more distinguished. "You say you signed the divorce papers and those waiving rights to court approval to the executor's actions in dispensing your father's will, the executor being your brother. Am I correct?"

"I believe so. As I told you before, the time after my father's death was very trying for me. I'm afraid that I trusted my lawyer and signed whatever he told me to."

"Do you remember how many different documents you signed?"

Anne thought a moment, trying her best to pick a few pieces from within the jumbled mess of the weeks that followed her father's death. So much had been shock of betrayal and loss then, it was difficult to remember particulars.

"Four, I think. It all happened three days before I left Boston the last time. If memory serves me correctly, Mr. Martin drove me to the office himself to accommodate me."

"Four," he repeated to himself, again going over the papers in his hand. "You're certain?"

"No, I'm not certain of anything."

Judson nodded slowly in acknowledgment. "Would you have signed power of attorney over to your husband?"

This time Anne's answer was prompt. "Of course not. The last thing I would have wanted at that point was to leave him in control of my life. Besides, what would the need have been? Father left everything in Brad's and Tom's names. Father didn't consider women able enough to control their own money. I waived my chances to contest the will with the stipulation that Tom and Brad let me move back to the cabin without interference."

Judson was peering at her over his glasses in a curious way. "Did you read the will personally?"

"I had no desire to. It was read to me, and I found no surprises in it."

"By your father's lawyer."

She nodded. "By Mr. Martin."

He nodded quietly once again, contemplating the material in his hands. The lines of his face reflected only his concentration on the matter at hand, but the atmosphere in the peaceful office had somehow changed. Anne was beginning to feel a sort of electric charge and unconsciously shifted in her seat.

"There is obviously something of import in all of this," she said carefully, not feeling as self-assured as she sounded. Her hands remained frozen in her lap.

Judson looked up and smiled. "There is. I cannot, however, make any definite conclusion about it until I have a few more documents examined."

She stared, suddenly understanding. "There is a power of attorney, isn't there?"

Judson considered his answer a moment before nodding and handing over one of the papers to Anne. She examined it herself. When she again faced the lawyer, it was with eyes only a fraction as chilled as her heart. "What does this mean?"

"Did you sign it?"

"It certainly looks like it, doesn't it?" It was as if with the sight of this paper, all of the control she'd so carefully constructed shattered like thin ice. Tom was holding the strings as he had held them all along, and she felt outraged.

"Well, I'll find out for certain. If it is authentic, then your father's will ended up saying just what you thought, and I'm afraid that Tom can do anything he wants with the land."

Her head came up sharply. "Ended up?"

Why did it seem as if the clock was ticking more and more loudly in the unnatural hush? Judson removed his glasses and held them out before him for contemplation before he answered. "I have a copy of your father's will here. It does not read quite as you thought, I'm afraid."

Anne had no answer, unaware that her hands were now clasped together as if to better keep her balance, her knuckles white.

Judson continued. "Your father changed his will toward the end of his life and left the majority of his property and share of stock to you, my dear."

The silence became profound; the street below the window was filled with voiceless animation. Only the clock interrupted with its insistent heartbeat—ticking, ticking. Anne stood and walked to the window to hide her confusion. Forty floors below, an ambulance flashed through traffic, its shrillness lost outside the Plexiglas insulation. The sun lay somewhere behind the skyline, setting the windows afire in an evil blood-glow.

Anne drew a shaky breath. "The cabin?"

"It was left to you. The only direct inheritance your father left Bradley was the house in Boston."

She turned once again, facing the quietly concerned lawyer. "So I signed the power of attorney, just as Brad and Tom had been trying to get father to do before he died, and now they've had the time to legally transfer all benefits of the will to themselves."

Judson didn't have to answer. He waited silently for her to continue.

"What can I do?"

He answered matter-of-factly. "To reclaim the land you want, you must be able to prove that fraud was involved."

"Can I?"

"That remains to be seen. I have already begun to investigate the matter. We have a few avenues open to us."

"I'll have to be frank with you, Judson. I have my mother's inheritance, and most of that I have invested in a clinic to be built near where I live. I don't know how well I can afford your fee." Her smile was rueful as she reflected on the situation. "I'm afraid that's something I never had to consider before. But if I could prove fraud..."

"You will, in fact, control JCL. That was that I'm trying to tell you."

"I'm not concerned with the company." She returned to her seat so that Judson wouldn't notice the definite tremble in her knees. "I am concerned with being able to pay your bill. I have the feeling that you've already put quite a bit of work into this. Would you consider a percentage fee?"

"That would be more than generous, Anne," he allowed, "but I think I would rather simply donate my fee to that clinic of yours. At my age I have the luxury of being frivolous if I like."

Anne took his hand in thanks. It seemed to be more than enough for the older man.

"Will we be able to manage it all in so short a time?" she finally asked. "The Board of Directors' meeting is day after tomorrow, and that will be my last chance to contest the sale."

He shook his head slightly. "I have the impression that the meeting will be postponed so that we will end up with more time. But that is another matter entirely, one that I would rather take up over dinner."

Anne offered a tenuous smile. "That sounds like the best idea I've heard since we said hello."

With a return smile that showed a touch of relief, Judson stood to show Anne out. But before he did, he paused with yet another unsettling bit of advice. "Anne, there is one more matter that I feel bears mentioning."

Anne had gotten to her feet when Judson did, and now found that she felt uncomfortable before him. That he had to hesitate a moment to find the proper words to express himself unsettled her even more.

"Have you ever had cause to be . . . wary . . . of your husband?" he asked diffidently.

Anne's eyes widened ever so slightly. "Wary? Do you mean other than the fact that you'd have to drag me kicking and screaming into a partnership with him?"

Judson didn't smile at her little joke, which widened her eyes even more. She couldn't imagine a man like Judson Fredericks being forced to use clichés like this.

"It is simply a matter of a number of . . . well, unusual pieces of correspondence that we have received in the office since we've started to investigate your situation."

"Unusual . . ." Anne stiffened. "Do you mean threats?" She was furious. The idea that Tom could try to intimidate this kind man who stood before her made her want to walk right over to wherever he was and rearrange his classic features a little. She drew herself up very straight, her eyes like winter ice. "My husband tried to threaten you?"

This time she did get a smile. A quick flash of wry apology. "Only in a very civilized manner, I assure you."

Anne's own smile was brittle. "It would be the only way Tom would operate. He is powerful, Judson. And unscrupulous. If it makes you uncomfortable . . ."

Before she could finish the thought Judson brushed it aside with a small wave of his hand. "Not in the least, my dear. His rhetoric has only strengthened my own beliefs that this whole situation is at the least more than a little suspect. No, I was more concerned for you."

Anne didn't understand. "Me?"

Again propriety forced him to look around for his words before facing her with them. "You live alone and in an isolated area."

It had been so long since Anne had heard anyone so deliberately tap-dance around a problem that it took her a moment to understand the import of his words. She knew that her eyes once again opened, and that her mouth gaped in incredulous protest, but she couldn't manage an intelligent retort.

"Anne," he said slowly as if the whole subject caused him great pain. "If we are correct in our suspicions that your husband and brother defrauded you out of your rightful inheritance, the scope of their crime is immsense. JCL is one of the most powerful in-

dustries on the East Coast. Desperate men have been known to resort to desperate measures."

"Except for one thing," Anne said, smiling wryly. She had no
intentions of even entertaining a thought like the one Judson proposed. "Tom would never believe that he could lose the legal fight
since he never has before. His fatal flaw, I'm afraid, is that he be-
lieves too much in himself and too little in others."

"I would still feel less anxious about the matter if I were assured of your personal safety, my dear."

Anne saw the true concern in those warm brown eyes and wished
she could have walked around the desk to give the man a hug. "I'll
see to it, just for you, Judson."

For a moment he searched her eyes, only allowing the worry in
his own to ease after being assured by her promise. Then he held
out his hand. "In that case, Miss Jackson, I believe we have a dinner engagement."

Anne afforded herself the luxury of stopping at the Plaza to
change, claiming that the suit she once again wore was strictly
business attire. She arrived for dinner in an electric-blue Jack
Mulqueen shirtdress that flattered her figure as well as her color-
ing. Her necklace and earrings were plain gold, her hair pulled up
into a heavy sleek braid.

Her appearance on Judson's arm turned heads in the elegant
restaurant. She smiled deferentially to him to heighten the illusion
as they were seated by the magnificent two-story windows that
overlooked the park. Along the walls, matching mirrors illuminated the candlelight ambiance of the lofty white room. Waiters
moved silently in black, bending and nodding to the impressive
clientele.

"I have to admit that this is something I miss on the mountain," Anne said as she sipped her Manhattan. "There isn't one
good French restaurant in the entire town of Elder's Crossing."

Judson chuckled, his office manner relaxing to that of a
Southern landowner. Anne was still having trouble placing him in
Wyoming. Probably a matter of East Coast prejudices that still
tended to crown everyone west of Baltimore with a Stetson.

"This can be just as wearing," he assured her. "In point of fact,
I have given much consideration to moving to a small town when
I retire. I rather miss it."

"Home to Wyoming?"

He nodded, the silver of his hair gleaming in the candlelight.
"Very likely. I have visions of lazy summer days spent along the
Snake River with a fishing pole in my hands."

"I can attest to the benefits of that sort of life," she agreed.

"Indeed you can, my dear. Your life seems to agree with you immensely." His appraising eye was gentlemanly and flattering. Anne enjoyed it all the more for the time she'd spent with the taciturn people of the hills who wouldn't consider doling out compliments so easily.

Judson claimed the privilege of ordering for them both, and they settled back to chat about his children and grandchildren, the wife he'd lost two years before and the contrasts between Wyoming and the Appalachians. They did not talk of Jonathan or of the business of the day. Anne knew that that would be served up over coffee.

She enjoyed the meal immensely, from the rack of lamb that arrived pink and succulent with a side of mint jelly to the cherries jubilee that ended the meal in grand style. Judson was the perfect host: attentive, considerate, and well versed in the sophisications of the city. Yet he had never lost the frank honesty life in his native state had instilled in him. He was able to bring Anne up-to-date on the latest in theater, opera and symphony offerings around town and offered to escort her if she were in town long enough. She thought that she would enjoy that very much.

The thought didn't escape her that this was the relationship she'd always longed for with a father who had never had the time to relax away from the demands of his empire, and who hadn't realized his mistake until it had been much too late to do anything.

It was almost eleven before coffee was poured, and Anne was served her Frangelica. Outside her window couples strolled along the street, and a hansom cab clattered into the darkness of the park. Streetlights illuminated the trees as they swayed in a fitful breeze, their limbs skeletal and gray. It made Anne appreciate even more the rich warmth of the restaurant as she sipped at the smooth liqueur.

"Dinner was lovely," she said, smiling at her host. "I'll remember this evening for the rest of the winter as I plod through the snow on my rounds."

"And I will remember it as I spend my winter attending boring meetings with lawyers and CPAs," Judson returned with genuine warmth. "Come spring, I might just visit your little town."

"I'd be delighted." Anne meant it. She'd love to see what happened when she introduced Judson to Silas. She probably wouldn't see either of them for a month as they sought out the area's finer fishing holes together.

"How long do you plan to remain in New York?"

Somehow Anne knew that this was Judson's introduction to business.

"Well, I'll stay for the meeting. I'd love to spend a few days here, but I do still have a patient to attend to."

Judson nodded. "Yes, I did want to ask after him. He sounds as if he's getting along quite well. Is it still impossible to move him?"

"For at least a little while longer. We still have some three feet of snow up there."

"That's quite unusual, isn't it?"

"I believe insurance companies refer to it as an act of God." She grinned. "My horse is about to go out on strike. He's been on rounds three times this week."

"Jonathan wouldn't be able to ride down?"

"Not yet. The nearest rest stop is seven miles down."

He thought a moment. "What about a helicopter?"

Anne shook her head. "I've thought of that, too." She didn't tell him that she had thought of it most frequently when Jonathan had still thought that cynicism was the way to her heart. "The nearest rest stop is also the nearest sizable clearing."

He nodded again as he sipped at his coffee. "I see. Well, at least I know he's in good hands. I have been in contact with his family, and they have been asking after him."

Anne waited to answer until the waiter refilled her coffee and faced away again. "Tell them that he's up and around on crutches, and if he's there much longer I'm going to send him out to milk the cows. And since you have my number, please feel free to give it to them. I have a feeling they make more phone calls than Jonathan."

"Well, he has most definitely been on the phone with me," Judson admitted. "He has insisted on being involved with every step of your case. I have employed several of his suggestions, in fact."

Anne had assumed that Jonathan had been apprised of what was going on, but for some reason she hadn't anticipated this. She'd only seen him on the phone two or three times. But if he knew about the will, he wouldn't discuss that in front of her until something was settled. He obviously had compassion. Why should that still surprise her?

"In any event, my dear," Judson continued, "you must let me know if there is anything I can do to help. Jonathan's parents are old and dear friends of mine, and you have given them an invaluable gift by helping Jonathan as you have."

"I will of course, Judson." She smiled as she decided to finally press the matter. "There is one thing you could do for me now, if you would."

"Of course."

"Well," she said, then hesitated, fingering the delicate lines of her liqueur glass. "As a matter of fact, it's about Jonathan. You've known his family for a long time." He nodded. Anne took a breath to gather enough tact together to continue. "I would ask you to be indiscreet, Judson, and tell me what you know about Jonathan."

Judson allowed himself a small frown of hesitation. "I don't understand."

She grinned wryly. "Since he's been staying with me, he has displayed some curious . . . oh, contradictions that make it difficult for me to understand him. There have been some incidents that make me think that he's a lot more troubled than he likes to pretend." She gave a small shrug. "I think it's important that I know all I can about him."

"He hasn't said anything himself?"

"No. Only that his family was from Wyoming and his business in New York. I do know that he was in Vietnam." Judson's eyebrow rose. "A nightmare he had one night," she explained, seeing no need to elaborate. "He seems to prefer to play the mysterious stranger."

Judson nodded absently to himself as he studied the hands he'd placed before him on the snow-white tablecloth. "I have not been in real contact with Jonathan for some time," he admitted, looking back up with a sober expression. "My heavens, it's been since before he was in the service: maybe eleven, twelve years ago. He was, I think, a different person then."

Anne recognized the tension his words ignited in her. "How so?"

Judson considered her for a minute as if estimating the risk of further disclosure. Anne thought that he was a very worthy friend.

"Permit me a moment of explanation." At the next table a woman giggled, a shrill, silly sound that seemed to shatter the restrained atmosphere of the room. Judson never noticed. His eyes were at once on Anne and on the past. "Jonathan was born and raised near Jackson, Wyoming. I grew up with John, his father. A fine man. At one time, many years ago, I courted his mother Helen. You would enjoy Helen, I think. She is very much like you. Well, when Jonathan was old enough, he came east for college. He wanted to make a name for himself away from his father's influence, which is, of course, not terribly unusual for an oldest son. Jonathan is the oldest of three.

"Soon after college Jonathan met someone who went into a partnership with him, some type of sales venture, I believe. I never understood the details. I was in Europe on extended holiday when it happened. Evidently a loan was taken out to finance the business. When the venture went under, the partner managed to default, leaving Jonathan holding a rather large loan along with no money and no business. To make matters worse, his father had helped by putting a second mortgage on the ranch and lost it. The family had to move in with Jonathan's brother who lived nearby.''

He paused to sip from a refilled cup of coffee. Anne followed suit without really paying attention to what she was doing. A quality of pain had slipped into Judson's voice that presaged the import of a nightmare.

Judson couldn't quite keep his eyes impassive as he continued. "Not long after that, Jonathan enlisted in the marines and put in a request for duty in Vietnam. His mother has always equated the action to a type of suicide note, and it is very possible that she was right. Jonathan shouldered a great amount of guilt for what he'd done to his family. He served two tours of duty and came away with a Silver Star, DSC, Purple Heart, malaria and six months in hospitals for injuries he received.''

"No one could prove any wrong on the partner's part?" she asked.

"It seems that the gentleman in question had a certain amount of influence and Jonathan, at the time, had none.''

"And he had no other alternatives to take?''

Judson smiled apologetically. "As I said, I was in Europe at the time. I was about the only person Jonathan could have come to for help. In point of fact, when he first called me about taking your case, I was surprised. I have always been afraid that he held my unavailability against me.''

Anne shook her head numbly. It was almost impossible to conceive that this had happened to the Jonathan she knew. She understood now, though, what he had meant about being in the same position as her. She couldn't imagine having to face that kind of situation, or having to bear that kind of responsibility. No wonder he dealt so badly with the memories of Vietnam. He'd used his time as his own private purgatory for what he'd done to his parents, and had ended up failing again, at least in his eyes.

"You say you haven't kept in touch with him since then. Do you know what he's been doing?''

He nodded, sipping again at his coffee and then carefully setting the cup down on its fragile saucer. "Jonathan went to law school on the GI Bill. I attended his graduation, but when I saw him then he had changed. When I had known him before, he had been a bright, independent, enthusiastic young lad: very open and honest, and out to conquer the world. When we spoke at the graduation, I could not help but notice that he had taken an almost cynical tack. Hard. He had lost that fine enthusiasm, and was instead ... well, driven. That much is easy to see in what he has accomplished since. He has founded and built a rather formidable empire in New York: Bradwell International. They deal in management turnaround. Four years ago he was able to buy back his father's ranch. Since then I expected him to relax a bit. Instead, he has devoted his time even more strenuously to advancing the position and influence of his firm.''

There was much from what Judson said that Anne had to digest. Jonathan's story was not unusual in a city like New York. It was merely another tale of a young man trying to make a name for himself and failing. The values he had brought with him from Wyoming had become engulfed within the alien code of ethics he'd been confronted with, and he'd been overwhelmed.

It didn't surprise Anne, for as she'd told Jonathan, she'd cut her teeth early on that sort of thing. She'd seen better men than him fail. She'd seen her own father, who'd invented the rules, fall a lot harder. It at least helped her understand Jonathan's time in Vietnam and its repercussions. She could better appreciate his attitude and the contradictions that so baffled her. The cynicism, the slick act, the sudden glimpses of compassion. Anne represented everything that he'd once battled against in vain. This was the story behind the first time he'd been helpless to save someone he'd loved from being hurt.

And whether or not he admitted it, Jonathan was still fighting between those two sets of disparate rules. Anne was afraid that he would finally convince himself that in New York the honesty and integrity he'd brought with him from Wyoming had no place.

She could well imagine that he didn't see Judson that often, either. The older man had somehow survived with his scruples intact. That would certainly be salt in a raw wound.

Anne wished that there were some way she could make Jonathan see that he had to keep fighting. The longer he stayed with her, the more she saw the boy from Wyoming in him. It had been that side of him that had attracted her to him in the first place. She was afraid that if Jonathan went back to New York without something to reaffirm his faith in the gentler side of himself, it would finally die out, leaving him in the end no more than another Tom McCarthy. Anne was beginning to realize how important it was to her that that didn't happen.

For a moment she allowed herself to consider the memory of Jonathan as he'd slept in her arms, his face so relaxed and almost young again. But the picture brought with it pain, a sharp regret for what he'd hidden so carefully behind those brittle blue eyes. She found that she had to force it away again.

"Thank you for telling me, Judson. It does help me understand."

"Happy to do it, my dear. I only hope that spending some time with you might help him somehow."

She couldn't help but grin. "Well, if nothing else, it's helped rebroaden his horizons. Tell me something, just for curiosity's sake. Has anyone told his company where he is? He certainly hasn't."

"Oh, I imagine not. They manage quite well without him, from what I understand, because of the excellent organizational system he set up. He is often away without notice. They've become quite used to it."

"What do you mean he goes away without notice?"

"It seems that it is supposed to be his way to test the efficiency of his people. Sometimes he goes home, from what his mother has written, although more often than not, no one knows quite where he goes. My theory is that he camps alone somewhere near his home. There is much wild country where a man can be by himself with his thoughts."

"I would have thought that he wouldn't have wanted to be caught there," Anne said more to herself.

The waiter appeared silently again, the silver coffeepot in hand, but Judson held up his hand. The man nodded with a small bow of well-bred servitude and melted away.

"As I said," Judson continued, "Jonathan has not confided in me. But the tradition is one his father was fond of employing. The two of them used to camp together when Jonathan was a boy." Carefully folding his white linen napkin by halves, Judson placed it next to his empty coffee cup. "Now, my dear, I am afraid that this old man must be getting on his way. But before we go, I wanted to explain a bit more about the meeting with Amplex."

Anne nodded in silence.

"As I said before, I have reason to believe that the meeting will be postponed. It would seem that there is a request that all the board members be present and two or three of them seem to be detained. From what I have been able to ascertain, it may be a matter of weeks." Anne moved to protest, but he held up a hand with a quiet smile. "Think of it this way. The delay is to our advantage. It gives us more time to find a case against your ex-husband and brother."

"I know." Anne sighed, the evening's enjoyment dulled a little. "It's the idea that I'll have to live with this hanging over my head for so long. I never did learn to wait with grace."

So it was that when Judson saw her to the front door of the Plaza, Anne felt deflated and a bit frustrated by the lack of control she had over the whole matter. Somehow it seemed to be getting further and further away from her until she was beginning to feel like a pawn.

As she stood in the ascending elevator she slowly rolled her head to relieve the tension the idea of upcoming weeks of uncertainty had given birth to. The more she thought about it, the more she thought that the only thing that would help right now would be a long hot shower.

The idea of the hot, stinging, muscle-relaxing water got her through the walk down to her room and the ritual of undressing once she'd gotten inside. Lights dotted the black park below her room, and the music of traffic battered at her window. Anne's mind could go no further, though, than the anticipation of a twenty-minute marathon without the hot water running out just as she was getting relaxed.

Only minutes later she stood in the tub savoring the hot water like the strong hold of a lover. Steam rose in lazy clouds around her, fogging the mirror and saturating the small errant tendrils that clung to Anne's neck and forehead. The persistence of the city noise had been silenced by the waterfall of cleansing bliss, and she could almost imagine that she was home enjoying the soul-saving quiet of the mountain.

Finally giving in to temptation, Anne lifted her head to the water and let it drench her hair and flood her face. She would have preferred to stand in a mindless trance, letting the water wash away the tensions that ate at her, but images of Jonathan nudged insistently at her. His hands, the stern lines of his face that so belied his wry, offhand humor. His laugh, so sharp and crisp it sounded like limbs snapping in a dry tree. But most of all, when she closed her eyes, his opened, and she felt herself once again mesmerized by the shifting, settling blue that had unnerved, fascinated, infuriated, and finally overcome her. Eyes that could withdraw completely into themselves to protect the kind of secret that had scarred Jonathan as permanently as the shrapnel that had opened his side, they had also reached out to her without hesitation. She had been seduced by the life-giving fire in his eyes long before she had succumbed to the magic of his hands.

She had never known any man like him before. The comparisons were certainly there to make, because he bore enough of a resemblance to them all. But he alone went beyond resemblance, not only to the men she'd known as Anne Jackson McCarthy, but the ones she'd met as Annie Jackson.

It was fascinating to her. Almost without exception, the men she had known in the city had been typical to the environment with their Hart, Schaffner & Marx mentalities and upwardly mobile outlooks. Only some of the medical personnel she had met had been unique, but she had been firmly restricted from socializing with them. On the mountain where men fashioned their lives around survival, their energies were used on farming and families and sometimes pool down at the hall in Elder's Crossing. Only Jim and a few of the other new homesteaders stood out as ever having known another way of thought.

Jonathan, though, was a real dichotomy. He straddled the two worlds like a man balancing on a knife-edge. As much as he presently loathed to admit it, he was a child of the mountain, raised on the Wyoming version. But he'd also managed to come back after his initial disaster and conquer the city.

It was no wonder to her that he had to disappear to repair his gyroscope from time to time. No matter how badly the city had burned the part of him that had been forged in Wyoming, he still considered it worthwhile to some extent or he wouldn't continue grappling with it.

How Anne would have liked to see him take what he had been taught in his own mountains and make it work in the city. Judson had proved that it would work. Anne would have tried it if things had turned out differently. If only Jonathan could match the drive the city had given him with the scruples his father had taught him, he could make a difference. A real difference. And the Jonathan whom Anne was falling in love with wouldn't have to be lost.

With a weary sigh, Anne stepped out of the tub and dried off. How she wished she were back home before her fire letting the heat from the flames dry her hair, her only problems being those of the people of Elder's Crossing. Her friends. No stranger in her life, no lawyers, no way for a special delivery letter to ever reach her from Boston. She thought that maybe when she got home she'd ask Granny Edwards to teach her to quilt. It was such a peaceful pastime.

Her robe hung on the closet door. She reached for it and caught her reflection in the mirror. For the first time in what seemed like so very long, she actually found it interesting, something she could be pleased with. She could still feel Jonathan's touch kindling life in what had become merely a tool, and remembered how it was to view herself for more than just her work capacity.

She had to admit that where she once nudged at plump, with full curves that Tom sometimes frowned upon a little, she had grown lean with the work she'd done. Her hips were small, her waist smaller, her breasts still high and firm. The times she'd stolen away to enjoy the secluded peace of the sun had left her skin with a rich glow. Ah, the benefits of the outdoor life, she could hear Jonathan say with a smug smile.

Unaccountably, the thought made her feel a bit breathless. She donned her robe and belted it, bending to sweep her hair up into a towel. Straightening, she reached out and opened the door to the other room.

"Well, Anne, I see you're also still a slave to tradition."

Anne stopped short, a cry caught in her throat. Her first thought was to run.

Tom smiled lazily at her from where he lounged on the bed.

Chapter 11

"What are you doing here?" Anne hissed.

"Why, I came to see my lovely wife," Tom answered smoothly. "By the way, Anne, you are more lovely than ever. Did I tell you that?"

He stood slowly, languorously, his words and movements making Anne uncomfortably aware of her nakedness beneath the short flannel robe. "You finally lost that weight, didn't you, pet?"

She instinctively took a step back, her composure threatened. "How did you get in?"

Tom's smile broadened with self-satisfaction. "It was painfully easy. I simply told the very pretty young lady at the desk that I was your husband and that I had managed to get to town to surprise you. She was most accommodating." He moved closer, his eyes roving her body in frank admiration. "I suppose that I must admit that there must be something to that backwoods life of yours after all," he admitted smoothly, still approaching without hesitation. Anne knew that she was breathing more quickly, his presence crowding her. "You may have calluses on your hands, pet, but your body is finally the way I always wanted it. I'm glad you came back to me."

Two bright pink spots flared high on Anne's cheeks and she stopped retreating. "You think I came back here because I couldn't live without you?" she asked with a smile that didn't touch her eyes.

"You'll always love me, Anne," he purred, his eyes boring through her. "You'll always need me."

With shattering clarity, Anne suddenly saw through him, to the very core of what drove him. And she finally admitted that his lust for power governed him even with her. She'd always thought that he had at least wanted her, if not loved her. It was more likely the truth that he'd enjoyed her, like a game. Like any game he played in his life. It was only fun as long as he had the control, the power. How it must have infuriated him when she'd walked out.

"Why did you really come here tonight, Tom?" she asked, her voice suddenly chilly. He stopped, an eyebrow arching in mock surprise. The action suddenly reminded Anne of Jonathan, and it was all she could do to keep from shivering. Jonathan wasn't like this man; he wasn't amoral. And yet, if something weren't done soon, he might be. He and Tom could be carbon copies all the way to the sneer.

"You want me to be honest?" Tom retorted, his hypnotizing eyes darkening as if he were giving serious consideration to the question. He walked closer, standing so that Anne had to look up into his eyes. A sly psychological move of dominance, but it was effective. He was so close, the faint smell of his cologne overpowering. "I came to take you back, Anne. You belong with me. You always have. I want to take care of you. To give you a real home. I was wrong before to have let you leave. I didn't realize just how much you meant to me." He laid a hand on her shoulder, gently stroking in rhythm to his words. "Anne, together we could have it all."

Anne steeled herself against the electric shock of Tom's touch, the smothering sensation Jonathan's hands had reawakened after so long.

It didn't come.

Tom caressed her arm slowly, watching his hand as it moved, something that had once set Anne off like dry kindling. But nothing happened. She watched with disbelief, waiting for something to change, for the inevitable to happen. She wanted to cry, to sing and laugh. Her knees remained rigid and her heart cold. She was finally free of Tom McCarthy.

The exhilaration was heady enough to make her smile. Tom saw the change and returned the smile he mistook for excitement, a slow seductive gaze touching the green of his eyes.

Anne's eyes hardened. "If you don't back out of this room right now, I'll start screaming rape at the top of my lungs and not stop until the entire hotel staff and the New York press corps are up here." His grip tightened on her arm, the warmth in his eyes dying. Anne looked down at his hand and then up to those cruel, hypnotic eyes she'd loved as much as she'd hated. Their power had disappeared; the glint in them was no more than selfish. "And then I'll slap an assault and battery charge on you. I'll have bruises on my arm inside an hour. Do you really want to chance it?"

For the first time since she'd known him, Tom was at a complete loss. He seemed to freeze where he was, his expression concealing any emotion he might have been battling.

"Anne, you can't be serious." His voice was strained with the effort. "I can take you back to the places you deserve to be."

Anne eyed him steadily, her feet planted a bit more solidly beneath her. The act of paralyzing him had released her. She had won; she had finally beaten his game. No matter what happened now, she had her freedom from the Anne Jackson that Boston had molded and Tom and her father had controlled as their right. She was free of them all.

"I said leave, now, Tom. Don't make me ruin your reputation."

His mouth curled into a sneer at her words. "You can't make me believe that you don't want me." Grabbing her roughly to him, he kissed her, his mouth harsh and brutal, his hands punishing. Anne stood still and waited, wanting to laugh and hit him at the same time.

He raised his head, not letting go of her, his eyes smoky with rage.

"More bruises, Tom," she said evenly. "If I were you, I'd quit while I was only a little behind."

For a moment she thought he was going to strike her. She'd never seen him so angry that he couldn't speak. The fact that she didn't flinch from him seemed to taunt him even more. He held her for a long moment, his fingers viselike, his mouth a bitter slash of scorn.

"Don't congratulate yourself too soon, pet," he hissed. "You just made a bigger mistake than you'll ever know."

And then he was gone, slamming the door hard behind him.

For a minute Anne could only stand where she was, staring after the closed door as if she'd seen an apparition. She hugged her arms tightly around her and massaged her sore shoulders with gentle fingers. She'd been right. There would be bruises: ugly, appropriate reminders of Tom's visit. She took slow, deep breaths, in through her nose, out through her mouth to ease the trembling that had set in once the fear had died.

Then slowly, inexorably a smile dawned. Rising from the corners of her mouth, it swept along the laughter lines that dimpled her cheeks to the gray eyes that sparkled with a new light of triumph. Anne had a sudden urge to call Cassie and tell her that the ghosts had been dispelled, the crutches thrown away. Mixing metaphors, she thought absurdly, not really caring. She had just stood toe-to-toe with her personal devil and overcome him. Tom McCarthy would never again intrude into her life as an unwanted obsession. She had proven to herself that she didn't need that kind of man anymore. She didn't have to fear his power or allure ever again.

Anne smiled even more broadly at the thought that he'd offered to take care of her. Once that would have been a powerful temptation. Once, maybe, before she'd been forced to go against everything she'd been taught since childhood and had learned to take care of herself.

It had always been a foregone conclusion that she should be taken care of all her life, like an objet d'art or a helpless animal. If she'd held onto that logic, she would have remained Tom's property. She would, indeed, have given in to him tonight and gone back to the prison that had once been her home.

Knowing no other hands than Tom's, she would have succumbed to them. But as if to seal the transformation that had taken place, Jonathan had reawakened her self-awareness as a woman when he'd taken her into his arms and made love to her. He had not only made her feel wanted, but treasured in a way Tom had never thought of.

There was a special exhilaration in rediscovering something you thought you'd lost for good. Within a period of weeks, Anne had stumbled back over not only her self-esteem but the wonder of how it felt to be reflected beautifully in a man's eyes. It was too bad it was so late. She suddenly wanted to call Jonathan, too. She wanted to thank him, to tell him that no matter what, she could never be able to return in kind the precious gift he'd given her.

Anne dressed for bed and dried her hair, listening with new contentment to the discordant city pass far below her. Until tonight she hadn't really realized it, but she was a free woman, able to go wherever she wanted or do what she pleased. She could count on not only her own worth and pride, but on the fact that she was worth the love of a good man. And waiting for her like a lifeline to her strength, a symbol of her resurrection, was her home, tucked comfortably away within the mountains and her memory. It seemed that as long as she had that symbol of her past and future, she could do anything.

As long as she had it.

A brief surge of fear flared and then waned as she remembered again the victory she had just savored. The impossible did happen. She would get her home back and from there be able to make the new beginning she very much wanted.

Settling into the big, comfortable bed, Anne wondered in passing whether Tom had really meant to threaten her when he left or whether he'd just badly lost his composure. Even so, it was a relief to know that she would be escaping the city tomorrow to the safety of her cabin. Judson might have just been correct when he told her that Tom might resort to desperate measures, and Anne knew better than most what kind of influence he could manage to wield in this city.

As she fell asleep the thought occurred to her that as much as she wanted to get back to the cabin, she anticipated seeing Jonathan again even more. It didn't occur to her to feel her customary caution.

The next afternoon Judson did, indeed, tell her that the meeting had been postponed and that she would be notified of its new date in due time. Amplex Corporation sent its regrets in hopes that it hadn't inconvenienced Miss Jackson too much. Miss Jackson scowled at the statement and told Judson that she would be back home doing some real work should they feel the need to get in touch with her. And then she made the arrangements to do just that.

Jim was in the store when she pulled in. He still had some difficulty getting used to her in city attire, and was shaking his head when she walked up to him.

"Oh, stop it," she said, laughing. "In five minutes I'll be back in my jeans and you won't be impressed anymore." She walked on through to the house, where she always changed before making the trip up on Andy.

"Why are you here, Annie?" Amanda demanded in her shrill four-year-old voice. "My mommy's at your house. With David." David was her six-year-old brother who never had much of a reputation for being able to sit still for more than two minutes at a time. Anne couldn't help but grin. Jonathan would probably be having the time of his life, considering how well he seemed to get along with small children. At least she could be sure he'd be glad to see her.

For at least the first third of the journey up the mountain Anne found herself puzzled by an odd tightness in her chest, a sense of unaccustomed urgency. Her ride home had always been her favorite time to meditate. Andy preferred a slower attack on the steep path, and Anne usually enjoyed the pace he set. It gave her the time to watch the wildlife and consider the way of the world. She would think about the people she'd come to know, the grannies who held the power of folklore in these mountains and maybe the serpentine family ties that seemed to bind the hollows she crossed. The road home was Anne's chance to unwind, to catch the first shattering of ice as the creek began to thaw or watch the spiraling flight of a hawk as it dipped and soared in among the shadows of afternoon.

After flying in from a place like New York she knew that she needed the time to unwind even more than usual. Instead she found herself nudging at Andy's flanks, urging him on at a steady pace. For the first time in memory, the cabin seemed to be too far away. When she actually caught herself toying with the idea of getting a real road up to the cabin, she began to wonder what was wrong with her.

It wasn't until she topped the ridge that it actually dawned on her. She'd never hurried to the cabin before because she'd never had someone like Jonathan waiting for her. She reigned Andy in just beyond a long stand of birch and sat staring sightlessly out over the soft gray-and-white folds of winter land that stretched away from her in never-ending succession.

Jonathan. Could he make that much of a difference? Could he be the reason that her chest felt constricted by an iron band and why she had to take deep breaths to ease the alien sense of fluttering in her? Safely encased in their gloves, her hands had begun to perspire. She had never experienced this kind of delicious dread before. But then she'd never been the person she was at this minute.

She had only been gone two days, and already she felt as if a different person were approaching the cabin. When she'd left, she'd done so as a cripple, emotionally hobbled by the manipulations of the man who'd stolen her trust. She'd made love to Jonathan out of desperation, certain that she could never profit from falling in love with him. It wasn't just that she hadn't trusted Jonathan—something she could hardly consider after the example set for her by Tom—it was that she truly didn't believe that she deserved to be loved. She'd really half believed what Tom had taught her.

She returned now having taken the cure. Tom had lost his decisive power to haunt, and Anne had found hers to take charge. The scene with him the night before had illustrated that without qualification. And that, she thought, was the first step to rediscovering the conviction that she had a right to be loved.

So she was back to the question of the moment. Was Jonathan that man? Or was he nothing more than a combination of attraction, infatuation and loneliness? Was love what bound them, or was it need, something that would vanish once the snow melted and they weren't isolated and dependent on each other anymore?

Anne allowed herself a moment to consider what the cabin would be like once Jonathan left and she found at least her own answer. Once he did go, the company of memories and familiar routine would no longer be enough to fill her life. He had changed that life and had changed her.

With a wry smile she realized that she was hungry for the sight of those eyes that had once so frustrated her. The multifaceted personality delighted her where it had once only confused her. Her discovery of that specially guarded place in him had set her tumbling from the safe niche her prejudices had so carefully carved. She'd been drawn to Jonathan as if the fuel that fed him could also revitalize her. If she weren't in love with him, she decided with an odd giggle, she should at the very least tap into him as a source of natural energy.

Anne took a deep breath, filling her lungs with brisk air to try and calm the growing clamor in her. It had been so much easier when everything was hopeless and finite. She had a chance for happiness now but the uncertainty of it unnerved her. What if she were in love with Jonathan? What guarantee was there that she'd be any luckier than before? What in the end did she know about Jonathan Bradshaw Harris? She knew that he had money, a tragic past to overcome and a knack for awkward tenderness that made her want to cry. She knew that he'd made love to her with a fire and sensitivity that had brought her back to life.

Yet he had just as surely lashed out at her more than once without real explanation. It was as if every time he got too close to her, some part of him revolted, rejecting her with a venom that was frightening. She could guess all she wanted about the reasons for it, and the conclusions she had reached all seemed to be sensible. But it was possible that she was wrong; there was a deeper, darker place in him that she hadn't found. Perhaps there lay the animosity that tended to flare unexpectedly. If that were true, if there was more to Jonathan's conflicting persona than even Judson knew, Anne was afraid that she would never find it in time to save her from repeating her mistakes.

Andy turned to eye her, impatiently stamping in the wet snow. His breath rose in swift clouds that dissipated quickly. Anne patted at him absently for a moment as she gathered the courage to go on. She hated uncertainty. For the last two years she'd patterned her entire life-style to avoid it. Yet here she sat in the throes of indecision, certain that she wanted nothing less than the conflict that awaited her when she got home, and yet knowing that she had no other choice but to go on anyway. She took another careful breath, wishing she could think of a more effective way to calm down and amazed that she needed one. Then she nudged Andy in the flanks and turned him for home.

When she reached the front porch, Anne found herself hesitating with her hand on the door. She made an unconscious point of stamping the snow from her boots with just a bit more noise than usual, as if in giving the people inside some warning of her arrival she could better set the stage. A small frigid breeze found her neck and provoked a chill Anne couldn't seem to stop.

Just as she'd anticipated, she found Jonathan seated comfortably in the wing-back next to the fireplace. In the instant before he looked up to greet her, Anne struggled to control her own reaction. The sight of his bent, tousled head sent her heart skidding unnaturally and set her hands to trembling. Instead of feeling more secure for the time spent away from him, she felt as if her balance were suddenly in great peril. Getting away from him hadn't accomplished in the least what she'd hoped. The independence she'd gained the night before was in imminent danger of crumbling before the anticipation of his sharp blue gaze. Any objectivity she'd prayed for in handling this scene seemed to have been left in that quiet office in New York. Her future would rest on Jonathan's response to seeing her.

The hard lines of his face shifted oddly as he raised his face. Momentarily they softened with an almost painful pleasure, then froze with restraint. After what seemed like hours, he allowed her a genial smile of welcome.

"Well, if it isn't Miss Fifth Avenue." He dropped his book in his lap, his eyes bright with measured amiability. Probably mirrors of what he saw in her own eyes, Anne thought. She could envision them both facing each other with strained civility, waiting for a clue from the other before proceeding. She'd been steeling herself against Jonathan's acceptance or rejection, the indications he would deliver about the fate of their future. Now here he sat waiting for the same from her.

"You're going through that library pretty fast." She smiled back a bit uncomfortably. "There's no other room to work your way up to, ya know."

An eyebrow arched minimally. "Isn't there?"

"Annie, what are you doing back so soon?"

Anne started at the sound of Cassie's voice, her eyes leaving Jonathan a brittle warning of discretion before turning to greet her friend. Cassie stood in the kitchen doorway with David like a shadow behind her. Cassie missed very little and couldn't have possibly missed the static atmosphere of the room, but she refrained from allowing herself comment.

"You keep coming home early," she protested with an easy grin. "How are Jonathan and I ever going to get any time alone?"

"Take him home with you," Anne retorted more easily as she began to discard her over clothes. "I'll keep David up here with me. I'd get more cooperation and less back talk."

Cassie laughed as she walked in, drying her hands on a towel. "Jonathan, you've been insulted. If I were you I'd demand satisfaction."

"Crutches at ten paces," he said dryly.

"I'm afraid it's going to have to be something else," Anne told him. "I only have one pair." It was already easier to talk. It was always that way when Cassie was there with them to buffer what they said to each other. If only she didn't have to leave.

"Well, if you're looking for something you have plenty of, throw muffins at each other," the tall brunette offered. "You have enough in there to fight off a batallion." She stood behind Jonathan with a hand on his shoulder. Anne envied her her natural ease.

"No," she obliged. "I'd end up eating the ammunition."

"What are you doing home so early?" Cassie asked. "You told us not to expect you for another few days."

"I'll explain over some hot tea," Anne answered, hanging up her coat. "It's kind of a good-news bad-news story."

Cassie turned, almost bumping into David and preceded Anne into the kitchen.

"Don't I get to find out?" Jonathan demanded.

Anne patted him on the head in mock patronization. "Maybe when you're a little older." Then, blithely ignoring his unhappy reaction, she walked into the unusually spotless kitchen and took a seat across from Cassie. Tea was already poured and steaming from the earthenware mugs.

"David," Cassie said, her arm around the little boy's waist, "why don't you go on in and talk to Jonathan?"

"Aw, Mom," he whined, scrunching up his face, obviously afraid that he'd miss something interesting.

"Don't 'aw, Mom' me, go on," she answered evenly with a small push to the backside. David went, the look in his face leaving no doubt as to his opinion on the matter. Anne sipped at her tea to hide her smile.

"Are you sure that Jonathan wants to talk to David?" she asked under her breath.

Cassie grinned. "I think you'd be surprised. Jonathan has been teaching David to play chess all morning. David thinks that he's the neatest thing since Spiderman."

Anne's eyebrows went up. "The same Jonathan who took one look at Mary's brood and almost made it down the mountain under his own power?"

"The same. He has almost as much patience as Jim. I think that if he learns to control that nasty streak of his, he'd make someone a good father... if he hasn't already, that is."

Anne shook her head. "That's part of my New York report. I found out all about him from Judson." She went on to give Cassie a detailed accounting of her trip.

Much later, they walked into the living room together to find David carefully replacing the chess pieces in their case.

"I almost won today," he beamed up at his mother. "Jonathan says I'm good."

"Deadly," Jonathan agreed with an impressed nod. Anne walked over to help David, staying carefully away from Jonathan as if she could more easily remain objective at a distance.

The tension in the room leaped the minute she walked in. She and Jonathan didn't even have to look at each other. The unspoken emotions that had been building between them begged for release, and neither could do it in front of company. Anne wasn't even sure that she had the nerve to confront that kind of conflict once Cassie and David had gone. Again she was assailed by the urge to ask them to stay, until she had the chance to straighten out the turmoil that had erupted in the last few days.

Anne looked up from her little task to see Cassie regarding her evenly. It was as if she'd been reading Anne's thoughts and had come to her own conclusion.

"Come on, David," she said, smiling quietly. "We have to get home in time to help Daddy deliver the mail."

"Thanks for keeping me company," Jonathan said to the little boy, his voice a little tight. "When I get better we'll have to go hiking together. I bet you know the best trails around here."

"Okay." David beamed, making a great show of shaking hands like a man. Anne once again caught that flash of gentleness in Jonathan's eyes as he participated in the ritual, a quick softening at the corners of his face. She physically restrained herself from reaching out to it, as if the warmth in his expression could be soaked up through her fingertips. The tension was mounting in her chest. She could hear it reflected in her own voice as she said her goodbyes to David and accepted his overenthusiastic bear hug.

Cassie delivered her own farewells outside where she could bestow Anne with a smile that at once called up the trust of friendship and offered an almost maternal concern. Her eyes twinkled with their familiar humor.

"Are you going to be safe if I leave?" Cassie asked. Anne had told her about the messages Judson had been receiving from Tom.

Anne's smile was her thanks for her friend's empathy. "I told you. Tom's far away."

Cassie's smile broadened, her teeth gleaming against her olive skin. "Maybe I should have asked Jonathan that question instead."

"That's entirely possible," Anne conceded, trying her best to match Cassie's studied ease. For the first time since she'd made the momentous decision to leave Tom, she knew the paralysis of indecision. She was actually terrified to walk back into the cabin to face Jonathan's judgment. Smiling anyway, Anne gave Cassie an extra hug for her unstated support. She watched in silence as Cassie and David turned their horses away from her and proceeded down the path. Then with a sigh she opened the door to face Jonathan's measured gaze.

"I think," she said with enough force to surprise herself, "that you and I need to talk."

Chapter 12

Jonathan allowed one eyebrow to rise in dry caricature. "Is this going to be one of those little domestic chats I've heard so much about?"

Anne's first impulse was to slap him. She came very close, stalking up without a word to where he sat and even opening her mouth to deliver a correspondingly biting retort. But suddenly, she saw the tension on Jonathan's face was as brittle as hers. He was as shaken as she was by the sudden shift in their relationship. And just as surprised.

She realized with some astonishment that she'd begun to soften. "Would you like some tea while we talk?"

His eyebrow lifted even higher for a brief moment before returning her rueful smile. "Unless there's something more potent. I have a feeling I'm going to need strength."

"Just a keen wit," Anne retorted evenly. "And yes, I have the perfect thing. My Aunt Adelaide used to sweeten her tea with it."

Jonathan pulled a very expressive face, but kept his silence as Anne walked by to the kitchen.

A few minutes later she returned to set the tea things on the coffee table. Curling her feet beneath her, she settled onto the couch next to Jonathan's chair. Her heart was still in her throat. She noticed that her hand shook as she poured the tea and handed Jonathan his blue earthenware mug. She also noticed that his hand was a little damp as he accepted.

"I have sugar if you'd like," she offered, "but usually Aunt Adelaide's tonic is enough."

Jonathan nodded absently and took a solid drink out of the steaming mug. He swallowed convulsively and then coughed. With tears in his eyes, he turned on Anne, his breath still coming in dramatic little gasps. "What the hell was that?" He had hold of ribs that seemed to protest all the activity.

"Tonic," Anne answered evenly, sipping her own tea very carefully. The well-remembered fire of the Jackson all-purpose elixir bit at her throat with a vengeance.

"Tonic, hell," he accused, still wiping at the tears in his eyes. "That's moonshine!"

She considered the accusation quietly, finding it hard to refrain from grinning. "Oh, I guess you could call it that, too."

The next drink Jonathan took was more modest. Even so, he still found it necessary to pause after swallowing, eyes closed, breathing suspended for a moment. "Did you make this, too?"

Anne did grin then, knowing that the two of them would at least start the renegotiation of their relationship on equal footing. "No. This particular jar was payment from a lady I helped with the pleurisy."

"She should have taken this. She never would have known she was sick."

Anne savored the wood smoke flavor of the liquid in her cup. "She did. And you're right, it worked wonderfully. You see, there are some benefits to the backwoods after all."

Jonathan took another taste of his quickly disappearing tea and nodded. "I'll certainly drink to that."

"I think you are."

They both spent the next few minutes in careful consideration of the jet fuel that spiced their mugs. The fire snapped before them, and the clock marked the passing of the silence with soft staccato.

Anne listened to the rhythm of accumulating time with growing unease. There could be no more putting off the talk they badly needed. She couldn't bear to spend another night in the house with Jonathan and not come to a resolution of some kind for the strained emotions that leaped between them. She studied the solid lines of her mug without ever seeing them as she feverishly turned over opening gambits in her mind and equally quickly discarded them. She was so afraid of what she'd find in Jonathan's eyes that she refused to look up at him at all. Suddenly she felt like a high school freshman searching in desperation for a mature introduction to a summer crush. By the time Jonathan did speak up, Anne had gotten so wrapped up in a futile attempt to ease into the answers she needed that she didn't even hear him.

"Anne."

She sat like a statue, the only betrayal of her tension a vein that stood out against her temple.

"Annie." Her head snapped up, but Jonathan's smile was solidly noncommittal. "How about a little more tea?"

It took her a few seconds to answer. "Tea or tonic?"

He grinned rakishly. "Sure. Have some yourself."

She did. Only this time she went into the kitchen and poured herself a small snifter of brandy. She spent the time there as she had on the couch, with no better luck. The longer she agonized over her next move, the more foolish and frustrated she felt.

Never in her life had she found herself at such a loss for words. It was as if in the last few weeks she'd been granted a whole new life with a new set of expectations, problems and guidelines. The difficulty was that she wasn't familiar enough with the new guidelines yet to be able to use them effectively in solving the problem. The problems weren't waiting patiently for solutions until she was ready. If only Jonathan could have waited to come into her life until she'd worn her freedom a little longer.

Returning to the living room, Anne reminded herself that if Jonathan hadn't been here already, there would never have been any freedom in the first place. Whatever else happened, she still had to thank him for that.

"Jonathan," she started to say as she walked in, "I wanted to thank you for sending me to Judson...."

The words trailed limply away when she caught sight of Jonathan. He was on the floor, propped on pillows he'd pulled from the couch. Legs stretched easily before him, he patted to the matching nest of pillows he'd built beside him between couch and fireplace.

"What are you doing?" she asked without thinking.

"Making us both comfortable," he said easily, the crinkle of his eyes warm. "Come on down and join me."

Anne cast a suspicious eye even as she moved to set the tray down on the already rearranged coffee table. "You certainly have been busy."

"Profitable use of time and resources is one of my company's hallmarks," he assured her.

Before she did join him, Anne stoked the fire and turned off the lights. Immediately the shadows crept close and danced rhythmically with the firelight over the walls. The night grew comfortable and intimate, its wind only a suggestion.

Anne pulled off shoes and socks and stretched her feet out toward the fire before she took brandy in hand and leaned back next to Jonathan's companionable warmth.

"You must be an idea man," she said. "This was a great one."

He slipped an arm around her and brought her head to his shoulder. "Well, I had a feeling we weren't going to get anything accomplished on the furniture. You looked like you were waiting to go in for oral exams up there."

"That bad?"

"Worse. I was beginning to feel completely at a loss."

"You?" She instinctively snuggled closer, the strength of his arm about her an exhilarating elixir that put the glow of the brandy to shame. She felt them both ease up, as if this were the prefect position for confessing truths: in intimate contact, but safe from the uncomfortable possibility of allowing revelations to be caught in unsuspecting eyes. Anne smiled at Jonathan's uncustomary admission. "I can't imagine you ever being at a complete loss."

His answering laugh was sharp. "Well, it's happened to me more since I've been here than ever before."

Anne took a sip of brandy and thought of how Jonathan's eyes held their own source of heat. His hand was rubbing at her shoulder, an absent gesture of easy familiarity that kindled its own energy. "Has it been so bad?"

For a moment there was only the answer of a patient fire. Then Jonathan nuzzled her hair, his own head now resting against hers. "Terrible."

Without really knowing why, Anne found herself testing their closeness.

"You don't really do that well, do you?"

He looked over. "What?"

"Being at a loss. Not being in control."

She felt him stiffen a little as he turned back to consider the fire again. "No."

Anne nodded to herself, trying her best to remain noncommittal. "You haven't told me yet about the other time you said you were helpless to keep someone you cared for from being hurt. It was before Nam, wasn't it?"

Jonathan's answer was a rigid, profound silence.

"It takes a lot to make a person so . . . obsessed," she said gently, careful to not push. "That's the only word I can use for how you've pushed yourself to get back on your feet." She shrugged offhandedly and offered a slight smile. "Anybody else would still be demanding breakfast in bed."

Still he didn't answer, didn't move.

She kept on, feeling even more unsettled. "What happened to you in Vietnam was terrible, but I have the feeling that it was the coup de grace. The final straw."

"Why is it so important to you?" he finally asked.

"Because it's important to you. And because it might help me to understand you better," she offered tentatively. "Your mystery-man image has its drawbacks."

When she felt him relax a little, she knew this particular moment of challenge had passed.

"You didn't ask Judson?"

"Of course I did. He told me what a beautiful woman your mother is and how he used to call on her back in Wyoming."

"That's all?"

"That took two hours. I figured that it would take another four weeks to span the next forty years." She supposed it would have been easier to admit her knowledge, but it was important to her that Jonathan volunteer the information about his past on his own. He had to want to share it with her or it would end up being nothing more than emotional blackmail to hold over him.

"It was a long time ago," he said quietly without moving, his voice pensive.

"It's not that long ago when it still bothers you so much," she insisted, then carefully backed off. "Judson worries about you."

Jonathan moved then. Anne knew he was looking down at her. "He worries, does he?"

She nodded, her eyes passive.

"Do you?"

Anne took a slow breath and turned to him, her eyes honest. "I don't want you to end up like my ex-husband. And I'm afraid something's driving you down the same road."

Jonathan considered her a moment in silence. Then, his features settling into a soft smile, he moved back next to her again, his embrace closer.

"In that case, someday soon I'll tell you all about it."

"Why not now?"

He shook his head a little. "Because this is not the time or place. Soon."

She nodded. His reply was both more and less than she'd hoped for. It was a promise of a future in carefully impressive words, but not the revelation she'd hoped for.

"Jonathan?"

"Mmm?" He was sipping at his tea, his good leg drawn up as a prop for his elbow. His fingers were lacing through her hair, their touch alive.

"You're going back to New York, aren't you?"

He stroked her hair for a little while longer. She closed her eye against the naked hunger such a simple gesture aroused in her.

"Yes, Anne," he finally said. "I'm going back."

Her voice became progressively softer. "Where does that leave us?"

He bent to kiss her forehead, the touch of him yearning and un certain all of a sudden. "I don't know. I don't suppose we could hope for another blizzard."

She grinned tremulously. "I could push you back off the cliff."

He kissed her again, his lips lingering on her cheek. "I don' think that would be a good idea. I couldn't stand being in a snow bound cabin with you any longer if I couldn't touch you."

"Is this going to end up being a cheap, tawdry affair?" she de manded, trying very much to sound flippant. She only succeeded in sounding frightened.

At that, Jonathan set down his mug and turned to take Anne' face in his hands. His eyes, half in shadow and half filled with firelight, sought her with an almost physical intensity. Anne fi nally found in them what she'd so long hoped for.

"I don't think I even want to joke about that, Anne," he said softly. Anne saw the clean, hard lines of his face and thought how they lent sincerity to his words. Her heart thudded and tears stung at her eyes. His hands held her face like a wild bird that might shy away. "Would you agree to take it one day at a time?" he asked "I want to promise you anything you want right now, but I'm no sure I can."

She felt even more unsteady than before. "Your seven children need you?"

He made a face at her. "I know Judson better than to think he would have forgotten to clear up that small detail within five min utes of meeting someone as lovely as you. There is no wife, no children; no one in my life." A grin tugged at the corners of his mouth, softened by his admission. "At least there wasn't anyone until I woke up to find you hovering over me like something out of a Raphael painting. I fell in love with you long before I wanted to."

Anne found herself smiling back, the light brighter in her eyes a certain determination in her voice. "Isn't that always the way If you hadn't been so darn stubborn, we could have been enjoying ourselves all along."

His eyebrows shot up again. "Me? I've seen murderers treated with more courtesy by the jury that hung them!"

Anne had no choice but to admit the truth of his charge as she snuggled back into the comfort of his arm. He immediately encir cled her with the other. "I guess I was a little prickly. I had a small problem to work out."

"So I heard. A husband who talked like me. What ever became of him?"

Anne grinned again with triumph. "Oh, I gave him his walking papers. Once and for all."

Jonathan moved against her. "You don't say. Well, I'll have to check that out for myself."

Anne looked up to see what he intended and was met by a kiss. At first slow and exploratory, Jonathan's mouth gentle on hers, it began to build of its own accord. Before Anne knew it, she was completely within Jonathan's embrace, his lips crushing hers, his tongue searching hers feverishly. His beard chafed her cheek. His breath tickled her ear. By the time he drew back over a minute later, they were both out of breath.

Jonathan's eyes gleamed with satisfaction. "You know," he said softly as he brushed Anne's hair over her shoulder, "it would certainly be a shame to waste such a good fire."

Anne couldn't refrain from a wicked grin. "What do you have in mind," she said just as suggestively, "a wienie roast?"

Jonathan didn't even blink. "Only if we get too close."

She chuckled, a low throaty sound that Jonathan enjoyed. "But you have a broken leg. Wouldn't that be awfully cumbersome?"

His hand was beginning to drift from her shoulder. Anne could have sworn he'd dipped his fingers in fire. They seared easily through her blouse as he moved to her top button.

"You didn't seem to find my leg cumbersome the other night." Bending down, he kissed the flesh he had exposed by freeing her buttons. Anne was having even more trouble breathing. His fingers had almost reached her waist. Jonathan seemed to find particular pleasure in the soft mounds of Anne's breasts where they swelled above the restraint of her bra.

"The other night I was...in a...rash..." she admitted weakly, her head far back into the pillows where Jonathan's other arm cradled her.

"A rash."

She could tell that he was grinning as he deftly slipped her shirt off and teased her nipples through the filmy material that held them. The suggestion of his touch was almost more than she could bear.

"You think you'd have to be in a rash to make love again?" Rather than remove her bra, he began to undo her belt, his lips leaving blazing trails across her throat. He was taking so long it was torture, teasing her with his touch, the promise of taking her, and then holding back.

"Oh... I think the... idea... shows promise..." she managed. She opened her eyes to see his face etched in firelight, his soft lips and laughing eyes, the small cleft in his chin. Then she reached up to draw him to her.

He waited a moment, his face very close to hers, his breathing rapid. "You let me know when you think you're in a sufficient... rash." His kiss was quick, a temptation. "Okay?"

She caught his head with her hands and pulled him to her for another kiss. A long kiss that left him with no illusions as to her intentions. "Okay."

The firelight bathed them, casting their skin in living bronze as they settled into each other's arms and the luxury of discovering each other. Jonathan slipped Anne out of her jeans, his hands painting her legs with fierce chills. Then Anne helped him out of his clothes, both of them laughing at the difficulty they had getting around his homemade splint and Anne kissing his ribs when he complained that laughing made them hurt. She allowed herself to run her hands over the thick hair on his chest and then trace the scars that stood out oddly in the soft light. This time she tasted his belly, the hard, flat plane so well developed that she could trace every muscle with her tongue.

For a long while, Jonathan refused to remove her bra and panties, as if he loved the temptations of secrets not seen. The scintillation of his fingers against the silk shocked Anne to a sharp aching. Taking her own time in exploring the exhilaration of his sinewy body, she surprised moans from him and set him to gasping when she teased him with her teeth.

She took his buttocks in her hands, so firm and tight, and pulled him against her so that she could enjoy his excitement. Then she pushed him back on the pillows and took great pains to teach him how to kiss, telling him so and laughing with him. Aroused by the soft strength of his mouth, she let her tongue slip in to taste the pleasant roughness of his, the smooth curve of his teeth, the sweet warmth of his lips. It all seemed a revelation. It was as if she'd never tasted a man before, and each new place she found set her to smiling with the delight of discovery.

"Well," he finally asked, his hands teasing her so that she almost cried out, "are you in a rash, do you think?"

She paused as if in consideration. She was on fire and freezing at once, her muscles quivering with the effort of control. "I think so."

He dropped a kiss on her nose and grinned, the spark in his eyes one of tender exhilaration. "About time."

Letting his hands slide carefully down from her throat, he undid the clasp between Anne's breasts. Her bra fell away, though the straps were still on her shoulders. Jonathan didn't bother with them. He bent to her breasts, taking first one in hand and then the other. Anne had never known such gentle attention. Tears reached her eyes as she cradled his head to her, his hair so wildly black against the milky whiteness of her skin. The core of her own arousal coiled like a tensed animal within her, her love for Jonathan an exquisite pain. Yes, she guessed she'd have to take it one day at a time. She could never have asked more in life than the delicious intensity of this moment.

As he eased toward capturing her breasts, first with his tongue, then lips and finally the sharp thrill of his teeth, Jonathan slid her panties down and away. Anne allowed his hands to part her thighs, searching upwards to find her long since accommodating.

"Doesn't...all this...hurt your...ribs?" she found herself demanding, ever the nurse.

Jonathan raised his eyes to hers, his fingers trailing new, even more unbearable fire. "Not really. I guess I must be in a rash, too." He punctuated his grin with another lingering kiss.

Unable to wait even longer, Anne took him in her hand, surprised again by the power of his arousal, and led him to her. From that moment, whatever control they had managed between them vanished. They clung to each other as if terrified of their parting and reached their peak together, shuddering and murmuring, their lips bruised from the hunger of their meeting. Again Anne cried out, wondering that she could be so overwhelmed. She felt her body become electrified, even to her toes, her scalp tingling as if she'd been hit by lightning.

Lightning had never happened quite like this to Anne before. Suddenly she wondered what she'd ever found so provocative about Tom. It occurred to her that he'd treated her exactly as she'd expected to be treated. Tom had been exciting, but had never really known how to give excitement. He had taken a woman rather than cherished her.

For a long while Anne lay silent in Jonathan's arms, her head nestled in the hollow of his shoulder, her old blue-and-white afghan helping to ward the creeping chill from both of them. She would have given anything to never have to move from this spot and not have to face the uncertainty of the future. She knew that Jonathan loved her just as she loved him, but she knew too that wouldn't answer all of their questions. He still didn't seem able to trust her with the responsibility of his troubled past and had refused to address their future. He wanted to return to the city, and she wanted to stay in the mountains. And she wasn't at all sure that either would find cause to change their minds. The impasse seemed too great to overcome, and it frightened her.

"You never did tell me what happened in New York," Jonathan said lazily.

Anne had been absently running her fingers through the hair that trailed from Jonathan's chest down to his navel, a dark line that begged exploration. She moved her head to take in his eyes, sleepy and content in the dying light, and decided that she loved them more than any other of his features. She could watch them forever.

"I told you," she answered. "I exorcised myself of the ghost of one ex-husband."

He shot her a wry look. "You didn't tell me," he corrected. "You showed me. And, may I add, with great conviction."

"And enthusiasm," she added.

"Overwhelming enthusiasm." His kiss of appreciation took a minute longer. "What else happened?"

She shot him a mischievous grin. "You mean you didn't ask Judson?"

Jonathan was all innocence. "Me?"

She nodded. "I figured you'd be on the phone ten minutes after I got out of his office."

"Well," Jonathan demurred with a wry smile, "I tried. The phone's out again."

Anne nodded with a self-satisfied smirk. "Serves you right for not telling me sooner about what Judson told you about the will."

"I did that for a reason," he protested.

She bestowed her own kiss of appreciation. "I know. It would have been torture on me to have been stuck here with only half the information. Thank you."

Jonathan's eyes sparkled darkly in the firelight. "So, what else happened? Besides the exorcism?"

Anne shrugged happily. "Nothing nearly as important as that."

Jonathan made a face at her. "You were saying something about Judson before."

"Oh," she said lightly, "that. I was thanking you for sending me to him. I don't know what I would have done otherwise."

Jonathan nodded, his eyes contemplating the glowing embers. "I'm glad he helped. I wasn't even sure he'd take a recommendation from me. I haven't seen him in a long time."

Anne held her breath, hoping for more. When it didn't come, she stifled a sigh and turned to the fire herself. "Stick around. He's coming for a visit in the spring when the new clinic opens. In fact, I may name it after him. He's donating his fees to it."

Jonathan's voice still had a faraway sound when he answered. "That's Judson all right."

"He seems to think very highly of you."

"Rank prejudice. He's my godfather."

Anne turned to him in surprise. "You never told me that."

Jonathan shrugged. "You never asked."

"I suppose you're going to tell me that you went to law school because of him."

It wasn't until she'd said it that she remembered that Jonathan had gone to law school after Nam. After he'd changed.

He looked down at her, his eyes suddenly unreadable, with a hint of the old animosity flashing through. "No" was all he said, leaving her even more troubled. "No, you can't blame that on Judson."

"Well," she said hurriedly, trying to cover her confusion. "He thinks I can get the cabin back. But then, you know that. You've been helping him, from what I hear."

He shrugged easily. "Judson doesn't have as keen an acquaintance with the devious mind as I do."

Anne couldn't help but grin. "Can't argue with you there."

"Tell me what happened," he said, scowling.

So she told him, leaving out only the now shoddy-sounding threat situation. It might have been that Judson didn't tell him about Tom's boorish behavior, or maybe Jonathan didn't make much of it, because he never questioned her about it.

At the end he nodded quietly, his eyes once again beyond her, and lapsed into silence. Anne couldn't help but wonder where he'd drifted, somewhere far beyond the walls of her small home.

Was he thinking about Judson, she wondered, or the time he'd stood impotently by as his own home was lost? Whatever it was he was remembering, it brought a hard, flat sheen to his eyes. They seemed almost emotionless, as if the memory had long ago lost its power to move him to passion, and left only pictures and sounds behind. She didn't like it, or the fact that he wouldn't share it with her. Well, she thought with new purpose, I can only keep on trying.

"Tell me about Wyoming."

He started. "What?"

"Wyoming," she persisted. "I want you to describe it for me."

"Didn't I?"

She took up a thoughtful pose. "Let's see. You mentioned the Tetons, I believe. The sky and mountain climbing. Is there any more?"

His gaze was at once amused and tender. "Maybe. But if I tell you about Wyoming, does that mean you'll tell me about where you grew up?"

She took in the room with her hand. "I grew up here."

"What was Boston, a field trip?"

She looked into his eyes a moment, realizing that the tables had been turned and not sure that she was any readier than he was for confessions. "Are your memories of Wyoming painful?"

He shook his head.

"My memories of Boston are. I don't feel like digging that all up tonight, if you don't mind."

Jonathan reached down to gently stroke the pain from her eyes. "It's a deal. Tonight's for the good memories. What are yours?"

She didn't hesitate. "My mother. And the mountain."

"Your mother, then. I've seen a bit of the mountain, but you've never talked about your mother."

Anne smiled a bit wistfully. Her mother had lived in the privacy of her memory for a long time now. "No, I guess I haven't."

They ended up talking through two more hours and another pot of tea. Jonathan spoke with reservation at first and then, warming to his topic, opened up with an expansiveness that surprised Anne. He described at length his boyhood home where mule-ear deer would mingle with the horse herds to get at the winter hay; where trout flashed in a thawing spring-fed river that rushed along behind the stone ranch house his great-grandfather had built near the south end of Jackson Hole. He described it in the different seasons with the words and recollections of a small boy's awe, his eyes alight with the pictures.

His father had taken him on pack trains high in the mountains twice a year to fish and camp. This was where his great lessons in life were learned. His father had taught him self-sufficiency, Wyoming style, and how to live off the land. Jonathan even admitted the veracity of Judson's theory that he returned often to challenge the mountain much as he had in his childhood.

Anne lay still, listening intently and encouraging him with cautious questions and observations. She never was able to push him beyond recollections of his boyhood. He never even admitted to an education beyond eighth grade. She didn't mind, though. The places he'd described to her were the ones she had wanted to find, to share with him so that he could rediscover their worth. It was at least a beginning in bringing their seemingly incompatible life-styles closer. By the time he turned to hear her part of the bargain, he looked as if ten years' weight had been lifted from his shoulders.

When Jonathan did exact the price for his admissions, Anne balked. It had been too long a time since she'd talked to anyone but Cassie about herself. It was a chance she suddenly wasn't sure she wanted to take.

Jonathan, with unusual tact and gentleness, drew the story from her. Before she knew it, she was describing her mother, the shy, blond beauty who had preferred her adopted home in the mountains to the strain of the Boston social life into which she'd been born.

Anne wasn't sure if she'd ever really forgiven her mother for dying three days after Anne's ninth birthday. Elizabeth Harrison Jackson had died in the cabin with the Millers and her children in attendance to ease her pain. Silas, so tall in Anne's young memory, had shepherded Anne and Brad in and out as he'd thought necessary, never once leaving the children in the final day of their mother's life. Anne's father had arrived too late.

One of the things Anne held in memory of her mother was the baking days in the cabin. The smell of fresh-baked bread, her gentle singsong laugh and hands as delicate as porcelain.

It took Anne a moment to realize that she'd been silent for quite a few minutes. The picture of her mother dressed for a big benefit, glittering with family diamonds and cleaning Anne's bicycle-scraped knees lingered in her mind. Suddenly she had the urge to walk up to the small graveyard above the house. She hadn't been there in so long.

"I'm sorry," she said, smiling quickly. "I got a bit lost for a moment."

"That's all right," Jonathan assured her, his voice so close that his breath swept her cheek. "I was enjoying the sight of your eyes."

"My eyes?"

He nodded. "I'd always thought that gray was such a cool color. It isn't really."

She smiled up into the endless depths of blue. "Rank prejudice."

He never answered, but bent to gather her back to him, his eyes brimming with his delight in her, his lips more gentle than his touch.

Late in the night as a brittle moon shed its light through the window and time became lost in its own rhythms, Anne and Jonathan made love quietly, their passion saved for another time. As the fire once again ebbed at their feet, they explored and thrilled in each other, offering each other the salve of friendship and tenderness. Celebrating their new intimacy, they brought their bodies together comfortably, softly, their sounds of satisfaction more like the music of night breezes.

Anne slept that night where she was, covered only by Jonathan's arm and her afghan, the cadence of his breathing beside her as soothing as the murmur of the sea. It had been too long since she'd slept peacefully in a man's arms. It seemed as if she'd never slept so contentedly before, happy to enjoy the moment as it greeted her without recriminations from the past or dread of the future. She refused to consider the fact that since she'd stepped back into the cabin her emotions had vascillated more often than a wind sock in a thunderstorm. For these few hours in the cocoon of a warm house, she felt whole and happy and wanted no more than that.

She decided to momentarily ignore the uncertainties of her future: the threat to her home and life-style, the theatrical doom predicted by a vengeful ex-husband. For the hours she lay protected in Jonathan's arms, she could avoid the doubts she still had about him and concentrate only on the delicious comfort of his embrace. Tonight, she was happier than she could remember. Anne decided to let tomorrow take care of itself.

Chapter 13

Four days later when Silas returned to help with the chores he spent a good deal of the time sniffing and snorting to himself, something that amused Anne to no end. That was Silas's way of expressing paternal concern and disapproval. He was trying to let her know that he'd been a lot happier when Jonathan had been unwanted and confined to the guest room. According to Silas's solidly suspicious mountain upbringing, now that Jonathan was able to spend his day with Anne, there was too much chance for immoral hanky-panky, if not imprudent relationships. Especially now that Anne no longer seemed to object to Jonathan's presence.

It seemed to particularly gall Silas that Jonathan could spend the majority of the lunch hour in the kitchen making Anne laugh. She could actually see the old man's contemplative eye on the crutches that were propped behind Jonathan's chair. Given half a chance, there was no doubt that the old man would walk off with them in an attempt to confine Jonathan to the sickroom where he belonged.

Anne did not think it prudent at the moment to point out to Silas that that was the last room he'd want to confine Jonathan to in an attempt to keep Anne's virtue safe. She also decided with a grin toward his disapproving frown that now was not exactly the time to tell him that her virtue hadn't been safe for a few days.

So distracted was he by the way Jonathan seemed to fit so nicely into Anne's life that it wasn't until he was almost ready to leave for the day that Silas remembered the package he'd brought for her. Bundling into his heavy jacket, he walked out to rummage in his saddlebag. Anne followed to the front porch where it seemed that the cold wasn't as biting as it had been. She watched Silas with arms wrapped around her chest.

"This come for you yesterday, Annie," he was saying as he tugged a fat manila envelope from the cracked leather pouch. "We didn't know as it'd make any difference if it waited a day before I got it up to ya. You haven't really cared much for the last letters ya got."

Anne grinned, hearing Jonathan hobble out behind her. "You're right, Silas. I haven't been too crazy about any of that mess."

Jonathan filled his lungs with air and peered up into the breath-taking blue of the sky that made his eyes look like mirroring lakes. "So, this is what it feels like to be on the outside. I'm going to have to ask the warden to let me out more."

Anne flashed him a withering look. Silas turned to see him standing by her and took a long, meaningful look at the sky himself. "Gonna thaw soon," he said, nodding a bit as if to seal his verdict. "That snow'll be off this mountain in no more than a few days."

"All of it?" Anne asked, taking in the monstrous drifts that obliterated the angles of the barn.

Instead of gauging the snow as Anne had, Silas turned his speculative eye on Jonathan. "Enough." Then he nodded again, just once, and stepped back up onto the porch to hand Anne the envelope.

It was all Anne could do to keep a straight face. She had never seen Silas this upset, at least not since Ef Tate tried to make unpopular advances toward his daughter Rose. Once again Anne recognized the kinship between Silas's family and herself. His clan had been more of a family than her own since her mother and father had died. Now, they were the only family she had.

"Will you be going by Jim's on your way home?"

He nodded in his slow way.

"I may have a reply to this. Come in for a little more tea and let me go through this really quickly. Please?"

Silas could never refuse her anything. Still grumbling, he followed her back into the cabin and once more shed his jacket. The protest did ease considerably when he saw what Anne had set out to sweeten his tea. His wife Sarah, a Bible Baptist, took no hold with drinking. Silas, who attended church with her on Christmas and Easter and the odd revival, had much more liberal views on the subject.

Anne took up the best defensive position right between Jonathan and Silas at the table and tore into the package Judson had sent her. The kitchen fell into silence without her participation in conversation. After the first few minutes the only sounds to be heard were the rustle of paper, the clock in the living room and a tentative clink of china.

From the first line she read, Anne completely lost contact with the other people in the room. Judson wasted no time in telling her that he was delivering an emotional bombshell, and he didn't go far to apologize. Anne must decide, he told her in carefully reserved language, whether she wanted him to proceed further or not, since her legal option had become an all-or-nothing proposition. He had tracked down all of the information to her case and more besides. He had also obtained the proof that she had not, in fact, signed the power of attorney paper. Because of that and the provision of her father's will, everything Tom and Brad had orchestrated from the time of her father's death had been not only unethical, but illegal. Copies of all documents were enclosed for her elucidation.

The bottom line, Judson wrote succinctly, was that if Anne wanted her house back, she'd have to accept the whole empire. Before she made that kind of decision, he suggested she read the enclosed copy of her father's will. It would, he hoped, help her better assess her position.

Anne picked up the accompanying forms, separating the will out to be read last. Judson had arranged everything chronologically from the power of attorney to the futures deal Brad had made. The documents were all in tortuous legalese, but it didn't take Anne long to recognize the pattern Judson had outlined. By the time Brad had made the mistake that brought the situation to a crisis, he and Tom had acquired complete control of the entire Jackson empire, leaving Anne no more than the family jewelry they knew she would never sell and her mother's small trust that they couldn't break anyway. As she'd told Judson, they'd contrived to create a situation she'd assumed had already existed. Frustrating yes, but no bombshell. They'd already come to these conclusions.

She looked down at the will and didn't notice how profound the silence had become in the bright kitchen, or that Jonathan and Silas watched her with identical expressions. Afraid of what the will would tell her, she picked it up as if it were alive.

It took no more than four paragraphs for Anne to be dealt the blow.

The will had been made before the last time her father had returned to the mountain, at the height of the power struggle. Anne could suddenly see again the gray of his face in those days, the stubborn refusal to disbelieve his son. She remembered his increasing dependence on her, and that he'd almost reached a point of expressing a love for her she'd sought as long as she'd remembered. He'd died still searching for the way to bridge a lifelong gap. And she had been left behind still wondering, as it always was with children of a hard man.

She wondered no more. What he had never been able to say, he'd expressed eloquently in his gift to her.

... to my daughter Anne, the only member left of the Jackson or Harrison families worth the honor of those names and histories, I leave all that is her inheritance, both in fortune and in heritage. I leave her the responsibility of directing both of these in the honorable, farseeing fashion she so often suggested to me. And in bequeathing my entire estate to her with the exception of the house and furnishings in Boston, which I know she wouldn't want, I have every belief that she will carry out her responsibilities in a way that will justify the pride her family has always had in her.

For long minutes Anne stared at the words, unable to focus on them, unable to move beyond them. Why hadn't he told her? Why couldn't he have, just once before he died, verbally expressed the love that echoed from these stringent pages? She could see now that it had always been there, though expressed only in a manner he could manage. Money and schools and opportunity. It was a tragic thing when the most important words a man can give his child could only be offered in his will.

Without a word to Jonathan or Silas, Anne stood and walked toward the door. She didn't see Jonathan move to follow, or Silas hold him back with a hand on his arm.

"Leave her be," he said, his eyes on her retreating figure. "She has business to attend that you got no part of."

The evening air was softer than it had been in a long time, the sunset less crisp at the edges. Beneath Anne's feet the snow folded into shadows cast in a painter's blue. Anne stumbled along, blind to the beauty around her, her eyes clouded with the tears of futility. The graveyard was only a short pathway up beyond the house, nestled in among pines and the oaks her ancestors had planted. Her parents were buried here together, their headstones as simple as the rest with only names and dates on the slim rounded stones.

Just the sight of their names brought back the pain, all of the different unresolved aches of their leaving. Her mother, so frail, fighting so hard to stay with her children, the apology in her eyes still fresh in Anne's memory. And her father.

It was because of her father that she'd avoided the graveyard so assiduously. It was a hard thing to face someone who caused anger and guilt at the same time. It was harder still when death had removed the chance to explain or be understood. Anne stood at the foot of her father's grave as if she could absorb there the feelings he'd never been able to share face to face. She wanted to understand the man who had written the words of that will.

She stood as the sun disappeared over the next ridge and pulled most of the light with it, until the first of the stars came to life in a peacock sky. She couldn't say for sure that she felt any great relief in the time she spent alone with the memories of her father. A lifetime of ambivalence didn't disappear like shadows with the flick of a light switch. But she did know that she felt different. Now, when she asked the questions she'd asked herself for so long, she found answers. Someday, she thought, they would be enough. She knew at least that the love she had so frantically tried to lavish on her father had been in its own way returned. She hadn't been the fool she'd feared.

When Anne returned to the kitchen, she found Jonathan and Silas where she'd left them. She could tell by the empathy in Jonathan's eyes and the pride in Silas's that they'd read the will. It didn't upset her in the least. She smiled at them with watery eyes and sat down to finish her tea.

"Silas, would you ask Jim to send a telegram for me?"

He nodded, more animation in his eyes than she could ever remember. "Ya goin' for it?"

Her smile widened, and she cocked her head at him in mock disbelief. "Well, what do you think?"

When he answered, his eyes were dead serious. "I think he had a right to be proud of you."

Anne couldn't think of anything to say, but as Silas left, she stood on tiptoe and delivered a hug that had him crimson.

That night Anne slept quietly in Jonathan's arms, savoring his silent understanding and companionship. In the morning she invited him outside to help her with the chores. He followed gladly, precariously balancing himself in the snow, his head on a constant swivel to take in the scenery he'd only viewed from the porch below.

"It's not the Tetons," he said as he worked his way through the door Anne held for him, "but it has its points."

"Why, thanks," Anne retorted dryly. "You've made it all worthwhile."

Due to obvious restrictions, Jonathan took over the less strenuous chores of feeding, milking and grooming. That and, when the mood struck him, kibitzing. His company taught people efficiency, he said, and it was the least he could do to teach Anne some. He also said that Anne's rather ascerbic retort was not unusual for someone who refused to see that they needed professional help. Anne's reply to that was a simple but effectively threatening display of the fertilizer she was in the process of mucking out. Jonathan took the hint and kept his peace.

"When do you think I'll be going down the mountain?" he asked a little later as he sat milking the cow. Bessie swung her head lazily around at the question, munching her hay as if in calm consideration of answering herself.

Anne looked toward the animal's back from where she was cleaning some tack to see what had prompted Jonathan's question. His eyes betrayed nothing as he rocked easily back and forth with his task.

"Silas almost dragged you down yesterday," Anne told him, going back to work.

Jonathan chuckled. "Does he not like me for the same reason you didn't like me?"

"More or less."

"Him and how many others?"

She shrugged noncommitally. "Let's say that the older people in the valley feel compelled to look after me."

"Would they mind if I didn't go back down at the first chance?"

Anne smiled more to herself than to him. That kind of scandal would be consumed with relish and condemned with fervor. She could almost hear the whispers already: "...that fancy gigolo taking advantage of our Annie..." She would have to stock up for all the curious and concerned visitors.

"They would," she finally admitted, "frown on it."

"So I figured. Well then, how much longer do you think I can successfully hide out in Shangri-la?"

Anne looked up at him and saw the genuine regret that was taking shape in his eyes. For a long moment she stood very still, sharing it with him as she saw the consequence of his trip back to civilization. Unable to face new pain, she said quickly, "Oh, a week at best. That's if Silas's thaw doesn't come. But I've never known Silas to be far wrong."

They would now measure their time left in hours, hoarding it like water on a desert. The uncertainty of the future colored the present with bittersweet light. Anne rubbed slowly at the soft, fragrant leather, using the activity as an antidote for the fear.

"Tell me something." Jonathan spoke up after a long silence. Anne turned to him. His eyes, gemlike in the morning light, were laughing, the crow's feet at their corners wrinkling suggestively. "Have you ever made love in the hay?"

Anne stopped what she was doing. "What?"

"You heard me." With a brisk twist of his hand, he indicated the loft, spilling with winter hay. The warm, fragrant hay was suffused with animal scents and age-old illusions.

"Jonathan," she objected instinctively, "I've just finished chores. Cleaning chores."

He would not be deterred. "Your cheeks are glowing and you have bits of straw in your hair."

"And I smell like horse . . ."

"Anne," he objected gently, a hand out in invitation. "Don't you want to find out what all the notoriety is about?"

Now her eyebrow arched, the enticement of his offer already waking tremors of excitement. "Do you mean that *you've* never made love in a hayloft?"

"No. I mean that I've never made love to you in a hayloft. And right now I want to. Very much." His hand was still out to her, his face still inviting much more than even his words as he got slowly to his feet. Anne only hesitated a moment longer before she walked over and held out hers in kind.

"Tell me one thing and I'll say yes," she said grinning. "How do you plan to get up the ladder?"

By now Jonathan had a tight enough grip on Anne's hand that she knew he wasn't going to let go, no matter the answer. "Very carefully."

He did, too. Balancing on the injured leg, he hoisted himself up with the good one, using his phenomenal set of chest and shoulder muscles.

What had begun in fun ended in earnest. Anne barely had the time to spread out an old blanket over the hay before Jonathan pulled her over next to him and took hold of her with an intensity that startled them both.

"This . . . is what happens to you," she panted between heady kisses, "in a barn?"

His smile was rakish, his eyes alight with their peculiar fire. "This is what happens to me," he amended, holding her beneath him and burying his face in her throat, "with you."

His impatience infected her as his hands undressed her. In no more than a few minutes she lay naked in the sweet, soft hay as Jonathan got out of his own clothes. Anne couldn't wait though. With an aggressiveness she wouldn't have recognized in herself before, she pushed him to his back and finished the job.

The sight and feel of his strong body beneath her hands set her pulse rocketing. Suddenly she was damp with perspiration. She couldn't seem to hold still, moving against him as if the friction of their bodies could further feed the flame that raged in her. She reveled in the coarseness of his hair against the smooth skin of her thighs, stomach, chest. She rubbed her cheek against him and nipped at the tight skin of his belly. And when she took him in her mouth, full and throbbing with power, she heard him groan with pleasure.

Jonathan could only take so much of that before he pulled her back to him, trapping her beneath him as if afraid she'd escape somehow. His excitement fed hers until it seemed unquenchable. His lips found her neck, the back of it where the small hairs anticipated pain and pleasure, and his tongue teased her unbearably. When she moved to meet his lips with her own, seeking the delicious heat of his mouth, his hands sought out the small, special places of her body that brought her even closer to the precipice.

Anne had never remembered such abandon, such fierce primal release. It was as if between them she and Jonathan had found a uniquely kindred energy source, a passion neither of them had ever really realized. They had also learned, instinctively, how to prolong their pleasure in each other until they were both drenched and gasping, eyes uncannily alike in their intensity. Together they teased and held back, promised release and then withheld, until they could bear it no longer.

"Please," she begged for the first time in her life, her voice shrill and breathless with the intensity of him inside her. "Please . . . now . . ."

With her plea, Jonathan took her to him almost brutally, his arms all but crushing her, his mouth ferocious. Captive within what could have been a prison, Anne met her freedom head on, the brilliance at the pinnacle so overwhelming that its delight was agony. Unbelievably, when Jonathan reached the same peak moments later, Anne followed again, wide-eyed and trembling.

For a long while later they lay exhausted in each other's arms, too spent to even marvel aloud at what they had shared. Anne supposed that she dozed for a while once the delicious fire that had coarsed through her limbs finally ebbed to a pleasant glow. She lay for a long time savoring the feel of Jonathan against her, the heady aroma of him and the slightly scandalous comfort of the hayloft. When she should have been inside her house making preparations for going out on rounds, she curled into the curve of Jonathan's hip and tested the texture of his chest with lazy fingers. All the while she found herself smiling and thinking that this sort of thing could easily become a habit.

"They were right," she finally said.

"Who?" Jonathan's voice sounded sleepy and content.

"Whoever decided that haylofts were so notorious. They should be."

He chuckled, his fingers just as lazily exploring the softness of her breast. "It's something about losing your inhibitions," he suggested.

"Inhibitions, hell." Anne grinned back at him. "That's not what's usually lost in haylofts. When I'm a parent, my daughter's not going anywhere near one."

It didn't occur to her until after she'd said it that until only a few days ago, she had given up the idea of children for good. The realization would have been more exciting for her if it weren't for the fact that she just as quickly understood that she had meant parenthood with Jonathan. She knew what her chances were there. A little of the light died in her eyes.

Jonathan must have sensed her feelings. "Tell me something, farm girl," he said, neatly changing the subject. "What do you plan to do if you win the suit?"

She didn't hesitate. "Stay here. Help run the clinic like I'd planned."

He shook his head. "What about the rest of the family holdings? Do you think that if you ignore them they'll go away?"

Anne thought a minute before moving up to her elbow. Leaning over to talk to Jonathan, she let her hair fall in a curtain to his chest. Her eyes were cautious. "I'll find someone to run them."

Jonathan's eyes were patiently amused. He didn't move. "Where did you say you cut your teeth? I suppose you think you can simply have everyone send résumés to the cabin so that you can pick the person to run seven industrial divisions and all the other subsidiaries right here from the mountain."

A new wariness crept into Anne's voice. "Applying for the job in person?"

The hint of a smile brightened. "That's the Anne Jackson I know and love. No, I'm not applying. I'm trying to tell you, my lusty wench, that no matter how you try to avoid it, if you win, which I think you will, you'll have to spend some time in the big city settling your affairs. And that I will also happen to be in that big city.''

There was a moment of silence before Anne replied, unable to keep the memory of Jonathan's New York bred personality from her voice. ''We've passed the country test. Let's see if we can do it in a corporate boardroom?''

Jonathan reached up and kissed her firmly on the mouth. ''You do have a way with a double entendre.''

''Still no promises?''

It was Jonathan's turn to pause. ''Do you think it would be wise?''

Anne knew what would be wise, but a hayloft was not the place for common sense. She stifled the new uncertainty his words had given rise to and smiled provocatively. Without a word, she began to slowly rock back and forth, her hardening nipples grazing against Jonathan's chest, the shower of her honey-colored hair enclosing them from the world.

Jonathan groaned in mock exasperation. ''What do you think I am, Superman?''

She grinned down at him, her movements more pronounced. ''I was thinking that it takes you such a lot of exertion to get up and down from the loft, we might as well make the most of our time up here.''

''Much more of this kind of exertion, and I won't be able to get back down at all.''

Anne's eyes lit up with an even more wicked light as she looked over to see that Jonathan wasn't nearly as nonchalant about her advances as he made himself out to be. ''Another double entendre? If it is, I can't wait.''

He groaned at her humor and pulled her back down to him.

Anne wasn't the least surprised when Cassie showed up the next day. When she opened the door to find her friend on the front porch, Anne hugged her warmly.

''Silas came to see you, huh?''

Cassie's grin had frozen into surprise the minute she saw Anne. ''My God, Anne,'' she gasped. ''What has happened to you?''

''What do you mean?''

''You look positively pregnant.''

''I beg your pardon.'' As yet, neither had made the first move to go inside.

''I never thought I'd say anything so trite, but you're honest-to-God glowing!''

"Get inside, Cassie," Anne suggested dryly, moving to accommodate her. "You're getting snow-blind."

Cassie walked in, never taking her eyes from Anne as she shed her coat and hat. "Annie, I mean it. You look wonderful. No wonder Silas was so indignant."

Anne had to laugh at that. "You should have seen him."

"Oh, don't worry. I got the whole show. He snorted and stomped around the store for a good twenty minutes before he decided that he didn't need to buy anything at all. I've never seen him so upset.

"He thinks that I'm about to repeat my mistakes." They headed as usual toward the kitchen, and Anne stopped a moment to throw another log on the fire.

"Are you?"

"I doubt it. Coffee or tea?"

"Coffee. Where's Jonathan?"

"He's still asleep. He's been pushing himself pretty hard the past few days." Even before she got the words out, Anne was struck by her latest unintentional double entendre and found herself grinning like a high school girl.

Cassie didn't miss a bit of it. She allowed a half smile to touch her eyes. "Before I forget about it, I have a good reason for visiting. A telegram."

Anne reached for the envelope with a scowl. It wasn't until she saw the return address that she relaxed. "Oh good, it's only from Judson."

Anne had hardly begun to read before Cassie saw the relief in her eyes grow to puzzlement. "What's the matter now?" she demanded.

Anne looked up, quickly trying to cover the worry that must have shown through. "Oh, nothing. It seems that we've stirred up a bit of a hornet's nest."

Cassie's eyes became immediately suspicious. "How, and what nest?"

"I'm sure that Silas told you about the papers that he delivered yesterday."

"And your decision to do unto your husband what he's done to you. Yes, and I think that congratulations are in order. What nest?"

Anne used her hand to brush away the concern in Cassie's expression. "Just Brad. He overreacts. Judson says I should be careful around him." Anne saw Cassie's expression sharpen and held out a threatening finger. "Don't you dare tell anyone in town," she admonished. "I'll have 'em all up here sitting on my front doorstep with their shotguns."

"Maybe that's not such a bad idea."

"Don't be silly. This isn't the Hardy Boys. Judson said that Brad had been 'visibly upset.' That means that Brad's been a jerk. I'm sure he stormed into the office and made a few vague and silly threats, and that Tom had to pull him back off. Brad never did know how to handle a threatening situation."

Cassie didn't give up easily. She was leaning forward now. "But this is a threatened jail sentence and a loss of everything he has, Annie. Maybe you should move in with us until this is all resolved."

Anne reached out and took her friend's hand. "Cassie, I grew up with Brad. He's all bark and no bite. Believe me." But Tom wasn't, she reminded herself uneasily. How threatened would the two of them have to be to do something spiteful like a little trumped-up blackmail or sabotage at the clinic? Damn it, she was tired of having to worry about those two. It was about time she let them know in no uncertain terms that she'd had about enough of their neat little squeezes. She wasn't impotent in the face of their attacks anymore. For not the first time, she realized that she was glad that she'd thrown down the gauntlet.

"You weren't going to let me have any of the coffee cake?"

The two of them started at the sound of Jonathan's voice. Looking up, they found him lounging in the doorway, clothed in Brad's old plaid shirt and corduroy pants, crutches propped against his sides. Again Anne noticed that his frame strained the material of the clothes.

"I didn't know you were up," Anne greeted him, darting a warning glance at Cassie.

"Congratulations, Jonathan," Cassie said blithely. "You look great."

Anne decided that Cassie had meant that to be significant and ignored it.

"Thanks," he said warmly. "Getting dressed only took me forty minutes start to finish this morning." He hobbled in and gently lowered himself to the seat next to Anne. "If it were a competition, I could beat every little old lady in Miami."

"You do in my book," Cassie retorted offhandedly. "None of them looks that good in their work clothes."

Anne ignored her again. Jonathan laughed, holding his chest to support irritable ribs.

"Cassie, I'm going to miss you."

Cassie shrugged with a mischievous grin. "Don't go."

Jonathan returned her grin, but with an odd loss for words.

Chapter 14

Three days later Anne stood at the front window watching the melting snow drip steadily from the eaves. Silas's prediction had come true with particular vigor, almost as if nature itself were conspiring with him against her. Jonathan would be gone in another day.

Anne sighed and rubbed at her eyes with a hand as she tried to hold off tears that had threatened all morning. It wasn't fair. Just when they were becoming really close, when the tentative forays into commitment had begun to gel into something tangible.

Jonathan had begun to find a new ease with the softer side of himself, content in the evenings to do no more than talk in the comfort of a fire lit room or read a good book. He'd lost much of the restless impatience that had marked his early days in Anne's home. More than once she caught him in moments of amused surprise as if he found it hard to recognize himself anymore.

Anne, watching him grow, had discovered a new matching place in herself that flowered within his reach. She was beginning to tap into a reservoir of love that she'd never known existed. Her time with Jonathan only fed a hunger for him that grew instead of diminished. Anne Jackson realized that for the first time since her mother died, she could love someone selflessly and completely.

Now, however, Jonathan would return to the city and the life that had forged and still supported the part of his character she wished she'd never seen. No matter how hard she'd tried in the last few days, she couldn't seem to move past that idea, past the picture of the man he'd been when he'd first arrived on her doorstep. Because of that, she couldn't seem to see her way to anything but an all-or-nothing relationship. New York or West Virginia. Choose, Jonathan.

And she knew what he would choose.

"Annie." Jonathan put a hand on her shoulder.

She jumped, not having heard him, his touch burning with new unquenchable fire.

"You're getting pretty good with those crutches," she said, not turning away from where the sun lit her strained face. "I didn't even hear you."

The night before they had made love in front of the fire again, but their words had had a ring of desperation, their laughter an uncomfortable shrillness. The snow had begun to melt yesterday.

"You weren't paying attention," he said easily. She didn't answer. He stood just behind her, a hand now on either shoulder as he looked out above her head. "Two weeks ago I would have paid any amount of money to see that sight."

Anne sighed wistfully. "Me, too."

Jonathan chuckled. "You mean you were about to throw the toast of New York out in the cold?"

"Right on his ear."

It was a moment before he asked the next question. Anne faced the silence like a penance. "When are you throwing me out?"

She took a long breath, the weight of his hands almost unbearable. "If this thaw keeps up the way it is, Jim and Silas could be up here tomorrow."

Say you won't go, she begged silently, the knot of unshed tears choking her. Change your mind and make a commitment to me, please. I can't let you go and survive.

Jonathan's voice, when it came, was quiet and strained. "Come with me, Annie."

She shook her head, struggling to keep her voice under control. "I don't think so, Jonathan. I don't think I'd like you in New York."

"You're locked in too tightly to those preconceived notions of yours," he argued quietly. "I might surprise you."

Still she didn't turn, but stood very still, her hands shoved deep into her pants pockets. "I'd like to think you would. I just…well, it's hard to get past old disillusionments. I don't know if I could compete with the lure back there anymore. I don't know if I really want to try."

"Then what do you think we should do?"

She could only shake her head. She felt his leaving already, and a great gap widened in her, a void where the life-giving force of his love had laid.

With gentle pressure, he turned her around to face him. She could hardly bear to look up at the sky-blue of his eyes.

"What do you think we should do?" he repeated, never releasing her from her gaze or grip.

"I think you should probably go back as you planned. Then you can give yourself some time in the real world to balance out your time here. Maybe we'll see each other when I'm there on business. Then if you want, you can come back for a while and we can decide what to do."

He drew her even closer until the ache of desire grew indistinguishable from the sharp pain of loss. "What about you?"

"I'll be here." She looked down, control almost impossible within the range of his eyes.

His one hand moved against her cheek, his touch caressing. Barely suppressing a moan for the agony of his touch, she lifted her head away from him, her eyes closing against the tears that began to spill. He followed and kissed her, his mouth searching hers with tender yearning.

"I love you, Annie."

Anne opened her eyes and thought that the morning sun in Jonathan's eyes would blind her. His face shifted and melted beyond her tears, and she saw the pain in its lines. What he had to do was no easier for him than it was for her. She was so afraid that when he walked away from her, he would walk away from himself. If that happened, he would have to forget her or never be able to live with himself. She wanted to tell him that. She wanted to be able to bribe or coerce or beg him to stay. She could only manage a half smile.

"I love you, Jonathan. You've given me back my freedom."

"No," he said with a slow shake of his head. "You did that, Annie. I happened to be around when it happened. That's why I think you'd survive in New York."

It was becoming increasingly difficult for her to answer without giving way to pain-wracked sobs. He wouldn't change his position. No mention yet of his staying. And she couldn't change hers. There were only so many steps she could manage at one time. "I'm not that strong yet, Jonathan. Until I am, I have no business back there with you."

"You're stronger than you think, Annie."

She couldn't answer at all. She could only look up at him, the eloquence of her turmoil glinting in tear-filled eyes. Without another word, Jonathan gathered her into the strong comfort of his arms, his lips finding that hers tasted of bitter salt. In her quiet desperation, Anne threw her arms around him, clinging to him as if he could save her. The kiss deepened as Jonathan eased her lips apart. His hands were around her waist, sure and sustaining, his hard body easing gently against hers. Slowly, inexorably, as his mouth took command of hers, his embrace tightening until the two of them swayed with the power of their need.

Anne felt his hands against her skin, fingers exploring and remembering, their touch igniting her own hunger. An obsession, a sure, sudden knowledge that she had to be next to him right now, to touch him and rouse in him the same unbearable tension he had sparked in her. Right now she needed him more than anyone or anything else in her life. She needed to know that what she'd given him had not been wasted or foolish, and it seemed to her that his most beautiful statement of that had to be made without words.

Jonathan understood as if her thoughts were telepathic. With his arms tight around her, he lifted his head a little and smiled. Anne found no guile there, none of the smugness that had once ruled their relationship. She saw only tenderness, the warmth of his love like the sun in the endless sky of his eyes.

Her tears still fell without restraint, but she smiled tremulously back. "Well," she managed in a throaty, hesitant voice, "it's probably a good thing you are leaving tomorrow. I haven't been able to get a thing done for a week."

"Yes you have, farm girl," he said. "You've made me fall in love with you. And for the first time in fifteen years, you've made me wonder whether I really want to go back to New York."

Jonathan took her to her own bed, the high old four-poster with the goose down mattress that overlooked the sunlight and felt the firelight. In the bed that had been her grandmother's and hers before her, Anne lay next to Jonathan in much the same way her ancestors had, giving and receiving the same timeless gift. Jonathan's eyes smoldered as they ranged the length of her body, their gaze raising goose bumps as surely as if they'd grazed her skin. The strong light from the front window threw him into a soft kind of relief, shadows outlining the taut muscles of his chest and arms and settling into the planes of his face.

Anne thought of the chiaroscuro of the painting masters, the dramatic play of light against dark. It couldn't be any more breathtaking than the pattern of white sunlight against Jonathan's skin. Without thinking she used her fingers as imaginary paintbrushes, stroking the rich, healthy colors into the contours of his body, the rounded edges of his shoulders and arms, the hairy coarseness of his chest. Along to narrow hips and strong, muscled thighs.

Still the tears came, as if contact with him were as painful as it was essential. Jonathan kissed them as they fell, following their traces to her throat and breasts, tasting the saltiness in her hair as she lay. With gentle hands he untangled her braid and fanned her hair out beneath her like a gilt frame. His eyes were tender but his touch hungry, impatient, and it was the contrast that was compelling to Anne.

She drew him to her breasts and begged him to savor them. She felt his fingers flutter against the sensitive skin of her thigh and invited them to explore. When they found her, their touch so light as to send her gasping, she arched against him, aching for union with him.

Jonathan whispered into her hair and nuzzled her ear, his hands driving her to a new, more urgent rhythm. The nerves in Anne's skin jumped to acute life, teased by the soft, curling hair of Jonathan's chest against her taut nipples, enticed by the scratch of an hours-old beard against her cheek and tortured by cool fingers against hot flesh. Unable to remain apart any longer, Anne led him to her, begged his arms to enfold her, his legs imprison to her. He waited long enough to capture her eyes with his own. Then together they moved in a like rhythm to a world beyond the finite one they inhabited. The sun was an explosion within them; the day, for a moment, endless; the future contained within a heartbeat and the gasping cry of release.

After Jonathan had drifted into a contented sleep, Anne lay wide awake within his embrace. She couldn't sleep, couldn't relax into the mindless peace Jonathan had found. Comfortably enclosed within his arms, she was even more painfully aware of the relentless passage of time. By tomorrow night she would once again sleep alone in her big bed. She would reclaim the isolation of her world only to find that it no longer gave her comfort.

When Jonathan left, her home, the haven she'd come to treasure for its secluded severity, would become for the first time a lonely place, a place not so much safe as empty. Another voice had become ingrained into the memories of these wooden walls. Another presence had become incorporated into the essence of what Cedar Ridge was. Only this presence would not easily relegate itself to the past.

Moving quietly so that she wouldn't wake Jonathan, Anne slipped out of his grasp and got dressed. Without any conscious intent, she made her way back down to stand before the big front window to look out on the softening snow.

The sun was rising high, and it glittered metallically. Small rivulets were beginning to cut paths into the white lawn that sloped away from the house toward the road. Soon its brown would be visible, parallel lines of sodden mud that wound down the mountain toward the town. The river would rise with the melting snow, and the trees, so deformed with the weight of the heavy snow, would begin to spring back up at the sky. As she watched, a large mound tumbled off a pine to the left of the porch and thudded to earth, the tree straightening a little. It wouldn't be long.

Anne couldn't exactly decide why she always brooded at this window. It seemed that the serenity of the scene before her helped to settle her so that she could gain a better perspective on the priorities in her life. The world around her home was always the same and always would be. It was stable.

More snow fell, the sound like a body falling. Anne watched it like the approach of a flood.

She tried, one last time, to find the resolve to follow Jonathan to New York. Looking back carefully she assessed her time there, the scant days she'd spent testing the city and corporate waters. She'd done well, she knew that. The old demeanor had slipped on as easily as the new clothes. She knew that if she went back with Jonathan now, she'd probably end up enjoying the games she would resume playing. At least to a certain extent. And she truthfully thought she could live anywhere as long as she was assured of his love.

The dilemma rested not so much in her own reaction to New York but in Jonathan's. She had to know what it would do to him before she could make a commitment. The drug of that world was far more alluring than any chemical known to man, and far more lethal. It had changed Jonathan before the eyes of his friends and family and left scars more unforgettable than those he carried from Vietnam. Anne knew all about that drug. She'd seen firsthand too, what it could do to a person.

Jonathan was going back to see how he would handle the kind of power that moved the nations of the world. It had beaten and claimed him once, altering him so thoroughly that Anne knew his parents must look at him now with the eyes of frightened strangers. She had no more guarantee than they'd had, those who'd loved him so much, that he wouldn't succumb yet again. She had known him for only weeks out of his life, and no matter how much she wanted, she couldn't hope that that time would automatically protect him.

If she went with him as he'd asked, it would only be worse. There she would be, the constant reminder of what she thought he should be, nagging at him with silent, anxious eyes. If he were going to hold onto what he'd gained here he'd do it on his own. If he weren't, her being with him would do no more than make their final parting resentful and bitter.

If she were to lose him, she would much rather it be while they still loved each other. If he had to go, better she saw him turn from her with regret.

Anne was so preoccupied that for a few minutes she lost track of what was before her. She didn't see the visitor approaching until he was through the clearing. Startled, she shifted her concentration to him.

It was a man, but not one of her neighbors. They didn't dress like that. She couldn't see him very well yet, but she wondered whether it might be one of Jonathan's corporate executives come to pay a social visit. He was attired in a manner suspiciously similar to Jonathan's when he'd arrived. Maybe, she thought dryly, it was a kind of corporate uniform for the woods.

She supposed that she should go out to greet him, wondering half-heartedly why anyone would make a trek like that on foot in snow that was still a good foot deep. The man was either very determined but stupid, or just plain stupid. Someone in town would surely have lent him a horse with the directions to her cabin, if only he'd asked.

Anne was about to turn for her coat when something caught her eye. A familiar posture to the visitor's walk. He looked as if he were denying the fact that he was walking up a mountain even as he did it, as if he wouldn't be caught dead here if he didn't have to be. She wanted to laugh.

It was Brad.

No wonder he didn't have a horse. After what had been going on in the last few weeks, no one in his right mind in Elder's Crossing would go out of his way for Bradley Jackson. In fact, she was surprised that Silas wasn't giving him an official escort to make sure he didn't give her any trouble.

Brad was the last person Anne expected to see. After all, the only time he'd been to the cabin in the last five years had been to bury his father. Brad believed that if a limo or air service couldn't get you there, it wasn't worth going. Now, looking at his rather clumsy approach, Anne desperately wished she could get her hands on a camera. Pictures of this would make delicious blackmail material, if for nothing else than to remind him in his worst moments of megalomania what a fool he really was.

She waited until she heard him on the porch before throwing the door open, the grin on her face not so much welcoming as smug.

She decided it might be a lot more fun than what she had been doing to gloat over Brad's discomfort instead. When he looked up from stomping his two-hundred-dollar L.L. Bean boots on the porch, he had nothing but malice in his eyes for her, his mouth twitching irritably. Her grin broadened in delight.

"Well, if it isn't the prodigal son," she greeted him. "What brings you so far from the big city?"

He straightened and smiled in return, the light in his eyes brightening oddly. "I'm glad you're here," he told her almost amiably. "It'll save me some time."

"Time for what?"

He motioned to the door. "Can I come in?"

"Why not?" Anne moved in to allow him by. "Coffee, tea? I have some semistale cake, if you like."

He stood inside looking around as if reorienting himself. "I'd almost forgotten how very...rustic this all was." He spoke as if the words had a slightly bad taste to them.

"I kept it just the way you left it," Anne assured him dryly. "I knew some day you'd come back."

He looked over at her with the same attitude of distaste with which he'd considered the cabin.

"I'll take some coffee."

Anne nodded agreeably. "Convention usually dictates that one remove coat and hat before sitting at the table."

"I'm still cold. It was a long walk."

She couldn't help but grin again. "I'll bet it was. What was the matter, all the horses already hired?"

He wasn't amused, but Anne certainly was. She wanted to go and get Jonathan. It would probably do him good to see what the other side of him could resemble. Maybe he hadn't been as bad as Brad—few people were—but he'd certainly worn that look of disdain when first considering life in the boonies. It was lucky for him that she didn't have the heart to wake him just for Brad.

Anne sat across from her brother as he sipped the steaming liquid in his cup and thought about the time she'd spent with him in this house. His memory should have been imbedded in this place like everyone else's. There should have been pictures that popped into her mind when certain things were handled, or aromas sensed. Like the way she could still see her father fishing down at the stream, his back sunburned and hair bleached blond, his pleasure in the silence brightening his stern features. Or her mother's delicate hands as she and Sarah worked over the wedding ring quilt that hung highest on the living-room wall. Sometimes, she even felt a pull of Tom's personality, filling the rooms like heady smoke.

But try as she might, she could not conjure up any kind of special feeling for Brad here. Even as he sat at the table where he'd eaten so many meals and worked so many jigsaw puzzles, he didn't conjure up any sensation that he had once belonged to this place. It was as if he were truly a stranger in his own house. What saddened Anne was that he didn't care in the least.

By the time he finished his cup of coffee, he'd lost much of his original antagonism. The side of his face had calmed to slow fluttering motions along the side of his mouth, and his lips didn't curl back so much in that perennial sneer. Anne knew that it was because he was anticipating the bombshell he obviously planned to drop. He wouldn't have gone to all the trouble of getting to the cabin for a trivial matter, and they both knew it. What pleading he might have done for leniency from his sister, he would have left up to Tom and adept lawyers.

She exchanged monosyllables with him, willing to play his cat-and-mouse game for the time being. She didn't want him to know how frustrated and worried his sudden appearance was beginning to make her, how very much she wanted to ask where Tom was while Brad made the jaunt up the Appalachian Trail.

Judson's carefully worded warning was still too fresh for her to take Brad's casual arrival lightly. He had something unpleasant up his sleeve, something like another legal paper Judson hadn't unearthed that would negate Anne's hold over her own destiny. But if she were going to get Brad's goat, she couldn't allow him to start with any kind of advantage.

"So tell me, Brad," she finally said quite civilly into her coffee cup. "Have you come up here to reacquaint yourself with historic architecture?"

"Just a leisurely stroll in the woods," he retorted.

"Of course," she said with a bright smile. "Well, it's always nice to see you. Oh, I'll tell you what. Since you're here, there are some clothes that you might like to take back with you."

"No, thank you."

Emptying his cup, he set it down before him and allowed Anne a measured gaze almost completely free of tics before a slow, sporadic smile caught at his mouth and made Anne uneasy. His look was anticipatory. He considered her leisurely, then took hold of his coffee cup with a corner of the tablecloth and slowly wiped its surface. Anne couldn't help but stare at the odd behavior. Brad's eyes turned to his work.

"Well, Anne, I'm afraid that I'm too greedy to put this off any longer, even for you. I have a tight schedule, so I don't have the time I'd like to sit and socialize about old times." His eyes sprang

n her, their look of expectancy now boiling uncomfortably. Anne
ecognized the look. He was feeling cornered, and thought he'd
ound a way out. Brad simply couldn't help gloating. What wor-
ied her was that there was very little control in his eyes right now.

"Put off what?"

He smiled again, his one eye blinking absurdly. "Simple, Anne
y dear. The solution to my problem. This cabin has become a
illstone around my neck, and you're the one who put it there."

She couldn't help but laugh. He'd taken his juvenile attempt at
evenge too far. "Brad, honey, how long have you been rehears-
g that? Why you sound almost threatening. It must be a line you
ead in one of father's mysteries. Just what does it mean? You've
alled in someone new to handle the case?"

Her sarcasm didn't seem to bother him. It had always awak-
ned a storm of facial irritation in the past. Instead, he continued
o smile as if relishing some private joke. Anne was becoming hard-
ressed to sit still.

"No lawyers, Anne. They seem to have come up empty-
anded." He paused to let her carefully digest his words. "Just like
om did when I sent him."

"You sent Tom?" she laughed. "Be realistic, Brad."

"I sent him."

There was a mad kind of glee in his voice now. Anne watched
im, realizing that he was serious. He really thought that he had
ent Tom to bribe her. Brad might have had his petty delusions in
e past, but Anne had never known him to completely lose his
ouch with reality.

"Brad," she tried more gently, suddenly very uneasy with the
icture that was forming. "What did you come here to say?"

"Say?" he echoed hollowly. "I didn't come here to say any-
ing. That's all finished."

Within the space of his words, something else appeared in his
es, something Anne had never seen there before. Beneath the
arice, the sarcasm and disdain, a new glow began to flicker: a
anic purpose, a look of hungry malevolence.

A real madness.

Anne froze, suddenly very afraid of her brother. He watched her
ith eyes that seemed to see something else altogether, something
he didn't recognize. With uncommon perception, she under-
tood that he was acting out a scenario he had practiced many
imes. He was living a dream he had created within the walls of
solation he had built long ago.

She could see now the revenge he had plotted and savored
hrough the long, ineffectual years when he had lived on jealousy

and resentment. The revenge was to have been carried out against
her father. And now, because he was out of his reach, against
Anne. Whatever he was about to do, Brad had done a thousand
times before in his fantasies. Now he had lost the ability to comprehend the difference.

Anne noticed again that the facial twitches had stopped. Brad
was in perfect control. She suddenly realized how far the game had
gone when Brad pulled a gun from his coat—a short, ugly little .22.
The famous Saturday night special, whose availability was legend
and whose bullet did an obscene little dance inside the human chest
cavity. And this gun was pointed directly at her.

Chapter 15

"Brad, this is absurd," Anne protested without thinking. "What do you think you're doing?"

Brad smiled giddily, his mouth an almost perfect crescent, and leaned comfortably back in his chair. "Actually, I think I should be grateful to you for bringing this whole mess to a head. You can't imagine what a pleasure it will be to put a match to this white elephant." He looked around with a little giggling sound, as if savoring the thought. "Pete Jackson's place. The legacy, the symbol of history and family, everything that he preached ad nauseam but never practiced. 'The tie that binds.'" His lips curled into a sneer and his gaze returned to his sister. "But Bradley didn't belong. He wasn't the bright, the gifted, the beautiful. He was only second best, and old Pete didn't even acknowledge his existence until he made good his threat to usurp the throne. You know, Anne, you never knew what you missed. You were never in the contest for the real world, at least not as far as Pete was concerned. Women didn't have to compete for something that could be theirs. So it was safe to lavish the worldly goods on you as the royal princess. The household pet. Weren't we all surprised when ole Pete decided to get back at Brad by leaving the household pet everything."

Anne's mouth was dry. Her heart raced painfully. All she could think of doing was trying to run. Every tactic she'd ever used with gun-wielding patients suddenly disappeared and she was afraid she'd lose control. The sense of unreality was increased by the fact that a part of her still refused to believe that it was Brad who sat so nonchalantly before her with a gun in his hand.

"So what are you going to do," she challenged instinctively, still reacting as she always had to him, "shoot me because I was cute and cuddly? Or is it that I'm the only one left to blame?"

His silent, smiling shrug made her want to scream. She didn't know how to talk to him, what to do to defuse him. Looking at him now, she knew with a sinking finality that he was long past reason. He was acting out his cruel fantasy, and try as she might, she couldn't get beyond her feelings of disdain. She wanted to scream at him, to insult him for the stupid way he was handling this. She also realized that she wanted to beg for her life.

"Brad," she said, her voice barely in control. "If it means that much to you, I'll forget the lawsuit. Take the land. Do whatever you want with it."

He shook his head with a smug grin of satisfaction. "Too late. That fine lawyer of yours didn't waste any time before contacting the authorities. I've been checking on it, you know, and I figure that if Tom and I were convicted, maybe we'd serve eighteen months in minimum security. I'd come out of it with the house on Beacon Hill and a comfortable living. But Anne, with you dead, I'd inherit the estate anyway, so I'd walk away from the whole thing in under two years in an even better position than when I went in. And Tom wouldn't have his fingers all over my money anymore." He waved the gun at her, punctuating his enthusiasm.

"Now, here's the fun part. I have an alibi. At six tonight, as usual, Tom and I will be waiting for Louis to seat us at our booth. And I've been seen going into my room earlier today to work on our unfortunate financial setback that could well cost me my ancestral home. Every once in a while my voice has been throwing recorded tantrums just loud enough to be heard and noted." He was enjoying himself immensely, like a small child getting the last piece of cake. Anne was frightened. The gun was once more leveled very steadily at her chest. "You know," he went on blithely, "I can't thank you enough for showing me such a good time today. Being able to see the look on your face right now is worth all the trouble I've gone through. I've been dreaming of something like this for years." He looked around the room with malicious glee. "As for the cabin, well, let's call that a settlement of old debts."

"What an interesting turn of phrase."

The interruption jolted Anne. She whipped around to find Jonathan lounging in the doorway. Even knowing that he gave them no physical advantage, she breathed an instinctive sigh of relief. Jonathan would know what to do. He would help defuse the situation by just being there.

Then she noticed that something was wrong. Jonathan seemed to not even notice that Anne was in the room. He gazed passively at Brad, but the light in his eyes burned eerily. A new, unexplained tension suddenly exploded.

Anne instinctively turned to Brad, maybe for some kind of explanation. The sight of him only added to her confusion.

Brad had turned white. His mouth hung slack as if he'd been hit, and his expression, which had only moments earlier been smugly pleased, caught fire. The left side of his face contorted madly. An evil enmity Anne had never seen before glared in his eyes as he struggled for control.

"What are you doing here?" he hissed.

Jonathan smiled lazily. "Waiting to run into you, it would seem."

There was a moment's silence Anne somehow couldn't break. It was as if a field of physical malevolence had sparked between the two men that no one could interrupt. They were two men Anne didn't know, consumed by something she didn't understand but instinctively feared. She watched each in turn, seeing a similarity in their expressions. She wasn't sure which one to be more afraid of.

Brad got slowly to his feet, the gun still steady, still poised at Anne. His eyes never left Jonathan.

"So it was you all along," Brad finally said with some wonder. "I should have guessed."

Jonathan shrugged with that strange smile that made Anne chill. "You've been outclassed, Bradley."

Brad nodded absently, still pondering something. "You managed to hide yourself well in that dummy corporation. It was, wasn't it?"

Jonathan nodded with a small grin. "I'll take that as a compliment. I went to a lot of trouble."

Suddenly Brad turned on Anne, his malice threatening to consume her. Still too stunned to comprehend what was taking place, she flinched from him.

"And you, little princess. Your part in this was a stroke of genius, especially after the wonderful act you put on two years ago. You like your revenge served cold, too, do you?"

Anne was too overwhelmed to react. "What are you talking about?" She turned to the stranger in the doorway. "Jonathan, please tell me what's going on. How do you know Brad?"

Somehow she'd gotten to her feet, though she didn't know how. She faced the two of them as she held the back of the chair for support, her hands sweaty.

Brad came after her and she started away. He looked from her to Jonathan, amazement dawning.

"She doesn't know," he breathed, again facing Jonathan and ignoring her in her small corner. He actually smiled at the man in the doorway, shaking his head with grudging admiration. "My God, what a masterful game. Jonathan, you have my respect. It was a brilliant move." He was really beginning to enjoy himself again, that little giggling sound escaping from him. It was as if he'd just remembered that he was the one with the gun in his hand, and that his new victim was far more amusing than the old.

Anne turned on Jonathan again. "What didn't I know?"

Brad wouldn't be denied the pleasure. "Anne, my dear, you know that Amplex Corporation Board of Directors you've been waiting to hear from? I'd like to introduce you." He made a show of indicating Jonathan with a grand wave of the gun, and then giggled again.

Anne blanched, trying to understand. Reality was fast leaving her behind. When she turned to Jonathan for explanation, he merely acquiesced with a passive shrug. She felt herself go deathly cold. The last of her foundations was beginning to crumble away beneath her.

"Why?"

Again he shrugged. "A story too long to tell in the time we seem to have."

She turned on Brad as if expecting help, but he just grinned. Her helplessness seemed to delight him all the more.

"An old score to settle," Jonathan added evenly, his eyes noncommittal.

His words set off a chain-reaction in Anne. A flurry of disjointed memories clicked together into place like a slot machine: Jonathan's odd trek back into the winter mountains in a custom suit, his animosity, the bits of out-of-the-way knowledge he'd collected about the family. His interest in Peter Jackson's daughter, Brad Jackson's sister.

Anne realized that she'd stopped breathing. She faced Jonathan and tried to discover some of the affection that had filled his eyes when he'd looked at her only hours ago and found none. His eyes were as cold as treacherous ice, a fragile covering for dangerous emotions below. His emotions were directed only at Brad. She challenged him to look at her again, her eyes bright with disbelief.

"Brad? Brad was the man who swindled you?" She knew she'd struck home even before he answered.

His answer was conversational, his voice as unemotional as the surface of his eyes. "Then Judson did tell you?"

"He told me. And because of what Brad did twelve years ago, you engineered the futures deal so that he would be sure to lose his family's home, too?"

He didn't offer an answer.

She swung on Brad. "Did you do it on purpose, Brad? Did you set out to ruin him?"

"Of course I did," he sneered, his reaction classic. His eyes gleamed maliciously as he looked at Jonathan and remembered whatever had set him off twelve years ago. "He was always so perfect, so *right*. So I outclassed him, didn't I, Jonathan? I got him caught between a rock and hard place to teach him a little lesson in where the real power lies."

Jonathan didn't bother to answer Brad either. Anne found that she was shaking her head as if she could deny what was happening. She wanted to lash out and didn't know at whom. It was too much to accept. Brad probably couldn't even remember what incident had been the catalyst for sending him after Jonathan. Jonathan had spent over a decade in return to exact his own brand of revenge, and Anne was the one caught in the middle.

Anger crowded her almost as closely as the terror of Brad's eyes. She lashed out at Jonathan for deceiving her, for according her a false security and then callously stripping it away again. She attacked him because she loved him.

"Was this all your quaint idea of Biblical justice, or did you think that I had a hand in what Brad did?"

She got no reaction. Jonathan was watching Brad.

"God, this is too good to be true." Brad giggled, his face jumping erratically. "It seems that I'm about to have my cake and eat it, too."

Jonathan finally gave Anne her answer then, his eyes still rigidly veiled. "I think Brad plans to make the point moot."

Brad laughed, the sound grating. "Indeed I do. But you sure have helped make this a most unforgettable afternoon. It's just too bad that I can't tell Tom how I found Jonathan Harris playing house with my sister, and that she didn't even know that he'd come to steal her precious home." His excitement was peaking as he considered the two people he held at bay.

At that moment Jonathan moved slightly to ease his bad leg. Brad jumped, swinging the gun around at him. "Don't you move, Harris," he shrilled a bit too loudly.

"Don't worry, Bradley," Jonathan answered calmly. Tugging at his pant leg, he revealed his homemade splint. "I'm not in good enough form for heroic gestures today."

"Why, Jonathan," Brad said with new delight. "I think you're keeping something from me. What happened to you?"

"I fell."

"You don't say. That's too bad. Hope it wasn't anything serious."

"I'll recover." Jonathan smiled evenly.

That seemed to appeal to Brad's sense of humor. His laughter was strident and loud. Then, abruptly, he stopped, his attention newly diverted. "Well now, let's see. Jonathan, you do complicate matters a little. I guess I'll have to get Anne to tie you up first. You see, the robbers tied the victims and ransacked the house before they...well, you know. It was too bad that Mr. Harris had suffered his injury and was able to offer no help to his hostess." He giggled again. "Really, Jonathan, you appeal to my sense of poetic justice. But remember, I have the gun. I'll be just as happy to shoot you now as later."

He backed up to the pantry and opened the door, never turning his back on his hostages. "Anne, I assume you still keep the clothesline in the same...ah, here it is. I should thank you for being such a creature of habit." He showed the roll to Jonathan. "It's been in the same place for the last twenty-five years at least. This place always has been a shrine to the fallacy of permanency. And Anne, as the dutiful daughter, has served it quite well, I think. Something like a vestal virgin." Still watching Jonathan, Brad flipped the ball of twine at Anne. She caught it instinctively.

When it seemed that Brad was about to head off on another self-serving tangent, Jonathan interrupted with a small, rueful smile.

"I hate to be a bother, but could we continue this when I'm sitting down? I'm wearing a bit thin."

Brad stared oddly at him, as if his concentration had been broken. Then he smiled. "All right. I guess the next act takes place in the living room anyway. Please proceed."

Anne walked over to the door to see that Jonathan's crutches leaned against the wall beyond him. He moved now to reach for them. Edging aside enough to let her through, he slipped them under his arms and leaned heavily over. If Anne hadn't been so close when he turned to follow her, she never would have heard him.

"Can you tie something I can get out of?"

She nodded automatically, just enough, and moved past him.

Jonathan turned to follow, walking very carefully, just as he had the first few days he'd been up. At first Anne was confused. He had been careful all along, putting as little weight on his injured leg as he could. But she knew darn well that he had no reason to be having so much trouble. He was breathing heavily as he lurched a single step at a time across to the couch. When he lowered himself very carefully to a sitting position, a small gasp escaped that sounded very real.

"You're not telling me everything, Jonathan," Brad accused with relish. "How did your accident happen?"

"I . . . told you . . . I fell."

Brad shrugged. "Be that way. All right, Anne. I'd like your best Girl Scout knots. Hands behind his back. And even though I doubt sincerely whether it would make any difference, tie his ankles together. Jonathan, you do look awful. I guess I can assume that more was injured than just your leg."

Anne piped up, beginning to get a glimmer of Jonathan's strategy. "Quite a lot more. He shouldn't be anyplace but bed." Absurdly, she thought of how she sounded like an old English movie.

"Ah." Brad nodded, his eyes wide. "Compassionate to the bitter end, Anne? This is the man who made you the fool of the century, and you still think of his welfare. Good instincts, you nurses. All right, Jonathan, after she ties you up, feel free to lie down." He shook his head with glee. "To think that you went to all that trouble just to surprise me."

"You know . . . me . . . any little . . . revenge . . . I can . . . get. . . ."
Jonathan still seemed to have trouble breathing, his chest heaving with exertion as he tried to speak. Anne was impressed, even though, as Brad had said, Jonathan had just finished making a fool

of her. His quick thinking could still save her life. Even now he was putting on the act of a lifetime as he wiped away nonexistent perspiration from his upper lip with the back of a trembling hand. He even managed somehow to look gray. Anne decided to ask him later how he did it.

"Isn't there some kind of . . . code," he gasped, his eyes coldly amused, "about taking . . . advantage of . . . an . . . injured man?"

Brad stood by the front door, alternately watching Anne's work and the scene outside. Anne's pastoral landscape. The sun rode straight up in the cold winter sky, glittering brightly off the snow so that the glare from the window cast the house in an uncomfortable gloom. Brad blinked repeatedly as he turned his attention back on them. His expression had frozen into disinterest, his smile faded. "None whatsoever, Jonathan." Anne couldn't see his eyes well, but she thought that the tic was worse.

Jonathan did smile, a chilly and rueful sight. "Funny . . . I had a feeling that would be . . . your attitude."

Anne straightened, hoping that Jonathan could manage to get the knots free and wondering what he intended to do once he did. She thought as she watched the tableau before her how dim the big fire in the fireplace appeared in contrast to that of the sun, how its dull red glow seemed almost evil.

Brad moved close enough to give Anne's work a half-hearted check and nodded, again motioning to her with the gun. The fact that she flinched again amused him. "Now, Anne," he directed, his voice businesslike and distant, "if memory serves me once more, there's a big can of gasoline in the barn. You'll walk there ahead of me to get it."

The band that constricted her breathing tightened. She stared at him, still fighting the belief that he could really carry out his threats. She was still not able to accept the fact that Brad was doing this, enacting a well-planned murder, torturing them like a great, slimy cat with his prey. Jonathan tried to catch her eye and nod, attempting to calm her, but she couldn't even accept his assurance. She didn't, after all, really know him, either. What did he want from her after all this? What had he wanted all along? The ground was falling out from under her, and she had nothing left to grab onto. She couldn't function anymore.

"Anne!"

She started, Brad's voice cutting into her. She looked over at him, at the tic that pulled again at his eye as if he were winking at a lewd joke, at the absurdly small gun that he wielded so ungracefully, and at the inappropriate walking boots he'd bought new to make the trek up here. It was at that moment that somehwere deep within her mounting terror a black rage was born.

This was all wrong. There had to be something she could do to stop him. He was lost up here in these mountains. His arena was the inside of a corporate office. This was her home, her world. Brad couldn't walk into it from his world of climate control and lawyer-spawned courage and expect to overcome her with such a silly little gun. He was on her turf, and it should have been to her advantage.

She caught Jonathan's eye and found reassurance in his calm gaze. They'd make it. Together they would be able to outwit Brad. She'd have to fight the bitterness of Jonathan's betrayal long enough to manage it, work with him until they were free and then rip his lungs out. He'd help to save himself if nothing else, and he was as comfortable in this world as she. They just had to get Brad to stumble.

She had to keep her head. Oh, God, if only she could keep the picture of Jonathan's eyes at bay long enough. She had to forget the soft blue of a mountain stream.

"I'm going, Brad," she said evenly, trying to hide from him the deep breath she had to take to steady herself. As she walked by him, the tic pulled again, more spastically. Maybe he wasn't as controlled as he seemed. Unless Anne were even more wrong than she'd been so far, he probably hadn't even had the courage to pull the official strings of Jonathan's ruin those long years ago. How could he possibly be expected to retain the temerity it took to do something this awesome face-to-face? She didn't want to think of the real power that obsessions gave to the delusional person. She didn't think she could survive the idea that Brad was invincible.

Anne walked ahead of him into the brittle afternoon air, the clean touch of it helping to settle her a little. Brad said nothing as they traversed the way to the barn, but the gun never wavered far from the center of her back, the feel of it a very unpleasant reminder.

Stepping into the barn calmed her even more. Andy whinnied over to her and Bessie stamped in her stall. The smells were familiar and warm, the sounds muffled. Somewhere in the back, melting snow dripped steadily from the rafters. Wanting to give Jonathan as much time as possible, she stopped as if to orient herself to the dark building.

"Don't play games, Anne," Brad warned irritably. "The gas is in the old tack room. At least that's where Pete used to keep it, and I can't imagine you defiling the sacred memory by moving it."

"I had my canning equipment in there this year. I moved the gasoline." She paused as if in thought. "The question is where..."

Brad shoved the gun into the small of her back, his patience wearing. "I'd rather not shoot you here, but that's always an option, Anne. Does that help you remember?"

"Oddly enough, it does." She led the way to the back of the barn.

Only five minutes later, unable to stall any longer, Anne started back, the half-full ten-gallon can heavy in her hands. Brad had checked it when she had pulled it out, evidently convinced that she'd also kept a gas can of water handy on the off chance that anybody would come up and force her to set fire to her house. His tic was becoming worse with the passing minutes and now pulled sporadically at his mouth. He'd begun to finger the gun like worry beads, which didn't encourage Anne at all. It was still pointed straight at her back.

She opened the door to the cabin and had to once again adjust her eyes to the gloom. At first all she could see was the fire to her right, still burning steadily and making the air close. Then, she was able to make out the furniture. it wasn't until Brad stepped in behind her that she realized that Jonathan was gone. It took no more to galvanize her. Almost without hesitation she dropped to the floor, the gas can landing upright in front of her.

"What the hell are you...?"

Then Brad saw, too. His eyes shot open as he began to swing around. He never got started. A poker whistled out of the darkness and caught him on the left shoulder. He cried out and fired, the sound deafeningly close. Anne rolled away from it without giving another thought to the can by the fire. She saw Jonathan lunge from behind the door. Brad saw him and screamed, the sound a mix of fury and fear.

From where she'd taken cover Anne watched the struggle, the two men's shadows against the throbbing glow of the fire. For a moment they were one silhouette, indistinguishable. Then Jonathan moved. Getting a hand on the gun, he tried to force it away from Brad. The two of them fought for it in silence. Jonathan still had the poker in his other hand. He brought it up to strike and lost his leverage on the gun. Anne could see it, small and deadly, caught high between the two of them and glinting dully in the light. The shadows still wavered in sweating silence, the only sounds now oddly the melting snow and the crackle of the fire. She watched impotently, unable to move or even breathe for the fear. Jonathan couldn't take this much longer.

Suddenly Brad lunged hard. The two men crashed against the wall, sending the hall tree over in a clatter. Jonathan lost grip on the poker and gave a sharp cry as he hit the wall on his weak side, his bad leg buckling beneath him. He never let go of the gun. Sweat glistened on his face as he brought the other hand up and pried at Brad's grip, trying to slam the gun against the wall to loosen it. Jonathan was losing his balance. His right leg was almost useless, and Brad was trying to aim for it in an attempt to cripple him. Frantically, Anne looked around for help.

The poker lay exposed by the door. Quickly, she scuttled out from where she'd taken refuge by the chair and scooted over to get it. She could help Jonathan with it. He was rapidly wearing out. She could hear the rasping of his breath as he struggled.

She got hold of the poker as Brad shot an elbow at Jonathan and caught him at the ribs. Jonathan gasped; his hold loosened. Brad began to edge the gun down toward him. They didn't see her. Crouched behind them, Anne had just enough time to warn him.

"Jonathan!"

She made her move. Swinging with everything she had, she caught Brad flat against the kidney. He screamed and reeled around, pulling the gun with him. Anne dove away in an effort to put the couch between them. He fired seconds later. The bullet thudded into the couch inches from Anne's head. Already flattened, Anne peered out to see the astonishment in Brad's eyes.

"Damn it!" Jonathan lurched away from the wall to keep Brad from getting to Anne. He caught him against the couch. The gun rose between them again, glinting oddly like a sacrificial offering. Jonathan pushed and pushed more, bending Brad back at the waist. Anne was so close to them now that she could almost smell Brad's terror, and Jonathan's rage. She brought the poker up again, moved just beyond Brad's field of vision and stood waiting.

Jonathan's eyes were fire, their only color the terrible glow of blood and fury. He had a hand around Brad's throat and began to squeeze. Anne could hear the gurgling noises as Brad fought for air. The gun wavered between outstretched hands, slimy with sweat. Jonathan was gasping almost as loudly as Brad.

Brad kicked hard and Jonathan jerked upright, his mouth contorted in soundless agony. Anne raised the poker above her head.

Brad got ahold of the gun. He slammed it against the side of Jonathan's head. Then he swung it point-blank at Anne.

She froze.

Jonathan staggered, unbelievably still on his feet, trying to clear his head. Blood streamed down his face, glittering blackly in the light.

"Brad..." Anne saw him pulling at the trigger and couldn't move. She couldn't move. Brad's breath came in sobs. His hands shook and his face contorted cruelly, but he pulled steadily, almost casually at the trigger, ignoring Jonathan as if he didn't exist. He was enjoying the realization of his fantasies, feeding on the blank terror in Anne's eyes. A split second that filled an eternity.

"Anne!" Jonathan lunged. His football tackle caught Brad at the waist and sent him over backwards. The gun clattered hard against the chimney as Brad fell back over the couch, his body buckling oddly at the waist. He slammed to the floor, knocking into the gas can.

Anne screamed. Jonathan seized Anne at the knees and pushed her over. They hit the floor together behind the couch just as the can fell into the fireplace and exploded. The blast deafened her, knocking the wind out of her. She lay stunned and disoriented. With a rush, flames shot straight up, their brilliance consuming the chimney. Anne could only lie and watch, detached. Through the sudden roaring that filled her ears she thought she heard a long, terrified shrieking and wondered who it was. Then she saw the roaring flames, leaping along the walls and dancing patterns across the ceiling. She couldn't breathe.

"Anne, get out!"

Jonathan was pushing at her, yelling in her ear. She could only see one of his beautiful eyes. The other was caked shut. His eyebrows were gone. He was coughing and choking, his face washed in sweat and blood.

"The window! Come on!"

He jerked her up and she turned to look. The shock stunned her anew. The whole cabin was engulfed, the fire already devouring the loft and staircase and turning the furniture into kindling. She doubted they could get to the door. Even the hall tree, wedged at an angle against the wall, blazed, her down jacket melting into bright liquid. The quilts, generations of Jackson heritage, were already almost gone.

Jonathan had her by the arm, his hand a vise. She couldn't move and couldn't keep trying. There was nothing left, nothing to fight for. It was coming down around her, like another house of cards. Her beautiful bed, the one her great-grandfather had made, was burning. Lost.

"Annie, come on!" Jonathan screamed at her, his face almost hideous in the blood-red light of the flames. "We have to get out now!"

"No..." She pulled at him, trying to get free, but she was too numb, too overwhelmed to move. She wanted to curl back into a ball and give in. She couldn't do any more.

Jonathan never hesitated. Grabbing her around the waist, he pulled her back down and literally dragged her across the floor. "Keep your head down."

Thick black smoke blocked out the brilliant sunlight. It looked like a halo, a far-off streetlight in the fog. Anne kept her eyes on it as the terror woke in her. She was coughing, tears streaming down her face as she stumbled along next to Jonathan. Cinders, bits of wood and quilt fell around them. The heat was terrible. Anne could hear Jonathan's coughing, sobbing breath and wondered how he thought they could get out of this furnace alive.

Halfway across the floor, Anne had to rip through Jonathan's shirt to get a flaming piece of upholstery from his back. He never felt it. He never stopped moving, head down, his leg dragging painfully behind him, his arm tight around Anne.

Anne followed him blindly, looking up only to try to find the window again. It was getting harder to see. Harder to breathe. God, they weren't going to get out. She could hardly move. Where was the window? Had they gone the wrong way? The room couldn't be this far to get across.

Then the smoke shifted, just enough. There it was, a few feet ahead. Jonathan stopped, his back heaving with the exertion of just breathing.

"A little farther!" he screamed above the din of the fire that sought them. She nodded, sobbing now with the effort to breathe. He moved on and found the chair, still miraculously whole. Next to it was the floor lamp.

Pushing Anne's head down to the safety of the floor, he grabbed the lamp and swung it through the window. Cold air rushed in with the shattering of glass and the fire exploded over their heads. Anne felt the heat across her neck like a scald. She brought her head up, terrified.

"Jonathan?"

He was out, reaching back in for her. She climbed, the light of the sun hurting her eyes. She wondered why. Nothing was more brilliant than the orange of the fire. She took Jonathan's hand, and he pulled her through the broken glass. Good old jeans. They kept her from getting cut.

Anne tumbled out onto the snow-packed ground, landing next to Jonathan. She couldn't get a breath. It seemed enough to stop there and heave in great draughts of air, but Jonathan pulled at her again. She looked up to see that his face was black and wondered offhandedly if hers was too.

They made it to the door of the barn and fell, gasping and choking to the cold dirt floor. Anne thought her ears were still muffled. She couldn't hear anything but her own labored breathing and a dull roaring sound. She shook her head, trying to clear it. Then she heard the slow dripping of the snow back at the far side of the barn. She realized that nothing was wrong with her ears. The world outside was quiet. She looked up to see that it was a beautiful, crystal winter afternoon, the white light almost surreal. Even the brushing of the wind was silenced. There was only the dull rush of the flames as they consumed the cabin.

She looked over at Jonathan as he leaned against the other side of the doorway, his legs outstretched. His breathing was harsh and loud, and he wiped at the sweat on his face with a trembling hand. Immediately, Anne slid over to him.

"Can you breathe?" she demanded. He nodded, not very convincing. "How is your leg?"

"Fine... broke a... couple of... ribs... again, I... think."

He was clutching at his side and leaning to favor it. She tried to get his shirt up so that she could better check him, but her hands shook so badly she couldn't work very well.

Jonathan shook his head at her, not enough breath for words. She took the hint and let what was left of his shirt go. Jonathan managed a grin and carefully lifted an arm in invitation. Hesitating only a second, Anne accepted his offer and stayed within the comfort of his embrace.

"Do you... believe I never... wanted to hurt you?"

"We have plenty of time to discuss that," she said. "Concentrate on breathing right now."

"Whatever happens," he insisted, still breathing with short, painful gasps, "you won't ever... lose Cedar Ridge... I promise."

Anne looked over at the inferno that had once been her home and realized with some surprise that she forgave him. "You saved my life," she said quietly. "The rest, I think, is gravy."

"I... wanted you to... know."

Anne turned to him, to see the genuine regret in his eyes, the pain of a man who saw the woman he loved suffer, and she found a smile for him. "I know."

Farther inside the barn Andy stomped and whinnied, the smell of the smoke unsettling him. Jonathan turned at the noise.

"Do you think we... should try and get down to... town?"

Anne shook her head. "No. I have the feeling that the town will be coming to us." The roof of the cabin gave way with a long crash that demanded their attention. A wide column of thick black smoke lifted straight up into the sky. "They'd never pass up an opportunity like this to tell me how much I need a real road up here."

She watched the destruction a while longer, her mind still too stunned to sort it all out.

"Anne?"

She turned to him with a crumbling, watery grin. "All of my Nancy Drews are gone. I had the... whole collection... for... when..."

It was a long time before her sobbing subsided. And an hour later as the sun impaled itself on the western trees, twenty riders crashed into the clearing at a dead run to find Anne and Jonathan sitting together at the side of the barn door watching the last of the fire as it licked the charred ruins of the cabin.

Anne stood in the cabin doorway and watched the new spring sun warm the top leaves of the trees, the first light refreshing and clear. It had been her first night home since the fire. Since that time she had been living the life of a Gypsy, traveling to Boston to settle family and business affairs, New York to consult with Judson and then back to Elder's Crossing to oversee the clinic construction and her practice.

It had only been a week since she'd closed the door for the last time on the house in Boston. She had dreaded that especially, anticipating the pain and remorse of selling it. She had, after all, spent much of her life there. But when it was over, she'd stood in the echoing marble foyer to look around at the sterile surroundings and felt only the emptiness of the place. She had left nothing behind.

It had been while she had been on that final trip to Boston, flying out as the last of the snow had given way to crocuses on the mountains, that the cabin had been finished. A completely new modern structure, with a lot of glass, whose design had been decided the day she'd buried Brad next to the father he'd so envied and hated. It had been at that moment that she'd realized with inescapable finality that her family was gone. All her childhood memories and dreams had been put to rest beneath white headstones and black ashes. It was time now to move on to a new life, symbolized by the radically new structure on her ancient mountain.

Anne turned from the door and walked back through the house that still had a loft and a high wall for the quilts her friends had already begun to collect for her.

She'd made it into the shiny white kitchen where she was pouring herself coffee from a new pot when she heard the sound of a vehicle approaching. A smile of anticipation lit her features. Pouring a second cup, she slipped out of her thick robe to reveal a pale pink lace-and-silk teddy. Then, picking up the cups, she walked to the front door, golden hair swinging gently down her back.

"You up already?"

"I'm a farm girl." She grinned lazily, leaning against the open door and waiting for him to turn to her.

When he did, Jonathan dropped the box he'd been lifting with a flat thud. "Good God, woman," he gasped, "you're not supposed to shock a man like that." His eyes didn't seem to mind so much. Anne couldn't get enough of the sight of him, so tall and handsome and whole. He had not dealt well with the hospital, nor it with him.

"And you're not supposed to run out on a woman the day after she's married."

"Important mail," he assured her, bending to pick the box back up. "Special delivery."

Anne scowled a little. "I was afraid you'd run back off to New York."

"Not for six more months." He stomped up onto the porch and nudged her backside. "That was the deal. And may I say," he leered, depositing a quick kiss on eager lips, "I can't wait to see what it's like to ravage the chief executive officer and chairman of the board of Jackson Corporations Limited.''

"You ravaged her last night," Anne reminded him, settling onto the couch and putting the coffee cups on the glass-and-wood coffee table.

Jonathan set the box down before her and grinned. "No. Last night I ravaged the finest rural nurse in West Virginia. Open the box."

"What is it?" She studied it before going to the masking tape.

"Your wedding present."

Anne eyed him suspiciously. "The pearls were my wedding present."

"Open it."

When she reached into the packing a few minutes later, Anne drew out a book—a small book, no more than one hundred and ninety pages. Then came another. The rest were packed lovingly beneath, some new, some originals, all familiar and treasured.

Anne looked up at Jonathan, tears in her smiling eyes. "How did you . . . ?"

Jonathan's eyes were bright and happy, the pain at their depths long since exorcised. "You once said something about collecting Nancy Drews for our daughter to read."

She put the books down and eased herself into Jonathan's arms. "Did I tell you that I love you?"

Jonathan kissed her with a gentleness that brought more tears. "Seems to me you did."

She grinned suggestively and stretched against him, the silk whispering against denim and flannel. "Did I show you?"

"Yes." He kissed her again. "But I think it would be okay if you showed me again."

She did.

* * * * *